MVFOL

P9-CKR-532

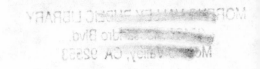

Books by Herman Wouk

NOVELS

Aurora Dawn

City Boy

The Caine Mutiny

Marjorie Morningstar

Youngblood Hawke

Don't Stop the Carnival

The Winds of War

War and Remembrance

Inside, Outside

The Hope

The Glory

PLAYS

The Traitor

The Caine Mutiny Court-Martial

Nature's Way

NONFICTION

This Is My God

INSIDE, OUTSIDE

HERMAN WOUK

INSIDE, OUTSIDE

OUTSIDE

A NOVEL

LITTLE, BROWN AND COMPANY
Boston New York Toronto London

FIRST BACK BAY EDITION

LIBRARY OF CONGRESS CATALOGING IN PUBLICATION DATA

Wouk, Herman
Inside, outside.

I. Title.
PS3545.09815   1985   813'.54   84-26087
ISBN 0-316-95504-3 (hc)   0-316-95529-9 (pb)

MV-NY

*Published simultaneously in Canada
by Little, Brown & Company (Canada) Limited*

PRINTED IN THE UNITED STATES OF AMERICA

To my sister Irene
with love

Rejoice, young man in your youth, and let your heart pleasure you in the days of your young manhood; and walk in the ways of your heart, and the sight of your eyes; but know that for all these God will bring you into judgment. So remove trouble from your heart and put away wrongdoing from your flesh, for boyhood and youth are a breath.

ECCLESIASTES 11:9–10

PART I

The Green Cousin

1

Introducing Myself

ALL hell has been breaking loose around here, and my peaceful re-treat in the Executive Office Building may be coming to a sudden rude end.

I suppose it was too good to last. It has been a curious hiatus, unimaginable to me a few months ago — first of all, my becoming a Special Assistant to the President, especially to this President; second, and even more surprising, my finding it no big deal, but rather an oasis of quiet escape from corporate tax law. I've at last pieced together the mysterious background of my appointment. The haphazardness of it will appear absurd, but the longer I'm in Washington the more I realize that most people in this town tend to act with the calm forethought of a beheaded chicken. It gives me the cold shudders.

Fortunately for my peace of mind, the bookcase in this large gloomy room contains, amid rows and rows of dusty government publications, the seven volumes of Douglas Southall Freeman's *George Washington: A Biography,* and Churchill's six volumes on the Second World War. I dip into these now and then to reassure myself that things were not very different in the days of those great men. Churchill calls the Versailles Treaty, the product of the combined wisdom and long labor of all the top politicians of Europe, "a sad and complicated idiocy." From what I see here, this description can be extended to almost all politics. No wonder the world is in such a godawful mess, and has been, it appears, since Hammurabi ordered his cuneiform scribes to start scratching his great deeds on clay tablets.

Let me describe the jolt I got the other day, to give you my feel of things at this world hub. When I first flew down from New York and briefly met with the President in the Oval Office — the one time I saw him until this recent jolt — I explained that if I did take the job I wouldn't work on Saturdays, and would make up the time Sundays or nights, if required. The President looked baffled, and then calculating. He pushed out his lips, widened his eyes, raised those thick eyebrows, and nodded gravely and repeatedly. "That's splendid," was his judicious comment. "I'm impressed, Mr. Goodkind." (He pronounced it right, with a long *i*.) "May I say that I've had numerous Jewish associates, but you're the first one who's made that stipulation, and I'm impressed. Very impressed. That's impressive."

I'm hardly a super-pious type, I hasten to acknowledge. What I do Saturdays, besides the usual praying, is mostly lie around and read, or walk a few miles along the tow path with my black Labrador, Scrooge. I wouldn't give up this inviolate chunk of peace in my week for anything. It has kept me sane at my Wall Street office down the years, this day of sealed-off Sabbath release from the squirrel cage of tax law.

But that's not the point of the story. The point is that for much of my life I've been a Talmud addict. I don't spend day and night over its many volumes as my grandfather did, but even at the Goodkind and Curtis office I used to arrive early and, with four or five cups of strong coffee, study for an hour or more every morning. I won't go deeply into this. Just take my word for it, under the opaque Aramaic surface the Talmud is a magnificent structure of subtle legal brilliancies, all interwoven with legend, mysticism, the color of ancient times, and the cut-and-thrust of powerful minds in sharp clash. I can't get enough of it, and I've been at it for decades.

Once I'd settled into this office and realized that I'd fallen down a peculiar well of solitude, I saw no reason not to bring the Talmud here and resume my usual routine. So there I was, day before yesterday, sitting at my desk with a huge tome open, puzzling my skull-capped head over the validity of a bill of divorcement brought from Spain to Babylon, when the door opened, and without ado in walks the President of the United States.

Startled embarrassment on both sides.

Up I jump, snatching off the skullcap and slamming shut the volume. Sheer reflex. The President says, "Oh! Sorry. Did I interrupt something? Your secretary seems to have stepped out, and —"

Awkward pause while I collect myself. "Mr. President, you're not interrupting anything. I'm highly honored, and ah —"

We look at each other in silence. I'm telling this ridiculous and unlikely little scene just the way it was: a goy walking in on a Jew studying the Talmud in the White House, and suitably apologetic. I knew the President had a hideaway office on the first floor of this building, but his barging in like that was a stunner. Well, the moment passed. In his deep Presidential voice, one of several he produces like a ventriloquist, except that all the characters talk out of the same face, he asked, "Ah, just what is that large book, Mr. Goodkind?"

"It's the Talmud, Mr. President."

"Ah, the Talmud. Very impressive."

He asked to look into it. I showed him the text, told him the dates and nationalities of the commentators, the printing history of the Talmud and so forth, my standard quick tour for outsiders. It's not a dull tour. On one page of the Talmud you encounter authorities from many lands, from the time of Jesus and even earlier down through the ages to the nineteenth century, all discussing or annotating a single point of law. I know of nothing else like it in the world. The President has a quick and able mind, though not everybody gives him that, not by a long shot. His face lit up. He shot me a sharp glance and said in his most nearly natural voice, "And you really understand this stuff?"

"Well, I scratch the surface, Mr. President. I come from a rabbinic family."

He nodded. The momentary relaxation faded from his face, leaving deep-carved lines of concern. The man looks ten years older than he did when we met two months ago.

Presidential voice: "I'd like to talk to you, ah, David. This impressive background of yours is very relevant. Let's chat right here for a bit. It's quiet."

That it was, to be sure. Sepulchral. He sat down, and so I did. The upshot of this exceedingly strange "chat" was that I wrote a TV speech for him about Watergate; a decidedly unlooked-for turn in the life of I. David Goodkind, counsellor-at-law and lifelong Democrat, though no more bizarre than the way I got here.

But rest assured, this Watergate business is going to take up no space in these pages. If it dies off, as I expect it soon will — that's certainly what he's hoping and trying for — well, that'll be that. Just one more sad and complicated idiocy scratched on the clay tablets. Somehow it's beginning to remind me, the whole Watergate caper, of the first time Bobbie Webb and I broke up; when I rebounded to a brief affair with a screwy but goodhearted dish named Sonia Feld.

As the affair began to cool down, Sonia knitted me a sweater, a loose ill-fitting thing. With it came a sentimental note that did the trick, warmed me up to her again, intravenous glucose for a terminally ill liaison. Well, Sonia left one long loose thread hanging from the sweater, which I cut off with a scissors, but the same thread would work loose as I wore the thing, and I'd cut it off again. Once when I was drunk for some reason — I think, after a snide telephone call from Bobbie Webb, an art form at which she was peerless — I saw that damned thread still dangling loose. I began to pull on it. I pulled and pulled, and poor Sonia's work began to unravel. That infuriated me. I pulled in alcoholic obstinacy, until I was left with a mess of white wriggly wool over the floor, and no sweater. It was gone.

The President was reelected not long ago with the biggest majority ever. There's only this one dangling Watergate thread, and he can't seem to cut it or tie it off. But I daresay he will. He is a tough and resourceful bird, and the Presidency is a mighty close-knit sweater.

Two things happened a while ago to create the hole in the White House entourage which I have filled. A speechwriter who specialized in quips resigned, and Israel sent over a new ambassador. The President and the previous man, a blunt ex-general, had gotten on almost too well; the ambassador actually came out for his reelection. At a cabinet meeting, the President said he wished there was someone on the staff who knew the incoming diplomat well enough to talk to him with the gloves off, until he himself could feel at home with the man. The Secretary of Defense brought up my name. Some time ago this same diplomat had spoken at a United Jewish Appeal banquet where I got the Secretary to come as a guest of honor, and SecDef remembered that the speaker and I had hugged each other. Nothing unusual, the general counsel for the UJA naturally gets to know and hug all the Israeli star speakers. SecDef described my background to the President, who had never heard of me (so much for newspaper notoriety, breath on a windowpane). The President said, "Sounds okay, let's contact him," and so it happened. Just like that.

A detail of my background much in my favor was my radio experience. Long, long ago, before the war — as I sometimes feel, before Noah's flood — the Secretary of Defense and I romanced these two girls in the chorus of a Winter Garden musical, *Johnny, Drop Your Gun.* I was then a gagwriter of twenty-one, and my girl was Bobbie Webb. SecDef was a lawyer a few years older; very married, and having a final boyish fling. I was discreet, and he appreciated it. We've been friendly ever since, as he too is a Wall Street attorney, though at the moment he's every inch the good gray statesman, a straight arrow with five kids and a house in McLean. Only last week my wife Jan and I had dinner at SecDef's house, and he made clumsy jokes about the time we hung around the stage door together. Mrs. SecDef gaily laughed; mainly with her mouth muscles, I thought, and her eyes kind of looked like glass marbles.

Anyhow, at the cabinet meeting SecDef mentioned my jokewriting past, and the President perked up at that. All politicians are desperate for jokes. Very few can deliver them, and he is not one of those, but he keeps trying. I have fed him a number of jokes since coming here, but the way he delivers them, they just lie where they fall, plop, like dropped jellyfish.

SecDef also told the President about the obscenity trials. That gave him pause. Like most red-blooded American males, the President is a horseshit and asshole man from way back. His packaged flat image, however, is entirely that other face of American manhood: dear old Mom and grand old flag and heck and golly and shoot, pretty much like an astronaut. He said that he'd never even heard of Peter Quat and *Deflowering Sarah,* or of Henry Miller and *Tropic of Cancer* — the President is not big on modernist literature — so he doubted that many people had. Anyway, he allowed that a bit of liberal input might be useful around his White House, at that. So I was in.

And I think I've already been of some use. Not that I've helped him feel at home with the ambassador. This President is never really "at home" with anybody, possibly not even with his wife and daughters. He dwells in a dark hole somewhere deep inside himself, and all the world ever sees of the real man, if anything, is the faint gleam of phosphorescent worried eyes peering from that hole. I did ease the first meetings of SecDef and the President's chief of staff with the ambassador. Since then I've become a sort of cushion for carom shots on touchy Israel matters too small to engage our superstar National Security Adviser. I'll get an idea or a position thrown at me by the ambassador or the administration, quietly and casually, and nobody's committed, and there's no body contact; and I bounce it along, and the play either continues or stops. I've furthered several minor matters in that way.

My official handle is "Special Assistant to the President for Cultural and Educational Liaison." In this political rose garden, Special Assistants and Assistants to the President are thick as Japanese beetles. I'm just one more of them. The job is a real one, of sorts. I'm on the board of the National Endowment for the Arts. Also I meet with delegations of teachers and artists who descend on Washington; I listen to their problems, and get them passes for special White House tours, and so forth. And I shepherd around foreign visitors, like a group of Soviet professors of American literature, who showed up last week, and greatly embarrassed me by insisting on being taken at once to a topless bar, and then to a dirty movie. I may be the noted defender of artistic freedom, but that was the first porn film I'd ever seen. Jan won't hear of paying money to pornmongers, and I won't go by myself. Suppose I had a fatal heart attack right there in the theatre? Jan would have to bury a husband carried out feet first from *The Devil in Miss Jones.* Nothing doing.

Well, escorting the Soviet professors made it all right for me to see a thing called *Hot Dormitories,* but it was disappointing. I was bored out of my mind, and mainly felt sorry for the poor actresses. The Russkis ate it up, however, and wanted to go to another dirty movie right away. I took them to the National Gallery instead, and they gave me the impression that they were displeased by that. Indeed, they were decidedly snotty about the National Gallery. They said they didn't have to come to America to see paintings, the Hermitage in Leningrad made the National Gallery look sick, and what about another dirty movie? I fobbed them off on a pallid State Department man, Soviet section, who displayed warm interest in showing the Russian professors, at government expense, all the examples of American artistic freedom now playing in the sleazy dumps on F Street.

Then there was this committee of authors who came here recently to pester Congress and the Treasury for relief from an adverse IRS ruling, something about authors' research expenses. Whenever an IRS mole has an idle hour, he whets his tearing fangs and has a go at actors, athletes, and authors. The few big ones make a packet, you see, and get hoggish and try to dodge taxes with slick contrivances which the IRS loves to dismember. Out come these adverse rulings, which play hell with the small earners. Well, that's my field, so I took charge, and actually got Internal Revenue to back down. The authors went in a body to thank the President; and as I saw them off on the Eastern shuttle for New York, they were remarking in wonderment at his approximately humanoid appearance. The cartoons do give a peculiar picture of the man.

Why on earth did I ever accept this job? Well, I can only say I did it out of the same quirk which led me at other times to take on Henry Miller, and the United Jewish Appeal. I would be a lot more affluent than I am, if I stuck to my business. Tax law satisfies me as a hardball mental game, an exercise in concentration and scholastic hairsplitting like some Talmud passages, though utterly devoid, of course, of Talmudic intellectual charm and moral substance. I enjoy the work, but it's all a mean fight over money; the heavy hand of government, versus the nimble wits of us lawyers hired by the fat cats. It pays very well, if you are good at it, but it is demanding drudgery. You have to dot every *i* and cross every *t* yourself, and not leave it to junior lawyers. The IRS will drive a Patton tank through a pinhole. I am paid for perfection.

So I can always be tempted to do something else, if my wife will agree to my indulging myself. She is an astute, beautiful woman, and I am the most happily married man on earth. You'll learn little about Jan or my marriage in these pages. She is the treasure that lay beyond Bobbie Webb and all my other racketing adventures, and as Tolstoy says, happy families are all alike, so there's nothing to tell, and Jan will remain a shrouded figure. It just occurs to me, thinking about it, that in my observation happy families are all about as different as faces or fingerprints, but I defer to Tolstoy. Very big of me.

I must disclose, however, that my wife was originally a Californian, and loathing the President is her long-time hobby. This dates back to when he ran for Congress early on, against a liberal ex-actress. During that campaign he doggedly kept hinting that his opponent was under direct control of the Kremlin, and was planning to blow up the White House, or pass Stalin all our atomic secrets, something unpatriotic and pinko like that. Jan worked in the lady's campaign, and thought these allegations were underhanded and base. Jan has no feel for serious politics.

My big problem, once I decided to consider the President's bombshell offer of a job, was Jan. When I broached the idea to her, she inquired how I would like a divorce. She too has voted Democratic all her life, and her idol was and remains Adlai Stevenson. She really could not digest the notion that I would even think twice about working for that baleful lowbrow who was so unkind to Adlai. I let her simmer for a day or two, then did my best to explain.

I had just banked a hefty fee from a big corporation for beating the government in tax court out of a massive sum. Was my client right or wrong on the issue? Who knows? I won, that's all. Where do right and wrong lie in taxation, anyhow? Politicians write laws for confiscating other people's earnings to use as their free spending money. That's the long and the short of it. The rest is trying to limit one's losses to the politicians. It was going on under the pharaohs, and it will be going on when we colonize Andromeda, no doubt, with regrettable waste of public funds by the Andromeda Agency. You can see I'm biting on a sore tooth of conscience here. No more of that.

I was financially able to accept the President's offer, and I felt like doing it, to my own surprise. Several considerations swayed me. The strongest was curiosity. Most of my friends are like Jan, dyed-in-the-wool eastern liberals content to sit up nights hating the President, and wishing that he would drop dead, and that Adlai would rise from the grave. Okay, but the man holds our present destiny in his hands, does he not? He worked his way into that position despite a singularly unattractive personality, and the political record of a polecat. How come? To observe him at close range, I thought, would be illuminating, and conceivably broadening.

The other consideration I inherited from my father. Pop was your typical young Russian Jewish immigrant, full of idealistic fire, disgusted with Czarist oppression, in trouble because of his clandestine socialist speeches, haunted by yearning for America. My father never changed his mind about the United States. To the end of his too-short life America remained the *Goldena Medina* (GOLD-ena me-DEE-na, you say it), the golden land, the freedom land. Pop loved the Goldena Medina. So do I, though I don't hang out flags on Memorial Day. Here was the Medina — my only relationship with which, except in wartime, has been to fend off its grasping tax claws — asking me, man to man, to lend a hand. Wait till it happens to you. If you have an American bone in your body, however you swathe it in cynicism, you'll feel the tug. And far back in my mind was something Pop or my grandfather would have thought of: placed here, I might somehow, at some moment, do something for our Jewish people. The Talmud says, "A man can earn the world to come in a single hour."

Certainly neither the supposed glamour, nor the nearness of power, had any attraction for me, and you can believe that or not as you choose. In this regard, too, I may have a screw loose, because those inducements seem to animate the entire place. I don't think anybody is more beguiled by the glamour and the power than the President himself. He acts in the Presidency, after four years, as though it's his glittering brand-new birthday bicycle which he adores, and which the big guys will take away from him if he isn't extra wary. It's amazing.

Obviously I won the argument with Jan, because here I am. Jan perceived that this was something I wanted to do; and that my motives, while possibly quixotic, were not unworthy. She spends a lot of time on the phone these days assuring our New York friends that I haven't sold out, or been terrorized into doing this by the FBI, or been thrown out of orbit by the male menopause. I don't care any more, and neither does she. She's beginning to laugh at the whole business. When Jan laughs it's all right.

She knows I've been killing empty office time by writing, and my chat with the President was so odd that I decided to tell her about it before putting it on paper. Her reaction rocked me. I thought the man came out crooked as a worm writhing on a hook; but she flew into a tall rage at me for making him sound so sympathetic. I'll have to think about it some more. If I'm falling under the spell of the President — to me, a ridiculous notion — I want to know it.

Meantime, the big television speech baring all has come and gone. Of the draft the President asked me to write, only a paragraph here and there survived. I expected nothing more. If confusion reigned around here before, we now have unadulterated chaos, for the two ousted German shepherds, as the columnists dubbed them — the chief of staff and the assistant for domestic affairs — had been running everything. Now the press is worrying their corpses on the bloodstained snow with hungry howls and snarls, while the President lashes his sleigh horses to carry him off to safety — if this isn't laboring the image. I don't think of many, and when one comes along I tend to wring it out like a dishrag. Old Peter Quat throws them off thirteen to the dozen, but there's only one Peter Quat.

Incidentally, his new novel is finished and I believe we're all in for some fun. Nobody has yet seen it except his agent. I'll be reading it soon, since I'll be drafting the contract. The agent, a white-haired, corrupt old sinner who has read and done about everything in the sexual line, shakes his head and will disclose nothing, except that "even the title will blow your tits off."

To be honest I feel a bit futile, fumbling on with this attempt of mine at a book, when such a stupendous blockbuster is shortly to detonate upon the world. But many lawyers are frustrated writers. I've been one since I left law school, and I've been enjoying the solitary scrawling in all these free hours here. I once made a sort of living by writing, if you can call a gagman a writer. Last year, laid up with a wrenched back for a while, I started a book about my April House days; about Harry Goldhandler, Bobbie Webb, Peter Quat, and the storms that boiled up in my family; that whole dizzy and dazzling time. Recently I dug it out. It commences too far along, and I'm backtracking to the beginning. There's nothing Presidential cooking at the moment. I can't just sit here in my tomblike office, in the false calm at the eye of the storm, waiting for some frantic dummy in this place to press the wrong button and end the world. So on I go with my book. Mainly I'll tell the truth — with some stretchers, as Huck Finn says, but the truth — and I start this time far, far back, with The Green Cousin.

2

The *Ploika*

WE begin with a stout woman in a Russian blouse and long dark skirt beating up a girl, slapping at her face, her arms, her shoulders, while the girl tries to protect her head and face with her arms; not crying, just covering up like a boxer in trouble. All at once the girl uncovers a very pretty face and counterattacks, battering bang-bang-bang with small fists in her stepmother's face. Stepmother reels back in amazement and pain, shrieking, "Help! Help! She's gone crazy! Help! She's a murderess!" while Mama — because this is going to be my mother, this blonde red-cheeked girl of fifteen or so, with bright angry blue eyes — bats her big cringing stepmother all over the front room and follows her out into the muddy street, still pounding that fat retreating back. Stepmother goes trampling off down the wooden walk between the houses to fetch my grandfather from the synagogue, squealing like a sow chased by dogs, "She's crazy! Help! Sarah Gitta is trying to murder me! Help!"

Mama goes back into the house, shaking all over with joyous shock at her own rash act. From a bedroom, her half sisters and brothers peep in alarm at crazed bloodthirsty Sarah Gitta. Ah, an audience! Mama marches to the table and, feigning great calm, sits down and methodically eats the PLOIKA.

Anyway, that is how Mama tells it. It is the only version of the event that I will ever know. The victor writes the history. The stepmother is gone from the earth, gone from the memory of man, surviving only in this tale. For all I know, she was an angel of patience, a perfect rabbi's wife, the most beloved woman in Minsk. I doubt that; but then I also doubt Mama's version.

Mama has never been easy to get along with. She once picked up a brick and went for a watchman on a Bronx construction job, who slapped my rear to chase me off his lumber pile. I fled blubbering, not hurt but scared. Mom saw it all. She belted the man with the brick, and then called a cop and had him arrested for assault and battery. I went along to the police court as a witness. The judge was sort of baffled by the whole thing, since the accused assailant's head was bloodily bandaged while neither Mama nor I had a scratch on us. After some confused questioning he threw us all out. That is as I dimly remember it; but I recall perfectly my mother's melodramatic cry, as she crashed the brick down on the watchman's head: "How dare you strike my child?"

Let me not ramble, though. Mama is not going to loom large in this story. On the other hand, if not for the ploika incident I would not be here. Occurring when it did, it unquestionably led to Mama's emigration, and hence to the stark fact that I exist. So there we start.

Okay. When you boil milk, as everyone knows, a skin or scum tends to form on top, and that, in Lithuanian Yiddish, is the *ploika*. In childhood I would gag on it. Mama had to remove it from my cocoa; which is how she first came to tell me this story, and I heard it a hundred times. In Minsk, or maybe only in my grandfather's house, this ploika seems to have been the rarest of delicacies. Caviar, truffles, pheasant under glass, white peaches in champagne — mere nothings to that oozy sticky yellow ploika. Mama's stepmother, a rabbi's daughter from the nearby small town of Koidanov, had borne my grandfather several children, and the story is that they always got the ploika and Sarah Gitta never did. This Koidanov harpy not only showed such mean favoritism; she hated and persecuted Mama without cease for being so much prettier and cleverer than her own children. (I quote Mama. She also reports that the town of Koidanov was notorious for the nasty natures of everybody who came from there.)

Well, this ploika business really ate at my mother, and that is the one element in the tale that rings like gold. Nobody deprives my mother of anything without sooner or later regretting it. On this memorable day, it appears that Mama — grown bigger than the Koidanov woman quite realized, and evidently feeling her full fifteen and a half years, and possibly her swelling bust, too — decided by God to boil herself a ploika and eat it. The other children were smaller, and no doubt more entitled to what milk there was in the house; but

Mama was redressing a long injustice. Koidanov caught her at it, ignored the larger issue, and started slapping her around.

"Why did you hit your mother?" my grandfather inquired, upon hurrying home from the synagogue.

"She's not my mother, and I didn't hit her," Mama replied. "I hit her *back*."

And that is how a rabbi's daughter not yet sixteen was allowed and in fact shoved out to set forth for America alone. Mama was beautiful then — a slip of a maiden, all but cut in two at the waist by a corset. I have seen her faded shipboard photograph. I don't know how a poor adolescent lass in remote Minsk managed it, but she really looked like a Gibson Girl: all bustle, bosom, luxuriant hair, and cartwheel hat, leaning on a rail by a life preserver. Some version of the ploika incident must therefore be true. I will say this, if any Russian rabbi's teenage daughter could have done such a bold thing as travel to America by herself, it would be my mother. I talked to her before I accepted this bizarre job, and she opined, "Why not? Say yes! The world belongs to those who dare and do."

3

The Steamship Ticket

Hold it. Now, there is a specimen of the unreliability of memory, of memoirs, and probably of all written history. I am honestly trying to tell the truth here. Yet the fact is — when I stop to think — I never even asked Mama about this job. She uttered that gem another time. We were all in a mountaintop Caribbean hotel, some years ago, my wife and kids, myself, and Mama. In a gross violation of security, my sister Lee had disclosed my vacation plans to Mama, who had instantly phoned and invited herself along.

Well, on this day, on that Caribbean island, it was raining, pouring, a steamy blowy deluge. We feared it might be a hurricane. Still, it was beach time, and my mother wanted me to drive her to the beach. Mama claimed that it was "just a shower," and would pass over. My wife and kids thought it would be insane to venture out in that howling storm, but it was simpler for me to go, and risk being washed into the sea by a flash flood, than to argue with Mama. So off we went in a rented Volvo, slithering in cascading muddy waters down the hairpin turns of that mountainside, Mom and I bouncing about in swimsuits, the thick rain hammering the car like hail. Just about the time we reached the beach, the clouds rolled away and the Caribbean sun blazed out in an azure sky. Mama plodded into the gentle surf of the deserted beach, sat down in the foam in the sunshine, and paddled her legs and arms like a child. "The world belongs to those who dare and do," she said. She was too old and fat and clumsy to swim any more. Maybe I thought of those words years later, when the phone call came that led to this job. I don't know.

Anyhow, it was no simple matter for her to go to America. What about the money for the steamship ticket? Most rabbis in Russia were dirt-poor. Here is how my mother got the ticket, and this will tell you something about Mama, and about the Russian Jewry from which I stem; and above all about my grandfather, who will play quite a role in this chronicle as Zaideh (*Zay*-deh). Mama drops out soon, the sooner the better. She is obtruding herself unbearably, as usual.

Well, then, when a rabbi died in the old country, his pulpit by custom passed to his son or son-in-law. Here in the Goldena Medina, where a temple is apt to give its rabbi a high five-figure contract, complete with house and car and sundry fringe benefits, the trustees naturally interview and hire anybody they please when the incumbent dies or moves on. It is strictly business, like recruiting a football coach. None of that went in Minsk. By marrying Mama's mother, my grandfather had fastened a strong lien on one of the best pulpits in Minsk, the Romanover Synagogue. The eminent Rabbi Yisroel Dovid Mosessohn was occupying it, and since neither of his two sons were rabbis, Zaideh was right in line for his post.

This Reb Yisroel Dovid, the great-grandfather after whom I'm named, was a man of scholarly note. He wrote a book called *Migdal Dovid*, that is, *David's Tower*, a super-supercommentary on *Lips of the Wise*, a supercommentary on Rashi's commentary on the Torah. Not your runaway best-seller, *David's Tower*, but an esteemed rabbinic work published at Reb Yisroel's expense in one edition of seven hundred copies. Mama brought a copy to America as evidence of her high pedigree. I still have it. The pages have gone all brown and brittle with the passing decades, but they are readable. I have browsed in the book, and it is fine stuff if you are into Talmudic subtlety.

Reb Yisroel Dovid usually slept four hours, studying the rest of the night, but while writing his super-supercommentary he cut his sleep allowance to two hours. That was overdoing it. He was mighty weak and unwell at his daughter's wedding; they had to carry him in to the ceremony. So to be cold-blooded about it, things were looking pretty good for Zaideh. However, a flood of learned praise for *David's Tower* restored his father-in-law to blooming and very discouraging health, and Zaideh had to go back to the great Volozhin Yeshiva to resume his studies and wait. Wives of young rabbis in Russia had to expect such pious abandonment, sometimes for years, while their husbands waited for the Angel of Death to scare them up a steady job.

Of Mama's mother I know only one thing; how she happened to wed Zaideh. One Sabbath when Zaideh was a poor young student passing through Minsk, he stayed at Reb Yisroel Dovid's house. My ancestress fell for him hard and let him know it; unseemly, such forwardness in a rabbi's daughter, but it happened. Zaideh was a poor match for the daughter of "David's Tower," the sobriquet by which Reb Yisroel Dovid was widely known. Though a brilliant Talmudist, Zaideh was dead broke; the son of simple devout country tavern-keepers who could scarcely rub two rubles together. Still, my grandmother must have had a touch of Mom in her, for one thing led to another, and a nervous matchmaker brought Zaideh's proposal to "David's Tower." Thundering trouble ensued. Reb Yisroel took the high ground, objecting that Zaideh lacked sufficient command of the Jewish legal code, the *Shulkhan Arukh.*

From that vanished house on Romanoff Street in Minsk, across the gulf of almost a hundred years, across seas and continents, echoes the defiant snap-back of my grandmother to her august father, as our family tradition reports it. "*So? Am I supposed to marry the Shulkhan Arukh?*"

In giving birth to Mama, this doughty shadow died. That retort of hers, passed down in family lore, is the chief testimony that she ever existed. It suffices to bring her to life for me, and perhaps for the reader. Her name was Leah Miriam, "Laya-Mira." My sister Lee, whom you'll meet in due course, bears her Yiddish name.

But we still have to get Mama out of Minsk. We are talking about two hundred rubles for the all-important *shiffskarte,* boat ticket, and how on earth was Zaideh going to lay hands on a fortune like that?

Zaideh burst into my life a stern-faced gray patriarch in his sixties, but that was not the Zaideh of Minsk, who married one rabbi's daughter and then another; nothing but the cream for Zaideh, and with no spacious interval as a widower. He was then a tall burly jolly brown-bearded young stalwart, so my Aunt Sophie has told me, his zest for life utterly undimmed by long immersion in the Talmud. He wanted a woman in the house, obviously, so he married the Koidanov rabbi's daughter; and why not? I never heard Zaideh say a word against the stepmother. He even — I thought — sometimes took a wistful tone about her, but never when Mom was around, that is for sure. And now for the two hundred rubles.

It's clear, I trust, that by marrying two rabbis' daughters, Zaideh had acquired a claim on two pulpits. This sounds great, but there can be too much of a good thing. When the eminent "David's Tower" did die, fairly young, and Zaideh hastened back to Minsk to embrace his fortune with grief condign, he ran into a snag named Reb Yankele.

Reb Yankele had been the rabbi's assistant for years. You have to understand the star system in our old-country religion. A luminary like "David's Tower" would deliver two sermons a year, and give judgments on very knotty legal questions. Otherwise he shed lustre on the congregation by his mere awesome presence, while the assistant rabbi ran things, taught the men the Talmud, decided for housewives whether chickens were kosher or not, and the like. The star rabbi himself meanwhile studied, prayed, meditated, and wrote. Thus Reb Yankele had gained a following, and his faction wanted him to get the vacant post. The Yankele faction argued that Zaideh, as the Koidanov rabbi's son-in-law, was in line for *that* pulpit, wasn't he?

True enough, and Zaideh was in real trouble, but he had an ace in the hole: to wit, Mama. Mama was the synagogue pet, beloved by one and all for her wit and beauty, as she herself explains; and a Mama faction rose to do battle against the Reb Yankele faction. When the fog of war cleared, the Romanover Synagogue had *two* rabbis, in two seats of honor on the eastern wall. Two congregations under one roof! Seems unbelievable, but there you are; and this standoff went on for years.

Then the Koidanov rabbi died.

I suppose Zaideh would have liked to speed off to the Koidanov pulpit, but again he ran into a snag. Few things involving livelihood went smoothly among the Russian Jews; most of them were too hungry, poor, and desperate. There was another son-in-law, a local Koidanov man, who wanted the vacant post. Zaideh had the senior claim, no question. However he was an out-of-towner, and he already had a pulpit — or half a pulpit, anyway — in Minsk. So argued the anti-Zaideh faction in Koidanov. His claims on two posts had in effect left him hanging in the middle.

After some terrible carryings-on, the Koidanov people offered Zaideh two hundred rubles — a handsome settlement in those days, make no mistake — to stay in Minsk and forget the whole thing. As destiny would have it, this offer came hard upon the ploika crisis. Zaideh had already heard his wife's ultimatum about the crazy stepdaughter who had tried to murder her, a formula familiar in many languages, in many contexts: "She goes, or I go."

But sending Sarah Gitta away just anywhere would not have worked. Mama had leverage in that Minsk synagogue, and like Samson, she might have brought Zaideh's whole edifice crashing down, just to bury her stepmother in the ruins. However, Mama said well, yes, she would consent to leave, providing she could go to America. So Zaideh took the Koidanov cash, bought Mama's steamship ticket, and resigned himself to leading half a flock for the rest of his days; for Reb Yankele was a young man, and hardy as a camel.

On the morning of her departure, according to my mother, all was warm sentimental regret. Neighbors and synagogue members gathered to watch the sensational departure of a lone teenage girl for America. Given an audience, Mama seldom fails to deliver. As she walked out the door after the farewell embraces — so she tells me — she turned to Zaideh, and, streaming tears, she cried out, "For the last time, I pass over my father's threshold!" With that, amid great lamentations of all onlookers at this dramatic exit, straight out of Yiddish theatre, she climbed into the wagon waiting to take her to the Brest-Litovsk station; and Mama was off to the Goldena Medina.

It wasn't the last time she crossed that threshold, though. Nobody gets shut of my mother for any two hundred rubles. Koidanov and Zaideh saw her again.

4

Uncle Hyman

Now for my father's departure from Minsk.

Talk about your mobile society; that was something Jewish Minsk was not. My mother and father grew up within a few streets of each other, and never met over there. How could they? She was the granddaughter of the rabbi of the big Romanover Synagogue; he was the son of the humble sexton — the *shammas* — of the small Soldiers' Synagogue on Nikolai Hill. No, they had to uproot themselves, cross an ocean, and meet on a new continent in a new world to engender our hero, I. David Goodkind.

And at this point, I must briefly turn over the narrative to somebody else, my father's younger brother, Uncle Hyman. I will not paraphrase Uncle Hyman's story of the ice-cake episode, a clue to Papa's early yen for America. My uncle tells it better than I can. Uncle Hyman should have been a writer, not a businessman. Many Russian Jews had their talents crushed by poverty and by the Czar's laws which kept them out of the universities, the professions, the big cities, and even out of large sections of the country. That may be why we, their offspring, in the freedom of the Goldena Medina, have tended to be exuberant overachievers. But that is a passing one-generation thing. Our children, American as apple pie, show a healthy and reassuring tendency to dog off.

Uncle Hyman scrawled this account in his late old age, very shortly before he died. I had asked my uncle to write his reminiscences, but not until recently did I find out that he had actually made a start on them. At his funeral, some five years ago, neither Aunt Sophie nor my cousin Harold said anything about it. Aunt Sophie was too weepy and stunned, and Cousin Harold was in bad shape, too. Not from grief, not at all; Harold is a cool customer, a psychoanalyst in Scarsdale, doing a land-office business in unbalanced teenagers. Not much fazes Harold, but he had a hard time with the body of Uncle Hyman.

Uncle Hyman died in Miami, you see, and the whole family lives up north in or around New York. Aunt Sophie and Uncle Hyman owned burial plots in Queens, which they had bought sixty years ago, so Cousin Harold had to fly down from Scarsdale to bring Uncle Hyman's body back for burial in Queens. This was in February. The weather was awful. Harold made it to Florida, but flying back, with Uncle Hyman in the baggage compartment of the plane, they were forced to land in Greensboro, North Carolina, by a blizzard. The airport closed down, all snowed in. There Uncle Hyman sat, or lay, for two whole days. He clearly was past caring, but Cousin Harold wasn't, what with a wailing mother of eighty or so on his hands, who would eat only kosher food — not readily available in the Greensboro airport — and endless telephone calls back and forth with the undertaker and our relatives, putting the funeral off, and on, and off again. Also, Harold had several unusually screwed-up Scarsdale teenagers who had to keep talking to him at all hours. His office gave them the number of a telephone booth in the Greensboro airport, and Harold hardly stirred from that booth for two days except to answer calls of nature. He had skycaps bringing him coffee and sandwiches, newspapers, everything but a chamber pot.

In short, it was a hell of a mess, and so Harold forgot about Uncle Hyman's fragment of reminiscence, which he had found in a manila envelope beside my uncle's deathbed in Miami, addressed to me. It got tumbled into a trunk with a lot of detritus of Uncle Hyman's old age, including Yiddish books that Cousin Harold couldn't read and wouldn't if he could, a collection of 78 r.p.m. records of the cantor Yossele Rosenblatt, a photograph album of Uncle Hyman as a World War I draftee in uniform, and an enormous heap of programs from the East Side Yiddish theatres, which Harold now thinks may be valuable Americana. He's trying to sell them. That's how he happened to go rummaging through the old trunk, five years later; and so he came on the envelope. It arrived in the mail some weeks ago, full of scrawls in a shaky hand on the backs of bills, the blank sides of old circulars, and random sheets of paper of different sizes.

I put the thing aside. If it had not rained like the devil one Sunday, the envelope might have gotten mislaid or buried, and moldered for another five years, or until I died. But it did rain, and I started cleaning my desk, and I came on Uncle Hyman's scrawl, so I read it. Anything rather than clean my desk. That was when I decided to make another start on this book; when I read Uncle Hyman's anecdote of Papa's slide on the ice cake. Why? Well, I'll try to tell you. An old buried awareness surfaced and hit me — hit me very hard — of how much I loved my father, how strongly he influenced me at turning points in my life, and yet how little I really got to know him. Mom has lived on and on, and mainly these days she makes me laugh; though it is a big help that I now live in Georgetown, three hundred miles from Central Park West. The other day I told her on the telephone that I was writing a book. "Good," she said. "Write about me." Fat chance, Mama.

But Uncle Hyman says, quite rightly, that I never truly knew my father. I guess I am searching for him with this story. The clues are there in my memory, and that's why I keep dumping out my recollections helter-skelter in these pages; the way you do when you are frantically searching all your pockets for a mislaid key to your home.

So here we go, down that hill in the vanished Minsk of my father's childhood, that Jewish world of eastern Europe, obliterated like Carthage; here we go, whistling downhill on an ice cake, on the fresh brilliant snow of a Russian winter, past the soldiers' barracks, past the synagogue, straight toward the river, straight toward that broad black hole cut by the peasants in the ice.

Uncle Hyman, you're on.

5

The Ice Cake

I am not endeavoring to write. The following is not an auto-biography . . .

When I open up the book of my memories, I find some pages outstanding in our family history. One such incident made an in-delible mark. The scene comes to me as though it happened yesterday. This is going back more than seventy years . . .

In the recesses of our minds there are indelible events or inci-dents which lie dormant until . . .

UNCLE Hyman backs up and begins again in this way several times. He gets going at last on the backs of pages torn one by one from a calendar. Inspiration evidently struck when no other paper was handy, maybe late at night. I get a picture of him sitting in the little kitchen of his Miami condominium in his bathrobe, scrawling away on ripped-off calendar pages.

One note: Uncle Hyman presumes the reader knows that pious Jews do not work on the Sabbath, kindle fire, or do other workaday acts. That is the premise of the whole story.

It is the 31st of July, 1968. I finally am getting started on what I have meant to write for many, many years. This is the second time I have started. The first was fifteen or more years ago. After work-ing on it for some time, I destroyed all I had written. Of what in-terest would all this be, I thought, to anyone today? In this so swiftly changing world, the lives of people who have gone before us, their ways, their conditions, their beliefs, the heritage they have left us, all seemed to have gone into eternity without attracting any atten-tion, having no practical use in the "new world" that was being built, on new foundations.

But these illusions of a "new world," these air balloons, began to pop, and the past came back to view. I began to hope that some day there would be one in the family who would want to know about his ancestors, what influence they had on the next generation, and what their accomplishments were. And then my nephew David came and asked that I write my memoirs. And so I am sitting down to do it.

The starting point will be the first thing that comes to my memory. It has left an indelible mark. Nothing else comes to me before that time. My father once found a whole treasure of family records, but to everybody's sorrow they were destroyed; all those people, gone forever.

A scene in midwinter. Saturday. Late afternoon, the home where I was born and lived till my departure to the U.S. at seventeen. The place is the city of Minsk, Russia. My home is part of the Soldiers' Shule, just a section of the foyer entrance to the synagogue, partitioned off to make a home for the shammas, my father.

By the end of September the rains grow colder in Minsk with the dropping temperature. About the middle of October the rain turns to snow. The earth freezes, and the snow does not melt any more. A couple of days, and there is enough snow on the ground to discontinue wheeled vehicles and turn to the sleighs. This changeover comes fast, almost at the same time each year. For Minsk is far inland, away from any ocean, or even a sea. The only water in the city is a narrow river, about a hundred feet across, but very deep. It passes the bottom of the street on which our synagogue stands, a very long steep hill. This hill ends in a cross street and the bank of the river.

In winter the river freezes up. The ice runs a foot thick or more. The peasants cut the ice out in cakes, and pack it between layers of straw in their ice houses, deep holes in the ground with little huts over them. The ice then holds through the whole summer. When the peasants are finished with the day's ice cutting, there are always some cakes left. Boys that have no sleighs use these cakes for sleds. It is a daring feat, and some boys even sleigh all the way down the long hill, across the street, and down the bank on to the river. This is extremely dangerous, for there are big holes in the ice left by the peasants. Mainly the boys who do that are well grown, and never Jewish boys, all gentiles.

Now I will describe our home, if one wants to call it that. It was just one room divided by a partition, in which a curtain served as a door. The smaller space had no window and no furniture but a bed where Mother slept. The rest of us, sometimes even my father, slept in the main room on doors taken off their hinges and laid between two chairs. My mother had a feather mattress, a remnant of her dowry, but we all used an old overcoat or anything else to soften the discomfort of bare boards. There was no plumbing. For water, there was a barrel in the synagogue foyer, filled by a water carrier with water drawn from the river; the same river where everyone bathed, where laundry was washed, and all the rain and melting snow from Minsk's streets ran down. An outhouse in the courtyard served everybody, even the worshippers.

The shule was built of logs. The main building was plastered inside, but in our apartment the walls were just the logs. The two small windows had double frames, to keep in as much heat as possible. Right inside the door there stood a big oven reaching almost to the ceiling, which was used for cooking, baking, and heating. Another small fireplace beside it gave extra heat in the winter. Both led into one chimney. Together they formed an L-shaped nook where one could sleep in cold weather, or else just sit there to keep warm.

On Friday afternoon the two fireplaces would be heated up almost to a glow. That evening the house would be warm, even in the coldest winter weather; but by Saturday morning it had already lost the first heat, and with the passing of the day it cooled more and more. The only heat one could feel was by leaning right up against the big oven, and it was not real heat, only warm bricks.

So as I say, the scene is late Saturday afternoon, midwinter. The sun is beginning to set. The lone kerosene lamp which has been burning since Friday is using up the last of the oil, giving but a dim light. I am alone with my mother. Father is next door in the shule, which is full of worshippers and their children. My brothers are there also, playing games with other boys their age. I am too young to be left alone, or perhaps I am tired of playing. So I am in the house with my mother, perhaps dreaming that the Sabbath will soon be over. Father will come in and say, *"Gut vokh,"* a good week. He will take out the *havdala* candle and light it, and let me hold it. (I always liked to watch the havdala flame flare up, trying to light the whole gloomy house.) He will bring out the wine, fill a glass, say the havdala prayer, and let me taste the wine, because I am the youngest. Mother will walk over to the frost-covered windows and rub some moisture on her hands — which you have to do before praying — and she will say the prayers to welcome the oncoming week. Father will fill the lamp and it will burn up bright, spreading light all through the room. He will throw dry logs into the small fireplace and put a light to it. The wood will burn fast and heat will begin to spread again through the house.

All this will be very welcome. But *Shabbess* is still not over, perhaps another half hour before the stars will be seen in the sky. The house is very quiet. Only the voices of the boys going sleigh-riding down the hill, you hear their happy outcries now and then.

I and Mother were sitting close to one another, leaning against the lukewarm oven. Maybe she was telling me stories about her childhood days: the big house she was born in, where everyone had his own room, beautifully furnished, chandeliers with large lamps and hanging crystals reflecting dazzling light everywhere. The house was full of servants who answered all your calls and needs. Mother would go out each day, riding through the countryside in a coach with a team of horses, she said. A few years later, when I visited my aunts and other relatives, I saw they really did live in such big houses and I compared these with our one room with log walls in the foyer of the shule. . . .

So Mother was talking to me, or else we were both sitting quietly, dreaming our dreams. Suddenly the door opened, and my brother Elya came running in with a great cry. After him came my father with a belt in his hand, hitting him and shouting, "My boy sleighing on Shabbess, and on a cake of ice! You, Elya, about to be *bar mitzva*! And to enter as a clerk in Oskar Cohen's lumberyard! You the best choir singer of Reb Mordechai! What will Reb Mordechai say when he hears it?"

With every sentence he belted Elya. They were both crying, and I cried too, and Mama cried. Never had I seen anything like this. It took Mother some time to calm Father down, but then he put his belt away, and went back next door to the shule. My brother Elya, after crying some more, also left for shule. Nothing was ever mentioned about it by my parents afterward. At least not in my presence. Only Mother said that she never before saw my father so excited, or striking one of his children.

As the years passed, and I grew up and began to understand things better, this incident kept coming back to my mind. I kept asking myself what made my father get so aroused? Was it the sin of sleighing on Saturday? I could hardly say so. He was not a fanatic; a believer in tradition, but I cannot imagine him punishing his son so severely for this sin. He would have admonished Elya and that would have hurt him more. No, that was not the reason.

Was it fear of losing his job? He did all the manual work of a shammas, taking care of the place and keeping the building and courtyard in order, also chanting the Torah, the haftoras, and the megillas. My father did not have a strong voice but it was melodious, and he had a great ear for music. There was nothing but praise for his chanting. Still, there were some who were jealous of him and always looking to find fault. Father knew who they were. Perhaps he feared this act of Elya's would stir up a tumult, and cost us our livelihood.

But there was something more. He deeply loved his children. The mere thought of an accident, of Elya getting crushed by a cake of ice which overturned, or skidding into a hole in the ice and drowning, probably threw him into a frenzy. Never again did he strike one of us, for no matter what cause. This was probably the real reason.

Elya only commented on it once, that same night, when we were snuggled down on our boards to go to sleep. He said to me, "I'll show them. I'll go to America."

I was so young I didn't understand. I asked, "Where is America?"

He said, "It is far, far away, across the ocean, and it is a free country, a *Goldena Medina*."

How could I recall such a conversation after so long a lifetime? Yet I remember it all as if it were yesterday. It left an indelible mark.

6

The *Porush*

WELL, that's it. There is a lot more of Uncle Hyman's memoir on lined pages in Aunt Sophie's neat handwriting, which he must have dictated. Actually, his yarn about the fights in the synagogue between Hesele the water carrier and his wife, who had one arm turned backward, might well divert you, but it has nothing to do with the birth of I. David Goodkind. However, the *Porush* does. The Porush takes up a good half of Aunt Sophie's pages, and he got very involved in my father's emigration, so I will just sum up the Porush story. This will shed a little light on Shaya Goodkind the shammas, my other grandfather, whom I never knew; who lived out his life and raised a large family in a log-walled anteroom of the Soldiers' Synagogue in Minsk.

Until I read Uncle Hyman's pages I scarcely thought of myself as having two grandfathers, because Zaideh was such a monumental presence in my life. I don't know what my other grandfather looked like, or how and when he died. He was still alive when Mama went back to Minsk, long before I was born, to cross her father's threshold again. She then met Shaya Goodkind for the first time. So she once told me, adding that her father-in-law was "a nice man." Nothing more. A rabbi's daughter doesn't dwell on her kinship to a shammas, I guess, or on her spouse's origin in a log-walled room.

Now you may well interrupt to ask, how about those reminiscences of my grandmother's? How did a woman from a wealthy family — big house, servants, horses, crystal chandeliers, and all the rest — come to be married to a shammas, and to be living in a log-walled hole? Haven't we said the Russian Jews were poor? Was it all my grandmother's fantasy?

Not in the least. There were a few merchant families that did all right, a very few, and Grandma came from one of those. Grandma had a short leg. A lame girl with a dowry and a pious shammas in a log-walled hole; as old-country matches went, a fair deal. But one thing at a time here. We will get to Grandma soon enough. (I smell the wintergreen odor of liniment, just mentioning her.)

So, about the Porush. When I describe him you may realize, by contrast, how far from a fanatic my grandfather the shammas really was. Otherwise you'll know Shaya only by the glimpse Uncle Hyman gives us, in which he is lashing a child for sliding on an ice cake on the Sabbath; when in truth, from the little I know, Shaya Goodkind had as sweet a nature as any man ever had. Now the Porush was something else. There was a fanatic, a type from the Old Country!

You have to understand what a Porush was. A Porush separated himself from all worldly concerns, to devote himself to holy studies. This Porush was the real thing. He slept on a bench in the synagogue. He lived on crusts and water. He was a wisp, a wraith, a dim bearded scarecrow. Uncle Hyman gives no details of who he was or how he came to be haunting the Soldiers' Shule in Minsk. He was there, and he was the Porush. He studied the Talmud by a window as long as there was daylight, then he lit a candle and studied till exhaustion stretched him on a bench. When he woke long before dawn from this wretched repose, so hard on his fleshless bones, he lit the candle and studied again.

Since God has said that it is not good for a man to be alone, the Porush had a wife; and since the Sabbath is a time for material enjoyments, even for a Porush — not to mention the clear commandment, "Be fruitful and multiply" — he would leave the synagogue Friday afternoon, spend the night at home, and come back Saturday to resume his studies. So, with one thing and another, he had four children. His wife, frantic with poverty, would sometimes break into the synagogue and create scandals, compared to which the scenes between Hesele the water carrier and his wife with the arm turned backward were mere billings and cooings. Apparently her reproaches just rolled off the Porush's back; I'm not sure he even quit studying while she was berating him.

Shaya the shammas held none of this against the Porush. In that lost world a Porush was a familiar, even an admired, figure. Still, some minor traits of this holy layman were vexatious. For instance, he would instruct people on points of religious law; which, Uncle Hyman points out, only an ordained rabbi has a right to do. Then there was his concern over his mental purity. He was ever on guard against impure thoughts, but this was a losing battle. Setting aside his human weakness and imperfection, the fact is that the Talmud is full of sex; quite naturally, since it takes all human experience as its domain. The Talmud on sex is wise, broad-minded, and to tell the truth, goddamned explicit; so the poor Porush was between a rock and a hard place, trying to plow through the Talmud and avoid impure thoughts.

Now whenever he did have an impure thought, what he would do was rush over to the font and wash his hands. The font was not capacious, and remember, the synagogue had no plumbing. If the Porush hit a hot page in the Talmud, he could empty that font in an hour. The font was the shammas's responsibility. My grandfather had to go to the big barrel in the foyer which Hesele the water carrier kept full, draw more water, lug it into the shule, and fill up the font. The worshippers assembled twice daily, and washed their hands before prayers. It was worth the shammas's job for the font to go dry. So all in all, there was a little bad blood between the shammas and the Porush over this matter of the Porush's mental purity.

Yet my other grandfather never asked the Porush to take his business elsewhere, but put up with him. Such was Shaya Goodkind, my shammas forebear on my father's side. I don't regard it as such a humble background. I lack Mama's condescending view of a shammas, being half shammas myself, so to speak.

"*Porush*," incidentally, is a Hebrew word meaning *dedicated, separated, ascetic*. In the New Testament it is transliterated "Pharisee."

Papa left Minsk in a big hurry. He had to.

Under the Czar, as I've mentioned, Jews were pariahs penned into small outlying provinces, shut out of cities, universities, professions, and the government, but the Czar conferred two inestimable privileges of citizens on Jews: paying taxes, and getting drafted. Nor was this any eighteen-month hitch, my young readers. You could be in for twenty years. You could be sent to Vladivostok or Novaya Zemlya in the frozen north, or to Sevastopol or Baku in the steamy south. All those years you might never see another Jewish face. As for diet, two choices: you could eat what the prophet Isaiah picturesquely calls "the swine, the abomination, and the mouse," or you could starve.

The Jewish soldiers in the Minsk barracks were in that respect very lucky, for the local Jews fed them. Nowadays when so many enlightened Jews eat the swine, the abomination, and the mouse without batting an eye, this diet problem may seem trivial, but to these old-world Jewish youths their religion was a life-or-death thing. So the call to the colors, all in all, rather failed to stir their manly blood quite as Czar Nicholas hoped.

When my father got his draft notice, all was confusion in the house of the Goodkinds. The family resolved on a desperate ruse. Papa's older brother Yehuda had been exempted from military service. Never mind why. The fact is I don't know why, and nobody is now alive who will tell me why, but it all turned on that. The idea was to hide Yehuda, pass Papa off as "Yehuda," show Yehuda's exemption papers, and tell the police that young Elya was out of town. Then Pop would obtain money for a steamship ticket one way or another, and go over the hill to America. Once he was safely away, the real Yehuda would surface, and the family would take whatever rap was forthcoming. No matter what, the shammas's son was not about to eat the swine, the abomination, and the mouse for the greater glory of the Czar of all the Russias; who, by the way, had just then been shellacked by the Japanese, so serving him was not only uninspiring but dangerous.

We skip enormous patches of the story here — the false Yehuda being marched to the police station, insisting he wasn't Elya, the whole family following to back him up, and so forth — to get to the Porush. Russian officials could hardly tell one Jew from another, so I don't know why the draft officer became suspicious, but he did. He brought Papa back home, the family trailing along, and dragged him inside the synagogue, empty except for the Porush, who as ever stood by a window murmuring over his Talmud volume. The Russian police knew of the Porush. They were superstitious about their own holy men, and they had the word that this Jewish anchorite haunted the Soldiers' Shule. Catastrophe! Nobody had thought of priming the Porush about the substitution, a fearful oversight. But would priming have worked, anyway? Who could get a Porush to lie, even to a Czarist policeman?

Straight up to the Porush the draft officer pulled my father. The family — and by now a mob of ghetto onlookers — came crowding in behind. It was high drama, on the brink of tragedy. Draft fraud was a grimly serious crime.

"What's this fellow's name?" the policeman barked at the Porush.

The holy man chanted and swayed over his Talmud, unheeding. The officer laid a hand on him. "*Starets* (holy man), what is this fellow's name, I asked you!"

The Porush glanced around at him, at the trembling family, at the white-faced mob behind them, and at Pop. "You mean Yehuda?" he inquired in Russian offhand, as though it was the silliest of questions, and he resumed murmuring and weaving.

That is just how it happened, according to Papa. The nonplussed draft officer gave up. The Porush never referred to the incident afterward. Nobody ever found out why or how he was inspired to answer that way. I volunteer to explain. The Russian officer, the quaking family, the pale young man, the scared and fascinated onlookers, must have made a clear picture. To rescue Pop with a planted lie might have been beyond the Porush; but did he lie? Not at all. He just asked the policeman a question: "You mean Yehuda?"

Okay, okay. You'll hoot at such rabbinic hairsplitting. You'll say his question was the most quick-witted sort of misleading response. Look! Through that split hair I marched into existence, as the children of Israel once marched into freedom through the split Red Sea. Don't run down rabbinic logic to I. David Goodkind.

Now then. Where could a shammas's son get two hundred rubles for a steamship ticket to America, in one hell of a hurry? I don't mind telling you. Pop was the straightest man I ever knew, but he took that money from the till of the lumberyard where he was a trusted stock clerk. The proprietor, the old Jew named Oskar Cohen, was neither a giver nor a lender. Pop always intended to pay Oskar Cohen back, and he did, with interest; but when he proposed to Mama he hadn't begun to, out of his meager wages. All that comes later. What comes next is myself, and high time.

7

My Name

M Y sister Lee is a quite a character, but she will have to write her own book. She was born first. And fast. Nobody says that she was premature, exactly, yet she did arrive three weeks early, reckoning back from her birthday to my parents' wedding date. I worked out this embarrassing piece of higher mathematics when I was thirteen or so. When I mentioned it to Lee, while she was washing and I was drying the Sabbath afternoon dishes, she commented, "Oh, shut your big stupid mouth." Lee was then seventeen, and in a bristly frame of mind.

Zaideh had arrived and was living with us, you see. As a first order of business, he had required installed, on the main switch of our apartment, a timer which on Friday night blacked out all lights at half past ten. This was so that nobody would switch off lights by hand. Electric lights were not known in Talmudic times, but the nineteenth-century rabbis had proven quite equal to this wonderful development. They ruled that electricity was just a form of fire and forbidden on the Sabbath. No problem.

But Friday night was Lee's big night for entertaining boy friends in the parlor. The sudden blackout at ten-thirty should have encouraged romance, you would think, but it did not work out that way. It scared her cavaliers out of their socks. Lee would not warn them in advance; I suppose, because she was embarrassed by such quaint goings-on in her home. Later on I will get into the curious religious adjustments of my family to the Goldena Medina. We lived what I would call a supersaturated Jewish life, but it was still news to Lee and me, when Zaideh showed up, that light switches on Friday night were taboo. Yet Goldena Medina or no, Mom and Pop were not going to contradict Zaideh about the timer.

Well, Lee took it hard. She is now a gray grandmother past sixty, but she can still get hot under the collar recalling those Friday night blackouts. She will snap and snarl on and on about Zaideh's timer, especially if she is once again trying to quit smoking, when she tends to rake up old grievances. (Two packs a day is Lee's habit. She is nevertheless healthy as a horse.) Not one of those Bronx Jewish swains, it appears, ever had the presence of mind to grope his way to Lee and get a little action in the sudden dark. No, they fumbled and stumbled to the front door as fast as they could, every one of them, ran downstairs as though devils were after them, and never returned. So Lee tells it. I should mention that Lee married a perfectly fine doctor from Port Chester, New York. She owes gratitude to Zaideh, and should stop grousing about the timer after fifty years. Those Bronx types she attracted, all sweaty hands and rampant pimples, were going nowhere.

Like Uncle Hyman, I too have an indelible first memory. I am swinging back and forth on the little iron door next to the kitchen window, behind which Mama puts the garbage pail. It is the cold time of year, so the window box outside holds the milk, eggs, butter, and such. The window is open, and I am just deciding to reach for the milk, when a terrifying din starts up out there: whistles, gongs, auto horns, sirens. It sounds like the end of the world. I shout at my mother in fright, "What is that?"

"The war is over," she says, not stopping her work at the sink. In my earliest memories Mama is fixed at a kitchen sink in the Bronx, peeling or washing something: an immortal posture, like the Marines raising the flag on Iwo Jima.

World War I ended on November 11, 1918. I was born on March 15, 1915. Three and a half years old, I was by no means as precociously retentive as Uncle Hyman. In a part of the fragment I didn't quote, he asserts that when the ice-cake episode occurred, he was only two and a half. I asked my mother about that. She had never heard of the ice-cake affair, questioned Uncle Hyman's dates, and scoffed at the idea that my father would have threatened to go to America. "It's all Hyman's nonsense," she said. "The whole thing never happened. Papa was too sensible to go sliding on an ice cake, and if he did, Hyman wouldn't remember. Hyman couldn't remember what day of the week it was. He was a dreamer. Maybe he dreamed this. He would have liked to see Papa beat up. Papa was the smart one."

Well, there you are. The past, especially the past of immigrant Americans, is fog. Clutch at it and it wisps through your fingers.

I have just read my chapter this far. Lee's early arrival on the scene is a curiosity, I hasten to note, and nothing more. Hanky-panky between my mother and father was inconceivable. Mama has never forgotten for one hour that she is a rabbi's daughter, the granddaughter of Reb Yisroel Dovid Mosessohn, author of *David's Tower,* who in turn descended from the *Minsker Godol;* literally, "The Great One of Minsk." The Minsker Godol was a rabbi of olden times renowned all over Russia for his wonder-working grave. I know Mama secretly thinks that I am a reincarnation of the Minsker Godol. My present job confirms that, for her. Maybe I am, for that matter, but I will have to cure the blind from my grave, or something equally conclusive, to prove it. What I am doing above ground doesn't qualify me — not yet — as the Georgetown Godol.

Mama read *David Copperfield* during her pregnancy, and decided that I would be a great writer. This I daresay was before I came to reincarnate the Minsker Godol. She was assuming, of course, that I would be a boy, and not another misfire like my sister. One grievance Lee really harps on is that her birth was nothing but a stage wait in our family before the grand entrance of myself. That is perfectly true. I was aware of it as soon as I was aware of anything. Lee's anecdotes of our childhood all turn on how I upstaged her, crowded her out, got the best of everything; that is, when she is not fuming about Zaideh's timer, or Grandma's blue spells, or the clambake. I will get to the clambake, but right now there is this matter of my name.

Not a complicated point, you might think; but you would be wrong.

To begin with, every Jew who has ever stepped into a synagogue or temple knows that we have two names: the outside name with which we go through life, and the inside name, the Jewish name, used in blessings and Torah call-ups, marriage and divorce ceremonies, and on tombstones. No shammas or sexton, even in the most Reformed of Reform temples, has ever summoned me to the Torah as "Mr. I. David Goodkind." Unthinkable. I am "Reb Yisroel Dovid ben Eliyahu." We usually are named in Hebrew after relatives who have passed on; then the parents try to find some outside name that will at least have the same first letter.

It is a far-drifted Jew who has forgotten his or her inside name. There are plenty of those nowadays in the Goldena Medina, and rabbis have taken to figuring backward from the outside names, by guesswork. So for the marrying or the burying, Mark becomes Moshe, and Gail becomes Gitta, and Peter becomes Pinchas, and everyone hopes for the best. Lately biblical names have regained some Christian chic, so, among us also, one encounters more Judahs and Sarahs and Josephs; in which case the inside and outside names merge, and there is one less acculturation problem for the harassed modern rabbi.

But my birth certificate reads "Israel David Goodkind," and no fooling around; no Ira, no Darrell, none of that acculturation stuff. Between *David Copperfield* and *David's Tower*, there was no way Mama wasn't going to call me David; and so Israel slipped in there too. A time bomb, as it turned out. Until I went to public school, where the bomb went off, I was just Yisroelke at home; that is, "Little Israel." The Frankenthal kids in the next door flat called me Davey, because whenever Mom talked to Mrs. Frankenthal I was "my David." Mama tried to remember to call me that in the house, too, but whenever any serious business was afoot, like dinner time or some discovered mischief, it was always "Yisroelke!"

I can hardly remember my father calling me David. I was Yisroelke to him first to last. I rushed to his hospital bedside after his heart attack, from the Army Air Corps school where I was getting officer training, right before Pearl Harbor. Mama was already there, trying not to cry. He gave me a smile that I still carry in my heart and whispered, *"Ut is Yisroelke, der Amerikaner offizier."* ("Here's Little Israel, the American officer.") His English was good though heavily accented; but he tended to talk Yiddish when tired or beset. I took his limp damp hand, and he got out a few more hoarse whispered words. *"Nu, mein offizier, zye a mentsch."* ("Well, my officer, be a man.") He was dropping off to sleep under sedation. Those were the last words I ever heard from him. I was not there when he died.

Still trying, Pop. Time's getting short, and it's uphill all the way, but I'm trying. You fooled me, making it look so easy.

* * *

8

The Partners

I HAVE to break off here, with my father on his deathbed, and the story not yet started; a strange way to tell it, but I'm writing it as it comes.

When I was describing Cousin Harold's adventures with Uncle Hyman's cadaver, some pages back, an under-secretary of State called me. I jumped clear out of my chair to grab the telephone. It had been days since I had done anything here but pass the hours scrawling. In spirit I was far away, at that funeral parlor. I was about to describe how the officiating rabbi, a smooth-shaven young divine who apparently worked there on a job-lot basis, puzzled all of us by eulogizing Uncle Hyman's extraordinary achievements as a dental surgeon. He was talking about the corpse in the next chapel, where the mourners were just starting to gather. One of the long-faced undertakers in tan satin skullcaps had to sidle up and mutter at him. This rabbi, a fast man with a eulogy, switched smooth as butter to a fine flowery improvisation on the social value of the dry-goods business. I didn't write that funeral scene because the phone call broke my train of thought.

Anyway, this under-secretary and I are now about to meet with the Israeli ambassador; agenda, the latest debate in the UN on Israel. I don't know what we'll accomplish. There's *always* a debate in the UN on Israel, and the vote always goes against Israel a hundred and seventy-nine or so to one or two. Stark Samuel Beckett elementalism. Reduce the drama to one solitary figure in a desperate, seemingly hopeless predicament, surviving by the sheer indestructibility of the human spirit. Yes, and didn't old Jimmy Joyce know what he was doing, when he made Ulysses one lonely little Jew amid the teeming hostile Irish of Dublin?

I was about to get to my father's start in America, and his two partners from Minsk in the laundry business. So as soon as I return to my story, on come the clowns.

* * *

REUBEN BRODOFSKY was short, stout, and sallow, with heavy hair parted in the middle, a thick grizzled mustache, and a narrow-eyed way of peering around as though looking for pickpockets; or for the cops, after picking some pockets himself. At age four I was deeply suspicious of Reuben Brodofsky. I was a wise child, as you will learn. Brodofsky had an American-born wife, quite a catch for a greenhorn. This Yankee spouse was a stout jolly woman, who sat around cutting serial novels out of ladies' magazines. Her apartment was piled high with stapled-up novels by Peter B. Kyne, Kathleen Norris, and Octavus Roy Cohen, under layers of dust; because as Mrs. Brodofsky liked to say, she didn't believe in housework.

This heresy thrilled and charmed my sister Lee when she first heard it. Lee rushed home and announced to my mother, "Mrs. Brodofsky doesn't believe in housework." My mother, a lunatic housecleaner, gave a loud sniff through a wrinkled nose, and I seem to remember her saying, "That's why, when you walk out of her house, you leave footprints on the sidewalk." I liked the easygoing fat lady, and her perpetual magazine clipping seemed no stranger to me than my mother's everlasting scrubbing of floors on her hands and knees. The Brodofsky children, three boys and a girl, fascinated me. They would come home from school and cook up whole meals for themselves from whatever was in the icebox, and give me some, while their mother sat clipping and stapling a *Cosmopolitan* serial. If there was nothing to cook they would eat bread with mustard. I thought that was ever so much more exciting than bread and butter, though now I wonder why they used mustard. Maybe Mrs. Brodofsky didn't believe in butter, either.

Brodofsky, like my parents, came from Minsk to Manhattan's Lower East Side, where he got a job in a small laundry, collecting and delivering bundles in a hand cart. Sidney Gross, the other partner, worked there, too.

Sidney Gross was very tall, very thin, very pale, and very hopeless. His pessimism about the laundry business, about his health, about the whole future was bottomless. Penury and fatal illness were ever-present in his mind. Sidney Gross outlived my father, outlived Brodofsky (who lived forever), and died rich, for he saved all his money and kept buying Bronx apartment houses. He smoked more than Lee does, but it never spoiled his fine baritone voice. He sang in the synagogue choir which my father led. Gross was courting a cousin of Mama's, my Aunt Ida, when Mama first came to the Goldena Medina. It was through Gross that my parents met. My father and Gross at the time were laborers in the same laundry; and one evening, at a café on Attorney Street, Gross introduced Pop to Aunt Ida's pretty cousin. His therefore was the hand of fate. Sidney Gross, and nobody else, turned the key that opened the golden door of existence to the nativity of I. David Goodkind; or, the Return of the Minsker Godol.

Gross ironed shirts. All his life long he was one of the world's great shirt-ironers. The Fairy Laundry grew in time into a three-story cement structure with a huge brick smokestack, covering a square block in the Bronx, and Gross was one of the three bosses. Yet he was only happy there showing one of the scores of perspiring girls at the presses how to iron a shirt. I saw him do it. This man had a deep mastery of shirt-ironing; it was his ruling passion, his Tao. He could do nothing else, except sing and smoke; and he knew it, and was never at ease as a boss. Hence perhaps his pessimism. I think he always feared being unmasked as just a shirt-ironer, and broken to the ranks. I also suspect he might secretly have liked that.

By the time my father came to America — eighteen years old, penniless, knowing no English — Brodofsky and Gross were Yankee Doodles. They could talk to policemen and streetcar conductors, and Brodofsky was even seeing a stout Jewish girl who had been born in America, or at least in Newark. My father had known Brodofsky in Minsk, so he too landed in that laundry; and so he met Gross, and so he met Mama. That is the story.

Pop started as a "marker-and-assorter"; that is, he undid the bags of soiled smelly wash, inked identifying numbers on each item, and threw them into piles or bins: shirts here, sheets there, ladies' drawers elsewhere. He did this for sixteen hours a day, in a damp cellar lit by one electric bulb, at the bottom of a chute. He did it for two years. That was his start in the Goldena Medina. Times were bad. It was do that or beg, or eat at some Jewish charity kitchen, so he marked and assorted at two dollars a week until times got better. There were no toilets in the cellar, and the proprietor did not allow the marker-and-assorter to waste time coming upstairs, not for a whole year. That year wreaked havoc on my father's insides. Brodofsky and Gross worked up on the street floor at five dollars a week. My father did not envy them their vast salaries, only their access to a john.

Reuben Brodofsky founded the Fairy Laundry, by supplying the hundred fifty dollars for the down payment on a washing machine, a mangle, and a press. That is undeniable. A hundred he had saved; the fat Newark girl's dowry furnished the other fifty. That cleaned out Brodofsky. Sidney Gross from his savings paid the rent of the little store on Attorney Street for the first year. My father was taken in as a partner, though he had no money. In lieu of capital investment, he worked for nothing. How long, I do not know. How he ate, I do not know. Possibly Brodofsky and Gross fed him. In the snapshots of Pop at that time that survive, he looks bushy-haired, fiery-eyed, and proud, but pitifully skinny and sleepless. The prints are in old-time violet ink, and under his eyes are deep purple pools. This spell of labor without pay for Brodofsky and Gross I believe puts Pop up there with Oliver Twist, as one of the great undernourished figures of literature. But at twenty, what can a man not endure?

The name "Fairy Laundry" came with the move of the enterprise to the Bronx. There used to be a Fairy Soap, a white perfumed oval cake, sold in a blue box with a little girl's picture on the cover, and the slogan, "Do you have a little Fairy in your home?" I believe that is where the partners got the name. Alas, by the time I was eleven, "fairy" had acquired a new meaning. I tried to keep it quiet that my father was part owner of the Fairy Laundry; but whatever neighborhood we moved to, and we were much on the move, the word always got out and caused me grief. Later, in boys' camp theatricals, I was cast in female roles, because of my soprano voice and genteel ways, and between that and the Fairy Laundry . . . well, I draw a curtain over those ancient horrors.

By the time the business moved to the Bronx, Papa was boss man. I don't write this out of fondness or pride. That he burned out his bright brief candle in the laundry business is a tragedy about which I'd prefer to be silent. He would have been good at anything. Given his rudimentary schooling, his uprooting, the chance that threw him in with Brodofsky and Gross, and the financial pressure on immi-

grants, he lived and died a laundryman. Investors often begged him
to drop the partners, leave the Fairy Laundry, and start a new large-
scale plant. I heard Mama urging him to accept one of these offers.

"What would Brodofsky and Gross do?" he said. "They would
starve."

"Are they your children?" said Mama. "Your brothers?"

"Sarah Gitta, you're just talking. Gross is married to Ida. He's family. If I can't drop him, how can I drop Brodofsky?"

"But they're dragging you down. They're killing you."

"They took me into the business," said Papa. "When Yisroelke grows
up, maybe we'll see."

That was it. In his own mind, he never did work off the hundred
dollars he didn't have when the thing started. In Brodofsky's mind,
Pop stole the Fairy Laundry from him, and his grandiose vision was
that some day, somehow he would regain his domain from the usurper.
As for Sidney Gross, he knew he could iron a shirt better than Pop.
I suppose that took care of his self-esteem.

Both partners came to my father's funeral, and went out with the
cortege to the graveside service. The rabbi had scarcely finished his
closing prayer when Brodofsky leaped at a shovel and threw the first
dirt into the grave on Papa's wooden coffin, thud thud thud, one
heaping shovelful after the other. I had to wrest the shovel from his
hand to throw some in myself. The family is supposed to do that;
there is nothing in the ritual about partners throwing earth on the
coffin. That was just Brodofsky's eagerness to pay his respects to the
dead.

At a business meeting right after the funeral, which I attended in
my Air Corps uniform, I learned that my mother was in danger of
being voted out of her widow's pension, due to incredibly tangled
bank loans and stock redistributions forced on my father by the
depression. This meeting took place in Mama's apartment, where we
were sitting around on mourning stools.

"I never voot against you, Sarah Gitta, dunt voory," said Brodofsky. His wife's Newark speech had not rubbed off on him in all the
years. "I never, never, never voot against you, dunt voory." He kept
repeating that.

Brodofsky did voot against Mama. He got Gross to voot against
her, too. Mama fought back and licked them; she didn't do it with

a brick, but she might as well have. "Don't let them spit in your kasha," was her word at times. Brodofsky wasn't man enough to spit in Mama's kasha, as it turned out. No way.

But all that is nearly forty years down the road.

9

The Green Cousin

MAYBE it was a dumb thing to do, but I took this manuscript to New York last Thursday (I went with the Israeli ambassador to the General Assembly meeting, though that's neither here nor there), and I read it to Mama. She smiled, now and then laughed, and sometimes looked pensive. She can't see to read any more, and she can hardly hear, and she creeps around on a cane, but there's nothing wrong with her head.

"Have I got the facts right, Mom?"

"Yes." Very disappointed tone.

"What's the matter?"

Pause. Sad headshake. "It's so *brief.*"

I might have known.

Look, just bear in mind, Mama, you were born well before the Wright brothers flew at Kitty Hawk. It's now four years since Neil Armstrong set foot on the moon, and here you still are. You're spanning the craziest, most crowded, most tragic, most incredible, most glorious, most dangerous stretch of years in the history of the world; a time so mad and risky and speeded-up that nobody can say that the curtain won't drop on both of us, on the whole wild show, in the next forty-eight hours. Literally! When I think about what I've already seen at the White House — when I contemplate the brute truth that the rope of the final curtain is really in those hands — I shake. I don't sleep. I get diarrhea. I've shut it from mind; which is only what the whole idiot world is doing, instead of applying some common sense to saving our skins while there's still time. Clearly, if I don't whiz through this tale I may not finish it while anyone is still left

alive to print and read books. So I will go right on being brief, Mama.
I must.

Still, I know — I could tell by Mama's look — what was troubling
her. I left out her courtship. Well, I did that on purpose. It would
make a book in itself, that romance of Alex Goodkind and Sarah Gitta
Levitan, or *The Green Cousin,* as the little circle of young Minsk Jews
dubbed Mama, when she showed up among them on New York's
Lower East Side. Her sad, "It's so brief" haunts me, so I'll put in at
this point, as baldly as possible, the story of The Green Cousin's
courtship.

This is for Mama, and for the world of her young love that is no
more; a small wreath that I toss from the Brooklyn Bridge, as it were,
to float down the East River, which still laves the place where it all
happened; where little is left of those rich years, and those lively crowds
of Jews, but boarded-up synagogues, failing kosher delicatessens, and
the decaying buildings of the Workmen's Circle and the *Jewish Daily
Forward;* where gray ghostly employees still sit around in dusty offices, drinking tea and talking disconsolate Yiddish.

When Mama first came to the Goldena Medina she roomed with
Reb Mendel Apkowitz, a former Minsk neighbor of Zaideh's, who
ran a furniture store in Brooklyn. I remember Reb Mendel well, a
genial gray-mustached old Jew with a swarm of smart sons. As I grew
up there seemed to be among my parents' friends a platoon of burly
doctors and dentists, all looking alike and all named Apkowitz. I had
my first tooth drilled, in fact, by Murray Apkowitz. Mama reports
that all the sons fell in love with her and proposed except Herman,
the stupid Apkowitz who flunked out of dental school and got a job
delivering chewing gum to vending machines, and collecting the
pennies. The family was ashamed of Herman. You didn't talk of
chewing gum around the Apkowitzes. But Herman ended up in the
jukebox business, stinking rich, with the laugh on all those doctors
and dentists.

To proceed, Mom met Pop through the *Kruzhok,* which you might
freely translate as the Circle or the Bunch, this crowd of young immigrant Minskers who hung out together. Sidney Gross brought her
into the Bunch at the Attorney Street café, where they would sit around
drinking tea and talking to all hours. Pop didn't propose for two years.

They then waited another year and a half to marry. Such was the courtship of The Green Cousin.

Pop's two-year hesitancy before asking for her hand has always been a puzzle to me. Not to Mom. She was the great beauty of the Kruzhok, she patiently explains, and of course frostily chaste. And she was also the big *yoxenta,* or girl of pedigree, descended from the great *David's Tower.* (More precisely, that's *yach*-sen-ta; but the guttural *ch* never comes off in English, so forget it.) The masculine term is *yoxen,* but believe me, that evokes not one-tenth the glamour, the worth, the sheer class of yoxenta. Pedigree was a feminine asset in the Bunch, like a beautiful bosom, and as with a bosom, there was no acquiring it, you either had it or you were out of luck. In Mom's photographs of the time you see her well fixed with both — the bosom by inspection, the pedigree by her bearing. Even in those blurry sepia prints the girl is all queenly yoxenta.

As a pearl of such great price, Mama points out, she naturally overawed my father. That was why he took his time about proposing. Meanwhile, several other young fellows in the Bunch wanted her, but she brushed them off. Alex Goodkind, also called Elya and Elitchka, was the promising one, the clever one, a joker, a singer, a delightful reader of Yiddish poetry and Sholem Aleichem's short stories, altogether the live wire of the crowd. Mama will say, with an incongruous touch of girlish coyness on her wrinkled old face, that from the start she had her eye on him, but she never gave him the *slightest hint.* Not she! Not the granddaughter of *David's Tower!*

So it was two years before he nerved himself to make his move. By then the Bunch was pairing off left and right. At one of the weddings where the wine flowed free my father finally girded up his loins, drew near, and so addressed my mother: "Well, Green Cousin! *Halevai af dir!*" (Roughly, "May you be next!")

Mom shot back saucily, "My blessers should be blessed!"

He proposed that night, and won the inestimable privilege of riding back to Brooklyn on the subway with the big yoxenta. He then had to lay out another nickel to return to his lair in the Bronx, some two hours away by BMT and IRT express. No doubt, to him, that night, those rumbling rattling subway cars were clouds of glory. You know the feeling. It doesn't matter too much at that moment in life whether you're in a Rolls-Royce or the IRT. Mom says my father was the first man who ever kissed her. I believe that, too.

In later years, Pop would account for one or another of Mom's odd ways by shrugging and saying to me in Yiddish, "Always remember, she's a rabbi's a daughter." *A* rabbi's *a* daughter, you will please observe. The reiteration of that little *a* had vast force. When I once asked him why he took so long to propose, he shrugged, smiled a far-off melancholy smile, and replied, "Well, you know, *a* rabbi's *a* daughter." Pop left a lot unsaid, waiting for me to mature, or something. I'm doing the same with my own sons and daughter, I realize.

Papa lived in a hole in the North Bronx that cost him almost nothing. The Bunch gathered on the Lower East Side on Saturday and Sunday nights. On holidays they would all go to Central Park to row on the lake, or to Coney Island, something like that. Their evenings sped by in talking politics and literature, singing Russian and Yiddish songs, going to the Yiddish or Broadway theatre, dancing, flirting, reciting, entertaining each other, sometimes into the dawn. They were young and merry in the Goldena Medina, out from under Czarist tyranny, cut loose from the rigid religious rules and social strata of Minsk Jewry, at home in the mushroom Yiddish civilization that had sprung up around Canal Street at the foot of the Williamsburg Bridge. When my mother talks of those times, her weak voice rings with a cracked echo of that long-gone joy of life, and I swear I envy her. Poor as rats, working sixteen hours a day, six days a week for a couple of dollars, riding the subways an hour or more each way to work or to fun, they lived lives vibrant with a hope of happiness in a new world of liberty. I've had most of the good things in life, including many things Mom and Pop never enjoyed, but a Bunch I never had, because I was never young in a new land, newly set free.

All the same, that was a damned long subway ride for Pop from Flatbush to the Bronx, once the first raptures had subsided, and that one goodnight kiss which — I don't know, but I bet — the big yoxenta allotted him, ceased to be quite such an explosive and celestial novelty. Soon he was pressing her to name a day. Her loving response was to inquire into his finances. Did he have enough money, for instance, to buy a bed, a mattress, a table, and two chairs? He did not. They added their bank accounts together. Still not enough.

"What," said Mama, "will two corpses go dancing?" She has a way of putting things sometimes. When Pop suggested getting a loan she vetoed that, loud and clear. No borrowing! Next, having noted Papa's happy-go-lucky ways with money (in that regard he never changed much), she inquired whether in fact he had any debts. Well, Pop told her about his emergency borrowing from the till of the lumberyard; made a clean breast of the whole thing to Mama, who then and there laid down the law. They would save up together and pay back Oskar Cohen every last ruble. Then they would save up and buy furniture. Then they would get married.

Hence the year and half delay after he proposed. Mama so far yielded to Pop's amorous importunities, and to his bone-deep weariness with two-hour subway rides, that she consented to buy furniture from Reb Mendel Apkowitz on credit, after paying down half the cost — no less, she insisted. A full fifty percent down before the crunching of glass at a wedding.

A year and a half! Eighteen months of young love foregone! Why? To pay back a prosperous old skinflint in Minsk who had long since written off the debt, and probably forgiven it; for young Alex had been a mainstay of the lumberyard office, and all Russian Jews understood about the draft. And to put down half the price of a bed, a mattress, a table, and two chairs!

A rabbi's a daughter. A big yoxenta.

She did something even stranger and rougher than that to Pop. My sister Lee arrived on the scene; you'll recall, a bare eight months into their wedded bliss. No sooner had Lee been weaned, than Mama picked up baby and baggage and went back to Minsk for a year. That is a most obscure business, and whenever I press Mom to explain, she comes up with some non sequitur like, "Yes, Papa was a wonderful man. He understood."

Maybe he did. I don't. It happened, and it almost resulted in cancelling the Minsker Godol's return for unknowable generations, because my mother was nearly caught in Russia by the First World War. She got out by a whisker, another terrific adventure, but that one I will skip. Enough! She made it, and I got born. But why did she go to Minsk? Possibly to cause the Koidanov woman to drop dead. There is no doubt that her stepmother did die shortly after Mom's visit to Russia.

Mom arrived in Minsk, you see, with a smashing American wardrobe, most of which she had sewn herself, but Koidanov didn't know that, and Mom wasn't letting on. The baby, I am told, had a wardrobe to match, the swaddlings of a princess. Mom's luggage, her millinery, her jewelry, were all American, all dazzling, all electrifying, to the neighbors who had seen the teenage Sarah Gitta tearfully depart six years earlier, an outcast stepdaughter setting forth into the great world penniless and alone.

By then, what is more, the Fairy Laundry was launched and doing relatively well, so Mama also brought money with her and gave it all to Zaideh. *Dollars!* Moreover, Oskar Cohen had already spread far and wide the tale of Alex Goodkind's refund of his borrowing, with six percent interest. The word was out in Minsk that Sarah Gitta Levitan had struck it rich with Alex Goodkind, the son of Shaya, the Soldiers' Shule shammas; and that Alex was becoming a big American industrialist. As I write this, it gets clearer and clearer why Mama went back to Minsk. Zaideh was always vague about the cause of Koidanov's demise, but I do believe that she choked on her own bile, exactly as Mama planned. It was a bit hard on young Elitchka Goodkind, that bachelor year or so early in his marriage; but Mama had to settle that ploika business, and by God did she ever. La Koidanov had spat in the wrong girl's kasha.

During this bizarre mission to Minsk, Mama also managed to reconcile Zaideh to her marriage with a shammas's son. Zaideh had sent many fiery letters forbidding the misalliance. Mama had returned indignant reams praising her choice as a learned, religious, altogether silken Jewish lad, quite worthy of a big yoxenta's hand. She wrote a short last note flatly announcing to Zaideh that she was marrying Pop, and asking Zaideh's blessing. His response was grumpy, his blessing on the curt side.

But Mom knew what she was about. Once she got back to Minsk, those American clothes, those American dollars, Mama's own Americanized yet very Yiddish self, and the enchanting baby Lee — Leonore, inside name Leah-Mira, after Mom's mother, Zaideh's long-dead first love — quite won him over. He even called on the shammas's family in their log-walled abode, invited the humble Goodkinds to the rabbinic residence, and wrote Pop a cordial letter about these visits. Zaideh was eventually pretty pleased with his son-in-law.

In her letters, as you may have guessed, Mama was shading the facts about Pop's piety. She was a girl in love. The Jewish immigrants had a saying, "When the boat is halfway to America, throw overboard your prayer shawl and phylacteries." To some, this meant a release from a galling yoke; to others, a sad yielding to the facts of the new world. In America in those days, you worked on Saturday or you didn't eat. For those old-country Jews, once the holy Sabbath went, the entire hoary structure tended to collapse. Some stalwarts like Reb Mendel Apkowitz fought the tide and kept the faith, all down the line. But lurid stories of new world impiety were rife in the old country. Some zealots called the Goldena Medina by another name: "Wicked America." This discouraged very few Russian Jews who could raise the steamship fare. Plenty of the zealots, even, were willing to chance the wickedness for a shot at the gold and the freedom. They found out soon enough that the streets weren't paved with gold. But the freedom was real. You made of it what you would.

Mom and Pop never got around to the swine and the mouse. They did have a sort of brush with the abomination, as I will report when we get to the clambake. Still, from my earliest moments, I not only knew that I was Jewish; I understood that this meant everything to them. The first music I remember hearing was the High Holy Day liturgy, which Pop would sing as he dressed and shaved, before setting off to the Fairy Laundry; and I can still sing most of his Yom Kippur service by heart. On the whole Mom and Pop did all right with this knotty business. Once Zaideh came, that was that. You couldn't have told our household from Reb Mendel Apkowitz's.

But the Jewish thing from the start was inside the walls. Outside, breathlessly awaiting the appearance of I. David Goodkind, was the Goldena Medina, or Wicked America.

10

Paul Frankenthal

M Y first encounter on the outside was Paul Frankenthal. He wasn't very far outside. We lived in Apartment 5-D and the Frankenthals in 5-A, on the top floor of a tenement house on Aldus Street, in the Southeast Bronx.

How did Mama cope with the hazard of small children loose in a fifth-floor flat? Keeping the windows shut was no answer. Mama believed in fresh air, and anyway in the summertime we would all have choked. No, what Mama did when we moved in was to take Lee and then myself by the ankles, hold us one by one outside a window head-down, and let us scream and wriggle in terror for a good while at the sight of the drop to the concrete yard five stories below. That did it. I have no recollection of this strong medicine, I have only Mama's word for it, but I believe her. To this day I can't lean out of an open window without getting a queasy feeling which locates itself very insistently in my scrotum. Joyce writes of the "scrotum-tightening" sea. A high window has it all over the sea in my book for scrotum-tightening, but then I have this singular background.

At some point Mama took me to the nearest public school, where Lee already was in the second or third grade, and enrolled me in the kindergarten, lying about my age with the blandest good conscience. Mom had no patience with this goyish foolishness of waiting until the Minsker Godol was six before starting him in school. I could already sound out Hebrew sentences, and she figured public school would be my meat. In fact, I had a rapid ascent, which turned into a horror not unlike hanging out of a high window by the ankles. The principal scrotum-tightener in this matter was Paul Frankenthal, and that is his entrance cue.

I can't remember not knowing Paul Frankenthal. I close my eyes and there we are sitting by a window in the Frankenthal flat, Paul, Lee, and I playing casino while a furious summer thunderstorm *c-r-r-racks* and crashes and rages outside on Aldus Street. Jagged blue-white lightning makes me wince, rain lashes the tenements opposite us, and on the sidewalk far below gray stars splash up in myriads. The bright colors of the cards, the flat-faced kings, queens, and knaves, the joker in his yellow and red hunting costume, fascinate me. No cards in our apartment! Mama in her latter days became a terror of the Miami Beach canasta set, but at that time she retained "*a* rabbi's *a* daughter's" objection to playing cards. Vulgar. The Frankenthals lived in the front. Our apartment looked out at the back yards, where tall bare poles supported five stories of clotheslines. You would wake in the morning to the squeak of clothesline pulleys. From the Frankenthals' windows you could see cars and people going by, a more interesting view than wet sheets, shirts, and union suits multitudinously flapping.

I may be doing Paul an injustice by attributing to him the memorable first beating I got. Still, I don't think it would have occurred to me on my own to go playing doctor with the girl in Apartment 5-C. I was four, and not that much interested in girls. Her mother caught me examining her bare behind as she lay prone on her bed, little skirt up, little pants down. A scandalized caterwauling broke out, a horde of adults came trampling into 5-C, and I was summarily removed to Apartment 5-D; where Mama then and there did her best, using my father's razor strop, to whomp voyeurism out of her jewel.

Instead, she beat into me the perception that there is something both marvellous and forbidden about a girl's bare behind. That is strictly true, to be sure; but she was rushing matters, pressing the point at my tender age. Now, I distinctly recall Paul Frankenthal among those invading adults. Question: what was he doing there? My guess is that he set me up and then sandbagged me, thus establishing the theme and tone of our long relationship. Possibly not. He did me enough damage later, and I will waive this count as not proved. To Mama's credit, she never told the story to Pop; not to my knowledge. I watched his face closely for the next couple of days. I'd have known, if he found out.

In the silent-film serials of my childhood, the bad guy could be spotted straight off by his mustache. Take Mr. Deering, the bad guy who pursued Pearl White through fifteen episodes of *Plunder,* trying to get the map for the diamond mine away from her. What a monster! What a mustache! Paul Frankenthal's father looked a lot like Mr. Deering, and he had exactly the same style of mustache: thick, slick, black, pointy. Later on, Paul too grew a Mr. Deering mustache, and in point of fact he landed in the pokey like his father, and for the same reason: kickbacks and whatnot in the construction game. Yet at the outset Paul was a sort of hero to me, and to most of the boys and girls in our neighborhood.

When Faile Street had a rock-throwing fight with Hoe Avenue, for instance, Paul was right up front, heaving and ducking stones, while I manned the far rear. Faile Street meant nothing to me, nor had I anything against Hoe Avenue. Our tenement was near Faile Street, and this accident of geography obliged us to show up on the field of honor, a vacant lot between Faile and Hoe, to show our manhood, or boyhood. The neighborhood girls flocked to watch, you see. The battle station I selected was fairly close to the girls. Any Hoe type who beaned me at that range would have had a throwing arm worth money in later life. I wasn't a conspicuous coward, the Faile Street rear was crowded with cannon fodder of weak convictions, but I was no Paul Frankenthal, either. My sister Lee admired the hell out of Paul for his valor, and talked on and on about the rock fight afterward until I was sick of it.

To my best recollection nobody — I mean not one combatant — was injured in that fight. Nobody fell. Nobody even bled. Not in the large rear clump of the hesitant, not in the hardier midfield boys yelling, ducking, and scurrying about, not even up front among the few like Frankenthal. A huge hubbub, a lot of stones flung randomly — such was juvenile combat in those days of the Bronx's lost innocence, before the ethnic gangs made a serious bloody business of it. A born street boy, Frankenthal perceived that a show of dash in rock fighting was a high-yield, low-risk activity. I wouldn't have acted on this insight if it had occurred to me, and I take nothing away from Paul

Frankenthal; but his subsequent swagger did not rest on a very broad base of exposure to death, and it riled me that this fact escaped my sister.

On the whole, I will call Paul the first of the villains in this epic. Like Iago, like Uriah Heep, like Richard the Third, like most of the heavies in literature, Paul Frankenthal was of a jealous and envious disposition, and therefore determined on villainy. He inherited the trait from his mother. Mrs. Frankenthal comes and goes in this story like Rosencrantz or Guildenstern, but this is her moment, and she can have her own short chapter.

11

The Glories of Starving

THE Frankenthals had more money than we did, right to the moment when Frankenthal père went up the river, leaving his family to wait for him in a fine private house off the Grand Concourse. So what on earth did Mrs. Frankenthal have to be envious about? She was a pretty woman with shiny dark eyes, curly black hair, and a nice white-toothed smile. However, she was no yoxenta, and the man with the mustache was no yoxen. Maybe that was it. There was an absence of breeding about the Frankenthals. Paul Frankenthal drank coffee. My sister Lee and I obeyed the doggerel rule Mama had taught us,

> *M is for milk*
> *And you should drink plenty*
> *But not tea or coffee*
> *Before you are twenty.*

But Mrs. Frankenthal just across the hall tried to tempt me, leading to my second memorable beating.

We were in her kitchen, Mrs. Frankenthal and I. Paul came in, panting from running up five flights of stairs, sweaty and thirsty. She offered him milk. "With coffee," Paul ordered. His mother gave it to him, half and half. Paul drank it off, eyeing me with contemptuous triumph, and out he swaggered, back to his street game, full of that rich tan abomination.

Mrs. Frankenthal offered me milk. I accepted. Cookie. I accepted. A white-toothed smile. "Coffee in your milk?"

"No, thanks, Mrs. Frankenthal."

"Paul likes it."

"I'm not allowed."

"Oh. Well, bring your milk and cookie to the parlor."

I followed her into the front room with the street view, carrying the milk and a lovely marshmallow-filled chocolate cookie out of a box. I could get these only at the Frankenthals', which may be why I was hanging around that kitchen. Mama baked her own cookies. Store-bought cookies were bad for your teeth, and anyway might have lard in them. I was rapidly learning not to worry about abominations where candy or cookies were involved. Wicked America.

"So, your mother is very strict about coffee," said Mrs. Frankenthal, settling down beside me on a long soft sofa.

"Oh, yes."

"Just about coffee?"

"Oh, no. Also tea."

"Really! About other things, too?"

"Sure. About lots and lots of other things."

"What else are you not allowed to have, David?" inquired Mrs. Frankenthal, smiling like Grandma in Little Red Riding Hood.

Locking my fingers behind my head — something I had seen grown men do — I leaned back in the corner of the sofa and proceeded to tell Mrs. Frankenthal all about the austerity of the Goodkind household. My main point was that Mom starved us to improve our characters. Mrs. Frankenthal kept mentioning various foods and beverages, and I kept saying that why no, we couldn't have that, or that, or *that;* and at each forbidden item she grew more humble and impressed at Mom's moral grandeur. How exalting it felt to sit there, leaning back with my hands behind my head, fascinating this adult with every word!

"And does your mother let you eat bread?"

"Well, maybe one slice a week."

"Really! One slice of bread a week! You're sure? No more?"

"Sure. Sometimes not even that."

The whaling I got afterward has sort of blotted many details from memory. Yet to this day — and the thing happened fifty years ago — if I happen to catch myself leaning back and locking my hands behind my head, a warning red light flashes in my brain, and a hollow computer voice intones, "You are about to make an asshole of yourself." So the beating clearly took hold. But it did not catch up with me at once. I played all day outside. Only when Lee came to fetch me did I gather that trouble was afoot.

Lee still complains, by the way, white-haired and arthritic as she is, that it was a rotten imposition on her to have to go out every night to fetch me home for supper. "Day-veed! Day-veed!" she would scream all over the neighborhood, she says, and in the back yards, and in the vacant lots, sometimes for an hour. She gives me a pain, Lee does, with her hoarded ancient grudges. That one is ridiculous. I was at home and ravenous for dinner most nights, long before Pop returned from the Fairy Laundry. Lee thrives on her grudges; I guess they generate adrenaline, which is good for her arthritis, and it's free, unlike cortisone, which costs like the devil. At any rate, on this occasion she didn't have to come far. I was sitting right there on the stone stoop of our Aldus Street tenement, talking to the other kids. With a funny look, Lee said, not that it was supper time (we called dinner "supper" until we moved to Manhattan), but just that Mama wanted me.

Well, I trudged up those five flights of narrow stairs sensing that I was in for it somehow. I found Mama at the kitchen sink in great wrath.

"*Yisroelke!*"

"Yes, Mama?"

"Mrs. Lessing told me that you told Mrs. Frankenthal that I starve you."

(Oh, *God.*)

"She did?"

"*One* slice of bread a week. *One slice!* Is that what you told Mrs. Frankenthal? Is it or isn't it?" Thus Mama, glaring at me from the sink, and continuing to peel or slice or wash something. She seldom wasted time, and could stage a heavy emotional scene while picking the eyes out of a potato. Mrs. Frankenthal, it developed, had spent the day spreading the story of the starving Goodkind children through all five stories of the tenement; and over into the house next door, where dwelled Mrs. Lessing, one of Mama's old friends from the Bunch.

Well, I had to admit it. Nor could I plead that I'd been bamboozled, by Red Riding Hood's grandmother next door, into believing I was praising my mother. I didn't understand this myself. I was just trapped. Childhood is a sequence of such traps, basic training in the dreary facts of life.

"Why did you lie like that? Why are you always telling such big lies? Don't you know what happens to liars? Don't you get plenty to eat in this house? Just wait till Papa hears!"

"Mom, please don't tell Papa."

But when my father came home he was recruited by Mom to wallop me for the crime of telling lies. Young as I was, and much as it hurt when Pop struck me, I could see that he was suffering more. He went through the beating as though he himself were being flogged. It was the ice-cake episode, reprised a generation later. We Goodkind men are not built to hit our kids. I can't bear to think of the one time I struck my daughter Sandra, and as for my sons — well, to hell with all that. I crawled off crushed and bawling to the davenport in the parlor, which Lee and I would unfold and sleep in at night. There I lay down on the cold imitation leather to weep myself out. Soon Lee came and laid a hand on my shoulder. I looked at her. She was offering me, half-concealed in her palm, a chocolate-covered marshmallow cookie.

It was one of Lee's great moments. I would have understood her gloating over my disaster. Instead this offering, and the soft look that went with it, and the wetness of her eyes, told me much about what a sister is; much, in fact, about the feminine heart. It made up for the snowstorm episode, my one dimly persisting grudge against my sister, and it revealed that Lee too was bending the rule against outside cookies. I divined that Paul, not his mother, must have given Lee the cookie, and that instead of devouring it instantly like any rational person, she had saved it, from some grotesque girlish motive.

And as I sat up, much comforted, drying my eyes and wolfing the cookie, while Lee noisily set the supper table in the kitchen, and Pop and Mom talked as usual in there about the Fairy Laundry, my mind cleared, and I realized that I had been unjustly drubbed. Sure, I had lied. But hadn't an adult gulled me into it? Mama wasn't all that upset about the lie, *she just didn't like being made to look silly by Mrs. Frankenthal.* The lady in 5-A had done the big yoxenta in the eye, and she had ordered my father to take it out on me. It was that simple. Why, it was on the level of the bickering between Lee and myself! My tail still warmly throbbed from poor Pop's open-handed whacks, but I found myself feeling sorry for him, and resentfully superior to my mother. I had gotten a lot older in one day.

Now for the snowstorm story. I've never once thrown it up to Lee. I've not forgotten it, either.

I was in the first grade, and Lee in the third or fourth, in a school about ten blocks from home. We would walk there in the morning together. On this day the weather looked bad, so Mama gave Lee an umbrella. Of course I tumultuously demanded an umbrella, too, but there was only one in the house. All the way to school Lee flourished the umbrella, and kept talking about it, and said she felt raindrops though the sun had come out, and she opened it, and complained that I was crowding her under it, and altogether made an unbearable nuisance of herself about the umbrella. I resolved that, one way or another, I'd get hold of that umbrella to walk home with, or die.

The weather worsened during the morning. It began to snow. Early in the afternoon a wonderful announcement: school cancelled! Nickels distributed by the teachers, *free for everybody,* for carfare home on the trolleys! By this time a gale was blowing, the snow was whirling down thick and white, and it lay piled on the streets. In the line of bundled-up kids at the trolley stop I encountered Lee with Paul Frankenthal, and he was eating an unkosher hot dog, which cost a nickel. I'm not making any of this up, I can see Frankenthal standing there just as plain in his snow-flecked plaid jacket, gobbling that hot dog from the vendor's cart. And Lee is giving me some complicated story about how he has lost his nickel; and wouldn't I like to walk home with the umbrella, and lend Paul the carfare? Then he'd pay it back, and I'd have a whole nickel to spend.

You can argue that I was a fool to make the deal. But she was my big sister, wasn't she? Oh, she assured me, what fun walking home with the umbrella would be! Why, there I'd be under it, no snow would fall on me, and all that. So I said okay, we did a swap, Lee and Paul boarded the lamplit trolley, and off I marched into the white storm with the umbrella.

Well, I was blown this way and that by the wild wind, staggering and tacking on the slippery sidewalk, hanging on for dear life to that black round mainsail with both hands; until a gust whirled me clear around, and in an eyeblink turned the umbrella twanging inside out. It was just as well, otherwise I might have sailed up in the air like Mary Poppins. I struggled to put the umbrella right, but the wind tore it clear out of my hands and it fluttered off upward, into the sky and out of this story, and there I was about eight long blocks from home, trudging head-down through a blizzard in a foot or more of snow, amid drifts taller than myself.

The going was easier without the umbrella. I plowed along, sinking deep into fresh snow with every step, rather enjoying the huge footprints I was making; only, getting colder and wearier and not much closer to home. Soon I was making not footprints but round holes in the snow, since with each step I went in up to my thighs. I became a bit scared. A blue twilight was descending, and the street lamps in the snowfall, mere lines of blurry yellow haloes, confused me. I was getting drowsy, too, from the fatigue of pulling up one leg and the other, and plunging them up to my hip sockets in chilling snow. I decided to lie down on a snowbank and rest; rather a mistake, if you know your Arctic narratives, which I didn't.

There in that snowbank, half-covered with freshly fallen snow, I was found by a Fairy Laundry wagon driver, Jake the drunk. He woke me with a shake, and a blast of breath like ignited Sterno. It was black dark. Jake picked me up, put me into the wagon, with its familiar mixed smell of horse manure and dirty laundry, and brought me home. Such rejoicing! Pop, Mr. Brodofsky, and all the drivers had been out looking for me, and the police had been called. I was given tea with rum to drink, stripped, and put into a hot tub. During the welcoming commotion, while Mama was mixing the tea and rum, and Papa was pouring a second slug for Jake the drunk, Lee managed to whisper to me, "Don't say anything about the umbrella." My parents had asked Lee plenty of questions, and she had improvised a cock-and-bull story which a word from me could have shattered.

Now I admit I was a chronic pain in the neck to Lee; a blatant competitor, a shameless upstager. I took for granted the extra petting and treats I got just for being "my David," as Mama knew nothing of impartiality. If Lee had taken an ax to me, it would have been an understandable bit of testiness. Yet at least I did not tattle on Lee; not then and very seldom, if at all; and there was much occasion to do so, for mendacity came naturally to Lee. It may be in the nature of the female predicament; Bobbie Webb was probably as big a liar as I ever knew. We will come to that, but meantime we move beyond Aldus Street and the Frankenthals, to the very matrix of my long destiny: the *Mishpokha*.

12

The Tribe

BY now I hope you've grasped that in this tale *inside* and *outside* don't merely mean Jewish and non-Jewish. Nothing that simple. Paul Frankenthal was Jewish. So was the little girl who bared her behind for medical evaluation. So was almost everybody in that neighborhood, aside from teachers like Miss Regan, Miss Dickson, and Miss Connelly, who were of course aliens from outer space. In our little street gang Paul Frankenthal spoke of non-Jews as "Krishts." He knew obscene songs and jokes about Krishts which at first baffled me, because I didn't even know what they referred to, so encompassingly Jewish was our part of the Bronx.

The old neighborhood is now a desert of abandoned burned-out tenements. Hoe Avenue and Faile Street look like wartime Stalingrad. Of the hundreds of synagogues which dotted the South Bronx in those days, only one survives: the Minsker Congregation, founded by my father and a very religious man named Morris Elfenbein. They just about financed the start-up between them. Elfenbein was the haggling giant of the Lower East Side clothing district, before he made his mark in West Bronx real estate. In due course I must tell you all about Elfenbein and the Purple Suit, a combat adventure right up there with Jason and the Golden Fleece. Anyway, as a small boy I laid the cornerstone of that shule, slapping on the plaster with a gilded trowel engraved with my name, which Mama still has somewhere in a closet. I went up there last year after the shule was vandalized again, and talked to the cops, and gave my Aunt Ray money for heavy iron grates on the windows and doors. So far, she says, they're holding.

Aunt Ray has the key to the synagogue. She lives in the one inhabited building in a long burned-out row, where the black glassless windows stare at you like eyes in skulls. Every Saturday morning Aunt Ray creeps to the shule and opens it for the ten or twelve old Jews who chance getting mugged and come tottering to pray. We'll have a scene or two in the Minsker Shule's heyday, but first you have to meet my *Mishpokha*. (There's the old unspellable guttural, the Indian "ugh" sound with no English equivalent. Call it mish-*pugh*-a, and you've about got it.) The word is classical Hebrew, taken over into Yiddish, and what does it mean exactly? Well, let's have a look right now, shall we, in my big *Lexicon of the Old Testament*, edited by the Reverends Brown, Driver, and Briggs? Here is how the Reverends define *Mishpokha:*

> 1. CLAN. Family connexion of individuals.
>   In a loose popular sense, TRIBE.
>   In a wider sense, people, nation.

Okay for Brown, Driver, and Briggs, Krisht lexicographers! Right on.

Our Mishpokha had settled in the South and East Bronx, with outposts in Brooklyn and New Jersey. The tribe comprised Papa's Goodkinds and Mama's Levitans, with all sorts and conditions of cousins, uncles, aunts, and in-laws. When Zaideh came over, bringing Koidanov's daughter Faiga, that activated a whole new connection of Koidanov kin, whom Zaideh, a total Mishpokha man, quickly tracked down. A far-flung tribe, with the Bronx as its base, its new Minsk.

In the Bronx, close by, were the families of Uncle Hyman and Uncle Yehuda. Pop had brought both his brothers over and set them up in business. Uncle Hyman limped through life in a dry-goods store, but Yehuda never quite got the hang of Goldena Medina commerce. He started out with a music shop, selling victrolas, records, and sheet music; a thing I never understood, since Uncle Hyman was the music lover, while Uncle Yehuda cared no more than a clam about music. Moreover, Yehuda was a low-spirited misanthrope, unsuited to retail business. He even had a Mr. Deering mustache. Customers sensed that besides knowing nothing whatever about music, Yehuda disliked people, and wished they would leave him alone. So they did. You never saw a place as deserted as Uncle Yehuda's music store. It was spooky, those rows and rows of dusty new victrolas, those neat stacks of unsold records and music sheets, and in a corner behind the counter on a stool, Uncle Yehuda glowering at his vacant emporium and stroking his mustache, as though plotting a new scheme to bilk Pearl White of the diamond mine.

Yehuda married a fetching American-born girl, Aunt Rosie. It was a lightning match. They met, fell in love, and wedded, all within two weeks after Uncle Yehuda opened the store. Rosie had no pedigree, she was irreligious, she was penniless, she didn't work — so Mama reports — but she certainly was an eyeful. Mama never liked Aunt Rosie. This Rosie happened into the music store a few days after it opened. She saw the array of shiny victrolas with which my father had staked Yehuda by borrowing from a bank, and she figured that Yehuda must be rolling in money. So she cast a hook for the surly greenhorn and hauled him in, no sweat. Marry in haste, you know; Aunt Rosie had plenty of leisure to contemplate those unmoving victrolas, those untouched stacks of Caruso and Galli-Curci records, and to perceive that she had been had.

By a transference that your friendly neighborhood psychoanalyst can perhaps explain to you, Rosie's reaction was to conceive a deep animosity, not for her husband Yehuda, but for my father. She couldn't forgive him for all those misleading victrolas. Yehuda she more or less ignored for the rest of her life. They are still together, Rosie and Yehuda, shuffling past each other in a Miami flat. After a long period as a Yankee-Doodle atheist Yehuda has turned religious. Whenever I encounter him at tribal bar mitzvas or weddings, he pours hot scorn on the evil ways of Wicked America. Aunt Rosie goes right on eating the swine, the abomination, and the mouse, seeing no reason to change her infidel ways because of her husband's nutty regression, as she regards it. Uncle Yehuda (his outside name, by the way, is Gerald) has got himself a milk pot and a meat pot, cooks his own food, eats off paper plates, and spends most of his time in a little storefront synagogue as a shammas. Full circle for Uncle Yehuda. Not an ideal couple, but there they are, still yoked after fifty-nine years.

Well, that music store failed; then a dry-cleaning store failed; then a hardware store failed. On the rare occasions when Yehuda did get hold of money, says Mama, he at once put it on Aunt Rosie's back in the form of a fur. Mama asserts that Aunt Rosie had a fur scarf, a fur jacket, and a fur coat years before she had any fur at all. Possibly an exaggeration; then again, it could account for the three children they had. As I reconstruct it, my father would borrow money from the bank and put Yehuda into business; Yehuda would gradually sell off the stock at a loss, living on the proceeds and meantime jollying up Aunt Rosie with another fur. When the collapse came this process would begin again in another enterprise, and Aunt Rosie meantime would have another kid.

About the time Pop brought over Zaideh and Aunt Faiga, a costly business, Yehuda failed once more, this time I think in bathroom fixtures. He had a great idea for a new start in costume jewelry, and wanted another grubstake from Pop. Mom put her foot down; no more furs for Aunt Rosie out of Pop's earnings! My father took Yehuda to the bank, and had Yehuda borrow the money himself, on a series of promissory notes. But Pop had to guarantee the notes, so it all worked out just as before. Yehuda regularly defaulted, and Pop regularly paid the notes plus interest. As a matter of form the bank each time requested payment from Uncle Yehuda first, and Yehuda took this as the most incredible affront, and all my father's fault.

Pop had made it to America, in my uncle's view, only by impersonating him so as to dodge the Czar's draft. If not for his, Yehuda's, military exemption, Pop might still have been in uniform, eating pork in Novaya Zemlya or Omsk, if indeed he would have survived the World War at all. Yehuda was his deliverer, his savior. How then could Pop allow a goyish bank to pester him with nonsense about promissory notes?

Uncle Yehuda had a point, but actually he had not suffered much after Pop's escape from Minsk. The end of that story is that when Yehuda cautiously surfaced, the draft officer accepted a five-ruble bribe to forget the whole thing. After all, the bird had flown. I once asked Uncle Yehuda why in fact he had been exempted from the Russian army. He flew into an incomprehensible rage, raving about victrolas, pork, and promissory notes. I have never raised the topic again, and it has to remain a missing element.

Anyway, Yehuda's dudgeon reached such a pitch that he and Aunt Rosie moved to Washington Heights, breaking all diplomatic relations with the bank and with Papa. After that we saw them rarely. At my son Alexander's bar mitzva, about thirty years later, Rosie was crooked with a spinal affliction, they were both white-haired, and Yehuda had gotten religion. He cross-examined our caterer's headwaiter fiercely and loudly about the after-dinner cookies, and refused to eat them, shouting that they had either butter or lard in them, I forget which. Pop had been dead by then for almost twenty years, but Mom was on hand. She gave Yehuda holy hell, and at last he grudgingly ate seven or eight cookies.

A move away from certain Bronx neighborhoods, in short, meant a break with the tribe; almost total, as in Yehuda's case, and real enough when we ourselves moved to Manhattan. For the "inside," as I look back on my childhood and youth, was the family, the tribe, the Mishpokha. You might or might not like some of them; you might infinitely prefer the company of one or another outsider; but the Mishpokha had a blood claim on you. To some extent this still works. I am writing this book only because I recently went up to Scarsdale for the circumcision of Cousin Harold's second grandson. I hadn't seen Harold since Uncle Hyman's funeral five years ago. He mentioned that he had found that envelope, I asked him to send it to me, and here I am scrawling away.

That was, by the by, the first circumcision of any son or grandson of Harold. Cousin Harold is very down on the Jewish religion. Not only does he never step inside a temple; he hasn't given a dollar to the United Jewish Appeal or any other Jewish charity. He told me that at the circumcision, with what seemed to be pride in his own cool common sense. He did not mind when two of his three children married non-Jews. Yet at this same circumcision Cousin Harold wept during the Hebrew blessings, and then got drunk and sang many Yiddish songs, capering about and snapping his fingers like Zero Mostel in *Fiddler on the Roof,* lavender satin skullcap askew, tears streaming down his usually expressionless face. Afterward Cousin Harold explained that he is emotionally labile, and Jewish ceremonies and music affect him that way, but it doesn't mean anything.

In truth I suspect I am responsible for Cousin Harold's disaffection from things Jewish. He ascribes it to early reading of Mencken, and then to his profession; a Freudian analyst, he explains, can no more believe in "that stuff" than in leprechauns. Still, he does not discourage his patients from adhering to Jewish religious fantasies, if these — as he puts it — make them feel more "comfortable." Such is his pitch, all very detached and rational. But I think Harold's godlessness really traces to his bar mitzva, and to the awful part I played in it, which soon I must reluctantly confess.

Cousin Harold and I were very close when we were young, and an early bond between us was our shared loathing of a certain green soup, what you might call the Mishpokha soup. Tribal custom required incessant visiting back and forth among the relatives. Not for fun, or to transact business, or out of love. We just did it, riding in my father's Ford for long distances, or walking to nearby Mishpokha homes. For us kids it meant long stupefying waits for the adults to finish blithering in Yiddish and get to the green soup: a cloudy bile-colored fluid, with chopped sour grass floating in it. It had a Russian name like a harsh sneeze — *shchav,* I think — and it was the usual table treat for these gatherings of the clan. Cousin Harold and I vied in making ghastly faces at each other over this old-country delicacy.

Then we took to sneaking out when it was getting to be greensoup time. By that time the adult parlay in Yiddish would be well under way, with everybody shouting at once, a usual cheery mode of Mishpokha chats. We could go and come without being missed. Once outside, we would produce what coins we had — pennies, a nickel, seldom as much as a dime — and we would buy a cream pastry or a bag of candy and divide it up. The Bronx had a red-fronted candy store or a white-fronted pastry shop, so it now seems to me, on every block. By the time we got back, the green-soup menace would, with luck, be past.

Being almost of an age, and living only a few blocks apart, Cousin Harold and I were drawn into a companionship that lasted long after Paul Frankenthal had sunk into the oblivion from which memory now keeps dragging him. Frankenthal doesn't figure in the main story, but he certainly mattered at the start. In his disclosure of what the big guys did in the lots, he also revealed himself for what he was: the first true herald of the Outside.

13

The Outside — or, What the Big Guys Did in the Lots

You might call the big guys the samurai of Aldus Street. Some were older brothers of boys in our gang. To the big guys, fourteen or fifteen years old, we kids were like grasshoppers. They would stand on the corners on warm nights, smoking cigarettes and kidding the big girls. Some days they would preempt the gutter for a rough ball game, and we would get out of their way. The caste system based on age in city streets is real grist for sociologists; possibly already worked up on federal grants, the reports stacked in the Government Printing Office like Uncle Yehuda's unsold Caruso records. Anyway, what the big guys did in the lots was abuse themselves.

Now at that time I knew no more of sex than I did of Planck's constant. I had a sister, we slept in one davenport and bathed separately, and I was aware of my body's singularities; however, Mom and Pop were extremely modest and prudish. Nothing was said in our household of sexual matters. I was occasionally attracted to girls (I've got to tell you about Rosalind Katz, at least, before we leave the Bronx) but I was truly innocent. I did not know where babies came from, and it was no burning question. I was much more interested in where my next ice-cream cone was coming from.

Paul Frankenthal fixed all that.

I see the scene before me as though I were looking at a movie. It is a twilit scene on Aldus Street, Sabbath eve, Friday night. When Papa enters he will be in his best suit and hat, which means that he is coming home from the synagogue, but the memory replay commences before he appears. We kids are not sitting on the stone stoop as usual, but huddling to one side of it in the shadows, around a metal pipe that projects from the sidewalk. I am resting a foot on the pipe. Don't ask me why I remember that, but I'll remember it till I die. Probably we're off the stoop because some girls are sitting there, and this is strictly man talk, the first I have ever heard.

Paul Frankenthal is telling us with total sneering authority where babies really come from. He crushes our shocked skepticism by disclosing that he has watched what the big guys do in the lots. The big guys have told him that this is how babies are made. The big guys go through motions which Paul describes in some detail, and which sound to me like very grubby foolishness, and after a while, says Paul, this "greenish-white" stuff comes out of them, and that's what makes the babies. Your pa sticks his dicky boy in your ma, see, and shoots this stuff into the hole that your mother pees from. That's how it all happens. That is Paul Frankenthal's revelation. We are all the result of our fathers defiling our mothers, by excreting into them.

At this point Papa appears through the twilight in his Sabbath best. "Suppertime, Yisroelke," he says affectionately, illumined by the lamp over the stoop, and he mounts the steps. "Coming upstairs?"

Scraping my foot on the pipe, I reply in a sort of strangled voice, "Coming in a minute, Papa."

Something makes him pause under the lamp, and look down over the metal rail at the huddle of boys in the gloom around the pipe. Paul Frankenthal has shut up. Nobody else is saying anything, and I imagine we all look embarrassed. I know I do. After a moment Papa gives me a weary little smile. "Well, don't stay long," he says. He goes inside, and I can hear his steps commencing the five-story climb.

"That's exactly how they do it," resumes Paul Frankenthal in a secretive voice. "Your father does that to your mother, see. He shoots this greenish-white stuff into her, and after nine months, out you come from that same hole. That's it."

Friday night in my home was the inside core of the core. In that fifth-floor Bronx flat, my parents created *Shabbess,* the old-country Sabbath. I see it through no softening mist of sentiment. I see it as it was. I see the scrubbed kitchen linoleum covered with newspapers and lit by flaring gas jets — for Aldus Street was not yet electrified — and I see one or two bold shiny brown roaches, undiscouraged by the harsh soap and fresh-scattered roach powder, scuttling across the paper. I smell the cooking fish, the noodle soup, the boiled chicken, the stewing prunes and carrots, and the newly baked cookies and *hallahs,* the egg loaves. That menu did not vary for the first fifteen years of my life. There is a golden light on the Shabbess table, and it comes not from any bathos of memory, but from the candles. The faces of my dressed-up parents and sister shine in that light; and as I write this, I hear the Shabbess songs, and I taste those unchanging foods.

By the time I was fifteen the monotony of that Friday night supper had driven me and Lee to mutinous sarcasm, and Mama was giving us stuffed veal, pot roast, and such, but on Aldus Street we ate the same Shabbess meal week in, week out, all the year round. I don't think Papa ever wanted any change. We ate Friday supper and Saturday dinner at the oval dining table in the parlor; otherwise we ate in the kitchen. With this shift in setting went different talk. The incessant weekday laundry chatter — what Brodofsky said, what Gross did, the repairs to the boiler, the threat of a strike, the troubles with Jake the drunk — all this endless, endless business drivel — was shut off. My parents told stories of their Minsk childhoods, sang old songs of the old country, played little table games, games as simple as trying to slap a hand before it was snatched away, or they asked us about our Jewish studies, Lee's at an afternoon Yiddishist school, mine with a Hebrew tutor. After supper Pop would read Sholem Aleichem aloud, and Lee and I would roll around on the davenport screaming with laughter, tears streaming down our cheeks, while Mama too laughed like a fool. Or he would vary it with the powerful tales of Y. L. Peretz.

I have no recollection of learning Yiddish. Mom and Pop now and then spoke it, but mainly they talked English. These Sholem Aleichem readings were probably decisive. Sholem Aleichem was a Yiddish Mark Twain, just as funny, just as easy to understand, and just as deep under the hilarious surface. *Fiddler on the Roof* has made Aleichem an outside name of sorts, but his writings do not translate well, layered as they are with Bible and Talmud phrases, and with types and touches of shtetl life. All that depth flattens out when you translate him. Nevertheless, the Soviets have translated all of Sholem Aleichem and claim him as a major Russian writer. Crude gall can go no further. Anyway, that night I couldn't wait for Pop to get to Sholem Aleichem and cheer me up.

But it was a bad night, the night of the famous schism in the Kelly Street synagogue which led to the founding of the Minsker Congregation. I don't know about churches, but in synagogues the tangle of politics is unbelievable. It doesn't matter how small the shule is. Ten members, five factions; I say five, since the minimum for a cabal is two. Morris Elfenbein, who had started the Kelly Street shule, had been voted out as president; ingrate newcomers had ganged up and overwhelmed him. All this Pop told Mama over the gefilte fish and the noodle soup.

And Mom chose that night to play the one wild card in the Shabbess meal that occasionally showed up. Like the green soup, it had a name like a hay-fever spasm — I think, *ptcha* — and because of this, and because it was so terrible, I am never positive whether this stuff was called shchav, and the green soup ptcha, or the other way around. A plague on both those dishes, anyway. Ptcha, if that's right, was calf's-foot jelly, Minsk style, which meant cooked in equal parts of hoof and garlic. Served hot it was liquid, but barely. You never in your life tasted anything like it. I'd take a spoonful and only half would go down; the rest would coat my teeth, tongue, gums, and throat with warm pungent glue. At Saturday lunch this delicacy would be served congealed. Cut up in squares, it would tremble on my plate; but not as much as my stomach would tremble at the sight and smell of it. Anyway, that night we had ptcha.

"Will it poison you?" Mama snapped, forcing a plateful on me.

I ate it. I was so numb and sick from Frankenthal's disclosure, I didn't much care what was going into my mouth. The candles seemed to be burning greenish white. My inside world was coated with nastiness, as my mouth and throat were with ptcha. I kept sneaking glances at my mother and father — somewhat as though I were peeking at a little girl's bare behind — and wondering if what Frankenthal had said could possibly be true. If not, where in fact had I come from? I recalled Pop once telling me, when I was much younger and asked him this very question, that my mother had been very sick in the hospital, and that I had "saved her life" by appearing. Casting me as the hero had sufficed to make the answer entirely satisfactory and complete. I hadn't pressed him for details.

My mother was beautiful that night, at least to me. Anyone might have called her a pretty woman, with her red cheeks, sharp blue eyes, and full figure going a bit to plumpness. Papa was tired and abstracted, but even so he was the man I admired above everybody on earth: fair-minded, good-hearted, hard-working, funny, a sallow slightly paunchy man of medium height with clever subtly sad brown eyes, and a wonderful kind smile. Could it be true? Could this man have done to this lovely woman the odious thing Frankenthal had reported — done it *twice*, so as to produce both Lee and me? And would he ever lower himself to do it once again, so as to make us a brother or sister? Such was the dazed ignorance of a city child. I had no barnyard knowledge whatever. All I had to go on was Frankenthal's story.

"Sunday we'll go and see the uncle in Bay Ridge," I heard my father say, as I slumped over the stewed prunes at the end of the meal.

We had an uncle in Bay Ridge, and an uncle in Bayonne. I could never keep those two places straight, any more than I could be clear about shchav and ptcha. One uncle was in Brooklyn, the other in New Jersey, and both meant long fatiguing rides in the Ford.

"Aren't you going to read Sholem Aleichem?" I ventured.

With the same tired little smile he had given me from the stoop, he said, "Not tonight, Yisroelke," and he left the table.

Whether I should allow this narrative to wander off to Bay Ridge I don't know. Maybe. Anything to get away for a while from Paul Frankenthal.

The beauty, the mystery, the sublimity, the glory of sexual love, and of conception and reproduction, those wondrous mechanisms by which biologists are only the more awed as they cloudily begin to grasp how it all works; my love for my father and mother, and theirs for me; the supreme sweetness of existence, the way of a man with a maid; the golden glow of Shabbess, the painful gallant laughter of old-country Jewry; all sullied, all quenched, all silenced by Paul Frankenthal. "He sticks his peeing thing into her hole, see, and shoots this stuff into her, and that's how babies are made. That's all there is to it."

Right, Paul Frankenthal. Right, cynics and reductionists of all stripes and breeds. Right, positivists. Right, determinists. Right, materialists. Right, Marxists. Right, Cousin Harold. Right, Peter Quat. Right, all you big guys out there in the lots. That's all there is to it.

14

The Haskalist

OKAY, short visit to the home of my Bay Ridge uncle, the Haskalist, the most forlorn outpost of the Mishpokha.

My sister Lee and I never liked being dragged out to Bay Ridge, God knows. It killed a whole Sunday, starting with the toilsome drive through the South Bronx, all down Manhattan, and over the Brooklyn Bridge. Now, that one moment was nice, crossing the high windy span arching over the sparkling river and its hooting steamships; but then, those dull grimy featureless wastes of Brooklyn! Lee and I, in the high narrow back seat of the open flivver, would try every way we could think of to pass the time, invariably ending up by fighting, getting yelled at, and dozing off.

Well, this time we drove to Bay Ridge, spent a few hours there, and drove home, same as always. You have to "hollow out the canvas" in painting the flat surface, as Cézanne or somebody said; introduce the receding dimensions of reality to achieve a picture that matters. That will take a bit of doing with my uncle in Bay Ridge, since the dimensions of reality recede maybe to the fall of the Second Temple, but I'll try.

Uncle Yail Mosessohn (Yail is Lithuanian Yiddish for Joel) repaired watches. He was the younger son of Reb Yisroel Dovid, of *David's Tower* fame; therefore my mother's uncle, and actually my great-uncle. But we all called him Uncle Yail. Yail should have been a rabbi, too, Mama says, for he was a superb Hebraist. But Yail went in for the *Haskalah,* the enlightenment movement which started in Russian Jewry about a hundred years after the rest of Europe got enlightened. The best Russian Jewish minds were steeped in the Talmud, you see, and the Jews were isolated in shtetls and ghettoes, so it took a while for those outside ideas to penetrate. Young Haskalists like Uncle Yail wanted to read the books of Darwin and Voltaire, and to write belles lettres in Hebrew and Yiddish — stories, essays, poems — instead of dwelling exclusively on the Talmud. But they were bucking a system many centuries old, bulwarked in oaken tradition that looked on the world wholly through the Talmudic prism. The rabbis' idea of dangerous outside reading, fit only for a few mature and superior minds, was Aristotle. Plato was a subversive radical altogether to be shunned. As for Darwin, his name was spoken around the yeshivas only in whispers, like a cabalistic term for the Devil which could raise Old Nick smoking and grinning through the floorboards.

Well, as I say, Uncle Yail was a Haskalist. It's a paradox, no doubt, that I have ended up a Talmud addict, whereas to my great-uncle the Talmud was a prison. Times change. I can certainly understand why the Haskalists had to break out and look beyond the old learning, but that fight is over. I've read all the Voltaire and Darwin I ever want to; and as an undergraduate of seventeen I had Plato and Aristotle coming out of my ears.

Now Yail's brother Asher, who never left Minsk, was really a red-hot Haskalist. Asher read every unkosher book in Russian, Yiddish, or Hebrew that he could lay hands on. He never married. A warm pleasant man of iron principles, he lived at home with Reb Yisroel Dovid, who ate his heart out over his son's profane reading. Asher showed no interest in his father's masterwork, *David's Tower*, or in the Talmud altogether. The Germans got Asher, as they did all my Minsk relatives, when they crashed into Russia in 1941. Mom loved Asher, whom she always called "the philosopher," *der filosofe*. I wish I could have known him.

Uncle Yail rebelled and left home. Once in America, he was at loose ends, broke as a tramp, free as air, with nothing more to rebel against. And he was hungry. He landed in Bay Ridge, and there he came upon this remarkably ugly religious girl with a dowry of three hundred dollars. Yail married her, and with the three hundred set himself up in watch repairing. Anything but synagogue work or Hebrew teaching. He was a rebel, you see.

A rebel of sorts, that is. Yail's house was kosher, as a matter of course. He kept the Sabbath and other rituals. Indeed, that was why he took up watch repairing, so as to be free on Saturday; but the work ruined his eyesight, and his scholarship went by the board. The woman he married was very fat, ill-favored, unsmiling, and by all odds the worst cook in the Mishpokha. Her green soup defies description. There was something truly lugubrious about that Bay Ridge apartment. The visits were long, with long silences. Uncle Yail's two daughters were sad bony girls who wouldn't play, just sat around gloomily swinging their legs. They were decidedly odd, those girls. What became of the younger one I don't know, but the bigger and bonier daughter, Evelyn, as she grew up developed a crush on Rudy Vallee. We heard a lot about that from Uncle Yail. Evelyn spent several years locked up in her room in that Bay Ridge flat, playing Rudy Vallee's records and writing him letters. That was pretty rough on my uncle and aunt, hearing "The Maine Stein Song" and "The Vagabond Lover" crooned through the walls day and night, feeding Evelyn on trays left outside her door, and getting nothing from her except snarls, and batches of letters to mail to Rudy Vallee. Then someone started a Rudy Vallee fan club in Bay Ridge, and that was a deliverance for everyone. Evelyn got out of her room, out of that apartment. She became a stenographer, lived alone, had nothing to do with anybody except the Rudy Vallee club, and eventually moved to San Francisco and drifted from the family view. Why she went to San Francisco I can't say. Possibly that was the national headquarters for Rudy Vallee fans.

I realize now that the pall over our Bay Ridge kin was compounded of poverty and unfulfillment. Watch repair was no more congenial to Uncle Yail than selling victrolas was to Uncle Yehuda. Mama rightly says Yail should have been a *klay kaydesh,* a holy vessel; a rabbi, a shammas, a cantor, a Hebrew school principal — something in that line.

Why wasn't he? Well, I can't hollow out that canvas. I don't know why Yail persisted in watch repairing until his eyes went bad, and then took a job as a night watchman; or why, in his last years, he did become a klay kaydesh after all, a sexton in a Conservative temple in Los Angeles. He still remembered the whole Torah by heart, with perfect cantillation, from his boyhood, so he pretended to read it from the parchment holy scroll. Nobody knew the difference, and he got by for a while, but then he went stone-blind and that game was up. The Torah is supposed to be read, not recited from memory. By that time I had had some dealings with Hollywood, and I got him into a Hebrew home for the blind in Los Angeles.

The last time I visited him he lay stretched supine on his bed, sightless, wasted, inert. His face barely flickered when I took his hand and told him who I was. In our halting talk, I mentioned my Talmud study. The faded lips wrinkled in a pitiful grin, and he quoted feebly from its text: "*The Torah seeks out its old lodgings.*" Then he whispered something I didn't hear. I bent over and asked him to repeat it.

"Speak to me in Hebrew," he gasped.

It's not my forte, but I did it. I forget what I said. He nodded, his face showing ghostly pleasure. He corrected a mistake I made in grammar, and he murmured, "They read me a newspaper story about you. You're a famous lawyer."

"Not all that famous, Uncle Yail."

"Very successful. Full pockets."

"Well, I have done all right."

He caught his lower lip between his false teeth in a sudden short sob, turned his sightless face at me, and whispered, "Now do something for our Jewish people."

This was right after Israel's victory in the Six-Day War. I was planning to take my family there to see the Wall and Mount Sinai and so forth. It seemed to me that "our Jewish people" were doing pretty well for themselves. I didn't reply. Later on, when I got so involved in the United Jewish Appeal, and a hundred times wished myself out of it, I would think of Uncle Yail's last words to me. He spent his little strength running away from our Jewish people, and turned out to be running in place.

Such was the impact of the Haskalah on my Mishpokha. It cut short the long rabbinic line of Mosessohns at Reb Yisroel Dovid and his *David's Tower,* of which ten or fifteen moldering copies may remain in the world. One of the great Haskalists said in his old age, "We wanted to escape from the Yeshiva and raise a generation of freethinkers. We raised a generation of ignoramuses." That, the Haskalists perhaps could not foresee.

Still the Haskalah was inevitable. It was a hell of a cultural riptide, and my Bay Ridge uncle went down in the whirling waters. It was one thing for Pop to come to the Goldena Medina and busy himself making it here, ignoring all the intellectual problems of the transition. Uncle Yail was a thinker, a son of *David's Tower.* He had to think about what was happening to our people. That took its toll, and he elected to go blind repairing watches.

The long ride back to the Bronx would end, the flivver would stop. Pop would reach into the back seat and shake us both awake. "We're home." Those are perhaps the sweetest words in human speech after "I love you"; at least so they would sound to me, after the greenish-white glare of Bay Ridge, and the long dark uneasy doze in the flivver. Greenish white? Yes, the street lamps in Brooklyn in those days burned a weird greenish white. I suppose they were gas-lit. I remember that cold glare in the night more than anything else about Bay Ridge, and now you know why I thought of it and dragged you there. Frankenthal.

15

Rosalind Katz and the Coo Coo Clan

How did I first become aware of the Coo Coo Clan? Again Frankenthal.

That's how we pronounced it on Aldus Street: Coo Coo, two words. The "Coo Coo Clan" was no joke; I still feel faint fear, just writing out the name. Dimly I picture a vacant lot in the twilight, and Paul scaring the devil out of us as we sat around a fire roasting potatoes; warning us to eat the potatoes and beat it out of that darkening cold weed-choked lot before the Coo Coo Clan got us. Frankenthal was talking about the Ku Klux Klan, of course. He was a great one for snooping out harsh facts of the adult world, and relaying them to us in garbled form.

As Paul told it, the Coo Coo Clan was a huge gang of Krishts all over America who dressed up in long white sheets and pointy hoods, so they looked just like ghosts. Sometimes they rode around on horses. The main thing was, they hated Jews. The Coo Coo Clan killed, with horrible tortures, by the light of burning crosses, any unwary Jews they caught. This so shocked us Aldus Street kids that for once Frankenthal encountered skeptical hoots at his wise-guy disclosures. I myself was sure he must be lying, even though my blood turned to ice water at this nightmare vision of Jew-killing ghosts on horses. We jeered in a body that it was all *bushwa,* a Bronx gutter term equivalent to, though not meaning, bullshit.

"Okay," said Paul Frankenthal, "you'll see," and he led a group of us to Southern Boulevard. "Look at that!" *That* was the poster of the coming attraction at Loew's Boulevard, our biggest movie house: a huge luridly colored picture of the Coo Coo Clan, a whole band of them in the night, complete with pointy hoods, white sheets, horses, and flaming crosses. They lacked only the Jewish victims, for which they appeared to be out on the hunt. *"Bushwa,* hey?" sneered Paul Frankenthal. I don't retain the name of the movie. I never saw it. I wouldn't have dared to see it, even if I'd obtained the price of a Loew's Boulevard admission. No monster movie could have been half so terrifying in prospect.

So Frankenthal's fearsome revelation stood confirmed. The Coo Coo Clan existed. There was a movie about it! The Krishts could never again be mere objects of Paul Frankenthal's dirty rhymes and jokes. They were the enemy; and being different from them, being Jewish, was no longer the most natural state in the world; it suddenly meant being an object of hate, a hunted prey, for absolutely no reason. Though the shock passed, my childhood remained shadowed by the Coo Coo Clan. In the presidential campaigns of 1924 and 1928 the Ku Klux Klan became an issue of sorts, so the newspapers helped me to understand what Paul Frankenthal had been alarming us with. In time I and my friends even managed to joke about the Klan, and about anti-Semitism. In a humor column I wrote in my college newspaper when Hitler first came to power, I thought of and printed a funny headline that I can never forget:

NAZIS BEAT JEWS, 21–19.

I was then a sophomore, you see, a liberated humanist of sixteen. I knew perfectly well that the noisy German politician with the mustache was a clown like Charlie Chaplin, and that there was really no such thing as a Coo Coo Clan.

Now, about Rosalind Katz, and after her the clambake. The shadow of the Coo Coo Clan fell athwart both.

What can I tell you about Rosalind that will bring her to life? The little bell of black hair that swung about her face? The pretty frocks she wore, her thin pink-white legs and arms, her bright hazel eyes, her remote cryptic smile? How do you describe falling in love with a girl years before puberty; years before there are the rounded breasts and the quivering thighs and the throbbing this and the hard that of the liberated housewives' novels?

As for Frankenthal's greenish-white loathsomeness, it had nothing to do with my feeling for Rosalind, nothing. I never even made the connection. I would no more have thought of lifting Rosalind's dress

and baring her behind than of stabbing her. She was perfection.
She was almost holy. Rosalind Katz was the first female I was ever
infatuated with. Everything adorable in a woman was there in Rosalind, in pristine purity; in that little black-haired girl in a white blouse
and a plaid skirt, holding my hand on a May walk in the early 1920's,
when not only I but all the world was still innocent.

Class 1B-3, led by our big-nosed teacher, Mrs. Kraus, walked two
by two, hand in hand, through vacant lots near Public School 48 on
May Day. Mrs. Kraus lectured us about the wild flowers we passed,
the butterflies, the grasshoppers, and the trees, and for a whole hour
I held the hand of Rosalind Katz, after nearly a year of silently ador-
ing her, of finding ways to be near her, to look at her, to catch her
eye and exchange shy smiles. What I felt, when I was able to hold
her hand for an hour, was fully as sweet an emotion as a grown man
can feel for a woman. Perhaps it burned the more bright and clean
without the smoky rich fuel of physical desire. That hand was alive
and electric during the whole May walk. Nothing limp or passive about
Rosalind's hand, in that golden hour! And as it ended, she gave me
her whispered consent to walk with me after school in the Dickeys
estate.

The Dickeys estate was an anomaly, a big white farmhouse on a
hilltop just a little way from Public School 48, set amid rolling greenery
and woods. That whole part of the Bronx had once been large farms,
but with the coming of the elevated trains, booming overhead along
Westchester Avenue and Southern Boulevard, the South Bronx had
gone all to hell in crisscrossing lines of tenements. Here and there
abandoned farmhouses still stood, weatherbeaten wrecks stinking of
excrement; "haunted houses," which none of us, not even Paul Frankenthal, would enter except in bright daylight. But the Dickeys estate
had survived in good condition as a Krisht orphanage; so we were
told, and pupils of P.S. 48 were strictly forbidden to trespass. Mostly
they didn't, but I did. I loved the solitude and the greenery. Legend
had it that you could find bullets from the Revolutionary War in the
Dickeys estate, and that was my pretext for inviting Rosalind to come
with me to the forbidden ground. We would hunt for bullets.

Well, it should have been the most delicious episode of my life.
There I was, alone with Rosalind Katz at last, wandering in the woods
in Maytime, holding her hand to help her climb rocks, sometimes

even putting my arm around her, whether truly needed or not. She did not object. Now and then as we leaped and climbed on the wooded slopes, I would catch glimpses of her white drawers, dazzling as the sun. I'd swear they left shimmering pink after-images, those blinding little undergarments. Agile little devil, after a year and more of poised mysterious remoteness, Rosalind turned out to be!

Now, as I say, all this should have been absolute Paradise, and it was, it was. But there was a snake poisoning it all, and that was the reviving thought of the Coo Coo Clan. The visit to Loew's Boulevard was fresh in my mind. This Krisht stronghold, on which I was trespassing for the first time since then, bore a new evil look. Was the estate a big Coo Coo ambush? Was that big "orphanage" up on the hill really full of slaughterers in white sheets and pointy hoods? Thoughts like that kept troubling my intoxicating idyll with Rosalind.

And not without reason! Through the woods came suddenly crashing three colossal Krishts. One of them roared at us, like a giant in a fairy tale, "WHAT THE HELL ARE YOU DOING HERE?" What made this worse, if anything could be worse, was that they were above us on a slope, these three men in rough clothes. They looked fully fifteen feet tall, glaring down at us.

"ARE YOU FROM PUBLIC SCHOOL FORTY-EIGHT?" bellowed another, as Rosalind and I clung to each other, tongue-tied and terrorized.

"Wha — wha — where's that?" I managed to babble. Ghetto presence of mind, transmitted in the genes; me and the Porush, the quick deflecting question.

But poor Rosalind caved in. "Yes, we are," said she in a sweet pleading little voice. "But we didn't know we weren't allowed. *He* brought me here." A little pink finger darted unnecessarily at me. There was no one else around to finger.

"Come with us," grated the third one, who had a terrible red face. As we walked up to the white building the three men talked about the infestation of the estate by P.S. 48 kids, the damage to the flower beds and trees, and the need to report us to our principal, a fat old bogeyman named Mr. Blume. To my first-grade intellect, being reported to Mr. Blume was the next thing to being electrocuted; yet even that was not as scary as being in the grip of these Krishts. I clung to the comfort that they hadn't asked us yet if we were Jews, and that, for the moment at least, they weren't wearing hoods and sheets.

In the white building we saw lots of children, so it was a sure-enough orphanage. And it was full of very strange cooking odors. What was cooking had never cooked in my home, or in the Frankenthal flat, or in any other Aldus Street apartment, or in any Mishpokha home. Krisht food. The three Krishts went into an office, leaving us shaking with fear on a bench in a corridor, smelling those alien odors, while the orphans came and went, giving us curious glances. Then out of the office catapulted a man dressed all in black, with a round white collar and no tie. Around his neck on a chain, a *cross;* not burning, but a cross. This was *it!*

"You're not allowed to trespass on the Dickeys estate. You know that, don't you?" he thundered.

"It was my fault," I managed to gasp. "She didn't know. We won't do it again." And then I suicidally blurted — and to this moment I don't know why, except that I could think of nothing else — "We're Jewish."

He stared at me, his eyes crinkling, small wise eyes; eyes of a strict teacher, after all, not of a hooded killer. He flung one arm toward a door that opened on a flowering garden. "Go home, both of you. Never come back!"

We rushed out into the sweet odors of May down a gravel road to a gate; ran out to freedom on Spofford Avenue, and went our ways without exchanging a word.

Rosalind avoided me after that until the school term ended, when I skipped a grade and lost sight of her. But I happen to know that Rosalind Katz is dead. In my memory, and in yours, I want to preserve her as she was on that May day, in a little plaid skirt and a short-sleeved blouse, leaping the rocks in the Eden of the Dickeys estate; Eve in all her God-created loveliness, six or seven years old.

16

The Clambake

Dㅁ it happen at all, the clambake?

Not according to Mama. When I asked her about it, she developed trouble with her hearing aid. When I managed to get through to her, she wrinkled her whole face at me and said, "Clambake? What clambake? Are you crazy? What could we eat at a clambake? You're remembering wrong. Maybe Reuben Brodofsky had a clambake, in that garden of his all full of weeds and tin cans. He was nothing but a goy, and she was worse. They would eat anything. Cats, rats, dogs. We never had a clambake."

My sister Lee has been carrying on about the clambake for decades, so I reported this to her. She became so mad that she smoked; I mean, literally. She was off cigarettes, but she marched to a bureau, unlocked a drawer, and yanked out a pack of Camels. She lit one as though setting fire to the Reichstag. Gray smoke jetted from her nose.

"Mama said wha-a-AAT?" Half a growl, half a scream.

"Mama says there never was a clambake."

Lee dropped to the sofa, gesturing to Heaven with both arms for patience to endure. She smoked in silence, staring at the air, gnashing her teeth. Lee does take on about these long-past things.

"Do you remember much about it?" I ventured.

"Remember? I remember *everything.*"

Chain-smoking until her ashtray overflowed, Lee reminisced wrathfully about the clambake, quite a graphic description. Let me point out that Lee loves seafood. Clams, oysters, lobsters, shrimps, scallops, frogs' legs — you name it; if the thing lives in water and doesn't have fins and scales (only the finned and scaled creatures are kosher) then that's for Lee, mmm! Mind you, it's not my business *what* Lee eats. That's between her and, as they say in show business, the Man Upstairs. She keeps a kosher home, goes to a temple on the High Holy Days, and loves seafood. Let her live for a hundred twenty years, leaving a trail of clam shells. I am only pointing out that for obvious reasons she hoards the memory of that clambake.

So where are we? You can believe Mama's denial that it ever happened at all, nothing wrong with that; except that, as Lee said at one point, Mama revises history like a Soviet encyclopedist. Not that she needs to, on this matter. She and Pop were young immigrants, after all, struggling with the riptide of change that pulled down Uncle Yail. What was so terrible about an experiment with seafood? Let the record show that Mama enters a general denial. I'll give my version, which is much like Lee's.

The clambake was the first annual outing of the Fairy Laundry employees. By then, after several moves to ever-larger quarters, the firm had made the big jump from hand laundry to steam laundry. Pop bought the required heavy machinery on credit. In a space vacated by a Woolworth five-and-ten-cent store those machines now tumbled, groaned, hissed, clanked, roared, spewed foam, belched steam; oily pistons thumped back and forth, driven by huge flywheels; and workers in starchy white smocks fed wet wrinkled stuff into satanic contrivances, which vomited neat piles of smooth laundry. The place was perpetually clangorous and vaporous, perpetually stank of chlorine, soap, and dirty underwear, and perpetually streamed foamy water in concrete gutters, splashing and slopping on the slippery floor.

Papa liked to take me around the laundry, show me the machines, explain in shouts how they worked, and introduce me to the employees, who tended to yell brutishly at each other in foreign tongues. Few seemed to be Jewish. I remember a fat girl who worked at a thing called a mangle, which sucked in and flattened sheets and towels, and in my view threatened to suck in and flatten me. A bird flew into the store when I was there, and this fat girl deftly caught it in her hands. With friendly pantomime, she offered to let the boss's son have the bird. I eagerly nodded; whereupon, to my thunderstruck horror, she seized huge shears, spread the paralyzed bird's wings, and crunch, crunch, clipped the feathers. I see, as I see the paper on which I'm writing, those shears cutting bloodily through those brown wings, while the girl chatters in German or Polish, and the bird stares at me with frightened bright eyes. I am a wildlife fanatic, and for all I know it traces to that moment. But I wander. My simple point is that for such non-Jewish workers a clambake was in order. They could eat seafood, or whatever they pleased.

The clambake took place at Orchard Beach, in a big white house on a lawn. At low tide on Orchard Beach, where we often bathed in summertime, I'd seen lots of clams. But eat them? I'd as soon have eaten the driftwood. Now there at this long table, in this big white house — which in fact smelled very like the Dickeys estate orphanage — Fairy Laundry workers were eating and drinking and joking in a great noise; and I saw wire baskets full of clams, popped open like dead men's mouths, exposing white rubbery-looking lumps at the center. Left to myself, and feeling hungry, I tried poking at a lump with a fork. The prongs rebounded as though I had tried to spear a tennis ball. I tried forking it out of the shell. It wouldn't come.

I had had no food for hours. I don't know where Mom and Pop were; I suppose as Boss and Mrs. Boss they were socializing, being good hosts. Nor do I recall where Lee was. I know I next found myself alone with a lobster, trying to eat it. Left and right the laundry workers were devouring lobsters with popping eyes, gustatory grins, and smacking lips. I turned the big red armored corpse here and there, looking for a place to dig in. Its stalked dead eyes, feelers, many hairy spider legs, and ragged claws disconcerted me, but I was getting ravenous, what with Pop's employees all around me putting lobsters away like lamb chops. Where to start? I turned the lobster over. Its underside looked a bit more vulnerable, a sort of wrinkled greenish-white stomach. The shell resisted a push of the fork, but it did seem to give. I clasped the lobster firmly in one hand, and with the other jabbed the fork down as hard as I could. The stomach yielded. The fork plunged in. Greenish-white stuff squirted all over me, with a strong Coo Coo Clan smell. I gave up trying to eat the lobster.

After the meal the whole party moved to the lawn and lounged in the sun, eating ice cream and drinking soda pop, and that was all I had at that clambake. High on a white flagpole a big American flag fluttered in the sea breeze, and on the grass the younger men played ball, and there was dancing to a wind-up phonograph with a horn. Jake the drunk took me to the lockers down at the beach, for a dip in the sea.

Jake was a wagon driver and a friend of sorts. He rescued me in the snowstorm, you remember. Aldus Street was on his route, so I saw him often. When he came to pick up our laundry bundle, Mama would produce a brown bottle and pour Jake a shot glass full. Nobody drank from that bottle but Jake the drunk. Once I sneaked a taste. Wow! Fire and brimstone! I never went near it again. Jake always had a three-day beard, more or less, and his stubbly face was lean, old, and sad, except right after he tossed down that shot, when he would smile like a baby. Jake was Jewish. He had to be, he had an accent like my father's. Anyway, he *felt* Jewish. I don't know how else to put it.

Well, you know public beach lockers: sandy mildewy little plasterboard cubicles with a stool inside, hooks, and a lock. I guess we had a paddle in the surf, but when memory, like a badly cut movie, fades in again, we are drying ourselves in the locker, Jake and I, talking about nothing much. We fall silent, and through the plasterboard, from the next locker, we hear two boyish voices burlesquing Jake's Yiddish accent. Half-dressed, we look at each other. His face is bitter, and peppered with gray and black stubble.

"Don't pay no attention," Jake says.

Through the partition, vaudeville Jew voices in singsong: "Ikey, dun't pay no atten-sheen!"

Jake puts his fingers to his lips.

Silence on our side of the partition. On the other side some giggles. After a while we hear their door open and close. We finish dressing and comb our hair. When we emerge on the long wooden locker platform in the sunshine, we see them: two kids about Frankenthal's age, in kneepants; ordinary street kids, standing a few yards off. As we head for the staircase, we hear singsong calls behind us: "Clip cocks! Clip cocks!"

Jake is holding my hand, hurrying me along. They follow us, their steps thumping on the boards. "Clip cocks! Clip cocks!"

"Never mind," Jake mutters.

"Clip cocks! Christ killers!" Then, close behind us, "Ikey, dun't pay no 'ten-sheen!"

Jake stops and turns, so do I. The kids are halted about ten feet away, grinning. In a voice such as I have never yet heard from a human throat, Jake roars, "GERRADA HERE," taking a step toward them. The grins change to quick glances of cowed fear. They scamper off down the platform, out of sight. Jake puts an arm around my shoulder. We go up the stairs, across the lawn, back to the outing, where the Fairy Laundry people now sit around under the waving Stars and Stripes, singing to a concertina.

That's how, and why, I remember the clambake.

Frankenthal's Coo Coo Clan story was just a rumor, after all. Even the Loew's Boulevard poster really proved nothing; mere movie nightmare, perhaps. Here was the thing itself, the first time I ran into it; the living voice of the Outside in broad daylight, in the pleasant salt breeze, the piping of a couple of kids in kneepants by the Orchard Beach lockers.

17

Izzy

I'VE mentioned that I had a fast rise through public school. My Minsker Godol blood worked for me, and I also had luck. A new school, P.S. 75, opened in our neighborhood in the field where our haunted house had stood; the watchman my mother clobbered with a brick (*"How dare you strike my child?"*) had been guarding that construction. Kids were transferred there *en masse,* and in the disorder, I tended to float upward. A class would get crowded, and I would be spot-promoted to make room. The higher class would be learning something strange like fractions, or the subjunctive mood, and I would have to sweat to get my bearings; but I was doing all right, until I overtook Frankenthal.

Frankenthal had made considerable noise on Aldus Street about being promoted to the seventh grade, where pupils changed classrooms and teachers every hour; no more of that kid stuff, said Frankenthal, all day with one teacher! "DEE-part-mental! Wow!" My sister Lee had reached the seventh grade a year before, and ever since had put on airs about her DEE-part-mental status. Frankenthal mouthed on and on about this, though he professed contempt for the whole school system. Paul abounded in dirty rhymes, rumors, and jokes about teachers; as, "Mrs. Hennessy is suing the city for building the sidewalk too close to her ass"; also, about a big-bosomed one who dealt out "zips," or zeroes, wholesale:

> *Tramp tramp tramp*
> *The tits are bouncing,*
> *Lizzie Reed is at the door,*
> *We will take her book of zips*

And we'll throw it at her tits
And Lizzie won't be dizzy any more.

Paul had a mind that sieved out knowledge and collected crap like that. My memory may appear similar, but it more nearly resembles an attic where everything accumulates, precious or worthless.

Anyway, Paul was mighty impressed with his seventh-grade status, and for once he had nothing but praise for a teacher. Mr. Winston, his home-room teacher, looked just like Douglas Fairbanks, he declared, and moreover was a regular guy who fucked all the lady teachers. Paul boasted of this as though he were doing it himself, a clear case of identification with his hero. He was comfortably ahead of all of us, thirteen years old, secure in his double eminence as king of Aldus Street and "departmental" pupil; when into Mr. Winston's room, led by Miss McGrath of the sixth grade, ambled none other than Davey Goodkind of Apartment 5-D, short, noncombative, something of a religious mollycoddle, nothing of a rock thrower, obtusely innocent, aged nine and a half. "Here's your new pupil," said Miss McGrath, with whom I was then in love, to Mr. Winston, who indeed had a Douglas Fairbanks dash about him. I noted the gleam in his eye at my dear Miss McGrath, and the way she flirtatiously bridled as she left. Hmmm! Was he — was she — perish the thought!

Mr. Winston sat me down in a vacant front seat. I was brokenhearted at being parted from Miss McGrath. Mr. Winston's talk at the blackboard about square roots was pure scary Chinese. I'd been in Miss McGrath's class only one month, earning a C in effort for dreaming in class, mainly about her. I was not happy at being shoved upward again, and at home that night I did not mention my new rise. I was all grief over Miss McGrath, and loathsome suspicion that she and Mr. Winston were "doing it," probably that very night. Why, I'd seen the lascivious looks they had exchanged! And there was my fear of Frankenthal, too. I'd have done well to concentrate on that, and not on Miss McGrath's hideous fornication with Mr. Winston.

Next day I thought I caught on to the idea of square roots. Patiently and wearily, Mr. Winston was going over and over the ground to an uncomprehending class, calling pupils to the blackboard to struggle through simple examples. I began to work the problems for myself on a scratch pad. Frankenthal's turn at the board came. Mr. Winston wrote

$$\sqrt{625}$$

and handed the chalk to Paul, who stared at the board with blank hostility. I raised my hand and blurted, "Teacher, isn't the answer twenty-five?"

"Excellent, David!" Mr. Winston flashed me such a charming Douglas Fairbanks grin that I instantly changed my mind about him. This fine clean-cut man couldn't possibly be "doing it" to Miss McGrath. In fact, I didn't care all that much about Miss McGrath, anyway. "David, come up here and show Paul how you figured that out." Frankenthal gave me the chalk, with a mutter. Also a look. He stalked off to his desk; and as I worked out the problem on the board he sat glaring at me. Talk about the evil eye!

I may be blowing all sympathy for myself with this disclosure. We have all known such obnoxious little smart-asses who jump in with the answers. Okay? Now just a word in my own defense. You have to envision my peculiar status on Aldus Street. Inside Apartment 5-D I was the petted jewel, but on the outside I was a nobody, a dud at one-a-cat and stickball, by no means the worst of the kids — there was always Howard Rubin — but among the dregs when it came to choosing up sides. A minor Paul Frankenthal hanger-on, I admired him, and despite his faults, felt a sort of affection for him. He was our leader. That he was number one seemed to be in the way of nature. And yet I felt that my own street ranking was off the mark. Maybe I had absorbed Mama's *yoxenta* spirit. Small and street-inept though I was, I thought myself a *yoxen*. The square root of 625 gave me my first chance to meet Paul Frankenthal *mano a mano*, and I leaped to the contest.

That afternoon I told Mama about my square root coup. For once I had bested the mighty Frankenthal, and I was feeling pretty good. Mr. Winston had patted my back when I finished at the board and said, "That's remarkable." I told Mom this. I told her that Paul Frankenthal was in my new class, and that it was Paul I had floored. Mama made me repeat the whole story, asking a lot of questions. "The square root of 625, eh? And where do you sit? And where does Paul sit? And he couldn't figure it out? What an overgrown dope! Here's a quarter for skipping, I'm proud of you. Hm! The square root of 625, you say? I have to borrow a cup of sugar from Mrs. Frankenthal." And she was off like a race horse. Her sugar jar was in plain sight, brim full. I guess she overlooked it.

A quarter! Half the Aldus Street kids trooped with me down to the Woolworth's on Southern Boulevard, to share my haul of five-and-ten cent sweets, while a hard core stayed behind with Frankenthal when he sneered, "Who wants your shitty candy?" God, how heady that was, leading Aldus Street kids away from Paul Frankenthal! And in those days, what piles of candy you could get at Woolworth's for a nickel! After loading up my followers with chocolate twists, gumdrops, and sugar corns, I left them, to gorge by myself on a strawberry ice-cream soda and a charlotte russe. Never before had I experienced such sheer joy of life. At nine and a half I was as innocent as Adam before the fall. I thought I had simply come into my own, a big yoxen, and high time!

Right after the lunch hour a few days later, the white-coated school doctor came in with two nurses bearing trays, swabs, bottles, and syringes. A diphtheria scare was on. We Bronx kids had been through these mass inoculations before, an awful business of getting stuck with needles at school. The burning lumps on our arms could ache and sting for days, but go fight City Hall! The pupils unhappily trudged up and bared their arms, as the doctor called names from a bundle of health records. They shrank under the puncturing and returned to their seats, trying to smile. Paul Frankenthal of course made a great grinning swagger of his turn. I sat in a funk. I had a deep horror of needles.

"Israel Godkin," called the doctor.

He had to mean me, nobody else had a name remotely like that, but I sat frozen. Mr. Winston struck in, "That must be Good-*kind*, Doctor."

The doctor squinted at the miswritten card through thick glasses. He had been stabbing wincing children for days, and the strain seemed to be telling on him. "All right," he grumbled. "Good*kind*. Israel Goodkind."

"And that should be David," said Mr. Winston.

"No David here," snapped the doctor, brandishing the card. "Israel! Just Israel." By now all the eyes in the class were directed at me. "*You! Are you Goodkind?* STAND!"

I stood. "I'm Goodkind."

"Well? And are you David or Israel?"

I was mute; struck dumb by the Dracula gaze of Paul Frankenthal, in the direct line of sight from me to the doctor. In those eyes was the glitter of sunset, and in his white smile were fangs. On Aldus Street I was Davey, and always had been. Nothing else. My father's ⌒ pet name for me, "Yisroelke," had never registered among the kids.

"Well? Do you have a brother named Israel here in school, or what? Speak up, child."

Child! The man who had solved the square root of 625!

"My name is Israel David," I choked out.

"Well then, Israel David, come on up here." I stood still, embarrassed and paralyzed. In a tremendous burst of medical wit the doctor added, "Don't be afraid, Izzy. You may have two names, but you'll only get one needle."

An insane gale of classroom laughter! Even Mr. Winston — I forgive him, he's undoubtedly in his grave — even Mr. Winston laughed. Frankenthal's face lit up in a frightful smile, as I passed him on the way to the needle. "Hi, Izzy," he hissed.

A SHORT disquisition on "Izzy," reader. This happened back in the 1920's. You have to grasp what "Izzy" meant then, or the rest of this part will make no sense; the whole rest of this book, in fact.

In 1948, as all the world knows, the State of Israel was reborn. Five Arab states at once invaded it, and Israel won its War of Independence. American Jews like myself — I was then just starting law practice — were stunned by this military miracle, and filled with a new wondering pride in our people. At the time, Jewish nightclub comedians worked one joke hard.

Fine thing, the new Jewish state. Just great. Only it's a shame they called it Israel. Why didn't they name it Irving?

The attitude is so dated that the joke is no joke any more, but it does suggest what "Izzy" implied in the 1920's. And not only Izzy; Abey, Ikey, Jakey — that is, the three patriarchs Abraham, Isaac, and Jacob — were the standard Jew names in cartoons, vaudeville routines, and dirty jokes.

Izzy comes home and finds his best friend Abey in bed with his wife, see? He says, "Vot's dis? Abey, mine bast frand, you! Und you, Reba, mine own vibe! How could diss heppen, und — say, you could at least stop, vile I'm talking to you!"

And so forth. Hundreds, hundreds of jokes and songs. Always Izzy, Abey, Ikey, Jakey. There was even a comic popular song about Izzy, at the time I entered Winston's class; in a burlesque Jew accent, a wife who suspects she has a rival wails, *"Whose Izzy izzy, izzy yours or izzy mine?"*

Nobody worried about ethnic sensitivities then. Nobody thought about them. There were Jew jokes, Irish jokes, wop jokes, nigger jokes, ad infinitum, and all, *all* the Jew butts were Izzy, Ikey, Jakey, or Abey. The immigrants, arriving with old-country biblical names, had fixed the stereotypes. Their children and grandchildren, in protective mimicry, took to using Irving and Irwin for Israel, Arthur and Alan for Abraham, and so on; what I've called the inside and outside names. Nowadays, of course, Abraham, Isaac, Jacob, and Israel are perfectly fine American names once more; they can even have a tart New England ring to them, if they go with suitable manners, dress, education, and possessions, instead of with beards, skullcaps or derby hats, thick accents, and pushcarts.

Now you are ready to hear what happened on Aldus Street that night. It was Halloween.

18

Hollooeen

I LEFT school with a sore arm and a sorer heart. The usual witch and pumpkin cutouts decorated the classroom walls, and in the candy stores you could buy masks and orange-colored Halloween candies and such. But on Aldus Street, I must tell you Halloween took an odd form. Maybe it still does. Childhood folkways are ancient and persisting. There was no trick-or-treat. Dressed in old clothes, pieces of chalk in hand, we roamed the neighborhood marking each other and shouting "Hollooeeen!" Tough kids would show up on our block swinging stockings filled with flour, and they would shout "Hollooeen" and belt the unwary. *Them,* you avoided. That compacted flour hurt like a flung baseball, and the white splotches made a hell of a mess.

Sunk in misery, I forgot about Halloween as I trudged homeward. Howard Rubin, the mama's boy, sprang at me from the stoop. "Hollooeen!" he sniggered, chalking my back. So I was reminded. The adenoidal dumbbell was doing it all wrong, of course, marking me while the sun still shone. The whole world knew that you didn't "Hollooeen" anyone until the street lights came on. No use battering Howard, which anybody could do. A kid who showed up on the first warm April day in short pants and socks — as we all did — but with long yellow underwear showing in the gap, was beneath reprisal.

Hollooeen, eh? Well, that might help. Chasing the girls was usually fun, they would run squealing and shrieking, nymphs fleeing satyrs. My sister Lee in recent years was staying indoors on Hollooeen, for the stocking marauders were a sort of menace to girls. While I waited for nightfall I did homework, and when the windows darkened, I put on a ragged sweater and filled my pockets with chalk. Lee sniffed that I was an idiot to go on taking part in that baby stuff. What did she know about my grief, and my need for diversion? I hurried down the stairs and out into the chilly night.

"Hlloo*eeen!*"

From the shadows Howard Rubin jumped, giggling through his nose. I felt his chalk slide down my sore arm. Halfheartedly I chalked him back. "Hollooeen! Where's everybody?"

"Paul and the gang went to Hoe Avenue. I have to stay by the stoop, Mama says." A pitiful case.

Afar off, around the corner of Hoe, I could hear the oncoming shrieks of girls and yells of boys. So Paul and the kids had flushed the game, and all I had to do was wait, chalk in hand. Sure enough, three girls rounded the corner, laughing as they screamed and ran from Paul and his followers. Nobody was making much speed, it was all clearly in play; when suddenly the screams turned piercing and the girls were gone, vanished into an apartment house. At the other end of the block strangers with stockings had appeared.

Just then Paul Frankenthal spied me. "Hey, fellas, it's Izzy," he shouted. "Everybody get Izzy!"

The pack came at me behind him, with yelps of "Izzy! Izzy!"

The way Paul shouted "Izzy" and the others took it up boded no good. This year Paul was carrying a stocking, what's more. From the other corner the strangers were approaching. I had a queasy moment of decision: stand my ground? Run back up the stoop and into the building? But why? Why do that? Why scuttle for safety like Howard Rubin? These were my friends, the Aldus Street kids. Paul Frankenthal was my leader. I grinned like a good sport as they came. Paul cut off any thought of retreat by darting between me and the stoop; and so doing, he began to sing, "*Whose Izzy izzy, izzy yours or izzy mine?*"

The kids in no time tightened a capering ring around me, as we would do when teasing a girl. One and all they joined in the song, cavorting and laughing. The stocking-armed strangers stood by, silently observing. I was no longer sure who was the greater menace, my own gang that had turned on me all at once to Izzy me, or the tough guys watching in the gloom. Instinct took over. Howard Rubin was part of the ring, and when he came opposite me, I leaped at him with a howl. He flinched and I was through the gap on the instant, plunging for the passageway to the back yards. "Get him!" I heard Paul yell. "Everybody after Izzy!"

Those back yards, bounded on all four sides by rows of tenements, formed one large concrete-paved enclosure, full of clothesline poles and trash cans. Through years of playing hide-and-seek I knew the terrain well.

"*Iz-zee! Iz-zee!*"

The cries reverberated in the yards. Peeking out of a hiding place between ashcans, I could see strangers whirling their stockings and gleefully chanting "*Iz-zee! Iz-zee!*" in the exact singsong of "*Clip cock! Clip cock!*"

Far down the yards there was one janitor's passage out to Hoe Avenue that was my secret exit. Most of the passages were locked at night, but I had discovered that by jiggling the loose screws on the lock I could work this gate open. In many a game it had been my saving trick. I slid from shadow to shadow and made one short desperate dash in moonlight. Somebody shouted, "There he goes!" But I was back in shadow by then, worming along a wall. I slipped into the passage, ran up the steps, and with shaking hands I loosened the screws on the lock. Behind me voices were closing in: "*I saw him go in here! . . . No, stupid, he went in this one! . . . He's over there! . . . Iz-zee! Where are you, Iz-zee!*"

The gate worked free. Saved! I pushed at it. It opened a few inches, and stuck with a jangling sound. Then, and only then, I saw the new padlocked chain that had been hung on it.

"IZ-ZEE!"

Frankenthal: "Hey, guys, here he is!"

A blast of light in the passageway! A hurly-burly of voices! My back to the gate, I face into a blinding flashlight.

Strange voice: "Is that him?"

Paul Frankenthal: "That's him. That's Izzy."

Shadowy form of Frankenthal advances into the light, swinging the stocking.

"Paul, what is this? Why? What did I ever do to you?"

"Izzy, you've got plenty to answer for."

I dart past Paul and jump headfirst at the flashlight. It falls. Crash of glass! Darkness! Cursing, shoving! I wriggle through the pack and try a forlorn run up the yards, but they are upon me, Paul Frankenthal in the lead, his voice above the others: "Izzy! Izzy!" His stocking

strikes me hard on the side of the head. My ears ring. I stagger. Frankenthal: "HOLLOOEEN!"

Another stocking on my head. Another, another, another.

Thud. "HOLLOOEEN!"

Thud. "HOLLOOEEN!"

Thud. "HOLLOOEEN!"

I go down.

Stockings beating on me; chalk scrawling and streaking all over me;
giggles, guffaws, as I lie with my face on concrete, trying to shield
my head with my arms from the flailing stockings, coughing and
choking in a cloud of flour. "Hollooeen! Hollooeen!"

Voices fading off, laughing and chorusing like marching troopers,

> *"Whose Izzy izzy,*
> *Izzy yours or izzy mine?"*

Such was my farewell to Aldus Street. My grandmother arrived shortly
after that, and we had to move.

＊ ＊ ＊

ALDUS Street, Aldus Street!
This is no way to leave those scenes, at the worst moment, the
moment that brought down the curtain on my childhood, so let me
tell you some of the good things about Aldus Street. I cannot go
back there. It no longer exists, though the street signs and the tenement shells still stand. Anyway, who can ever go back to childhood
scenes and perceive them through the same eyes? This is the last time
I will ever visit Aldus Street; here and now, as I scrawl these few
words. Let them be words of love, then, because I loved Aldus Street.

When I think of Aldus Street, I think first of winter twilight, and
of the vendors of hot roast sweet potatoes, who came by through the
snow with tin handcarts in which wood fires burned. I could buy a
potato for a penny or two. The vendor would pull out a trayful of
potatoes, and fire and sparks would fly up through the little flue, as
he put a scrap of newspaper around a scorched potato and handed it
to me. I didn't care much for sweet potatoes; I was happier when
the jelly-apple vendor came around with his glass-enclosed cart, or
best of all the charlotte-russe man. *There* is something that I can no
more recapture than Bobbie Webb's first kiss — the taste of the char-

lotte russe of Aldus Street, that bit of sponge cake in cardboard, topped with spiralling ridges of sublime whipped cream. But a charlotte russe cost a nickel. Maybe that was the charm of the sweet-potato man; usually I had a penny on me, and could buy something from him.

But there was more to him than that. He was warmth in the cold, fire in the dark, sparks ascending to the moon past squat tenements. He was heat in hands chilled by making snowballs. If a potato was no charlotte russe, it still felt warm and good going down. Call the charlotte russe poetry, and the sweet potato a legal brief . . . or, hell, never mind the metaphors! Just remember the sweet-potato man as I do, and his tin cart full of fire in December gloom amid falling snow: my primal after-image of Aldus Street.

Well, shall I go on about the fragrant summer fruit in the horse-drawn wagons, the rich look and smell of the sweet butter blocks the grocery man sliced out of a tub, the hundred other memories and pictures and tastes and smells of Aldus Street? Peter Quat would no doubt offer a comic chapter on peeking into the girls' toilet in P.S. 75, before they found the hole and plastered it over. Why force the note? Why imitate? I'm writing out my thoughts as they come, I have no idea whether they're "literature." I don't care. I've told you about the lots, about Southern Boulevard where the grand shops and movie theatres were, about the haunted house, about the sweet-potato man, and about the kids. True, the outside was rougher and colder than the inside. True, I was never as admired and petted and happy in the street as within the sheltering walls of Apartment 5-D. But I did have a place out on Aldus Street, a society, a rank, and a leader. *I was at home on Aldus Street,* as I have never been since. And when that Halloween night Aldus Street turned on me, and I was thrust into the exile which remains my true condition, my childhood ended.

19

Alienation

Paul Frankenthal fades off in memory after the Izzy night. In fact, he went on haunting me for years, and he'll show up again. But the pot is boiling over again in the White House, and I may have to break off at any moment, and who knows when I'll get back to my story? So if I seem to skimble-skamble through the next part you'll know why. So far, I've narrated mainly the outside, the Aldus Street strand of my childhood. Now a brief necessary word about the inside existence which paralleled my street life. In retrospect, these simultaneous things seemed to happen on different tracks of reality.

We start back when I'm about six, with the half-dollar. It fell on the open book as I sat with old Mr. Horowitz, starting on my Bible studies. "*In . . . the . . . beginning,*" I was painfully translating, "*God . . . created . . . the heavens —*"

Thump, clink, roll! The big silver coin hit the page and bounced to the parlor floor. I was on it like a cat. From nowhere, in midday, my father had appeared behind the Hebrew teacher's chair. "An angel dropped that from Heaven," he said, slightly smiling. "Keep it, and study hard." And back he went to the Fairy Laundry.

Did I believe the angel story? At age six, hard to say. I pocketed the half-dollar, no questions asked, and resumed the Hebrew work, highly motivated. It's an old Jewish custom, this coin that falls from Heaven when you start learning Torah. A yet older one was a touch of honey on the Bible page, which the child got to lick off. Same idea, but in the Goldena Medina, money beat honey hands down.

Well, is it playing on the credulity of a child, the coin from overhead? Why, sure, it's a sort of variant on the Santa Claus theme, I guess. When I found out, in the first grade at public school, about hanging up your stocking on Christmas Eve, I couldn't wait to try it. I did hang one up, though Pop gently advised me not to bother. Next morning there was something in my stocking all right, an anonymous note: *Dear David, you are a great big stupid dope to believe in Santa Claus.*

Guess whose handwriting. Mama has never had a light touch. A case in point, about the same time: the incident of the window shade. It happened in the Kelly Street synagogue, on the eve of *Simkhas Torah,* the Rejoicing of the Law.

That was our merriest religious night of the year. It still is, among the pious. The men marched with the Torah scrolls seven times around the synagogue, singing and dancing between the circuits, and we children paraded behind them bearing paper flags. On the sticks of the flags apples were impaled, and in the apples candles were burning; an unbelievable fire hazard, since the Kelly Street shule was just a wooden store, and the dancing jostling children kept dropping burning candles all over the place. "God watches the simple," says the Psalmist. The little store never did burn down. Maybe the spirit of Sholem Aleichem, who died in a house next door back in 1916, stood guard over the Kelly Street shule.

Now I was quite content to march around with flag, apple, and flaming candle. Naturally I yearned for a mantled Torah scroll all aglitter with sequins, or at least for one of the smaller velvet-mantled scrolls that the bar-mitzva boys carried: Ecclesiastes, Isaiah, Jeremiah, and such. But I knew I didn't rate that, not at the age of six. Mama, however, had a great idea. The shule possessed one prophetic scroll for which nobody had as yet contributed a mantle. The long slender rolled-up bare parchment was visible in the open Holy Ark, and Mama came bustling out of the women's section, and asked Pop why Yisroelke couldn't carry that thing around. It was a sacred book, too, wasn't it? So Papa got out the naked white scroll. "Here," he said to me with not much enthusiasm, "wouldn't you like to carry this?"

"That?" I exclaimed. "Why, that's a window shade."

"No, no!" He glanced over his shoulder at Mama, back in the women's section, nodding and smiling eagerly at us over the curtain. "Take it, Yisroelke. It's just as good as a Torah."

He was my father, so I believed him. I fell in behind the last of the bar-mitzva boys who carried a mantled scroll, ahead of all the kids with flags, apples, and candles. The marching and singing for the next circuit began. Behind me a child's voice — not mocking, just inquiring: "Say, Davey, what are you doing with a window shade?"

I, over my shoulder: "It's not a window shade."

"Oh."

A synagogue crowds up on Simkhas Torah. The congregants line the aisles, and mothers hold their children up, and all kiss the scrolls as they go by.

"Mama," piped one of these tots when I had hardly started out, "do I have to kiss the window shade?"

"Of course not," said the mother, looking down in puzzlement at the little pudgy lunatic marching with this silly object.

"It's not a window shade," I said. "It's as good as a Torah."

"Go along," she said to me, and to her child, "never mind the window shade."

Well, so it went. Some jeered, some wondered, some whispered, some shook their heads in disbelief, but all along the line of march, there was unanimity on one point — I was carrying a window shade. Soon I was desperate to get rid of the thing, but how could I? It was holy, so I couldn't throw it down; yet it was so ridiculous no other child would take it off my hands. I tried, but they shrank from it.

No, even when the circuit was over I still had to dance and dance and dance with that blasted bare scroll, the target of innumerable pitying or amused looks and pointing fingers. "Is he crazy, that kid? Why a window shade?" But Mama was clapping away in the women's section, beaming around proudly with a look that proclaimed, "Look at my Davey! Six years old and with a scroll already!" Only she, of all the people in that synagogue, failed to see that, like a clown whose heart is breaking, I was dancing before God with a window shade.

What I'm getting at here is that, all during the Aldus Street years, I lived this other Hebraic life of which Paul Frankenthal and the kids knew almost nothing. Sure, they were Jewish, but none was a yoxen like me, stemming from a rabbi on one side and a shammas on the other. Possibly this explains — or helps to, anyway — why I've never had much of a hang-up about being Jewish, never felt the "alienation" which has been getting such a ride in the books and magazines nowadays.

That is, of course, old Peter Quat's turf, alienation. There's this heavyweight Jewish magazine that once ran an entire issue about alienation, and Peter himself generated that issue. Such a scandal broke out about a short story of Peter's which appeared in the magazine that he wrote a long, learned defense of it in the next issue, arguing that the story was a parable of alienation. This brought on an avalanche of learned letters in reply, lauding Peter or lambasting him, and so next came the issue wholly devoted to these letters on the alienation theme. All this was marvellous for business, since Peter was just coming out with his first novel, *Deflowering Sarah*. The fuss got the book off to a jackrabbit start, and then with the obscenity trial in Cincinnati, which I fought and won, Peter was home free. There wasn't a rabbi in the land, hardly, who didn't either praise *Deflowering Sarah* from the pulpit as a brilliant and profound treatment of alienation, or denounce it as a mere lurid wallowing in sex. How could Peter lose? The Jews buy about half the hardcover books in America, and they went rushing out in battalions to snap up this profound novel about alienation that wallowed in sex, and Peter Quat was launched as a literary lion.

If you're curious about the scandalous short story — mainly rabbis and professors read this magazine, so you may not have come across it — I can summarize it for you. It was called "My Father's Farts," and it was all about a kid on Yom Kippur eve. As everyone knows, Jews fast on Yom Kippur, starting at sundown the evening before. Prior to sundown they usually eat a huge meal; though I myself have learned down the years that the less you eat before the fast the easier it goes. Anyway, this kid's father gorges himself, and the heavy meal disagrees with him. He drags the kid to the synagogue to sit beside him, and Peter has a lot of raw fun about the contrast between the solemn music of *Kol Nidre*, the rabbi's long passionate sermon about repentance, and the father's incessant rumbling and breaking wind, as the boy is sincerely trying to repent.

Well, we Jews love to laugh at ourselves in an acidly self-critical way, and we put up with a lot of such stuff; but somehow this particular alienation gem went too far and got nearly everybody sore. A huge ruckus ensued, and for months you heard nothing in literate Jewish households but Peter Quat, pro and con. It was the making of Peter, a real breakthrough, sort of like Charles Dickens's *A Christmas Carol*. When you think about it, old Scrooge was a pretty bad case of alienation himself. That is an absolute literary gold mine, alienation. Maybe I can work it in here somewhere, though at the moment I can't see just how. I'm about to tell you about my own Yom Kippur experience, and it's a far cry from Peter's short story. But at least it's true, and Peter just made all that up. He told me so. Awful stuff, but remarkably vivid, and ludicrous as it could be.

A jump to age nine and a half in my Hebraic life, about the time of the Hollooeen horror. Pop and Mr. Elfenbein, thrust out of the Kelly Street shule, had organized the Minsker Congregation and started a building. The contractor dug a big hole, but they ran out of money, so they finished off the basement as a synagogue, and above it erected a handsome facade, a stone stairway to ornate double doors that led nowhere. Behind the doors there was only the basement roof. This was supposed to be a temporary thing. I've mentioned that the Minsker Congregation is the last synagogue left in the desolate burned-out South Bronx. It is still a basement, topped by a facade with nothing behind it.

My father decided to lend cheer to that chill basement by forming a choir for the High Holy Days. I was the boy soprano. We practiced at the gloomy apartment of the rabbi, a forbidding old-country sort with a long black beard. He had this enchanting blonde apparition of a daughter, who would go wisping by in the hallway. During that choir practice I was a very religious boy, eager to please the rabbi, showing off my Yiddish and my Hebrew, and keeping a sharp eye out for his shadowy flitting Rapunzel of a daughter. One evening I managed to shake loose in mid-practice and corner the wraith in a bedroom. She was very shy, though clearly not unwilling to be cornered. Having nothing to talk about she showed me a *shofar,* a ram's horn, soaking in a tin basin, and explained (in Yiddish) that Satan sometimes got into the horn during services, so that no sound came out when her father blew it. The horn was soaking in vinegar. Vinegar, she said, discouraged Satan, or something to that effect.

Well, I was dying to impress this Yiddish-speaking blonde angel. My father, the backup shofar blower, had been practicing for a week at home, and he had taught me how to do it. "There's no such thing as Satan," I announced to her, lifting the horn out of the vinegar. "I'll show you." It really stank, and the first taste of vinegar puckered up my mouth, but I was in it now, and I blew — a loud, wet blubbering breaking of wind, right out of old Peter's short story. The rabbi's daughter vanished like a spectre at cockcrow. I never saw hair nor hide of her again. My father came and collared me, and from then on it was all choir practice and no flirting.

The choir, I must say, was a hit. We had no music to read, for from his years as a choirboy in Minsk, under the great Reb Mordechai the cantor, Pop had retained the a cappella music of an entire High Holy Day liturgy. He had been singing the melodies around the house as far back as I could remember. Sidney Gross was our baritone, Pop tenor, and a stout bearded old man called Solly the Bass, from Pop's old Minsk choir, thundered the deep harmonies. Another tenor, a remote member of the Mishpokha named Uncle Shmuel, a thin sad little man who smoked even more than Sidney Gross, picked up Pop's melodies and after the holidays sold his cigar store and became a full-time cantor, playing wedding chapels and funeral parlors. The choir itself fell apart after that first year. The laundry ate too much into Pop's time and energy.

Now as to the music itself, give me a moment to tell you about it. The compositions of Reb Mordechai the *Hazan* are the sound track of my childhood. Not long ago I dug into the matter and found out that Reb Mordechai Shavelson's choir music had been admired not only in Minsk but all over Russia, though there had been some purist carping at his composing waltzes, mazurkas, marches, and unmistakable love songs to set to the High Holy Day texts. But that was the very magic of Reb Mordechai's melodic gift. His High Holy Day service was something between a Broadway musical and a grand opera. Obviously, he was a brilliant composer; but Russian Jews were shut off from the art and culture of the big cities, so he poured all his talent into the synagogue liturgy. At least he was appreciated. Pop told me that when Yom Kippur ended the worshippers would carry Reb Mordechai on their shoulders through the streets of Minsk, cheering.

My big solo came on a line from Isaiah:

> *And it shall be on that day*
> *That a great shofar shall be sounded*
> *And the lost ones shall return*
> *From the land of Assyria*
> *And the scattered ones*
> *From the land of Egypt*

To bow down to the Lord
In his holy mountain,
In Jerusalem.

That melody! That sweet, painfully yearning, long-breathing line of song, ending in a burst of joy from the whole choir behind me, on the words, "In his holy mountain, in Jerusalem!" I tell you, even in rehearsal when those male voices roared out around me my hair would stand on end; and in the packed basement of the Minsker Congregation, when my piping voice floated out above the silent mass of men in white prayer shawls and shiny-eyed women in their curtained-off section — where I could see Mama looking at me with tears rolling down her face —

And it shall be on that day
That a great shofar shall be sounded . . .

I rode on a wave of exaltation, of hot prickling thrills, that I feel again as I write these words.

* * *

CAPTAIN Abe Herz of the Israeli Defense Force reserve was at our house the other night, calling on my difficult daughter Sandra. Because he's attending the Army Industrial College here outside Washington, he was wearing his parachutist uniform, red beret and all, which gets our Sandra all glassy-eyed, though she's a fire-eating pacifist who once marched on the Pentagon right behind Norman Mailer, carrying a six-pack for him. I told Abe about the Minsker Congregation, the hole in the ground, and the facade above that led nowhere. "American Judaism," Abe growled. The son of Mark Herz, an old college chum of Peter Quat's and mine, Abe emigrated to Israel in 1968, and has since been getting more and more Israeli by the year.

Then I got to reminiscing about Pop's choir, and Sandra urged me to sing this same Isaiah melody for him. An unpredictable screwball, she loves Reb Mordechai's music, and can pick out a lot of it on her guitar. So she accompanied me and I sang, *"And it shall be on that day."* Abe listened with a fixed, rather stony expression.

"Well?" said Sandra.

"Very nice."

"What's the matter with it?"

"Nothing. Very nice."

"Don't be like that," said Sandra with an edge in her voice.

"Holocaust music," said Abe Herz. "Music to march into gas chambers by. Very nice."

What kind of fellow would say that? Bit of background on this young American-Israeli lawyer, who is Sandra's current swain, though they both dissimulate about it. Abe's father, Mark Herz, has become a high-powered, low-profile scientist; no Einstein or Oppenheimer yet, but up there among the gray eminences. Abe is his only son, from his first marriage. I first met Abe on a gloomy November morning, right after the 1968 election. He sat across the desk from me in the Goodkind and Curtis office, looking me in the eye.

"Mr. Goodkind, do you like what you're doing?"

Now, get the picture. Editor of the *Columbia Law Review*, tall weedy young devil, lean bright sallow Jewish face, looking a hell of a lot more like Mark Herz, the big man on campus of 1933, than Mark himself does today. Hated Mark's present wife, hated (and still hates) Mark. Disgusted with the swelling tumor called the Vietnam War. Cousins, aunts, uncles in Israel. One of the uncles — now retired Brigadier General Moshe Lev — was on the command staff in the terrific Six-Day War victory. This fascinated Abe Herz.

His father Mark's opinion of Israel was — and remains — that the whole country is a Jewish mistake, preposterous and suicidal, and that the Six-Day War was a fluke; his arguments are convoluted and vehement, but that's what they boil down to. Another reason why Abe detests his father. Or possibly he's for Israel because Mark isn't. Anyway, what with my being a heavy Zionist practicing law on Wall Street, I was supposed to straighten out Abe Herz. My job, to persuade him not to *make aliya,* that is, emigrate to Israel, but to settle down to a remunerative law career here.

"Do I like what I'm doing?"

Awkward question. Keen Herz eyes boring at me. Small room for maneuver.

"Very much, yes. I'm a happy man. The wife I wanted, the sort of children I wanted, the standard of living I wanted, challenging work."

"The work you wanted?"

"The work that came to my hand."

"Because you wanted to make money."

"So will you, Abe, and there's not much to be made in Israel."

"Mr. Goodkind, I appreciate all this." Honest shrewd smile. "Maybe you're right. I just think I can do something more with my life than be a Wall Street shit-eater."

The way he said it, believe it or not, miraculously inoffensive. A pleasant blaze of idealistic light on his face. Across the gulf between age twenty-three and age fifty-three, he pulled no punches, didn't handle the old codger with kid gloves, talked straight. Made the candor seem a rough-edged compliment . . . almost.

That finished me. What did I owe Mark Herz, anyway? I stood up and stretched out a hand. "I envy you, Abe."

And so I did then, and so I still do. But I don't want to make aliya, any more than my wife does. If I finish this book, maybe Abe Herz will read it one day. It should answer in full his question: "Do you like what you're doing?"

First he has to know me better. I am not just his father's old one-dimensional college friend, the staunch UJA and Israel Bond lawyer who wouldn't think of moving to Israel; the American Jew, in short. I am my father's son. Elya Goodkind emigrated from Russia, not to Palestine but to the Goldena Medina. A Jewish State was then the remote dream of a few contentious idealists, most of them in Europe, only a few pioneering in Turkish Palestine. What Pop wanted was a good life and freedom. These he achieved, and so here I sit in the White House, six thousand miles from the beleaguered Jewish homeland, about to write down more of my story as fast as I can. For events both there and here threaten to run wildly out of control, if the intelligence reports are true.

* * *

20

The Sauerkraut Crocks

WE never called my grandmother anything but Bobbeh, a Yiddishizing of the Russian "Baba," so let's launch her here by that name.

Bobbeh arrived shortly after the Hollooeen disaster. Lee and I had been hearing talk about Bobbeh long before that, and also about one "Uncle Velvel," both of whom my father was bringing over from the old country. Bobbeh was Pop's mother, of course. Uncle Velvel was Mama's half brother, son of Zaideh by the Koidanov stepmother. The Koidanov strain may help to account for Uncle Velvel's peculiarities, as they unfold.

Pop's father had by now died in what had become the Soviet Union. Bobbeh was alone and miserable, for the workers' paradise was no place for a shammas's pious old widow. So Pop decided to bring Bobbeh to America. Velvel would come over too, the plan was, and share a little apartment with her. Velvel was in his twenties, unmarried. Bobbeh would keep house for him, and he would work at the Fairy Laundry, or teach Hebrew or something. This was all Mom's idea, the Velvel part. I am not saying, exactly, that Mom was maneuvering to avoid having Bobbeh under her roof; though if she was, why not? That would have been simple prudence, based on long human experience, even if she thought her mother-in-law sheer joy to have around. Mom had gotten to know Pop's mother in Minsk. I don't know what impression of Bobbeh she had brought away with her, but she was powerfully anxious to get Uncle Velvel to America.

So at supper for a while we heard more about Bobbeh, and Uncle Velvel, and shiffskartes, and visas, and passports, and money orders, and Ellis Island, than about the Fairy Laundry even; and most of all, about money orders for Uncle Velvel. Uncle Velvel was having a hard time settling his debts, bribing the Soviet immigration authorities, and buying clothes and luggage for the journey. Always something. Bobbeh's arrangements went smooth as oil, but importing Uncle Velvel kept getting more and more expensive. Still, Mom was steely in her resolve to be reunited with her half brother. With every letter or cable that came from Velvel, another money order went shooting over to Minsk. At last all was arranged. Mama's desperate push to have them sail on the same boat from Riga fell through, but Uncle Velvel was booked on the very next ship, leaving three weeks later.

Bobbeh arrived. Lee and I, peering down the narrow tenement stairwell, saw her come hobbling up step by step, assisted by my father. Our first impression was of a little old lame bewigged lady smiling shyly over her brown fur collar. She entered our flat talking old-country Yiddish, and in fact never did talk anything else. Bobbeh moved in with us then and there. No alternative. Uncle Hyman had no room, and Uncle Yehuda had recently broken off communication, in his disgust with the bank's crass greed about the promissory notes. It was only for three weeks, after all, until Uncle Velvel came. Mom had already lined up a flat that would do very nicely for Velvel and Bobbeh.

So Mom and Pop made the best of it; gave Bobbeh their own big bed, displaced Lee and me from the davenport, and put us in the kitchen: Lee on a cot, and me on the floor. Things became fairly snug in Apartment 5-D. Snug, and pungent. Bobbeh used some old-world liniment for her stiff limbs, which it seemed that I could smell over in the public school, though that may have been an olfactory delusion. But as Mom kept repeating like a striking cuckoo clock, it was only for three weeks, three weeks, three weeks.

The three weeks passed. Lee and I went along with our parents to meet Uncle Velvel's steamship. We all stood on the wharf behind a railing, watching the immigrant families throng down the steerage gangway of a huge rusty liner. Mom kept saying, "There he is! That's Velvel. No, Velvel is shorter," and so forth, running frantically back and forth to get a better look at the arrivals. The stream of immigrants slackened. No Velvel. Pop went aboard the boat, and returned with a very strange expression. He and Mom began talking in Russian. Whenever some topic was not fit for our ears they would talk

Russian. This time the cover failed. Their gestures, their tones, their looks, said everything. Thus, more or less:

PAPA: He's not on board.

MAMA: What! It's impossible! *(looking desperately about)* Did we miss him when he got off?

PAPA: His name isn't on the passenger list.

MAMA: But I called the company. His name *was* on their list.

PAPA: He didn't sail. He wasn't on board. The ship's officers told me that.

MAMA: They're crazy! He's stuck on Ellis Island. You go over to Ellis Island and get him.

PAPA *(with great patience):* I'm telling you he's not on the ship's list, Sarah. Something happened, and he never left Riga. He's still over there. With all that money.

MAMA *(close to a scream):* Will you stop arguing and get on the next ferry to Ellis Island? Velvel is on Ellis Island. Maybe he has sore eyes, or a bad back. You go and get Velvel off Ellis Island, you hear? Don't take no for an answer. If there's trouble call Assemblyman Bloom. He gets everybody off Ellis Island. I'll take the children home. You telephone me from Ellis Island, so I can talk to Velvel.

PAPA: But suppose he's not on Ellis Island?

MAMA *(wild-eyed):* Go! GO! He's on Ellis Island!

Ellis Island was the screening point in New York harbor for incoming immigrants. Quite a few who made it past the Statue of Liberty never got beyond Ellis Island. I have an uncle in Minsk, now about ninety-three years old, who was turned away for an ear infection; he glimpsed the Manhattan skyscrapers, and sailed back to live out his life in the Soviet Union. We still correspond in Yiddish. Only he was left alive of all the Goodkinds and Levitans, after the Germans occupied Minsk. He somehow escaped and sat out the war behind the Urals.

Velvel was not on Ellis Island. When Pop came home with this report, Mama was beside herself. Gloom thickened the liniment-laden atmosphere of Apartment 5-D, and Bobbeh turned blue. Not literally, but still spectacularly. Bobbeh's blue spells were to become a part of life in 5-D thereafter. I'd come home from school and Lee would whisper to me, "Bobbeh is blue." This meant that we had to steer clear not only of Bobbeh, but of Mama, and that it was no time to get in Pop's way, either.

Ordinarily Bobbeh was a smiling, almost chirpy little old thing. Her well-groomed white hair tucked under the prescribed brown wig of pious ladies, she would busy herself around the kitchen, possibly getting in Mom's way, but turning out some very superior coffee cakes, egg breads, noodles, and strudels, which it seemed to me Mom never properly admired. But when Bobbeh turned blue, all changed. She was a fright. A bitter disconsolate look on her face, her wig discarded, she would stump here and there, endlessly combing white hair that fell loosened past her shoulders; she would not speak, and would not answer when spoken to; or she would hole up in the bedroom, silently emanating waves of misery and liniment. This ghastly business could go on for days; and it was triggered for the first time by Mom's obvious agitation at Velvel's non-arrival. Until then Mom had been sweet as pie around Bobbeh, but with this blow the mask slipped, and Bobbeh turned blue.

I'll interject here that the Velvel mystery was cleared up months later by a long letter in Yiddish which came to the Fairy Laundry from Riga. Papa read it at the supper table. Bobbeh wasn't blue at the moment, but Mama, as she listened, turned pretty blue herself. It went something like this:

> Much respected and beloved Sarah Gitta, brother-in-law Reb Elya Alexander, and children Israel David and Leah Miriam, live well and happy, amen!
>
> You owe me congratulations, I'm a bridegroom! It was a God-thing, decreed from Heaven. I met my destined other half in Riga, while I was arranging for the shiffskarte, and I knew at once that it had to be. She comes from one of the finest Jewish families in Riga, her father is a very well-to-do dealer in hay and feed and very learned, and her mother is distantly related to the Vilna Gaon. The dowry is very generous, though we are still discussing details and I haven't collected it yet, and meantime we have settled down in a nice little flat in Riga. Malka, that is my beloved bride, does not want to go to America, she says people are not religious enough there, so we will stay in Riga.

The letter went on and on about the bride's family, about the flat, about Velvel's gilded prospects of becoming a partner with his fa-

ther-in-law in the hay and feed business, and about the splendid Riga
Jews. There was no mention of the large sums my father had sent
Velvel. That I recall, because Pop said in a puzzled tone when he
finished the reading, "Isn't it strange? And what about all the money?"
Mama barked, "Money? He's from Koidanov!"

And so the kitchen scene fades out. There is more to tell about
Uncle Velvel — this was just his first move — but all in good time.

There was no way anybody could snap Bobbeh out of a blue spell.
She usually did it herself, by making something: an unusual pie, a
complicated soup, or some major old-country recipe, like home-brewed
wine. Early on she made some superb wine, jugs and jugs of it. Prohibition was on then, and the only wine one could buy was purple
slop with no kick. Bobbeh's wine was the sensation of Aldus Street.
Mom passed a sample to Paul Frankenthal's mother for Sabbath use;
not that the Frankenthals did much about the Sabbath. The next day,
all white-toothed smiles, Mrs. Frankenthal was in our apartment,
flattering Bobbeh in her discordant Galician Yiddish, praising the wine
to the skies, and dropping hints like brontosaurus footfalls that she
would appreciate a jug or two, and might even pay for it. Her husband just loved it.

Bobbeh sweetly referred her to her darling daughter-in-law, for
whom, she said, she had made the wine. It was all up to Mama. So
Mrs. Frankenthal had to start all over, and fawn on Mom. She carried on about what a brilliant boy I was, and how Paul said that I
was the star of Mr. Winston's class, and that her husband was always
after Paul to be more like Davey Goodkind, and that I was breaking
the hearts of all the girls in Class 7-A because I was so handsome.
Mom's appetite for such stuff was gross and insatiable, and I rather
enjoyed hearing it myself, though we both knew that it was hogwash; that — in respect to us Goodkinds — the apartment across the
hall was the next thing to a Coo Coo Clan lodge, and that Mrs.
Frankenthal was just sucking around for some of Bobbeh's wine.

Her rough spouse must have ordered her not to return without
the goods, because she wouldn't leave. Mom let her grovel and crawl
until she was visibly worn out. Then Mom said that Bobbeh had of
course made the wine for Passover; that the whole family gathered
then and drank gallons and gallons of wine; but that if any was left
after Passover she would gladly give Mrs. Frankenthal a jugful.

Meantime, her compliments to Mr. Frankenthal and Paul. Mrs. Frankenthal gave up and left, with a Dracula glare much like her son's, evidently a hereditary trait.

With this wine triumph of Bobbeh's, tensions eased in our tight quarters. Still, Mama put heavy pressure on Pop to bring his married sister Rivka, husband and all, for Bobbeh to live with. Correspondence was already going on between Pop and Rivka, but Rivka's husband was objecting to the capitalist system, and that needed some working out. Meantime, Mom had her eye on a big vacant flat on Longfellow Avenue, several blocks away but still in the P.S. 75 district. She wanted to settle the Aldus Street lease and move there at once. My sister Lee was getting on, she argued, and I was no infant, and we couldn't go on sharing a davenport; or a kitchen either, even though I was on the floor and Lee in a cot. But for once Pop dug in. Velvel had drained our savings, he protested. Bringing over Rivka and her husband would cost another fortune. Moreover, things were not good in the Fairy Laundry. It was no time to take on a bigger flat at a higher rent.

A major crisis was in fact on at the laundry, just then. A Mr. Susslowitz, a lean choleric real estate man, very religious, had bought into the laundry as a fourth partner to relieve the debt load. He soon perceived that Brodofsky and Gross were dead weights, but it took him some time to get on to Brodofsky in all his dim-witted grandeur. The matter of horses versus trucks tore the veil.

The laundry bundles were still being collected and delivered by wagons such as Jake the drunk drove. Mr. Susslowitz figured out that two trucks could do the job of all seven wagons, bring in more business, and cost less to run. He offered to advance the money for the trucks. Brodofsky resisted. His interminable and incoherent arguments boiled down to two: (a) the wagon driver Morris was his brother-in-law, and Morris was too nervous to handle a truck; (b) the stable owner, Samuel Bender, was his cousin, and Brodofsky's cry was, "Ve not shet Sam Bender's bloot! Ve neffer shet Sam Bender's bloot!" One night the partners met in our Aldus Street flat, and Brodofsky kept Lee and me awake for hours, pounding the dining-room table and bellowing, "Ve not shet Sam Bender's bloot!"

Mr. Susslowitz remained after the partners left that night, and he and Pop went on arguing in Yiddish. Susslowitz had a way of throwing around Aramaic terms from the Talmud. "They're both idiots!" Susslowitz shouted. "Idiots! The one difference is, Gross is a common-law idiot, and Brodofsky is a statutory idiot!* An animal in the form of a man! How can you put up with them? How have you lasted this long, without turning into an idiot yourself?"

"They started me in the business," Pop said mildly.

"That statutory idiot goes," fumed Susslowitz, "or I pull out."

"We can't buy you out, Susslowitz. You know what condition we're in."

"Then get rid of Brodofsky. Brodofsky goes! What kind of business is this? Morris, the nervous brother-in-law! Sam Bender's blood! An animal in the form of a man! A statutory idiot!"

"You're asking me to do a very hard thing, Susslowitz."

"Goodkind, you can die young, that's your affair. You can eat your guts out, arguing with that statutory idiot. I have high blood pressure. I go or he goes, I say."

Susslowitz went. Pop would not force out Brodofsky. To save the Fairy Laundry, he tried the banks, the moneylenders, and finally the big downtown firm that sold the laundry its soap and chlorine. To keep a good customer going, the boss of the soap company, a German named Mr. Kornfelder, bought out Susslowitz, and became a silent partner on harsh terms; and so partial control of the laundry passed into Outside hands. One of Kornfelder's terms was an immediate switch from wagons to trucks. It was done forthwith. Brodofsky did not bring up the question of Sam Bender's blood. Mr. Brodofsky never did open his mouth much around the gentile partner.

Morris, the brother-in-law, took over supervision of the boiler room, and in a month or so scalded half his skin off by turning the wrong valve. The Fairy Laundry had to pay him compensation, and when he recovered he went to work in Sam Bender's stable. Brodofsky now had a new grievance against my father, the scalding of Morris. It would never have happened, he said over and over, if Pop had not yielded to Mr. Kornfelder in that weak-kneed way, and shed Sam Bender's blood.

Well, with the buy-in of Kornfelder the crisis was over. Mom prevailed. The move to Longfellow Avenue was on. Rivka's husband was

---

*The Aramaic, for the curious: statutory idiot, "shayteh d'*ooreissa*"; common-law idiot, "shayteh d'ra*bon*an."

still having problems with the capitalist system, and Mama's back was breaking from the sag in the davenport, so she said; and she also kept complaining to Papa that the davenport was "too public," a description that baffled me. I asked Lee what that meant, and she replied that I was a *shayteh d'ooreissa*, that is, a statutory idiot. Lee didn't understand Aramaic, but she had gathered the import from Mr. Susslowitz's tones, and she liked the snappish sound of it.

And so I found myself leaving Aldus Street and the hegemony of Paul Frankenthal at last. With this came the cataclysm of Bobbeh's sauerkraut.

To make her wine, Bobbeh had required a number of crocks: huge clay vessels with extra-heavy lids. Pop knew just what she needed, bought them on the Lower East Side, and one by one hauled them up the five floors. Mama grumbled all through this effort, and she grumbled more when the crocks were lined up in our hall. We had to slide along the wall just to get into the flat. Bobbeh's activities with cheesecloth, sugar, and grapes generated some curious odors, once fermenting set in. But as I've said, the wine was a hit, and all was forgiven.

However, there were the crocks, now clean and empty, and Bobbeh took it into her head to make sauerkraut. She asked Pop to buy her a few dozen heads of cabbage. At that Mom put her foot down hard. Nobody in the family liked sauerkraut! She could buy all she ever needed at the delicatessen, for ten cents! So what was the point? The right thing was to get rid of those big crocks; sell them, or even give them away. Bobbeh turned blue. It was a terrible weapon. Mom caved in, and my father bought the cabbages, an astonishing pile, and stacked them in the parlor, great round objects redolent of the great outdoors and of Mother Earth, an agreeable novelty on Aldus Street.

And Bobbeh turned to making the sauerkraut.

* * *

21

The War Alarm

May 1973

EGYPT is about to attack Israel. It's set for mid-May; secret intelligence, and evidently hard fact. So I've sat up all night, scribbling away, trying at least to finish the great sauerkraut affair before what looks like a long break in my peace. Couldn't make it. If those last pages seemed more helter-skelter than the rest, that's why. The dawn is streaked pink outside the library window of our rented Georgetown house. The street lights just went out. I've got to snatch some sleep.

I hope this isn't the end of my book, but I hardly see how I can go on writing, in that tumbling cement mixer of a White House down on Pennsylvania Avenue. On the other hand, if I resign and go back to my law firm — a step I'm considering — that'll be curtains. My mind will sink again into the muck of legal English, and to attempt narrative in odd hours with such a bemired instrument will be futile.

The fact is I was beginning to love that big dark dusty half-forgotten office in the Executive Office Building, and the solitary hours of roaming in my past, piling up the pages. I imagined that by now I'd be reliving those iridescent brief years with Bobbie Webb, yet here I am, no farther than Bobbeh and the sauerkraut. Long haul, Bobbeh to Bobbie! I can only plug on, and hope to get there if I find the time and retain my wits. But for the moment, the scroll of remembrance has to roll up, while I blearily turn to the day's abrasive realities.

Abe Herz has been called home. He telephoned Sandra very late at night, woke her up to tell her he was "going back to familiar scenery." Abe served a year on the Suez Canal line during what the Israelis call the War of Attrition, the little-publicized but very costly border conflict at the Canal after the Six-Day War. Sandra came into our bedroom and stirred us up. I'd already heard, at the White House, and from the Israeli ambassador, about the war alarm, but I didn't let on. Jan sat with Sandra drinking scotch and talking most of the night, while I wrote and wrote.

My troublesome daughter Sandra is twenty-one, upsettingly beautiful in a darkish way, with large overpowering eyes which I can resist only by laughing at her. She cuts men down with those eyes as though with twin-mount lasers. I don't mean young men, I mean any men. She slops around in patched rags, looking marvellous, and if she wants to, she can groom herself up to dazzling formal chic in half an hour. To a possibly fond father Sandra looks like a Jewish entry for Miss Universe; at any rate, she is a smart tough sort, a straight-A Wellesley graduate: informed, positive, and out to make old I. David Goodkind's life miserable, for reasons obscure. About the time I took on the tax problems of the United Jewish Appeal and became chief counsel, Sandra brought home an Arab, a Saudi attending Yale. Imagine, if you will, a young Arab in preppy garb sitting at our Friday night candle-lit kosher table on Central Park West, listening politely as we sang Hebrew songs! That gives you an idea of Sandra Goodkind and suggests her range, since Abe Herz is her current interest, though neither of them outright acknowledges it.

Well, dear Sandra does seem to have put her shapely little foot in the door, doesn't she? There is only one way with Sandra Goodkind. Firmly but gently I shove her pretty foot back outside, and I clang the door shut. I have enough on my mind.

If the war does break out, I don't see how this President can handle it. The main question about him now is whether — or indeed when — he will resign. The newspapers and the television carry almost nothing else, it seems. Every day there are new scoops, new leaks, new accusations. Small fry and medium fry have been indicted right and left, and now the hue and cry is narrowing in on this one personage. It has become a public manhunt, a colossal and eerie national spectator sport. The press is in full cry. The hounds are leaping and snarling at the quarry treed in the White House. Anything goes. The wildest rumor, the most farfetched story, gets attributed to faceless "sources" and plastered all over the front page. I'm not talking about the yellow rags but about *The New York Times* and *The Washington Post*. The TV anchormen vie for hot lead-off stories about the President. Like as not the stories turn out within the week to be exaggerated or phony, but nobody minds, nobody notices, nobody apologizes.

We lived through the same kind of hoo-ha twenty years ago, the McCarthy business; a rabbit shoot of frightened little bureaucrats who in their dim pasts had gotten caught up in depression radicalism, a few to the extent of joining the Communist party. It was all lunkheaded nonsense, first to last, kicked off by the trapping of one sizable bureaucrat, Alger Hiss, in lies to a congressional committee about his Communist past. The press and television went baying in exactly this way after every new name that cropped up in Senate hearings launched by a Senator McCarthy of Wisconsin. It was nightmarish. It had all our liberal crowd in a tizzy, not a few of them getting rid of their old copies of Karl Marx and John Strachey, just in case the FBI would come knocking at midnight. Quite a few lives and careers were blasted in all that malignant tumult. McCarthy uncovered nothing, nothing at all.

The irony of all this is that the President, then a congressman, was the very man who trapped Hiss in perjury. It made him a national figure. Of course he cheered on the McCarthy hullabaloo, right up to the moment when the Senator got condemned by the Senate and fell out of sight. Now he himself is the target of just such a hue and cry, and in my obscure office I hear wails echoing through the White House about the unfairness and irresponsibility of the media. The poetic justice of it all escapes everybody around here: to wit, that this is the Hiss-McCarthy thing in reverse, assailing the very man who touched it all off twenty years ago.

And the richest irony, maybe, is that our liberal crowd — and my dear wife Jan leading the pack — snatch up the newspapers, gloat over the Watergate headlines, grin and giggle at the television stories, happy as pigs in clover with the whole thing; we, who were so indignant and horrified at the way the media were trumpeting Senator McCarthy's accusations, hounding his targets with sensational stories, and being so horridly unfair. All over the political spectrum, I guess, human nature is much the same.

I've said I'm keeping the Watergate mess out of these pages, and it still goes. That the President and his inner crowd got involved in some very rancid misconduct, indeed subversion, and that he has now been caught lying in his teeth about it, seems evident to me, as it does to the newshounds and their public. Everyone smells blood. Everyone is caught up in the thrilling daily serial melodrama of bringing down a President. Behind it all, it seems to me — though nobody is saying this yet — is the anger over our Vietnam flop. Americans don't like getting licked. Somebody's head has to roll, and he's the President. Three other Presidents backed us into that war, but our crawl-out happened on his watch. The poor fellow poses with the returning prisoners of war, thinking it does him some good in the Watergate mess; and he just paints himself tighter into the corner as the crook who bombed the poor Asiatics and lost the war anyway.

I have *got* to get to bed, the sun's shining on my desk. But I have just referred to the President of the United States, the most powerful politician on earth, as a "poor fellow," and that's revealing, isn't it? It may be why I'll decide to stay on. Here is the original Horatio Alger figure, the American dream incarnate, the nobody who rises by sheer drive and grit out of poverty and obscurity to the Presidency. I don't think any President since Lincoln has had more lowly beginnings. There he is in the White House; and nobody loves him, and legions hate him, and that has been true ever since he got there. To be forced to resign from the Presidency almost seems to have been his fixed fate, the star he has unknowingly been following, all his days.

Well, I have a front seat at this melodrama. With the rising Watergate sewage, the smell of which seeps through the place, I have nothing to do. Jan would claw me for saying this, but if I could I'd help the bedevilled bastard. I keep trying to do that, in the snippets I contribute to his speeches. Meantime it's a glorious morning out there, and the magnolias are in bloom. A few hours' sleep, and then a walk to the White House, my chief pleasure in these dismal and scary days.

Will Egypt really attack?

* * *

Two weeks have passed since I penned those weary hasty pages. Let me pick up the pieces quick-march. Abe Herz is back. False alarm. Either that, or the Israeli mobilization made the Egyptians think better of it. Stand-down on the Egyptian side of the Canal, anyway, after a massing of troops and equipment that looked like D-day minus one.

First thing Herz did when he returned, practically, was to get into a fight with Sandra. That romance is off for now. Sandra's views on Israel are strong and negative. The Arab boy friend, I've always believed, was an expression of Sandra's opinion of Israel — and of me, for taking on the UJA — made as explicit and as jarring as possible. Since the Six-Day War I've come to believe, like most Jews, that the destiny of our ancient people now turns on the fulcrum of Israel. If my little New Leftist Phi Bete can't grasp that, okay. I myself once thought Zionism was for the birds. *Il faut que la jeunesse se passe,* as the wise Frenchies put it.

The Israeli ambassador scared the hell out of me, two weeks ago, by confiding that the Israeli defense line along the Canal is paper-thin. In effect nobody is there, just a handful of troops moving around to give an impression of being ten times as many as they are. How can Israel take this risk? Answer, a damn sobering one: no choice. Israel has a very small standing army. Its military strength lies in its reserves. The whole country can spring to arms in a matter of days, and the reserves are remarkably well trained. The economy can't stand any other arrangement. Abe Herz says that even the swift brief mobilization from which he has just returned cost Israel twenty to thirty million dollars. Rough, on such a poor and tiny country.

Abe says — and at lunch yesterday the ambassador, now much less tense, made the same point — that the Israeli victory in 1967 so over-awed the Arabs that a skeleton force of a couple of thousand along the Canal can face down the whole Egyptian army, unless it masses at the Canal on a full war footing. I hope that's right. When I visited the Israeli installations along the Canal a few years ago, they seemed damned meager to me, but I told myself, "What the hell do I know about land warfare?" Sizable Egyptian formations moved in plain sight on the other side of that broad ditch. The handful of Israeli soldiers facing them seemed cheerful and self-confident, though pretty lonesome out there in the sand, the blazing sun, and the flies, living on field rations and anxious to get relieved; tanned brawny kids in green fatigues, nearly all of them younger than my own two sons.

Brezhnev's due here, so the media are momentarily letting up on the President. The howling storm that burst over him after his "clarifying statement," a revelation of some long-hidden White House misdeeds, is starting to die down. The statement was forced on him, obviously, because someone on the inside was about to squeal and seek immunity. It'll all be in the history books one day, this shocking Presidential confession of surreptitious crimes, committed by goons in his secret employ, to get evidence on people he considered malefactors. No wonder the cartoonists now show the White House collapsing, as in an earthquake; or the President on a ship in a typhoon, rolling two steel balls; or else he's standing on a sandspit labelled *Presidency,* that's awash and melting in a tidal wave; or he's cowering in a fierce beam of light, stripped to his jockstrap. All sorts of jolly representations of our Head of State fill our press, as he prepares to meet the boss of the Soviet Union.

I was in the thick of that "clarifying" bombshell. I couldn't contribute too much, not knowing exactly what was going on. But the startling thing I'm beginning to perceive is, *nobody may know the whole truth about Watergate, not even the President.* The affair is so complicated, and it was so secretive to begin with, and so many people are now lying, and everybody's motives are so desperate and so suspect, and there's so much buck-passing, that it's all becoming a hall of mirrors; a hundred images and half-images bouncing around and receding into an infinity of prismatic shadows, until you can't tell where you are, or what's an image and what's real. The President may even be groping among the mirrors himself. Still, he knows more than he's letting on to the public. He once said to me, very soberly and earnestly, "David, it's too bad national security precludes our going the hangout route, because that would be the easy way." In advertising-man patois — the chief legacy around here of the departed German shepherds — "going the hangout route" means telling the truth.

He said that at the time he found me studying the Talmud. Somehow the glimpse of that exotic tome got to him. He sat down and talked about his parents, especially his mother, whom he reveres; and about his Quaker upbringing, and his unchanged fundamental belief in a Supreme Being, and his practice of praying for guidance in difficult hours, and his respect for the tenacity and brilliance of the Jewish people. "I know something about tenacity," he said with a far-off look from under those heavy cartoon eyebrows; and he added wearily, with a twisted little smile, "also, about being disliked." I've been glancing again at the description I wrote down of that strange chat, and I can now understand why Jan saw red. He does come out sort of sympathetic, and to her he is a loathsome tricky knave who must fall. Nothing else. She doesn't want to be confused with light and shade, or with multiple mirror images.

When the "clarifying statement" reached its final form, word went down to "run it past Dave Goodkind for the ethical angle." You can believe that or not, but it happened. What with my yarmulka and my Talmud, I was evidently counted on to detect and correct ethical sour notes to which he and his staff might be tone-deaf. In fact, I did suggest changing a few phrases and sentences; and they were changed, and I got from him a scribble of praise and thanks.

Around this White House nothing seems to be in itself right or wrong, you see, moral or immoral, law-abiding or criminal. There's only one standard: things either work or they don't work. Vaguely sensing the limits of that viewpoint, they run the statement past me for "the ethical angle." It all has an Alice in Wonderland sound, but even Lewis Carroll couldn't have thought up the fantasy of running a speech past me — I. David Goodkind, tax lawyer, artful dodger and wriggler for hire — for the ethical angle! Well, the White House staff tried to laugh off Watergate as a caper, and now one by one they're capering over a precipice. The boss man seems about to caper off into the void himself, and free-fall. If so, I'll help him with the ethical angle till he hits. I don't know exactly why, but I want to. A hell of a way for a President to face Brezhnev, stripped to his jockstrap.

Meantime I turn back to *April House*, as I've decided to call my book. It's becoming my refuge and my fun. I've never wholly buried the urge to write, that's becoming obvious. Maybe I just envy Peter Quat. Law was my game, regret is vain, and I've done good things in the law, whatever Abe Herz thinks. (He, by the way, when he's not abroad for special training or out on reserve maneuvers and call-ups, now practices tax law in Tel Aviv. Not the first fire-eater to turn shit-eater, I daresay.) But I'm still happiest writing, preferably to make people laugh.

And why not? It was always my bent. My high school and college yearbooks both show, in the senior class vote, "Wittiest — Goodkind." More to the point, it was the way I earned my first dollar. It was the vocation of Molière and Twain, so who can knock it? I believe I'd rather write about my Uncle Velvel, and amuse a few people in these gruesome times, than be a Supreme Court justice. That doesn't mean in the least that jokes are better than law; it simply defines me as a frustrated funny man.

A propos of old Peter, I have at last read a typescript of his new book. *Whew!* Words fail me! Then there's a letter from Mark Herz. About the time his son Abe got called back on the war scare, Mark was invited to lecture in Israel this summer and he may go, just for the money; it's one of those endowed things. Maybe he'll meet his son again in Israel, after long cold estranged years. In all the time Abe's been here, they haven't even spoken on the phone.

Herz, Quat, and Goodkind! The three comic musketeers of Columbia in the 1930's; you'll read all about us soon. Meantime, here we go with Bobbeh's sauerkraut.

* * *

22

The Sauerkraut Crisis

FIRST, can I say a quick kind word about Reuben Brodofsky? I've been bad-mouthing the man right along. He did shorten Pop's life, and he was a small, small person, a midget in mind and soul, shrivelled and soured by jealousy; truly a statutory idiot. I take back none of that.

But there was another side to Reuben Brodofsky. To this day, when I happen to eat kosher delicatessen — pastrami, corned beef, rolled beef, salami, especially with coleslaw and sour pickles, and a certain kind of lumpy white Bronx-style potato salad — I think of Brodofsky and his family. I've told you about his beefy wife, the magazine-clipper. I've skipped over his kids, but in them lay his redeeming side, the obverse of his hate of my father: his love for those three boys and one girl.

Why delicatessen? Well, the partners and their families used to come together on Sunday nights in the shut-down Fairy Laundry for a supper of cold cuts from paper plates. The adults would talk business, and of course Brodofsky talked the most. As his strident Yiddish accents reverberated through the darkened place, we kids would climb over the cold canvas-hooded machinery, play hide-and-seek in the soapy-smelling gloom amid the stacks of laundry, even descend to the black scary boiler room and slosh through the greasy puddles.

Felix Brodofsky was my special chum in these gambols. Once Felix and I, poking around with a flashlight in a storeroom, came on some piled-up dusty boxes under wood trash; and when we opened them, behold, they were full of glittering gold and silver! Having just read *Tom Sawyer*, I thought we had found treasure and were rich for life.

We rushed our find back to our parents, who said they were worthless old tin spangles left by the Woolworth tenant; and they went on talking business and eating cold cuts and potato salad. A hundred Sunday nights like this impregnated kosher delicatessen for me with an everlasting echo of Reuben Brodofsky's voice.

Felix was the youngest Brodofsky boy, about my age, with a wall eye; stout like his mother, and easygoing by nature. We were pretty good friends until once, in Hebrew school during recess, he made fun of me for botching a translation from the Book of Samuel. I'm afraid I overreacted a bit and called him a "fat fuck." This was surely in questionable taste, but Felix made it worse. Like other fatties, when he got mad, he really got mad. He chased me all over the benches in the classroom, out in the hallway, up and down the stairs, threatening murder, throwing off the restraining arms of students and teachers alike, yelling as we ran, "He ain't gonna call me no fat fuck! Ain't nobody calls me no fat fuck!" He sounded very much like his father, objecting to the shedding of Sam Bender's blood. He kept shouting about fat fucks in just the same unnecessary repetitious way. The school was an old wooden house, and Felix's galloping after me made a thunderous racket. The whole place was in an uproar.

Captured at last by two male teachers, we were hauled up before the principal, a very solemn Hebrew scholar named Mr. Abramson. With his wall eye, Felix stared off to one side of the principal and bellowed at vacancy, "Ain't nobody calls me no fat fuck!" Mr. Abramson's thick glasses fell off. He picked them up, and silently waved us out of the office. Neither of us was punished. I guess Mr. Abramson was too numbed to take action. As you can see, Felix was rather a statutory idiot himself, though not a bad guy. In that school he was known thereafter, unfortunately, as that fat fuck. I suspect even Mr. Abramson thought of him as a fat fuck. The alliteration tended to stick in one's mind.

Anyway, the Brodofskys were a clan, a very close Mishpokha all to themselves. As the kids grew up I attended several Brodofsky weddings. The three boys and their sister all married young, and those weddings were incandescent with family affection. They weren't big costly affairs, nor even especially religious in tone. But when those young Brodofskys hugged and kissed each other, and kissed their mother, tubby in pink lace and gardenias, and kissed their grizzled father, all weeping and red-eyed with joy, you were in the presence of the real thing, the hot ties of blood. Brodofsky was a good father, or he couldn't have had such a family.

The old-country friendship, and the immutable truth that Brodofsky had taken Pop into the laundry, were factors, but it was Brodofsky the family man that Pop couldn't throw off his back. I don't know whether to admire Pop for that or to regret it. Either way, it's thirty years too late.

Well, now, about the sauerkraut. Bobbeh's mulish resolve to make it overlapped our move to Longfellow Avenue, otherwise there might never have been such a disaster. A woman on moving day is a dragon. Two women in a move, especially when one is the other's mother-in-law, are virtually the secret of the fusion bomb. Add the fact that Bobbeh, knowing that we were moving because she was cramping Mom's style, had turned deep blue again; and add what I'm about to tell you about the process of making sauerkraut, at least as Bobbeh did it; and you can begin to understand the blowup.

Even piled in the living room, those cabbages ripened fast. Maybe it was because they were stacked against a steam radiator. I only know that when Pop first brought them in they had a pleasant farmland smell; but the very next day, when I came home from school and walked into Apartment 5-D, I was struck with the silly notion that a horse had died there. The Bronx had quite a few dead horses scattered about its streets. The overworked old beasts would collapse, and the wagon drivers would unhitch and drag off their vehicles, leaving the stiffening flyblown carcasses for the municipal authorities to worry about. Dead cats and dogs also abounded, and they had their individual fragrances, but it was the dead horses that you had to hurry past, exhaling all the way.

Well, what I smelled was the cabbages, though Bobbeh hadn't even gone to work on them. The following day, she chopped them up into an amazing quantity of shreds. When I returned from school, heaps of shredded cabbage filled the hallway and the kitchen, and there was a pile in the parlor. I don't know how we ate supper that night, and I can't imagine how Lee and I slept, unless we bedded down on chopped cabbage. But at least the shredding had aerated the stuff, and the smell had calmed down. Also, Mom had opened all the windows. It was very cold in the apartment, except right up against the hissing and whistling radiators, but the air was passable.

A day or two later when I got back from school all the cabbage was gone. So was the smell. This was a big surprise. Somehow Bobbeh, with her old-country magic, had managed to stuff those heaps into the crocks, and to seal the crocks. They were big crocks, but still that was a feat. The flat was clean and normal; not a shred in sight, and no odor. Bobbeh had no doubt mixed in traditional additives which had reduced the vegetation in some drastic way. At any rate, it was all gone.

I think it was I who first noticed the noise. It woke me in the middle of the night; a low grumbling bubbling sound. In itself it wasn't frightening or even obtrusive. It was just strange and new. I got up, wandered through the apartment, trying to locate it, and finally traced it to the crocks. They were still sealed, still odorless, but no longer inert. Things were going on inside the crocks. They were sort of alive. Mystery solved, I went back to sleep. I knew that peculiar things happened with Bobbeh's crocks. The wine had never grumbled, or indeed made any sound, but the crocks had foamed like mad dogs, and had smelled odd. I figured that we could settle happily for a little grumbling from the sauerkraut; not too unlike, actually, the noise Bobbeh made when she walked around in a blue spell.

What follows now should be told in Yiddish. The word for "mutter" in that language — *boorcha* — exactly reproduces how the crocks sounded next morning. In a steady quiet way, they were going *boorcha, boorcha*. Again, the noise was not disagreeable, just unusual. To a nervous or touchy person — certainly Mama's state, for she was packing up for the big move — I daresay it seemed threatening. She confronted Papa at breakfast.

"*Die kroit boorchet*," she said; that is, "The sauerkraut is muttering."

"Muttering?" Papa said absently, drinking coffee with the strained, abstracted look that meant trouble at the Fairy Laundry.

"You can't hear it? You're deaf?"

The soul of patience, Pop put down his coffee, went and listened, and returned. My sister and I, heads down because of Mom's nerves, were hurrying through our oatmeal. "So it's muttering," he said with a shrug.

Mama would not let it go at that. "And why is it muttering?"

"Sarah," Pop said, "I'm not making the sauerkraut, and I have to go to the laundry."

"Go ask her."

Her was Bobbeh. She and Mama were hardly speaking, since Mom had lost her battle against the kraut. Papa was their interlocutor. Things were not good just then in Apartment 5-D.

"Muttering? Of course it's muttering," we soon heard Bobbeh's querulous shout from the bedroom. "What is she, a gentile? Didn't her mother ever make sauerkraut? How do you tell it's working, if it doesn't mutter?" (A weak approximation of Bobbeh's vigorous Yiddish. I'm doing my best.)

Papa returned to the kitchen. "She says the muttering is a good sign. It'll be the finest sauerkraut she ever made."

"I heard what she said. She said that I was a gentile, and that my mother was a gentile. And you didn't answer her a word! Do you realize that makes your children gentiles? Go tell her to apologize!"

This was an unserious rhetorical demand. Papa left for the laundry, and Lee and I slunk out past the crocks *(boorcha, boorcha)*, to go off to school. I seem to remember already detecting a whiff in the hallway, as we passed through, of a new and very horrible odor; but I may be inventing that. By the time I got home in the afternoon, though, the emergency was definitely on. The smell was reaching clear down to the stoop and out into the open air, and kids were gathered on the sidewalk talking about it; talking, too, about the green truck parked at the curb, with NEW YORK CITY HEALTH DEPARTMENT in big gold letters over the city seal.

I am trying to reconstruct something that happened half a century ago. Who summoned the health department? I'll always believe it was Mrs. Frankenthal, taking her final revenge on the departing yoxenta. Certainly she was there on the fifth-floor landing with Mama, Bobbeh, and the lady from 5-C with her daughter, whose bare behind I had inspected years ago, all of them yammering at the health inspector. The smell was really awful when I pushed my way up there through the curious neighbors crowding the stairway; the stench of hell itself, if we're to believe Dante, though the door to our flat was closed.

I took aside Bare-behind to try to find out, through the discordant din, what was going on. She was now a stout plain girl, incidentally, with a stout plain well-draped rear, and we were just good neighbors. I gathered that whoever had called the health department had used her mother's name. Her mother was angrily denying that she had made the call, and was accusing Mrs. Frankenthal of the deed; Mrs. Frankenthal was accusing her of lying, and also complaining about the smell; and Mama and Bobbeh were protesting the inspector's visit in two languages, while he, a big red-faced kindly man in a green uniform, was trying to pacify the ladies in an Irish brogue like a third language. The whole thing was approaching vaudeville, but at the time it was harrowing. My mother seldom yelled, but she could outyell Mrs. Frankenthal without even turning up the volume, and she was in a mood for yelling; it was a real outlet for her dangerous head of steam. Mom might in fact have been glad to see the crocks condemned as a health hazard — a broken sewer line leaking gas wasn't in it with that sauerkraut — but she was embarrassed, naturally, at the way it was happening.

I vividly remember all three fifth-floor women stabbing their fingers at each other and simultaneously screeching, "She — *she* —SHE —" while Bobbeh, who wasn't quite in the picture, kept shouting in her weak voice that of course the sauerkraut had to *boorcha*, if it didn't *boorcha* it wasn't sauerkraut, and were they all gentiles? And what was this big gentile with his big red face doing here anyway?

At last Mom brought the inspector into our apartment, and we all went sidling in after him past the muttering crocks: Bobbeh, Mrs. Frankenthal, Bare-behind and her mother, and I. The inspector sniffed around and lifted one of the lids, releasing some yellow growling vapor; whereupon he burst out laughing and closed the lid tight. He didn't say these words, but this was the tenor: "Faith and begorra, sure 'tis only that the puir auld soul is making sauerkraut, and divil the foin sauerkraut it looks like to me and I'll take me oath to that, bedad and bejabbers." He went off down the stairway laughing fit to kill.

Well, the jeers Mom had to endure from the neighbors, above all from Mrs. Frankenthal, were devastating. All her yoxenta prestige in that apartment house, accumulated over years of fanatical housekeeping, good neighborliness, and blowing her horn about her pedigree and her David, were going up in the mad stink of Bobbeh's crocks. Said Mrs. Frankenthal on one occasion, "My husband still has his gas mask from the war, dollink, if you need it." Stuff like that. It didn't call for wit. Any neighbor could raise a laugh at Mom's expense just by saying something about the price of sauerkraut. Poor Mom!

And it went on to the last. Even when the two vans arrived and the movers were carrying out our furniture on a bright cold morning in March, the neighbors, huddling on the sidewalk to watch and to bid her goodbye, couldn't resist sly digs about the health department, sauerkraut, and mothers-in-law. For Mom it was not just a move, it was a defeat, a rout; and presiding over her ignominious downfall, in a new squirrel coat and muff, was Mrs. Frankenthal, white teeth gleaming in the morning sun shafting down Aldus Street.

"Well, dollink, we'll miss you," said Mrs. Frankenthal, "and we'll miss your smart boy, Davey, and of course we'll miss your mother-in-law. But anyway, whenever she makes sauerkraut over on Long-fellow Avenue, I know we'll think of you, because we'll smell it."

How can I ever forget the words, or the burst of laughter among the neighbors, or Mama's speechless choked response, a sniff and a toss of her head, as she went on with her orders to the movers, swarthy burly Italians gabbling at each other and piling our household goods into the vans? Never before had I seen the big *yoxenta* so utterly put down.

That morning Pop had to go to the laundry as usual, and Lee had to be in school for an exam. I was elected to stay home and assist Mom. My job was to escort Bobbeh to the new flat in a taxicab. For this I was entrusted with a stunning one-dollar bill, a green fortune. My instructions were to give the driver a dime tip, "And don't you dare to keep any of the change, do you hear? I know just how much a taxi costs to Longfellow Avenue, to the *penny!*" Thus Mama, flushed and wild-eyed and mussed up, as she climbed in beside the driver of the first van. I don't know why there were two small vans instead of one big one. Maybe Mom planned it that way. Or maybe this was just a small cheap moving company.

Anyway, off Mom went in the first van, to begin getting our things into the new flat. The two men of the second van were still grunting down the stoop with our old leather davenport, which looked very queer in the sunshine: cracked, shabby, a different color from what it was in the parlor. Bobbeh and I stood on the sidewalk, watching. My orders were to find a cab and come straight to Longfellow Avenue, but of course I wanted to enjoy the loading to the last. The sweating and groaning of the men, and their guttural Italian yells as they wrestled our furniture into the truck, were as good as a movie. When one got behind the wheel and the other chained up the rear door, I started off to Southern Boulevard to find a taxi, but a feeble wail in Yiddish from Bobbeh brought me up short.

"What about my sauerkraut?"

I had quite forgotten the crocks. Without a doubt they had not been brought down. They were still sitting up on the fifth floor in the emptied flat, muttering. Bobbeh hobbled over to the boss mover at the rear door, shook his arm, and in Yiddish — screaming at the top of her little old lungs, to help him understand — she pleaded, "My sauerkraut! Go back and get my sauerkraut!"

He wrinkled his bristly face at her and at me. He wore a ragged red sweater and a knitted cap, a cold cigar was stuck in a corner of his mouth, and he looked like Al Capone. "What's-a she say, kid?"

I told him.

"She's-a mistake," he said. "That stuff-a no go. You tell-a her."

I translated to Bobbeh. She began to cry. That seemed to disconcert Capone. He yelled something in Italian to the fellow at the wheel, a swarthier and still more bristly character in a leather windbreaker. This gorilla jumped down, came to Bobbeh, and said to her in flawless Yiddish, "What's the matter, Grandma?"

I couldn't have been more astounded if a real zoo gorilla had spoken Yiddish. Yet it was really not strange. A simple sort like Jake the drunk, he had evidently gone to work as a mover, so he had learned to bawl in Italian the phrases that movers use. His name was Hymie, and he was as Jewish as Bobbeh, and could talk to her better than I could. Here was the hole in Mama's plot, if it was a plot; the one thing she never foresaw. From then on my problem was mainly to keep up with the rapid-fire exchanges between the boss, Hymie, and Bobbeh.

What came out was this:

The boss had told Mom that getting the full crocks down all those flights would take an extra hour and would cost accordingly, yet he couldn't guarantee against spilling or breakage before delivery to Longfellow Avenue. Whereupon Mama had told him that, as a tip, she was making him a present of the valuable crocks. He could pick them up as soon as the move was finished. She had no interest in the sauerkraut. He could keep the stuff, pour it in the Bronx River, flush it down the toilet, whatever he pleased. He sensibly told that part to me in English, while Bobbeh stared bright-eyed at us, wrinkling up her tearstained face in suspicion, trying to understand.

Belying his looks, Capone now revealed a heart of mush. He kept glancing at Bobbeh, and ended by shouting angrily at Hymie that his own mother was just like this, crazy; these old ladies were all crazy; imagine, crying over some shitty sauerkraut! He would bring the shitty crocks down and not charge for the extra time. Hymie told the decision to Bobbeh, leaving out the obscenities. She kissed him and then, smiling through a stream of tears, hobbled over and kissed Al Capone. Capone said never mind-a that shit, and began to cry, and went tromping up the stoop with Hymie, cursing in Italian and wiping his eyes on his sweater sleeve.

I found a cab, and Bobbeh and I took off for Longfellow Avenue. The new flat was only six or seven blocks away. We could easily have walked it, except for Bobbeh's short leg. This handicap, by the by, was not a birth defect, according to family legend. Rather, in the wealthy home in which Bobbeh had been born, a maidservant had either dropped the newborn baby, or poured scalding water on her, I'm no longer sure which. Growing up deformed, she had been married off to a learned but lowly shammas, and had raised four children in that one log-walled room. So Bobbeh was entitled to her blue spells. The wonder was her usual good cheer. My father was responsible for that. Pop could make his mother laugh with his random drolleries until she was helpless, and he was always working to keep her amused. He could make Mom laugh, too, but he knew when there was no use trying. He hadn't been jollying her much since the arrival of the cabbages.

The new flat was a knockout. I had never seen it before. My first impression when I walked in was a flood of sunshine on dazzling white walls and brilliantly varnished floors. The next was the remarkable change in my mother. Her mood was as sunny as the apartment. She had shaken the dust of Aldus Street from her feet, moved far up in the world, and that was that! Mom actually threw her arms around Bobbeh and kissed her, and they exchanged Yiddish incantations of good luck. Mom proudly led Bobbeh through this vast sunlight-drenched apartment smelling delightfully of fresh paint, to a back bedroom. This, she said, would one day be Lee's room. Meantime, it was all for Bobbeh. A new bed was already in the room, and Mom had unpacked Bobbeh's things and hung them in the closet. All disarmingly solicitous and very canny, for this was the flat's remotest chamber, and Bobbeh was out in Siberia. Yet she was all smiles and Yiddish compliments, as she at once prepared — at Mom's suggestion — to take a nice hot bath in the big glossily tiled bathroom. Bobbeh bathed every morning before applying her liniment. She had missed her bath in the move, and had groused about it very bluely. Now she went hobbling into the bathroom in the highest spirits.

Mom resumed ordering the movers to "put the table here, no, let's try it there," female fashion, while I wandered through this new abode in an exalted daze. She must have worked on the place before the move, because new curtains and draperies were already up. With much of our furniture already in place, it was really a home, our old home, the cramped dark Aldus Street fifth-floor back, miraculously expanded into a spacious radiant front apartment; much nicer even than the Frankenthal flat, because it was so bright. It looked out on vacant lots, not on another tenement front. Except for billboards and a cigar store, the view was sunshine and green fields. Splendid! Magnificent! Lordly! Farewell to Aldus Street, to Izzy, to Frankenthal! So I was thinking, as Hymie and Al Capone came grunting into my bedroom, a huge white empty space, carrying the davenport.

"Pretty nice place, huh?" I said to them, but they only grunted and went out.

I must now ask old readers to recall, and young readers to imagine, the worst moment in the most frightening movie ever made: the silent version of *The Phantom of the Opera,* with Lon Chaney. It comes when the beautiful young singer sneaks up behind the masked Phantom, who is sitting at the piano coaching her. She flips off his mask. Wow! Chaney leaps up, glaring with a face that is no face but a gruesome living skull, and the girl screams and screams and screams. A generation later, Alfred Hitchcock recreated the moment, in *Psycho,* when the girl touches the old lady's shoulder, the chair swivels around, and the old lady is a skeleton in a shawl and a gray wig, and the girl screams and screams and screams.

Well, Mom was in the big front room, still ordering the furniture moved around, when Al Capone and Hymie came groaning into our glorious new apartment, each with a sloshing crock full of sauerkraut slung on his back. I was there. I observed it all, and I'll never forget it. Mom saw the crocks. Her face distorted in the exact horror-stricken expression of the girl who pushed off Lon Chaney's mask. She screamed and screamed and screamed. I had never heard my mother scream before, and it really made my hair stand on end; I could feel it stinging and rising. The boss mover and Hymie stopped where they stood, and the boss hurriedly but carefully lowered his crock to the floor. Hymie tried to do the same, but Mama's screams shook him up so that he couldn't help staring at her. His crock hit the floor at an angle. The top slithered off, and a bubbly mess sloshed out on Mama's newly varnished floor. Hymie caught and straightened the crock, and clattered back the lid, but the damage was done. The apartment filled with the explosive stink of an overturned privy; and there on the sunny hall floor lay a spreading puddle of yellow-green vegetable slop like camel puke, and little blisters were forming in the varnish at the edge of the puddle, in some malignant chemical reaction. What a disaster, and Mama's own fault! What on earth was the point of those mad screams?

And her poor face, suddenly gone pale and distracted! She pounced on a telephone, called the Fairy Laundry number, and began wailing and bellowing at my father in Russian. Meanwhile, the boss mover and Hymie, who shrewdly gathered that she was a little upset, rushed out and rushed in again with bundles of rags. All four moving men began mopping up the spill. They did get it up, and where the stuff had been, they left a broad eaten-away blotch of leprous bare wood. The apartment still smelled frightful, and Mama started struggling to open a window, but it was stuck by the new paint. So the helpful moving men began wrestling with windows, and one of them fetched a crowbar and gouged a lot of paint off a sash, and Mama screamed at him, "*Stop that,* STOP THAT!" At this point Papa arrived, looking pretty pale and wild himself.

He had made good time. He tried to tell Mama that an auxiliary boiler in the laundry had burst so he had to go back at once. Mama overwhelmed him with a torrent of angry Russian, in which three English words kept incongruously recurring: "*old age home.*" Papa's placating Russian responses were getting him nowhere. He briefly disappeared, then reappeared with a grumpy dusty man he called "Superintendent." I knew at a glance that this was a janitor, a wrestler of garbage, who would whomp a boy with a stick as soon as look at him. So, on Longfellow Avenue a janitor was a superintendent! We were truly rising in the world.

Just then through the sauerkraut miasma came wisping a suggestion of liniment. Bobbeh had finished her bath, and would soon be joining the discussion! My beset father ordered me out into the street to play. What would ensue, he probably felt, might not be entertainment suited to minors. I was not sorry to get out, but I hadn't dared move across Mama's range of vision in her berserk mood, past those crocks and the horrid hole eaten in the new varnish of the hallway floor.

Under pressure, I later found out, Papa came up with a stroke of genius. The janitor — pardon me, the superintendent — agreed to let the movers put the crocks up on the roof. Mama accepted that, and Bobbeh didn't mind, once she was reassured that the door to the roof was kept locked. Papa had to cross the superintendent's palm that morning with a hefty bribe, to get him to go along. The superintendent had a nose and was not eager to accommodate this marinating horsemeat, or whatever it was, even on his roof. But money answereth all, the Good Book says, and Pop was truly desperate.

When Bobbeh's sauerkraut finally matured it was, in fact, the best I've ever eaten; none of your limp gray wet tangles of strings they sell nowadays under that name; firm chewy kraut, with something of the farmland tang we had smelled at first, sour but remarkably appetizing, so that you kept eating more and more and more. Lee and I loved the stuff, and Bobbeh loved to watch us eat it. I'm sure Papa was crazy about it, too. But he never took more than a small helping, and always glanced guiltily at Mom first. She wouldn't touch it, claimed it raised lumps on her tongue. The Mishpokha in their visits devoured it, and carried away large quantities. It was as great a hit as the wine.

* * *

HAVE I given my mother a hard time, in this truthful account? Look, who hasn't had a brand-new car scratched, or a fender bent, or a tail-light broken, and gone into an insane rage? It's only the child's grief over a damaged toy, but in an adult it can generate homicidal urgings. That sunny second-floor apartment was Mom's escape from the Frankenthals, from the dingy back flat and grimy five flights of Aldus Street; her first step of upward mobility, which would take her at last to the Central Park West flat where she creeps about today.

When she was about twelve, her stepmother sent her to work —

so Mama once told me — in the best store in Minsk, Levinson's department store, as a delivery girl. The Levinson home, which she often visited, seemed to her a palace: great spaces, elegant furnishings, and an inside toilet with running water! So, Jews could actually live this way! She says she made up her mind at that time that she would one day go to America and have a home like the Levinsons'. I believe that in the Longfellow Avenue apartment that brilliant morning, in the brief time before the crocks came, Mama felt she had arrived in the Levinson house.

But with that awful moment of truth, the slop of Bobbeh's old-country sauerkraut all over her American dream, Longfellow Avenue became just another place to climb away from. In time the smell cleared out, of course; the floor was revarnished, and Bobbeh moved away. But Longfellow Avenue was stunk up for good.

23

Mr. Winston and the Big Yoxenta

I MENTIONED to Mr. Winston that my mother was coming to the school to re-register us with our new address. Flashing that Douglas Fairbanks smile, he said he would very much like to meet her; and he did, the very next day after the sauerkraut cataclysm.

And now, to describe the next great turn in my life, I'm compelled to disclose the affair of Mama and Mr. Winston. That is a most bizarre passage. I haven't bothered to ask Mom about it, her hearing aid would simply go out of commission for a few days. Mysteriously, my sister Lee doesn't treasure this oddity of Mom's early years, and I'm not about to remind her of it. Lee would only improvise a scurrilous fantasy about poor Mom and Mr. Winston, and go on embellishing it for years. In time Mr. Winston might even eclipse the clambake. So let's have none of that.

You understand, of course, that throughout Mama remained pure as the driven snow. Surely I don't have to tell you that about the big yoxenta. It was just foolishness, foolishness on a grand scale, on a Mama scale. Mama seldom did things by halves.

"Send him to a camp? What for?"

We were at supper. Papa looked more pale and abstracted than usual. It was before he gave up smoking, and he had smoked cigarette after cigarette and eaten nothing. A crucial meeting he was about to have that evening with the gentile money man, Mr. Kornfelder, and a new personage, a Mr. Worthington, was much on his mind. I had heard worried talk about this meeting for weeks.

Mama: "Why, he'll grow strong and healthy at a camp. He'll learn all kinds of things."

Pop (not belligerent but baffled): "What sort of things, Sarah?"

"Oh, everything. Canoeing, diving, horseback riding, weaving baskets. Everything."

"Weaving baskets? What for?"

"Why shouldn't he learn to weave baskets?"

"When is this teacher coming?"

"Half past eight."

"Sarah, that's when I meet Kornfelder and Worthington."

"So I'll talk to Mr. Winston myself."

"But what's wrong with Feder's farm?"

"Feder's, again? So he can run wild all summer with that no-good Harold?"

"No-good" Cousin Harold and I, with Mom and Aunt Sophie, had been spending summer vacations for years at Feder's farm in the mountains; a heavenly place enlivened by several frisky Feder daughters. Last summer there had been a shadowy incident involving Harold and one of those daughters. Cousin Harold got a horrendous licking, and now he was "that no-good Harold." The daughter in question had a receding chin and pinkish eyes, and Harold was always throwing windfall apples at her and calling her "Andy Gump," after a chinless comic-strip character, now extinct. Harold was then only a little over nine like me; too old for the doctor game, and hardly up to anything spicier. As I recall, "Andy Gump" got a licking, too, so maybe she did entice Harold into some precocious foolery. In any case, a prime argument for Mr. Winston's summer camp was that I would not be with that no-good Harold. There was no way Mama could foresee, of course, that I would be getting to know Peter Beater Quat.

Papa left. I rushed through my homework, all excited because Douglas Fairbanks was coming to our house, though about summer camp I was dubious. I did not feel suited to the outdoors life. That no-good Harold, now, was a real outdoorsman, a Boy Scout. He had tried taking me along with his scout troop on hikes in the wooded Palisades. It had not worked out. The first time, I stumbled and rolled down the Palisades through brush and brambles, fetching up against a rock with my head. The scoutmaster had to drive me to a hospital in Hackensack to have my head stitched. He was ungracious about this. The next time, using Cousin Harold's scout knife to cut a steak I cooked over a wood fire, I laid my thumb open, and pulsed a lot of blood into my handkerchief, trying to hide the gash, not wanting to annoy the scoutmaster. Still, I trailed blood all over the ground. He noticed it and got very upset, until he found out that the blood was mine; then he cheered up a lot, I guess because I was a visitor, and not in his troop. Or possibly he wanted me to die.

The third time did me in. A can of baked beans, when heated in a fire, needs a hole punched in it to let out the steam. Nobody mentioned this to me. Outdoorsmen know it. We were gathered around a big fire, toasting frankfurters on peeled sticks, and the cans were all heating up in the flames, when my can went off like a grenade. It was an amazing explosion, and it aborted that outing. We were all bespattered head to foot, the scoutmaster's ear got cut by flying tin, and he shed much blood himself; and I do believe people were picking beans off themselves in Hackensack. I was not invited again. Harold said the scoutmaster told him not to invite me any more, said I was too clumsy. In fact he referred to me as "your clumsy little fairy of a cousin," which I think was inappropriate language. I don't remember what he looked like, but he did not have the equable temperament for a scoutmaster.

So, all this talk of Camp Eagle Wing made me apprehensive. I liked Feder's farm, and asked nothing better than to while away my summer days there. But the doorbell rang when I was finishing my arithmetic, and here came Mr. Winston.

As I scribbled off the last problems, I could hear him and Mama talking. That in itself was strange, Mr. Winston's voice within our walls. Stranger yet, when I came into the parlor, was the way Mama looked. I had last seen her at supper in an apron and an old house dress. I found her transformed: remarkably thinner in the purple dress reserved for weddings and bar mitzvas, her hair all done up as on Friday night, the long gold-and-pearl earrings from Russia dangling in her ears. And her eyes sparkled, and her cheeks were flushed, and she and Mr. Winston were laughing merrily. Her lips looked bloodshot, or something. I had never seen them so red. A beautiful scent diffused from her, almost like the smell of Feder's apple orchard: sweet, fresh, powerful. Mom sometimes wore perfume, but this was a new fragrance. Had she bought it so as to make a special impression on my teacher? Why? She knew I was in pretty solid with Mr. Winston.

"Speak of the devil!" giggled Mama. "Here he comes! Were your ears burning, Davey? *Somebody* has been saying some very nice things about you."

"Hello, there, David." Douglas Fairbanks grinned and ran a thumb across his mustache, exactly as he did in the movies. He crossed his legs, in dark trousers pressed razor-sharp, and I saw buttoned gray cloth casings on his shoes. Spats! A pure film touch. I had never seen anything so dashing on a live man. He and Mama sat together on the sofa. On the low table before them photographs, booklets, and papers were spread out.

"Come and see," said Mama. "It's so exciting!"

I obeyed. Camp Eagle Wing in the pictures looked all too out-doorsy: kids swimming off a dock, or marching in a line through woods, or playing ball games, or eating at long tables, or gathered around campfires toasting frankfurters (!), or canoeing in a squad-ron, or weaving baskets. Scoutmaster types hovered everywhere.

"Girls' camp, too?" I asked, because there were a couple of all-girl pictures.

"Oh, yes," said Mama eagerly. "Camp Nokomis. That's where Lee will go."

"Nokomis? Is that Hebrew?"

Mr. Winston smiled. "It's Indian, David. 'Daughter of the Moon, Nokomis.' You'll be reading Longfellow next year. That's who your street is named after, Longfellow."

"The camps are Jewish, of course?" asked Mama, a shade thought-fully.

"Mrs. Goodkind, I'm Jewish," said Mr. Winston with a jocund grin and a thumbstroke at his mustache.

"You *are?*" Mama's eyes opened wide and brilliant. "Who'd ever know it?"

This was a surprise to me, too. I assumed all teachers were gen-tiles, certainly including this charmer; nor in those days was I far wrong.

"Why, my grandfather was a rabbi."

"You don't say! Where?"

With a vague gesture toward, I guess, the Atlantic Ocean, Mr. Winston said, "Oh, Europe."

I don't think he was pretending. In those days they used to say that movie stars like Douglas Fairbanks, Mary Pickford, and Ramon Novarro were actually Jews named Cohen or Horowitz or Goldstein. In that sense I'd guess Mr. Winston was Jewish. As for his rabbinic grandfather, you meet few American Jews whose grandfathers weren't rabbis in the old country. By this is meant an elderly gent in a skull-cap and a beard, scowling from a dim old photograph.

Anyway, Mama turned yoxenta in an eyeblink. "My father is a rabbi from the Volozhin Yeshiva, that was the greatest yeshiva in Lithuania. And my grandfather was a chief rabbi in Minsk."

"Now we know where David gets his brains from," said Mr. Winston, "and his mother, too."

They both laughed and laughed, looking playfully at each other. I began to feel oddly in the way.

"Maybe David can help us conduct Friday night services at Eagle Wing," said Mr. Winston.

"Gosh, a sand beach," I said, thumbing the pictures.

"We have a great sand beach," said Mr. Winston. "The best."

"What do you think, Davey?" said Mama. "Doesn't it look wonderful?"

"I won't know anybody there."

"We'll put you in my bunk," said Mr. Winston. "You'll get to know everybody."

"Oh, my David is a good mixer," said Mom. "He'll make friends."

Over Mama's perfume, I smelled liniment. Bobbeh was usually asleep by now; but she was an inquisitive old thing, and the strange male voice probably stirred her up. She came hobbling into the parlor in a shapeless brown sack, her wig plopped on her head any old way, so that all the white hair showed. She halted and stared at Mr. Winston, who stared back at this apparition.

"What does the gentile want?" Bobbeh asked Mom in Yiddish.

Mom darted an embarrassed look at Mr. Winston, but he was smiling obliviously. Bobbeh might as well have spoken Swahili as Yiddish.

"Nothing, Bobbeh, nothing," murmured Mom, jumping to her feet. "The man is just visiting us. There's some tea in the kitchen, and . . ."

"What does he want? Is he from the police?"

"Bobbeh, *you should be healthy*," hissed Mama. Yiddish has these inside-out imprecations. "He's not from the police, and he's not a gentile, he's a Jew. Go have some tea."

"A Jew? With those things on his feet? He looks like a priest."

I can't imagine why Bobbeh said that, but I suppose she took any outlandish garb as a vestment. Peering at Mr. Winston, not taking her eyes off him, she hobbled to an armchair and sat down.

Silence. Thick awkward liniment-laden silence.

"This is my mother-in-law," said Mama.

"How do you do?" said Mr. Winston.

"He probably wants money," said Bobbeh. "Give him money and he'll go away. You'll see. That's all any of them want. I have some money, if you need it."

"Bobbeh, he's Davey's teacher!" snapped Mama. "I know him, and he's a fine man."

"A teacher from Hebrew school? With those things on his feet?"

Mama asked Mr. Winston through gritted teeth whether he wouldn't like some tea. He said he would. She disappeared off to the kitchen, where we could hear her clanking and slamming around, while I explained to Bobbeh that Mr. Winston was my teacher in "English" school. That she understood. Her suspicious expression relaxed, and Mr. Winston noted with admiration my mastery of Yiddish. "Boy, you really sling that lingo around, don't you?" was the way he put it. "Tell your grandmother that I think you do very nice work in school."

I translated.

"Ask him what those things are on his feet," said Bobbeh.

This seemed slightly personal on short acquaintance, so I hesitated.

"What does she say?" asked Mr. Winston.

"She says she's proud of me."

"She's such a fine-looking old lady," he observed.

"What did he say?" asked Bobbeh.

"He says they keep his feet warm," I said.

"Cold feet, hah?" Bobbeh asked. "Like by a frog."

I broke into whoops of laughter. I was still doubled over in my chair when Mama came in with a clattering tray. Bobbeh and Mr. Winston were regarding me with puzzlement as I howled and writhed, picturing Mr. Winston's frog feet inside the spats.

"So? What's so funny?" Mama inquired, setting the tray down so hard that cups, saucers, spoons, sugarbowl, and cookies all jumped.

I couldn't reply, in my mad fit of the giggles. The amount of subtle disdain Bobbeh managed to cram into that one word, *jabba*, "frog"! She just didn't take to Mr. Winston.

Mom didn't enjoy the stump of that evening. Bobbeh's intrusion had clouded the delight of Mr. Winston's visit. Mama was quenched, her gaiety gone, her high color faded, her eyes dulled. She seemed much too dressed up in contrast to Bobbeh's homey brown sack, and her red lips were like a clown's. Her peculiar playfulness with my teacher was all over. Mr. Winston too sobered, under Bobbeh's questioning gaze, into his severe classroom self. He drank a cup of tea, bolted a cookie, and took himself off, leaving all the Eagle Wing stuff. Mama saw him to the door, and I guess went downstairs with him, because she was a while getting back. Bobbeh drank tea while I flipped through the camp pictures.

Tying on her old apron as she marched into the parlor, Mama began slinging the tea things back on the tray with jerky gestures.

"He wants money," said Bobbeh. "You'll see. Otherwise what was he doing here, that English teacher? He wants money. Maybe to give Yisroelke good marks. Don't pay him a penny. Yisroelke can get good marks by himself, he has a Jewish head."

"Bobbeh, you should be healthy," snarled Mama. "YOU SHOULD LIVE TO BE A HUNDRED TWENTY YEARS."

I couldn't sleep. Much later I heard my father come home, and I jumped out of bed and went to the parlor. I wanted to hear how Pop had made out with the money men, and I had only to look at him to know. His pale face shone, his dark-shadowed eyes gleamed, and the tired smile he gave me lifted my heart.

"Yisroelke," he said, glancing at his wristwatch, "why aren't you asleep?"

"Papa, did you lick Kornfelder and Worthington?"

He and Mama guffawed. Mama wore her old pink bathrobe, her lips were their usual color, and her hair was combed out for bed. On the low table, amid the scattered Camp Eagle Wing pictures and papers, stood a whiskey bottle and two glasses. Amazement! My parents drank strong spirits once in a blue moon, and then only for a toast or a good-luck wish.

"Mr. Kornfelder and Mr. Worthington are fine gentlemen, Yisroelke," said Papa, trying hard to be solemn, "and we had a nice meeting. So go to bed."

"You bet Papa licked them," said Mama, adding in devilish Yankee slang, "Papa licked the pants off them."

Again they both laughed with joy.

"Oh, boy! I knew it!" I hugged Papa, and I could smell the whiskey. "So we'll build a great big place, just like the Splendid Laundry, won't we?"

"We'll see. We'll see." Papa patted my shoulder. "Go back to bed."

"And I've got wonderful news for you, Davey," said Mama. "You're going to Camp Eagle Wing."

You have to know what happened at Pop's meeting, since all our futures hung on it.

I've mentioned the boiler that burst at Pop's place. Such breakdowns were all too usual. The Fairy Laundry had started with no capital, and bled by two dead-weight partners, it was still gasping along without capital. Pop had had to buy old machinery on credit from the General Laundry Machinery Corporation, for the move into the vacated Woolworth store. Meantime, a rival Bronx firm, the Splendid Laundry, had expanded into a grand concrete structure with all-new machinery. The boss of the Splendid, Sam Solomon, had moved down to West End Avenue in Manhattan, among the rich gentiles. Sam Solomon had no partners. Mom was keen for Pop to build a big concrete plant so that we too could move to West End Avenue. Wasn't he every bit as good a laundryman as Sam Solomon?

Mr. John Worthington thought so. Mr. Worthington, the boss of the machinery corporation, had been urging Pop for years to ditch Brodofsky and Gross and start a new steam laundry. As you know, Pop wouldn't do that. He did ask Mr. Worthington whether he would back a concrete plant for the Fairy Laundry, and the man was all for it. Kornfelder, too, was favorably inclined.

So most of the talk at supper for weeks had been about an impasse with the two money men, Kornfelder and Worthington. They wanted Brodofsky and Gross dropped with lump-sum settlements; otherwise, no financing for a concrete plant. Papa was equally stubborn. Brodofsky and Gross might accept the settlements, he told Mama, but they would never cease thinking they were partners. Once they ran through their lump sums, he would wind up supporting them, as he did Uncle Yehuda. Surprisingly, considering how she despised the partners, Mom was backing up Pop this time. "Listen, you've come all the way with those two fools," she said as he left that evening for the showdown meeting. "Now the goyim want you to throw them out. Nothing doing. They'll finance the new plant, anyway, you'll see."

As you know, Pop won the showdown, and so the big plant was on, partners and all. That victory was probably Pop's death warrant, but who foresees such things? Immediately, because he went to that meeting, I went to Camp Eagle Wing. On the matter of Mr. Winston, I'll bet Pop would have sided with Bobbeh.

Anyway, that was it. I never saw the Feder farm again. I can't imagine that it still exists. I don't remember where it was. I know we took a coal-burning train to get there, and I never hear the chuffing of an old-style locomotive or the wail of its whistle but I remember that gritty sooty ride to golden summer days; to an apple orchard where the wormy windfall fruit lay sun-warmed on the grass, sweetening the air; to a wool hammock where I swung under the apple trees, reading Penrod and Tarzan books; to green meadows where big monarch butterflies went flitting through the milkweed and the goldenrod; to a dung-smelling barn buzzing with flies, and to the taste of warm raw milk right out of a stamping cow's rubbery teats; and to rose-spotted little lizards scuttling on the rocks by some unnamed river. The Feder farm, like the Aldus Street that was, lives only in my memory; and now perhaps in these meager words, if they ever see the light. I went to Camp Eagle Wing that summer, and to other camps for years and years, until I freed myself from camps by starting to work for Harry Goldhandler, the gag czar.

And right here my story starts moving on the main line, with a faint last whiff of smoke from an old coal-burner, and the fading echo of its whistle, as it disappears down a branch track I travelled no more.

24

Peter Quat

SITTING with some big guys on the bus to Camp Eagle Wing was Paul Frankenthal. Now, *there* was a surprise. Mr. Winston hadn't let on, and at school, since our move to Longfellow Avenue, Frankenthal had been ignoring me. On the bus he still ignored me. As I halted in the aisle and waved, he just went right on holding forth about Babe Ruth and Lou Gehrig, with all his old masterful Aldus Street air, maintaining his running lie that his father knew them both.

One of Paul's listeners, a good-looking boy with thick curly dark hair, was measuring Paul with an incredulous narrow-eyed look, his upper lip curled in a sneer. He sat by the open window, hands loosely clasped, dressed in long pants, bright plaid socks, and a dandyish jacket and tie. I saw this boy raise his clasped hands to his face, then blow smoke out of the window. Wow! Frankenthal sneaked smokes in our schoolyard. But to do it on the bus under the noses of the counsellors! Who could this tough guy be? I moved on up the aisle, and that was my first glimpse of the celebrated novelist of the American Jewish experience.

The bus arrived at the camp about noon, and we were all marched in our city clothes to the "mess hall." I remember well my first meal in that big clattering raw wood structure: stringy brown roast beef, with mashed potatoes and green peas; and what I remember most is — surprise — the sight of jugs of milk and plates of butter on the table. Hoping that this epic will be read by a vast public of non-Jews, I will explain why I was surprised. We religious Jews never eat dairy products with meat. Never. The prohibition is found in the Bible, and the Talmud elaborates it. My mother has dishes and cutlery for milk meals, and other sets for meat. So does my wife. So, for that matter, does my sister Lee. She slakes her passion for shellfish outside her home, but in her kitchen milk dishes and meat dishes are separated. Okay? And there sat the Eagle Wing campers and counsellors, thickly buttering their bread, and washing down roast beef with hearty gulps of milk.

At this distance in time, it's hard to say what my reaction was. I move in the Christian world. I don't eat meat and dairy products together, but I'm used to seeing others do so, Jews as well as gentiles. It's a secular age. A lot of our people have lost touch with our traditions, especially the rich ones who need tax lawyers. When a client named Goldberg, let's say, at lunch in a restaurant casually orders pork chops and a glass of milk, I don't make an issue of it. I have no directive from on high to change the world as I find it, though I may cool off a bit toward brother Goldberg, and even fob him off on another lawyer. I have no directive to give all comers my services, either.

Well, to my best recollection, I felt no moral dismay at that first Eagle Wing lunch. Mr. Winston had assured Mom that the camp was Jewish. The milk and butter must be there for those who weren't religious and wanted them. I would make no holy noises about that. Live and let live. As for the meat itself, Douglas Fairbanks couldn't have lied about such a serious thing, could he? It had to be kosher. So spoke my hunger to my conscience, and I fell to with gusto on the roast beef. I didn't eat the ice-cream dessert, and I ended up feeling well fed and virtuous. Still, it was a major surprise. Where had Mama sent me?

Next surprise. Blaring bugle notes shock me out of sleep. I am under a coarse blanket on a low cot, breathing sharp cold air in a wooden hut amid strange boys. Sleepy kids in pajamas and bathrobes, Yisroelke among them, pour out of a row of such huts and line up, shivering in chilly mist. A burly scoutmaster — all right, counsellor, though I put in three hard years of law school to earn that title, but okay, counsellor — a counsellor in bathing trunks and a sweatshirt bellows an exercise chant through a megaphone: *"One-two-three-four! Bend, stretch, touch those toes! One-two-three-four!"* Fifteen minutes of this distasteful harrying, then a megaphone bawl, "All juniors, *morning dip!*" We are juniors. So back to the hut, change from pajamas to bathing trunks, throw on a bathrobe, grab a towel, and march to the swimming dock.

Another surprise! The sand beach isn't there. Yet I saw the photograph with my own eyes, and Mr. Winston said himself — remember? — "We have a great sand beach. The best." No sign of it. Thick
thorny bracken grows to the water's edge, and a rickety dock extends
over the brush into muddy shallows. Megaphone: "Last one in is a
rotten egg!" Megaphone man dives, and comes up snorting. "It's great!
Great! Everybody in!" The dock is jammed with hesitant contenders
for rotten egg. One by one we leap or dive. Among the last, I hold
my nose and stiffly jump.

Next surprise. As I knife down feet first into icy water, my ankles
sink in cold slime, and tangle in water plants, or snakes. I struggle
free and splutter to the surface, amid many boys gasping and thrash-
ing in the brown water, which smells like rotting leaves. We all
flounder to the mossy ladder, slip and slide up, and dart for our towels. Uncle Phil, my counsellor, stands there in his bathrobe with the
other counsellors, dry. They are not juniors. We frantically towel
ourselves and fling on robes. Last out of the water, Megaphone springs
about the unstable dock with dull booms. "Great! Great! Nothing
like it! Makes a new man of you!"

That was the morning dip. It went on all summer. Camp Eagle
Wing, for my money, was one long morning dip. Great! Nothing
like it! Makes a new man of you! A cold dismal baptism, but I learned
like the other kids to slap my chest and yell, "Great! Great! Nothing
like it!" Children are simians, and they will mirror the doings of their
elders. But the imitation may have no more heart in it than a monkey's wave back at you, from behind the bars of his cage.

As we straggle back to the huts, I spy Mr. Winston on the lawn in
shorts and a T-shirt, very hairy-legged, a whistle on a thong around
his neck. I dart to him. "Mr. Winston, I thought you said we had a
sand beach."

"I said the girls' camp had a sand beach," he replies over his shoulder, hurrying away.

Talk about surprises! To be lied to in this barefaced way, by a
grown-up, and a teacher at that! And by Douglas Fairbanks! This
second lie — that he had said Camp Nokomis had a sand beach —
was worse than the first one. This time Mr. Winston *knew* that *I knew*
he was lying, *and he didn't care.* I was trapped for the summer. If I
didn't like it I could lump it. He had lied to me, that night on Long-

fellow Avenue, because as Bobbeh said, he wanted money. Now he had the money. Wise Bobbeh.

It crossed my mind, as I trudged back to my hut, that Winston was the counsellor of Bunk Eight. Paul Frankenthal and the tough guy who had smoked on the bus were in that bunk. How could Winston have told Mom he would take me in there? The camp was divided by age. I was a junior. Bunk Eight was for intermediates. Another Winston lie!

Well, then, what could I believe? Was the camp even Jewish?

In the days that followed, the doubt nagged. The camp owner, a Mr. Seidman, was a small round shiny personage, with a shiny bald head, shiny face, and persisting shiny smile. I thought Mr. Seidman might be Jewish. He had a large wife, reputedly an opera singer, with a big jaw, a huge bosom, a rear to balance, and a stiff corseted walk. I wasn't so sure about her. Frankenthal was a Jew. In my bunk one kid was named Levy, another Goldenheim, and Uncle Phil's name was Kahn. Yet — what about the butter, the milk? I had nobody to consult or to turn to; certainly not Mr. Winston. There was no rabbi in the camp. There was no minister or priest, either. Nobody said grace at meals. As for Hebrew lessons, not a trace. No prayer books. No Hebrew Bibles. Nothing!

Mind you, this perplexity didn't keep me awake nights. I was swamped in novelty, hustled from one activity to another: morning dips, ball games, dramatic tryouts, glimpses of the girls at canteen time, when we could line up and buy candy, my best moment of the day. Such things, much more than religion, were my concerns. There was just this low-grade nag: *where was I?* I figured the Friday night services ought to tell the story. Or had Winston lied about them, too?

Well, on Friday night, sure enough, all the campers marched in uniform to "the chapel," a one-story wooden building full of rough benches. The nature counsellor, a soft white bespectacled rather maggoty man, passed out brown booklets containing Indian prayers to the Great Spirit. As he led us in reading these, the campers yawned, blinked, and dozed. Things livened up when he went to the piano, and Mrs. Seidman stood up to sing a hymn, hands clasped against her stomach. Nobody could have dozed through that. She wailed that hymn like a fire alarm, rounding her mouth so you couldn't understand a word. I listened hard for Hebrew, but heard nothing like it.

After that Mr. Seidman spoke, and you couldn't understand him, either. Mr. Seidman had the sort of voice that turns off your mind; no sense formed from his singsong oily noise, certainly no discernible Bible message. Mrs. Seidman then caterwauled "America the Beautiful," and we marched off to the bunks. That was Friday night worship at Eagle Wing. I did not pursue Mr. Winston's notion that, in view of my rabbinic background, I assist at services. I didn't want to seem pushy. Had I been a full-blooded Iroquois, descended from an orthodox medicine man, I might have given it more thought.

Now, all during those services, a dark-haired pretty girl about my size had kept glancing at me from the Nokomis side. Next day at canteen time I spied her off by herself, throwing a stick for a little black dog, and I went up to her.

"Say, what kind of dog is that?"

"Scottie." A pert look sized me up. "I'm Betty Seidman."

Betty Seidman! So a princess of the blood had an eye for the Minsker Godol! This was more like it. "Hi. I'm David Goodkind." Bashful pause. "Does your camp have a sand beach?"

"Sure. Like to see it?"

"I'm not allowed on the girls' grounds."

"Oh, pooh." She called the dog. "Come, Laddie."

We slipped into the wild woods between the camps and walked down a narrow path, the dog gambolling after us. "There's the beach," said Betty Seidman, as we came out on a big gray rock above the water. There it was below, sure enough, the long sweep of sand I had seen in Winston's brochure. We sat down on the cold stone. Puffy white clouds, low sun, still lake, pretty girl. Groping for conversation, I said, "Look at that cloud. It's like an elephant."

"Look at that one." She picked it right up, pointing and laughing. "It's a monkey."

"Ha, ha!" I pointed. "I see a whale."

"And I see a horse."

"I see George Washington," I said, rather stretching it.

"I see Jesus Christ," giggled Betty Seidman, startling me almost out of my skin.

Jesus Christ?

Jesus Christ had not been a name bandied about on Aldus Street. Only once had we ever talked much about Jesus Christ. The newspapers at the time had been making a to-do about an evangelist who predicted the world was about to end. The evening before the announced Judgment Day, we kids sat around a fire in the lots, discussing Jesus Christ in low worried tones. We agreed that Jesus Christ had not really been such a bad guy, that he had only been trying to help people. We were all hedging against the risk that, if the world ended, there might be something to this Krisht business, after all.

Now what about Betty Seidman? Could she possibly be a Krisht?

Laddie followed us back to the boys' camp, on a shortcut through thick brush that Betty showed me. "Nobody sees you when you come this way. Remember that." She squeezed my hand and vanished.

As the summer wore on I found out that Eagle Wing had started as a Christian Science camp, but times were tough, and so Seidman had gone after the Jewish trade, too, with Winston as Bronx recruiter. Hence Friday night services, and the absence of ham or pork. On the other hand, many of the campers were Christian, or Christian Scientists, or nothing; hence butter and milk with the meat. It never was clear what the Seidmans were, but Camp Eagle Wing was American as apple pie: heterogeneous, easygoing, noncommittally spiritual once a week. I was the maverick, to be worrying about it.

One morning I was lying alone on my bunk with a Baseball Joe book when in walked the tough intermediate who had smoked on the bus. Jimmy Levy's brother in Bunk Eight had told us all about him: a wise guy named Peter Quat from a Manhattan private school, hated by all his bunkmates. Quat broke rules and got the other fellows in trouble. He claimed he was trying to get kicked out of camp. The gossip was that his father, a rich doctor, had given Winston a big tip to put up with him.

"I hear you have a copy of *Les Misérables,* kid," he said, with that same narrowed-eye sneering look. It's still Peter's trademark, visible on all his book-jacket pictures. "What the hell for? To show off?"

"To read."

"Let's see it."

I got it out of my trunk. My public library card, I should explain, was the joy of my life. I had long since read through all the fairy tales and boys' books, and lately had been taking out the fattest books I could find — I guess, to impress the librarians. In that way I had come on *The Three Musketeers* and *The Swiss Family Robinson;* so fat books seemed a good bet, and *Les Misérables* was the fattest in the building.

The lady librarian had blinked down at me in heartwarming amazement, checking it out on summer loan. *Les Misérables* was a slow starter,
but then I got all in a sweat to find out what happened to Jean Valjean, and I finished it by flashlight under my covers after taps, snivelling
over Valjean's death.

"Lend it to me," said Quat.

"Got anything I can read?"

"Come to my bunk and we'll see."

The campground was deserted. Rowdy baseball noises echoed from
the far playing fields. I had never been in Bunk Eight before, wanting to steer clear of Frankenthal. Quat picked a book off an unmade
bed — all the others were army-neat — and said, "How about this,
as long as you've read *Les Misérables?*"

It was *Portrait of the Artist as a Young Man,* by one James Joyce.
The first page seemed to be gibberish, so I declined it.

"Tell you what," said Quat, "try this, but don't let your counsellor
see it, and let me have it back tomorrow."

With that he pulled a magazine from under his rumpled blanket.
Le Sourire was the name. I remember the cover well, a drawing in
twenties' style of a pretty girl in frilly lingerie, with perky breasts plainly
showing through, pink nipples and all.

"I can't read French," I said. I was intrigued and faintly scandalized.

"You don't have to read French," said Quat with an evil grin. "You'll
enjoy this magazine. At least I *think* you will."

At this moment Laddie came bounding into the bunk. "Hey, Laddie! Lunch time, hey?" Quat pulled a salami from his trunk and hacked
off pieces with a scout knife. Keeping food in the bunks was against
the rules. So was feeding the Seidman dog. Laddie had once almost
choked to death on a chicken bone, hence the edict. But the dog leaped
and caught Quat's salami morsels in a practiced way. Quat knelt and
hugged the animal. "I love this dog," he said. "There's nothing else
in this camp worth shitting on. Well, maybe I'd shit on Mr. Seidman, if he asked me in a real polite way. I sure wouldn't shit on Bill
Winston. I don't believe in pampering counsellors."

I left with *Le Sourire* all rolled up. I didn't know much, but I knew
it was contraband. Back on my cot in Bunk Four, I leafed through
Le Sourire with mingled feelings of guilt, delight, and ever-rising warm
disturbance, all shot through with visions of Betty Seidman, Rosa-

lind Katz, and my old neighbor Bare-behind. A new world of sensation was opening to me, and Quat was quite right, a knowledge of French was not essential.

Now mind you, *Le Sourire* was pitiably tame compared to what's around nowadays, all these glossy magazines with pictures of girls showing their hairy crotches under klieg lights, interspersed with short stories by Nobel Prize authors, and interviews with eminent politicians. We live in peculiar times, or at least they strike me as peculiar. I don't fight the trend, in fact I helped bring it about by winning the obscenity cases; but I will have my senile headshake at such goings-on. *Le Sourire* had, I now realize, a sort of quaint art deco charm. All illustrations, no photographs; and for my money those colored pen-and-ink sketches of naughty mamselles, in various stages of peek-a-boo undress, had it all over the stark genito-urinary closeups which today's adolescents get off on, as I believe they put it.

Anyway, Uncle Phil came bounding into the bunk very much like Laddie, with much the same gaping jaws and hanging red tongue, and he frightened me by roaring, *"Where the hell did you get that?"* To Uncle Phil, *Le Sourire* was of course the hottest of hot stuff.

Unnerved, I spoke the simple truth. "I got it from Peter Beater."

"From WHO?"

Shakily I repeated, "Peter Beater. Peter Quat. In Bunk Eight." Jimmy Levy's brother always referred to the rebellious oddball as Peter Beater. To me it was just an innocuous nickname.

Uncle Phil took the magazine from me, sat down on my cot, and shifted to a clergyman voice. "Davey, do you know what that means?"

"What what means?"

"What you've just said."

A Talmudic mind can put two and two together. My disquieting sensations over *Le Sourire,* Frankenthal's tales of the big guys in the lots, and some other things I had heard at camp fell into one squalid picture. Naturally, I said I hadn't the slightest idea. Uncle Phil left, thumbing through the magazine, and he stumbled in the doorway and fell down the steps. He picked himself up and made off toward Bunk Eight.

All kinds of a crisis ensued. *Le Sourire* was confiscated. A solemn meeting took place in Bunk Eight, chaired by Bill Winston, ranging from sex matters to the need for harmony in the bunk. Quat offered to give a wienie roast and make his bed thereafter, and the other guys agreed to stop calling him Peter Beater. Bill Winston was delighted. They had the wienie roast next night after taps, and Frankenthal got hoggish and demanded a fifth or sixth frankfurter, and Quat told him to go to hell, and Frankenthal said, "Okay for you, Peter Beater," and Quat laid his head open with a mustard jar. That chilled the new era of good feeling. The story got out all over camp that Quat had put Paul Frankenthal, the star athlete, in the infirmary with many stitches in his scalp. Quat still didn't make his bed, and they still called him Peter Beater, only now they did it in front of Winston. *Le Sourire* passed from one counsellor's hand to another, until Mr. Seidman himself collared and kept it. Remembering Mrs. Seidman, I'd say *Le Sourire* ended up where it did the most good.

Meanwhile, my romance with Betty Seidman flourished. We would slip off at canteen time to the gray rock above the lake, and hold hands and talk, and maybe I'd beg a kiss or two. Nothing more. After-images of *Le Sourire* were haunting me, and I would daydream of trying every lascivious devilry with Betty Seidman. But when she was right there in the flesh, in big thick green bloomers and a white middy blouse, with those dark eyes sparkling at me, I fell apart. All my indecent intentions dried up. The fact is, I've never changed much. Women awe me. I have to nerve myself after nearly thirty years, if you'll believe it, for every pass I make at Jan, my own wife. Some say women prefer rough tough guys who yank down their panty hose without a by-your-leave, but I'll never know. I'm not saying I've done badly in the long run with my reverential approach — I'm not complaining, shall we say — but it got me exactly nowhere with Betty Seidman.

I was returning to my bunk from one of these tender meetings, via the short cut through the woods, when I noticed a peculiar black thing swinging in the air. I literally didn't believe my eyes, and for a second or two stood dumbfounded. Laddie was dangling from a heavy clothesline thrown over a high branch of a tall tree, with the other end knotted around a white birch. I snapped out of the daze and reached for him, but he hung too high. With shaking fingers, I tried to untie the hard knots at the other end. The dog was alive, whining and gagging, his head bent to one side, his jaws open, blood trickling from his thrust-out tongue. He looked straight down at me, beseeching help, then the glazed eyes drooped shut.

Peter Quat came crashing through the brush with a scout knife, his clothes torn, his face all bloody and swollen. "Okay, you catch him!" He hacked through the thick line and the dog fell into my arms, the rope coiling around him. He opened dim eyes as I laid him on the ground. Peter cut the noose around his neck, and he feebly wagged his tail. But his head fell to one side, the life went out of his eyes, and he lay still. Peter felt for the dog's heart and called, "Laddie, Laddie, come back, Laddie! Don't die!" His bloodstained face was streaming tears.

If you ever wonder, now and then in the rest of my story, why I put up with Peter Quat, remember this, it's all true. He is now what he was at Camp Eagle Wing, an *enfant terrible* with a very nasty streak, but there is forlorn bottled-up love in him somewhere, if he seems to have none for his parents or his people. He lay embracing the dog, and howling, "Laddie! Laddie! Don't die!" He turned his blood-streaked face up at me. "That moronic criminal son of a bitch did it! Just because I love the dog! I caught him at it!" The inert dog uttered a strangled cough and barely moved his head. "Christ, he's alive!" Peter stood up and glared at me, tears and blood running down his dirty face, and lifted the dog in his arms. "I'll handle this. You don't know anything, do you hear? Don't say a word to anyone, ever. Beat it!"

Next day, Frankenthal left the camp. The last time I ever saw Paul Frankenthal he was crossing the lawn in his city clothes, a real big guy, with a cigarette dangling from his mouth. A few days later, Quat also departed. Betty Seidman avoided me after that. I did not know for a while whether Laddie had survived, until I sneaked up to the Seidman house and saw him moping in a small pen of tough chicken wire. All sorts of rumors flew for a few days, and then the fuss died down.

A week or so after this, my parents drove over from Feder's farm to visit me, bringing along that no-good Harold; also my sister Lee, who with rare good sense had fought off being sent to Camp Nokomis. Poor stumblebum Minsker Godol, in goyish exile! I didn't want to admit how miserable I was. I bluffed it out. I showed Lee and Harold the canteen, the social hall, the lake, the tennis courts, the playing fields. I told Harold about campfires and overnight hikes. I boasted to Lee that the camp owner's daughter was in love with me. Mr. Seidman and Bill Winston raved to Mom and Pop about their brilliant son. In that whole orgy of phoniness, there was one mo-

ment of truth. I was showing Mom and Pop the mess hall, where
the waiters were setting up for supper. I pointed out the milk and
butter on the table. "We always have meat for supper," I said. "And
see what they serve, every night."

My father looked at Mom, without a word.

My mother was dressed to kill in a silk frock and a big picture hat.
She had lapped up the praises of Seidman and Winston, smiling, bridling, behaving like an intermediate girl at canteen time; while Pop,
who appeared gray-faced and thin, had listened impassively. But when
Pop gave Mom that look in the mess hall — just a roll of his wise
brown eyes — I realized that he had not for a moment been taken in
by Camp Eagle Wing; that he held her accountable for sending me
there; but that he would not put her down in front of me. Mom
shrugged at his look and dropped her eyes.

"Don't eat the butter or drink the milk, Yisroelke," Pop said.

"I don't," I said.

He put an arm around my shoulders and we left the mess hall. So
I served out my sentence in Camp Eagle Wing, and I went on eating
the meat.

When I read this part to Jan, she said, "Do you realize how *awful*
your mother is coming out?"

Poor Mama!

Look, remember how young she was, an immigrant in a strange
new world, and remember those sauerkraut crocks, will you? Is it really
so awful that Mama was bemused by a handsome young fraud of a
teacher who flattered her and flirted with her because — as old Bobbeh knew at once — he wanted money? Camp Eagle Wing in those
brochures, with Bill Winston flashing his manly smile and his pearly
spats at Mama, looked so much like the ploika that she hadn't the
heart to press Douglas Fairbanks with the old Jewish nag: "*But is it
kosher?*" Too redolent of sauerkraut, eh, Mom, that dull old-country
query?

Green Cousin, poor Green Cousin, not so awful, and there is
nothing to forgive. Eagle Wing was my first stop on the way to April
House, and it had to happen. The thing I will remember is the nickel-
plated flashlight. The camping list called for a flashlight, so before I
left for Eagle Wing we went to a hardware store. The black flashlight

cost a fraction of the nickel-plated one. They both gave the same light. Frugality was your middle name. But you saw Yisroelke yearning over that classy nickel-plated flashlight, and that was the one you bought. Okay, Mom.

25

The Five Medals

"SKIP Camp Maccabee," I wrote in my notes on this part of my life, "nothing important happened there, and it's all unspeakable." But I was forgetting the medals when I wrote that. The five medals became a buried dynamite charge that, touched off by my bar mitzva, blew my life apart like a land mine. There is no leaving out Camp Maccabee.

This camp in the Catskills, where I won the medals, was the brainchild of one Mr. Dresser. If Peter Quat were telling this, he could make of Samuel Dresser the most loathsome literary Jew since Fagin, but Mr. Dresser was just another paunchy little cheeseparer like Mr. Seidman. He hired Charles Strongfort, "the world's most perfect man," as director. The camp featured body-building, and was called Camp Strongfort at first. That didn't go, so after a losing year Mr. Dresser changed the name to Camp Maccabee, and made it kosher. Strongfort stayed on, and since he was a devout Catholic who always wore a crucifix on his gigantic hairy brown chest, Mr. Dresser took on a former Jewish boxing champion, Benny Leonard, as "athletic adviser." He also cut his prices in half. Everybody in the Bronx knew about Benny Leonard, and I was netted, with some three hundred other boys and girls. Mama, penitent over the Eagle Wing botch, jumped at the kosher inducement; and Pop was in financial hot water again, so the cheap fee got him.

I am compelled, however, to draw a curtain over the incredible doings at Camp Maccabee. I can't compete with Peter Quat or his Jewish-housewife imitators in the fearless candor racket. I'm shooting for the family trade, and you'll have to admit I've stayed pretty genteel so far. *April House* is right in there with *Little Women,* and I mean to keep it that way. The camp was something of a Dotheboys Hall — and Dothegirls Hall, too, because there were hordes of girls — except that we weren't oppressed, not at all. We could do whatever we pleased. There was no barrier of any sort between the boys' and the girls' camps, and what pleased all of the counsellors, and most of the campers past puberty, was sex. It was something wild, Camp Maccabee, and not what my parents had in mind in giving me a kosher summer.

I trust the family trade will put up with my merely mentioning, for instance, that the head counsellor, one Uncle Jack, a tall lean bespectacled fellow, was known to one and all as the Scumbag King. This was not meant in derogation. It was descriptive. He pressed one of the seniors into service as a sort of batman, and this kid got into Uncle Jack's trunk and found an astonishing number of the things, several thousand of them. They could not have all been for personal use; the camp season was too short. I must presume that Uncle Jack had the concession, and sold them to the other counsellors and to selected campers; in which case Mr. Dresser certainly had a piece of the action. Mr. Dresser would not have overlooked such a profitable spin-off from Camp Maccabee.

In my bunk the campers were too young to patronize Uncle Jack, but they displayed such a lively interest in sex, all the same, that I had to move out. I couldn't stand it. I wasn't a prude then and still am not, but there was this stout boy named Whitey that my bunkmates kept trying to bugger, when they weren't comparing lengths of erections, and doing other things even old Peter would have trouble making believable. It was like living in a monkey house with a lot of depraved orangutans. I didn't know when they might tire of Whitey and cast their hot eyes on me. So one day I just packed up my trunk and carried it over to the tent of Uncle Sam, the dramatics counsellor, where the circumstances seemed quieter.

They were quieter. It was a senior tent, and the campers were away in the girls' area most of the time. When they came back they were all worn out and just slept. It was days before I was even noticed. Uncle Sam must have been a night prowler, because he slept nearly all the time. I don't remember seeing him get up for meals. We all tended to eat at odd times, going to the mess hall and foraging around when we got hungry. The scheduled meals were poorly attended, because Mr. Dresser's menus really were right out of Dotheboys Hall.

But there was a canteen, and down the road a ways a sandwich place. Both were open day and night, did a roaring business, and undoubtedly were dummy corporations wholly owned by Mr. Dresser; for the worse the camp meals were, the more he was bound to rake in from those two gold mines.

I came to Uncle Sam's attention during a week of heavy rains. The seniors kept moving their beds around to get out from under the leaks and a bad leak sprang over Uncle Sam's head and woke him.

"What are you doing here?" he asked, sitting up and mopping his head with a towel. I was, at the moment, the only camper in the tent. I was pretty wet and bedraggled, because there were no unoccupied dry spots left. I was lying on my soaked bed in my raincoat, reading a book.

"I'm your new camper."

"What? But you're just a little kid." Uncle Sam got up as he talked, shoved a camper's bed into a puddle under a heavy leak, and moved his cot into the dry place.

"I'm interested in dramatics."

"Who put you in here?"

"The Scumbag King."

"Well, that's all right then. What do you do?"

"I can sing and recite."

"Good. I can use you."

But let's get out of Camp Maccabee fast. I'm just accounting for the medals. I rather enjoyed the anarchy of Maccabee, the freedom to read all I wanted, the absence of athletics — there were casual choose-up games, but no schedules — and to be honest, the sex carnival also entertained me. I think it would have entertained the emperor Caligula. A sort of blithering innocence kept me from any participation in it, but the summer was a great eye-opener.

There were two Parents' Days, one in July and one in August, when we had fine steak dinners. For the July day Benny Leonard showed up. It was the only time we ever saw him. He gave a mass boxing lesson to two hundred boys, while the parents looked on. A patently silly fraud, it was. That same night Uncle Sam put on a show, and I did a takeoff on Benny Leonard's boxing lesson. I'd been amusing the kids at rehearsals with such clowning, and Uncle Sam saw this and put me on as a solo act. It made a hit. Benny Leonard in the front row was rolling around, guffawing and wiping his eyes, though my scurrilities were all about how fat and old he was, and how the whole thing was a farce staged for the parents. The parents were laughing, too. Clowns can get away with a lot of truth. Next day Leonard called me into the camp office and gave me the Benny Leonard Proficiency Medal in the Manly Art, picking one out of a large box full of these on Mr. Dresser's desk. So that was one medal.

At the second Parents' Day Strongfort did his standard act: rippling his enormous muscles, tearing a telephone book in half, straightening a horseshoe with his bare hands, and all that. It was made for parody, and I was blossoming out as the camp funny man. So that night I lampooned Strongfort. Another hit, and nobody in the audience was more amused than Mama. She and Pop were sitting up front. They had missed the first Parents' Day, but here they were, and she laughed so loud that my act could have been ruined. Luckily, the campers were starved for some amusement besides lust — the season was winding down and they had all about had it — and they ignored the berserk lady in the front row. After the show, Strongfort invited me and my parents to his tent, and there presented me with the Strongfort Correspondence School Medal for Body-Building Prowess.

Would you believe that Mama took that award seriously? Body-building prowess! I was a physical ruin. That was half the fun of my burlesque. I had been living on candy bars and peanut butter sandwiches, lying indoors and reading day and night. I had scarcely broken into a run the whole time at Camp Maccabee, and I had given up swimming because of the leeches in the lake. I looked like a stunted eunuch, all white and baggy and puffy. But Mama glowed over the medal, and thanked Charles Strongfort, and gave him a kiss. Papa did not say much during the whole visit. When they left next morning in the car, he remarked only that I should try to get a little sun. Mama was gloating over the two medals in her lap, for she had collected the Benny Leonard award, too. "My prizewinner!" she exclaimed, as Pop started the car. Pop looked at me, slightly shook his head, and drove off.

Well, Uncle Sam then awarded me a medal for dramatics, which made three, and one in journalism, for a total of four. There wasn't much food at Maccabee but medals abounded. About the journalism: Uncle Sam put out just two mimeographed editions of the *Maccabee Menorah* for the Parents' Days. Before each occasion he took me to a dusty little office, sat me at a typewriter, with lists of parents who were expected, and a few stencils; and told me to write some gossip about their kids, anything that came into my head, with all names in capital letters. It was fun pecking out words on a machine, and I enjoyed writing up the campers. The hardest part was keeping it clean. I had to press my imagination hard for sex-free items; it was my first try at serious fiction. Toward the end of the second edition I got tired and absentmindedly referred to our head counsellor as the Scumbag King; meaning no harm, I just forgot I was writing for the parents. This caused a few puzzled inquiries, but the summer was waning and nobody really cared much.

A strange experience, Maccabee, and it's all been coming back to me as I write. Uncle Sam had a long sad face, and Mr. Dresser had a big belly and so did Benny Leonard, though he kept remembering to suck it in. Years later I interviewed Strongfort for one of Harry Goldhandler's radio shows. I was startled to find him a head shorter than I was. At Camp Maccabee he had seemed a giant.

And the fifth medal? Well, that was on the up and up. When I graduated from public school, I got the gold medal for Excellence in English. I still have it, the gilt is untarnished, and it reads

I. David Goodking
for Excellene
in English

In my lifelong quest for excellence, I've usually ended up with that crippled "excellene."

26

Money Troubles

I'VE said Pop was in financial hot water. How come, when the big new plant was going up and business was booming? Well, I have to put you in the picture, because Pop was a strong and able man, and you will not understand why he went down — for that is the whole key to my life, his early fall — unless you know all about the weight he staggered under. He had come far from that cellar chute on the Lower East Side, with Brodofsky and Gross riding on his back all the way, but they were just part of the load.

I never gave any thought at the time to Pop's affairs. He took me now and then through the huge new Fairy Laundry, an echoing concrete shell filling up with great gleaming machinery, three stories high on a whole square block near the Bronx River, its brick smokestack rising up higher than anything in sight. Why did I act so bored, though I could tell it hurt Pop? I suppose above all things I didn't want to be a laundryman and spend my days in a stink of soap, chlorine, and dirty clothes. I shut the whole subject of laundry from my soul. Yet I do know — I heard it from the attorney who fought and won Mama's lawsuit against the partners after Pop died — that my father thought up and installed original systems which were adopted by other major laundry plants. Pop had a natural engineering gift, no doubt of that.

He would bring home copies of *The Laundry Age* and show us pieces about the new Fairy Laundry. My sister Lee, who was then getting on to seventeen, and therefore looking for ways to impress her admirers, made much of those articles. Recently I got her to dig out one yellow brittle clipping from a box in her attic. It half crumbled as I read it, but that lawyer had told the truth. It was all about Alexander Goodkind's ingenious production systems. My God, how young

Papa looks, squinting into the sunlight, posing as always with one hand in a jacket pocket, smiling with visible pride in front of the unfinished building! Much, much younger than I am now, yet pitifully harried and worn. The clipping is dated in Papa's neat, steeply slanted handwriting, about a week before my bar mitzva.

It was a very bad time, and Papa's back was sagging badly. He was still paying off Uncle Yehuda's promissory notes; which Yehuda had walked away from, you remember, in high dudgeon at the crass and unfeeling bank. That payoff stretched over years. Bobbeh was living with Aunt Rivka, whom Pop had finally brought over with Uncle Peretz, the one with reservations about the capitalist system. Uncle Peretz, a soft-spoken little man with red curly hair, had overcome these scruples to the extent of accepting two steamship tickets to capitalist America, an apartment in the Bronx for which Pop paid the rent, and a small hand laundry which Pop bought for him with another bank loan.

Then there was Uncle Velvel, who by now —

But wait. Am I portraying my family as a gallery of grotesques? My story compels me to dwell on the ones who wore my father down. Now my Aunt Sophie, Cousin Harold's mother, was an angelic woman. She raised her kids quietly and well, ever sustaining Uncle Hyman's tender ego. Sophie was infinitely hospitable, radiating a natural sweet warmth, the true atmosphere of my family. In fact, whenever I write the word "Mishpokha," I think of Aunt Sophie. When Bobbeh wasn't blue, she was a lot like Aunt Sophie. So was Aunt Rivka, a little rotund woman, with clever brown eyes like Pop's, working like a field hand in Uncle Peretz's laundry, forever cheery as she poured sweat at the press. With Bobbeh, her mother, even at her bluest, Rivka was unfailingly kind and smiling. The so-called Lithuanian Jews, the Litvaks from the western Russian pale, did have this pure warm nature about them. My Pop was a sort of ultimate Litvak. Perhaps this trait was a survival mechanism. However, your Brodofskys and your Uncle Velvels were also Litvaks, so where does that leave us? Pretty soon Zaideh will be making his entrance, and you'll meet a man and a Litvak.

But about Velvel. Pop had been sending him a lot of money. What about the rich father-in-law in Riga, you may ask, with the hay and feed business, into which he was taking Velvel? Well, Velvel's letters were now full of the rascality of this pious hypocrite, this cold and heartless grandfather, who was about to turn out his daughter, his own flesh and blood, her two beautiful babies, and her husband into the streets of Riga. I couldn't follow all the details. Velvel's letters, while rich in Yiddish imprecations and rabbinic quotes, tended to skitter around all facts, except the fact that he needed money.

Velvel had sued the father-in-law, in whose home he and his family were living. This made for a strained situation, wrote Velvel, but he put up with it for his wife's sake. The father-in-law won the lawsuit, and offered to shake hands with Velvel, forget the whole thing, and take him back into the business. But Velvel saw through this clumsy trick, so he wrote; it only showed his father-in-law knew he would lose on appeal. So Velvel appealed. Then a big shock! The appeal was thrown out of court! But only, Velvel swore, because the father-in-law bribed the judges. Papa had been sending Velvel money for his legal costs, but Velvel wrote he was now broke, his children were in rags and crying for bread, and he had decided to emigrate with his family to Palestine.

The Holy Land was calling him, wrote Velvel, as it should every Jew. Besides, an old friend of his from Minsk was raking in a fortune on orange groves, and wanted him to come and be a partner and a foreman. In addition to the fare from Latvia to Palestine, Velvel also required a loan of two thousand dollars to buy into the orange groves. Mom and Pop had many an argument over this, so I remember the sum. Driven into a corner, Pop refused, saying he was more broke than Velvel. He had just sent a large sum to Zaideh for his passage to America with his daughter Faiga; this required, besides the steamship tickets, bribe money for the Soviet officials who had to stamp the passports and exit visas.

So Pop wrote Uncle Velvel, in effect, "Nothing doing." Velvel wrote back that in that case he was applying to a Jewish immigrant aid society for a loan to take his family to America, and all he asked of Pop was to sign a paper, a mere formality, guaranteeing that Velvel and his family would not become public charges. Pop immediately got another loan from a bank, and wired Uncle Velvel all the money he needed to go to Palestine.

So there you have an idea of what was draining Pop.

Yet on the other hand, since the laundry was flourishing, why wasn't he earning a much higher salary to cover these outlays? Yes, he was making more money. But never forget that Brodofsky and Gross were equal partners. Whenever Pop took a raise, *they had to get the same raises.*

And that wasn't all. The soap man, Kornfelder, was a tough bird. He and Worthington had failed to make Pop shed the partners, but they kept vetoing salary raises for them, so Pop's salary was frozen, too. At last, Papa forced a showdown, in desperation; and Kornfelder said all right, if Goodkind wanted to go on carrying those incompetents and give them raises, that was his problem; but the money was coming out of the pockets of himself and Worthington, the cash investors, and they would have to be put on the same weekly salaries, as silent partners. Pop could not resist. The building project was rolling. A pull-out by the money men would have meant collapse. There was no going back to a small place any more. So from then on, every dollar of increased salary my father drew cost the laundry four more dollars for Worthington, Kornfelder, Brodofsky, and Gross. This crushing leverage never changed until Pop died.

Pop and Mom would sit up late at night going over their accounts, trying to pin down why they were chronically short. Mom would say he needed a bigger salary. Pop would wearily point out the leverage problem. Mom would say something helpful like, "Well, why did you give in to Kornfelder, then?" I can see the scene before me, the two of them at the dining-room table going over their checkbooks and records by lamplight, Pop writing out a balance sheet, and Mom quoting an old-country saw, "Yes, Alex, *'The account balances, but there's no money.'* " I prefer not to describe the look on Pop's face when she would trot out that pearl of wisdom.

Brodofsky, by the way, opposed the idea of the big building from the start, fought it tooth and nail, calling it a "ruination." Gross followed Brodofsky's lead, pointing out that the way the price of starch was going up, it was risky to iron shirts on too big a scale. At a wild late-night meeting in our flat, Brodofsky grandly announced that he and Gross had decided to *voot* against the ruination; so it was two to one, and Brodofsky called for a voot of the partnership to end the matter. I was wide awake listening to all this, and I heard Pop say, "All right. I'll buy both of you out. Name your price."

It was a great moment for me, lying there in the dark. At last, at last, Pop was going to shake those two! I knew Pop could obtain, from the money men, whatever he needed to get rid of the partners.

After a silence Brodofsky said, "I'll have to talk to mine wibe." That ended the meeting. "Mine Wibe" was Mrs. Brodofsky. Whenever Brodofsky had to scuttle for cover, he would say he had to talk to Mine Wibe. Mine Wibe seemed to have told him every time to stop being a statutory idiot. Nothing more was ever heard from Brodofsky, once he had to take something up with Mine Wibe.

Brodofsky wanted to live on in the Bronx and stay small, you see. Pop and Mom had visions. Pop knew he could build and manage a great laundry. He had probably already worked out the new systems in his head. Anyway, this was the Goldena Medina, and he was on the move! Rowing with Mama in Central Park during their courtship, he had pointed to Fifth Avenue and said, "One day that's where you'll live, Sarah Gitta." Mom never forgot, and she knew her one shot at downtown Manhattan was the big plant; so she spurred and urged Papa on, in his down moments.

Mom does live on Central Park, but Pop did it the hard way. Her investment of his insurance money, and the proceeds of her lawsuit against the partners, made it possible. She didn't move there until she was in her seventies, when Pop had been dead twenty years.

It occurs to me that, in this day of laundromats and washing machines, you may not even be able to picture what the Fairy Laundry was like in its heyday. Well, this fleet of blue and orange trucks with a cute sexy fairy painted on the sides, a fairy with bigger breasts than wings, fanned out from the plant all over the Bronx, and into Manhattan and the suburbs, too. They would pick up your dirty clothes and deliver them back in a couple of days: wet wash, rough dry, semi-finished, flat work finished, full finished, deluxe finished, any way you wanted. This kind of service for the private home was an ephemeral feature of American big-city life, lasting in all about forty years, the span of Pop's own life in America. With many good things of other days, it is gone. The whole industry didn't long outlive him. Like Papa's career in the Goldena Medina, it was a mushroom.

Well, enough sad stuff. I will leave out Pop's many night meetings about Minsker Congregation affairs, and about organizing the Hebrew school, and — most remote and incomprehensible to me — about the "Bronx Zionist chapter." I hadn't the foggiest idea of what Zionism was. The very word filled me with acute boredom. It was the only thing in Pop's life actually more boring than the laundry.

27

Morris Elfenbein and the Purple Suit

TOWNSEND HARRIS HALL was a free high school in Manhattan which got you through four grades in three years. Like home-delivered laundry service, it was a plus of the good old days. It has been extinct for decades. When I passed the admissions test for this elite school Mom and Pop were enchanted. It meant a long daily trip to Manhattan by trolley or subway, and there were high schools close to home. But we never considered my passing up Townsend Harris Hall, and for my leap up in life to a Manhattan school I acquired the purple suit.

Those rides in trolley cars and subway trains, by the way, much expanded my sex education begun by Frankenthal ("That's all there is to it"), *Le Sourire,* and Camp Maccabee. At rush hour I would like as not be jammed helplessly against helpless female flesh; and when there were seats poor Yisroelke, with glands barely stirring, saw wherever he looked skirts flapping in the breeze, displaying crossed legs clear up to gartered thighs. I don't understand how old Peter, in all his Rabelaisian oeuvre, has missed out on this erotic side of mass transport. I can only suppose he walked to that private school. I suf-fered some of the spiritual pangs of a Porush over my impure thoughts, I truly did, and I had no font in which to wash them away; alas for the torments of growing boys with religious consciences! No more of that, in this lighthearted gambol; on to the purple suit.

Mom decided that a Townsend Harris yoxen was entitled to his first suit with long pants; so she took me to the cloak-and-suit dis-trict on the Lower East Side, where Pop bought his clothes. Clothes were cheaper there, and especially cheap at Michaels', a store directly under the rumbling El. A dark noisy repulsive location, but because the rent was so low, Mr. Michaels could cut his prices to the bone. Not that he did, unless he had to. The first time I saw myself in a three-way mirror, in long trousers drooping around my ankles, I did get a thrill, but it soon wore off. Mom had me putting suits on and off for an hour while she haggled. Soon I was yearning for Mama to pick a suit, any suit, and get us out of there. To me a suit was a suit, and those bombinating elevated trains were giving me a headache.

Then Mom spied the purple suit off by itself on a high rack. She asked about it. Mr. Michaels warned her that it was too dear: jacket, vest, two pairs of long pants plus a pair of kneepants; too much material, a line he was discontinuing because customers wouldn't pay the price. Never mind, Mama wanted me to try it on. So he took it down, and I trudged into the narrow dressing booth and got into the suit. Seeing myself in the three-way mirror, I was not pleased. I had no sense of style whatever, but even I could see that it swam on me, and that the color was disagreeable: bold dark purple stripes on a dull purple background.

"It's too big," Mama said.

"You don't expect him to grow?" asked Mr. Michaels, a plump pale bald man, with big sorrowful eyes.

Mom felt the material.

"Iron," said Mr. Michaels. "Steel. He will never wear it out, he can't."

On this point Mr. Michaels was not just talking. The suit lasted like chain mail. It must still exist somewhere, and some unlucky kid must be wearing it.

Mom reluctantly nodded. She did know material, and she recognized the texture of eternity between her fingers. "How much?"

"Missus, you don't want this suit. It costs too much," said Mr. Michaels, sizing her up carefully with his grieving eyes. But he named a price. Mama offered him about half. Mr. Michaels groaned, and proposed to give her the suit as a present. He had a heart condition, he said, the suit was the last of the line, and she was welcome to it. He didn't have the strength to discuss her offer seriously, it wasn't worth risking another coronary attack.

Mama stood her ground. Half.

Mr. Michaels came down about a dollar. Mama went up about a dollar. The gap remained wide. Long dickering ensued, mostly shouted over train noise, while I stood staring at three images of myself, com-

paring my two profiles to pass the time. Finally, wincing and clutching at his chest, Mr. Michaels gasped that to end the matter, he would
make one last offer; and he came down another dollar.

"All right, David," said Mom, "take off the suit and let's go home."

I headed for the booth, the pants slopping over my shoes. Mr. Michaels began to cry, and to beg Mom to take the suit as a gift. I mean
he cried real big tears out of those sad eyes, mopping them with a
handkerchief. It was a very upsetting sight. To console him I said,
"Anyway, it doesn't matter. I don't like the color."

"The color? What's wrong with the color?" sobbed Mr. Michaels.
"It's a beautiful color. All the college boys are wearing that color."

"Take off the suit, David," Mama said.

"Do me a favor, David," Mr. Michaels wept, grasping my elbow.
"Come and look at the color by daylight. It's a very sporty color."
He led me outside. There wasn't much daylight under the El, but the
suit if anything looked worse. There were two sets of purple stripes,
I now discerned, one fainter than the other, making for a very muddy
effect.

"I don't like stripes," I said.

"WHAT?" he wailed, for a train was crashing by overhead.

"I HATE STRIPES," I screamed.

Mama was now in the doorway. "You wait here," she shouted at
me. "I'm going to get Morris Elfenbein."

Mr. Michaels didn't have much color in his face, but whatever was
there faded away. His jaw dropped, his melancholy eyes bulged, and
he said in a plaintive voice, "Elfenbein? Why Elfenbein? Missus, I beg
you, never mind Morris Elfenbein."

But Mom marched off around the corner.

"You're wrong about the stripes, sonny," said Mr. Michaels, as we
went back into the store. "Stripes are the latest fashion. Nothing but
stripes. Take the suit, don't take it, but if you want to be real
collegiate, you want stripes."

He sat down at a shabby desk and wrote in an account book, drying
his eyes. I perched myself on a box, for walking around in those
dragging pants was hazardous. So a little time and a couple of trains
passed, and Mama returned with Morris Elfenbein.

I knew the man very well, from all the synagogue trustee meetings
that had taken place in our home. He was also our main holiday *ba'al
t'fila*, lay cantor. On Yom Kippur, when Morris Elfenbein, with his

silver-collared prayer shawl framing his head, his voice cracking with emotion, his face red with strain, his tall sturdy body swaying far up and down, poured out in the old minor mode that great Psalm

> *Lift up your heads, ye gates,*
> *And let the everlasting doors open*
> *And the King of Glory will come in!*

I tell you, you didn't have to know what the Hebrew meant to be stirred to your bones. He was terrific.

He was terrific now, too, but this was a different Morris Elfenbein; different from the rousing lay cantor, and different, too, from the worrisome synagogue trustee. Morris Elfenbein entered Mr. Michaels's shop like a matador; erect, eyes flashing, shoulders back, the champion ready for the supreme act, the hour of truth, the kill. As dramatic, as exciting, and as somber was the demeanor of Mr. Michaels, as he rose to encounter Morris Elfenbein. Mr. Michaels was a brave bull, who knew his time had come; but he faced the sword with defiant grace, head down, eyes tragic, his bearing uncowed as he waited for the blow. It was pure ritual, and seeing the scene now in my mind's eye, I almost hear the phantom crowd noise die away to a hush, and the matador music sound forth, even over the crashing of the elevated train.

The contest was short, fierce, and mostly in rapid cloak-and-suit Yiddish. I could barely follow the words. The question of whether or not I liked the purple suit dropped from view. Of course I was going to get and wear that purple suit. When Morris Elfenbein entered the arena, there was only one possible outcome. The suspense and the thrill lay only in his skill at weakening his adversary, and his timing of the final thrust. Mama watched the master perform with her face aglow. Down, down, a dollar, and a dollar, and then half a dollar, came Michaels's price. These men were both well-off merchants, you realize. The money gap had shrunk to very little, and anyway there was nothing in it for Elfenbein. They were zestfully playing out a contest as old as the ziggurats of Babylon, and as fresh as the bagels being vended outside on Canal Street. Michaels, as he sank to his knees, so to speak, had almost lost his sad look. His eyes glittered with the exalted despair of the end.

"He's being ridiculous," said Elfenbein to my mother at last, with a wonderful hitch of his broad shoulders, a fantastic flourish of both

hands, and a three-quarter turn to the door that was pure body poetry. "I'm going back to my store. Take your son home."

"All right, Elfenbein." The sword was in to the hilt, and Michaels
gave up the ghost with a noble groan at Elfenbein's back. "I'll
take it."

On the instant, Elfenbein turned and struck hands with Michaels,
who still looked tragic, yet sheepishly amused, like Hamlet when he
rises for a bow after being slain. He stayed in character to shake his
head dolefully at Mama and tell her she was getting the bargain of
her life, but by the time he accepted her check and wrapped up the
suit he was all smiles. I suspect he had waited years to get rid of that
suit, and was a very happy man; but at any rate he got bottom dollar
for it. Morris Elfenbein saw to that.

They broke the mold when Morris· Elfenbein passed on; but I think
he'd have liked the way I handled the president of Paramount Pictures in the deal for the film rights to *Deflowering Sarah*. This executive looked a little like Mr. Michaels: short, pudgy, same bald head,
tragic style, and sad eyes. Time after time when he said the deal was
off, and even mournfully walked out on me, I bethought me of the
purple suit and held fast. The fact is, Internal Revenue plays the purple-
suit game all the time. I've won a lot more than I've lost, because in
me the IRS faces a man who knew Morris Elfenbein. We all risk vanishing in smoke one day, because our Russian friends seem to think
thermonuclear war is just another purple suit; and may the spirit of
Morris Elfenbein watch over us, if that apocalyptic showdown comes.

28

Biberman

A ND now to the melancholy outcome of my acquiring the purple suit.

I don't know whether high schools nowadays still have honor societies called Arista — ΑΡΙΣΤΑ, in the Greek letters they affected. Possibly the tide against "elitism" has swept the Aristas away. What a laugh that is! They will eliminate elites when they standardize chromosomes, and issue the same set to all customers. There are elites now, there always have been elites, and there always will be elites. The problem with elites, which in our topsy-turvy times has got people all churned up is this: who defines the elite? And then, who decides that you or I do or don't meet those superior requirements? Such queries can drift us into minefields like racism and genocide, which this easygoing amusement will bypass, thank you.

Certainly in the Arista Society of Townsend Harris, an elite within an elite, a cream of the cream, the standards of superiority were slightly arbitrary. For instance, if you didn't live in Manhattan, you were screwed. If you lived in that borough above Ninety-sixth Street, especially on the West Side, you were still in bad shape. Whereas, if you lived on the *East* Side, above Fifty-ninth Street and below Ninety-sixth, oh boy! Ruffles and flourishes! As in former times you could be noble or royal simply by birth, so at Townsend Harris you were Arista by residence.

Which brings me to Abby Cohen and Monroe Biberman. Monroe Biberman's father was in the construction business, with an apartment on Park Avenue below Ninety-sixth Street. Monroe was taken into Arista about the time he crossed the threshold of Townsend Harris Hall. He also joined at once the staff of the *Stadium,* the school paper, an Arista hotbed. Abby Cohen lived in the Bronx and rode down to school on the trolley, as I did. Abby Cohen and other Bronx troglodytes sweated for years, some of them in vain, to win a place on the *Stadium* masthead. Abby coveted election to Arista, too, but you had to be invited to apply, and nobody asked Abby to apply.

Abby Cohen's father was a heart specialist, but in the Bronx, alas, on Prospect Avenue. Dr. Cohen had broken with Orthodox parents to go to medical school, and in consequence was a red-hot atheist. Abby echoed his father's views, and I held out for the old-time religion, and we argued for years on the trolley, and also at lunch time, when Abby would eat hot dogs from the vendors' stands, pallid, rubbery-looking things, laughing off my suspicions that they were solid pork, possibly with some cat and dog thrown in. Abby knew all the inside dirt of Townsend Harris politics, and it was he who revealed to me how unfairly the Arista elite ran things. I was unmoved. I just didn't care. It never occurred to me either to try out for the *Stadium* or to apply for Arista. Don't ask me why. Maybe all that seemed like unnecessary trouble.

I have more or less gone through life that way, like the goofy hero of a film comedy who strolls through perils unaware of his close shaves; the villain drops a safe on his head and it just misses him, tries to blow him up and the fuse fizzles, puts poison in his food and the waiter tastes it and drops dead. I wasn't aware at law school, for example, that a cabal of Goodkind-haters worked overtime to keep me off *Law Review,* and failed. I heard about it years later, and could scarcely believe it. In the same way, I hadn't the foggiest notion that the Arista crowd despised "that kid in the purple suit," and made sharp inside jokes about me.

The reason for their dislike was, I guess, the same as Paul Frankenthal's: that irritating Minsker Godol facility of mine. I waltzed through Latin and geometry tests, and I would scrawl A-plus English themes at lunch time between chess moves, all in my hideous purple suit. But this aptitude was decidedly spotty. I came close to flunking history, time after time, for I was a dullard at memorizing dates and facts; also, I barely scraped by in art, a major subject at Townsend Harris, where we had to produce a couple of "plates" — patterns or pictures — each month, and I was as blind to design and perspective as I was to style in clothes. No doubt I had my square root of 625 lapses which angered one or another Arista type, but I never knew when or how I offended; and whatever I did wrong, the purple suit made it worse. I was a marked man.

Honestly, I can recollect only one real offense of mine at Townsend Harris, and I will tell it now to clear my conscience, and to indicate how harmless I must have been otherwise. Once I stole a French grammar from a fellow named Baum, by no means an Arista man, a trolley peasant like me. Baum knew I had done it, and accused me of it, but I brazened it out. "If I can ever prove it, Goodkind," Baum threatened, "I'll have you kicked out of school." His very words; my memory retrieval system throws them up at me an aeon later. I did this fell deed because I had already lost two such textbooks on the trolley, and to apply for a third meant a heavy fine and twenty hours in "the jug" — office detention after school. I couldn't face Mom and Pop with news of such a sentence. If Baum is still alive and happens to read this book, I'll return him the cost of a tenth-grade French grammar, with interest compounded over forty-five years. I don't know what else I can do, and I'm sorry, Baum.

Never before have I revealed this sordid crime to a living soul, except to Bobbie Webb. Once when Bobbie and I got very drunk at the Golden Horn restaurant on Armenian brandy, I poured out the tale of Baum's French grammar. Thereafter, whenever I would turn maudlin in her company — and it happened all too often, as you will hear — I tended to start up on that French book again. Bobbie was a tolerant sort, and she listened sympathetically the first dozen or so times. Then once when we were lying together in bed, in my suite in April House, and I fell into a low mood and began moaning about Baum's grammar, Bobbie put her naked arms around me and said, "Yes, yes, darling, but why not forget it now? I'm sure God has forgiven you long ago." And when I protested that I could never be sure, Bobbie responded, "Well, *I* forgive you, dear, and for Christ's sake shut up about Baum and his French book." It was one of the early warning signs that her patience was not infinite. I might have paid more attention.

Monroe Biberman one day approached me and offered to collaborate with me on a short story. Amazement! The yearbook ran an annual contest, funded in memory of an editor who had died of meningitis, and the prize was twenty dollars. Monroe and I were both top scorers in English, but he was out front because he would read through things like *Rasselas* and *Il Penseroso,* and get A's for reciting on them; whereas I fudged my recitations, merely glancing at what I thought was opaque rubbish revered by fools. Monroe knew I could write, purple suit or no purple suit. We went to his home that same afternoon, and in an hour or so we worked up a story.

Ye gods, what a rise for Yisroelke! Why, the great Monroe Biberman, the haughty and darkly handsome assistant editor of the *Stadium,* Arista pin glowing in the lapel of his fine downtown-looking jacket, took me on as a collaborator; brought me past a uniformed Park Avenue doorman, magnificent as a general, who saluted and smiled at us; led me through a palatial lobby with thick carpets and gilded marble columns, and then into a wood-panelled elevator, and so into an apartment of huge, richly furnished rooms, with bathroom upon bathroom! Like Mama in that merchant's home in Minsk, I had not believed that Jews could live like this. And we ate exquisite puddings out of the giant refrigerator in the giant kitchen, and the great Biberman rolled around laughing at my jokes!

I fell in love with Monroe Biberman. I can put it no other way. Sex had nothing to do with it, and my psychoanalyst friends can wisely grin at this till their mouth muscles ache; a schoolboy crush, yes, violent but innocent. I rode back to the Bronx on the East Side subway for the first time that evening; and as I watched stations slide by with unfamiliar numbers and names in their differently tiled walls, I was one exalted little purple-suited Bronx plebeian. If there were any gartered thighs, I didn't notice them.

We kept meeting in his Park Avenue home to exchange drafts. It was unthinkable, of course, for Monroe to go to the Bronx. I doubt he'd have drunk the water. Soon he invited me to apply for Arista, strongly hinting that I was a shoo-in. Nor was he faking. Monroe and I had taken a real shine to each other. He thought I was very funny, and I thought he was godlike; he basked in my admiration, and I in his laughs, and it was roses, roses all the way. We submitted our story to the yearbook, sure of a win, newly fast friends. This was noticed around the school, of course. Monroe may well have taken some heat from his Arista friends, but if so he shrugged it off in his lordly fashion. Abby Cohen was badly upset, and kept warning me to keep away from "those guys." I didn't ritz him, I liked Abby no less than before, but that wasn't enough for him, and he pretty well turned his back on me.

Soon I must bring on an excessively disagreeable Arista character; a villain, but not an elemental villain like Frankenthal; a cringing, smiling villain, a whispering side-glancing villain — Seymour Dreyer. Dreyer was that rare bird, a Bronx member of Arista. How could that be? Well, there were a few of these freaks, each with a story. Terence O'Donnell, for instance, was a Christian, which put him almost in a class by himself in Townsend Harris. Jules Wachtvogel lived on the Grand Concourse, as classy an address as you could have in the Bronx, and his father managed the Loew's movie houses in the city, and so Jules had access to passes, and it was said that he had met Clara Bow. As for Seymour Dreyer, his father owned the small printing plant that produced the *Stadium*. Maybe the old man was printing the newspaper free of charge: a small price at that for sliding a creature like Seymour into Arista.

Anyway, Bronxite though I was, I applied for Arista, invited and urged by Monroe Biberman. Once I had done that, my pride was engaged. This honor to which I had once been indifferent became something of which I dreamed, for which I gasped, the absolute shining goal of my life, much more so than the short-story prize or even my bar mitzva, now only a week or so away.

29

The Bar Mitzva

BUT I don't intend to make a great to-do over my bar mitzva. It's the horrendous effect on my standing in Townsend Harris Hall that I must chiefly narrate.

Jewish nightclub comedians have long since rung all the changes on bar-mitzva low comedy with their various versions of the bar-mitzva speech, generally known in the trade (I once was a gagman, remember) as "Today I am a fountain pen." That is not worth explaining to the non-Jewish reader, take my word for it. I'm not saying there was nothing funny about my bar mitzva. On the contrary, much of what happened was awfully funny, as I look back on it. At the time, as the star of the thing, I just thought it was all rather splendid, except that I wasn't getting a party at the Chateau Deluxe like Cousin Harold.

Pop just couldn't afford a catered affair, you see, beset as he was. Maybe Uncle Hyman and Aunt Sophie couldn't either, but they were determined to shoot the works. And don't think Cousin Harold let me forget that he — and not I — was having a Chateau Deluxe reception. Harold wasn't the sort to crow, ordinarily, but Aunt Sophie had given him no peace for years with her everlasting "Why can't you be more like David?" This was Harold's one shot at outshining me, and he rubbed it in every chance he got.

And don't think Aunt Sophie let Mama forget it. And don't think Mama wasn't determined so to manage things that — Chateau Deluxe or no Chateau Deluxe — it would remain clear in the family who was the yoxenta, and who had the Minsker Godol for a son. *Hinc illae lacrimae,* if I remember my small Latin from Townsend Harris: "Hence these tears." It was Mama's determination not to let Aunt Sophie have even her one pitiful day in the sun that brought my

Townsend Harris career crashing down. My bar mitzva itself was a wonderful moment in my life. Mama's frills were what made for the comedy, the pain, and the crash.

It's important to interject here that Cousin Harold never really was religious. His father, Uncle Hyman, was not a serious Haskalist like the uncle in Bay Ridge, but he loved to listen to opera broadcasts, read novels, go to plays, and talk about them. Nobody who grew up in that log-walled room in Minsk could help being deeply Jewish; however, Uncle Hyman didn't heave and pant about his Judaism.

Harold went to Hebrew school, all the same, as a matter of course. At the school's Sabbath services, Harold would slump beside me, prayer book open, muttering, "Onions and potatoes, onions and potatoes," since as long as his lips were moving, teachers wouldn't bother him. Harold could read Hebrew, but he preferred to repeat "onions and potatoes, onions and potatoes." I, on the other hand, not only read every Hebrew word, I sometimes conducted the service or gave a little sermon, alternating with a much more eloquent older kid, Julie Levine.

Julie later became an Orthodox rabbi, by the way, and then rebelled, and changed his name to Judah Leavis, and is now an eminent Reform rabbi in Manhattan. I once went to his temple for the funeral of a Columbia philosophy professor of whom I was very fond, Vyvyan Finkel, a rabid agnostic. Given the choice, Professor Finkel wouldn't have been caught dead in a temple, or in any other house of worship; but his sister was a congregant, so there he was, caught dead in fact, in a nice blue suit in an open coffin, looking resigned. Well, the way Julie, or Judah, wove quotations from Vyvyan's writings into the eulogy to make the deceased out a religious man was truly stylish. I half expected Vyvyan to get up out of the coffin and leave, but he just lay there looking more and more resigned.

My bar-mitzva *melamed* — the word means teacher — was a white-haired man named Weil, formally addressed as Mar Weil, who smelled not unpleasantly of the Turkish cigarettes which he smoked all the time. Mar Weil cut each cigarette into short pieces, I think four, and would smoke each piece on the end of a pin until it crumbled away in ash and smoke, leaving no butt whatever. Either Mar Weil had very tough lips, or this pin trick somehow cooled the burning tobacco down to where he could endure that last glowing puff before

the whole thing vanished. There was a man who got his money's worth
out of a coffin nail. The principal of the small Minsker Hebrew school,
Mar Weil had to watch his pennies.

I would go to Mar Weil's home for my bar-mitzva drilling, and
we'd sit out in a little back yard where sunflowers grew. Mar Weil
loved Isaiah, and was a fine Hebraist. I remember the way he parsed
each word and phrase of my bar-mitzva passage for me, his eyes
lighting up, his gnarled hands dancing in precise little gestures. When
I come on this chapter of Isaiah even today, I see those dancing hands,
holding a bit of a cigarette smoking on a pin.

But I mention this only in passing. Mar Weil is no literary competition at all for Peter Quat's famous Hebrew teacher in his sensational novella, *The Smelly Melamed;* Shraga Glutz, with his bad breath,
garlicky body odor, thundering belches, and celebrated habit of picking his nose and parking the snot crusts under the seat of his chair.
Peter is justly proud of Shraga Glutz, whom he made up out of thin
air. Peter never had a bar mitzva. The part where the boy comes upon
the bearded skullcapped Shraga abusing himself while peeking through
a bathroom window at the boy's mother on the toilet has caused much
serious academic discussion, pro and con. Professor Levi Silverstein
of Amherst, in a massive essay in *The New York Review of Books,* made
the definitive defense of old Peter, calling the scene "the ultimate epiphanic moment of alienation in the fiction of the American Jewish
experience." Mar Weil could not have conceivably done anything so
picturesque or epiphanic.

But then, Mar Weil couldn't have kept whacking me over the
knuckles with a strap until — as in Peter's masterful climax — I threw
the Bible in his face, kicked him in the testicles, and leaped out of a
second-story window into a garden, shouting à la John Wilkes Booth,
"I'm not a Jew, I'm an American!" Mar Weil was a gentle old scholar,
and there was no literature in him. I just thought he rated a paragraph, if Shraga Glutz rated a whole novella, since at least Mar Weil
existed.

And now about a bar mitzva that really happened.

I might as well start with the *Bronx Home News,* a sizable daily paper full of local doings; mainly social events, fires, robberies, and rapes.
Rape was always reported enigmatically in the *Bronx Home News* as a

"serious charge." I puzzled for many boyhood years over the high number of unspecified serious charges. Well, that gives you an idea of the *Bronx Home News.* The Fairy Laundry advertised in it all the time.

So it occurred to Mom that my bar mitzva was hot news and rated a write-up, and Pop had no trouble arranging for a reporter to come to our flat for the scoop. The man was supposed to interview me, but I happened to get jugged that day, so he talked to Mom. I had been of two minds about the interview, half-dreading it and half-flattered. On the whole I was relieved that the reporter had come and gone in my absence. Still, I was a bit uneasy, for I knew that where I was concerned Mom was inclined to exaggerate. I asked her what she had told the reporter. "Oh, I just answered his questions," said Mama, already up to her elbows in kishka-stuffing at a huge vat in the kitchen. So she did, God help us all.

The kishka was Mama's second way of whittling down Aunt Sophie, as the newspaper story was the first. There would be nothing about Cousin Harold in the *Bronx Home News,* of course, and whatever the Chateau Deluxe might serve at the banquet, nothing was going to equal this historic kishka. No doubt the whole world knows that the dish called kishka is stuffed cow gut. Mom got hold of an entire intestine, yards and yards and *yards* of it, and stuffed it whole, instead of stuffing a short piece as she sometimes did on Sabbath. I believe this spectacular whole kishka was an old-country custom for great occasions. I know Bobbeh and Aunt Rivka both worked on it, as well as Mom and my sister Lee.

Lee still grouses, in fact, about that kishka, because she ended up in charge of it. Lee was seventeen and becoming very beautiful. A number of boys she liked came to the synagogue, but she had to stay home and mind the kishka. My bar-mitzva party was laid out in a vacant flat above our own — tables, chairs, food, soft drinks, and many bottles of Bobbeh's wine — but the kishka was the *pièce de résistance.* It went twisting all through the place, in and out of the rooms, sort of like a fire hose, brown and spicy-smelling, truly the damnedest kishka anybody ever saw; and Lee had to drape and work it here and there, and keep it off the floors, and arrange it so that guests when they arrived wouldn't get all tangled up in the kishka, or roped off by it from the drinks. I myself don't think the kishka eclipsed Cousin Harold's Chateau Deluxe banquet; and it gave my sister Lee another everlasting complaint, to wit, that only she in the whole Mishpokha didn't hear me do my speeches and my Isaiah chant.

But that is a phony peeve. Lee knew the whole performance by heart from hearing me rehearse it. If she gets sufficiently pie-eyed she can still launch into that Isaiah passage, and my speech too, more than forty years later, and reel them off, glaring the while at the sheer injustice of life. Nobody gets more mileage out of a grudge than my sister Lee, but she has really worn that kishka out. Anyway, the kishka was much admired and praised by the guests at the party. I was the one to make the first cut, which sent it writhing off in two directions, dropping stuffing, to great cheers. Every inch of it was eaten up, and it was the talk of Longfellow Avenue for a week, so maybe it was worth the trouble, at that.

As for the great day in the synagogue, Mama simply outdid herself. Poor Aunt Sophie, poor Cousin Harold! They never had a look-in. When I say Mama I mean Papa, too, of course. He put her grandiose visions into execution, and probably gloried in them as I did.

To begin with, Mama engaged Cantor Levinson and his choir. How can I convey to you what it meant to us Bronxites to have Cantor Levinson — a great old-country cantor who made popular records, a cantor so much in demand that no congregation could afford him on a year-round basis — appear in person in the Minsker Congregation's modest cellar, with his awesome purple pom-pom hat, and his full-length prayer shawl with its glistening gold-work collar, and his choir of twelve in purple robes? It was just stunning. But that wasn't all. She also got hold of the famous itinerant Yiddish preacher, the Bialystoker Maggid, to deliver the sermon. Mind you, these superstars cost less by far than the seven-course roast beef banquet at the Chateau Deluxe, complete with little American and Jewish flags stuck in the grapefruit; but for impact, there was just no comparison.

And speaking of flags, Mom brought off a pretty good effect with flags, too. Old Mr. Weil had about forty kids in the Hebrew school, and Pop was the chairman of the school committee, so putting the kids to work as extras was no problem. When the services began, all those kids sat lined up in the first two rows, the boys and the girls separated. I sat on the front platform by the eastern wall, between Pop and the Bialystoker Maggid. The synagogue was jam-packed, of course, standing room only, as on Yom Kippur; for a large sign in

Yiddish and English outside proclaimed that Cantor Levinson was officiating, and the Bialystoker Maggid speaking, at the bar mitzva of I. David Goodkind. I had a mother who thought of everything, and she wanted to be sure of a full house.

Well, the time came. Cantor Levinson, a small but leather-lunged man, rose on his tiptoes with pom-pom trembling, to belt out the traditional call to the Torah:

"Stand, Yisroel Dovid ben Eliyahu, the bar-mitzva youth, for the closing reading. Be strong!"

And the purple-robed twelve roared in rich harmony:

"BE STRONG!"

Whereupon the boys and girls of the Hebrew school stood up, formed two lines along the aisle from the eastern wall all the way to the raised reading desk in mid-synagogue, and crossed thirty flags, American and Jewish, to form a triumphal arch; and under that arch Israel David Goodkind, in a new gray Michaels suit, marched up to the Torah to do his thing. You never saw such a gaudy effect as that canopy of crossed flags. Cousin Harold was sitting in a front row, and he may well have given up the religion then and there, once and for all.

I read my Isaiah. I spoke in English. I spoke in Hebrew. Mar Weil had prepared my discourses, and they were heavy, but I sailed through them. The Bialystoker Maggid followed me — forty minutes of witty singsong Yiddish, rich with plums of parable, fable, plays on Scripture texts, and Talmudic twists, all leading up to his presenting me with a Bible. Cantor Levinson and the choir concluded the show with a gorgeously florid closing service, and a couple of hundred guests trooped to Longfellow Avenue to regale themselves on kishka, and drink and sing and dance.

All in all, a knockout of a bar mitzva. I proceeded to get pretty drunk on praise and Bobbeh's wine; I had far too much of both, and they went to my head and had me giggling and reeling, but I was the hero of the day and could do no wrong. I seem to remember doing a jig up on a table at one point inside a ring of kishka while everybody sang and clapped, but I hope that didn't really happen.

Now let me leap ahead two weeks to finish the Cousin Harold part, before we take up the Arista catastrophe.

Harold had his bar mitzva in the Minsker Congregation cellar, too.

He had his prophetic passage down pat, but his heart wasn't in it. If he had dared, he would have chanted fifteen minutes of "onions and potatoes." He just slouched up to the reading desk when Morris Elfenbein called his name, and went through his chant like a robot with dying batteries. He made a speech, too, which Uncle Hyman had written, a good speech, but his delivery was lacklustre, and the half-empty synagogue buzzed all through it. Silence fell, however, when I ascended the platform.

Why, yes, here came the old Godol himself. Encore! There was no Maggid to give Harold the Bible, so Mama had persuaded Aunt Sophie that it would be nice for David to do that. Aunt Sophie, a sweet and guileless soul at bottom, was so taken by this notion of Sarah Gitta's David playing second fiddle to Cousin Harold for once, that the poor thing agreed, and even asked me to introduce Harold at the Chateau banquet!

There is more of The Green Cousin in me, possibly, than I care to admit. I ad-libbed an oration in handing Harold the Bible in shule, and then another that night at his banquet, which just shut him out with goose eggs. I don't know why I'm telling this in public, but you may as well know all. Just don't forget how Harold had been lording it over me with his Chateau Deluxe catered affair. It was bad business to start up with me on my home turf. Here in the Bronx, in matters Hebraic and ceremonial, I was Charles Strongfort; if down in Manhattan I was just the kid in the purple suit, passionately yearning to get into Arista.

But there is much of Aunt Sophie in Cousin Harold. He never held those goose eggs against me, not at all. I may have cast a soul adrift from Israel with this mischief, though I think Harold was already well on his way out, muttering "onions and potatoes." Harold was and is a born skeptic, except he does believe that every word Sigmund Freud wrote was first uttered on Sinai. We can all use a revelation of sorts.

30

The Newspaper Story

THE morning after my bar mitzva, I returned with Pop to the synagogue. What a contrast! Gloomy, silent, all but empty; down front, Morris Elfenbein and a few old men putting on prayer shawls and phylacteries, *t'filin*. I had my new phylacteries, and Mar Weil had taught me how to tie them on. Before my bar mitzva I had been ineligible to utter God's name in the blessings; I now recited them as I fastened on the black leather boxes, with Pop's eyes shining at me. That was good, but otherwise, what a letdown! Without me they'd actually have lacked the *minyan,* the quorum of ten men.

We American Jews have strange ways. Most of us tend to take the bar-mitzva blowout as a sort of graduation from religion until we get married or die, something drastic like that; when what it signifies is that observance is supposed to start in earnest. That was certainly how my father took it. I went with him to the Minsker shule every morning for weeks, arising at an ungodly hour to drive there. Afterward he would drop me at the subway, and ride off to the messy building site for his day's aggravation and aging. It was hard going for both of us. It didn't last. Eventually I was rushing through morning prayers at home, in an abbreviated format which my sons have irreverently dubbed "Straps on, straps off," and which is the way they still do it, so far as I know. I don't inquire.

This chapter is about the story in the *Bronx Home News,* but since I've wandered this far afield, let me add one thing more. The drop from the packed bar-mitzva Sabbath to the meager little service Sunday morning was in retrospect the crux of the experience. If Pop hadn't made the effort I'd have missed the whole point. Anybody can stage a big bar mitzva, given a bundle of money and a boy willing to put up with the drills for the sake of the wingding. The backbone of our religion — who knows, perhaps of all religions in this distracted age — is a stubborn handful in a nearly vacant house of worship, carrying it on for just one more working day; out of habit, loyalty, inertia, superstition, sentiment, or possibly true faith; who can be sure which? My father taught me that somber truth. It has stayed with me, so that I still haul myself to synagogues on weekdays, especially when it rains or snows and the minyan looks chancy.

When Pop and I got home from shule that first Sunday, my sister Lee, sitting in the kitchen in a bathrobe with a cup of coffee, grouchily told us that there was a big story about the bar mitzva in the *Bronx Home News,* and Mama had taken the paper over to Aunt Sophie's. Pop telephoned her there. I could hear Mom's excited voice declaring that Sophie and Hyman agreed the write-up was marvelous, and Cousin Harold was reading it right that minute, and laughing like anything.

"Why is Harold laughing?" Papa asked. "Is there something comical in it?"

"No, no," I heard Mom say. "He's just so happy for David. I'll be right home."

Papa hung up and asked Lee whether the story was in any way funny.

"Funny? I'd call it tragic," said Lee, evidently still burned up over the kishka affair.

"Why?" Pop wrinkled his forehead. "What's wrong with the story?"

Reluctantly, after a long leisurely gulp of coffee, she answered, "The mistakes."

I felt sick.

"*What* mistakes?" Papa insisted.

But Lee, if pushed too hard, can move fast from enigmatic evasions to her spitting treed-leopard vein, and then she fears no man — father, brother, husband, it's all one to her. You just have to leave her alone, and give her time to climb down out of the tree.

She now spat at my father, "Look, was I supposed to MEMORIZE the damn story? I wasn't even THERE for the damn bar mitzva, you know, Papa? One thing I know is, he sure spelled 'kishka' all wrong. Not that *I* give a damn!"

Three *damns* in a row, straight at Papa. He blinked and let them pass.

"What? He mentioned the kishka?" I faltered.

"MENTIONED it? It's all ABOUT the kishka!" Lee snarled, setting down the cup with a crash. "You'd think it was the kishka that got bar mitzva'd! You'll soon see for yourself! Leave me alone!" And away she flounced, wrapping the loose bathrobe close around her sexy young figure.

I went out into the hall and leaped up the stairway, hoping to come on a copy of a delivered *Home News*. I did find one and was frantically turning the pages, when the door was opened by a frowsy fat lady with practically nothing on, glaring at me and clutching modestly at herself here and there. I dropped the paper and went galloping out to the nearest newsstand. No *Bronx Home News*. When I got home Mom was there and Pop was looking at the paper.

"Where have *you* been, David?" said Mama affectionately. "Don't you want to read all about yourself?"

"What about the mistakes?" I asked Papa.

He turned large sober brown eyes at me. "It's a very nice write-up. Don't worry, Yisroelke. People don't pay attention to what they read in the papers." He handed me the paper and left. In a fever I laid it out on the table. The story spread over three columns of the social news page, full of pictures of ill-favored brides and engaged girls. There was a picture of me, too, just my face, fat and squinty, blown up from a camp snapshot.

ISAAC GOODKIND BECOMES BAR MITZVA; BOY GENIUS WON FIVE GOLD MEDALS.

The shock of that headline I will never forget. My memories of the story are otherwise fragmentary. I have permanent amnesia about it. Too bad; it was a gem of the journalist's art. I've since had some experience with reporters, including the widespread coverage of the obscenity trials, and have learned to shrug at what newspapers print. But this was a first, and a humdinger. Mama and the reporter between them had really done for me; paragraph by paragraph, as I read the thing, I felt myself being disembowelled with a rusty saw.

All through the story, I was Isaac; just once Isaac David. In the lead paragraph I was identified as the outstanding genius of Townsend Harris Hall, a school for brilliant students, where I had already won five gold medals — for English, dramatics, newspaper work, perfect physique, and boxing prowess. One sentence does swim up through my amnesia after all: *"Young Isaac will chant the entire service from beginning to end, assisted by Cantor Levinson and his choir of twelve."* There was also a very garbled reference to the Bialystoker Maggid; he came out the Bubbleheaded Mugger, something like that.

I tell you, this was quite a news story. Young Isaac was descended from a long line of famous rabbis on his mother's side, and his father was the laundry giant of the Bronx, and also the president of the Muenster Synagogue, of which young Isaac had laid the cornerstone; also the chairman of the Hebrew School, and the Bronx Zionist Chapter, and so on and on and on. Lee had exaggerated about the kishka, but at the end there was a short final paragraph stating that Isaac's mother had prepared for the occasion a traditional religious dish called a pushka, forty feet long, by far the largest pushka ever cooked in the Bronx. In a final burst of creative accuracy, the reporter wrote that the recipe for the pushka had been supplied by the Bubbleheaded Mugger.

Staggered, appalled, shaken to my soul, I looked up from the newspaper at Mama. There she sat, radiating happy pride, feasting her eyes on young Isaac, the boy genius of Townsend Harris Hall.

"A pushka," I managed to choke out. "A pushka."

"Oh, what can you expect from a goy?" she said. "He got it all mixed up. I certainly never said it was forty feet long. He put that in. But what does it matter? It's such a nice big story!"

"Mama — Mama, did you tell him I won those medals at Townsend Harris Hall?"

"Of course not." Mama turned a shade irritable. "Did you hear me say he got all confused, or didn't you? I never said that, and I never said they were all gold, either. I just said the English medal was gold, and it was, wasn't it? I told him you won the others at Camp Maccabee. I just answered his questions and gave him the facts. He mixed them up. What's the matter with you, anyway? Why do you look so upset? Everybody wants their name in the papers, don't they? You've got a whole big story about you! Only the stupid fool calls you Isaac, God knows why, but everybody knows what your name is. The rest is fine, who doesn't know that papers always get something wrong?"

Even as she spoke, I was calculating my chances of surviving this horror. I myself had never looked at the social page before. It was an inside page opposite the classified ads, and conceivably not a single Townsend Harrisite would notice the story. It would be a close thing, and I'd have to hold my breath until Friday, when I was coming up for my hearing before the Arista Society. Till then a sword would hang over my head.

My mother began to look concerned. My shock and alarm must have been written on my face. The misstatements hadn't seemed all that serious to her. Why, there was her David's picture in the paper, with a great big write-up, three columns, all about his wonderful achievements. What more could you ask for? She still glowed with her recent joys. Her color was high, her eyes brilliant. She looked beautiful and very young. To her the whole confounded business — the bar mitzva, the cantor, the maggid, the kishka, the news story, the one-upping of Aunt Sophie — had been a grasp at the ploika, and this time she really thought she had it in hand. I didn't understand that at the time; yet seeing her turn anxious, I suddenly felt sorry for her. Another first! Sorry for my mother; realizing that any attempt to explain how I felt would be wasted words. A gulf had opened between The Green Cousin and her Minsker Godol. It has never closed.

"It sure is a big story, Mom," I said cheerily, "and it sure was a great bar mitzva. I don't care about the mistakes." I kissed her, and went to my room. The walls swam, but I brushed my tears aside and sat down to Cicero's second Oration against Catiline. Six days to the Arista meeting.

31

The Arista Meeting

I ARRIVED at Townsend Harris Monday morning in a state of advanced dread.

On the trolley Abby Cohen had not referred to the *Bronx Home News*. For once his echoes of his father's views — of the Talmud as a futile waste of time, of kosher butchers as a guild of irreligious fakers and thieves, and of God as a Stone Age bogeyman — were music to my ears, so long as he said nothing about my bar mitzva. He didn't know it had taken place, because I hadn't told him. You may find this hard to believe, but I kept my Townsend Harris life and my Bronx life rigidly compartmented, and Abby belonged in the Harris compartment. I had invited nobody from the school, not even Monroe Biberman, though he had a fair Jewish background. I had been moving between two planets, the Inside and the Outside. The horror of the *Bronx Home News* story was that it leaped the interplanetary void; and "my David," the synagogue paragon, was proclaimed in public print as the mental and physical giant of Townsend Harris Hall. That was what I had to live down, unless by a miracle it escaped notice.

I passed through the morning periods, through the chess-playing in the crowded lunchroom, and through the afternoon classes, and heard not a whisper of the *Bronx Home News*. Was the miracle happening? Was God — in whom, unlike Dr. Cohen, I unreservedly believed — overlooking my small thieveries and the serious matter of gartered thighs, and giving me this incredible break as his bar-mitzva present? Even Seymour Dreyer, as we met going down into the subway at the end of the day, cordially waved and smiled. *Not* what I would expect from Dreyer if he had anything on me; and Dreyer, remember, was from the Bronx.

Now let me fill you in on Dreyer. Early in our first term, he and I had been partners in petty crime. Once when I was going down into the subway, he approached me and proposed that we crowd through a turnstile together. I had no compunction about gypping the subway system, and we did this regularly, each time saving a nickel. (Doesn't that put the patina of a lost golden age on my youth? Five cents to ride anywhere in New York!) Dreyer next sought to improve our acquaintance by inviting me to see how easy it was to steal books from the library. I was curious enough to go with him to his neighborhood branch. Sure enough, he checked out two books and left with a third under his coat, beaming in triumph. When we reached the street, he offered me the pilfered book, but I wouldn't accept it. I was capable of mulcting the transit system of a nickel a day, but there was something rotten to me in stealing a book from a library. I took a distaste to Dreyer, and backed off from our subway arrangement.

Once he joined the *Stadium* staff and got into Arista, Seymour Dreyer had no time for me. Dreyer was a born side-glancer, winker, and snickerer behind his hand. Every now and then I'd see him with some *Stadium* fellow, the back of his hand to his mouth, glancing toward me sideways with those half-closed Dreyer eyes. At the time, in my naive obliviousness to the whole Arista thing, I wasn't bothered. Chances are he was proving how superior he was to his Bronx origins, by making jokes about the Bronx butt in the purple suit. You know such people, we all do, and that was Seymour Dreyer, the long and short of him.

Well, nothing is as stale as yesterday's newspaper, and I awoke Tuesday with my spirits reviving. I had another uneventful day at the school. Ye gods, I thought, was I going to make it?

No.

When I got home, a letter awaited me from Seymour Dreyer. He congratulated me on my bar mitzva and my five gold medals. He expressed his wonder at the journalism award, since he wasn't aware that I had joined the *Stadium* staff or even tried out for it. About my physical perfection and boxing prowess, he said that he'd have to be more careful around me hereafter; he hadn't realized that such a powerful body lurked beneath my purple suit. I was bound to get into Arista now, he concluded, since there weren't many boy geniuses around, and the honor society was always eager to raise the level of its membership.

Next day I approached Monroe Biberman and said I was withdrawing my Arista candidacy. He was dumbfounded. "Why?" he asked. "What's bothering you?"

How could I tell him? I said the first lame thing I could think of: I had heard there was talk against me in the *Stadium* office. Biberman pooh-poohed the notion, said I shouldn't get cold feet now, my election looked all set. Only, he casually suggested that I wear a different suit to the meeting. He didn't criticize the purple suit; that was all he said. I densely let that go by, even after the Dreyer dig. And so, an ox to the knife, in the gray bar-mitzva suit in which I had marched to glory under the arch of crossed flags, I came to the Arista meeting on Friday afternoon. When I entered the classroom where they held it, about twenty members were lounging in the chairs. Several of them were smoking, and a few had on their laps copies of the *Bronx Home News*.

"Mr. Goodkind," said the president of Arista, a dark, mature, and not disagreeable lordling named Jerry Bock, who was the editor of the *Stadium,* and who by general school whisper actually knew and frequented a whore, "will you please tell us why you think you should be elected to Arista?"

He sat at the teacher's desk, a copy of the *Bronx Home News* open before him to the society page. Seymour Dreyer had gone to a lot of trouble, all right. He might have just passed one clipping around, but no, he was driving this nail to the board, establishing once for all his credentials as a Bronxite who despised Bronxites. Dreyer sat in the front row with a hand over his mouth, leaning toward the ear of Monroe Biberman, in the seat beside him, and on his face behind the hand was the beam of triumph with which he had stolen the library book.

— I wish I could break in here to tell you that Seymour Dreyer came to a bad end, but the fact is I've never heard of him since I left Townsend Harris. Dreyer was buried deeper in my subconcious than even Frankenthal was; but as soon as I began writing about my bar mitzva, the *Bronx Home News* came bursting through the six feet of mental cement with which I've overlaid it for forty years and more, and so this inconsequent snickering sneak has moved center stage.

But how much of this ordeal do you really want me to describe? It all happens in Lilliput, and who cares that I am back there, one of the tiny people, in a desperate situation? Well, okay. I stand with my back to the blackboard, my sweaty hands behind me clutching at the shelf where the chalk and the erasers lie, confronting those Arista kids and actually attempting to say why I should be elected. That was my mistake. I should have found a few dignified words and walked out as soon as I saw the newspapers, because I was sunk. I could see that in the smirks all over the room. Only Biberman and Bock seemed to be somewhat embarrassed. I hadn't gotten far when one grinning face interrupted and asked me please to describe my journalistic achievements. Even as I drew breath to try to account for that accursed write-up, another grinning face declared he was more interested in my boxing record. Was I a welterweight or a bantamweight? Giggles. A third grinning face observed that a perfect physique was a rarity; would I consider stripping to the waist, so that the Arista members could all admire my award-winning body?

Raucous laughter, and the pillorying was on. Such questions and crude jokes shot at me from all sides. Adolescents aren't kind, they put each other to the test all the time, and they'll peck a downed one to death. It was my second Halloween. I faced it in silence, and let them joke and laugh themselves out. I didn't say anything. I just stood there and took it. My knees were shaking, but I'm glad to say, even across this gulf of years, that my face remained calm and my eyes dry.

The noise died down.

"Mr. Goodkind, is your first name really Isaac?" Jerry Bock asked in a sober, almost apologetic way, as though trying to get the meeting back on the track.

"No."

"Ignatz?" said someone. That someone was Monroe Biberman. He piped up "Ignatz" in a funny voice, and set them all laughing again.

And then, as the hee-haws subsided, Seymour Dreyer said, in the crude Jew singsong of vaudeville, "Tell us, Iggy, where's your purple suit?"

("Clip cock! Clip cock!")

That did not get a laugh. I found my voice and said to Jerry Bock, "My first name is Israel. Any other questions?"

He didn't answer. He looked out at the Arista members. So did I. No one said anything. Biberman wouldn't meet my eye, and his face was turning red. Perhaps he was regretting "Ignatz," now that the thing was done. For a laugh, one laugh, he had finished me off. The other faces were blank, except for Dreyer's, whose eyes were almost shut in the happy book-stealing look. His kike imitation had over-shot the mark and ended the fun, but he didn't realize it.

"Thank you, Mr. Goodkind," said Jerry Bock.

I walked out. Though I had a jug sentence to serve, I went to my locker, got my books, and hurried the few blocks to the trolley, so as to arrive home in time for the first Sabbath after my bar mitzva. That night I intended to go to the synagogue with my father.

For the rest of my time in Townsend Harris, which is truly a blur, I was Iggy. The name caught and stuck. I don't remember being bothered by that. The school just ceased to matter to me. Biberman and I scarcely talked again, and we didn't win the short-story prize, by the way. As a matter of fact, Abby Cohen did. It didn't help Abby on the *Stadium,* though. He worked like a dog till the end, yet got no higher than associate editor. But then, rather to my surprise, Dreyer didn't even achieve that. Seymour Dreyer never did quite make it across the bridge.

* * *

32

The Art Plates

Aloft, Washington–Tel Aviv
August 17, 1973

M AYBE it's the hour or the altitude. The plane is black dark, I'm
writing by a cone of light from the overhead hole, and the
bouncing is making these lines straggle and wander like my thoughts.
I should quit and try to sleep, but I'm wide awake. So okay, let me
get a slug of booze from that fetching little El Al stewardess with the
flirty dark eyes, and I'll try to close out Townsend Harris with Mama's audacious art plates coup. If not for her, I might never have
graduated from Harris; certainly my transcript would have been a
crippling disaster. The Green Cousin rescued me, brick in hand, so
to speak, and she is entitled to this credit item after the hard time
I've been giving her, and considering the shape she is in at the moment.

I still suspect Mom will bury all the doctors now waiting on her,
and Lee and me, too, but at the moment she is hospitalized in Jerusalem, and I've been summoned to her bedside. She took it into her
head to visit Zaideh's grave on the Ninth of Av. That's an old custom, praying at one's parents' graves on this day which commemo-
rates the fall of the two temples, but one isn't expected to fly six
thousand miles to do it, not at her age. That was strictly my mother's
idea. That she can't see, hear, or walk worth a damn, and keeps coming up with mortal symptoms, is for the doctors to worry about. She
just bashes on.

Of course I'm concerned as hell.

*   *   *

WELL, about the art plates. I've mentioned the lunatic impor-
tance of art at Townsend Harris. All students, semester after
semester, had to turn in designs or pictures called "plates." There's
no way I can tell you why a student's career hung on his ability to
draw and color pictures. Art was called a "diagonal" subject, like Latin
and English. I can't account for that label, either, but if you failed a
"diagonal," you couldn't graduate.

Now, I never could draw or color for sour apples. I still can't. After
the Arista fiasco, I stopped caring about Townsend Harris, and as for
the art plates, I just didn't do them. I had to turn in eight plates in
my senior year; and as I fell behind in art, doodling while the rest of
the students daubed out still lifes, posters, landscapes, and whatnot,
the teacher, a cold-eyed blond prig named Langsam, warned me that
I was heading for my doom. Nobody could fail art and escape a ghastly
fate, said Mr. Langsam. A few days before final exams I awoke to
this predicament, and sat up nights at home doing desperate things
with crayons and watercolors. Maybe Mr. Langsam would even have
liked what I concocted. I never knew what pleased that ice-blooded
fusspot, and my stuff did have a Picasso grotesqueness about it. But
there's no saying, because on the last day they were due I absentmindedly left those eight plates on a trolley-car seat.

When I realized this I got excused from school, took a cab to the
car barns, and raised a hullabaloo, but the plates were gone. I told
my sad story to Mr. Langsam, shedding genuine tears, and he listened, glacier-faced, and flunked me. He really couldn't have done
anything else, but there was no compassion in the man. We were alone
in his office, and he took out his marking book with an arctic smile.
"Well, Mr. Goodkind," he said, "this is some kind of record, anyway.
Your final semester mark in Art Diagonal A-Four is exactly zero."
His pen swooped in a round flourish. "There we are. Zero. I regret
that you cannot graduate. You may go, Mr. Goodkind."

He never dreamed, of course, that that wasn't the end of it; but
then, he had never dreamed of a person like my mother. Next morning there she stood with me in Mr. Langsam's office. The night before, preparing my parents for the shock of my first school failure
since kindergarten, I had warned them that with this black mark on
my record I could scarcely hope to get into Columbia or any other
good college.

"We'll see about that," said Mama. "I'll go and talk to him. You made the plates, didn't you? Why, I saw them myself. They were beautiful. I never heard of such injustice. What's this man's name again?" She wrinkled her nose at me.

"Langsam," I said.

"An anti-Semite," Mama said, stabbing a stiff forefinger in the air.

"Oh, for God's sake, Mama," said Lee. We were all at the supper table. "What are you talking about? How could the teacher pass him? Without even seeing the plates?"

"Is that David's fault? Somebody stole them on the streetcar."

Gray-faced and weary, Papa said to Mom, "Maybe he can draw more pictures. Or maybe they'll let him go to summer school and make it up."

"Why should he? I'll talk to that man tomorrow," said Mama. "That Mr. Langsam."

And so there she was, bright and early, confronting him. I must say that, in this context, Mr. Langsam did look extremely gentile, though the notion had not struck me before. He was also a thoroughly thunderstruck gentile. He had a lot of trouble taking in Mom's purpose, which was to get him to pass me in Art Diagonal A-4. "Mrs. Goodkind," he said in a cautious quiet way, as though soothing a madwoman with an ax, "your son didn't do the work, so how can I pass him?"

"He did do the work. All of it. He did eight beautiful pictures — what do you call them?"

"Plates," said Mr. Langsam.

"Plates, yes. Plates. Eight fine plates. One of flowers, one of a wonderful red horse, and the Empire State Building, and —"

"He did not submit any such plates in class, madam. He sat at his desk for five months, doing nothing."

"So he did them at home. That was allowed, wasn't it?"

"Yes, but I didn't see the plates."

"Mr. Langsam, would I lie to you? He did them, and they were fine, take my word for it."

"Madam, how am I supposed to mark eight plates I never saw?" Mr. Langsam ran both hands through his thick blond hair, staring at Mom with appalled watery eyes.

"Am I asking you to give him A-plus? I'm asking you not to wreck a boy's whole career, just because some thief stole his briefcase. My son has never failed any subject in his life. Not once."

Mr. Langsam at last said she'd have to talk to Mr. Hutchison. If Mr. Hutchison wanted to take the responsibility of passing me, that was all right with Mr. Langsam.

Hutchison, head of the art department, was the toughest marker in the school. Mom didn't know that. She marched me straight across the hall into his office, and went through the whole thing again. Mr. Hutchison, a dour long-jawed man, sat shuffling art plates, chewing on a cold pipe, and shooting me disbelieving looks from under shaggy iron-gray eyebrows.

"Madam, Mr. Langsam is absolutely right. I can't possibly order him to pass your son," he growled when she finished. "I never heard of such a thing. He didn't submit the work, and that's that."

"Then who do I talk to?" Mom inquired.

Hutchison's jaw sagged open, showing big yellow teeth. He stuffed his pipe with tobacco, staring at Mom as though she had horns or tusks.

"Well, it won't do you the slightest good," he said, "but you can take it up with Mr. Ballard, if you want to."

So down we went to the school's main office, though I well knew we had come to the end of the line, and that it was hopeless. It's hard to say just what Mr. Ballard's position was. He wasn't the director of the school. That was Dr. J. Hampton Hale, a remote presence in an inner office never profaned by student feet. Dr. Hale's name appeared on school proclamations and on diplomas, but he showed up only at rare assemblies, in the form of a little gray pharaoh-visaged man who did not speak. Mr. Ballard did the speaking at assemblies.

Mr. Ballard was a mountainous fellow with great shoulders and bulging eyes. The students in the school believed that Mr. Ballard regularly copulated with the two school secretaries, Miss Reichman and Miss Jacoby, and also with the librarian, Miss Jamison; and not because he was irresistible — on the contrary, he was a repulsive blubbery hulk, any way you looked at him — but simply because they were frightened of him and had to submit to his horrible advances. Mr. Ballard was the man who sentenced you to the jug, and sneered away your excuses for tardiness or other crimes, and summoned parents to discuss your failings, and, in short, gave the final decisions in all school matters. There was no appeal from Mr. Ballard, and he was a steel wall of total contemptuous negativism. He had heard every possible sob story and alibi a student could produce in every conceivable tight spot, and his invariable replies were two: "No," or "Jug."

Well, he couldn't jug Mama, but he could say "No," and he did, loud and flat, popping his eyes at her in the terrifying way which dried up students' excuses and tears, and undoubtedly caused Miss Reichman, Miss Jacoby, and Miss Jamison to yield their poor bodies to him.

But this time he was dealing with Sarah Gitta Goodkind, the big yoxenta, an entirely different breed of female. Mama faced him, waited until his eyes sank back into their sockets, and then asked, "Are you the head of this school?"

The eyes popped out again in amazement, and I believe Mr. Ballard answered before he thought. "No. That's Dr. Hale."

"All right," said Mama, "I'll talk to Dr. Hale. Where do I find him?"

"No! You can't talk to Dr. Hale."

"Why can't I? My son is a student in his school, isn't he?"

Mr. Ballard forced out his eyes to their farthest bulge, like a batrachian's, and he powerfully croaked, "Dr. Hale is a very very busy man, and nobody sees Dr. Hale unless —"

"Is that Dr. Hale's office?" Mama interrupted, pointed at a polished wooden door with a highly visible sign on it:

DR. J. HAMPTON HALE
DIRECTOR

For once in a long career, Mr. Ballard could not reply either "No" or "Jug," so he mutely nodded, and Mama made for that inner office. For such a huge and heavy man, Ballard moved with surprising quickness to block her, and in an instant there they stood toe to toe at Dr. Hale's door.

It must be clear to all readers of this narrative that my mother by and large has been, down the years, something of a trial to me. My feelings about her are mixed. But as that picture rises in my mind's eye — Mama, red-cheeked, middle-sized, buxomly pretty, her bright eyes blazing up at that King Kong of a No-sayer; and Mr. Ballard looking down at her with shaken wariness, his eyes shifting at his harem slaves, Miss Reichman and Miss Jacoby, who were taking in with fascination this brave challenge to their insatiable sultan — I have to tell you that I admired her, that I saw she was a mother of the old school, a mother like a mother bear or tigress, a mother with enough

fight in her to face down half a dozen Mr. Ballards in order to see a
Dr. Hale. What did it matter that she was in the wrong, preposter-
ously in the wrong, that her nerve was incredible, trying to get me a
passing mark in Art Diagonal A-4 when I hadn't turned in any art
plates? She was magnificent. She was MAMA.

And Ballard — Ballard gave way before Mama! With an indistinct
mutter like, "I'll have to talk to him first," he disappeared inside the
door. A long wait ensued. Mama stood there at the closed door, I
stood beside her, and Miss Reichman and Miss Jacoby pretended to
busy themselves with paperwork, while they kept glancing at each
other, at Mama, and at the door, clearly thrilled to the bone by this
high moment in their sexually harrassed lives.

The door opened.

"The answer is NO," thundered Ballard, appearing in the opening.
Under the arm that held the door, I could see Dr. Hale at his desk,
head down, writing. "You son has FAILED in art, madam. That is
Dr. Hale's decision, and it is final."

Ballard's mistake was holding the door ajar instead of shutting it
behind him. He did not yet realize that he was dealing with a woman
who at fifteen had beaten up a stepmother twice her size, who had
once taken on a big watchman with a brick, and who, where her jewel
was concerned, did not know manners or fear. Mama ducked under
his arm, dragging me along. "Just let me explain something to Dr.
Hale," she said, and there we were inside the holy of holies of Townsend Harris Hall. Too late Ballard groaned, "No, madam, you can't
go in there. No!"

The gray head at the desk lifted. The pharaoh visage stared lifelessly and wordlessly at Mama, and then at Ballard. Mama plunged
straight into the story of the lost plates. Dr. Hale listened without
changing either his expression or his position: an arm on his desk, a
pen in his hand, a school director in sandstone. At these close quarters this immobile figure frightened me more than Ballard did. He
was Ozymandias, King of Kings. I looked on him and despaired.

Not Mama. With the most cheerful rectitude in the world, she appealed to him to pass me. As she summed it up, the choice was simple: mar an unblemished record, wreck a brilliant career, destroy a
possible future President's life, or pass I. David Goodkind in Art Diagonal A-4.

Dr. Hale's visage turned slowly to Mr. Ballard, who stood beside the desk in ill-contained fury. "Well, the circumstances are unusual," he said in a weak, mild, high little voice. "If the boy has never failed anything, it would be a shame to let a mishap mar a perfect record, wouldn't it? Let us give him a D minus in Art Diagonal A-Four."

Mr. Ballard's eyes popped out bloodily. It was awful to behold. He was struck speechless, but Mama wasn't. She at once interjected, "Is that a passing mark, Dr. Hale?"

"Well, it isn't failure," said the director in that same meek small voice, "but it's nothing to be proud of."

"You're a great man," said Mama, and we left.

So it was that, besides passing Art Diagonal A-4, I learned the dread secret of Townsend Harris Hall. Dr. Hale was not Ozymandias, King of Kings. He was Oz, the great and terrible, actually a softhearted fraud; and that was why he had that bug-eyed raper of secretaries and librarians in his outer office.

* * *

A ND so it is that I sit here in an El Al airplane en route to the Holy Land, more than a little swozzled by the three scotches I have downed while scrawling out that scene. The little stewardess with the black eyes either has taken a shine to me, which I find hard to believe, or else she has nothing else to do but spring at me with a fresh drink as soon as I empty my glass.

Who can say how my life would have changed, had I failed that diagonal? I would have spent an extra semester at that school, might never have gotten into Columbia College, let alone the law school; never met Mark Herz, never joined Tau Alpha Epsilon, never worked for Goldhandler, or lived in April House, or met Bobbie Webb. It all turned on Mama's great moment at Townsend Harris, which happened exactly as I've described it; except of course that I don't know that Mr. Ballard really had his will of those three meager females. Anyway, they are surely gone, all four of them, their rumored orgies over, their dust buried who can say where, their very names forgotten, except in this tale. I'm glad I wrote out the story in drunken haste. I owe it to Mama; swift recovery and long life to her! She has the virtues of her faults, or she could never have overborne Langsam, Hutchison, and Ballard to get at the wonderful wizard of Oz.

Now for some sleep before we land in Israel and I find out how she is. The airplane windows are growing light. Sandra's eyes just fluttered, and she muttered in her sleep and turned on her side. That's right, Sandra. She showed up yesterday morning in dirty jeans, carrying a duffel bag — she'd been attending a summer writing workshop in Idaho — and said she heard I was going to Israel and she wanted to come along. No explanation, and here she is.

Maybe before this short trip is over I'll find out what Sandra is up to, and then again maybe I won't. Sandra plays a devious and dirty game with me, which you might call "Sweat Blood, You Old Bastard." We have an exceedingly tangled relationship, and I love her too much to write another word about it. I suspect she loves me. Consult your local psychoanalyst on why some daughters enjoy breaking their fathers on the wheel. Oddly, reclining there in the next seat in the dawn, Sandra reminds me a lot of The Green Cousin.

PART II

Manhattan

33

Golda

THE Green Cousin met me at the airport. I almost fell down from the shock. The last word had been, after all, that she was lying in an oxygen tent, in an intensive care unit of the Hadassah hospital. There she stood beside a wheelchair, leaning on the arm of her companion, smiling and feebly waving, in the no-admittance area where they stamp passports. She had bulled her way past the Israeli security barriers, an impossible feat except for my mother. So we hugged and kissed, and she explained in weak gasps that putting her in a hospital was all foolishness, she felt fine; while the companion she brought from New York, an infinitely patient Puerto Rican girl who hardly speaks English, shook her head hopelessly at me.

Sandra gave Mom a big hug, and helped her back into her wheelchair. Sandra had a spell of hating Mom for nagging her about finding a nice Jewish boy. Once Mom gave Sandra's phone number to a friend who had a nice Jewish grandson, and a yeshiva student in a black hat and vestigial earlocks showed up; a warm and witty young fellow, actually, but a jolt to behold. There was a harsh blow-off, we got Sandra a new number, and Mama quit the matchmaking. Now Sandra admires her grandmother in a rueful way, but keeps her distance.

Well, I fetched the bags and we made our way out of the terminal. When I first visited Israel in 1955 Lod Airport was a dusty, disorganized primitive installation: just a few runways, palm trees, and shanty-like buildings. First-timers used to kiss the ground. I've seen that only once in recent years, when I watched a group of Jews arrive late at night from the Soviet Union. A couple of the old folks got down and did that.

The glossy new terminal is a big crush: crowds coming, crowds going, joyous crowds greeting the newcomers, tearful crowds seeing off the departing; crowds of bearded Hassidim with their kerchiefed women and swarming children; crowds of sunburned bareheaded Israelis in shorts and sport shirts, or in army uniform; and of course the two-way crowds of Americans, mostly Jews but also many Christian innocents abroad on Holy Land pilgrimages. A few bronzed young Nordics, skin-divers and hikers and such, haul heavy sporting gear off the baggage belts. Nobody is kissing the ground.

Naturally the first order of business was what to do with Mama. The companion was no help, babbling in Spanish. I asked Mom what the doctor's orders were. She said the doctor was a scoundrel *(paskudnak)* who charged a fortune for nothing. Mom's desire was to celebrate my arrival by dining at a kosher Chinese restaurant in Tel Aviv, a very bad idea. My mother can't eat anything with sodium in it. If she does, an ambulance is on the way within the hour. But in a Chinese restaurant everything is full of sodium, down to the very lychee nuts.

Nevertheless, Mom loves to go to a kosher Chinese restaurant — you find them in Israel, and in New York, too — summon the head-waiter, and work her way down the menu, trying to order a meal with no sodium. Cross-examining him item by item through the entire bill of fare can kill a lively half hour, and meantime she has a couple of gin and orange juices, on which she thrives. Invariably she settles for steamed fish and boiled rice without salt. When these arrive she barely tastes them, says they're full of salt, and has another gin and orange juice. It's a favorite treat of Mama's, this Chinese restaurant routine. It's only a complicated way to tank up on gin and orange juice, but she does enjoy the long byplay with the head-waiter.

However, I couldn't indulge Mama in that delight this time. She looked wizened and white, and I was scared. Sandra and I bundled her, wheelchair, companion, and all, into a taxicab. Off we sped to the Hadassah hospital, a vast complex outside Jerusalem. When Mom realized that we weren't heading for Tel Aviv she protested, but not with quite the old fight; and soon subsided, placidly holding my hand clasped in her withered paws, as the car climbed the hills to the Holy City.

It was a while before I tracked down her doctor to his office. When I introduced myself, he gave me a hunted look. He appeared young, but worn out from overwork: a bushy-haired dark little man in a crumpled white coat, with a crumpled white face, a stethoscope dangling from his neck, and a reflector on a band around his head. Clearly the man needed sleep. When I remonstrated with him for turning Mom loose to go to the airport, he said in weary Israeli accents, "Where is your mother now, Mr. Goodkind?"

"Downstairs in a taxicab."

"What does she want to do?"

"Go to a Chinese restaurant."

"Take her."

"What? Doctor, my mother looks awful. She's barely alive."

"You should have seen her last week. Your mother is amazing, Mr. Goodkind. I didn't give her seventy-two hours to live. That's why we cabled you. When we told her you were coming, her blood pressure dropped to normal, her pulse stabilized at seventy-five, and she sat up and started eating like a horse, complaining that everything was full of sodium. But she ate all she got. Next day she was walking up and down the corridors."

"Well, I'm not taking her to any Chinese restaurant. That's madness."

"It's up to you." The doctor shrugged. "Just don't leave her here. We're crowded. She kept her hotel room, you know. She didn't want to come to the hospital at all. Take her back to her hotel, please. She's a bad patient, she makes the whole staff nervous. She keeps claiming her food's full of salt, which is preposterous, and calling for the chief administrator, insisting she's a founder of the hospital. I've checked that, by the way, and it's not so. She's a patron. Founders give a quarter of a million dollars apiece, Mr. Goodkind. Patrons give a thousand. I told her that, and she said, 'Patron, founder, why argue? Your food is full of salt.' She did once raise a lot of money for an electron microscope we needed, and we're grateful, but she really is a difficult person."

"Doctor, what about my mother's health? Her chances?"

"Right now she's all right. All right, I mean, for a person who medically shouldn't be alive. It's all willpower. I'll keep in close touch."

So Mom is now down the hall, in her favorite King David room, with a balcony facing the Old City, in fair shape, and there she'll stay through Yom Kippur. Now that she's here, she's decided there's no way she'll leave Israel before the High Holy Days.

The puzzle of what Sandra is doing here has cleared up. My notion was that, girl-fashion, she was in undeclared pursuit of Abe Herz. But no, apparently not; or if she is, her technique is a new benchmark in female deviousness. I talked to Abe on the phone today, in his Tel Aviv law office, and he didn't know Sandra was here. Their windy quarrels back in Washington had extinguished, or so I thought, any spark of that unlikely little attraction, yet he was plainly annoyed that he hadn't heard from her.

Abe Herz is about seven years older than my daughter, and except when in army uniform with decorations, not especially prepossessing anymore. His hairline is retreating, and he has a hint of a mid-bulge, possibly because of the starchy Israeli diet. His resemblance to his bony father has blurred. But he's a hardy specimen, scuba-dives in the Red Sea, has even tried hang-gliding, and goes on tough field maneuvers so often that his law practice suffers. The reserve call-ups in Israel fragment everybody's career, but I suspect there's some demanding secret aspect to Abe's reserve status. Not that I would inquire, or that he'd tell me anything.

It was Abe, it turns out, who gave Sandra the idea of coming here. During one of their combative dates in Washington, when she was spouting her valued New Left views on Israel, he stopped her cold by remarking that his uncle, an ex-general of the Israeli air force, held much the same opinions, and lived on a kibbutz where everybody thought that way. Sandra responded, with her accustomed civility, that she didn't believe a word of it. All the same, she made a few inquiries, and decided to freeload on my trip, so as to see for herself these peace-loving anti-imperialist Zionists. I found that out last week while registering in this hotel. Sandra, at the desk beside me, suddenly said, "Don't check me in, I'm going to Sde Shalom."

"And where and what is Sde Shalom?"

"A kibbutz down south." Taking no notice of my amazement, she added, "Let me have my return air ticket now, okay?"

"Aren't you flying back with me?"

"I'll probably leave before you do. I'm not staying here any longer than I have to."

"How will you get to this Sde Shalom?"

"Don't worry."

"You don't know a word of Hebrew."

"I'll be all right."

"Have some dinner first, at least."

"Okay."

We drank a lot of Israeli red wine with the six-course kosher dinner, and she loosened up. She liked the noble proportions of the King David dining room, and the Levantine decor dating back to the British mandate. What a pity it was, she said, that imperialism was finished, however immoral it had been. She then disclosed the purpose of her trip; nothing less than to get a leg up on her M.A. in political science at Johns Hopkins. She's enrolled for the fall, and she already has a theme and a title for her master's thesis: "The Israeli Peace Movement: Progressive Countercurrents in a Proto-Fascist State."

What the enterprising young baggage had done, bypassing Abe Herz, was to write directly to his uncle at Sde Shalom, General Moshe Lev. Lev at once answered warmly that she'd be welcome there any time. She has brought along in her duffel bag books and articles about the peace movement, and already has a head full of undigested ideas on the subject. The trip to Sde Shalom is field research. Now what the little dear doesn't know — has no way in the world of knowing — is why General Moshe Lev fired back such a friendly letter. Only two other people in the world would know beside Lev: my sister Lee and I. In the interest of truth and art, I'll now briefly rattle a family skeleton.

There's a big branch of the Herz family here; Herz is Yiddish for *heart,* and the Hebrew word is *Lev,* hence the name change long ago in the Palestine branch. Mark Herz's cousin, Moshe Lev, practically started the Israeli air force, and Moshe Lev is the man my sister Lee fell in love with when she visited Palestine back in the dim thirties. Mark and I were then college friends, and Mark mentioned that he had relatives in Jerusalem. He gave me the address. Moshe Lev was a much-married fellow with three kids, but these Israelis are sometimes free-wheeling types, the ones who aren't religious. Lee came home all shaken up and starry-eyed, whispering to me of a divorce cooking over there. In the end nothing happened. Lee settled down happily with her doctor in Port Chester, and just smoked twice as much ever after. Lee seldom speaks of Israel, but when she does there's a tremolo in her throat, to this day.

Just incidentally, Moshe Lev and Mark Herz are named after the same grandfather, who remained in Russia and was murdered by the Germans. In America Moshe, of course, became Mark. Israelis don't have outside names. If anything, they tend to switch to even more inside names, as in changing Herz to Lev. When I telephoned Abe at his office, I heard the secretary call him Rommy, short for Avrohom, Hebrew Abraham. How it happens that Abe wasn't named Alan or Aubrey I don't know. I'll have to ask his father sometime.

Mark Herz happens to be here, giving the Sir Isaac Something lectures at the Technion Institute in Haifa, no doubt for an exceedingly fat fee. Nothing else could get him to Israel. I read about the lectures in the *Jerusalem Post,* and when I talked to Abe I asked him whether he'd seen Mark. His gruff reply was that he hadn't seen or spoken to his father in five years, and intended to leave it that way. And so much for skeleton-rattling. General Moshe Lev was responding to the niece of the enchanting Leonore Goodkind, you see, when he wrote that cordial invitation to Sandra.

Typically, once Sandra took off to Sde Shalom I heard nothing from her for over a week. Had she arrived there at all? Had she left? I didn't know. Finding out the telephone number of the kibbutz took some doing. Getting through was next to impossible. The line was busy, hours on end. When I finally did reach her today, Sandra told me they have exactly one phone for their ninety-seven members; kibbutz policy, she thinks, to keep to a minimum contact with the decadent bourgeois society beyond the orange groves. She said she was ready to go back if I was. I told her that Mom was holding her own, and that I'd finally seen Golda Meir, so we could leave anytime. "Has it been interesting there?" I asked.

"Well, I've learned a lot. Say, why not come down here and get me? Meet a different kind of Israeli."

So I telephoned Abe Herz for directions to Sde Shalom, intending to drive there in my rented car. It didn't occur to me that he wouldn't know Sandra was in Israel. He said the roads south of Beersheba were confusing and he hadn't seen his Uncle Moshe for a long time, so he would take me there himself. I'm to meet him at his law office in Tel

Aviv, and it'll be a four-hour run south through the Negev. The Sde Shalom kibbutzniks farm the southeast corner of pre-1967 Israel, formed by the Gaza Strip and the Sinai border, thus asking for terrorist trouble from two directions. That's where these peace lovers have chosen to settle.

As for Golda Meir, I'd call her a political edition of Mama; not as whimsical or impossible as the big yoxenta, to be sure, but basically another nice Jewish lady with a brick, whom fate has made a world figure. She was in Europe when I got here, and when she returned she was tied up for days. I had to wait more than a week to see her and give her a verbal message from the President, about which I will say nothing. She did not comment on the President's message; just sat there sober and silent for a few moments, then told me to come and see her again before I left Israel.

It's strange that a nobody like me can go between two such world-famous politicians. So help me, I think the President's confidence in me started with the fact that I study the Talmud. Somehow that got to him. It couldn't matter less to Golda Meir. She thinks I'm some kind of religious nut. Once she invited me to her home for dinner, long before she became Prime Minister. I wouldn't eat her meat — she's a bone-deep old irreligious socialist — and she was amazed and slightly put out, then laughed it off and fixed me some hard-boiled eggs. Golda likes fussing in the kitchen. She's typecast for American television as the Israeli Prime Minister, old Mother Sarah herself. But she is, in fact, a cool-handed politician who, in the old saying, chews nails and spits tacks. I wouldn't want to cross her.

How am I acquainted with Golda Meir? Well, the legal counsel for the United Jewish Appeal gets to meet the people over here who count. The tax problems are tricky, and clear sensible advice is much wanted. I inherited a mess, and Mrs. Meir admired the way I straightened matters out. Later, when she toured the United States for the UJA and Israel Bonds, she asked that I escort her. You come to know somebody pretty well, doing a road show like that together. I've been out of UJA work for a while, and this is the first time I've seen Golda since she became Prime Minister, but everything was the same between us. Israeli leaders don't stand on ceremony. They can't. The Israelis would just laugh them down and vote them out.

Golda got right to business, cross-examining me about Watergate, chain-smoking nearly a pack of cigarettes. It worries her. What's behind all the uproar? What can it matter, that silly break-in to the Democratic national headquarters? Is that a reason to bring down a President? There must be something else going on. I tried to explain about the cover-up, and the new sensation of the tapes. She knows the details, but though she was born and grew up in Milwaukee, she's Israeli through and through. The actual outrage of it all doesn't register.

She thinks the President's the best we've had since Truman; and not just because he's been decent to Israel. They were edgy over here when he took office, since the American Jews were so dead set against him. But in foreign affairs, says Golda, he's proved himself a remarkable man. She thinks that he got us out of the Vietnam mess — left by three *other* Presidents, she points out — the best way any man could have done; that he's been handling the Germans and the Soviet Union very craftily; and that the turn to China was a masterstroke. I suggested that our celebrated National Security Adviser had performed those feats, pretty much. She cut me off. "He works for a boss," she observed very drily. And she said that when I see her again before I leave, she'll give me her reply to the President.

But will he still be in office by the time I get back to the States? A serious question. Our President is a very lungfish for surviving, but now he is surely done for. Ye gods, that electrifying moment on television when the scared little bureaucrat spilled the beans about the tapes! Those Senate hearings had been droning downhill. I thought the President might be escaping his harriers, after all, because they were getting so dull and boring. But wow, you could see all those sleepy senators stiffen and their eyes bulge, and you almost expected their hair, those who had any, to shoot out in all directions. "That's *it*," I said to myself. I've been planning my return to private life ever since. Not that I'm going to resign at this point. Not me. The rats are jumping ship in droves, it's getting to be a rodent stampede, and maybe that's why I've been digging in. He deserves to fall, and will fall, but until that happens I'll be there with the ethical angle, and any other way I can help him, as he does the stations of the political cross on his knees.

Surely this is the loneliest President that ever was, and the strangest. Foreign leaders admire him, yet I don't believe that at home even Andrew Johnson was more reviled, or Harding more obtusely and naively corrupt. What stuns me is his blind stupidity in this Watergate matter. You almost start believing the Freudian stuff about a death wish. I contributed some ethical touches to his second big Watergate speech on television, delivered with such fanfare just before I departed. His entourage, what's left of it, said it was a big success, turned the tide, and all that. I saw him right after the broadcast. He thanked me and shook my hand and looked me in the eye, even as the White House crowd was congratulating him on all sides; and I could see that he knew to a hair the difference that the speech had made — i.e., zilch. He is many men, the President, and none of those men is a fool, except for the one knucklehead who has stumbled into the Watergate quicksand, and is dragging down all the others.

"Enjoy Israel," he said. "I hope you find your mother better."

At odd moments here I've been reading the galleys of Peter Quat's new opus. Hair-raising! I'm halfway through them, and can hardly believe my eyes. I had them on the plane, and didn't get far when Sandra tried to collar them. I fended her off. My pretty little Sandra considers herself liberated and no doubt she is — too much so — but I'm damned if I'd let her read those galleys. Not while I sat beside her. I couldn't look her in the eye!

Yet I'll never regret fighting the obscenity cases. Airport bookstores may be lined with steamy paperbacks and crotch magazines as a result, and raunchy Jewish scriveners, male and female, like old Peter — Mark Herz calls them "School of Quat" novelists — may have been turned loose to write their comic scurrilities about the chosen people, but anyone can read Henry Miller and D. H. Lawrence who wants to; and when the new Twains and Dreisers and Dostoevskys come along, they won't have to pussyfoot about the facts of life. That was worth it. So I keep telling myself as I wander through airport bookstores, feeling vaguely guilty, or as I read the galleys of Peter's latest opus.

Mark is peculiarly censorious about Peter, and down on me for defending *Deflowering Sarah* in the Cincinnati bookstore case. Mark was in Israel when Peter made a triumphal tour lecturing about his sizzling Pulitzer Prize novel, *Onan's Way*. He still fumes about that.

Mark had come here to plead with his son not to sign up for a fighter pilot course he eventually washed out of. That was five years ago, and they had some kind of explosive bust-up on that occasion.

Well, bedtime. It'll be a long day tomorrow, getting to that kibbutz.

I've been asking around about Sde Shalom. The name means Fields of Peace. The members disapprove of the Israeli government as occupiers and oppressors, and advocate giving back all the territories and working out some nice friendly deal with the Arabs. The founders are anarchic malcontents from old collectives, who feel that prosperity is shooting the socialist dream all to hell and choking the kibbutz movement in fat. It's a young struggling collective, only about six years old. The members get out and demonstrate against building settlements or strong points in Sinai. When the government recently moved some Bedouins out of a desert area to build a fighter base, the Fields of Peace members went out *en masse* and lay down in front of the bulldozers. They also took the government to court on behalf of the Bedouins. You begin to understand why Sandra has landed there.

Kibbutzim can be far left, middle left, left religious, moderate religious, and so on. There are a few hundred kibbutzim all over Israel, but none is quite as far-out as Sde Shalom. It's a throwback to early Zionism, a split-off from the extreme socialist "Young Guardians." The members are purists, striving to return to the simple pioneer life and to keep the red flame burning, so to speak; hence their anti-imperialist rhetoric, their severe communal rules, and their demonstrations for peace. The other Israelis tend to admire and respect Sde Shalom for its old-fashioned austere idealism, while regarding the members as lovable cuckoos.

Kibbutzniks are Israel's low-profile elite, no doubt of that, and have been since the pioneer socialist days. I've heard that sixty or seventy percent of the army officers, for instance, are kibbutzniks. What they all do is cultivate the land. The stretches of fruitful green plains that mark off Israel from the gray sands of the Sinai and Jordan, seen from the air, are likely to be collective farms. Some collectives have failed, others barely hang on. Still others have become so wealthy, down the years, that as socialist believers they're nonplussed and embarrassed by their own riches.

"Kibbutz" and "collective" mean the same, but to me "kibbutz" happens to be about the ugliest word there is — in English, not in Hebrew. In Hebrew it sounds fine. *Key-boots.* But you link that harsh *k* to that low-comedy doubled *b* and that eructating *utz,* and you have got a word that Peter Quat himself might have invented, to suggest something Jewish and disagreeable, like his smelly melamed Shraga Glutz. The word embodies everything I resisted in Zionism when I was growing up.

Before I turn in, let me explain that resistance. I'm not sleepy; high energy charge of Jerusalem air.

34

Bernice Lavine

IT was on a Friday night that Pop and I walked to the first Zionist meeting I ever attended. I was fourteen. Zaideh was already living with us. Picture my reaction, then, at coming into a hall hazy with tobacco smoke, where the men sat chewing enormous black cigars and the few women puffed at cigarettes; and where, after the lecture, platters of sandwiches were brought out, which Pop muttered to me not to eat. The caution was superfluous. I had long since learned to recognize, in the Townsend Harris lunchroom, the pallid pink square look of sandwich ham. There was no mistaking what these Zionists were regaling themselves with on Sabbath eve: the swine for sure, and very likely the abomination and the mouse.

Well, I heard the word *kibbutz* for the first time that evening, in the lecture. The word stays in my mind forever associated with tobacco smoke and ham on Friday night. I'm not being censorious, I'm just describing how a fourteen-year-old boy, with a Hassidic rabbi for a grandfather, reacted to his first glimpse of that Bronx Zionist chapter. On our way home I asked my father about such goings-on. "It's not always like that," he said wearily. "That's Spiegel's doing. Spiegel would eat pigskin gloves on Yom Kippur, to make his point." Spiegel evidently was the chapter's arch-rebel, and in charge of that night's refreshments; which, I must say, rapidly vanished from the platters.

Then I wanted Pop to explain exactly what a kibbutz was. It's odd how little things stick in your mind. We were walking past Loew's Boulevard, where a Douglas Fairbanks picture was playing. Outside stood a big cardboard cutout of Fairbanks, dashing, mustached, grinning, the ultimate American hero. Papa was trying to explain the farm-collective idea; and he stamped on my young mind once for all the sense that a "kibbutz," whatever it might be, stood at the opposite pole from America and from Douglas Fairbanks, smiling at me on that cardboard cutout.

That summer I was sent to a Zionist camp. Camp Carmel, it was called, until early in August it suddenly became Camp Herzl, causing no end of confusion in things like camp banners, stationery, and marching songs. I believe this happened because of a fast bankruptcy proceeding. In money matters the owner, an impractical dreamer named Mr. Kapilsky, was the very opposite of Mr. Dresser. He bought and had hauled up to the Poconos, for instance, an enormous old motor launch, just to give the campers rides on the lake. This vessel, which he renamed the *Theodor Herzl,* sank on its maiden voyage. Forty kids had to swim ashore in their best camp clothes, and at least half of those campers were yanked home. Possibly that was why Mr. Kapilsky went bust and had to change the camp's name. It would be like him to rename it Camp Herzl, with that derelict *Theodor Herzl* still sunk in plain sight in the lake, its rusty deckhouse sticking out above some nine feet of water.

Mr. Kapilsky's whole caper was Zionism, and the camp was an offshoot of "Young Herzlians," an institute he ran in Brooklyn. I have no reason to believe Mr. Kapilsky's enthusiasm for Palestine was not genuine, except that he never went there in his whole life. I know that for a fact. When I was doing the UJA thing I encountered him at a meeting in Brooklyn, very shrunken and white-haired, still a hot Zionist, and looking forward — so he told me — to retiring to Israel. It was a pity, he said, that he had been too busy promoting the cause ever to get over to the promised land. "But as you know," he commented, "Theodor Herzl only spent a few days in Palestine, all in all."

Now at his Camp Carmel-Herzl, I hasten to say, the Zionism was not of the Friday night ham-and-cigars variety. On the contrary, we had daily prayers, kosher food, grace at meals, and long Sabbath services. Mr. Kapilsky's Zionism was a matter of hearty songs in modern Hebrew, galumphing sweaty round-dances, playlets about "building the land," the Star of David flying beside the Stars and

Stripes, and yawn-generating lectures. Kids are sharp observers, and something told me that it was all unreal; that Mr. Kapilsky, the lecturers, and the Young Herzlian counsellors did not in the least intend to emigrate to Palestine and settle in kibbutzim, and build the land, and plant oranges, and cavort in circles, but just to make a living talking about it. I couldn't have put it into words then, but that's how I felt.

Unlike Camp Eagle Wing, this camp did use me at Friday night services as the cantor. One day I received an unsigned fan letter on stationery of the girls' camp, a twittery gush. This got me all in a glow of vainglory. Next Friday night, I kept a sharp eye on the girls' section. One cute girl was throwing me, I thought, blushing little grins. After the services we exchanged a few snatched shy words. She confessed to writing the letter, and we agreed that we were in love. That was Bernice Lavine, about thirteen and a half, with a sweetly budding bosom. As cantor I was a sort of holy man, so I tried not to notice that.

Next morning at services, this girl's father, introduced as a great Zionist by Mr. Kapilsky, lectured about kibbutzim. He had just spent a week at a kibbutz in Palestine. Mr. Lavine was round and soft and white and bespectacled, like Eagle Wing's nature counsellor. He rhapsodized on and on about the brawny kibbutzniks, the beauty of the kibbutz, the charming children in the kibbutz nursery, the exquisite kibbutz fruits, the crystal kibbutz air, the fragrant kibbutz flowers, the delicious food in the kibbutz dining room, and the thrill of watching the kibbutzniks at night, singing and dancing in circles under the kibbutz moon. Mr. Lavine's voice cracked with ecstasy, describing the kibbutz moon. "You could read a newspaper by the light," he gurgled, tears standing in his eyes. That speech touched heights, never since reached in my hearing, of uncommunicated enthusiasm. We campers sat in dulled slumped rows, waiting for him to finish all that crap about the kibbutz moon so that we could go to lunch.

But I did not hold Bernice's father against her. After he left I happened on her, hammering at some flats backstage on a very hot day, in a sleeveless shirt. As we chatted and flirted, there was visible through the armhole this one exquisite pink rose-tipped breast, scarcely formed. Bernice seemed utterly unaware that it was on view. Well, if I wasn't in love with her before, that did it. Bernice Lavine's little breast haunted me. I covered pages of camp stationery with drawings of it, then tore them up. I went around in an amorous fog. Whenever I saw her again she was always well covered; but through her blouse, like Superman, I saw what I had seen and could never forget.

Across this aureate romance there fell the shadow of one Clarence Rubin, a super-senior of sixteen, who came to services in plus fours, enormously baggy knickerbockers popularized by the golf champions. There was a big dance one night in August, to celebrate the change of camp names; and — one of the great shocks of my life — I overheard Clarence Rubin say he was taking Bernice Lavine to the dance. She and I had talked about the dance, and I was sure we were going together. But she went with Clarence Rubin, all cock-of-the-walk in his plus fours.

Next weekend Bernice's father came back to lecture again. My resistance to his fruity talk about kibbutz, kibbutz, kibbutz, and therefore to Zionism altogether, got all kneaded up in my gut with my agonies over Clarence Rubin and Bernice Lavine. Alas, that breast! Bernice did not seem to grasp what she had done to me. After the lecture she approached me with the old intimate smile, and was hurt and baffled when I snarled something about plus fours, and held aloof. We never had it out. At the camp reunion in the dead of winter six months later, she came up to me and shyly said, "David, I didn't really care for Clarence Rubin." By then the summer seemed a million years ago. It didn't matter any more.

Bernice may have been the only Young Herzlian who ever did go to Palestine. She married there, and had a big family. And if you're wondering why Bernice is on my mind, okay, I'll tell you. When I'm in Jerusalem I spend hours walking the streets, and there are always neighborhoods I haven't walked in before. Today after my meeting with Golda I took such a walk, and came on something called the American Library, in an old stone building. I can't pass a library any more than a drunk can pass a bar. In I went, and there, by God, was Bernice Lavine.

Bernice Lavine, all plump and gray, but we recognized each other! Her father, she said, has been dead for thirty years. We talked about our children, and how our lives had gone; and at one point, with a wry wrinkling smile, she said, "You know, David, I didn't really care for Clarence Rubin." Bernice never worked on a kibbutz. I asked her. She's been a librarian all along.

*   *   *

Mais ou sont les neiges d'antan? I'd better take a heavy slug of my dwindling Jack Daniel's if I want to get any sleep before I go to that kibbutz.

35

Sde Shalom

King David Hotel, Jerusalem
August 28, 1973

W ELL, it was quite an experience, Sde Shalom.
   I found Abe Herz behind a small piled-up desk in a hot little
office, much smaller than any clerk's cubicle in my firm; the walls lined
with law books in Hebrew and English and file boxes hand-labelled
in Hebrew. A fan whooshed overhead, a window cooler rattled and
groaned, and Abe in a sport shirt was nevertheless shiny with sweat.
Telephone in hand, he said, "Sit down, this won't take long."

My Hebrew improves once I'm in Israel for a while, so I could
catch the drift of the call. A client in Switzerland wanted to form a
Liberian corporation to buy real estate in Beersheba, in order to lease
the land to South African contractors, who would build housing for
Russian immigrants, with Argentinian capital held in a bank in Australia. Abe was urging that the whole thing be done instead through
corporations in Hong Kong and South Korea, via an investment firm
in Dallas that had an Australian branch. According to Abe's boss, who
had just resigned as Israeli Treasury Minister to return to private
practice, that would be sounder taxwise, for some tangled reason.

"These Swiss Jews," said Abe, hanging up, taking off horn-rimmed
glasses, and shaking his head. "Kind of slow on the uptake. Let's go.
Why are you wearing a coat and tie? You'll die in the Negev."

The telephone rang. "*Zozti kvar* (I've already left)," Abe snapped,
picking up the receiver. "Oh! All right, put him on. . . . My boss,"
he said to me. "Calling from London."

He talked in English about import duties on bulldozers. I gathered that a deal involving millions of British pounds might get tax exemption if the bulldozers could be ruled a matter of national urgency. But the new Treasury Minister's view, Abe told his boss, was that Israel was about to slide into the sea from the sheer weight of bulldozers on hand. So where was the urgency? A senior partner was contacting the Minister of Defense, and there might be something more positive to report in a day or two. The army seldom had enough bulldozers.

"You could be doing this on Wall Street," I said, as we walked down narrow rusty iron stairs, "making a lot of money, and staying cool."

"Are you telling me I was crazy to come here?" said Abe a shade irritably, mopping his brow. "This country was created and is maintained by crazy people, and the tax system is crazier than anything that foreign lunatics could invent."

We emerged from a dark vestibule into blazing white glare. Abe put on sun glasses and led me to a decrepit Citroën. I peeled off coat and tie before I got in, saying, "It helps to look like a foreigner here, sometimes."

"Oh, we're wonderful to foreigners, just hard on each other. Close quarters." He threaded expertly through the twisting streets of old Jaffa, where the traffic noise made talk difficult, and headed south on a black-top road traversing farmland. "When I made aliya, this firm offered me a job," he spoke up. "I wasn't interested then. I told them that I hadn't left America to help fat cats dodge Israeli taxes."

"What changed your mind?"

"After I did my army years, I had to eat. I was having a rough time. Woman trouble, money trouble. They say if an American sticks it out here for five years, he stays. I nearly went back in year four. That's why I took the job. Actually, it's a service to Israel to do tax law. The people who beat the system are the ones who keep the country going. How's Sandra doing at Sde Shalom?"

"You'll have to ask her."

In Beersheba we stopped to eat. Dehydrated by the hot dry drive, we drank three or four beers apiece. Back on the road, I said, "Look, it's none of my business, but your father and I are very old friends. What's the trouble between you, and can I help?"

Things I already knew came pouring out as we drove: Mark's divorce from Abe's mother, his two marriages to gentiles, his philandering with college girls, and so on. Mark had not come to his first wife's funeral after her death from cancer. That, I didn't know. Abe was very bitter about it. The lecture by Peter Quat in Tel Aviv, I learned, had really occasioned the break. Mark refused to go, and afterward in a hot argument Abe finally told his father off. His exact words — which he quoted, staring ahead at a bumpy dirt road and clutching the wheel — were these: *"Listen, just do me a favor and leave me alone, now and forever, will you? You're envious, you're opinionated, you're a bad Jew, and you're a whoremaster."* At this Mark had walked out of Abe's flat. They had not communicated since. I didn't press my offer to help.

When we arrived at Fields of Peace, dinner was over. Sandra was in the kitchen with other girls, also some young men favoring beards and long hair, washing and drying vast stacks of plastic dishes in a steamy racket. She looked all sunburned and healthy. When she saw me through the vapor, she dashed up to me and gave me a wet hug and a real kiss. Sandra has to do something like that only once or twice a year to keep me in line, and don't tell me what a fool I am. If you're a man and you have an only daughter, you understand, otherwise forget it.

Abe came tromping into the big empty dining hall, his footfalls echoing. Sandra's eyes went wide, and gleamed at him like a cat's in the dark.

"Well, well! *Shalom!*" The tone put ironic quotes around the Hebrew.

"Hi," he said.

She brought heaping plates of fried chicken and minced-up salad vegetables with a basket of coarse bread, and sat us down at a long freshly washed table. "Got to get back to my chores. When you're through, Dudu is expecting you," she said to me. "He has some other visitors." With a sly glance at Abe she darted back into the clattering kitchen.

"Who's Dudu?" I asked Abe.

"Dudu Barkai. Chairman of the kibbutz."

He wolfed all the food, but I passed up the chicken. Kosher slaughtering by these radical peaceniks was unlikely.

"Okay," Sandra said, picking up our plates and grinning at my uneaten chicken, "I'll take you to Dudu's cottage."

"I know the way," Abe said, but Sandra came along.

There was a brilliant full moon outside. Maybe I could really have read a newspaper by the light, as Bernice Lavine's father had burbled half a century ago. The Negev air is remarkably clear, for a fact. At Fields of Peace it was sweet with the scent of flower borders along the walkways and the heavy fragrance of orange blossoms. One could see that this was a small young kibbutz. Some of the old established collectives are almost as imposing as American country clubs: beautiful gardens, fine villas, swimming pools, and tennis courts. This one was, as I expected, in the stark style of the pioneer days.

As we walked toward Dudu Barkai's cottage down a long row, Sandra told me that the chairman was now running the laundry, the dirtiest job on the kibbutz. Everybody took turns doing everything at Sde Shalom, it was a very idealistic place. Mrs. Barkai, for instance, managed the turkey-breeding pens, and also was in charge of repairing tractors. Music wafted from the cottage windows we passed, the same Beethoven symphony on the highbrow Israeli station, but from the chairman's cottage as we drew near, we heard a beautiful solo violin: Menuhin, at a guess, or possibly Isaac Stern. "So, friend chairman has got himself a shortwave radio," I thought, "and is listening to Paris or London. Rank hath its privileges even at Sde Shalom."

Sandra opened the door and slipped in, beckoning to us. In the middle of a small bleak sitting room, a curly-haired man in shorts and a T-shirt was fiddling magnificently. Seated on a sofa were Mark Herz and a man I knew from my UJA days, Professor Nahum Landau the physicist, the rumored father of Israel's rumored atom bomb. Sandra whispered to me that the white-haired man in shorts sitting cross-legged on the floor was General Moshe Lev, and the fiddler was Dudu Barkai. Mark Herz, usually impassive as Dr. Fu Manchu, started when he saw his son, and a strange look, half-pained and half-glad, crossed his face. I peeked at Abe to see how he took his father's presence. His irked glance at Sandra blamed her for not warning him. She returned a tart little smile.

So the reader now gets his first glimpse of the Man in the Iron Mask, as Mark Herz was known at Columbia College. Mark Herz remains today as lean as when, some forty years ago, he wrote Varsity Shows with Peter Quat. His close-trimmed hair is gray, his face is seamed, craggy, and very melancholy. That sad cast of countenance seldom leaves Mark Herz's face, unless he is momentarily amused.

His ascetic weighed-down air makes me think of J. Robert Oppenheimer, though his career, while including work on the bomb at Los Alamos, has not been that brilliant or controversial. Professor Landau by contrast has the smiling sardonic look of a Voltaire bust. Landau worked with General Lev on the Kfir fighter plane, but unlike Lev he is a flaming hawk.

The turkey farmer and tractor repairer, Mrs. Barkai, was pottering noiselessly in the kitchen; a small brown muscular woman, in a sleeveless housedress. When her husband finished and we applauded, she brought out tea, cakes, and cognac. Barkai said to Professor Landau, laying aside bow and violin and wiping his brow, "Nahum, this is the girl who is writing her master's thesis about our proto-fascist state." He shook hands with me. "Welcome to Sde Shalom."

"Proto-fascist, eh?" Landau said genially to Sandra. Laugh lines wrinkled his whole face, but his blue eyes were calm and penetrating. "Well, that's still better than some people give us."

"I have a lot to learn, I guess," said Sandra. "That's why I'm here."

Abe Herz, slouching on a wooden chair with a glass of cognac, asked her, "Well, have you learned anything yet?"

"Why, sure. For instance, that one can get the wrong impression from Americans who make aliya. Israelis aren't all gung-ho militarists, by a long shot."

"My dear," put in Mark Herz, "the Israelis are erasing a two-thousand-year-old image of the cringing Jew as victim. This calls for a certain high mettle, which can be mistaken for brassiness or arrogance. Especially in Americans who make aliya. They feel they have to out-Israeli the Israelis."

"Well, that could be it," Sandra said.

General Moshe Lev sat up very straight and began to lecture Mark. He clearly disliked that buzzword *arrogance*. Living in a sea of enemies, he said, having to prove in war after war their right to exist, Israelis had earned their self-respect the hard way. It was the backbone of the country, the secret of its survival. Self-respect was not arrogance. His crisp sentences caused Mark to raise both hands and say sorry, sorry, sorry, he withdrew the word, since it gave offense. He had simply made a joke, which hadn't quite come off.

"Now who's being a cringing Jew?" said his son. "That's what you really think, so why back down?"

"How do you know what I think?" Mark exclaimed. "When did you last talk to me?"

"The last time I wanted to."

A snappish exchange, very awkward for the rest of us.

Nahum Landau struck in with a smile. Very vivid and realistic, he said to Lev, that phrase, "sea of enemies." The dikes that held back this sea were the territories, of course. Sinai, the West Bank, Golan. Could Moshe please explain again his so-called phased peace plan, which would level the dikes and let the sea surge in to the walls of Jerusalem and the outskirts of Tel Aviv?

General Lev retorted that his plan would transform the enemies into peaceful neighbors, so there would be no sea and no need for dikes. An acid exchange ensued between these two old antagonists. They had a fresh audience — Mark, me, and Sandra — and they warmed up to it with sharp cut-and-thrust. Dudu Barkai broke in to declare that they both missed the real point, the decay of Israel's ideals.

"We have had a chance to create a just society here," he said, "the first true socialist country on earth. If we become just another capitalist consumer society, how can the Arabs ever befriend or trust us? Capitalism is aggressive and expansionist in its very nature."

"Proto-fascist," said Abe Herz, "in fact."

"Damn right," said Sandra.

With a dismissive wave at her, Abe said that the real danger in his view was Israel's loony electoral system. He had served on the Suez Canal off and on for many months. To come back to Tel Aviv from duty amid the sandstorms and the flies — with the enemy in plain sight across the Canal, killing Israeli soldiers in the outposts every day — was a shock; hotels full of fat tourists eating fat meals, streets streaming with cars, Israelis pouring in and out of cinemas and shops, eating ice cream and drinking coffee in the sidewalk cafés, with not a worry in the world! Either the politicians didn't have the guts to tell the people in what danger they still stood, or they too were living in a dream world, like the people. Either possibility was frightening. Abe became vehement about the evils of proportional representation. Mrs. Barkai, whose English was weak, asked him to translate. The discussion veered to rapid Hebrew. Mark Herz sat contemplating them all, drinking shot after shot of cognac, slowly shaking his head, with the face of a man of sorrows.

"What are you shaking your head about?" Abe abruptly asked him.
"Never mind."

"Let's hear, Moyshe," said General Lev, whose joke it was to call
Mark by the inside name which was also his own.

"This is all such futile talk in a void," Mark said.

"How, futile?" grated Abe.

Now came the crunch of the night.

Mark stared at his son for heavy seconds, and poured himself a
hooker of cognac. "Okay. You asked me. Now listen, all of you, to
some sense."

He spoke almost sepulchrally as he sipped. "Let us say that the
Japanese in World War II managed to gain a beachhead in California, okay? Never mind how. Let's say they took — oh, San Diego,
with a sizable patch of territory around it, and started to settle and
develop it. And let's say the war ended just the way it really did, Hi-
roshima and all, except that the Japs in the beachhead managed to
fight off the Americans. Caused enough casualties, let's say, to get
themselves a cease-fire and a truce. All right. How long do you suppose the Americans would tolerate that excrescence on the west coast?
How long could that beachhead last? Five years? Ten? *Fifty?* What
future would those Japanese have, but sooner or later to be thrown
into the sea?"

"It's a ridiculous analogy," said Abe.

"Not at all," shot back his father. "Israel is exactly that, an isolated
beachhead in an enemy region, an armed perimeter with its back to
the sea. Zionism has failed. No reinforcements are coming. The Jews
never did come here, except to escape some unendurable place. Even
then they've come in handfuls, never *en masse*. And how many stay
who can go on to America or Canada or Australia? The Israelis
themselves leave in droves for Los Angeles and New York, if only
they can afford to move."

"You're just dead wrong, on numbers alone," Abe bristled. "Israel
has kept growing and growing."

"I'm not wrong. Hitler made the beachhead swell briefly — Hitler,
and the Arab countries that expelled their Jews. Now it's shrinking
again. The British created the beachhead. They brought in the Jews
in World War I, with some notion of protecting the Suez Canal. In

1948 the Brits pulled out, leaving the beachhead Jews behind to have
their throats cut by the seventy million Arabs. Which is the only way
it can all end."

In a moment of quiet, the Israelis looked at each other. Abe slumped
on a chair, regarding his father with a drawn face.

"All wrong, Moyshe." General Lev calmly broke the pause. "The
Arabs aren't Americans, and Israel isn't a beachhead. The Arab countries are unstable fragmented provinces of the Ottoman Empire. They
have no cohesion. Their tribal enmities go back hundreds of years.
Their culture doesn't have an industrializing tendency. That's what
Israel brings to the region. As a people, as a culture, the Arabs can
be noble, and generous, and proud, and hospitable. Our future among
them will be secure once we make peace. We are a small country, but
solidly structured, very strong and stable, and they need us to help
them bury their ancient differences."

"Pipe dream," said Nahum Landau quietly.

"As to the weak sisters who go to Los Angeles," Moshe Lev went
on, ignoring him, "we can spare them. We don't want or need them.
We don't even blame them. Life here is a hard challenge, only for
the best. The ones who stay and the handfuls that come — like your
son, here — are the ones who count. Nothing can attract them away
from this land. It's home. Abe is right, the Suez line is a strategic
mistake that spells trouble. But we'll survive."

"You had better survive," I couldn't help saying, "because talking
of self-respect, the self-respect of every Jew that the Holocaust left
alive now rides on Israel."

"My self-respect rides on my work!" Mark Herz acidly turned on
me. "What your self-respect rides on, Dave, I admit I've never understood. You so all-fired Jewish, and religious, and Zionist, *you* defending Peter Quat —"

"Oh, God," exclaimed Abe. "Not that again!"

"Why not, if self-respect is the issue?" Mark snapped. "Peter Quat,
a one-man anti-Semitic movement, more effective than all the pro-
paganda put out by all the Arab countries combined!"

"Moyshe," said General Lev, "the man just writes funny books.
Don't get off the subject, and don't exaggerate."

"Funny books," said Mark, "restoring throughout the world, despite Israel and her victories, the comfortable image of the Jews as
foul grotesque degenerate people. No wonder the gentiles hail him.

But you, David Goodkind! You and your self-respect! You of all people, to defend this self-abusing kike comedian!"

"He's always been jealous of Quat, hasn't he?" Abe Herz said to me.

The father and son seemed to be picking up their fight where it had broken off five years ago. I wanted to cool it. As mildly as possible, I said, "Peter writes his truth, Mark, and if it's a sick truth, well, so was Proust's."

"Quat is the American Jew," said Abe. "That's why he's a success. He's nailed down the American Jewish experience. And that's exactly why I'm here, and not there."

"Really? And what about Peter's lecture that you went to?" barked his father. "You Israelis turned out for him as though he was Elizabeth Taylor, and all he did was shit in your faces. Told you that he didn't believe in Zionism, didn't feel at home here, didn't consider himself a Jew but an artist, and had no intention of ever coming back. What did that matter? You flocked, because he's an American celebrity. If you're here to get away from Quat's America, you're at the wrong address. Israel worships Quat's America."

"We went to see and hear Quat," retorted his son, "the way we'd go to look at a two-headed horse, or any other freak. For diversion. At least his Jewishness troubles him. It's a live nerve, not dead and gangrenous like yours. We've been through all this before, you know. Where do you stand, once for all? You despise Peter Quat, who tells exactly what it's like to be a rootless American Jew. You think Dave Goodkind's religion is an obsolete cop-out. You call Zionism a doomed regression to tribalist nationalism. What do you want the Jews to do with themselves, anyway? Build gas chambers and walk into them?"

"Maybe forget the whole thing at last," said Mark, "and join the human race."

"Assimilate, you mean," said Nahum Landau. "Excellent idea. Very successful in Germany." He yawned. "Do we drive back to Haifa tonight, Moyshe?"

"Are you crazy?" said Dudu. "We have a cottage waiting for you, beds made, everything."

Abe looked from me to Sandra. "Do we drive back tonight?"

"I have to," I said. "I have an appointment at noon tomorrow."

As we broke up, Abe went out without another word to his father.

Sandra and I walked to the cottage where she bunked with some girl volunteers from Canada. At the door she sprang her surprise on me, in her customary offhand way. I returned to Abe's car without her.

"So? Where's your daughter?" he inquired.

"She's staying."

On the long drive back to Tel Aviv I told Abe something about *April House* — the second person who knows, beside Jan — and he mentioned that he was keeping notes on his own experiences. I told him, too, that his remark about my Wall Street coprophagy, rankling for years, had perhaps been the starting point of these scrawls.

"Well, I'd like to read your book." Abe grinned. "Maybe I stimulated a masterpiece."

"I'm trying to show the American Jews I know," I said. "They're not much like School of Quat characters, as your father calls them."

"Oh, look, I was baiting him about Peter Quat. Quat is much the best of those university bellyachers. He gets boring with his repetitious sex-ridden schlemiehls, who can't stop picking their noses about being Jewish. Still, he can be damned funny."

"Peter always was damned funny. I once said to him that maybe it was too soon after the Holocaust to be making such raw fun of the Jews. 'We're barely up on one knee and bleeding,' I said. 'Give us a chance.' "

Abe's face brightened. "What did he say to that?"

"That once an artist started thinking that way, he was a goner. So I dropped it. We've never discussed it since."

To stay awake on the long moonlight drive, I probed a bit about Abe's reasons for making aliya. Meeting his uncle General Lev in New York for the first time, right after the Six-Day War, had been a revelation. Also his grandfather, Mark's father, had been an influence, although Abe got to know him only when he was in college. There, too, between the grandfather and Mark, an almost total father-son break had occurred. It appeared to run in the family.

When Abe stopped at the taxi depot in Tel Aviv, in the dead of night, he said, "I wonder whether Sandra just didn't want to ride with me. Better check with her tomorrow."

"Don't be a fool. She's going to Haifa to hear Nahum Landau lecture on the hawk position. Wants to get the other side, so she said. Also, the volunteer girls are finishing up a big orange-sorting operation at Sde Shalom. She doesn't want to fink out. She's staying just two more weeks."

"Sudden decision, though."

"That's my little girl." I got out of his car. "Thanks for the lift."

"She's the most attractive girl I've ever met," Abe said in a troubled tone. "She's stunning. She's paralyzing. She's so beautiful, and so sweet when she wants to be. But God Almighty, her head is screwed on backward! Where were you when she was growing up?"

"I'll tell you, Abe," I said, leaning on the open car window, "being a Jewish father is not all that easy in this day and age. Bear that in mind."

He stared at me. "Oh? And I'm a School of Quat son, eh?"

"Not you. You're here. I told you long ago that I envy you. It still goes."

"Well, I'll tell you," he replied, "it's easy to sit on Wall Street, and envy me here on Ibn Gvirol Street. You bear that in mind."

"You're suggesting," I said, "that I'm the American Jew. I don't deny it."

He offered me his hand for a firm handshake. "Shalom, shalom," he said, and drove off. I slept in the taxi all the way to Jerusalem.

And that is the story of my famous night at Sde Shalom. I will shortly be plunging back into that madhouse at the airport, homeward bound alone. No Sandra. I've said my farewells to Mama, who is in remarkable shape, considering. She is now having her nap.

"Tell the President to be good to Israel," she said sleepily when I left her, "and God will be good to him."

My plane leaves in four hours. My taxi is ordered. You have to get there early for the baggage inspection and body search. The Israelis are deft and polite about it, but there's not much chance of getting a penknife, let alone a gun or grenade, aboard an El Al plane. It's your one reminder that this is a nation at war with every country along its borders. Abe Herz is right; you'd never know it in the grill of the Tel Aviv Hilton, where sleek Americans quaff Israel's good red wine and eat fine kosher rare roast beef from Kansas; or in fact as you climb Mount Sinai or visit Jericho, Hebron, and Shechem, places where Jews couldn't set foot a few years ago. Junketing among the quiescent Arabs still seems a lark for the tourists, though lately it's made me uneasy.

At the moment I'm sitting in a seersucker suit and tie, on my terrace facing the Old City, waiting for the cab. When the sun rose I was down there praying at the Western Wall, after about an hour's sleep. Even that early, the walk back through the Arab market was a hot uphill pull. Peaceable as those Arab shopkeepers are, I never feel calm among them; and I hurried, and I perspired from more than the heat. Then I took my last random walk in modern Jerusalem, in the religious neighborhood called Geulah, that is, "Redemption." In a revelatory flash I realized, as I walked by the small shops and food stands, why I love to take such walks. To me, Jerusalem is Aldus Street. I can't put it any other way. I'm not sure that ten thousand words would say it better. *To me, Jerusalem is Aldus Street.* In a way perhaps it is to much of the world, and that may be the Jerusalem problem. Or one of them.

I've had a shower and I've packed up. Quat's galleys *(Kee-rist!)* are tucked away in a suitcase. My dispatch case is jammed with a heap of pages I've scrawled in these past two weeks about my Columbia years. The cork really blew out of the bottle here. I sat for hours on end in the hot sun on this terrace, getting a blistery sunburn and pouring it all out. I would write and write until the sinking sun lit up the Old City walls with the golden glow one sees nowhere else on earth. When that faded I'd go inside, have a few beers and a sandwich, or maybe eat dinner with Mama. Then I'd scribble more pages, sometimes far into the night. There wasn't anything else I wanted to do, once I took care of Mama and saw Golda Meir, and Sandra went her way. I know so many people here that I'd have killed the whole time just touching base with them. I asked the Prime Minister's office not to let on that I was in Jerusalem, and they were very decent about it.

Golda was in an ebullient mood when I saw her at noon today. She gave me an upbeat message for the President, and chatted about how secure Israel is at last, from the Suez Canal to the Jordan River, from the Golan Heights to Sharm-el-Sheikh; invincible and at peace, despite the formal war status. It's all true. If this happy state of affairs continues, Mrs. Meir looks to go down as one of the great mothers in Israel. But I was somewhat shaken last night by what I heard at Sde Shalom, and I now have a daughter here. Moreover, I still remember the false-alarm mobilization in May.

I asked Golda about that. A shadow passed across the broad rugged old female face. Fleetingly she looked like Mama, reminded of something she'd rather not talk about. "Well, the Egyptians naturally want to keep things stirred up. It's a problem. We've been handling it, and we'll continue to handle it."

*   *   *

36

Zaideh

IN show business they speak of an actor "taking stage." The curtain goes up, the minor players get things going with small talk, then on comes the star. There is no mistaking the moment. Well, when Zaideh arrived, he took stage.

I first saw him, as I did Bobbeh, ascending a Bronx staircase. But what a difference! Bobbeh was a bewildered little old lady, hobbling upward one step at a time. He climbed those Longfellow Avenue stairs quick-march, a vigorous gray-bearded giant in a heavy fur-lined black coat with a rich brown fur collar. When he reached our landing he towered above the lot of us: Mom, Pop, Lee, and of course me, just past my bar mitzva. Behind him came Aunt Faiga, a fresh-faced girl about Lee's age and size, wearing a Lenin cap and the red scarf of the Young Pioneers. So it was that Hassidism and Leninism entered the Goodkind household as a package. The consequences would be interesting.

"So this is Yisroelke," he said, right there on the landing (in Yiddish, of course), caressing my face with a firm yet soft hand. "Other children skip over benches, Yisroelke skips over classes."

No sooner had Zaideh settled in Bobbeh's former room and unpacked his library than he sat me down at a gargantuan brown volume, smelling somewhat mildewy from the ocean voyage, and opened it to a passage in Talmudic property law. The page is famed for difficulty, I later found out. I had had only a little Talmud in Hebrew school, and it had seemed an antique nuisance, mere puzzling rote drone. I was not bad at Bible study, by American standards, but Talmud was what Zaideh was after. Bible he took for granted. He told me what every Aramaic word of the passage meant, but not the idea, the point of it; and he said that if I figured it out he would give me five dollars. Thereupon he left me alone with the book.

Five dollars! *Five dollars!*

It was two months' allowance. It was a bloody fortune. When it came to motivation, Zaideh knew a thing or two. I pored over that volume, and after a while I figured I had it. I called him and began to expound the point in halting Yiddish. He listened eagerly, but then the light died out of his eyes. He shook his head and went away. No fiver. I crouched over the page again, and arduously thought, and thought, and thought.

Maybe I should stop and explain here how the Talmud works. The President himself once asked me to do that. I tried to tell him, citing quite a simple passage, as it seemed to me. His eyes soon went glassy, so I trailed off and quit. He said yes, thanks, now he understood, it was very interesting; and he changed the subject. So it's risky to get into this, but it's the key to what happens next. If I take a brief whack at it, please don't go all glassy-eyed on me. It's not that mysterious or difficult, I swear. The President just had a lot on his mind.

The Talmud is a rambling encyclopedia of religious and civil law of Second Temple times. When Jesus, as the gospels narrate, disputed brilliantly with the elders, he was arguing Talmud law. Throughout its thousands of pages, the rabbis debate every sort of legal principle, some practical, some abstruse, in elegantly rigorous give-and-take. The language is tight and gnarled. Half the job is fathoming what a few apparently plain words imply. Among other things, in fact, the Talmud is a perpetual intelligence test. Helpful commentators line each page, but at that time they were over my head, and couldn't nudge me any closer to the fiver. I was on my own, butting and butting that stone wall of text.

And yet I got it! I broke through the wall! I grasped the point of logic, I saw the light, and for the first time in my life I felt the rush of joy which is the soul of Talmud study. When you have got the answer, the idea of a passage, you *know*. Jews have pored over this literary inheritance for twenty centuries and more because — over and above the lore, the parables, the folk history, the Bible comment, the word pictures of Babylon and Rome, and the religious and legal substance — besides all that serious stuff, the Talmud is such incomparable mental fun. I am describing my love, or my hobby, so discount my enthusiasm as you please; I do believe I see some glassy eyes here

and there among you, gentle readers. But now you'll understand what
followed between Zaideh and me.

I called him again, and he stood over the open volume as I sailed
out on my explanation. Well, those bright piercing blue eyes! The
way they blazed at me! The way that bearded imposing countenance
nodded and nodded! "Yes, yes — no, *no* —" (when I wandered off
the point a bit) "yes, go on, yes! Good! Yes! Oy, God in Heaven!
Yes! That's *it*. Oy, HEALTH to you!" He sprang at me, embraced
me, and gave me a hairy kiss; pressed the five dollars on me, and rushed
off to tell my parents. It must have been a Sunday, since they were
both at home, and on Saturday, Zaideh would as soon have touched
a white-hot poker as a five-dollar bill. "A godol, he can still grow up
a godol!" I heard him say. "But he knows nothing, nothing. A fine
head. Now he has to start learning."

That was it. From then on, I studied with Zaideh two hours a day.
The novelty and the thrill didn't last, I must tell you. I paid dearly
for that first five-dollar reward. "*Koom* (come)," he would say, when
I got back from Townsend Harris. Weary, bored, I would trudge to
the table and open the volume. After a month of this, "*koom*" began
to sound to me like "doom." Those columns of abstract Aramaic were
hard cheese, friends, for an American boy used to Douglas Fairbanks
movies, Frank Merriwell paperbacks, and public library novels.

Instance: "*Reuben's cow kicks a stone, which breaks Simon's crockery in
the marketplace. What does he pay?*" Now, cow, stone, and crockery do
neatly pose the issue of extended liability in a public place; but at
thirteen I didn't find torts a spellbinding subject. I still don't. Besides, that would be expanding the text into comprehensible English.
The Talmud would say something like, "*Stone in market, what?*" I
suppressed yawns, studying with Zaideh, till tears rolled down my
cheeks. He seemed not to notice.

Still, I was allowed to drop Hebrew school; and I did enjoy the
blaze-up in his eyes whenever I caught on to a Talmudic idea. That
did wonders for my self-esteem. At Townsend Harris, remember, I
was just the Arista reject in the purple suit. Here was this genial
amusing colossus of a grandfather — for his way of teaching, as much
as possible, was to make jokes and draw comic comparisons — telling me and my parents that I could still be an *iluy* (genius), a *gaon*
(academy head, super-genius), a *godol* (you know that one), if only I
applied myself, and went to the right school. He did not mean Co-

lumbia College: my goal, my rainbow's end, the classiest college in New York, and so far as I knew, in the world. Zaideh thought that the only place for such a Jewish head was a yeshiva, an all-day Talmud school. Quite a difference of opinion; and if presumably the decision was mine, the star quality was his.

It was Aunt Faiga who tipped the balance, strangely enough. From the day she came, Faiga marched to her own music. She already knew some stilted English from a Soviet high school course, but she at once enrolled in night school. She was very bright and learned fast. She came and went as she pleased with her own latchkey, on the Sabbath as well as other days. Zaideh never said a word about that.

And this was odd, because with his arrival our household had much tightened up on religion. I've mentioned the timer which shut off the lights on Friday night, driving my sister Lee nuts, and panicking her suitors. There were other minor reforms: separate dishtowels for milk and meat utensils, sterner scrutiny of ingredients in packaged foods, and the like. Electricity on the Sabbath was finished, for Zaideh announced when he came that electricity was fire. Mom and Pop obeyed him. Star quality. Later on, when I learned a little physics, I argued this point with Zaideh. Electricity was a flow of electrons along a wire, I explained. It wasn't a flame at all, it was more like water running through a pipe.

He cheerily inquired, "Does the water give off light and heat?"

"Water? How can it? It doesn't burn."

"Exactly. Electricity gives off light and heat, because it does burn. And it burns because it's fire."

Aunt Faiga heard this exchange and winked at me. She was our resident unbeliever, but it didn't seem to trouble Zaideh at all. She could do anything with him: tweak his nose, tickle him, pinch him, and he would pretend to be harassed and offended, but he obviously loved it. She was the child of his old age. None of the rest of us, not even Mom, would venture on such liberties with the patriarch.

Faiga at once began bringing into the house *The Daily Worker,* the *New Masses,* and pamphlets by Lenin and Trotsky; this was before Stalin had had Trotsky brained and erased from Soviet history. She tried to interest Lee in this stuff, but Lee's mind was full of boys and clothes, with no room left for revolutionary economics. Pop, an ex-socialist, tried reasoning with Faiga. America was all different from

Czarist Russia, Pop said. Faiga would soon realize that. It was the greatest land on earth. The real revolution had already happened in America a long time ago, and everybody was free and equal, with all kinds of opportunities. The Soviet Union, by comparison, was just one huge backward prison.

But Faiga had at her fingertips the Negro lynchings, the Haymarket riots, the coal miners in Kentucky, and the horrors of Chicago meat-packing. Faiga ate up stacks of novels in red paper covers by writers like Upton Sinclair and John Dos Passos. I read a couple of those for the violence and gore, but they were too talky for me. America was built on the exploiting of slave labor, Faiga maintained. It was a collapsing society, the revolution was only a few years off, and she would be a fighter in the class struggle.

"Am I exploiting slave labor in the Fairy Laundry?" Pop tiredly asked one night. "They work eight hours a day, I work sixteen. They get the highest pay in the laundry business."

"Do you make a profit?" asked Faiga.

"We try."

"How can you make a profit, if you don't exploit slave labor? Profit is nothing but the margin of surplus value extorted from the workers. The whole world knows that."

"If we didn't make a profit, we'd go broke, Faiga, and all our workers would have no jobs."

"That's why it's an evil system," said Faiga, "and has to be destroyed."

"You don't mind eating an exploiter's bread," observed Mama. We were at supper, and Faiga was tucking into her second helping of lamb stew.

"It won't help the toiling masses if I starve," said Faiga.

These fiery abstractions notwithstanding, when Faiga finished her English course she asked Pop for a job. Mom was all for that. Faiga was underfoot, house expenses were way up, and Faiga was offering to pay rent and board, because she didn't want to exploit my parents. So Pop took her on as a shirt-ironer. Mr. Gross taught her the art, and soon reported that Faiga was a first-class girl, ironed a beautiful shirt; only the other girls complained she talked too much.

37

Boss Goodkind

S HE did more than that.

Aunt Faiga's wrecking of the Fairy Laundry's finances rendered moot the question of my college choice. Columbia was costly, about six hundred dollars a year (times have somewhat changed), and when Faiga got through with the laundry, Pop couldn't afford the six hundred. This is a story you may not believe, but it happened exactly as I will tell you.

The new building was now operating full blast, occupying a square block, with a smokestack you could see for miles, with three stories full of crashing, thumping, steaming, sloshing machinery, with a horde of employees in white smocks and caps turning out mountains of bundles, delivered by a fleet of new trucks all over New York. The Fairy Laundry couldn't have been more impressive, and it was going broke. Wall Street had crashed. Aunt Faiga's *Daily Worker* bubbled happily about the long-awaited death agonies of capitalism. The huge expansion had put Pop in a cash bind. The bank wouldn't renew the construction loans. Kornfelder and Worthington, pleading hard times, had put up such tough terms for more cash that Pop was desperately looking elsewhere.

Luckily, he had met at a laundryman's convention a wealthy Californian, who was moving to New York and wanted to buy into a laundry. They got on well at the convention, and the man liked the operating statements Pop showed him. Pop invited the man to come and have a look at the Fairy plant. He told Mom that this man would be arriving in a week; a millionaire, a gentleman, ready to put in, on reasonable terms, whatever new money the laundry needed. All of us could hardly contain our joy. It meant release from Kornfelder and

Worthington. It meant Pop could take a raise, we could move to Manhattan at last, and Lee could go to Cornell, instead of Hunter College. All our money pinches would be a thing of the past!

Well, Papa came home one afternoon looking greenish. I was reviewing the Talmud in the parlor, and I heard the whole thing.

"Why home so early, Alex?" Mom asked, her face anxious.

"The laundry's on strike."

"On *strike?*" Mama was flabbergasted. So was I. "On *strike?* You're joking. Why, there's no union. Everybody's happy."

"Faiga did it. She brought in organizers from downtown."

"Faiga? *Faiga!*" grated my mother. "Oy! Koidanov!" She waved her fists wildly in the air, and beat her temples. "*Koidanov!*"

"That man is coming day after tomorrow," Papa said, slumping down in an armchair.

"Settle the strike, then," exclaimed Mama. "Settle it! I'll talk to Faiga. Leave her to me."

"You don't know the demands. Those fellows from downtown are Communists. They want the workers to take over the plant, nothing less."

"Why did your people listen to strangers?"

"Brodofsky." Pop sighed in a heartbreaking way. "Brodofsky, again! Just before the vote, Brodofsky got up and made a speech. He said he would fire anybody who voted to strike. So the vote was unanimous to strike, and Brodofsky fired everybody, and they all walked out. I was at the bank, and when I got back, the place was empty. Outside, pickets were marching with signs. Signs about me! And they kept shouting a poem."

"Signs? A poem! About you? It all sounds so crazy."

"Faiga made up the poem herself. She was leading the march. She's proud of it. I remember every word."

And Pop chanted, in a mournful singsong,

> "*Boss Goodkind isn't good,*
> *Boss Goodkind isn't kind.*
> *Boss Goodkind sucks the workers' blood*
> *And steals the workers blind.*"

Aunt Faiga came home at her usual time, in excellent spirits, and asked Mama what there was for supper. Mama ignored her. That set the tone of the evening. There had never been such a supper in our household. We sat around the dining-room table, the six of us, hardly saying a word: the four Goodkinds in shock, Zaideh puzzled, Faiga happily downing chicken and noddles, remarking that she was awfully hungry, or requiring someone to pass the bread, the salt, or the ketchup. Faiga had developed a heavy ketchup habit, shaking out half a bottle at each meal.

At last Mama spoke out. "So, you had to start a strike, Faiga, did you? After Alex gave you a job, only because I asked him to? What's the matter with you?"

"I'm just another worker," said Faiga. "The workers are waking up. It's a historical process."

"Did you start the whole thing, or didn't you?"

"That's ridiculous. How can I start a world movement? Please pass the ketchup."

"No," said Mama, firmly clutching the ketchup bottle.

Faiga looked surprised, and a little disconcerted. "What?"

Mama recited,

> *"Boss Goodkind isn't good,*
> *Boss Goodkind isn't kind.*
> *Boss Goodkind sucks the workers' blood*
> *And steals the workers blind.*

Did you write that?"

"That's the voice of the workers," said Faiga. "I just gave it expression."

"And you can still sit there," Mom said with sledgehammer sarcasm, "and eat Boss Goodkind's food?"

Faiga shook her head and said very patiently, "Why not? Personally, I have nothing against him."

This reply so dazed Mama that she mechanically passed Faiga the ketchup. Faiga slopped great gobs into her chicken and noodles, and went on eating.

After a while Papa said, in the tones of Job on the ash heap, "Faiga, you've been in the laundry six months. Am I that kind of boss? Do I suck the workers' blood? Do I steal them blind?"

The faint flickering smile on Aunt Faiga's flat Slavic face might have been embarrassment. Then again, it could have been pride of authorship. "Alex, that's agitprop for the masses. Agitprop must be simple and strong."

Well, let me wrap up this painful scene. Mama told Faiga about the man from California, and the urgency of calling off the strike. Faiga insisted that Papa's situation was just part of the class struggle. History had caught up with the Fairy Laundry. You couldn't make an omelet without breaking eggs. (First time I ever heard *that* one was from Aunt Faiga.) And so on. They were getting nowhere, their voices were rising, and all this was in English. Zaideh was looking from daughter to daughter in bemusement. He struck in and asked in Yiddish what was going on.

Mama told him, with a free translation of Aunt Faiga's agitprop poem. As she explained, Zaideh began to glance at Aunt Faiga, with thunderclouds gathering on that majestic bearded countenance such as I had never seen there before. When Mama finished, he and Faiga were staring at each other, and Faiga was pouting like a naughty little girl.

"Did you do this?" Zaideh asked her.

She whined something about the bosses and the toiling masses. Zaideh's face grew sterner and darker. Faiga fell apart. She said the men from downtown were very tough. The strike wasn't her fault. She had just talked to them about the Fairy Laundry, and they had come on their own and organized the strike. There was nothing she could do about it.

"Papushka," she crooned, timidly stroking his hand, using her favorite endearment, "don't be angry with me, Papushka. I can't bear it."

Zaideh stood up, and wrathfully left the table.

The strike soon disintegrated. Pop's foreman told him that actually Brodofsky, more than Faiga and the downtown agitators, had precipitated it. But the man from California arrived at the height of the chaos. The machines were standing idle, the place was filthy, half the workers were back and milling uselessly around, and the others were absent, thinking that Brodofsky's dismissal was for real. So the man returned to California on the first available train. Pop had to submit to the crushing terms of Kornfelder and Worthington, to keep operating. Lee did not apply for Cornell. My chances for Columbia went glimmering. Papa installed Zaideh and Faiga in a small apartment near the Minsker Synagogue, and we moved to the Pelham section of the Bronx.

Not long after the Boss Goodkind episode, Faiga was arrested during a riot on Union Square. Faiga hit a cop on the head, with a placard protesting police brutality. Shades of Mama and the brick! That placard must have been mounted on a two-by-four, because it laid the policeman out, and he left the scene in an ambulance. Faiga's defense was that in the close quarters of the riot, the policeman had started to feel her up. Clouting him with the placard was not a political act at all, Faiga claimed, it was a reflex of offended female modesty.

Well, this was pretty thin stuff. Faiga was clad at the time in her Lenin cap, a leather jacket, and a wool skirt; a forbidding sight, not calculated to provoke a New York cop to lewd liberties. Faiga spent some six hours in jail with assorted shoplifters and whores before Pop got hold of Assemblyman Bloom and had her released. Some money also changed hands, to persuade the cop not to press charges; my father's money, of course. Faiga was sobered by her few hours in the lower depths, and grateful to Boss Goodkind for springing her; and her Soviet brainwashing began to fade. In time Faiga changed a lot, as you will see.

Meantime the damage was done. It hit my sister Lee hardest. She had been promised Cornell, but now she was graduating, and there was no money. Lee rode the subway to Hunter College for four years. Her indignation still burns at this, an eternal light. After college, my parents staked her to a year of travel abroad, by way of recompense, and that was how she came to meet Moshe Lev in Palestine; but Lee never forgets that Yisroelke ended up at Columbia, and she at Hunter. For some unfathomable reason she holds this against me, not Aunt Faiga. She has utterly forgotten — Lee, of the elephant memory — the Boss Goodkind affair.

I have not, because it landed me in a yeshiva.

38

The Yeshiva

Yes indeed, it really came to pass, Zaideh's dream: our hero sitting in the study hall of a yeshiva, the *bet midrash*, amid sixty or seventy skullcapped youths all swaying, chanting, and disputing over tall Talmud volumes in a great noise; and Yisroelke right in there with them, expertly stabbing a thumb in the air to emphasize a point, as they say in Yiddish, "with the fat finger."

How come? Well, my class graduated from Townsend Harris in February, so that we were at a loose end until the fall. Some of us planned to stay on to repeat courses, so as to raise our averages on the statewide Regents tests. New York gave out college tuition scholarships of a hundred dollars a year to the highest scorers. I appeared doomed like Lee to a free subway college; still, a hundred dollars a year might close a gap and make Columbia possible again.

Well, Zaideh got wind of this. He asked around, and heard about a new Jewish seminary, Yeshiva University; today a major institution, but forty years ago a little one-building affair gasping for survival. It had a lower school, called the Talmudical Academy, which gave the Regents tests. Why not repeat my subjects there, inquired Zaideh, and pick up some Talmud, too? His hope, of course, was that I would continue on and become a rabbi, a brand snatched from the burning of Wicked America. Pop was all for it, saying that a few months of intensive Talmud couldn't hurt. I casually agreed.

Little did I grasp what I was letting myself in for! Ten hours of English and Hebrew subjects, two hours of study with my grandfather, and four hours on the trolley; that was the daily schedule. I could hold my own in Talmud only if Zaideh drilled me. I rode a trolley from Pelham to his flat, then another trolley clear across town to the yeshiva. Now and then Pop came to Zaideh's flat to join in our study. How wistful his weary face would be, as he listened to our sharp exchanges, never cutting in, only listening! I had my moments of rebellious disgust with this burden, I must tell you. Once I told Pop in no uncertain terms how tired I was of this interminable Talmudic brain-twisting over laws two thousand years old.

"I understand, Yisroelke," he said. "But if I were on my deathbed, and I had breath enough to say one more thing to you, I would say, 'Study the Talmud.' "

Not Zaideh's star quality, I now realize, but Pop's attitude, kept me going. He had yielded me into Zaideh's hands, so that I would get more religion than he had the time or the learning to give me himself. Zaideh was a commanding personality, but in his quiet way, so was Pop. For a long time I thought of Zaideh as the one who shaped me most. Wrong. It was Pop, always Pop. All my life long, I have only been trying to be like my father.

Once I got used to it I rather liked the yeshiva. The students, though more religious than the Harris Jews, followed big league baseball, played street games, went to movies, swapped copies of *Amazing Stories,* and talked and talked about girls. Not all of them, no. A few pious ones frowned on idle chatter, but most of the fellows were like me. The pious ones and the rabbis did, however, generate something pretty new to me: *guilt,* a scarlet thread which ran through yeshiva life.

Take Coca-Cola, just at random. The pious few pointed out that the glue in the corks of Coca-Cola bottles could have come from horses; hence with your Coke you might consume a trace of an unkosher animal. I have no satiric intent here, I report a bizarre extreme just as it was. This contention lent to drinking Coke at the yeshiva a novel touch of bravado, of defying the lightning, and also a tinge of guilt. To these same purists, movies too were "*batlonus,*" wasting God's time, when one could be learning another page of Talmud. I knew that film-going on Saturday was wrong, but that a movie on an ordinary Tuesday could be offensive to God was a surprise.

With all that, there was something warm and homey about the yeshiva; no Bronx-Manhattan distinctions, no ham sandwiches in the lunchroom, no fiendish oppressors like Mr. Langsam and Mr. Ballard. The rabbis were gentle scholars, by and large, and we students were all good Jewish boys together, talking Yiddish over the Talmud, and English the rest of the time. This bilingual ambience brought back a feeling of childhood, almost of Aldus Street. None of the fellows were gilded snobs like Monroe Biberman, or jeering skeptics like Abby Cohen. They were my sort, cloistered though they were.

But that was it, in the end. That was decisive. They were cloistered. The yeshiva was a closed world, full of fugitive shadows of guilt, and I had come in from the blithe innocent American open air. I was different.

For instance, upon Zaideh's arrival, Mama had instituted separate dishtowels: red-striped for meat utensils, blue-striped for milk utensils, a new strict touch. It struck me as going rather far. One Sabbath I was washing up the dishes and my sister Lee was drying. She used the blue-striped towel on the meat crockery. I guess the yeshiva scrupulousness was getting to me, so I called this to her attention. It was a mistake. She was boiling over about something: Cornell, the timer, a tough exam, a romance gone wrong, a quarrel in her clique at Hunter. Something. Lee threw the dank towel in my face, screeched at me to dry the dishes myself, defied God to strike her dead for using the blue-striped dishtowel, and stormed out of the apartment. Lee was growing surpassingly beautiful, but hard to handle.

The incident troubled me. Next day at the yeshiva, I brought it up with my Talmud partner, a good-natured Brooklyn boy with whom I reviewed the lessons; no fanatic, in fact a Coca-Cola addict. "Really, will God strike me dead," I put it to him, "if I use the wrong dishtowel? What's the point?"

"Once you start to compromise," he said solemnly, "the whole thing will break down. You have to stick to the rules."

There had to be a better answer than that. I decided to approach the Kotzker Iluy.

Now the Kotzker Iluy — that is, "the genius from Kotzk" — was one fellow nobody would have suspected of drinking Coca-Cola. I doubt he had heard of the stuff. In the study hall we worked by a kind of buddy system, preparing our Talmud in pairs; but not the Kotzker Iluy. He studied by himself: a pallid chunky lad, always in black, always on his feet, swaying over a volume on a stand in a corner. He had no buddy, because nobody could keep up with him. They said he was going to finish the entire Talmud before he was twenty, a staggering mental feat. No matter how early you arrived in the study hall, there was the Kotzker Iluy, gesturing away at his book. No matter how late you left, you left him behind. He took no English subjects. He was a lone, privileged, awesome little celebrity.

Zaideh knew the Kotzker Iluy, or had known his father or grandfather. When he first brought me to the academy he introduced us. Like me, the Iluy had a hairless baby face, but his look was adult and somber. He did have a surprisingly sweet shy smile. As he shook my hand with a soft little paw, he smiled and wished me luck in my learning. That's the yeshiva expression. The students don't study and the teachers don't teach. Everybody learns.

Thereafter, if we happened to encounter each other, he was likely to smile and ask me how my grandfather was; all this in Yiddish, of course. If the Iluy knew English — and I suppose he could have picked up the language overnight, if he wanted to — he never used it. Zaideh, too, would inquire after the Iluy, and say I should spend more time with him. But I wasn't about to make friends with the Kotzker Iluy. He scared me.

I met the Iluy that day in a lineup at the water fountain outside the study hall. I was ahead of him, and offered to yield my place. He wouldn't let me. I said, "Look, can I ask you a silly question?"

He gently answered, "No honest question is silly."

As we walked back into the study hall I raised the problem of the dishtowels. Stroking his chin as though he had a beard, he looked at me for a long moment. "What are you learning?" he inquired.

A common yeshiva inquiry. You reply with the title of a Talmud chapter — nothing else, for nothing else ever matters — and it is always the first two or three words of the chapter.

"*How the Foot,*" I replied.

How the Foot is a section on the law of contributory negligence. The Talmud takes up the case of a herdsman whose cattle cause damage as he drives them along a public thoroughfare. The three words "How the foot" would need a long paragraph if expanded into English. You'll allow me to skip that, I'm sure.

The Kotzker Iluy's eyes lit up with pleasure. We were at his study stand. He opened his volume, and stood stroking his nonexistent beard and smiling at me. "*How the Foot!*" he said. "*How the Foot!* You're learning a marvellous chapter like *How the Foot,* and you worry about dishtowels?"

And he resumed his chant and his sway.

Now you remember Julie Levine, the Hebrew school orator who eventually became Judah Leavis, the famous Reform rabbi. Well, as I left the Iluy, whom should I run smack into but Julie! He was a sophomore in the upper school, or college; a tall lean handsome youth, whose small skullcap floated on a thick mane of red-blond hair. I was still short and pudgy, so he recognized me first. "My God, Davey Goodkind!" he exclaimed, looking horror-stricken. "What are *you* doing here?"

I explained about the Regents averages. He kept shaking his head, waving his hands at me as though warding off an apparition. "No, no," he said. "You don't know what you're doing to yourself. Get out. Get out! This place is hell on earth. Look, come over to my dorm room, Davey. God, it's good to see a face from the outside."

"It's Friday, Julie. I have to get home soon."

"Don't I know it's Friday? Come along."

A very queer smell pervaded the dormitory. Through open doors I could see students, their faces all coated with a mustard-colored muck, scraping the stuff off with spatulas of bone. Julie Levine took me into his room and, with the door open, ostentatiously stirred up a large bowl of this gunk.

"Some stink, eh?" he grinned. "That ought to keep old Steinbach happy."

He locked the door, put the bowl near it on the floor, and took from the bottom of his trunk a razor, a shaving brush, and a soap stick. "I have a date tonight," he said, lathering his face slowly and luxuriously. "Davey, what the hell were you talking about with the Kotzker Iluy?"

Steinbach was an assistant dean, the enforcer of rules, the nearest thing we had to a Mr. Ballard. Razors were forbidden by strict Torah law, so the yeshiva boys shaved with depilatories. Steinbach was known to prowl the dormitory halls on Fridays, sniffing at closed doors for the right smell. The bowl on the floor gave off very powerful fumes, so Julie seemed safe enough. Still, I wished he would hurry.

"Dishtowels, eh?" Julie laughed. "And what did the Iluy tell you?"

He began to shave as I repeated the exchange about *How the Foot.*

Rinsing his razor, Julie shook his head, and scraped a long pink swath down his cheek. "The Iluy is okay," he said. "An iluy's answer, that was."

"What? It was no answer at all. The fellow I learn with says that once you break a rule like that, the whole religion starts to fall apart. That's an answer, at least."

"Is it? Just ask yourself, Davey," said Julie, carefully shaving his chin, "what kind of religion is it that you can disintegrate with a dishtowel?"

The door burst open. The bowl went rolling, slopping yellow all over the floor. In the doorway stood Steinbach, a little dark mustached man in a black velvet skullcap, a ring of keys in his hand. Startled, Julie cut himself near his ear. Blood trickled through the white lather as he and Steinbach glared at each other. ·

"*So*, Levine!" said Steinbach. "Again!"

Julie sighed, shrugged, and went on shaving. "Oh, go ahead and report me, Steinbach," he said wearily.

"*Shaygets!*" said Steinbach. The term means unbeliever, heathen, abomination. The feminine form, with which the world is more familiar, is *shiksa*. "This, on top of the radio! You'll hear about this. So will your father. *Shaygets!*" He slammed the door shut.

"The radio?" I started to clean up the spill with a towel.

"Thanks, Davey. Oh, he caught me listening to the fight last Friday night. That's why I locked the door. Wouldn't you know he'd have a skeleton key?"

"Julie, why do you stay on here?"

"Do you think I want to? It's my father. He's a trustee. I could raise pigs in this room and they wouldn't throw me out. God, I damn near cut my ear off. Look at that blood!" He splashed cold water on his face. "Davey, I was valedictorian in my high school class. I had a straight-A average. I was admitted to Cornell and NYU. *I was waitlisted at Harvard.* And here I am, stuck in this hell for two more years. Don't let it happen to you, Davey! Get out! Get away from this dishtowel religion!"

39

The Little Blue Books

"Pop, I want to apply to Columbia," I told my father that night after dinner. "If I'm accepted, I'll try to get a scholarship. Also, there are student loans."

We were alone in the parlor. Mom and Lee were talking over crockery clatter in the kitchen. Pop looked at me thoughtfully. "You're not happy in the yeshiva?"

"I like Talmud, Pop, but I want a Columbia education."

"Go ahead and apply, then. You don't have to tell Zaideh, till we see what happens."

I already had the form. I had only to pull it out and get at it.

Under the question *What authors have you read?* there was a large white space. I could have put down a respectable list, but I wanted to fill that white space really full. We had in our flat a shelf of the Haldeman-Julius Little Blue Books, which Aunt Faiga had bought to improve her mind. A few readers in their dotage, like me, will recall these booklets. You bought them in Woolworth's for a dime apiece: slim selections from the great authors of the world, easily swallowed pastilles of culture. I had gone through the lot, for you could read a Little Blue Book cover to cover in fifteen or twenty minutes. Plato, Aristotle, Dante, Spinoza, it didn't matter, they were all there, hacked down to a few tiny digestible bits.

Well, need I say more? I crammed that white space with the name of virtually every giant of world literature, from Confucius to Kant, from Aeschylus to Shaw. You never saw such a dazzling list of classical authors, except maybe carved in marble outside a library. I asked Lee about citing those Little Blue Books as part of my literary background. She said sure, put down everything, why not? She was chronically sulky at being in Hunter College, she was painting herself up for a date, and she didn't give it much thought. Neither did I.

Oh, that trip from the Talmudical Academy to Columbia, when I went for my interview! Just a subway ride downtown; but that train was a rocket between planets, between galaxies, between incommensurable universes: in short, between the Inside and the Outside. I passed from the crowded bet midrash full of Talmud chant to the campus of a great American university; to green playing fields, broad lawns, and stately red and gray buildings. The domed library atop a sweep of stone staircases was in itself much bigger than Yeshiva University. The students strolling the brick walks looked to me like extras in a college movie: the boys all spiffy and gentile, the girls all elegant and gentile, their clothes all collegiate and gentile. Not a yarmulka in sight! A gilt Alma Mater statue held out welcoming arms.

But were they welcoming a Bronx yeshiva boy? I went into that awesome library to find out, and I confronted my fate in a small office, in the shape of a pleasant round-faced man with one arm. I didn't really need further unnerving by a one-armed interviewer, but that was how the ball bounced. My application was on the desk before him. I never did find out how he lost his arm, but it may well have been in hand-to-hand army combat. He went straight for the jugular.

"You've done some fine reading, I see, Mr. Goodkind."

"Well, uh, yes." Uncomfortable sense of trouble coming. Why pick on that one question?

"Aristotle, eh? Plato. Thomas Aquinas. The Venerable Bede."

"Uh, yes. Some."

"Fascinating. What have you read of Plato? The *Republic?*"

"Uh, no."

"The *Symposium?* The *Phaedo?*"

"Uh, well —" Trapped! Down in an elephant pit, writhing on the spikes, and the interview not one minute old! Clean breast; the only hope. "Well, uh, we have this little blue book of Plato at home, you see, and I read that."

"Ah, yes. Chaucer. Milton. Shakespeare. Beaumont and Fletcher. Molière. Ibsen. Chekhov. You're interested in the drama, I see, Mr. Goodkind, as well as philosophy." He wasn't being sarcastic, he was smiling in the friendliest way. Just asking.

"Uh, yes, I acted in plays some, uh, in summer camp."

"Really? Which plays?"

Somewhat demoralized, I truthfully spoke the first title that came to mind. "*Jerry Sees the Gorilla.*"

"How interesting. *Jerry Sees the Gorilla.*" Again he scanned my infernal reading list. "Pascal. Hobbes. Montesquieu. Spinoza." He looked up brightly at me. "What do you think of Spinoza, Mr. Goodkind?"

Anything, *anything*, to jar the interview out of this track! I said, "I disagree with him."

"You disagree with Spinoza?"

"Yes. Definitely."

The one-armed interviewer nodded, regarding me with a tinge of new respect. Not a bad stab in the dark, at that, I thought, disagreeing with Spinoza.

"With what aspect of his philosophy do you disagree, would you say, Mr. Goodkind?"

"Pretty much all of it."

"The ethics? The theory of God? Be a little more specific, if you can."

"Well, see, I read this little blue book of Spinoza at home, and whatever was in it, I disagreed with it."

Enough! You have the idea. He went through that whole accursed list of mine, wringing out of me admission after admission that I had read "this little blue book." It was a shambles. I was staring down a straight road toward four years of the yeshiva.

"Victor Hugo?"

Ah, a lifebelt to a drowning man. "Yes!"

"Another little blue book?"

"No. *Les Misérables.*"

He opened wide eyes. "Mr. Goodkind, you have read all of *Les Misérables?*"

"I have."

"What do you think of it?"

Well, I launched into a bar-mitzva speech on *Les Misérables*. I took that book from the opening scene of the bishop's candlesticks to the death of Jean Valjean, twelve hundred pages later, summarizing the plot, describing the main characters, and expatiating on Victor Hugo's version of the Battle of Waterloo. If I say so, it was a pretty good last flurry for a fighter out on his feet. The one-armed interviewer contemplated me in a stunned way; then he made rapid notes on my application, while I sat there panting and sweating.

"Mr. Goodkind," he said very cordially, "you are an unusual, ah, man, if a little young for college. I wish you well."

He offered his one hand to me, his left. I awkwardly shook it and went out, blinded by despair.

I couldn't have been less surprised by the contents of the long white envelope I soon received from the Admissions Office. I tore it open with shaking hands. My eyes went right to the horrible handwritten number in the printed form:

GROUP 4

Group 1 meant you were admitted; 2, probably admitted; 3, doubtful; 4, "advised to consider other possibilities"; 5 and 6 were the dustbin. I had to start considering "other possibilities," in Columbia's chilling words. Maybe Zaideh was wisest at that, I wretchedly wondered, and I ought to go on into the upper yeshiva. Why not? City College meant open defeat; that was where Cousin Harold was applying. Columbia didn't want me, Manhattan didn't want me, girls didn't want me, but I had a stalwart admirer in my grandfather. Why not just stay on in this familiar Yiddish-English world?

It was about this time that, in my depressed and anxious frame of mind, I decided I must be an invert. Homosexuality was then scarcely the commonplace of journalism and entertainment that it has become today, when fallen arches seem more unusual. It was a little understood, scarcely whispered about tendency in a very few, very strange individuals. I first found out about it in a long dismal novel called *The Well of Loneliness,* written by a lesbian named Radclyffe Hall. The book made a sensation at the time. I got hold of a copy and devoured it on those long trolley rides to the yeshiva. Radclyffe Hall's invert heroine was big, flat-chested, deep-voiced, and hipless.

Aha! That was my problem, only in reverse. I wasn't yet sprouting hair on my face, or anywhere else to speak of, except on my scalp. My voice stayed cracked and uncertain. The Talmud contained references to *androgynes,* twilight creatures not quite man or woman. I spent hours in the yeshiva library, hunting up everything I could find in the rabbinic texts about androgynes. Between these, and the disclosures in *The Well of Loneliness,* and my smooth body and hairless pubic region, I concluded that the fix was in. That was why Bernice

Lavine had preferred Clarence Rubin and his plus fours. That was why the Bronx girls ignored me and ogled Cousin Harold, who shaved, and was a foot or more taller than me, and spoke in a deep voice. That was probably why the one-armed man had put me in Group 4, come to think of it. Radclyffe Hall wrote that the world cruelly rejected inverts, because it didn't understand them. It might even be the reason Arista had turned me down. Of course! There you had it. I was one of those. Mystery solved.

Uncle Hyman's family had moved near us, and though things weren't quite the same between Cousin Harold and me, we still went out together girl-hunting. He had matured in every way; and in what finally mattered as evidence of manhood, I will only say, out of deference to the family trade, ye gods and little fishes! I could scarcely believe my eyes, and it so humiliated me that I confided to him Radclyffe Hall's reason for my being so different. Harold had never heard of inverts, but he certainly wanted to know more about this aspect of existence, in which he had it all over me. He went out and dug up all the available books he could find on the subject. He became a real authority on inverts, and on offbeat sex in general. He even once lent me Krafft-Ebing, which was no help at all. I just rediagnosed myself as an invert with a garter fetish. It was a sad time in my life and that's a fact. Cousin Harold, as you know, went on to become a prosperous psychiatrist; and he may not agree, but I think he owes his whole career, all unwittingly, to that book by Radclyffe Hall.

Well, my buddy and I were droning over the last page of *How the Foot* in the study hall about six weeks later, and I was worrying about the problems of inversion, when I was called to the telephone. It was Mama. Her voice shook. "You've been admitted to Columbia."

I stood in the school office, leaning against a secretary's desk. Otherwise I think I would have fallen down.

"Davey, do you hear me? The letter came in the mail just now. I *had* to open it. You're admitted. Admitted to Columbia!"

I gasped, "Well, Mama, are you glad?"

"Glad! I'm so proud I could bust. I called Papa. We'll find the money somehow. Oh, Yisroelke! Columbia!"

I did not return to the study hall. I just walked straight out of the building. Steinbach was coming in, and he gave me a puzzled frown. I walked out into the sunshine, into the American open air; strode a

few blocks away from the yeshiva to a little park, took off my yarmulka, and threw myself on the grass, in happy shock.

What had done it? My speech on *Les Misérables?* Or did heaven pay
attention, after all, to the prayers of a kid studying the Talmud month
after month, at the cost of four hours a day on the trolley? What did
it matter now? I WAS A COLUMBIA MAN. Whatever had wrought the
miracle, I was *in!* I was no invert. I was no reject. I was no yeshiva
boy. The June sun had never blazed more brightly on me, nor had
grass ever smelled sweeter. After a while I put on my skullcap and
went back to the study hall, which already had a strange look and
sound, to a Columbia man. On an impulse, I went up to the Kotzker
Iluy and told him the news.

"Your grandfather will be sad," he said, "but — *ess is nit g'ven bashert* (it was not destined)." He offered me his soft paw, gave me his
unforgettable gentle smile, and tapped his open Talmud. "You will
come back to it."

Everyone knows where Judah Leavis is. But where is the Kotzker
Iluy? My guess is that he heads one of the tiny obscure yeshivas in
Jerusalem, where the flame burns on.

When I told Zaideh about Columbia, he shrugged and managed a
smile. "*Ess is nit g'ven bashert,*" he said. "If only you could have made
friends with the Kotzker Iluy! But I came too late."

No, Zaideh, no. Just in time.

"I want you to go downtown and talk to Mr. John Worthington,"
Pop said to me when I came home rejoicing. "Tomorrow afternoon.
You have an appointment."

"What on earth for?"

"Never mind. Do it."

John Worthington was the first Christian I ever talked to man to
man, so to speak. I was then just turned fifteen. His wood-panelled
office on Wall Street was like a movie set to me, and he was like a
movie actor: portly, white-headed, beautifully tailored, scarily dignified, speaking fine downtown English. After throwing some severe
questions at me, he suddenly laughed. "You remind me of Elya," he
said. "You'll do well at Columbia." His use of Pop's Yiddish name
astonished me, for Pop was always called Alex in business. He handed
me a typewritten note. "Your father wanted you to see this."

Columbia University
Office of the President

Dear Jack:
Responding to your inquiry, Israel David Goodkind has been admit-
ted to the college.

Sincerely . . .

Worthington went on to talk at length of my father; said he admired Elya Goodkind, Elya was a man, and he'd back him in anything
he tried. I can hear him saying *"Elya,"* in that faintly condescending
yet affectionate Christian way. About the letter, he said not another
word.

"For the first time in I don't know when, I asked a gentile for a
favor," Pop said to me in Yiddish that night, "because I heard there
was a Jewish quota at Columbia. Now, Yisroelke, make them look
silly for putting you in Group Four."

*   *   *

40

Columbia!

September 1973

SANDRA telephoned this morning at nine A.M. Israel time. I guess she forgot that she would be startling us awake at three in the morning. I heard her voice as in an echo chamber, "Hello, hello — it's me, Sandra!" Then the line went dead.

Jan and I sat up in bed, pretending we weren't shaken, waiting for another ring. The Palestinian terrorists are on a rampage lately, blowing up Israeli buses, tossing grenades into marketplaces, and the like. They took over a school, too, recently, and killed some kids before the army got in, rescued the rest of the kids, and finished off the terrorists. And there our daughter sits in the Fields of Peace, right at the corner of the Gaza Strip and Sinai.

It was a damned long ten minutes before the phone rang again. Jan pounced on it. No problem. Sandra is fine. She has simply decided to postpone her graduate work for a year, and stay on there. She has talked to her department head at Johns Hopkins and has his okay. She hasn't changed her mind about Israel one whit, she assured us, but the material for the thesis keeps opening up. She is on to something, and doesn't want to scamp it.

I spoke to her and asked what she thought of the terror raid on the school. She hesitated, then said that most of the deaths were the army's fault, they botched it; and that anyhow, no such things would happen if Israel would give back the territories. I didn't argue, though before Israel won the territories, such things happened much more often. Sandra was then entering her teens, and falling in and out of love once or twice a month, which absorbed her attention. She has since mastered world affairs, and has nothing but contempt for my opinions. As for my working for the President, she has now and then hinted that I may be criminally insane. I thanked her for keeping us informed and asked her to give Abe Herz my regards. With an indistinct hostile mutter, she rang off.

There's nothing we can do about Sandra. At twenty-one she is off on her own steam. Nor, indeed, have we had much to say about her doings since she was seventeen. The power of our purse over her is nil. We tried that once. She merely went and got herself a job as a nighttime receptionist in a Boston restaurant. When we visited the place and saw all the horrible leers she was getting in her tight low-cut yellow dress — in my view the place was patronized entirely by rapists, sadists, voyeurs, and other assorted male sickies — Jan and I caved in and restored her allowance. No, let Sandra do as she pleases.

What troubles me about that phone call, beyond the chronic Sandra puzzle, is the thought of the terrific changes that have engulfed the world since my Columbia days. That was when Lee went to Palestine. By boat and train, it took her a month. Today you get on an El Al plane, have your dinner, read a book, grab a snooze, and there you are in Tel Aviv. We chat with our daughter, over there in the Holy Land, as though she were in her Wellesley dorm. Mark Twain described the land as a plague-ridden stony waste of ruins, and now it's as full of cars roaring on highways through lush green orange groves, farmlands, and vineyards, as Southern California; which indeed it is getting to resemble far too much. Of what interest, I'm wondering, can all that pile of pages about Columbia, the Columbia of forty eternal years ago, possibly be?

Columbia still looks almost the same. They've plugged up one side of South Field with a big new library, and stuffed in yet another building where the tennis courts were. That's about all. The whole *mise-en-scène* of my childhood has vanished — Aldus Street, Camp Eagle Wing, the Fairy Laundry, the Minsker Synagogue, Townsend Harris Hall — all gone, gone with the wind, gone like Twain's Mississippi of steamboats and slaves. But Columbia stands, and Mark Herz and Peter Quat are still part of my life. Last year I went to the Columbia commencement, because Mark got an honorary degree and spoke at Class Day. There was Alma Mater still holding out those gilded arms, and I sat in a back row on South Field, feeling like a character out of *The Time Machine;* especially when an occasional youth in a yarmulka ambled by.

Well, let's come to a decision here. I'll cut the Columbia stuff to ribbons, just give you a glimpse of my college years and race on. I can't entirely skip Columbia. Not possible. For what was our Yisroelke doing, living in a Central Park South hotel suite on his own at twenty-one, and squiring around an enchanting showgirl? Answer: he became a gagman. And how did the Minsker Godol undergo such a bizarre metamorphosis? Answer: through working for Harry Goldhandler, the gag czar. And how on earth did *that* come to pass? Answer: through my encountering Peter Quat and Mark Herz at Columbia.

* * *

TIME, September 1930, just before the college year starts. Scene, the Columbia gymnasium, where some four hundred freshmen are crowding into rows of wooden seats to take placement tests. Behind me, an amazed and displeased baritone bellow: "Iggy! What are *you* doing here?" I turn.

Towering over me, looking down at me with distaste — rather like Gulliver at a sassy Lilliputian on his palm — is Monroe Biberman. He looks taller and more pimply than Cousin Harold. He has the bluish jaws of one who shaves twice a day; indeed, he was already shaving his upper lip when we were collaborators. At all points he is dressed like a college-movie extra: obligatory contrasting jacket and slacks, woolen blue-and-red tie, dirty white shoes. I am only dimly aware of dress as yet, but I can recognize the fashion-plate effect, though I have no idea where one buys such clothes; certainly not at Michaels'.

"Hi, Monny." After all, we are now Columbia men together, aren't we? Formerly I called him Monroe, but he was always "Monny" to those Arista fellows.

"So! It *is* you. I'd know that suit anywhere."

The purple suit, of course. I take no offense. In this sea of giant strangers, I'm delighted to find an old acquaintance, though he too is now so huge. Happily I blurt the first thing that comes to mind. "I thought you were going to Harvard."

A black look crosses Biberman's face. He takes this as a riposte for the remark about the purple suit, for his next words — I remember this snatch of dialogue all too well — are uncalled for. "How the hell did they let you in here?"

And I in my obtuse innocence accept this as joshing, and adopt his vein. "God knows. I was in Group Four. Somebody sent me the wrong letter by mistake, I guess. What happened, Monny, didn't you get into Harvard? I thought it was all set."

"Decided I'd rather stay in New York," Biberman snarls down at me. "I was in Group One."

"I suppose your brother's pretty disappointed," I say — again, I swear, meaning no offense. Biberman's brother goes to Harvard. Monny had an early interview there, and afterward spread the word around school that he was in. Biberman's expression changes, suggesting Frankenthal's old Dracula look. He turns on his heel, goes off, and sits down. I think of following him and sitting beside him — after all, us Townsend Harris guys should stick together — but where he puts himself there is no room for me.

Columbia College must have been as thoroughly ruined for poor Biberman when he spotted my purple suit as Longfellow Avenue was for Mama when the men showed up with Bobbeh's sauerkraut. I daresay I embodied his rejection from Harvard. Monny had been president of Arista, and managing editor of the yearbook and the *Stadium*. He lived on Park Avenue, below Ninety-sixth Street. Why didn't he make it into Harvard? Peculiar place, Harvard. Cousin Harold's son Kris just got admitted to Harvard. Kris has bright wavy red hair down to his shoulders, he does a lot of sky-diving, and he stands on his head two hours a day. There is nothing he hasn't smoked, except possibly tobacco. He intends to practice child psychiatry, and — but I wander. No time for that.

Waiting in the wings are Peter Quat and Mark Herz.

"Iggy!"
Biberman again. Two months later. Same displeased tone. I have seen very little of him. No doubt he is having trouble, as I am, adjusting to the staggering load of work. We are in the Varsity Show rehearsal room on the fourth floor of John Jay Hall, where all student activities are centered. Freshman aspirants for the daily news-

paper, the *Spectator,* are crowding into the big barren cork-floored room. Biting on a big new black pipe, Biberman sends up a column of blue smoke and red sparks, and growls at me through the conflagration, "What are *you* doing here? The call is for guys with previous experience."

"I edited the *Camp Maccabee Menorah,*" I reply.

Biberman casts his eyes up to the ceiling, in despair at my imbecility.

Yet we are both accepted. Everybody is. We soon learn why. Freshmen serve as printer's devils, carrying the day's copy downtown to the plant on the Bowery, and then staying up all night, amid the rattling linotype machines and the thumping presses, to help a senior editor get the paper out. It is rough going. The freshman candidates dwindle in a month to about ten. Biberman hangs on. So do I.

It is easier for Biberman. He can ride the subway from his home to the printing plant in twenty minutes. I have to forgo my dinner, stay downtown, and subsist on tuna fish or peanut butter sandwiches, for I am still eating by the rules; or else I must travel to the North Bronx for a hot meal, and return all the way downtown to the press, and at dawn ride back to Pelham for a few hours' sleep.

Why, then, do I stick it out? Well, for one thing, the night work turns out to be fun. I smell printer's ink. I begin to smoke cigarettes. I come to know the deepest fatigue, and the wonderful surge of second wind that comes with coffee at two A.M. in an all-night diner, and a slice of greasy pie. (Made with lard? Oh, probably not.) Dawn turns the dirty windows gray. The *Spectator* comes off the press, with headlines I've improvised, pages I've helped the night editor to dummy up; and a line on the masthead, in boldface, *Associate Night Editor for this issue: I. David Goodkind.* Reward enough!

Jan persuaded me years ago to give up cigarettes. But if I light one now and jet smoke through my nostrils the way I did when I was fifteen — thinking that it made me look thirty — the sting in my nasal passages will instantly bring back the smell of the printer's ink, the taste of the coffee, the greasiness of that pie (probably made with lard, I can concede now); and the exaltation of seeing my name, freshly printed and still damp, above the editorial column of the Columbia *Spectator.*

But the main reason for hanging on is none of that. It is the "Off-hour," the daily humor column, a mix of wisecracks and light verse, alternately signed by two pen names: *The Man in the Iron Mask,* and *PDQ.* Very early on, Peter Quat's name on the masthead catches my eye. There can't be two fellows named Peter Quat. So that odd fish from Camp Eagle Wing is now a contributing editor of the *Spectator!* He must be PDQ, and I'm hoping this literary giant will remember me and be friendly.

I first catch sight of the great PDQ crouching in a blue overcoat at a corner typewriter reserved for contributing editors. I barely recognize him. The gaunt Bunk Eight misfit has become a young man. His face has lengthened, and the bones stand out. His head rests on his hand, and his forehead is clutched in two spread fingers, in creative agony. He sits up, pecks a few quick lines with index fingers, then falls back into the crouch. A showy performance, not unexpected from Peter Quat. His curly black hair falls down on his forehead when he crouches, yet two receding bays in his hairline already show.

I do not dare to interrupt the artist at work, but I am at the copy desk when he hands in his column. "Hi," I venture with a humble smile, taking the yellow pages, "I'm Davey Goodkind."

Peter Quat glowers blankly at me as though I have said something intolerably impudent, idiotic, and revolting; buttons up his overcoat and walks out. It seems my name has not rung a bell.

The Man in the Iron Mask is a junior named Mark Herz. He sends in his copy from the Beta Sigma Rho house, and it is midterm before I lay eyes on him. On a blizzardy day I come into the newsroom, shaking off snow, and espy somebody new at the contributors' desk. He sits up straight, typing steadily with both hands. A stained battered brown hat, the crown pinched into a triangle, is tilted back on his head. A cigarette droops in his mouth. I stand staring until he turns and squints at me, through smoke curling up into his eyes. He has a round face, short brown hair, and his look is cold and thin-lipped.

I keep sneaking glances at him as I work at my own little story. He blue-pencils his pages briskly and drops them at the copy desk. "Thanks, Mark," says the night editor. He begins laughing over Herz's pages, as the Man in the Iron Mask puts on a very ragged duffel coat and chain-lights a cigarette. I am staring again, and Mark Herz shoots me a keen glance, his head sideways as he drags on his cigarette. He leaves, and I sit at my typewriter unaccountably stirred up.

Freshman year whirls by. No doubt I am acquiring an education: Plato, Aristotle, Spinoza, Milton, Dante, John Stuart Mill, Thorstein Veblen, and none of your little blue books, either, but ponderous tomes; and zoology, and psychology, and trigonometry, and French drama, and God knows what else. But all that is by the way. The main thing is "Off-hour."

The Man in the Iron Mask and PDQ both accept contributions. I am in a hot race with Biberman to have a poem accepted. I have at last realized that Monny Biberman is down on me; not that I understand, but that seems to be the way he wants it. Well, as a Columbia freshman I may be a confused Bronx Jew, trying to get my bearings in this bewildering antechamber to the Outside; but man to man, I'm ready for Monroe Biberman. Let him understand, in due course, that he has taken on the Minsker Godol!

Clearly I need a nom de plume for my witty stuff. I consider "D'Artagnan," in Herz's Dumas vein. That seems too straight. I bethink me of "The Vicomte de Bragelonne"; and in a great flash of inspiration, I hit on my immortal Columbia alias — the VICOMTE DE BRAG. Even nowadays, if I go to some Columbia affair, one or another bald paunchy wag will hail me with, "Hi, Vicomte," and perhaps with vast wit add, *"Comment ça va?"*

Actually, Monny wins the sprint with six lines of doggerel, dully signed "M.B.," about an adored female who turns out to be a cow. I have been pelting both columnists with poems left on the message board. Quat drops them, after a glance, in the wastebasket. The ones that go to Herz at the Beta Sig house vanish into a void. One day the Man in the Iron Mask himself saunters into the news room, looking very weary and shabby in his pinched sweat-stained hat and ragged duffel coat, from which his wrists redly protrude. He takes a poem of mine from the message board and reads it. I guess he feels my eyes burning at him; for though the room is full of fellows clattering at typewriters, he walks up to me.

"Are you the Vicomte de Brag?"

"Yes!"

"Not bad. Keep it up."

A week later I break into his column with a ballade, a four-stanza French form with a tough rhyming scheme. My God, when I open the *Spectator* and see my poem there, taking up half the column, signed *Vicomte de Brag!* And a week later Quat runs a rondeau of mine! Life is beginning.

Next time I see Quat at his desk, I approach him proudly and declare, "Hi, I'm the Vicomte de Brag." He gives me that same blank freezing stare. I add, "Uh, thanks for printing my poem."

"*Sword* doesn't rhyme with *broad*," says Quat, "except in the Bronx." Wow.

For a long while after that I roll my *r*'s almost like a Scotsman, to mask my low origin. I'm self-conscious about that missing Bronx *r*, in fact, to this day, for I still tend to drop it when I talk quickly and naturally. Not that I really give a damn; but that barb the great PDQ stuck in me never has worked quite loose.

By the end of freshman year, the Vicomte de Brag is riding high in "Off-hour," and M.B. has fallen silent. In no other way, however, have I outdistanced Monroe Biberman. On the contrary, he is the leading freshman candidate. He gets assigned to big stories. He becomes assistant theatre critic, sees plays for nothing, and writes snotty reviews in imitation of George Jean Nathan, the preeminent snotty critic. The editor of *Spectator,* Randy Davenport, a remote short dour Theta Xi, and the managing editor, a pallid Beta Sig Jew who really runs the paper, always in shirt-sleeves and a green eyeshade, both show favor to Biberman: smiles, praise, and exemption from lowly errands.

As, for instance:

One rainy blustery day in March, Randy Davenport emerges from his inner office, when only Biberman and I are in the news room. "You," says Davenport, crooking a finger at me. "My mother is expecting this. Take it down to this address." He hands me a bulky envelope. Why me? Why not Biberman? But it couldn't possibly be Biberman. If I pronounced my *r*'s and lived on Park Avenue below Ninety-sixth Street, I might try facing Davenport down. This errand is not newspaper work. But *Spectator* is my life at Columbia, and Randy Davenport is the big cheese. As I struggle into my too-short yellow slicker, a relic of boys' camp days, Davenport genially commends Biberman on his snotty demolition of Eugene O'Neill's latest play.

The address is on West End Avenue, below Ninety-sixth Street. We are talking of forty years ago, when those handsome huge apartment buildings still had mostly gentile occupants. I take a trolley downtown, and trudge through the rain to Davenport's address. A uniformed doorman under the canopy looks me up and down, taking in my yellow slicker, my wet head, the bulky envelope under my arm, and — I suspect — my Minsker Godol features.

"Service entrance over there." He jerks a thumb at a side gate.

My reaction is from the gut. "I'm no errand boy. I'm a friend of Randy Davenport. This is for his mother."

He opens the door for me. I get another head-to-toe inspection by the elevator man before he admits me to his car. A little gray-headed lady opens the Davenport door a crack, and peers out with one eye, pokes forth a bony hand, and takes the package without a word. Behind her, I can just glimpse a huge apartment and a stained-glass window in the foyer, before she shuts the door in my face.

41

I Grow

As though freshman year at Columbia isn't tough enough, I have to cope with a surging onset of overdue puberty. When the semester starts, I am still the small plump baby-face of the yeshiva. Coming home to Pelham, my head spinning with Sophocles and Milton and John Dewey, I play sidewalk handball for an hour or so with any available street boy, before plunging into my heavyweight studies. The incongruity doesn't bother me, and the kid is never aware of it, for I talk street language with him, and I could pass for an eighth-grader.

But with the coming of springtime, as the earth begins to blossom, so at last does our Yisroelke. The Talmud defines the sprouting of two pubic hairs as legal evidence of the maturing process. I suddenly and abundantly run far over the minimum. I have erotic dreams, with startling results. Such things were not then the common coin of magazine articles, as they are today; even "hygiene" teachers pussy-footed around them, shedding as little light on the topic as possible. Consequently I hardly know what the hell is going on. I consult my mother's old *Home Medical Companion,* a fat red volume full of frightful descriptions of diseases, and anatomical pictures that fold out in three dimensions, in garish colors. I have not looked in this *vade mecum* since I read up on leprosy, and spent a week or two finding numb white spots all over myself and getting used to the obvious truth that I was a leper. Now I seek some clue to this erotic dream thing.

I find it amply discussed by the author, Dr. William Herkimer, under the heading, "Pollutions." I am told that I have probably been reading salacious books or seeing the wrong sort of plays, which is not a bad shot at my gartered-thighs secret, and I am advised to mend my ways, take very frequent cold showers, and discontinue eating hot red peppers, raw eggs, and oysters. Old Doc Herkimer undoubtedly means well, but I've got to keep using the subway, I cannot endure cold showers, and I've never eaten an oyster, a raw egg, or a hot red pepper in my life. So where does that leave me?

The thing is going on and on. In desperation I visit the doctor at the Columbia infirmary, a baldish white-coated gent in his late forties. He asks me how often the problem is occurring. When I tell him he looks impressed, and if I'm not mistaken, envious. He tells me not to worry, and to see him again if it happens thirty or forty days in a row. I stop worrying, or try to; but a new alarming symptom crops up. During a touch football game on South Field a huge blocker shoulders me aside as always, but this time my chest hurts like anything, especially my nipples. Now what? I look up nipples in old Doc Herkimer's *Companion*. There is a huge full-color picture of a female breast that folds out, showing absolutely ghastly structures under the skin; most disillusioning to one who still treasures the vision of Bernice Lavine's divine left bosom. But the doc says nothing about male nipples, that I can find.

This happens around Passover. When I see Cousin Harold at the seder in Zaideh's Bronx flat, the one occasion when the aging and scattering Mishpokha still gathers, I confide in him. Cousin Harold helpfully suggests that I may have breast cancer. This clue enables me to track down my case in Herkimer, who says, yes indeed, while unusual, it is by no means unheard-of for males to be so afflicted, and it is nearly always fatal. I endure hypochondriacal agonies for about a month — all the time composing the Vicomte de Brag's funny poems, you understand, and working as an associate night editor, and passing exams and writing themes — and at last fear drives me to the college doctor again.

He reassures me, not without a certain testy condescension, that sore nipples are an expected part of what I'm going through. He tells me to stop being so nervous, and asks me how I've been doing lately with the dreams. Somewhat annoyed, I pull an astronomical number out of the air. His eyes pop like basketballs. He writes me a prescription, and says I had better keep him informed for a while. Actually the dreams have been tapering off, so I throw the prescription away. After an incredibly long time on a plateau, I plainly am growing up. The purple suit is getting short in pants and sleeves, and before the semester ends I have to shave my hairy upper lip. I use Pop's razor, of course, not yellow depilatory powder and a bone scraper. I am already very, very far from the yeshiva, though I am still keeping to the rules on food — more or less.

The big event of the spring term is Peter Quat's Varsity Show, *Greek to Me.* The scene is ancient Athens after a stock-market crash. Socrates is selling apples, Plato and Aristotle are bankrupt stockbrokers, Pericles has moved into the tub with Diogenes, the chorus of dancing female impersonators forms a bread line, and so on. Zeus is a takeoff on Herbert Hoover, and Pallas Athena talks like Mae West. That sort of thing. Strictly collegiate, full of Columbia jokes and depression wheezes.

To me, the show is a glittering marvel. To think that one man could write it all! Peter himself, playing the god Pan, does a very off-color number with Aphrodite, capers around with her, and dances off to an ovation. I am consumed with admiration for Peter Quat. Football heroes, campus politicians, Randy Davenport — how can they compare with a genius who can do all this? The night I see *Greek to Me* my college course is fixed. I am going to write a Varsity Show.

And why not? Already I have emerged from the pack. "Who is this Vicomte de Brag?" I hear fellows ask, as they lounge about reading *Spectator.* Sweet music! The June issue of *Jester,* the comic monthly, contains two articles by the Vicomte de Brag. I am growing, I am shaving, I am getting into print, and in my dreams at least I am a man. In my waking dream, I am the next Peter Quat. As for the Man in the Iron Mask, while I feel peculiarly attracted to him, I see little of him. They tell me he is a science major, and works like a dog.

Sophomore year starts happily. The sparkling fall weather tingles in the blood. I have a warm sense of belonging, enhanced by the sight of callow-looking freshmen forlornly wandering about the Van Am quadrangle in their beanies. My name flowers on the mastheads of both *Spectator* and *Jester* as an associate editor.

There is a bit of a scandal about the *Jester's* new managing editor. Peter Quat fully expected to be elected to this Jewish seat, so to speak, on the editorial board, since he has been writing about half of the magazine for years. Peter couldn't be elected editor, the editor is always a Deke: immemorial custom. But another Deke nobody knows, an invisible goy named Preston Burton, has been elected managing editor, and that is that. Royally screwed by the outgoing board, Quat has resigned. I am too small-bore to be drawn into such intrigues, and it doesn't surprise or anger me that Jews can't be editors at Columbia, or that Christian fraternities run things. The way of the world; what else is new?

Fraternity rushing begins. The one for me, I know, is Beta Sigma Rho. Nearly all the Jews who matter on the John Jay fourth floor — writers, team managers, politicians — are Beta Sigs. At the Beta Sig rush parties, Monroe Biberman already acts like one of them. He passes drinks, makes easy jokes with the house officers, and remains behind when the rest of us leave. One night I decide to stay late myself, and give the Beta Sigs their chance to bid in the eminent and high-riding Vicomte de Brag. When Biberman sees me hanging around, he leaves. The members cleaning up after the party are polite to me, offer me more drinks and food, but say nothing about my joining. Mark Herz, who has hardly been seen during the rushing rituals, comes downstairs in his shirt sleeves. "Hey, Vicomte," he says. "There you are. Let's go up to my room."

There are moments in life that you never forget. They may be buried out of sight for decades, but when they rise up they hit you with the heat of life itself. So it is with this conversation, my first real one with Mark Herz. As I write, I am back in that dingy attic room, a slope-ceilinged hole lined with science and economics texts, smelling of shaving lotion and stale cigarette smoke. He asks me about my family, where I live, what my father does. I mention that my sister Lee is about to leave on a trip to Europe and Palestine. He scrawls on a bit of paper the address of his relatives in Jerusalem, the offhand gesture which will have such explosive consequences.

How plainly I see — at a remove of forty years — that Mark is knotting a worn tie at a mirror, not looking at me, when he mumbles that he supposes I've decided on some other fraternity, since Beta Sig is not my sort of crowd. It is a hint of sledgehammer subtlety; but as unheeding as a girl in love, exalted by this intimacy with the Man in the Iron Mask, I assure him that Beta Sigma Rho is just my style, and I know I'll be very happy here. Long silence. The tie takes a lot of knotting. He puts on his badly worn tweed jacket, leather-patched at the elbows. "Say, where did you get this nickname, Iggy, anyhow?" he very casually asks, his eyes on the mirror.

The sick flash comes after a puzzled instant. *Biberman!* He has managed to talk the Beta Sigs around against the Vicomte de Brag. I am not going to get a bid; and the Man in the Iron Mask has found the tersest, subtlest, kindest possible way to signal to me what has happened. He glances at me, his usually frigid face somber but friendly. I know I don't have to reply to his question. It's over. I yawn, stretch, look at my watch, and say I'd better get on back up to the Bronx.

"This room costs me half what a dorm room would," says Mark Herz, putting on his hat. "That's why I'm here. Otherwise fraternities are bullshit." For all his threadbare garb, he looks the perfect fraternity man.

I say, "Once you're in, maybe."

He darts me the sharp glance of our first encounter, and sticks out his hand. "Peter Quat and I are collaborating on the Varsity Show this year. You should start thinking of an idea for next year. There's nobody else."

I ride the subway home, nursing a bleeding ego, yes; but also thinking hard of Varsity Show plots. Couldn't I do something funny about Hitler, for instance, the German ranter with the Chaplin mustache? A title even occurs to me: *To Heil with It!* Not bad. And to heil with the Beta Sigs! They'll be remembered in Columbia history for only one reason: they passed up I. David Goodkind, the Vicomte de Brag, the author of the memorable 1933 Varsity Show, *To Heil with It!,* in favor of a forgotten nobody named Biberstein, or something.

Next day, out of nowhere, Peter Quat comes up to me at the fourth-floor water cooler. "You know what? I've decided to call you Tex," he says, with a charming smile that astounds me. "Come and have lunch at the Tau Alpha Epsilon house." I have never given that place a thought, having been told it's an "interfaith" house. Nonsense, Quat assures me, all the brothers are Jewish, great guys. Just a chapter or two down south may have mixed memberships. So I go to lunch. The long and short of it is, I'm invited to join Tau Alpha, and I do join. The initiation fee is hefty, but my Regents scholarship covers it. Besides, things are looking up a bit at the laundry, and Lee got all that money for the trip abroad; so Pop and Mom don't demur at Tau Alpha, nor do they make religious inquiries. Yisroelke is a Columbia man now.

Well, Peter Quat sort of adopts me as a protégé, and I respond with a spell of slavish adoration. Natural enough! Cast adrift at Columbia from Pop, from Zaideh, from the Bronx, from the yeshiva, I have no model, no pattern, no received set of manners, no role to play. I've already decided to be another Peter Quat in achievement, and when the great PDQ takes me under his wing, I decide to be Peter Quat at all points. I carry it to ludicrous extremes. He smokes Spuds, a mentholated cigarette, so I smoke Spuds. He has a way of gesturing for emphasis with his left hand, a cigarette in his rigid fingers, and that becomes my own emphatic gesture. When excited or angry Quat twists his mouth sideways, rolls his eyes upward, and addresses the air. I do the same, especially in my arguments about religion at home, which are becoming more frequent; so that Mom finally asks me to stop making those crazy faces when I talk to her. I prolong this preposterous aping for about a year. That is as long as Tau Alpha lasts.

For when Quat recruits me, the house is dying. Its few members are Manhattan Jewish snobs to end all snobs. The old Arista crowd isn't in it with these birds. But the Wall Street crash has cut down the number of Jewish freshmen with fancy East Side addresses, so Tau Alpha has wasted away, its members unwilling to compromise their lofty standards. This year, in a sudden convulsive clutch at survival, they are grabbing virtually anybody: a South American scholarship student for whom they have to waive all fees, two actual Brooklynites, and Goodkind of the Bronx. *Brooklynites!* A Bronxite! A pathetic haul. Nor does it help. Both Brooklynites soon depledge, ill at ease in that company. The South American has to go home when he fails all his courses, owing to excessive pool-playing at Tau Alpha. Only I hang on, because of Peter.

One day I remind him of our days at Camp Eagle Wing. "Good Christ!" he exclaims. "Of course. You were that *Les Misérables* kid. A million years ago, wasn't it, Davey?" He never does call me Tex. That was just his suave approach to a Bronx boy who rhymed *sword* and *broad*.

42

Quandary

THE Herz and Quat musical is about a Jewish bullfighter from Brooklyn: title, *The Kosher-Killed Bull*. Quat invites me to sit in with him and Herz as they work on their script. I hang around them as they write, and even contribute a joke or two, to my vast exaltation. Herz sits at the typewriter, and Quat roams around, sparking off jokes and ideas. They have a hilarious time, laughing hardest at Quat's obscene suggestions which they can't use. Peter displays gleams of his later form with those quips, and with that title; also with jokes about the Jewish matador's big nose, his cowardice, his circumcision, his distress at learning he is eating ham, and so on.

The Deke who manages the show makes them change the title to *Si Si, Señorita*. "Nobody knows what kosher means," says the Deke. The Deke house is some kind of ivory tower, obviously, but what the manager says, goes. The Deke manager also books a theatre for the two performances of the show on the two Passover seder nights. I find myself in a quandary. I've been counting on seeing both performances, but the Passover seders are sacrosanct, the one solid island of religion left in the year. Passover is Zaideh's great hour, with the whole Mishpokha crowded at tables zigzagging through the book-lined flat. No matter how the old Mishpokha ties are weakening, everyone who is alive and within a hundred miles shows up. That Yisroelke should absent himself is unthinkable.

Nevertheless, after agonizing for days, I announce flat out that I intend to skip the second seder. Mom responds that it's unthinkable. It'll be a scandal in the family. The shock to Zaideh will ruin his Passover. She won't be able to face him or the Mishpokha. I point out that in Palestine there is only one seder. The doubling up of the seder elsewhere is a mere survival of the moon calendar problem, from the days before exact calculation of orbits. So the second seder can't matter all that much, can it? My own sister Lee isn't going to two seders, is she? "No. So wait till you get to Palestine," is Mom's answer. "Now you're in the Bronx. Two seders, and stop rolling your eyes and making those crazy faces."

Protracted bickering on this topic comes to an abrupt end on Saturday, when Pop and I are walking home from the synagogue. He stops to catch his breath, and says, panting a bit, that he's always felt he and Mom owe us the best of everything: a good home, a fine education, a trip abroad for Lee, a fraternity for me, and whatever else can advance us in life. Maybe I ought to consider, he says, whether in return we owe them anything at all. With that, he walks on again. He says nothing about the seders, but I am done for. I sit through the dress rehearsals of *Si Si, Señorita,* a show I know almost by heart, but I miss the performances. Peter afterward tells me that a couple of my jokes got good laughs.

Yet sometimes it is better not to win a fight. In the end, Mom loses more than she gains.

My slide from Jewish observance, as the reader will surmise, is now well along. Joining Tau Alpha has really greased the skids. We eat lunch every day at the house. I ask no questions about the lamb chops and pot roasts and stews which a black butler serves us. One day as we are finishing the meal, Peter Quat, who handles our finances, inquires, "By the way, does anybody here object to eating ham?"

"I do," I exclaim. I may be a long way from worrying about the horse glue in Coca-Cola bottle tops, but I have never touched pork products.

"Well, you've just eaten it," says Quat, raising a merry laugh among my Jewish brethren. I stare at the remnants on my plate of the peculiarly pink corned beef I thought I was having. The scene ends right there in my memory, so I won't embellish it. Maybe that is what inspires Peter's ham jokes in *Si Si, Señorita.* So far as I know, I'm not served pig again at Tau Alpha, and I go on eating there.

Now I trust that my non-Jewish readers know of another Mosaic food edict, the prohibition of leavened bread on Passover — a rule more honored in the breach than in the observance, perhaps, by some of their Jewish friends, yet a stern decree of our ancient law, actually stricter than the ban on pork. It's the point of what comes next. The first seder passes off well enough, but the second is a bust. Mom has invited the Brodofskys, all six of them. Added to our growing Mishpokha, they jam Zaideh's small flat to gridlock. There is a shortage of prayer books. Zaideh's tranquil voice is drowned out in the din from the women in the kitchen, and the chatter of bored youngsters without books. Pop and I keep up with the limping service, nobody else. By custom I sit on Zaideh's right hand at seders, and for years I have made him happy by disputing fine points of the haggada text with him. Tonight I just mumble grumpily in Hebrew. My grandfather bears on in good spirits, all the same.

The big trouble comes at mealtime. Bobbeh's matzoh balls, her annual occasion for praise and applause, turn out stony. They are really no more edible than biiliard balls. The scoffers' section, presided over by Cousin Harold, fires off a stream of matzoh-ball jokes. We are all convulsed, until Bobbeh turns blue and begins to cry. A frantic uproar to comfort her ensues, and during this crisis the food gets cold. Anyway, there isn't enough to go around. Mama heaps up the Brodofsky plates; never let it be said the Brodofskys went hungry at a Goodkind meal! Young Goodkinds fare poorly.

The upshot is that Cousin Harold and I worm out of the jammed flat to take a walk; both ravenous, and I for once as full of heretical scorn as Cousin Harold. He proposes that we get ourselves hot dogs, and I am all for it. At a kosher delicatessen, we buy frankfurters on rolls. If a religious sophisticate breaks in here to ask how come a kosher place would serve leavened rolls on Passover, he doesn't know what a mess Bronx Jewish mores were then. We are devouring the dogs, when out of the washroom in back comes nobody but Felix Brodofsky, fatter than ever. "Well, whaddya know! Davey Goodkind eating bread on Passover! What will Grandpa say?" He leaves, leering, to return to the seder. So the jig is up, the fix is in. The Brodofskys will rub Mom and Pop's nose in this scandal, until they will wish they had never had a Yisroelke in the first place.

Cousin Harold, of course, is unperturbed. Wolfing another hot dog on the way back to Zaideh's flat, Cousin Harold explains that the Jewish religion is mere primitive nonsense. He urges me to read H. L. Mencken's *Twilight of the Gods*. H. L. Mencken proves that all religion is nothing but mankind's fear of the unknown, institutionalized as propitiatory magic, and perpetuated as a fat racket for priests. Cousin Harold is now a freshman at City College, majoring in psychology. But his real major these days, to hear him tell it, is fornication. Cousin Harold's tales of his conquests are long and lurid, going into explicit details of contraception, positions, the cries of the females, oral variations, and so on, in a manner remarkably anticipating Peter Quat's artistic breakthrough years later. It is a pity that Cousin Harold has no literary gift, and anyway is ahead of his time.

In point of fact, I never hear another word about the hot dogs. Did Brodofsky tell Pop? I get no hint of it. Pop has seen me go off to football games on Saturday. He has heard, in the way I argue about religion with Mom, abrasive echoes of my Columbia education. He himself was a rebel of sorts, a fiery young socialist who came back by degrees to his shammas father's religion. If Brodofsky did say anything, I'm sure Pop shrugged it off with a sad smile.

America!

But the thing eats at me. Not so much the incident in itself, as the whole snowballing oppressiveness of the religion. At every turn the faith is beginning to nag at my conscience, conflict with my schedule, and clash with my changing views. In my comparative religion course I have been taught that the Torah is a patchwork of several documents of different eras and regions — J, E, P, D, and whatnot — which if true makes a joke of the Talmud's minute analysis of the Torah as one seamless Mosaic unity. All religions, I now gather, are really a special sort of folkloristic literature. Whether you are a Christian or a Buddhist or a Jew or a Hindu simply depends on when and where you were born, not on the intrinsic content of this or that faith. Our comparative religion professor, a naturalized former Englishman named Dr. Vyvyan Finkel, vaguely Jewish, an amusing lecturer and a very tough marker, is clearly above being taken in by any of these naive myths — including, of course, Judaism — but thinks them all worth study, like the bones of dinosaurs.

My readings in philosophy, which Dr. Finkel also teaches, have further eroded the ground of faith. And a psychology course, in which we've spent a couple of weeks on the psychopathology of religious experience — that is, the study of nuts who think God talks to them — has cast something of a shadow on figures like Abraham and Isaiah.

In short I am becoming an atheist. I have read H. L. Mencken's *Twilight of the Gods*. Great stuff. Why should an atheist who has read Mencken feel guilty about eating a frankfurter on a roll on Passover? Preposterous.

43

I Rebel

THE holiday we call Shavuos (Pentecost) — which follows Passover by seven weeks — falls smack during the final exam period. In freshman year, by luck of the shifting Jewish moon calendar, I escaped that problem. Now I have three finals on the two days of Shavuos, when observant Jews don't write. In public school and high school, where there were so many Jews, the administrators avoided such conflicts. At Columbia the matter promises to be awkward. I have to appeal to each department head for a special test on another day. Logically, a man who rides to football games on the Sabbath should take exams on Shavuos without a qualm, but a collapsing religious commitment is not a matter of logic; it is a mishmash of pretenses, evasions, embarrassments, and inconsistencies. With these, I am fed up.

Final exams are a week away when I hear that all applicants for special tests are being turned down. One rabbi's son is appealing to the university's board of trustees. Monroe Biberman, of all people, approaches me with a petition to the dean. He is more religious, or more subservient to his parents, than I imagined. Maybe it's because of Monroe that I mulishly refuse to sign; and I ride home on the subway that evening seething with resolve to have this issue out.

Off at a Zionist meeting, Pop doesn't get home for supper. I do my homework, trying hard to keep myself at a boil. I have to stage this showdown tonight. I have built up the steam of righteous indignation which will carry me through; I may have trouble generating it again. By the time I manage to confront my parents, they are both in bed. Propped up on thick pillows, Pop is reading the Book of Psalms. That is how he goes to sleep, sitting up. Otherwise he has some trouble breathing. He is working through the Hebrew text with the commentaries, and has told me that he finds it full of marvels.

Well, I let them have it: a stark brutish summary of what human existence is all about, the real truth of the matter, displacing once for all the hoary and hobbling Jewish ideas drummed into me from childhood. Man is an animal, I inform them, like other animals. As for the soul, nothing exists of a person's consciousness or identity except what is inside his skull. The universe is a vast machine operating by natural laws. There is no heaven or hell, therefore, and no white-bearded God up there to keep track of our sins and our good deeds. We live and after a while we die, like the dogs and the pigs. There is nothing after death. Dead men are just machines that have stopped. That's the end of them.

Pop sits there listening, his head resting back on the pillows, his eyes brightly fixed on me; not angry, not even visibly upset. He has closed the Bible, and holds it loosely in his pale hands. I pause for breath. Having laid down the general principles of my newly liberated viewpoint, I am about to launch my bombshell announcement that, in the light of these advanced ideas, I intend to take my finals on Shavuos.

"So the universe is just a machine. People are just machines," Pop says, nodding. "But who put together the machines, Yisroelke?"

"Oh, that's the old argument from design, Pop," I say, trying not to sound too condescending. "It's fallacious. It was exploded long ago by Immanuel Kant."

"Why do you keep rolling your sleeves up and down?" Mama says. "You look so stupid."

I've been thinking how remarkably suave and self-possessed I am being in this crisis, but I guess I'm a bit nervous at that. It has taken the form of constantly rolling up and unrolling my shirt sleeves as I expound my new philosophy. I let go of the sleeve I'm about to roll up. I now have one sleeve up and one down.

"Immanuel Kant. Kant is a German philosopher," says Pop, "like Hegel. Isn't he? Karl Marx was a student of Hegel. Karl Marx said he stood Hegel on his head."

"That's right," I say, surprised at this scrap of erudition, retained no doubt from Pop's socialist days. "And Kant exploded the argument from design for good, Pop."

"He did? How?" Pop inquires with genuine curiosity.

I can feel my head of moral steam dissipating in these irrelevancies. I say sternly, "We can talk about that another time, Pop. There's something much more important to discuss —"

Mama says, "Roll both sleeves up or both sleeves down. Don't leave them like that. It looks funny."

"Mom, never mind my sleeves," I exclaim, a trifle irritably, "I'm not going anywhere, for God's sake!"

But I resume rolling up the down sleeve with jerky haste, so as to squelch her interruptions. "The point I'm making is, I have three exams on Shavuos. Maybe I can get them postponed, maybe not. They're very tough about such things at Columbia. But my *point* is, I don't want to get them postponed. I don't believe in all that any more."

My point sinks in. Mom and Pop look at each other with sober eyes. Pop asks, very tentatively, "What time are the exams? Can you go to shule first?"

"Impossible! Anyway, what kind of a hypocrite would I be, Pop, going to shule and then writing exam papers?"

"Now you're making crazy faces and rolling your eyes," says Mama. "Where did you pick up those habits, anyway? Does everybody roll their eyes and make crazy faces at Columbia?"

"Mom, I'm talking about something terribly serious, and you keep interrupting. It's not fair. I want you to understand me!"

"What's so hard to understand? You intend to take your exams on Shavuos," says Mom, "because you don't want to bother your Columbia professors to give you the tests another day. Is that it? Do I understand, or don't I?"

"No, you don't. Not in the least. It isn't that I don't want to bother my professors. It's a matter of *principle*. If you'd only listen to me for once —"

"Now you're rolling your sleeves *and* your eyes," Mama says. "What's the matter with you? Who can listen to you when you act like such a fool?"

I consider stamping out of the room in a rage. I know I imitate Peter Quat, but at the moment I can't help it. I shake my head and grind my teeth, utterly stymied.

My father says, "Well, you can come to shule the night before, at least, can't you, Yisroelke? You don't want to forget that it's Shavuos, altogether."

According to my new philosophy I shouldn't agree to attend the holiday eve service either. Still, my father is being a startling gent about this thing. I decide to meet him halfway, and H. L. Mencken can take a turn or two in his grave. I have the rest of my life to be a consistent atheist.

"Sure, Pop," I say. "We'll go together."

"Good luck on your exams," he says, opening his Bible. "But if you can still get them postponed, Yisroelke, by all means do that."

"You don't understand him at all," says Mom. "He has no soul, and we're just animals, and there's no God, so he doesn't have to tell the professors he's a Jewish boy who won't write on Shavuos."

Pop gives me a melancholy little smile, showing gaps in his teeth. "I understand him," he says, and resumes reading the Book of Psalms. I return to my room, scarcely believing that the great rebellion has come off so easily.

Next morning, as I open my eyes, the recollection floods over me. Free! What a relief! Old Mom, though she missed the main philo-sophical point, cut pretty close to the bone, at that, in her fashion. I have dreaded talking to my Columbia professors about Shavuos. After all, I am the Vicomte de Brag, the sophisticated wit, the campus ce-lebrity. Dr. Finkel himself has quoted my poems in his lectures, with many a puckish glance at me. My cadaverous English instructor, a Mr. Ludd, has read a rondeau of mine aloud in class, and then in-vited me into his office for tea and cookies; where, when I mention I am reading *Twilight of the Gods,* he lights up like a Times Square sign and says that book is his Bible. My psychology professor clearly holds that religion is a mild variety of mental disorder. These are not men to whom the Vicomte de Brag wants to go sniveling that he doesn't write on Shavuos.

But now that nightmare has passed away! So I am thinking, as I dress to go to school. What to wear on this happy day — the purple, the bar-mitzva gray, or the nondescript herringbone that Michaels sold me when I went to Canal Street by myself? Mama thinks the her-ringbone suit is disgusting, and the price I paid sheer robbery. She is all for getting Morris Elfenbein to make Michaels take it back; so naturally I have sworn that I love the garment, and that nobody is wearing anything at Columbia this year but suits exactly like this one: loose-hanging double-breasted herringbones, with collars that fall widely away from the neck, and sleeves that cover the knuckles. In truth I am ashamed of the herringbone. I wear it only on rainy days, or for my *Spectator* night-editor vigils.

I decide on the gray. I don shirt, gray trousers, striped tie. I'm standing at a full-length mirror, and it occurs to me, in my antic liberated mood, to put on the purple jacket, the sleeves of which have been lengthened more than once. I do it. *Wow! My God!* Stroke of genius! Jacket and pants that don't match; *at last* I have captured the collegiate look! In another inspired flash, I take my new brown synagogue-going hat bought for Passover, pinch it into a triangle the way Mark Herz does, and set it on the back of my head. Amazing! Perfect! Yisroelke is gone! Vanished! And there before me in the looking glass stands the Columbia big-man-on-campus, the Vicomte de Brag, at all points an absolute Deke! Well, not quite. Dekes wear dirty white shoes, and I have on my old shiny brown wingtips. A mere detail. I will immediately buy white shoes and dirty them up. The main thing is the stunning collegiate effect of the purple suit jacket, the gray suit pants, and the triangulated synagogue hat. A Deke, a Deke, I tell you, a palpable collegiate smoothie Deke! Yisroelke, thou art translated!

I emerge from the subway at the Columbia campus on a bright May morning in a daze of euphoric glory, on a crest of ineffable elation at belonging, at having arrived, at having crashed the last barrier between the Inside and the Outside, made myself over, taken on the total protective mimicry of a Deke. I go straight to the *Jester* office that morning. The May issue, due from the printer, contains four of my articles. With the defection of Peter Quat, I have become the workhorse producer of copy. Bob Greaves, a Deke in my class who draws cartoons, is there in the office. Without a doubt, he will become the editor in our senior year. Now Bob Greaves is not just a Deke, he is the ultimate Deke. Perfect! The very man on whom to test out my disguise — I mean, my new collegiate look.

"Hi, Bob," I say with true Deke nonchalance, lighting a Spud.

"Oh — hello, there," says Bob Greaves. He stares hard at me, raises one eyebrow high, glances at his watch, and lounges out of the office. A bit cast down, I open the coat-closet in the office to have another look at myself in a mirror.

Horrors.

Do I resemble Bob Greaves, in his heather tweed jacket, wool tie, flannel trousers, dirty white shoes, and pinched triangle hat? It is to laugh. My gray Canal Street pants are wide, floppy, and shiny-hard, not soft, narrow, and tapering, like Bob's flannels. My synagogue-going hat is enormous, gigantic, and a terrible bright reddish-brown color; Bob's hat, like Mark Herz's, is small, old, olive-brown, and sweat-stained, with a small hole at the peak of the pinch. I can poke a hole in this colossal glaringly new hat, but that won't help. Nothing will. It is just all wrong.

It is not nearly as wrong, however, as the purple jacket. No doubt this jacket has looked ill-proportioned on me for years, with those repeatedly lengthened sleeves; but set against the gray pants — no wonder Bob Greaves raised an eyebrow and left! Probably he barely made it out into the fourth-floor corridor before falling down in a laughing fit. What a sight! A jacket barely covering my navel, with those extended purple gorilla arms hanging way down! It is a sad moment of truth that I experience, alone there in the *Jester* office, a hard nasty fall out of the clouds. But ah, that brief illusion, that gloriously idiotic hour or two of my apotheosis, in gray pants and purple jacket, as a Deke smoothie!

I experience another moment of truth, on the morning of the first day of Shavuos in the Columbia gym, where rows of seats fill the floor of the basketball court. Proctors patrol the aisles, passing out to hundreds of students the mimeographed questions and the blue booklets for the answers. My first exam is in psychology. I glance over the questions. Not too tough, but the writing will take the full three hours.

I have never yet written a word on a Sabbath or a religious holiday. Has Monroe Biberman? I don't know. We have exchanged hangdog looks, on encountering each other coming into the gym, but we haven't spoken. He sits a few seats from me. I glance over at him. He is already busily writing, head down. Well, here goes! The blue-book cover has the usual lines to be filled in with name, class, and course. I unscrew my fountain pen, and after a slight hesitation, I write

I. David Goodkind '34

It seems to me, as I do so, that something invisible is breaking, something like a glass wall, breaking noiselessly, with the faint whisper of the pen.

And that is the true end of Yisroelke. He is really gone this time. I am by no means a Deke, but I am irreversibly I. David Goodkind, the Vicomte de Brag.

* * *

44

Dorsi Sabin

E VER since I started on this book, I've been wavering about Dorsi Sabin, damn her soul. Put her in? Leave her out? I'm blazing along here through some forty years, after all, from the start of Mama's tale in Minsk around 1900, to the end of my saga in April House at Pearl Harbor. What does Dorsi Sabin have to contribute? Why not leave her in the plushy Scarsdale oblivion into which she sank, way back in 1934, never to be seen or heard from again?

So I was thinking at ten o'clock this morning, here in my lugubrious lair in the Executive Office Building, wondering how to proceed with *April House* for want of something more sane to do, when my secretary buzzed. "Mr. Goodkind, do you know a Mrs. Pell? Mrs. Morris Pell of Scarsdale, New York?" Well, I want to tell you, it was frightening. My hair prickled. I wouldn't call myself superstitious, but I do believe in signs. I couldn't invent a thing like Dorsi's showing up this morning, it would be too farfetched. It settled the matter. Dorsi is in; and once I saw her I realized why. Talk about serendipity! Dorsi was crucial.

The Pells were visiting Washington, and had tickets for the White House tour. It was Morris, not Dorsi, who came on the line, sounding hearty, friendly, and wealthy. He said Dorsi was too shy to talk to me herself. Well, of course I said never mind the tour tickets, come along. I showed them around, and then brought them to my office. It's an imposing room — high ceilings, old-style moldings, huge mahogany bookcases — and it fostered their illusion that I was a statesman of consequence. Dorsi saw this pile of manuscript and asked about it. When I said I was writing a book in my spare time, she batted those unforgettable eyes at me and murmured, "You always did accomplish a lot, David, didn't you?"

Altogether, I had a sweet time of it with the Pells today, and with their unmarried daughter, whom they call "Daughter." I couldn't make that up, now, could I? That is exactly how Dorsi addressed the dour silent sallow woman of thirty or so who came with them. *"Daughter!"* Dorsi herself astounded me. She is a year older than I am, fifty-nine. Her eyes are wrinkled and the skin of her neck is crepey. But her black hair is only touched with gray, her face has held its heart shape and its strawberries-and-cream color, and her slim hips sway yet in that same intoxicating way when she walks.

Dorsi dressed for the occasion in a smart little flowered silk nothing that showed every well-preserved soft curve. Old beauties can't help, I guess, wanting to devastate old admirers. Her perky white straw hat was tied with a fluffy chiffon scarf under her chin, which took care of the turkey-neck problem. And with those big dark blue eyes flashing at me as always, why, I hardly noticed the crow's-feet after the first shock. Remember, I hadn't seen Dorsi Sabin in almost forty years. The effect was something out of Hollywood, a young charmer dissolving in an instant, through the trickery of makeup and film, into an old lady. Only, the trickster here was Time.

I took them to lunch at the White House mess. They were in luck. Both the President's daughters were there, and the Secretary of Defense came over and said hello. Were the Pells ever impressed! They regard me as the big celebrity in their life, that's obvious. They must really be out of it, in that costly Siberia called Scarsdale. Dorsi said that she couldn't imagine how Morris had mustered up the nerve to call me. She herself would never have *dared*.

She told me how she had kept clippings of the obscenity trials, and of all references to me in articles about the White House staff. How proud she was, she said, tinkling on and on in that unchanged voice like crystal chimes, to see my picture in *Time* (in that full page of White House assistant nobodies). Morris Pell beamed at her during all this, while Daughter stared around, eating nothing. I felt sorry for Daughter, and I understood her, too. She had given up early in the contest with Dorsi Sabin, and was just waiting to die, more or less.

Morris Pell wanted to take pictures, so we went out to the sunny rose garden. "Closer, get closer," he kept urging, the Leica to his eye, as Dorsi and I stood beside a blooming rosebush. Click, snap, click.

"Come on, *real* close now." Dorsi was keeping her distance; something at which, in all my experience, she never had a peer. At last, with a sidelong upward glance at me she moved nearer. Instead of roses I smelled Dorsi Sabin. Is it possible? I thought her hair still smelled the same.

"Can't you get any closer?" asked Morris plaintively, squinting through the sighter.

Dorsi gave me another look, and moved right up against me.

"Great! *Great!* That's it! Hold that!" Click, snap, click, snap.

Daughter was watching the pair of us sourly. It was she who looked fifty-nine years old.

Ah, Dorsi, Dorsi Sabin! That soft side pressed to mine, those eyes glancing slantwise and upward at me with an erotic gleam, for the first time ever! Forty years too late, and no more serious now than she ever was. Still playing games with the Big Man on Campus. Ah, Dorsi, Dorsi Sabin, damn your soul.

"One more, now. Close! Close as you can get!"

Close enough, thank you, Morris Pelkowitz.

For that was his name, you understand, when I heard the shattering news that Dorsi Sabin was getting married. *To whom, for God's sake?* Why, to that banker's son from Woodmere; that Beta Sig on *Law Review*, the tall fat one, Morris Pelkowitz. Of course, in retrospect the mighty events of the time reduce that calamity to a flyspeck. That is why I almost left Dorsi out. And that is why history is a cheat, and memoirs verge on fraud. Perspective lies. Dorsi Sabin outweighed and dwarfed the election of Franklin D. Roosevelt, the repeal of Prohibition, the worldwide economic collapse, the start of the New Deal, and Adolf Hitler's leap to the chancellorship of Germany.

*   *   *

At the end of the Yisroelke era, I firmly believed that success as a womanizer was measured by a single official yardstick. I entered my junior year at Columbia College without having successfully measured up, even once. That is why I have to say I got off to a wobbly start as a womanizer. I refer, of course, to fooling with a girl's thorax.

Meantime Cousin Harold was claiming a weary worn-out expertise in actual copulation, and in variations which left Lady Chatterley's lover at the post. Cousin Harold gave the impression that he hadn't bothered with mere breasts in years. At Townsend Harris there had been much bragging about bodice gropings, and more advanced intrusions under skirts; while I sat mute, my imagination overheated and my ego steamrollered. This sort of talk went on in college, too. Yet in my junior year I still had nothing to report. I was sitting in Comparative Religion, dreamily filling page after page of my notebook with drawings of Bernice Lavine's left bosom, while Professor Finkel expounded the views of Saint John of the Cross.

I have wondered much about my early retardation. My slow physical maturing, together with my being younger than my classmates, may partly account for it; but the real cause may have been a gift I uncovered back at Camp Maccabee. Uncle Sam, the dramatics counsellor in whose bunk I slept, once overheard me telling "The Monkey's Paw" in the dark after taps to my bunkmates. He made me get dressed at once and come to a party the counsellors were having in the girls' infirmary, where there were many beds but no patients, the doctor having quit or been fired. Uncle Sam introduced me as this wonderful teller of ghost stories. They turned out the lights, and I narrated "The Monkey's Paw," if I do say so, in a very scary fashion, judging by the sudden groans and gasps I kept hearing in the dark, and the creaking of the beds and twanging of the bedsprings, as my listeners quaked and shuddered at the frightening turns of the story. For the rest of the season I was in enormous demand at Camp Maccabee parties as a matchless teller of ghost yarns.

This reputation outlasted the summer, and spread all over the Bronx. I was deluged with invitations to parties, more than I could handle, and I went on telling these stories in the dark with great pride. I was somewhat obtuse about this popularity of mine at parties, I daresay. "Go ahead, kid," a hoarse voice would groan in the dark, when I finished a story, "Tell us another one." And I would oblige. All around me at these parties, while I declaimed "The Fall of the House of Usher" or "The Mezzotint," I would hear hard breathing, and nervous giggles, and little shrieks, and moans, and strange shufflings and slurpings, and squeaks of furniture, sometimes going on for hours, and I ascribed all that to the effect of my spine-chilling dramatic talents. It was at such parties that other fellows gained their expertise at groping, I maintain, while I polished up my renditions of "The Telltale Heart" and "The Monkey's Paw."

It will do as a theory, anyway. Mind you, I am not claiming that

I never tried, before my seventeenth year, to make a pass at a girl's chest. But the few dismal times I tried, mainly because I felt my manhood required it, the girl would knock my hand away with a snort, a growl, or a giggle, and so far as I was concerned, that would be that. Basically I was on the girl's side. I didn't think I had any business grabbing at her charms, as the Victorians put it. You are now in a position to understand, if not exactly to sympathize with, the great womanizer, Davey Goodkind, when he encountered his fate — installment number one — in Dorsi Sabin. We first met in my junior year, which even aside from Dorsi, was a jazzy year for me.

THE VICOMTE DE BRAG TRIUMPHANT! Editor of "Off-hour," assistant managing editor of *Jester,* author of a script submitted for the Varsity Show; and what is more, I could now look Monroe Biberman in the eye. I mean that literally. I had grown fully as tall as the pimpled giant who, at the freshmen placement tests, had bellowed down at me from a terrible height, "Iggy! What are *you* doing here?" His pimples were fading, and mine were just coming on, bloodily interfering with my daily shave.

Monroe too was strangely fading. He had dropped out of Beta Sigma Rho, and taken up with a solemn literary crowd, which put out an avant-garde magazine, *The New Broom,* full of opaque ravings in the vein of James Joyce, T. S. Eliot, and Ezra Pound. But Biberman wasn't writing much for *The New Broom,* having fallen besottedly in love with the plump Barnard president of the Jewish Students Society, called — believe it or not, I don't care, it's true — "Puss Puss" Ohlbaum. He had lost interest in his studies. We were both in a seminar on the World's Great Books, where he sat sucking at his pipe, wearing a deep *New Broom* frown, and evidently thinking not of Sophocles or Spinoza, but of Puss Puss Ohlbaum; for when called on, Biberman would offer vague general utterances, sprinkled with terms like architectonic, chiliastic, teleological, and antinomian. Columbia professors, alas, are world authorities on bullshit, and in the end Monroe never graduated; like an old soldier, he just faded away.

But if you're curious about what became of him I can tell you, because by chance I did find out. Monroe Biberman teaches Hebrew in Los Angeles. I haven't slipped a cog, and I'm not talking about my Uncle Velvel, but about Biberman. How do I know? Well, a few years ago, I was in Hollywood negotiating a film deal with Warner Brothers for *The Smelly Melamed.* It had just created a sensation in *The New Yorker,* and Peter Quat was all the rage again, and Warners had an idea of doing it with Zero Mostel; that is, until Mostel read the thing and called Jack Warner to his face a moronic asshole, and the deal fell through. It was an embarrassing moment. I was right there. Jack Warner's face turned plum-purple, and he ordered Mostel out of his office. Zero tilted his hat over one eye, danced a hilarious off-to-Buffalo exit through the door, and that was that. A pity; what a great clown! Nobody but Zero could have played Shraga Glutz; it was no role for Henry Fonda, let us say.

The anniversary of Pop's death occurred just then, so I went into a temple near my hotel to say kaddish; and damned if I didn't come on Monroe Biberman, stout and gray, smoking a pipe in the lobby. We recognized each other straight off. "Iggy!" he greeted me. "What are *you* doing here?" He told me that he was the principal of the temple's Hebrew school, that Puss Puss (he still called her that) was fine, and that they had four kids. He couldn't stop to talk much, because he was late for a bridge game. Exit Biberman, fading into the smog of Los Angeles, and of lost time.

It was Biberman who mentioned to me one day that a staggeringly pretty girl named Dorsi Sabin was showing up at the Thursday tea dances of the Jewish Students Society. But the word on this Sabin girl was discouraging. On a recent date some guy had made a pass at her, and she had clobbered him in the face with her pocketbook, breaking his glasses, and temporarily blinding him in one eye. So fellows danced with her, but were not asking her out much. Biberman had seen the pocketbook in question, heavy brown leather studded with copper. A menace. Still, she was a mighty fetching creature.

Now I had given up on those Thursday tea dances. The girls you found there tended to be stodgy and bulgy. Puss Puss Ohlbaum was the best of the lot, and she needed to shed twenty pounds. This Sabin girl must indeed be getting desperate, I thought, to be going to the tea dances. I had another girl on my mind, and I forgot about the purse-wielding iceberg.

This other girl was named Delphine Dowling. That's right, a Christian. I had never gone near her, let alone spoken to her. She and I sat in the same row in Music Appreciation class. When we passed

in our first quiz papers, I caught a glimpse of the name, Delphine
Dowling. What a cool neat gentile handwriting! And what a name!
How it matched this dazzler with a snub nose, black hair, big blue
eyes, silken skin, cupid's-bow red lips! The Irish colleen incarnate, very
reserved, no eye for the boys. One day after class, I was standing close
enough in the elevator to Delphine Dowling to touch her, and wishing I could, when another girl said to her, "Dorsi, can you lend me
your Psych notes?" Delphine Dowling responded with a voice like
heavenly chimes, "Certainly, Ann," and she handed this girl a notebook on which I could see, in Delphine's handwriting,

Dorothy Sabin, Psychology 304

Great balls of fire! Delphine Dowling was *Dorsi Sabin!* A bizarre case
of mistaken identity! Then she was *Jewish,* and all I had to do, to
hold this black-haired angel in my arms, was go to a tea dance! It
was a breathtaking surprise. As for the real Delphine Dowling, I never
found out what she looked like. From that moment I was a poleaxed
man, waiting for Thursday.

"So! You're the Vicomte de Brag," said Dorsi Sabin with an arch
upward look, as we danced.

"Uh, yes. How do you know?"

"Oh, I know. I knew the first day of music class. Somebody pointed
you out."

Dorsi was a bit hard to lead, perhaps because of the distance between us. In those days, my idea of hot sex was a snuggle on the
dance floor; but a small pony could have trotted between me and
Dorsi without upsetting us. She stood away from me, in her reserved
way, and I stood away from her, to show how different I was from
all those coarse kissers and snugglers and thorax feelers. I was steer-
ing Dorsi Sabin at stiff arm's length, like a nervous student driver.

"How do you think up all those things you write?" That voice again,
Scarlatti on harp strings. "They're so clever. Especially the poems."

Anybody could please me by praising the Vicomte de Brag. But to
have this homage from the most beautiful girl I had ever laid eyes
on, the girl I'd been worshipping for weeks as Delphine Dowling! I
blurted, "There'll be a poem to you in my next column."

She blushed. That rise of pink in her face, and a blastingly sweet look from her wide eyes, made my poor womanizing head swim. "To *me?* But you don't know me."

"Dorsi, let me take you home."

A slow careful blink up at me. A slow careful smile. "All . . . right."

It began as it went on to the last: with a long subway ride to the Grand Concourse in the West Bronx, and then a lonely ride back home. We stood hanging to straps in the roaring train until the crowd thinned, then we sat down side by side. Later on, when I got to know Dorsi better, we would shout in each other's ears, but this first time we were quiet. In fact, Dorsi tranquilly opened her psychology textbook and did some homework. Was I annoyed or put down? Not in the least. Just to be near that girl was perfect joy.

For a month or so our dates were magical. Unless I was out of my mind, the unmeltable Dorsi Sabin was warming to the Vicomte de Brag! Poem after poem to "D.S." was coming out in "Off-hour." When I would arrive at the music class on such mornings, Dorsi's eyes would gleam at me, and she would give me a secret little smile which, in my fevered state, was sheer pillow talk. When we were out on a date she bubbled. When I called her up her voice lifted. She never refused a date.

I can't imagine what we talked about in our hours together, for Dorsi was a plodding, studious sort, inside that blinding envelope of Venus flesh. I only know that there were never enough of those golden hours for me. I lived a whole other life of campus activity. I worked hard at my writing and my courses. I kept revising *To Heil with It!* I saw quite a bit of Herz and Quat, who had graduated, but all that was like sleepwalking, compared to the hours I spent with Dorsi Sabin.

Then we crashed into a stone wall — and of all places, at April House.

Ah, Dorsi! "Forever wilt thou love, and she be fair," the poet promises, and so it is. Though the shards of memory have lain buried under the detritus of forty years, when I dig them out and glue the pieces together, behold, there the two of us are again — Dorsi eternally in coy flight, just out of reach, and I everlastingly in pursuit of her, across the thousand cracks in the Grecian urn. In prosy fact, of course, Dorsi Sabin aged into the well-preserved old Mrs. Morris Pell in the white hat and chiffon scarf whom you have just seen. But in my mind's eye she is forever young, forever fair, and forever Delphine Dowling — damn her soul.

* * *

45

General Lev

September 1973

Now General Moshe Lev is here, and I have just taken *him* to the White House mess. That's the juicy part of the privilege, getting to bring guests there. Lev telephoned me from the Israeli embassy, and said he wanted to talk to me about Sandra, so I invited him to lunch. Lev was not as bowled over as the Pells. He found himself elbow to elbow with the Vice President at the next table, and he murmured to me, with a narrow side-glance, "That's him?"

"That's him."

His little headshake expressed eloquently how military men feel about most politicians. The Vice President was chatting cheerily, now and then laughing out loud, blithe as a skylark. A short week or two ago this man was a heartbeat away, as the newspapers love to put it, from the most powerful political office on earth, and from command of the world's most awesome air force, armed with enough hydrogen bombs to wipe out the human race; and there he sat, skidding out of office for taking petty bribes, with every prospect of landing in the penitentiary. His color was good, his laugh genuine, his bearing altogether jocund. The President looks much worse. Maybe once things are hopeless a man can laugh again; it is clinging to an eroding hope that sickens the soul.

It's quite a perquisite, at that, the use of the White House mess. The navy runs it, so it's a smart and tidy eating place. Its main function, however, is to feed not stomachs but egos. The White House staff can be divided roughly into those who have mess privileges and those who don't. Those who don't are employees, menials, ciphers, who keep their egos inflated to working pressure by casually telling people, "Give me a ring at the White House." Those who have access to the mess may be nobodies too, like me; but the excluded nobodies make us feel like somebodies.

The mess privilege was granted to me a few days after I got back from Israel, a spin-off of my surprising new intimacy with the President. I do very little honest work here otherwise these days. Arts-and-culture liaison has been languishing, since artists and cultured folks are avoiding the Executive Mansion like a cancer ward; and he makes few speeches, as he hunkers down to try to survive the typhoon howling over his head. At the moment, besides the nasty exposé of the Vice President, he is sweating out the wait for a court decision on the tapes. I am *not* writing about Watergate here, I am keeping that historic insanity out of these pages with great exertions of will-power. I am simply placing in time the strange development that has made me a confidant of the President.

This new status began, as I say, with my return from Israel, and it caused a bit of marital infelicity for a while. Jan and I jogtrot along in harness amiably through the days and nights, but lately I've been getting an acerb needle whenever I venture an affectionate pass at her; thus, "Are you sure, dear, that you won't be hearing from the President?" The night I got back, you see, she welcomed me with unusual demonstrativeness, for her; we opened a bottle of champagne, and a warm connubial reunion was in clear appetizing sight, when the telephone rang. President's secretary: if I wasn't feeling too jet-lagged, could he see me right away? Well, off I went, leaving Jan in her lacy negligee with half a bottle of champagne. When I came home hours later she was fast asleep, or giving a brilliant imitation of it. I clattered and thumped around, hoping to rouse her and collect that sweet reunion. No soap.

The President was impatient, you see, for Golda Meir's reply. "Amazing woman," he said, nodding gravely at the verbal message. "More balls than most men around here." He asked how my mother was. My description of our meeting at the airport really tickled him. "Sounds like my own mom," he said. "They don't come like that any more. Real moxie." He was sitting in a small air-conditioned room, with a fire going in the fireplace. That's one of his many peculiarities. He loves to sit and think by a fire in all seasons. If it's too warm for a fire — and it was above eighty outside, a heavy Washington summer night — he just refrigerates the place and has his fire anyway.

He began to reminisce about his mother. The inevitable clipboard with the yellow legal pad, on which he marshals his ideas, was turned down on his lap. He seemed to be warding off with chitchat the reality that glared from those yellow pages. He talked and talked, and we had a few drinks. Color returned to his wan face. His filmy eyes took on life, and he rambled all over the place, loosening up as the time passed. About two o'clock he came around to the subject of Israel again. Between jet lag and the booze I was getting droopy, but he shocked me awake with some secret and disturbing things he said, about the way Eisenhower and Johnson behaved during Israel's wars. I can't go into any of that, but I have to note one paradox. Not only have the Jews never liked this man, never trusted him, never voted for him; throughout his career they have shown solid hostility to him, led by the journalists, the academics, and the famous writers and performers. This is one President who owes the Jews nothing. Yet unless I am more wrong than I have ever been on any subject, he is a friend such as we have not had in the White House since Truman.

Oh, yes, he can toss off phrases like "All those eastern Jews and intellectuals," which can jar you. He is a friend none the less. He thinks Israel and the Jews have "moxie." I'm not saying that he likes us, or that if realism dictated it, he wouldn't let Israel go down the drain. He is a wholly cold customer. Acts are what count, and his acts so far have been helpful. Jewish history, if not the chic Jewish set, judges rulers by what they do about Jews.

Since that night he has taken to summoning me at odd hours, just to sit around and talk. This must be the way he relaxes with those bizarre millionaire cronies who ride around with him on the Presidential yacht. And I'm handier. I'm right here in the White House, at his beck and call. He does not ask my advice on his crushing problems. In fact, we scarcely talk politics; I say "we," but he does the talking. I am a congenial, and he thinks a trustworthy, ear. "You can wear that, uh, *yarmulka* of yours," he once said to me as I was pouring refills for both of us, "if you feel more comfortable with it on." He was plainly pleased with himself for knowing the word.

My study of the Talmud really is what got to him. He as much as said so. He feels he has struck in me some kind of exotic paragon of integrity, probity, and discretion. Of course it is absolute hogwash, but there you are. I am just another Wall Street tax lawyer, as devious, scheming, and self-seeking as the rest. He is far too impressed by a Talmud volume and a skullcap. I have known Talmud experts who gossiped like washerwomen, and whom I wouldn't trust with my telephone number.

I've read that Hitler used to blither for hours every night to his entourage at Berchtesgaden, until they were collapsing from boredom. The President doesn't bore me, at least not yet. He has had an interesting life. He does get a bit soppy about his family, especially his mother and his daughters, but I am a family man myself. I can put up with that. If by chance, just by sitting and listening to him ramble, I relieve this strange, isolated, very withdrawn person of some of the pressure that's destroying him, well and good.

I feel no shred of affection for him. He does not invite affection, being so utterly knotted up and shut in on himself. Yet I more and more discern, as he opens up, a keen pragmatic intelligence, which only makes his ham-handed Watergate blundering all the more incredible. What fatal flaw nullified all the "moxie" which raised a penniless loner to the White House? So I often wonder, as he sits there by the fire in a refrigerated room, bending my ear for no earthly reason but to get his mind off the Philistine temple he has pulled down on himself, now falling, falling, falling in on top of him, in agonizing slow motion.

But about General Lev. He is a little man. He looks shorter than my sister Lee. To my knowledge they have not met since their romance forty years ago. Still, I can understand her taking to him.

The Herz family tree has branches in America, Israel, and South Africa. The Germans got the grandfather, his wife, and all of their children — there were eleven — except for three sons who emigrated, much against their father's will, back in the early twenties: one to Tel Aviv, one to Cape Town, and the third to New York. To that extent the family survives. Grandfather Herz had strongly objected to his sons' leaving Poland, fearing they might become less religious.

Like Mark, Moshe has a thatch of thick hair, but his is white, not grizzled. They don't look much alike. Tall as Mark is, and hale and wiry as he has kept himself, I suspect Lev could break him in half.

Past sixty, Moshe Lev looks poured out of pig iron. His manners are abrupt, like most Israeli army men's. He is mild in conversation unless it turns to military matters. Then you get clipped sentences of hard authority.

He told me a lot about himself in such clipped words. I knew he was one of the most rabid doves in Israel, advocating returning the Sinai to Egypt, and setting up a Palestinian state in the West Bank and the Gaza Strip. I didn't know much of his background. He was a fighter pilot in the 1948 War of Independence; far too old, but they weren't fussy then. He was a sport flyer when Lee knew him. During World War II he went to Rhodesia, volunteered for Britain's Royal Air Force, and flew in combat against the Germans. He walks with a slight limp, because in 1948 he had a leg maimed in the crash of a Spitfire. The machine was assembled from pieces of scrapped planes the British left behind in Palestine, and it wasn't very good. When the ever-trustworthy French suddenly stopped selling Mirage fighter planes to Israel — slapped on an embargo, just when the Egypt dictator, Nasser, mobilized and announced he would annihilate the Jewish State — the Israelis decided they had better build their own fighter plane, the celebrated Kfir, the "Young Lion." Lev was in on designing and producing the Kfir. And that is a quick rundown on General Moshe Lev.

I did not ask him what he was doing in Washington. He volunteered not a word. We talked a bit about Watergate, which, like most Israelis, he finds a puzzling tempest in a teapot. My prediction that the President would fall saddened him. "Who knows what kind of guy you'll get next?" he said, with another quick glance at the jolly man at his elbow. "He has been very good on your foreign policy, you know. Very shrewd."

"Invading Cambodia to capture rice bags?" I said, in suitable low tones. "Bombing civilians in Hanoi and Haiphong? Shrewd?"

"How do you stop a war you didn't start," inquired Moshe Lev, "when your people decide they're sick of it? And your enemy knows they've lost the will to fight? And you have half a million men to get safely off a continent ten thousand miles away? And thousands of prisoners to recover? And an ally right there on the ground who won't fight? It was a mess. He hadn't made the mess, but it needed drastic action, and he acted."

"I thought you were a dove," I said.

Moshe gave me a quizzical look. "That's a stupid newspaper expression."

"Maybe you should meet him," I said. "He can use a kind word."

"Him?" Lev shrugged. "Not him. He's a tough guy. Your daughter's not for him, you know. Mention his name, and she hisses and spits. If she had fur, it would stand up."

"Sandra holds nothing but strong opinions."

"Naturally. She's very Jewish."

An odd thing for him to say, I thought, considering Sandra's attitude toward Israel, her refusal to go to Hebrew school or to have a bat mitzva, and her bypassing of all the rules at home as soon as she was too big to be spanked. To give you an idea: for years Sandra has been eating on Yom Kippur. Says she won't be a hypocrite. Shades of Yisroelke rolling his sleeves up and down! Jan and I talked that out long ago and decided to do nothing about it; a sapient conclusion, since there was nothing we could do but lock the girl in a closet all Yom Kippur, or clamp a dog muzzle on her.

Moshe Lev seems fond of Sandra. His tone about her is amused and warm. When I met him at the kibbutz he remarked that at first sight Sandra had shocked him, she looked so much like my sister Lee. He did not refer to Lee again, but that one time there was a wistfully wicked glint in his eye. I will never know, of course, what went on forty years ago, but it must have been something.

"I tell you, though," he now said, turning somber, "if there's anything you can do about it, make her come home. And if you can't do that tell her to go to Jerusalem or Tel Aviv."

"She seems to like it at Fields of Peace."

"She has no combat training," Lev said. "These American volunteers are good for kitchen work and sorting oranges. That sort of thing. If there's trouble, they're in the way."

"Are you expecting trouble?"

He looked at me without words.

"Israel is sitting pretty," I went on uneasily. "At least that's my informed belief."

"It's the informed belief in Israel," said Moshe Lev very abruptly, "up to and including the Prime Minister and the Minister of Defense. Well, now I can tell my grandchildren I've eaten in the White

House. Thank you. I have to get back to the embassy. By the way, where did you say your sister lives?"

"Port Chester," I said.

"Port Chester. That's New York, isn't it?"

"New York, yes."

"Does she have grandchildren?"

"Three."

"I have four. Well, give her my best."

Oh, Lee, poor Lee! The glimmering glint in old General Lev's eye!

Yes, poor old widowed Lee! All knotted up with arthritis, all gray, smoking three or four packs a day of unfiltered Camels, living alone in that big house in Port Chester, except when Mom "drops in" for a few weeks or months, or her married sons turn up with their wives and their runabout progeny. God in heaven, how beautiful she was when she first met Moshe Lev! But oh, that series of catastrophic boy friends before that, all of whom I remember: how they looked, the way they danced, the way they held their cigarettes or pipes, the times I came on them smooching with her in a hallway, or on a sofa, or — well, never mind, never mind, it was all so goddamned long ago. Most of them must be dead. What a parade of schleppers, though; what a wringer Lee put herself through! But the master schlepper of all was Frank Feitelson. If not for Feitelson, Lee would not have met Moshe Lev, and we might never have made the grand and fateful move to Manhattan.

When Lee graduated from Hunter and Mom and Pop offered to send her abroad, surprise! She was no longer interested. After four years of trying to get this Frank Feitelson to marry her, she thought she had him boxed in. At first Feitelson had pleaded that he had to finish medical school; then, that an intern had no time for marriage; then, that he had to save up for an X-ray machine before he could open an office and support a wife. Unbeknownst to my parents, Lee had offered to take the money for her trip and buy Feitelson the X-ray machine. Ha! She was trying to corner a greased pig.

Mama knew a slippery shoat when she saw one. For years she had tried to convince Lee that Feitelson was not a desirable doctor-husband. At last, evading Lee's offer to buy the X-ray machine, Feitelson slid squealing through her clutches again, and so she sadly let herself be shoved aboard a boat to Europe. A year later, mind you, when Lee returned from her encounter with Moshe Lev, Dr. Feitelson came crawling to Lee, snivelling and grovelling, telephoning her at midnight and so on, and finally offered to marry her, even without her buying him an X-ray machine! Despite this magnificent concession, Lee told him to get lost, and must have enjoyed doing it.

Actually, a move to Manhattan was as yet hardly within Pop's means, though his income was up. He was still supporting Bobbeh, Zaideh, Uncle Yehuda, and Aunt Rivka. He also had to keep sending money to Uncle Velvel. Blights repeatedly hit Velvel's orange groves, and with each blight he would hint that maybe he should try growing oranges in California. Any serious suggestion that Uncle Velvel might leave Palestine was always good for a fast thousand from my father. So, though Mom for years had been yearning to move to Manhattan, Pop was still resisting the costly plunge.

Also, Pelham Parkway was a five-minute drive from the laundry, and Manhattan would take an hour. At forty or so, Pop was slowing down. I'd been in the car with him when he'd pull over to the side and park to catch his breath. When we walked to the synagogue on Saturday, he would halt often on the way. The doctors said the shortness of breath was due to his irregular habits, and lack of exercise and vacations. Pop was not quite as hot as he had been to ensconce Mama in Manhattan grandeur; not just yet, anyway. What changed his mind, swiftly and radically, was a letter from Uncle Velvel about my sister Lee.

Lee was never a good correspondent. Since her departure we had received one postcard from her in London, and another from Rome. She had been due in Palestine in November. Late in January Mom frantically cabled the American consul in Jerusalem to track her down. Back came a cable next day: AM WELL NEED MONEY LEE. So they sent her money, and heard nothing more until they got this letter from Velvel. Next thing I knew, they were apartment-hunting in Manhattan. Velvel had written them — I pieced this together from their anxious confabs in Russian — that Lee was involved with a married man. There was nothing they could do about it, six thousand miles away, but they made up their minds that when she returned, it would be to the best Jewish neighborhood in New York. Their beautiful but unlucky daughter would make a fresh start on Manhattan's West Side. No more Feitelsons!

One Sunday I went downtown with them, and was startled by the size, elegance, and opulence of the flats they were looking at. Good God, I thought, can Pop afford this? He appeared worried, too. But Mama bubbled. Times were bad, and these luxury apartments were going begging. There was a wrinkle in the lease called a "concession"; the landlord let the tenant in rent-free for the first few months. When Mom figured out the year's rental, why, it cost less to live on West End Avenue than in our Bronx apartment, at least the first year. Mama wasn't looking beyond that. These apartments hypnotized her.

As it happened, one of the flats we inspected was not only in Randy Davenport's building; it was the very apartment. Randy's mother opened the door a crack in the same one-eyed way, and let in the rental agent and us with a silent bleak air. There was no mistaking that stained-glass window in the foyer, or the manner and look of this woman. The frozen-faced curmudgeon in a crimson velvet jacket, reading the Sunday *Times* in the big gloomy living room crowded with old furniture, had Randy's long jaw and thin mouth. So the Davenports were moving, and were pretty sullen about it, too. They didn't acknowledge our presence by a smile or a look or a word. Even Mama was chilled. We got out of there fast. When we were out on the street Pop said, in as bitter a tone as I ever heard from this amiable man, "*Mi hutt g'zen di penimer* (They saw the faces)."

Pop signed a lease for an awesomely large and handsome flat in a West End Avenue building above Ninety-sixth Street, across the street from a big temple. Occupancy, September first. The rent was more than twice what we paid on Pelham Parkway, but Mama got an unheard-of nine-month concession. She was in seventh heaven. Why, we were saving money by moving to Manhattan; and Lee would meet some worthwhile young fellows at last!

46

West End Avenue

LEE came down the gangway of the *Mauretania* on a cold blustery October morning, looking wild, sunburned, and strange. Her eyes had an exhilarated, almost crazy, light. She wore a soiled shaggy sheepskin coat, her hair was long and disorderly, and she was clutching a bottle. On hand to meet her were Mom, Pop, myself, Zaideh, and Aunt Faiga. Zaideh was anxious for news of his son, Uncle Velvel, so Aunt Faiga had brought him to the dock. As we all drove back to our new West End Avenue apartment in our twelve-cylinder Cadillac (I'll explain about *that*), Lee regaled Zaideh with Uncle Velvel's latest doings. Lee speaks perfect Yiddish to this day; seldom uses it, but can roll it off like Molly Picon if she has to. That one baby year in Minsk did it.

Lee talked in a breathless wandering way, blinking around at New York as though waking from a deep dream. Uncle Velvel was now out of orange groves, she reported, and into soda bottles. He and his orange-grove partner were suing each other, both of them were suing the Zionist land authority, Velvel's wife was suing him for divorce, and since his father-in-law had come to Palestine, Velvel was suing him all over again about the hay and feed business in Latvia. Legal costs were mounting up, and Velvel urgently required a cabled money order of fifteen hundred dollars; otherwise he might be compelled to come to America, family and all, to teach Hebrew in Los Angeles. He expected great things of his venture in soda bottles, but at the moment his children were in rags and crying for bread. Pop assured Zaideh, who took this report hard, that he would send off the fifteen hundred at once, and you can bet he did.

As for the bottle business, this is what Lee told us. A British soft-drink company operating a branch in Palestine had been paying for returnable bottles. Uncle Velvel had piled up a lot of these, figuring to turn them in all at once. Then the firm had announced a change of policy: bottles not wanted, no more payment for returns. Uncle Velvel considered this a moral outrage and a breach of contract. He was planning to sue the company for damages, as well as for the value of his bottles, and he was accumulating more and more bottles, convinced that there was a fortune in them. Nobody else had any use for them, and by the time Lee left Palestine Uncle Velvel had amassed some forty thousand bottles. I think that was the figure, though it does seem high. Four thousand, maybe.

Anyway, Uncle Velvel's flat in Tel Aviv was an extraordinary sight, Lee said. Glittery soda bottles were stacked floor to ceiling in every room and hall, with only narrow passageways through the glass to the beds, the kitchen stove, and the toilet; and the small yard out back was solid soda bottles, as high as a man could reach. Possibly Lee was stretching things, in her fashion; yet without a doubt Uncle Velvel had the Palestine corner in nonreturnable soda bottles, and was confident of making a big killing. But the law was slow, hence the interim request for fifteen hundred dollars.

Well, to look at our twelve-cylinder Cadillac, you'd have thought that Pop had at last hit it big, and Velvel's request was a mere bagatelle. Not so. Remember Brodofsky's brother-in-law, Morris, who scalded himself in the boiler room of the Fairy Laundry? It had been his Cadillac. Morris had married a young wife, and had taken to drinking, gambling, and generally living it up on borrowed funds. He had been riding around in this second-hand Cadillac when his brief fling ended in bankruptcy; and the Fairy Laundry got the car in lieu of money which Brodofsky had nagged Pop into lending Morris. It was a thing of beauty — long, sleek, tan, gleaming — but its insides were a mess, for it had been through all sorts of automotive hell. Pop took it over because it seemed to go with a West End Avenue address.

Luckily he kept his Model A Ford, because that was what he continued to drive. When the Cadillac wasn't up on blocks for major internal overhaul, it was in the body shop getting a fender unbent, for Pop could never get used to driving the dreadnought. Repair bills were murderous. The whole frame was out of whack, so that the car wore down fresh new tires to the white cords like a grindstone. After

a while Pop tried to give the thing back to Morris; who, according
to Pop, laughed "like a crazy one" and said his downfall had almost
been worth it because he had unloaded the Cadillac. Eventually Pop
did give it to a garage man, as payment for a back-breaking bill for
a new transmission; and he had to sweeten the deal with a hundred
dollars or so, to get the monster off his hands. But that was later.

Mom loved that Cadillac. Just to be able to meet my sister Lee at
the Cunard dock in that ailing dinosaur justified for her the trouble
Pop was having. I was crazy about it, too, and couldn't wait to become old enough to drive it. We once travelled to Florida in it, and
had to take the last part of the trip at fifteen miles an hour; anything
faster caused an infernal smell of redhot iron and melting rubber, and
tumbling black smoke from the twelve cylinders. But Mom arrived
at the Miami hotel in a Cadillac.

About the new apartment, though, there was nothing illusory. We
leaped to true high style: a canopied entrance with gilded ironwork
doors, a carpeted lobby walled in marble, doormen and elevator men
in brown uniforms gaudy with gold braid, wood-panelled elevators,
and a service elevator for the lower orders. What a change from that
slow small whining self-service lift in Pelham, crowded with vulgar
people like our former selves, carrying bundles of groceries! You never
saw that in a West End elevator. Mama caught on fast and had her
groceries delivered, at prices doubling those in Pelham. She was a
canny frugal shopper, but she was not about to brave our Irish doorman — actually named Pat, with an intimidating square red face, and
a thick brogue — by walking into the building with her arms full of
brown paper bags. Here was a woman who in the Bronx could brain
a man with a brick; yet before the haughty look of a West End Avenue doorman, her "moxie" failed her.

Or maybe that is unjust. Mama has never lost her fighting spirit,
not really. Only a couple of months ago I sat with her while she
crushed an IRS agent; a mean little ferret with a sneaky face and a
nagging whine, who kept his black raincoat on in her flat as he went
over her return. I myself would have let him disallow all my deduc-
tions, to get the creep out of my house. Not Mom. She kept arguing,
and explaining, and forcing him to add up his figures over and over,
until he plain quit; went cringing out of her apartment with his black
raincoat dragging, whipped by an ancient lady. I wanted to cheer. I
invited Mom to a kosher Chinese restaurant on the spot.

So, on second thought, in the matter of Pat, the Irish doorman, I suppose Mom decided she was now a Manhattan *yoxenta*, and wouldn't carry bundles. She remained quite capable of clouting even Pat with a brick, should the occasion arise.

Pat's eyes bulged as Zaideh got out of the car in his ankle-length black coat and round black hat; and, stroking his broad beard, contemplated the facade of the temple across the street, with its Hebrew legend carved in stone over high bronze portals, THIS IS THE GATEWAY TO THE LORD, THE RIGHTEOUS SHALL ENTER HERE. My parents had joined the temple. My father had been elected a trustee. Zaideh was not pleased.

"*O dos iddess?* (That's it?)" he asked my father.

"*Dos iddess,*" said Pop.

The expressions of my grandfather staring at the temple, and of the doorman staring at Zaideh, were much the same: hostile wonderment, more or less controlled by good manners.

"*Nu,*" said Zaideh.

"Nu" is a brief Yiddish word of infinite extension. This "nu" said: "Well, such things actually exist, I see. It's really true that Jews spend fortunes to build them, in crazy America. Enough already."

With an eloquent shrug, he turned to enter the building. Pat held the door open with belated deference, having meanwhile correctly sized Zaideh up as a Jew priest. In marched my grandfather. By his bearing, he could have been Randy Davenport's grandfather, so at home did he appear, entering those splendid alien surroundings. But then Zaideh always appeared at home everywhere, however exotic he might look to others; possibly because he knew God was everywhere, and he was at home with God; or to come off that high note, maybe it stemmed from being so utterly himself, from not trying to "make it," because there was nothing to make, and nobody to make it for. He had a kindly smile for the astounded elevator man; and as we all rode up in the gilded car with a full-length mirror he kept saying, "*Panski! Panski!* (Aristocratic! Aristocratic!)"

My sister Lee was a different story. She looked strange too in that shaggy sheepskin coat from Palestine, with her long hair all wild, and the bottle under her arm. The smile she returned to Pat's haughty stare was half-defiant, half-apologetic. In the lobby she looked around and said, "Wow, Loew's Boulevard," wanting to sound unimpressed, but betraying herself with a weak giggle. She tried chumminess with the short dark elevator man. "Hi, what's your name?"

"Jesus," he said. Lee blinked as though he had thrown something at her. Even Zaideh gave a slight start, but that was the man's name all right. He was a South American. I never quite got used to it.

Zaideh touched the mezuza on the doorpost of our new apartment and kissed his fingers. Proudly, Mom opened the door. "Come, Papushka. See how Sarah Gitta lives!"

"Panski! Panski!" Zaideh kept exclaiming, as Mama showed him, and Faiga, and Lee, through the place.

The rooms were twice as large as those on Longfellow Avenue. There were four bathrooms, counting the maid's little toilet. Gross luxury! We had come a long way, we Aldus Street Goodkinds. A chair or two retained from Pelham looked lost in this apartment, which Mom had furnished handsomely, arguing that when fine young Manhattan fellows came calling on Lee in a palatial apartment, they couldn't very well sit around on old Bronx sticks. The Aldus Street tables, chairs, and beds which had moved along with us for years were all gone. I heard much concerned talk, as my parents went over the bills. But Pop summed it all up late one night, in a resigned Yiddish byword: "Once you're eating pork, let it drip from your chin."

47

Holy Joe Geiger

"THIS is where you'll have your wedding," Zaideh said to Aunt Faiga, as the tour finished in the immense living room. "Panski!"

He stood on a flowered blue Persian carpet by a rosewood baby grand piano. Lee had given up piano playing at the age of eleven, midway through the "Poet and Peasant Overture." Mama hoped she would now resume her lessons. If not, the baby grand was still a rich touch, and Mom had got it cheap. In fact, buying at the bottom of the depression, Mama loaded up with amazing bargains. To this day she lives among those possessions. The carpet and the piano are worth about twenty times what she paid for them, but dollars were then harder to come by. Mama never bought anything on credit in her life; hard cash or no deal.

"Papushka," pleaded Faiga. "No! Not here! Boris won't like it."

"You'll get married here," said Zaideh, "and you'll walk around Boris seven times. Here there is room."

"I'm not walking around Boris seven times," Aunt Faiga exclaimed. "Not once, either."

Aunt Faiga and Zaideh were on a collision course in matters of ritual. Faiga felt that she and her groom, Boris, both atheists, were conceding enough by having a religious ceremony. I had met Boris, a sweet-natured youth, whose thick orange hair stood out in stiff waves from his head. Boris would not put on a yarmulka even in Zaideh's home. Gentiles did, but not Boris. It might not have remained long on that hair, but we had no way of finding out. Boris would not wear a symbol of the opiate of the masses on his head, so he explained. It was odd to see Boris sitting bareheaded, talking perfect

Yiddish to Zaideh. It was almost as though he had no clothes on. One wondered how he endured it. Zaideh was quite amiable toward him, but Boris himself looked ill at ease, and kept passing his hand over his springy orange hair where the yarmulka should have sat. He stuck to his principles, all the same, like an abalone to a rock.

Now while Zaideh might have preferred that Faiga marry, say, the Kotzker Iluy, he was above all things a genial realist. He liked Boris. Boris was a nice Jewish boy, except for the Communist loose screw, for which he was not to blame. Boris too had left Russia at seventeen, and Zaideh knew all about that, and could make allowances. Zaideh figured the blemish would pass off in the course of time, like warts.

Nor was he far wrong. Boris had a good heart. He had agreed, for instance, to put on a yarmulka for the ceremony, and had even okayed a canopy, a *khupa*. Now, I had heard Boris assail the canopy as a survival of the primitive open tent under which the groom, in Bible days, deflowered his bride in the presence of parents, relatives, and legal witnesses, so that all would know by the visible bloody evidence that he had got himself a virgin. Or, if there was no blood, she would be stoned to death then and there. I have no idea where Boris had picked up this colorful bit of anthropology, which Zaideh said was sillier *meshugas* even than his communism. How, then, could Boris have agreed to be married under a canopy? Well, in Pop's words, "Once you're eating pork, let it drip from your chin."

No, the clash was on what happened under the canopy. By Jewish custom, old as the Jerusalem hills, a bride walks around her beloved seven times. One can see in old Yiddish films how elaborately this was once done, with a procession of women holding lighted candles, accompanying the girl in her seven circuits. Aunt Faiga was digging in her hooves, saying this made no sense to her. When pressed for the logic behind the custom, Zaideh had explained, "Who doesn't walk around her groom seven times?"

Anyhow, said Faiga, there was no room in Zaideh's little parlor, which would be jammed with guests, for her to go circling Boris. Zaideh said there was plenty of room. Mama had suggested inviting fewer guests, so as to leave room. Papa's idea was that guests could step outside at circling time, to make room. I had jested that Boris could turn himself around seven times where he stood, which would give Faiga seven exposures to his perimeter, if that was the idea. Zaideh had commented on my proposal that it was all he could expect from a shaygets raised in Wicked America. And there the matter was deadlocked.

My sister Lee stood there in her sheepskin coat, a look of amused scorn on her face, as Zaideh and Aunt Faiga argued. "Zaideh, I went to three weddings in Palestine," she put in, "and the bride never walked around the groom. Not once."

"There you are!" exclaimed Aunt Faiga. "Even in the Holy Land they don't walk around."

"The Holy Land!" said Zaideh with scorn. "What kind of Jews live in the Holy Land?"

This may sound odd, but the fact is that the Zionist pioneers were held in low repute, by Jews of the old school, as irreligious rebels.

"Hell will freeze over," Lee said to Faiga, "before I walk around any man. Don't you do it."

"Over my dead body I'll do it," Faiga assured her. Faiga was fond of English idioms, but did not yet hit them right on every time.

"Don't talk Turkish," exclaimed Zaideh. It was his word for English. "What are you two saying?"

All during Faiga's truculent talk she had been glancing longingly around at this gorgeous room. Now she suddenly reversed her field. "Would you really have the wedding here?" she asked Mom. "Maybe Boris would agree. Not," she added forcefully, "that I'll walk around him. Let hell be frozen first!"

Mom and Pop assured her that they would be delighted. As excited talk sprang up about staging the wedding in our flat, Lee beckoned to me. She led me into the pretty bedchamber that was hers, all pink and flouncy and mirrored, and threw her sheepskin on the big bed covered in quilted pink satin.

"You've grown a *foot!*" she exclaimed, hugging me and giving me a quick kiss. "And you're an absolute stringbean, and your voice is so deep!"

"High time," I said to Lee.

"But Davey, what in God's name is the matter with Papa?"

"Papa? Nothing. He's fine."

"He looks awful. Terrible! He's aged twenty years. When I first saw him, I was frightened."

To me, Pop looked the same as always. I said so. Lee pulled cigarettes from the sheepskin and lit one with a nervous scratch of a wax match; the first of a billion cigarettes, or so it seems, I've since seen her smoke.

"So, you're hooked, too," I said.

She shrugged. "Ever tasted arak?"

"What's arak?"

"This." From the bottle she had brought off the boat, she poured big slugs of a clear liquid into two bathroom glasses. We drank, I choked, and she laughed. "Now, Davey, why on earth are we living in a place like this? With all this expensive furniture? And what about that Cadillac? Have they gone crazy? Is Papa making that kind of money?"

"It's all for you," I said, "so that you'll meet a nice fellow."

She reddened, drank off her arak, and plopped down on her bed. "Can you keep a secret? I've met a nice fellow." Her voice dropped almost to a whisper. Her flushed face was both troubled and radiant. "I'm going to be married, Davey. So Mom's wasted a lot of time and money. The only thing is, he's married now. He has to get a divorce, and he's going to."

And there it was, straight from Lee. Uncle Velvel had told the truth. I was floored. I was barely past telling ghost stories at parties, and my infatuation with Dorsi Sabin was just igniting. Such passion was over my head.

"Lee, do I have to know about this?"

"I've got to tell *someone*. Anyway, you're responsible." She laughed joyously. "He's Moshe Lev, the one whose address in Jerusalem you gave me. He teaches history at Hebrew University, and he can fly an airplane, and I've gone up with him, oh, several times." She poured herself more arak.

"Does he have kids?"

Her face fell. "Three." She drank in a swift swooping motion, emptying the glass. "But the kids like me. That won't be a problem."

Mom appeared in the door of the room. "So, what are you two hiding for? Come out, Lee, and meet Rabbi Geiger, from the temple. And since when do you smoke?"

"What, a rabbi? Christ, I don't want to meet a rabbi."

"Don't be like that. He's come to welcome you. Take five minutes to be nice to him. And get rid of that cigarette! He's very smart and handsome, and he's a bachelor." Mom left, raising her voice. "She'll be right with you, Rabbi."

"Gawd," Lee said. "What's Rabbi Geiger like?"

"Holy Joe Geiger?" I said. "He's indescribable. Go on out and meet him. Just tighten your chastity belt."

So out sails Lee to greet the rabbi, brandishing the bottle of arak, her hair wild as a witch's, her eyes flashing antagonism. She looked mighty pretty.

"Rabbi Geiger, this is my daughter, Leonore," said Mama, her genteel smile at the rabbi modulating into a horrible frown at Lee and her bottle.

"Hi, Rabbi," said Lee. "D'you like arak?"

"Love it," said Rabbi Geiger. "Lived on it for a year."

This stopped Lee cold. She stared at Geiger. He stood there bareheaded, holding a black derby, in a black overcoat with a velvet collar, into which a white silk scarf was tucked; a plump-cheeked man of thirty or so, with thick slick black hair, a neat mustache, and a look at once ministerial and faintly raffish; let's say, as though Errol Flynn had been cast as a priest, and was trying hard but not quite getting into the part.

"Really?" said Lee. "On arak?"

"Well, not a whole year, and I didn't exactly live on it." Rabbi Geiger smiled, spreading the mustache and showing a lot of Errol Flynn teeth. "I got my M.A. in Bible archaeology. I worked on the digs around Megiddo, and I did drink a heck of a lot of arak."

"So you've been to Palestine?" Lee's tone warmed.

"Yes, and you've just come from there, I understand, Leonore. I stopped by for a moment to say" — he switched to Hebrew — "*Brukhim ha'ba'im* (Welcome, newcomer)."

"Take off your coat," said Mom. "Stay a while."

"I have to conduct a funeral," said Rabbi Geiger, "otherwise I'd be delighted."

"Anyone we know?" Pop asked, looking somber.

"Oh, no. I didn't know the gentleman, either. The family is from out of town. The gentleman dropped dead last night at a performance of George White's *Scandals*. The funeral parlor has engaged me to perform the sad duty."

"Well, have some arak before you go," said Lee with grudging cordiality, pouring the stuff into glasses on a sideboard.

"Not too much," said Holy Joe.

Zaideh and Aunt Faiga, who had been off somewhere in the apartment, at this moment returned to the living room. When Geiger saw Zaideh his hand slipped into a pocket and whipped to his head, depositing there a small black yarmulka. The reader remembers my whipping off the yarmulka when the President caught me studying the Talmud. It was exactly the same motion, in reverse.

"And this must be your father," said Geiger to Mom.

Mama introduced them.

Zaideh gave Holy Joe a sharp quizzical glance as they shook hands. "*O dos iss der rebb-eye?*" he said to my father. ("This is the rabbi?")

He sounded friendly enough. But again, if you knew Zaideh, you heard the overtones. Neither Zaideh, nor anyone else of the old school, called a rabbi a "rabbi." Zaideh was a *Rov*, with a guttural capital *R* — R-r-rov; in direct address, *Rav*. When Zaideh said, "rebb-eye," he was talking about a strange and scarcely believable form of life. There was no animosity in it, just incredulity. Contemplating the smooth-cheeked mustached young man in the black Chesterfield and white scarf, holding a black derby and wearing a small black yarmulka, Zaideh might have been having his first glimpse of a platypus.

Holy Joe endured the scrutiny with aplomb, and said to Zaideh in tolerable Yiddish, "It's a great pleasure to meet you, Rav Levitan. I've just dropped by, to greet your granddaughter with the traditional, '*Welcome, newcomer.*' "

Zaideh opened wide eyes, smiled, and said to my parents with surprise, "*Er ret gor vi a mentsch.*" Rough translation, "Why, he talks absolutely like a man."

Aunt Faiga said brightly to Mom, "Let's ask Rabbi Geiger about walking around Boris seven times."

"Great idea," put in my sister Lee. "Rabbi, my aunt here is getting married soon. What about that business of the bride walking around the groom seven times? Is that really the law?"

With a side glance at Zaideh, Holy Joe said, "Well, it's a question that can be discussed on several levels. Basically —"

But Zaideh had caught Lee's swift rotary gesture with her finger, and his mind was not slow. "So? What does the rebb-eye say?" he asked Faiga. "Doesn't even *he* say you should walk around? Of course he does. What else can he say? He talks like a man."

Faiga had some trouble with "several levels," and she rather fudged Rabbi Geiger's answer. In her Yiddish paraphrase, Holy Joe said it wasn't actually necessary to walk around, it depended which floor you lived on. Something confusing like that. Zaideh turned a clouded-up glance at Rabbi Geiger, who hastily said in Yiddish that Faiga had misunderstood, that a young rabbi never gave a ruling in the presence of an elder, and that was all he had meant to say. He hadn't mentioned floors.

"Nu, nu," said my grandfather. Zaideh's doubled "nu" could mean a thousand things. In this instance it expressed skepticism, distaste, and a strong desire to drop the subject.

"Well," Rabbi Geiger said, "I must get along to my sad duty."

"You haven't drunk your arak," said Lee, offering it to him.

"Ah, yes. Well, it's a cold day." He accepted the glass and pronounced a flawless blessing in Hebrew.

"Amen," said Zaideh and Pop.

Rabbi Geiger tossed down the arak, slid off his yarmulka, and put on his derby. Smiling graciously at Zaideh, and indicating Pop with a nod, he said, "Your son-in-law is a very fine Jew."

With a smile quite as gracious, Zaideh replied, "How can he be a very fine Jew, when he goes to your temple?"

"Touché," said Lee, grinning at Geiger. "What do you say to that?"

Unperturbed, Holy Joe said to her as he buttoned up his coat, "That too can be discussed on several levels."

"What did the young man just say?" Zaideh asked Faiga.

"He says different people live on different floors," said Faiga.

"Again? Is he crazy?" said Zaideh.

"I didn't say quite that," said Holy Joe in Yiddish, with great good humor. "And let me repeat, Rav Levitan, it's a joy to have the Goodkind family in our midst, and to meet a R-r-rov of such great learning."

"Nu, nu," said Zaideh.

Geiger shook hands with Lee. "I hope I'll see you at services," he said ministerially, yet with a tinge of Errol Flynn in the tone. The door closed. Silence. We all looked at each other.

"He's cute," said my sister Lee. "Maybe I'll try the temple, at that."

48

Peter Quat at Home

"**M**y father is full of shit," said Peter Quat.
That jarred me, a nice Jewish Bronx lad not all that long
out of the yeshiva. Trying to adopt Quat's downtown irreverence, I
said with a debonair laugh, "I take it the old boy doesn't like your
story."

"He never likes anything I write. Not since I got out of college,
he doesn't." Peter slumped on the window seat, lighting a cigarette
with jerky gestures. "Say, ever been to April House?"

"Not yet."

"Dick Himber's in the Orchid Grill. Not a bad place to take a girl."

We were lounging in his bedroom in a tower of the San Remo,
looking south at skyscrapers silhouetted in purple by a fading sunset.
Atop the tallest hotel on Central Park South, red neon letters stood
two stories high:

APRIL
HOUSE

A strong wind whined at the window, forcing a trickle of icy air into
the smoky overheated room. While Peter leafed through my Varsity
Show script, I was reading his latest effort to crack *The New Yorker*.

Peter was low. He and Mark Herz had spent the summer vainly
trying to concoct a farce. Peter had scornfully told me that in three
weeks they would come up with a funnier hit than any of the rubbish
on Broadway. Not so, alas. Herz had gone to work with an uncle in
the fur trade, to save up money for graduate work in physics. Peter
was hanging around at home, writing short stories.

A paunchy bald man of stern presence appeared in the doorway.
"Peter, have you thought over our conversation?"

"Yes, I have."

"Good. This, I take it, is young David Goodkind. Welcome."

"Thank you, sir."

Dr. Quat certainly looked Jewish — big curving nose, large clever brown eyes — but his speech and his manner were dignified, forbidding, and altogether "downtown." He tilted his heavy head for a somber stare at Peter, said, "I trust you've come to a sensible decision, son," and walked off down the hallway.

"Fuck," muttered Peter, flinging aside my script. "Fuck, fuck, fuck."

Peter's conversation may create a problem here, at that. He gets into the action more and more, and I may have to write off the family trade, and just take this magnum opus straight to Grove Press. But let's grope along for a while and see. Maybe later I can change it all to "Shoot," and "Gee whinnakers," though that isn't much like Peter Quat.

Why the expletives? Peter irritably explained that a patient of Dr. Quat was the celebrated joke czar of radio, Harry Goldhandler. The doctor had spoken to Goldhandler about his son who had written Columbia Varsity Shows, and Goldhandler had offered to interview Peter for a job on his staff. Peter told his father that "radio garbage" didn't interest him, and Dr. Quat's reply was that Peter would not be allowed to idle at home when he could earn his own bread. He had given Peter twenty-four hours to think it over.

"Can you imagine me writing that crap?" exclaimed Peter. "I asked my father to wait and see if 'Mama Dunt Vanna' will sell. He says it hasn't a chance." Peter narrowed his eyes at me. "You don't like it, either, do you? Tell the truth."

"Peter, I grew up in the Bronx. To me the story doesn't ring true."

"It *is* true, word for word. Only it happened in Passaic. A guy in my Hebrew school there told it to me. He listened at his parents' bedroom door and heard it all."

The story was about a Jewish wife fending off her husband by pleading her period. Old Peter was right in there from the start with his unsparing candor. Peter quoted in the jeering clip-cock singsong of Dreyer, " '*Mama, dollink, you said de same tink last Toisday night.*' Davey, those were the exact words the guy heard his old man say! I once had to live with people like that in Passaic for a year. Don't tell *me* it doesn't ring true."

I now learned more about Peter Quat's background than I had in the two years I had known him. I guess he was proving, in his quick nervous gush of words, that his story was authentic. His mother had worked as a legal secretary, had fallen in love with her boss, and had divorced Dr. Quat; a protracted and messy episode, during which the nine-year-old Peter had been parked for a year in Passaic with an aunt, married to a man in the garment business. The mother had married the lawyer, and custody of Peter for some reason had fallen to his father, who had then remarried. Suppressed dreadful anger underlay all this. Peter bit out his words, twisted his mouth, and rolled his eyes as he talked. The Passaic relatives had forced him to go to a temple and a Hebrew school, though the Quats had been wholly irreligious. Peter had bought a crucifix and worn it to his Hebrew class, getting himself kicked out of the school for good. That incident, of course, is the famous opening chapter of *Deflowering Sarah*.

"Kikes," Peter summed up his Passaic relatives, as a buzzer cut short his bitter rambling. "Just plain kikes." He jumped up, tightened his tie, and put on his jacket. "Come on, Dave."

"Do you know," Dr. Quat said to me, breaking an excruciating long and heavy silence at the dinner table, "that Peter's mother is the grandniece of a very famous, ah, Yiddish writer?"

He said "Yiddish" with quote marks around it, as though it were an obscure tongue that I might have heard of, though I could be excused if I hadn't.

I shook my head. Seldom had I been so frozen and intimidated. I might be living on West End Avenue, but I was regarding the Quat household with Bronx eyes, and I couldn't handle it.

To begin with, there was this painting, glaring at me from the dining-room wall behind Peter's stepmother; a huge oil of an old gent in a Dutch cap, his mouth snarled half-open, showing a few stumpy teeth in red gums. The rheumy wrinkled eyes bored at me, as though incensed at the very sight of a Bronx clip cock in the San Remo. (Peter Quat was circumcised, but in a different downtown style.) There was the stepmother herself, a slim lady with the straightest spine I had ever seen, and a smile that went on and off unnervingly, like a traffic blinker. There was her daughter, a thin small girl with Dr. Quat's nose and her mother's ramrod back. There was Dr. Quat at the head of the table, imposing as the emperor Hadrian, eating in majestic silence. There was Peter next to me, staring down at his plate, radiating scary hostility. There was the cook-maid, a blonde gray-uniformed woman, passing the food with a terrified look. An actual white servant!

And there was the food: slabs of fish — fish and not meat, I gathered, out of courtesy to my kosher upbringing — each slab garnished with bacon. I didn't venture to object, or to decline, or even to shove the bacon off; not in the presence of Hadrian Rex. To Peter, I'm sure, the bacon was like parsley or capers; he didn't give it a thought. I did what I could to hollow some fish out from under the red-and-yellow curl and eat a scrap or two, to avoid trouble.

Above all there was the silence. The silence! In my home silence at table meant some bad trouble in the family. There was always talk: the laundry, religion, the new movies, *something*. The ever-lengthening silence tortured me. I kept racking my brain for something to say, and might have come out with God knows what imbecility, when Dr. Quat rescued me by bringing up the Yiddish author.

"Possibly your parents will be familiar with the name," Dr. Quat went on, and he enunciated with downtown distinctness, "Mandalay Mohair Serafin. You might mention this to them."

"Mandalay Mohair Serafin," I croaked, my voice not working well. "Yes, sir." It was an unrecognizable name, not in the least Yiddish-sounding, but I was keeping my horns drawn all the way in.

That was that. There had not been much mileage in the topic of Mandalay Mohair Serafin, but Dr. Quat had put Peter's ultra-Jewish friend at his ease; much as people entertaining a black will tell him how much they admire Ralph Ellison or Justice Thurgood Marshall. Long silence resumed, until the coffee. Then Dr. Quat launched a disquisition on the evils of idleness, and the obligation of a man to earn his keep. He made solid if not spellbinding sense, in a stately vocabulary and austere downtown diction.

At his father's first pause for breath, Peter said, "Okay, I'll go and see Harry Goldhandler."

Dr. Quat went on, developing at some length the parable of ants and grasshoppers. Peter repeated, at his next marked pause, "I said, I'll go to see Harry Goldhandler!"

Dr. Quat gave him a Hadrianic look, head aslant. "Well, I'll have my say," he returned, and so he did. He talked of selling newspapers as a boy, and waiting on tables in the college lunchroom, fiber-building experiences he would not have missed for anything. Then he took note of Peter's yielding. "You've made a wise decision, son. Now I would like your opinion, as a writer, on a matter of literary taste. Here is a Christmas greeting card I may order, to send to all my patients. What do you think of it?"

He drew from his pocket and handed Peter a thick square envelope. On the folded card Peter took out there was the usual Star of Bethlehem scene. When he opened the card to read it, he gasped and so did I, because a big paper butterfly came flapping up into his face, bounced off his nose and flew at me, then sailed around the room, hit the painting, hit the stepmother, and fell on the little girl's head. Dr. Quat shook all over with laughter, the stepmother giggled, and the girl turned the thing solemnly over in her hands, looking at the spring that made it go.

"My nurse brought it to the office as a lark," said Dr. Quat. "I found it amusing. Well, I shall have my brandy and cigar in the library. And Peter, you'll find working for Mr. Goldhandler more satisfying, I assure you, than accumulating rejection slips from *The New Yorker*. It's just a hoity-toity little magazine."

"It's an important magazine. I'll be printed in it," Peter said. "I'll be *featured* in it."

With an indulgent smile, Dr. Quat said, "Well, that's the spirit, son," and he left the table.

Peter didn't remind me of this when *The Smelly Melamed* took up almost a whole issue of *The New Yorker*. He didn't have to. My first thought when I opened that issue was, I wished Dr. Quat had lived to see it.

I have here pictured Dr. Quat as he struck me that night. He scared me. Beneath that formidable surface, I found out in time, was a warm good heart. He mended an elbow I broke in an absentminded tumble down stone stairs in Central Park, and the elbow works like new to this day. I grew quite fond of him over the years, but that first time only the butterfly hinted at his gentler side.

Back in his room, Peter said to me, "The thing is, he doesn't understand me. Truly he doesn't. I want to write novels. The farce thing was just to make money. I'd have taken my M.A. in English, gotten a college teaching job, gone the academic route, but the English departments are firing, not hiring. I hoped to get some stories printed, and then apply for a Guggenheim." He sighed and said almost plaintively, "Christ, I don't want to write radio jokes, Davey."

He returned to reading my libretto. I sat in the window seat, looking out at downtown Manhattan and the APRIL HOUSE sign, while he chuckled and turned the pages, and the wind whined at the casement.

"You know, you're the one who should work for Harry Gold-handler," he remarked. "Some good jokes here."

"Law school for me," I replied, though I warmed all over at what he said.

"You're a fool. Lawyers are a dime a dozen. Gagmen make fortunes. You better think again about law school, Davey. You're a funny man."

"I'll consult my girl friend," I said, half in earnest.

"Girl friend? Hmmm!" Peter wickedly grinned. "No kidding. Getting your end wet?"

I said stiffly, "You wouldn't ask, if you knew her."

"Who is she?"

"Barnard junior. Dorsi Sabin."

Peter was lolling on his bed with my script. He sat up. "Dorsi *Sabin*? Jesus Christ, you're not going out with the iceberg?"

"You know her?"

"I play bridge with the guy she half-blinded. He couldn't see the cards to play, for two weeks."

"Well, he got fresh with her."

"Davey, he wanted to give her a good-night kiss."

"She wasn't interested."

"He gathered that. Dorsi Sabin! Well, it's a challenge. Get a hand on her tits or her ass, and you'll be elected to the Explorer's Club."

"Mandalay Mohair Serafin?" said Papa. "No."

"But they said he was famous."

"Famous? Yiddish?" Mama repeated the name slowly. "Mandalay . . . Mohair . . . Serafin?"

"That's it, Mom."

Mom shook her head, whereupon my sister Lee struck in, "What's the matter with all of you? It's *Mendele Moykher S'forim!* It has to be."

"Ah!" Pop exclaimed. "Of course, Mendele." He patted Lee's cheek, and she preened. "You're a sharp one."

Mendele Moykher S'forim, "Mendele the Bookseller," is indeed considered the father of Yiddish literature, regarded even by Sholem

Aleichem as his master. Pop sometimes read to us from Mendele. Viking not long ago brought out Peter Quat's *Mendele the Bookseller Reader,* intending to cash in on the Yiddish nostalgia fad, with some pieces translated by a Columbia professor. Peter's long learned preface mentioned the family tie. The book didn't sell. Mendele doesn't translate well, though in Yiddish he is brilliantly readable, and often quite as bitter as Quat about Jewish life. Peter made much of that in his preface, claiming a sort of literary kinship with Mendele. But it won't wash. Mendele wrote an Inside language, addressed to the folk alone; and his bitterness only lends tang and honesty to an all-pervading, self-evident love for his people. The Quat fiction is different merchandise.

Peter got the name right in his preface, of course, but in casual talk he will still call him Mandalay Mohair Serafin. You can take the boy out of downtown, as they say, but you can't take the downtown out of the boy.

49

Dorsi in April House

AND now for that stone-wall crash. The tuxedo I bought from Mr. Michaels contributed to the calamity. I wasn't going to take Dorsi Sabin to our first formal Columbia dance in a fusty rented suit, you see, not on your life. So I went down to my old sad-eyed friend, Mr. Michaels, and he brought out from the back of the store an enormous tuxedo, super-stout size. He no longer carried formals, he said, and had just this one left. His price was very low, with alterations thrown in. "Feel the material," he said. "You'll leave this suit to your grandchildren."

"Mr. Michaels, it's miles too big."

"It will be tailored to you. Just like in London. You'll look poured into it."

The suit wasn't ready until the afternoon of the dance, but then it was in fact a nice fit, only tight under the arms. For all I knew he made a whole other suit out of the excess stuff. Michaels and his tailor assistant chattered in Yiddish as I tried it on. Their assumption that I couldn't understand them was flattering. Evidently I was taking on a bit of the downtown patina of Peter Quat. My newly rolling r's were great camouflage on Canal Street.

"What did you do to those armpits?" Michaels scolded at the tailor. "If the fellow understood tailoring, he would sue me."

"I'll fix the armpits," said the tailor.

"You can't. He needs it right now." Michaels switched to English. "What did I tell you, sonny? Poured into it, eh? Like a British lord."

While I waited in the Sabin parlor for Dorsi to finish dressing, and made small talk with her mother, those tight seams did bother me. But when at last she came swaying out in a black velvet dress that bared much of her white arms, and even a glimpse of those snowy breasts, I forgot my armpits. Her hair was massed in bewitching curls, clearly the work of hours. "Hi there, I'm ready." What a killingly casual entrance! What a sweet-scented vision she was, and how my heart raced at the sight of her! She had kept me waiting for nearly an hour, but my God, who cared? In the long taxicab ride to Columbia, I felt the underarm binding again. If we had been kissing or even holding hands I wouldn't have noticed, but with Dorsi? Ha. I just tried not to think about the discomfort. The dance was going strong when we arrived in the commons room of John Jay Hall. Dancing by us near the door was Sandy Wexler, a handsome Zeta Beta Tau, in a Brooks Brothers dinner jacket and flowered satin waistcoat. "Hi, Dorsi," he called. "You look smooth."

That was our jargon word of high praise then. The current translation would be *cool,* or *neat,* or some newer term I haven't overheard. Anyhow, Sandy Wexler was a too-smooth smoothie, who had recently been dating Dorsi Sabin.

"Oh, hello there, Sandy." Her eyes sparkled at him. As he danced away, Dorsi said to me, "Why, I didn't know Sandy would be at this thing. Where's the powder room?"

I escorted her there and waited for her. I waited three-quarters of an hour, chafed in spirits and under the arms. I must have seen half the girls at the dance come and go. One of them said to her waiting escort, as she came out, "I swear to God, the most incredibly beautiful girl is in there completely redoing her hair." Dorsi at last emerged looking exactly the same, with some slight relocation of a curl or two. "Have I kept you long?" she purred, making great eyes at me.

Well, we danced, and in the delight of holding Dorsi's supple velvet-clad body I overlooked the tight seams, the long wait, Sandy Wexler, everything. Snuggling on the dance floor was as unthinkable with Dorsi, of course, as fornicating with her at the foot of the Alma Mater statue during the lunch hour. Still, girls have their subtle little ways, and as we danced I could tell that she was feeling kindly to me. I asked for no more. My right armpit was pleasantly loosening, too, so the suit just needed a little breaking in.

Bob Greaves cut in on us, with a tap on my shoulder. Reluctant but unworried, I yielded Dorsi to him. Greaves was the ultimate super-smoothie on the campus, the Deke of Dekes, but no competition; for Dorsi was the ultimate nice Jewish girl, and would no more fall for a Deke than for a Ubangi. Greaves had come in white kid gloves, white tie, and tails, bringing his usual blonde date, utterly Aryan, with no nose to speak of. He had been dancing her vigorously around in his ultra-smooth if pigeon-toed style: left white glove high and stiff, head erect, a slight pitying sneer on his face. Before taking Dorsi off, Bob Greaves made a puzzling gesture at me and twirled away sneering into the crowd, that one white glove visible wherever he moved, like a submarine periscope.

Sandy Wexler, dancing by me, made the same puzzling gesture. I saw Biberman out on the floor with Puss Puss Ohlbaum, and damned if *he* didn't do the same thing, slapping a palm under his armpit. It occurred to me to feel and — ye gods. I went dashing up to the *Jester* office, turned on the light, and checked in the closet mirror. My white shirt hung out far below the seam, which had split wide open. Using long straight pins with which we dummied up our issues, I closed the split seam tightly over the shirt — not easy to do, with that battleship-steel cloth — cursing Michaels and his tailor, and I went back downstairs.

Wouldn't you know, Dorsi was dancing with Sandy Wexler. That one picture is eternally fixed in my memory: Dorsi Sabin and Sandy Wexler cheek to cheek, dancing like mad, both faces shining with fun. Between Wexler's pelvis and Dorsi's, and this was crucial, there was a space which a St. Bernard, if not a pony, could have trotted through. Their bodies formed an arch of chastity, closed only at the top by their two happy heads. The music changed to a slow number, and I confess I held back in the sideline shadows — Swann spying on Odette — but the gap did not close, not by a hair. Relieved beyond words, I was about to cut in on them when a big pale plump fellow in spectacles beat me to it.

This was a former president of Beta Sigma Rho, now in law school, Morris Pelkowitz. He had been cordial to me in that ill-fated rushing week, and I had nothing against Pelkowitz. It did not cross my mind to be jealous of this awkward shuffling dancer; too old, too stout, too splay-footed, his hair going, a solemn grind of another generation. Dorsi didn't laugh once as they talked and danced, and I could always make her laugh. No menace in Pelkowitz.

Can you grasp now what the deadly fascination was that this Dorsi Sabin had for me? Simple: if I could not get anywhere with her, *nei-*

ther could anyone else. That was the honeyed trap. Here was the girl of my dreams, the virgin who would yield an inch to no man until — overborne by my sheer wit, achievements, and charm — she yielded her all to me, *ME,* I. David Goodkind, in volcanic passion. Until that happened, her tits would be untouched by human hands, except her own. I was as drawn to Dorsi Sabin's notorious frostiness as normal fellows were to hot doings with kinder girls. It was an irresistible snare, a fatal encounter. It extended my inexperience, already much too prolonged by my ghost-story specialty, straight through college, and set me up for Bobbie Webb.

"What!" exclaimed Dorsi, settling back in the taxicab. "The Orchid Grill? *April* House? Oh, my! I've never been there. Can we get in?"

"We have a reservation."

On that lovely countenance, in those morning-star eyes, appeared a thoughtful look. Usually after a dance fellows took their girls to some eating place near Columbia, but I was going for broke. I felt masterful and strong, a gambler on a winning streak, and I reached out and put my hand over Dorsi's. As I did so, several pins stung my armpit, but I was past pain. She let her hand linger in mine for a long time — possibly as long as ten seconds — before she gently and laughingly withdrew it.

The huge red and gold lobby of April House was intimidating in its elegance and opulence. It smelled rich, and rich-looking people were moving through it, and bellboys in red and gold were rushing here and there. Dick Himber's music floated from the grill. Dorsi retired to the ladies' lounge to fix her hair, and I went to the men's room and checked the shirt. It was all stained red under my arm, and looked rather like a towel that had stanched a nosebleed. No matter. I reset all the pins tightly, picked up Dorsi outside the lounge, and on we went to the Orchid Grill.

All over the big multilevel grill room, and from the dance floor, people stared at my beautiful date. The headwaiter himself kept glancing over his shoulder at Dorsi Sabin, with a sad Italian look mingling memory and desire, as he led us to a little table right at the edge of the dance floor. And there I was! Blowing in a fortune, far over my head, but nervily riding my winning streak. Dorsi was impressed and excited, and in a glow. Why, the girl squeezed my hand as I led her out on the dance floor!

The paunchy band leader, bouncing up and down as he waved his stick, gave Dorsi an admiring leer. I was being ultra-smooth to my best ability, holding my left hand stiffly high like Bob Greaves, and probably dancing pigeon-toed like him. In matters of smoothness, having no standards, I tended to be suggestible. I cannot honestly recall whether I sneered, too. I do know I held my right elbow pressed hard against my side. No more mishaps!

"Dorsi, I've written another poem," I said, when we finished our sandwiches. I pulled a folded paper from my breast pocket, and handed it to her.

The youngsters who read this probably don't know what it is like to see a girl blush. The reflex must be extinct. What could my daughter Sandra possibly blush at? She makes *me* blush. Well, to see the color mount from those small white breasts, up her throat and neck and into Dorsi Sabin's exquisite face, was to look on a natural wonder like the aurora borealis. She glanced up at me from the poem, her eyes glistening; and the power in those stirred eyes shook me. "It's too serious for 'Off-hour,' Davey."

"*Jester* runs verse like that sometimes. That's for you. I have a copy."

Dorsi slipped the poem into her purse. "Strange. You're usually so funny."

"Do you prefer me funny, Dorsi?"

"You're all right as you are."

Back on the stand, the musicians began to play "Stardust," and the lights dimmed. Yes, children, the snuggler of snugglers is that old, and Dorsi and I got up and danced to it. I'm not saying that Dorsi cuddled up against me — of that she was incapable — but this time there was a difference, one hell of a difference. I felt Dorsi Sabin's thighs brush mine. I was drunk, and not from alcohol; for Prohibition was still on, if barely. Time ceased its flow. "Stardust" seemed to go on forever, and yet to be over in an instant. In some unknown dimension possibly I am still there in April House in 1932, with Dorsi Sabin's sweet thighs now and then touching mine as we dance to "Stardust." It happened outside all everyday reality, that I can tell you.

"Dorsi," I said as we sat down again, looking deep in each other's eyes, "let me ask you something."

"Yes, Davey?" Solemn, expectant, willing tones.

"It's about my future."

"All right."

I repeated what Peter had said about Harry Goldhandler, about my Varsity Show, and about gags versus law. I put the question to her. What was it to be — law school or comedy writing?

"But can you really make a living writing jokes, David?" Dorsi was drawn in, all right, dead serious, looking at me with concern and affection.

"Dorsi, Harry Goldhandler lives in a quadruplex apartment, and makes two thousand dollars a week."

"Wow." Dorsi pulled down her pretty mouth in awe. "Well — which would you rather do, David?"

"I'm thinking maybe I could do both. Get my law degree, and then try comedy writing."

"But when you graduate, you'll be twenty-four, twenty-five. Much too late to experiment."

"Dorsi, I won't even be twenty-two."

She smiled. "I mean graduate from law school, silly. You'll be wanting to settle down then, get married."

"I'm talking about law school, too, Dorsi. I'm barely seventeen now, and —"

"You're *what?*"

"Seventeen. I was seventeen in March."

She stared at me. "Cut it out. You're twenty. Or going on twenty. Somebody told me so. A girl in music class."

"Dorsi, I'm seventeen years old."

"You? It's impossible. You're kidding." She was flustered and stammering. "I mean, you're one of the most important men in Columbia, David. So well-read, so mature, so — why —"

"Dorsi, does it matter?"

"Why, why, of course not, David. It's just surprising. Is it really true? Remarkable."

If I had suddenly disclosed that I was a Deke or a Southern Baptist, I could not have chilled Dorsi Sabin more. The temperature was dropping by the second. The music was beginning again, and I held out my hand to her. She looked at her watch. "Well — shouldn't you get the check? It's awfully late, David. I still have homework. Well, all right. Maybe one more dance."

She was distant and stiff in my arms. I was stupefied. My age was self-evident to me, but of course she had known me only since the fall, and over the summer I had shot up, developed a real beard, and steadied in the baritone register. The subject had never surfaced before. Dorsi was a practical sort, and someone a year or two younger was simply not suited. The decision was written on her face. I could feel it in her lifeless dancing, in her limp hand. Before the music ended, we sat down. At the next table a grayhead in a dinner jacket, calling for his check, flourished a five-dollar bill at the headwaiter. I've said I was suggestible in such things. I didn't know what was vulgar and what was smooth. In a last magnificent gesture to reverse the tide, I too flourished a five-dollar bill at the headwaiter, waving my right arm high in the air. "Check, please!" I heard the pins loudly rip and pop, felt them stabbing and tearing at me, felt the shirt come flopping out.

"My God, David, look at you," cried Dorsi. "The blood, the *blood!* Your arm! What have you done to it? You're bleeding like a stuck pig!"

Forget the rest of that stone-wall evening. I have.

50

Holy Joe's Temple

WEEKS went by, and Lee did not go with Mom and Pop to Holy Joe's temple, or do much of anything else. They were woebegone at her glum idleness. What was the point of the whole Manhattan move, if Lee would not cross the street once a week to visit the temple? How else was she going to meet young men? She lay around reading rented best-sellers, now and then rustily playing Palestinian songs on the piano. Pop hinted that she could have a job at the laundry, but she did not respond. Virtually since puberty Lee had been mulishly bent on marrying one or another shlepper, so she had never thought of going to work, and had learned no gainful skill. Now she was counting on marrying Moshe Lev, but obviously she had not heard a word from him.

That subject was uppermost in all our minds, but never mentioned. We sat around the big costly new dining table, almost as quiet as the Quats. I had the deep-frozen Dorsi on my mind. Pop's forehead was corrugated with his chronic worries. Mom had Faiga's wedding, which was gathering complications, to fret about. Lee was far inside her shell. All in all, there was a cold gloomy stillness in that fancy West End apartment of ours such as we had never known in the Bronx, for all our spells of hard times.

I could now walk to Columbia and I had downtown status, which was all very fine, but the move was taking its toll of Pop. He was often missing at dinner, remaining uptown to work late, or to eat with Bobbeh or Zaideh, or to attend a board meeting of the Minsker Congregation, where Zaideh was now the Rov. Or he would be in a rush, when he came downtown, to get to a Zionist meeting, or a

Masonic meeting, or a temple trustee meeting. Half the time he either didn't show up, or he would bolt his food and leave.

Never, however, on Friday night. The candlelit Sabbath meal remained inviolate, and the menu had improved. In honor of Lee's birthday, Mom one Friday night made a rare rib roast. When Lee saw the red slices she inquired with a giggle whether we were still kosher. It was a happy evening, and she made Mom and Pop happier by volunteering that she would go to the temple next morning.

"Got to catch Holy Joe Geiger's act," she said, "sooner or later."

Whereupon Pop astonished us by saying he was resigning as a temple trustee. The board had voted to start taking up a collection at Sabbath services. Pop had told them that though he knew times were changing, he could not condone that. Mom was saddened. A rabbi's *a* daughter could hardly disagree with Pop, but she loved being a downtown temple trustee's wife. Lee just sat there glowering until I mildly remarked that since the women came to the temple with pocketbooks anyway, and the men with their wallets, why not? Well, Lee burst out at me as though I had endorsed the clubbing of baby seals. Pop was right, she snapped, and I was just a sneak and a hypocrite, playing up to Zaideh all those years, putting on my pious Talmud act, and now coming out with this! She turned on Pop and asked why on earth Rabbi Geiger hadn't put his foot down and forbidden it.

"He tried. He and I both fought it. He even talked of resigning. But nobody can do anything with E. F. Kadane."

"And who the hell is E. F. Kadane?"

"Come to the temple," said Mom, "and you'll meet E. F. Kadane."

"By God, I will."

Now, mind you, my sister Lee had been irreligious for years, so I can't say why she fired up like that. I guess she was spoiling for a fight, any fight, and took Pop's side. She had never been much of a synagogue-goer at best. Nor had Mom been, for that matter. In the Bronx the women's section of the shule was all but empty on Saturday because mothers, daughters, and grandmothers were at home, "making Shabbess." The women showed up in force on holy days to say Yiskor, the memorial prayer for the dead; to hear a maggid speak, and have themselves a good cry. The keening and sobbing behind the women's curtains really used to frighten me as a boy. "*Ooo! Ow-*

ooo-ooo! OOOO!" The saddest movie you ever saw was nothing to
one of those Yiddish Yiskor sermons by a maggid. It is a lost art form.
The women left the synagogue wrung out, drying their eyes, and
quite content not to come again until the next Yiskor and the next
heartrending sermon.

In Rabbi Geiger's temple things were different. The women came
every Friday night and Saturday morning, and sat right beside their
menfolk. Huge arched stained-glass windows gave a religious yet smart
tone to the broad auditorium, where the expanse of pink plush seats
could seat maybe a thousand in all. When there was a bar mitzva, the
place would fill up as for a hit play, otherwise two or three hundred
worshippers would come, and the empty rows made a forlorn picture. Two podiums on either side of the stage were manned by the
rabbi and the cantor. Behind them, an immense ornately carved Holy
Ark was flanked by thronelike chairs, where temple officers sat in high
hats and frock coats. A big change from that Minsker Shule in the
Bronx cellar, altogether; no women's section, and no good cries on
Yiskor days.

"I don't believe this," Lee said, or rather gasped, as the Holy Ark
opened by itself. "I simply don't *believe* it."

I myself was used to Rabbi Geiger's services by now, but I think
my sister Lee may never have been inside a temple before. All she
knew was the old-time religion of the Yiskor days, and she was full
of white-hot indignation at every departure from the familiar format.
She objected at the outset to sitting with Pop and me; said it "felt
wrong" to be with the men. She objected to the cantor's microphone, because it "used electricity." When for the Reading of the Law
the auditorium lights dimmed, and a rosy glow brightened the stage
and the Holy Ark, she muttered at me, "Davey, that rabbi is working
the lights himself. I can *see* him. He's *pressing electric buttons!"*

This from Lee, who had probably abandoned the religion because
of Zaideh's timers, and had never stopped railing against them, and
smoked like a fiend on Saturday in her closed bedroom. Of course
Holy Joe was doing the lighting effects, and making no pretense of
hiding it, though the broad sleeves of his bright lilac robe did cover
his hand at the control buttons on his podium. At the other podium,
the cantor, in a matching lilac robe, was pouring out in a rich baritone the traditional melody, "And when the Ark set forth," to a grand

swell of organ music. Holy Joe's hand moved under the sleeve, and the great carved Ark doors majestically and slowly slid aside to reveal sixteen lilac Torahs, banked four above four, exactly matching the robes of the cantor and Holy Joe. This was what brought the big gasp from my sister Lee, "*I don't believe this!*" The people in front of us turned to look at her.

Pop murmured, "Lee, respect."

She kept snorting during Holy Joe's sermon. Yet there was nothing to snort at. Rabbi Geiger's style was worldly, easy, sonorous, and witty. The sermons were cut to one pattern. They started with a Bible text, wound off for about half an hour into current events or a new best-seller, and curled back to the Bible text. Those sermons were popular. Latecomers all were in their seats before Holy Joe Geiger spoke. Maybe the religious content was something like an aspirin tucked inside a banana split, but I have to say that that was the dose his audience wanted, and how they wanted it. Zaideh's sort of old-country Talmud discourse was certainly not for these prosperous West End Avenue Jews. They liked Holy Joe's service just as it was, and they liked him. Over near Amsterdam Avenue on Ninety-fifth Street there was a big Orthodox shule with no organ or lighting effects, for others whose taste or convictions differed. Lee was all wet about Rabbi Geiger, and just being cantankerous. Mom and Pop kept looking sadder and sadder as my sister fumed, for they had hoped that Lee would go for Geiger's updated service. That was undoubtedly why they had joined the temple instead of the Ninety-fifth Street shule, where they eventually did end up.

After services they could hardly prevail on Lee to stay for the *kiddush,* the buffet brunch. "I've had it with this place," Lee said.

"The rabbi wants to say a word of welcome to you," Mom pleaded. "Why can't you be a good mixer?"

"I'll give him a welcome," said Lee. "I'll give him a purple eye, to match his sixteen Torahs."

Pop took her by the arm. "Come, Leah-Mira."

Crackling with hostility, she came. At the crowded brunch in the social hall, Holy Joe, still in lilac vestments, said a lot of nice things about Pop as he welcomed Lee. He also mentioned Mom's revered father, Rabbi Levitan, and got some giggles with remarks about Lee's beauty; but he said not a word about her having returned from a year in Palestine. He was still talking when a very portly, very red-faced man in a horsy tweed suit and a green polka-dot bow tie stood up. "Just a moment, Rabbi. I'd like to greet the young lady myself."

I whispered to Lee, "E. F. Kadane."

"Aha!" growled Lee.

"As president of this temple, and on behalf of myself and all the other officers, let me welcome you, Leonore — if I may call you that — to our midst."

E. F. Kadane was a bachelor who had hit it big in real estate. He would not wear a frock coat and top hat, so other officers sat in the places of honor, but he was the unchallenged boss man of the temple. He gave the most money, and he called the tune.

"You are not only a very beautiful young lady," he went on, "anybody can see that, but you obviously have rare common sense. For you have left behind that stinkhole in the Middle East, to return to the good old U.S.A."

Nobody reacted except Lee, who sucked in her breath with a hiss, like a Japanese. E. F. Kadane was somewhat touched on Zionism. All one had to do around E. F. was mention Palestine, or Chaim Weizmann, or Theodor Herzl, to set him roaring about the stinkhole in the Middle East. E. F.'s little foible was, by general consent at the temple, always ignored. Even a Zionist like Pop shrugged it off. A big giver like E. F. was entitled to his crotchet, especially as there was nothing anyone could do about it.

"That's about all I want to say, Leonore. Except that I'm sure the land of the free looks mighty good to you, after that stinkhole in the Middle East. And I want you to know that you look mighty good to us. Especially to the bachelors among us." With a wink at her, and another at Holy Joe, he sat down.

"Rabbi Geiger," said Lee, getting to her feet, "let me thank you and Mr. E. F. Kadane, and tell me, do you also regard Palestine as a stinkhole in the Middle East?"

Consternation in the social hall. All faces turned to Holy Joe, including E. F. Kadane's stern red balloon of a face. Slowly Holy Joe rose, gathering the lilac robe around him. "Well, Leonore," he said, "that can be discussed on several levels. And I'll tell you what, let's have a good discussion of it in my study soon, shall we? Just the two of us." It was perfectly done, with just a faint wag of the eyebrows and an Errol Flynn grin. He got a big laugh in which even E. F.

Kadane grudgingly joined, and he was off the hook. Fast on his feet, was Holy Joe.

The kiddush broke up. Both E. F. Kadane and Rabbi Geiger came over to shake hands with Lee. The yearning expressions on their bachelor faces made me realize again how pretty she was. To me she was just Lee, but I guess she was every bit as enchanting as Dorsi Sabin, if one could look at her that way. She went right on the attack. "I think it's awful," she said, "your taking up a collection on Friday night. I think it's disgusting. I don't blame my father one bit for resigning. I may not be all that religious, but I know what's supposed to be right and wrong."

E. F. and the rabbi looked at each other. Holy Joe said, "The idea may be reconsidered."

"We have a lot of respect for your father," E. F. said. "Maybe we'll find the money some other way. I have two fine tickets for *Of Thee I Sing* for tonight, Leonore. Do you happen to be free?"

"I'm not," said my sister.

"And tomorrow night?" inquired Holy Joe. "We are having a men's club dance, but alas, I have no girl, Lee."

Lee had heard plenty about the dance from Mom, and had kept declaring with rising tartness that wild horses wouldn't drag her to it.

"You have one now," Lee said. "I'd love to come."

To wind up this part of my story: thanks to Pop, Rabbi Geiger won the battle over the collection. E. F. Kadane had it in for him after that, and about a year later tried to terminate his contract, for immorality. Pop defended Geiger, and saved him from dismissal that time. But Holy Joe was no match for the all-powerful E. F. Kadane, and eventually he was ousted. His career suffered badly from that black mark. He went to a temple in Texas for a few years, then returned to the New York suburbs, drifting from one pulpit to another. After a while he had no pulpit, but continued to do funerals, weddings, and such. A widower in his later years, he married a wealthy widow, so he is okay, but rather sad.

Now I want you to understand about Holy Joe. At Pop's funeral several rabbis spoke, including both Zaideh and Holy Joe Geiger. Geiger broke down and cried. He was the only speaker who did, and he wasn't faking. I saw him conduct many funerals, and at none of the others did he lose his composure. If I have seemed here to be satirizing a man, I've missed the mark and done a wrong, while trying to paint a true picture. I've given the light and shade of Holy Joe Geiger, but I will never forget that he wept for my father.

I dwell on this because I fear I am partly responsible for that celebrated comical rabbi in *Onan's Way,* "Holy Moses Schmuckler," one of Peter Quat's more colorful creations. I made the mistake, if it was a mistake, of telling Peter about Holy Joe. He was convulsed and insisted on meeting him, so I asked Peter to Aunt Faiga's wedding, since Mom had invited Rabbi Geiger. It made quite an impression on Peter, that wedding, but I must say his portrayal of it is preposterous — all that business about the rabbi feeling the bride's behind under the canopy, and putting his hand up her dress under the table at the wedding dinner, not to mention that unspeakable scene in the hall closet. All that was pure Quat. Holy Joe Geiger was a good fellow, and the soul of decorum: only, like any bachelor his age, somewhat on the make.

I did once come upon him in the hallway outside our apartment late at night, trying to snatch a kiss from my sister Lee, holding his derby in one hand and pawing at her with the other. A pitiful sight, that was. Lee could have fended off an octopus holding seven derbys, if she had had a mind to. It was no more than she expected, and she did not hold it against him. Once we both got inside the apartment, in fact, she about died laughing. I think she led on Holy Joe. Lee always has had a mean ultra-female streak.

In any case, I will now tell you what really happened at Aunt Faiga's wedding. It was nothing like Quat's raunchy fantasy, yet lively enough, in all truth.

51

Aunt Faiga's Wedding

FAIGA and Boris had requested a small parlor ceremony, but Mom had ended up inviting the entire Mishpokha, in all its Bay Ridge and Bayonne ramifications. Otherwise, she argued, those left out would feel that the high-flying Manhattan Goodkinds were snubbing them, and the wounds would fester for life. Boris's relatives were also a sensitive clan; so he informed Faiga, and Faiga informed Mom; therefore all of them had to be asked, too, and the thing expanded to a large unwieldy affair.

More problems cropped up as the big day approached. There was the matter of Pat the doorman. Late in the game Boris casually mentioned that many of his kin spoke only Yiddish. How, Mama worried, would they communicate with Pat? Of course, Pat might well have sent all unidentifiable Jews to the Goodkind apartment, but such guesswork was not for our Pat. His job was to announce all visitors, and he was rigid about it. Moreover, to everyone's amazement, after cutting us dead for years, Uncle Yehuda had sent a last-minute acceptance. Here was a special worry! Aunt Sophie called Mama to warn her that Yehuda had grown a long white beard, that he wore a cast-off collegian raccoon coat and looked like a lunatic, and that he fully expected to be insulted and turned away by his rich brother's West End Avenue doorman. When this happened, he intended to call the police. No anti-Semitic downtown goyish doorman — so Uncle Yehuda was expostulating over the telephone, to everyone in the family but Mom — was going to push him around.

To calm Uncle Yehuda, and take care of Boris's relatives, it was decided to post me in the lobby downstairs. My sister Lee's Yiddish was much better than mine, but the wedding had become a high-

tension issue with Lee, and nobody dared propose that she do anything about it. This was entirely Mom's fault. Mom had taken to loud
sighing that if only she were doing all this for *SOMEONE ELSE* she
would be the happiest woman in the world, but why for Faiga? Each
time some new difficulty or expense cropped up, Mama would complain that she wouldn't mind at all if it were *someone else's* wedding,
but just for Faiga it was intolerable; and lest she be misunderstood,
every time she said *someone else* she would turn melancholy cow eyes
at my sister Lee. One evening Mom declared she would have to hire
a caterer, after all. It would cost a fortune, which she would gladly
have spent for *someone else's* wedding, but it annoyed her to have to
throw the money away on Faiga. If it were *someone else's* wedding,
Mom said, she would have happily gone to all the trouble in the world.
She would even have stuffed a kishka with her own hands, the longest kishka ever stuffed in America.

"I wouldn't advise that, Mom," snapped Lee. "*Someone else* might
wrap all forty feet of that kishka around your neck, and strangle you
with it." Whereupon she threw down her napkin and left the table.

"Go easier on her," Pop said to Mom.

"I don't know what you're talking about," said Mom. "Everybody
in this house is becoming a nervous wreck, and all for what? For who?
For Faiga. If only it was for *somebody else!*"

Just to keep Mom off her back, Lee had been going out on dates
with Holy Joe Geiger, and even E. F. Kadane. They bored her and
she intended to break off with both of them, but meantime Mom
invited them both to Faiga's wedding. Poor Lee! She listened for the
arrival of the mail every morning, hurriedly looked through the en-
velopes, and wilted as she cast them aside. She was languishing and
dimming by the week. She hardly ate.

On the wedding day, as I lurked in the lobby, shepherding Boris's
bemused uncles and aunts past the deadpan Pat to Jesus's elevator,
and lying doggo for Uncle Yehuda, I had my own problem. The ceremony was scheduled for three o'clock. Dorsi and I were going to a
party in Great Neck that evening — Puss Puss Ohlbaum's birthday
party, in fact — and I was to call for her at six. The wedding might
drag on for a couple of hours, I figured, but surely I could get out
of the house by five. Close, but manageable.

Well, wouldn't you know, that day there was a big storm all along
the eastern seaboard. At three-thirty, when only a handful of guests

had showed up through driving rain, the elevator man brought me a note scrawled by Lee: *Stay in the lobby, heavy snow in New Jersey, ceremony put off to five.* Five! Good God! How late would I be, calling for Dorsi? How angry would she be? Unquestionably, she had already laid out her clothes, perhaps was in the tub; Dorsi's lead time for a date was three or four hours. There was no way I could break that date. So I hung around that grandiose lobby, on the watch for lost-looking Jews, and for a raccoon coat and long white beard approaching through the rain; smiling at the guests and directing them to the elevator, explaining in a mutter to Cousin Harold, and later to Peter Quat, what on earth I was doing, and all the while my wristwatch showed the time melting away. Four! Four-thirty! Dorsi Sabin was out of the tub by now at her mirror, her nakedness imperfectly filmed by lace-trimmed peach lingerie — my head whirled at the shimmering picture — putting the last touches on her hair, which would take only an hour or so. The wedding would never even *start* at five, the way the guests were straggling in.

"Meestair David, telephone for you," called Jesus, the elevator man. I rode with him upstairs, and alerted Lee to watch through the window for Uncle Yehuda.

"David? It's Dorsi. David, I think I've got the flu. I feel *awful*. Don't I sound awful? I'm croaking like a frog."

Dorsi did not sound sick, not to me. She sounded as though she were *trying* to croak like a frog, and doing a piss-poor job of it. What a relief! I knew very well what was up. Dorsi had a big history exam the next day, and she was an obsessive pursuer of A's. The weather was lousy, it was a long way to Great Neck by subway and train, and she had decided to stay home and study.

"Oh, come on, Dorsi, you sound just fine." The Vicomte de Machiavelli, master womanizer, seizing lightning advantage of this development. "Take an aspirin. I was just leaving. I'll see you at six."

"David, I can't possibly go to that party."

"You're breaking our date? Again?"

She had broken one just two weeks ago. A nice Jewish girl didn't break two dates in a row in those days, not unless she was discarding a fellow.

"Don't put it like that. I feel terrible about it."

"All right, then, Dorsi, will you come with me to the Junior Prom?"

"What? The Junior *Prom?*" Taken unawares, Dorsi forgot to croak.

"Why, that's months away. I don't even know what night it is."

"It's February seventeenth. I'm on the committee."

Dorsi hesitated. The Prom was as steep a commitment as New Year's Eve. She had already turned me down on that one. Fish or cut bait? Drop the underage but glittery Vicomte, or hang on?

"Davey, I am really in a ghastly state." (Croak, croak.) "Give me a ring next week."

"Look, Dorsi, if you don't want to see me any more, just say so. You're too old for me, maybe, or the chemistry is wrong, or —"

Lee shouted, "Here comes a raccoon coat!"

"I don't *like* you when you're this way," exclaimed Dorsi in angry clear bell-like tones, "but all *right,* I'll go with you to the Junior Prom. Satisfied?"

"Marvellous, Dorsi! Bye." I hung up, and dashed for the elevator.

It was unmistakably Uncle Yehuda out there under the canopy; raccoon coat, white beard, and all, with Aunt Rose beside him, quite gray but still pretty. Yehuda was not making a scandal, however. Unless I was seeing things, he and Pat the doorman were having a friendly chat. Pat spied me. "Ah, there's your nephew, Rabbi," he said. "He'll escort you to the wedding. Enjoyed talking to you, sir." Pat smartly touched his gold-braided cap with two fingers.

"Can you imagine? That goy took me for a rabbi," said Yehuda to me in Yiddish as we walked inside. "Say, I could have been one if I wanted to. A very fine goy."

It was the raccoon coat. It had to be. Pat knew Zaideh was a rabbi. Zaideh had that fur-lined coat, with fur collar and cuffs. Yehuda's coat was all fur, and I guess the long white beard did the rest. Pat the doorman had solemn respect for men of God.

"A rabbi," said Aunt Rose, as we rode up in the elevator. "That's a hot one. The Porkville Iluy."

Uncle Yehuda growled something rude in Yiddish at Aunt Rose, and Yiddish expressions can be very rude, so I leave it untranslated. Pop was waiting at the door to embrace his brother. Uncle Yehuda submitted to the hug with good grace, all things considered, though muttering indistinctly about promissory notes and victrolas. Lee caught my hand and pulled me aside. "Big panic," she said. "There may just not be a wedding today, and I'm not kidding."

"What now, for God's sake?"

I followed her down the hall toward a wild commotion in the master bedroom. We could not get in. The room was jammed with women. So was the hallway outside. Because these were old-country Jewish females, they were mostly small, so I could see over them. At the center of the hullabaloo were Faiga and Mom, their voices rising over the babble. Zaideh towered out of this mass of noisy femininity, between Faiga and Mom. In a blue silk dress, and a blue veil pushed back on her head, Faiga looked lovely, though excessively red in the face. Mama, all gotten up in jewelry, lace, and satin, seemed calmer than Faiga, though not at any cost in audibility.

"*No candles!*" Faiga was shouting.

"Now, no more arguing, Faiga, do you hear?" Mama shouted back. "It's getting late. I'm paying the caterer by the hour, and it's costing me a fortune."

"*No candles,* I say!"

"There's nothing wrong with candles. I got married with candles, and *so will you.*"

A number of women in the bedroom, including Bobbeh and assorted aunts of both families, were holding tall unlit white tapers, and glancing uncertainly from Faiga to Mom.

"Faigeleh, be a good girl and come along," Zaideh put in. "Everything is arranged, Sarah Gitta has made you such a fine wedding. You look so beautiful. Who gets married without candles?"

FAIGA (*in frantic Yiddish*): NO CANDLES! Boris and I have put up with enough of these crazy old superstitions. I draw the line. NO CANDLES!

MAMA (*in Yiddish, distinctly louder than Faiga*): This is MY house! I've made you a wedding fit for a princess! You haven't lifted a finger! I've never seen such ingratitude. You'll come along *right now,* it's a shame and a disgrace the way you're holding up the wedding. And you'll come WITH CANDLES. (*To the women*) Light the candles and let's go!

FAIGA (*in Yiddish, top of her lungs*): I'M getting married, Sarah Gitta. YOU'RE not. (*English, fortissimo, to the women*) If you light those candles, I take off this veil and go home. That's final! Let hell freeze over!

What I'm not conveying here is the tone, the antagonism reaching back through the years and across the seas. It was Mama against a daughter of Koidanov, and this time it was to the death. Faiga had

already agreed to march around Boris; why then make an issue over
the candles, a usual part of the custom? But in the pre-ceremony hys-
terics, lifelong resentments had surfaced over this trivial detail. It had
become the Bloody Nose Ridge of Faiga's wedding.

Lee murmured to me, "This is bad, and getting worse." She shoul-
dered her way through the women. "Listen, Faiga," she cried, in pretty
good voice herself, "I couldn't agree with you more. You've been an
angel of patience. You've put up with a lot more primitive nonsense
than I would have. I don't blame you for not giving another inch!"

Faiga clutched Lee's hand. "Thanks, Lee. God bless you, and
thanks!"

"What is she saying?" Zaideh asked Mom. "Leah-Mira, don't talk
Turkish, please."

"Who asked you?" Mama yelled at Lee. "If this was *somebody else's*
wedding, you might have a say. Since it is not, you just butt out!"

Lee snatched a candle from a Boris aunt and lit it with a flip of her
cigarette lighter. The taper flared, and all the women suddenly shut
up. It was a remarkable effect, that silence. It couldn't have been done
better on the stage. Lee said to Zaideh in her perfect Yiddish, "Nu?
How many candles must there be, Zaideh? Twenty? A thousand?
Here's a candle. Is it enough?"

Zaideh looked from Mom to Faiga. Both were struck dumb. He
clapped his hands, and exclaimed in jubilant tones, "Come! Let me
marry off the daughter of my old age!" He started for the door, and
the women gave way before him with joyous shouts and hand-clap-
ping. The burning taper in one hand, her other arm through Faiga's
elbow, Lee followed him. With a last unyielding glare at Mom, Faiga
allowed herself to be dragged out of the bedroom, escorted by the
entire mass of singing, applauding, rejoicing women.

Well, after all that cliff-hanging foolishness, there was something
eerily impressive about Faiga's seven circuits of Boris, with Lee beside her holding one lighted candle. The small canopy of purple velvet was hand-supported on four wooden rods by four men Mom had
chosen: Uncle Hyman, Uncle Yail from Bay Ridge, Holy Joe Geiger,
and E. F. Kadane. There were sixty or seventy people there, but our
big living room might have been empty, so silent was everybody. Faiga,
her face obscured by the veil falling to her shoulders, paced around
and around her groom, who stood there grim and white-faced, a yarmulka perched precariously on his wild bush of hair. Four, five, six,

seven times. I had expected both these unbelievers to smirk if not to giggle during the circuits, but not a bit of it. Faiga's eyes were glittering through the veil, and her lips were pressed in a hard line, as she halted beside her groom.

Zaideh's masterstroke of tact was to give the long difficult Seventh Blessing to Uncle Yehuda. To Aunt Rose he might be the Porkville Iluy, but Yehuda, like Pop, retained all the old melodies of their shammas father. He chanted flawlessly:

> *Blessed are you O Lord our God, King of the Universe, who created gladness and joy, bridegroom and bride, merriment, song, happiness and gaiety, love and affection, peace and neighborliness.*
>
> *Soon, O Lord our God, may there be heard in the cities of Judea and the streets of Jerusalem the voice of jubilation and the voice of gladness, the voice of the bridegroom and the voice of the bride, the voice of grooms celebrating from their canopies, and the young men from their feasts of song.*
>
> *Blessed are you, O Lord, who gladden the groom with the bride.*

Through the white beard, as he was chanting, I could perceive as never before on Uncle Yehuda's face the lineaments of my own father, who stood nearby, pale and happy. Holding a stick beside Yehuda was Uncle Hyman, and there were those same lineaments, blurred by fat, and sagging with hard luck. In those three faces I was catching a glimpse, I realized, of the shammas of the Soldiers' Shule in Minsk, whose melody I was hearing, the other zaideh whom I had never known.

Boris smashed a paper-wrapped glass under his heel. *CRUNCH!* Oh yes, old Boris went through with the whole works. The place exploded. Cousin Harold jumped at the rosewood piano and banged out the traditional wedding song, just a few Yiddish words, "*Bridegroom, bride, good luck, good luck,*" endlessly repeated; and our Mishpokha one and all, old and young, including Lee and me, surged to sing and dance around the couple in a disorderly hand-holding ring. Boris stood grinning in a befuddled way, the yarmulka gone. Faiga, veil thrown back, clutched his arm, tearfully laughing. Boris's family, by and large antireligious socialists like him, and I daresay not feeling at home in the fancy apartment, stood aside looking on. Standing aside too were E. F. Kadane, Holy Joe Geiger, and Peter Quat, in a separate cool clump of three, commenting to each other as they

watched us; E. F. Kadane fiddling with his bow tie and staring, Holy
Joe with folded hands beaming sacerdotally, and Peter Quat taking
it all in through narrowed eyes. Ordinarily I might have felt embarrassed by Peter Quat's chilly scrutiny of my tribe in action, but now
I didn't give a damn.

The eating, drinking, dancing, singing, toasting, joking, and general whoopee went on and on. The caterer's men pushed back the
furniture and rolled aside Mom's Persian carpet, baring a ballroom
expanse of newly varnished floor. The wine, whiskey, and food
loosened up the Boris clan, until most of them, too, were dancing in
circles, not a yarmulka in the lot, but spirits high. Damned if E. F.
Kadane himself didn't at last select a plump little Boris cousin of
eighteen or so, and go thudding around with her, his face frighten-
ingly crimson but very jolly.

My sister Lee inveigled Holy Joe Geiger into a so-called handkerchief dance. Out of modesty the Orthodox boy and girl are not supposed to touch each other, so they hold a handkerchief between them
and step around. Holy Joe shed his ministerial poise to shake a mean
leg, and Lee flashed much more silk-clad shank and thigh than is called
for in this dance. Everybody else — except Peter — stopped dancing
and formed a large ring around them, laughing and singing and
cheering. When Holy Joe quit, puffing hard and guffawing, they got
a round of applause. Peter leaned against a wall, just watching it all
through those narrowed eyes, a pink caterer's yarmulka aslant on his
head like a funny little party hat.

From the piano Cousin Harold called, "Now! The bride and
groom!" Boris and Faiga waltzed out by themselves and clomped
about. Everybody in the ring clapped hands, and various aunts wiped
their eyes.

Faiga exclaimed, halting by Mom, "Now Sarah Gitta and Alex."
The half-sisters seized each other's hands, looked in each other's eyes,
kissed, and embraced. Pop came and took Mom in his arms. Boris
and Faiga fell back into the circle, and Cousin Harold began to play
a Mishpokha waltz tune of our childhood. Some Tin Pan Alley writer
once put words to this same tune, and made of it a standard called
"The Anniversary Waltz," but it is really a very old Jewish melody. I
don't even know if it has a name. Mom and Pop danced to that waltz
at Faiga's wedding, in the big living room of the new apartment, with
the whole Mishpokha and Boris's family, too, applauding. I mean

everyone, even Uncle Yehuda. If only for that fleeting moment, everybody was admiring them, wishing them well, forgiving them for making it to West End Avenue.

Pop and Mom seldom danced together any more. His steps were old-fashioned, quaintly graceful, and he looked so proud! But he looked tired, too, extremely tired. He had been the life of the revelry ever since the crunch of the glass, singing and capering with Boris, with Faiga, with Lee, with me, with the aunts, even drawing Zaideh into a grave little shuffle. So he was pretty well worn out. But he twirled Mom around smartly to that old tune, just the same.

I never dance to "The Anniversary Waltz." I would rather not hear it. If it comes on my automobile radio I turn it off. In those moments of the dance, with all the family applauding her, Mom came as close as she ever would to grasping the ploika; and because Pop wanted her to have it, and at least got her as far as West End Avenue, for me it was and remains his song.

Bobbeh wasn't Faiga's grandmother, but she was the grandma present, and the grandma is supposed to dance at a wedding. Mom steered Pop over to her. "Dance with Bobbeh!" So Pop embraced his lame little mother, who laughed like a girl and slowly, haltingly, began waltzing with him. As you can imagine, this brought a burst of clapping and cheers, but they went only a few steps and stopped, and not because Bobbeh was lame. My father stopped, stopped cold, his face gone gray. Smiling, he said very hoarsely, almost choking but waving his arms gaily, "That's it! Everybody else dance now." The ring broke up into dancing couples. My sister Lee and I pushed through to him, and we went with him to Lee's bedroom. He leaned heavily on both of us. His hand clasped in mine was greasily wet. In the bedroom he fell face down on Lee's bed.

"Go back! Dance! Have fun," he said, his head on his arms. "It's a wedding, see that the people enjoy themselves."

Mom came in. "Alex, Alex, what is it?"

Lee said, "I'll call Dr. Shiner."

"Don't call Dr. Shiner," Pop gasped. "I'm not dying yet. You kids go on. Sarah Gitta, bring me a glass of cold water." He turned his head and looked at us with heavy brown eyes. "Did you hear me? We have guests. Go!"

Lee said to me as we left the bedroom, "I'll start to work at the laundry. I'll drive him to the Bronx every day."

The living room was in a merry hubbub. The Boris clan had come to boisterous life, doing an old-country round-dance, with couples passing under upraised arms and snaking in and out as they sang a Russian song. The older people in our Mishpokha were joining in, and some of the young cousins, too. A Boris relative had taken over the piano, while Cousin Harold wolfed a heaping plateful of roast beef. E. F. Kadane and Holy Joe were gone. Peter Quat still leaned against a wall, the pink yarmulka atilt on his head, coldly watching. *Just plain kikes.*

That is how I guess we looked to him, since that is how Aunt Faiga's wedding comes out in *Onan's Way,* where he even has a distorted touch of the candles argument, which I guess he overheard. But that is not how I remember Faiga's wedding. Through those narrowed eyes, maybe that is how it looked to Peter. He wasn't one of us. I suppose he wouldn't have wanted to be, and yet his travesty has the forlorn note in it of someone bitter at being left out.

Soon after the wedding Pop went to see Dr. Shiner and took me with him. Dr. Shiner listened at his bared white sunken chest; listened much too long, and folded up his stethoscope with the expression of a hanging judge. Dr. Shiner had a big mustache and smelled of cigars and medicine, and childhood terror overcame me whenever I smelled him.

"You can dress now, Alex."

"Is it the pump?" Pop asked calmly, his forehead a mass of wrinkles.

"You're going to have to take it easier," said Dr. Shiner, with the faintly fiendish sympathy of the self-important healer, such as we all have known.

Easing off was not in my father's nature. My sister Lee did start to work in the laundry office. She chauffeured him to and from the place, and that helped. After a while Pop could again walk a few blocks without halting for breath. He came of sturdy stock. Uncle Hyman lived into his eighties, and Uncle Yehuda at ninety or so is still shuffling around in that small Miami shule as a shammas. Trouble was, Pop was mounting too high and too fast in the Goldena Medina, with too much dead weight on his back. Driving ambition and good nature are an unhealthy mix. Not one of us faced that truth at the time, least of all himself, and we all ignored the warning we got at Aunt Faiga's wedding.

52

"You Shall Have It"

DRUDGING in the laundry put Lee into a tailspin. Utterly dispirited, she did not even have a date for New Year's Eve, because she wanted none.

Peter, Mark, and I were meeting at the Quat apartment, to go down to Times Square and watch the ball drop at midnight. I invited her along, and she at once agreed, obviously hoping to pick up from Mark some news of Moshe Lev. That was the very first time I saw a Christmas tree in a Jewish home; a sure-enough small fir in a corner of the Quat living room, complete with silver tinsel trim and scarlet baubles, crowned with a gilt star. At a grand piano near the tree, Mark Herz was tinkling simple jazz. "Ah, the girl from the Holy Land!" He switched to *Hatikvah,* ending with a glissando and a standing salute.

Lee got her news, all right. Mark said straight off that he had regards for her from his cousin, who had written from South Africa, asking him to ring Leonore Goodkind and say hello. "Moshe Lev really took to you, I gather," Mark observed. "He said his wife and the whole family enjoyed your company." Lev had moved to South Africa on business, wife, kids and all, for a couple of years, Mark reported, staying with Moshe's wealthy brother, who had a huge house in Cape Town.

I had to admire the way Lee handled it. She made cheery small talk about Moshe's children, drank a glass of eggnog, and left, saying that she was going on to a party. I knew she was heading home to lick her wounds, but Peter and Mark hadn't a clue to how crushed she was.

We were debating whether to brave a thick drizzle and proceed to

Times Square, when Dr. Quat and his wife showed up. In his courtly way he said, "You will see in the New Year with us," and he brought out bottles of champagne which a bootlegger patient had pressed on him. So at midnight we stood around the piano, glasses in hand, and sang "Auld Lang Syne."

"I raise my glass," Dr. Quat said, "to a happy 1933, to our new President, and to Peter's gainful employment."

"It's a race for life," Peter said to us when the Quats retired. "Can I sell a story before I hear from Goldhandler? If I do, I'll tell him to shove it." His interview with the joke czar had gone well — too well, Peter said — and he might get a call any day, if a staff job opened up.

About one in the morning, Mark and I walked up Central Park West together. The rain had stopped. A misty moon shone through ragged clouds on late revellers, roistering along the wet black street, blowing horns. "How about that Christmas tree?" I said.

"Oh, well." Mark Herz shrugged. "Peter says his father believes Jewish children shouldn't grow up feeling deprived. As though *Jewish* and *deprived* weren't two words to describe one thing."

"Why do you say that? I've never felt deprived."

Mark gave me a sidelong glance in reply.

"What do you think Jews should do, anyway, Mark?"

"About what?"

"About being Jewish."

"Invent the space ship, and get off the planet while there's time."

A conversation stopper. We walked in silence. I had been waiting all evening for him to say something about my Varsity Show script, which early in the week I had given him to read. As we turned into the side street where we lived, I ventured, "I guess you didn't think *To Heil with It!* is funny."

"I don't think Hitler is funny. If the German situation falls apart and he takes power, I doubt anybody will stay amused for long." Outside his shabby brownstone boardinghouse, we shook hands. "Your show is full of droll things. I hope it's chosen. Happy New Year."

Well, the German situation did fall apart, Hitler got in, and among other grave international consequences, the Columbia Varsity Show judges rejected as out-of-date three competing scripts about funny Hitlers. If no acceptable new script were submitted in two weeks, there would be no show. I began beating my brain for an idea, and

I decided to call off my Junior Prom date with Dorsi. The dance fell smack in the middle of those two weeks. First things first.

"David," said Dorsi over the telephone, "if you break this date, I'll never go out with you again. I had other invitations, you know. I bought a new dress just for the Prom. I won't ever forgive you, David."

Obsessed as I was by Dorsi Sabin, here was one thing that mattered more. "Dorsi, I'm going to write a winning script, and I'll take you to the opening night."

"I won't go with you." Girlish slam of receiver.

Within the hour, the ringing telephone broke into my slow downhearted scrawling of notions for another script. Aha! Second thoughts, eh, Dorsi? Not quite ready to discard the juvenile but dazzling Vicomte, what? But it was only Mark Herz.

"Are you giving up on the Varsity Show?"

"I'm going to write a new one."

"In two weeks?"

"Yes."

"Any ideas?"

"A few, but I can't get going."

"Come over to my lab tomorrow."

The laboratory was a big bleak evil-smelling tiled room full of sinks, pipes, crooked glass tubes, and the like. No place, I thought, to try to be comical. It was odd to see Mark Herz in a stained laboratory coat, at home in these Dr. Frankenstein surroundings. I felt science and humor did not go together, and considered science altogether a grim dangerous nuisance. In required high school courses my attempts at experiments had produced only sparks, stinks, boilings-over, and explosions. I had faked the numbers callously to make the reports come out right. The Man in the Iron Mask was a paradox; at least by rumor something of a physics genius, yet undeniably a funny man.

Mark liked my notion of parodying *Anthony Adverse,* a big bestseller of the day. In a couple of meetings we cooked up a plot about a ham-handed aide of George Washington, who got all the orders wrong and accidentally won the Revolution. I went to work around the clock like a madman, and wrote *Oliver Obverse* in ten days and ten nights. In the doing, the characters seemed real, the comedy sidesplitting, the romance so beautiful and tender that I choked up on reading it over. I called the heroine Dorothea. And I missed the

Prom. Dorsi was the most popular girl there, could hardly dance twenty steps without being cut in on, and altogether had a swimming evening of it. So Biberman reported. He knew from Puss Puss about my fight with Dorsi, and was full of sympathy, rather like Dr. Shiner's.

1933 VARSITY SHOW ON!
GOODKIND SCRIPT CHOSEN

It was a three-column story in Monday's *Spectator*. On Tuesday I found on my desk at home a neat blue envelope. Here was the entire communication:

> *February 25, 1933*
> *Congratulations, David, on your Varsity Show.*
> *Sincerely,*
> *Dorsi*

So lovesick was I, this low-voltage billet-doux electrified me. Dorsi was sweetly magnanimous over the telephone. "You've apologized enough, David. Of course I'll go with you to your opening night."

So the romance of the century was on again, and I had to get myself a driver's license at once. My eighteenth birthday fell in March and the Varsity Show in April. I meant to take Dorsi to my opening night in rented white tie and tails, at the wheel of the twelve-cylinder Cadillac, which was then still in our possession. And if Dorsi Sabin could resist such 24-karat gold wooing then she was not an iceberg but a golem, a weird figure of animated stone, and I would have nothing more to do with her.

Pop was outside the laundry, squinting at me in the sunshine, when I first took the wheel of a dilapidated old two-seater Ford the business owned. Beside me was Felix Brodofsky, two years older than I, fatter than ever, a laundry marker-and-assorter now and a married man. He had the use of this car, so he was going to teach me to drive. I grinned with nervous pride at Pop and called, "Well, at last!" Tolerantly smiling, Pop called back, "Not this should be the ambition of David Goodkind." And so we chugged off.

I would have learned faster and better if not for Felix Brodofsky's conversation. Felix thought I was unlucky to be going to college. He was already earning money, he pointed out, and also "getting it regular." He inquired whether possibly, I, too, was getting it regular from one of them coeds, who he understood were hot stuff. I said no, I wasn't getting it regular from a hot coed. Next he inquired if I had *ever* gotten it. Concentrating on my shifting, clutching, and braking, I was too busy to manage reticence, and I said well, no, I had never gotten it.

That was my mistake. By God, Felix Brodofsky had me there. I might be the son of the usurper of the Fairy Laundry presidency, I might live on West End Avenue, I might be a Columbia smartass, but not only wasn't I getting it regular, I had *never* gotten it. As I drove around amid the vacant lots near the Bronx River, he kept regaling me with word pictures of what I was missing. Revelling in these X-rated descriptions of his marital joys, he brushed off the one really sticky maneuver, starting uphill. In those old cars, you had to engage the gear, let in the clutch, let out the brake, and step on the gas all at once, almost. Otherwise you rolled backward and were in trouble. Felix taught this trick to me on a gentle grade, let me start uphill a couple of times, and pronounced me ready for the test.

My driving skill, or lack of it, he then disclosed, wouldn't matter a damn. All I had to do was put ten dollars in the pocket of the door upholstery, and whisper to the inspector, "There's something for you in the door." That was all. Unless I drove the car into the Bronx River and drowned us both, I would get my license. But he recommended against telling my father. All Bronx drivers knew this, but my father would disapprove. Felix Brodofsky was letting me in on the secret, I daresay, for old times' sake; also out of sympathy with me for never having gotten it, the fat fuck.

Well, you have no idea how that jarred me. My first encounter with the majesty of the law, with admittance to adult society, came down to a bribe; here was a loss of innocence! I worried and worried about that bribe, and when it came to the test, I couldn't bring myself to do it. The inspector, a stout grayish man with a disgruntled face, said, "Go ahead, drive." It was then only two weeks before the Varsity Show opening night. The stakes were high, the pressure on me heavy. I had actually put the ten-dollar bill in the door pocket, but my nerve failed me, and I said nothing to him. I just drove. I did well enough until he abruptly ordered me to stop, halfway up a steep deserted hill. I pulled the emergency brake tight. It held, barely.

"Okay. Start."

Start? With the hood pointed at the sky? Damn Brodofsky, and his rhapsodies on getting it regular! Why had he never trained me on a real hill?

"Well, what are you waiting for? Start!"

"There's something for you in the door," I hoarsely whispered. I threw in the clutch, shifted into gear, let out the brake, and stepped on the gas. At least I thought I did all that, but it came out wrong. The gears screeched, the motor roared, the car trembled, and we began travelling backward.

"What the hell do you think you're doing?" the inspector barked.

"There's something for you in the door," I repeated louder.

"What? I can't hear you. Stop the goddamned car!"

I fussed with brake, clutch, gear, and accelerator in panic, producing grinds and roars and nothing else, while we gathered velocity in reverse.

"Stop this car, for Christ's sake!"

"THERE'S SOMETHING FOR YOU IN THE DOOR!" I screamed, as we backed down that grade at about thirty miles an hour, picking up dizzy speed by the second.

"You're a goddamned maniac! You'll kill us both! Out of my goddamned way!" The inspector thrust me aside, grabbed at the emergency brake and yanked it with all his might. The Ford slowly squealed and shuddered to a halt. Sudden silence, there among the weedy lots. The inspector stared at me, panting, speechless.

"Something for you in the door," I sobbed.

"I'll take that wheel."

He drove back to the Fairy Laundry, got into his own car, and departed without another word. When I felt in the pocket of the door, the ten-dollar bill was gone. A few days later, an envelope came from the Motor Vehicle Bureau in the Bronx, informing me that I had failed — so I assumed; until I opened it. It contained my driver's license.

So scorn not the humble tax man, reader, and his beagle nose for loopholes in the law. It is the way of the world, and I learned it early. Tax avoidance is not bribery, of course; it seeks out permitted dodges, and everybody does it. But I will say this. No Internal Revenue agent has ever found, at the Goodkind legal offices, something for him in the door. I learned disgust for that early, too.

And now for the Cadillac, I thought rejoicing! Impulsively I took the subway to the Bronx, and went galloping up the broad metal stairs of the Fairy Laundry to Pop's office, to show him my driver's license, and line up the twelve-cylinder white elephant, which was rusting away on blocks. I was sure Pop would get it down and running for the Varsity Show author. He was so proud . . .

All at once the recollection comes upon me in an overpowering wave — I smell the steamy soap-and-chlorine air of the laundry, and hear the machines clattering and rumbling, and see the sweaty women in white smocks out on the main floor, working the presses and feeding the mangles. Gone, all gone! The New England Thruway obliterated that Bronx neighborhood. The Fairy Laundry is as lost as Atlantis. And to think that that building was my father's life; that that was all he ever did with his mind and his gifts! Well, on his bent back I mounted and became a prosperous tax man in the Goldena Medina, and even a Presidential Assistant. Back to the Fairy Laundry, then, back forty years . . .

My sister Lee was at a desk in the outer office. The office looked much smaller, like the rest of the place. I could remember how grandiose the building had once seemed, with its smokestack reaching to the clouds, and its vast interior vistas of awe-inspiring machinery. Now it had the seedy sooty look of a common factory going full blast, and the spaces had shrunk. My sister looked seedy, too, in a brown skirt and brown blouse, shuffling stacks of frayed file cards. Pop's office door opened as I talked with Lee, and he came striding out, papers in hand, countenance stern, movements brisk, speech terse to the clerks. The Boss. The faces at the desks sobered, and all bent over their work, even Lee. But when he noticed me, his tough aspect softened. "Yisroelke! Come inside." His office was half the size I remembered.

"Well, congratulations," Pop said, nodding over my license and handing it back. "What can I do for you?"

Clear implication, without malice: Yisroelke doesn't travel up to the Bronx and visit Pop in the laundry, unless he wants something. The request for the twelve-cylinder Cadillac all but stuck in my throat. How dreary the laundry was, and how unhealthy! I was thinking that this was where my father made his money, after all; this was what kept us on West End Avenue; this was how I was being supported at Columbia, while Felix Brodofsky already supported a wife. Still, I got the words out.

"I see. When would you need it?"

I told him. He thought a moment, and then managed a smile.

"You shall have it."

53

Opening Night

"CAMEL'S hair?" said Lee at dinner. "For opening night? Are you out of your mind, Davey? Nobody wears brown with tails. You'll look like a gangster."

"Shows how much you know," I said. "At Columbia, nobody wears anything else."

Bob Greaves had taken to arriving at dances with a camel's-hair topcoat over his white tie and tails. Whether he had no money for a black coat, or just hit on this as a stroke of ultra-smooth reverse snobbery, I don't know. Maybe it was the thing that year at Yale or Princeton. In any case, our class had broken out in a rash of camel's-hair coats at formal dances, always with the collar turned up, because that was how Bob Greaves wore his. One day in the *Jester* office I glanced at the label inside Greaves's coat, hanging in the closet: *Finchley's,* with a Fifth Avenue address. That did it. I might be the author of the Varsity Show, the Vicomte de Brag, assistant managing editor of the *Jester,* I might have a twelve-cylinder Cadillac at my disposal; all that was as smoke on the wind, unless I could get a Finchley camel's-hair coat to wear over my rented tails on opening night, with the collar turned up. Only then could I be sure of sweeping Dorsi Sabin off her feet.

"Well, it's no problem," Mom said. "Michaels' has racks and racks of camel's-hair coats."

"The only place to get a real camel's-hair coat," I said, "the kind everyone wears, is at Finchley's, on Fifth Avenue."

"David," said Mama kindly to her unfortunate cretin son, "on Fifth Avenue you pay for the high rent, not for the merchandise. If you must have a camel's-hair coat to wear over white tie and tails —"

"It's completely ridiculous," said Lee.

"Do you wear a high hat," asked Pop, "with the camel's-hair coat?"

"He wears a lampshade with it," said Lee, "a brown lampshade. At Columbia nobody wears anything else."

Lee was an embittered soul. I ignored and forgave her.

"No hat, Pop. Just the coat. With the collar turned up."

"But must it be Finchley's?" asked Pop. "Mama is right, it will cost twice as much."

"Pop, Finchley's has the coat I want."

"Then that will be our present," he said, "for your opening night."

"The lampshade he can get at Macy's," said Lee.

I said, "Thanks, Pop. The author will be a real smoothie that night. You'll see."

"Smoodie?" he said, glancing up from his soup. Pop never quite lost his accent, and I can't forget his pronunciation of that word. "What's a smoodie, Yisroelke?"

"Oh, you know. A man of elegance. Chic. Smart. In the fashion. *Comme il faut.*"

"*Comme il faut,*" Pop said. "Yes. Tolstoy writes about being *comme il faut.* Good, then we'll be proud because you'll be so *comme il faut.*"

Next day I stood outside Finchley's, peering in as if it were a Catholic Church, and just as shy about entering. I could see the salesmen standing about inside, all so well groomed, so erect, so tweedy, so unlike Mr. Michaels! Finchley's appeared to be staffed entirely by old frozen-faced Dekes. I was not even sure they would take my money and sell me a camel's-hair coat like Bob Greaves's. Such a coat hung on a dummy in the window, the exact Bob Greaves coat, with the collar turned up. The dummy itself looked gentile, in fact not wholly unlike Bob Greaves, especially with that turned-up collar and the slight waxy sneer. I had to have that coat. I nerved myself and plunged in.

Well, Finchley's took my money, all right, and sold me a coat; though not before the salesman who waited on me, a sandy-haired patrician with a toothbrush mustache and a British accent, obviously a Coldstream Guard fallen on lean times, let me know just how out of place I was. The coat looked fine on me, in fact marvellous. I was faintly disappointed, I admit, standing at the three-way mirror, to observe that in that perfect coat, with the collar turned up, I bore a striking resemblance — which I had somehow never noticed before — not to Bob Greaves, but to my Aunt Faiga. Also, as I turned here and there, I noticed there was no belt in the back. I could have sworn Bob Greaves's coat had one. I mentioned this to the Cold-stream Guard.

"If you want a belt in the back, *sir*" — he spoke the word *sir* like a Shakespearean actor doing Antonio and addressing Shylock — "you will have to go to Canal Street."

I paid my money and escaped into the hazy sunlight of Fifth Avenue with a Finchley camel's-hair coat in a box under my arm, the Jew who never felt deprived. The salesman was right, by the way. There was no belt on Greaves's coat. All those coats at Michaels' had belts, no doubt, every last one of them. Now suppose I had showed up at opening night in a belted Michaels' coat? I might as well have worn phylacteries.

"The Cadillac is here." Lee burst in on me, as I toiled at my books.

I leaped up. "Where? Where is it?"

"Right downstairs."

I put on the Finchley coat and turned up the collar. Downstairs Pop was talking to Pat the doorman, and there at the curb was the Cadillac.

"Take a spin," said Pop, "Smoodie."

I got behind the wheel. Ah, this gigantic gleaming beautiful thing, smelling so rich, mine to drive! I started the engine. Ah, that low majestic powerful purr! In the Finchley coat, I felt invincibly competent and cool. I waved at Pop, and turned up the Finchley collar a bit more. He stood smiling, one foot in front of the other, his right hand in a jacket pocket. In photographs taken in his twenties, in his forties, in the last snapshot before he died, he is invariably standing just that way. For him that right hand in the jacket was *comme il faut*. You see it in old pictures of the Russian Jewish intelligentsia; the right hand either inside the jacket, Napoleon-style, or else thrust in a pocket.

The Cadillac moved like a cloud one rides in a dream. I arrived back in front of the house numb with euphoria. Dorsi Sabin was mine. Pop still stood there with Pat.

"It's wonderful, Pop."

"Smoodie," said Pop, "I'll take it to the garage."

Dress rehearsal. The cast, all painted, wigged, and costumed, milling on the stage in a great dither. Stagehands shouting as they move

flats into place. The shirt-sleeved musicians of the orchestra tuning
up. I stand alone, at the rear of the empty rows of chairs in the grand
ballroom of the Waldorf-Astoria; on tenterhooks, contemplating this
swarming enterprise taking final form. The curtain falls on the disorderly racket on stage. Overture time! The conductor has put together a potpourri of the show's tunes, but I have not yet heard this
overture, and the first notes send warm sharp thrills along my spine.
What I hear is a fife shrilly piping "Yankee Doodle," to the rat-tat-
tat of a drum. Nothing else.

God Almighty, the evocative power of music! It was all there in
those opening bars: the Minutemen, George Washington, Valley
Forge, the crossing of the Delaware, the Spirit of '76; I was almost
ashamed of having made fun of the American Revolution, so flooded
was I, at the sound of that fife and drum, with the naive copybook
patriotism of my childhood. Several drums took up the beat, and the
orchestra crashed into our opening number, the March of the Minutemen, which has since become a Columbia football song. Right now,
forty years later, as I write about that moment, pins and needles are
prickling all over my body. And that was the onset of the creative
fever; an infection of which I have never been wholly cured, it seems,
tax man though I am — or what are these hundreds and hundreds of
yellow pages all about?

What a turn in my life! The conductor knew the plot of my show,
and had simply stated the theme in the most obvious way. But "Yankee Doodle" hit me like a sledgehammer. I, David Goodkind, I was
the creator of *Oliver Obverse!* All those actors, all those costumes, all
those musicians, all that scenery, all these rows of empty seats that
would be filled for three nights running — all, all was *my doing.* Writing
for "Off-hour" and *Jester* had just been my way of becoming somebody at Columbia, but that fife piping "Yankee Doodle" spoke to my
soul. It told me that there was nothing on earth like authorship, that
a man could do nothing better with his life, and that few achievements were even comparable. I still believe that. But many are called
by that fife, and few are chosen. Peter Quat was called and chosen.
What he did with his talent is something else. I did not have what it
takes, so I became a tax man.

On that night of nights, in white tie and tails, I thought I looked
very like a Coldstream Guard out on the town, except for a fresh crop

of pimples, incompletely masked by powder. But a Varsity Show author was above such trivia. In the Finchley coat, the box with two white orchids under my arm, I said goodbye to my family. Lee's eyes glistened at me as she fussed with her evening gown. "Hi there, Handsome! Good luck!"

Mama said, "It's the proudest night of my life. You've made Papa and me so happy!" She added, in a voice that resounded through the apartment, "Now, if *someone else* would only get married!"

Pop accompanied me out to the elevator in his new tuxedo. This was his night, as much as mine; this was his triumph in the Goldena Medina, long, long delayed, and he was revelling in seeing it unfold in style. Such was my surmise, but all he said, as the elevator door closed, was "Smoodie!"

Dorsi came sashaying out into her parlor in a cloud of delicate scent, in a dazzling effulgence of white arms, white bosom, and sequined red floor-length dress. "Oh, my," she said, inspecting me up and down, "Don't you look *smooth!* And thank you for these flowers." The orchids nodded on her shoulder, a month's allowance, and cheap at the price. When I opened the door of the Cadillac for Dorsi, the thoughtful look appeared in those celestial eyes, which I had seen when I told her I was taking her to the Orchid Grill. If I could read the hieroglyphs of that uninformative face, Dorsi was having second thoughts about cooling the Vicomte. Young, yes — but God, what a conquistador!

"Your father's car?" She gathered up her skirt and cloak, and stepped into the Cadillac like the Queen of England.

"Well, it's not mine, Dorsi," I said. Dorsi burst out laughing, and laughed and laughed until tears stood in her eyes, while I started the Cadillac and drove down the Grand Concourse. "Oh, David," she gasped, "sometimes you're so priceless." Well, fine. I had bounced a hundred jokes off this girl and barely elicited giggles. Making Dorsi Sabin laugh heartily was as random a hit as a double jackpot in Las Vegas.

At the Waldorf-Astoria we rode a large elevator to the grand ballroom amid a crush of Columbians in camel's-hair coats with the collars turned up, and their sweet-smelling shiny-eyed girls, who were making a noise like an aviary. I was recognized. I was congratulated. The author's girl, cloak thrown back to show her white orchids, quietly glowed. As usual, she disappeared into the ladies' lounge. I lurked nearby in a mirrored hall, pacing among the potted plants, my palms wet, my heart thumping. The mirrors showed a white-faced spook in white tie and tails, staring back at me with tense triumph. Curtain in ten minutes. In five! At last, at last I had reached the mountaintop on which Peter Quat had stood. My picture took up a full page in the program, as Peter's had.

Not long ago I dug out that forty-year-old picture: a profile of a lean Jewish kid, so very young, with a prideful hint of mocking humor about the mouth.

I. DAVID GOODKIND

AUTHOR

For this I had waited and worked for three years; sharpened a knack for humor, written a two-hour show, had it rejected, and written another in ten days and nights. This full-page picture in the Varsity Show program was the laurel wreath I would now lay at Dorsi Sabin's feet.

As we walked together down the center aisle of the packed ballroom toward our seats, I was hailed left and right by well-wishers. The orchestra was already in place, tuning up. From a box Mom, Pop, and Lee waved to me. Two programs lay on our seats in the second row. The cover design showed the fife-player, flag-bearer, and bandaged drummer of the Spirit of '76, marching through smoke and flame cross-eyed. The title was spelled out in Old English lettering:

𝔒𝔩𝔦𝔳𝔢𝔯 𝔒𝔟𝔳𝔢𝔯𝔰𝔢
𝔜𝔢 1933 𝔠𝔬𝔩𝔲𝔪𝔟𝔦𝔞 𝔙𝔞𝔯𝔰𝔦𝔱𝔶 𝔖𝔥𝔬𝔴𝔢

We sat down. Dorsi turned the pages of the program, and came on my photograph.

"Ha! There you are," she said.

The lights were dimming. The audience was quieting down. "Not a bad picture, Dorsi, eh?"

"Well," said Dorsi Sabin, with a side-glance and a giggle, "at least it doesn't show those horrid PIMPLES."

Darkness. The fife and drum played "Yankee Doodle." But the music did not affect me this time as it had at dress rehearsal. What I heard this time was

Pimples Doodle went to town
Riding on his pimples,
Stuck some pimples in his hat
And called them horrid pimples.

The curtain rose on the chorus of marching Minutemen. The audience applauded. I glanced up at my family in the box. They beamed proudly down at me, and Lee gently waved her fingers. I had a sudden very faint inkling of what her pain must have been, at hearing that Moshe Lev was in South Africa; of what it was like to take the shock of offhand, instantaneous, bloodcurdling disenchantment. But there was a gulf of difference. She was a rejected woman in love. I was a mere doting fool, getting a casual kick in the teeth that I had asked for.

The show was a hit. Laughs greeted my jokes, applause and cheers the sweaty dancing of the hairy-legged chorus. Dorsi herself, totally oblivious to the ruin she had wrought, had a high old time. At the final curtain the audience generously applauded, though there were no calls for "Author," except for stentorian female cries from my family's box; and when I looked up in embarrassment, there was Lee vigorously telling Mom to be quiet.

One more memory of that evening so haunts me that I have to add it. After the show, the chairs were cleared for dancing. Dorsi disappeared to the ladies' lounge, of course, as couples filled the floor. I stood on the sidelines, accepting compliments right and left. Puss Puss Ohlbaum came drifting past me with a distracted air.

"Hi, Puss Puss. Dance?"

"I can't find Monny," she replied. "Monny was here a minute ago. Have you seen Monny?"

"Monny will show up, Puss Puss. Don't you want to dance with the author?"

"Oh, all right," she said. "But I wish I could find Monny." I took her in my arms. She lifelessly shuffled around with me, looking here and there over her shoulders. "Where can Monny be?"

"Did you like the show?"

"Well, Monny said he'll give you a good review. I wonder where — oh, *there* Monny is! Monny!" Breaking away from me, she darted for Biberman and threw herself into his arms. They danced past me. Her face was turned up to him with a love-light in her eyes that I had never known, that I had fully expected to see, this night of nights, in the eyes of Dorsi Sabin; and had learned instead — or should have learned, for there is more to tell — that in her eyes I would never see it.

I saw eyes shining like that for me years later, for the first time in my life, in the face of a professional beauty, a singing girl in a Broadway show, Bobbie Webb. It was my fate, I guess, that she was not to be a nice Jewish girl like Dorsi Sabin, damn her soul.

54

Pincus Forever

"DAVID, you are a pew-et," Professor Vyvyan Finkel insisted, as we drank champagne in his apartment, toasting my success the day after *Oliver Obverse* opened. (That was how "poet" came out, in his ultra-British diction.) "A true comic pewet. You can be the Mark Twain of the theatre! The American Molière! Mark Twain too was a pewet, you know, an unappreciated prose pewet. You are a *pewet,* David."

All this, from a man who seldom gave an A, who himself wrote sardonic essays and verse for *Harper's* and *The Atlantic Monthly!* Professor Finkel was a most imposing man, very tall, very lean, with thick graying hair and an enormous craggy nose. A demanding lecturer, a murderous marker, Professor Finkel had already taken quite a shine to the witty if pimply young Vicomte de´ Brag, but his admiration for *Oliver Obverse* was almost disorienting. Then Bob Greaves stunned me by remarking, after congratulating me on *Oliver Obverse,* that he thought I should be the next editor of *Jester;* after all, I had done the most work on the magazine, and I was a very amusing fellow. This was mighty decent and unexpected of Greaves. Was he feeling the impact of Roosevelt? We were in the famous first hundred days of the New Deal: the bank holiday, the Brain Trust, the fireside chats, the repeal of Prohibition, that whole carnival of swift gaudy change; and possibly a Jewish editor of *Jester* seemed in the spirit of the times.

Anyhow, elected I was. When I told this to Peter Quat, as we walked and chatted in Central Park, he made an exceptionally frightful face. "Ha ha! So it finally happened, hey? They couldn't come up with a Deke who could read and write." His eyes rolled in a fine frenzy. "Well, well, well! End of an era. The Dekes give way to the kikes.

Sorry I missed it by two years. Congratulations, Vicomte." Peter had
gone to work for Harry Goldhandler at fifteen dollars a week; good
pay in those days, but he was bitter and ungracious about it, and
about most things. He had not even come to see *Oliver Obverse,* which
hurt me.

As junior year ended, I was spending much time with Vyvyan Finkel at concerts and plays, and in his bachelor apartment too, listening
to Beethoven records and talking about my future as a comic pewet.
Vyvyan made all kinds of genteel passes at me, I realize now, but at
the time I thought he was just being warm-hearted, or possibly moved
by the music. Once a stiff ex-Briton dropped his reserve, I figured,
that must be the friendly Anglo-Saxon attitude. Anyway, I became
very fond of him, and of Beethoven, and of the notion of becoming
the American Molière.

Much the same thing, though in reverse, happened to me around
that time with Eleanor Kraft, the petite daughter of the Fairy Laundry's lawyer, Mr. Theodore Kraft, a grim rich West End Avenue type.
Eleanor was a flaming Communist, with braided fair hair and a big
bosom. One evening we were together on a sofa, and Eleanor was
saying that Roosevelt was a reactionary featherhead, his New Deal
pure economic applesauce, and revolution was around the corner. As
a shot of cowpox protects against smallpox, so exposure to Aunt Faiga
had long ago immunized me to all Marxist carrying-on, and meantime there was this bosom, obtrusive under a russet cashmere sweater.
So to vary the monotony I grasped at the nearer bump. Eleanor Kraft
went right on excoriating Roosevelt, allowing my hand to stay where
it was. No other reaction. I was dumbfounded. What next? I had no
idea. All my dates with Dorsi Sabin had been useless as field training.

Still, as things stood I had then and there escaped the iron grip of
adolescent gravity. I was in orbit, so to speak, with all systems go.
What were your feelings at this historic moment, Commander Goodkind? Please speak into the microphone. Well, frankly, I was embarrassed. I was not smitten with Eleanor and had no great carnal urge
to proceed. To reduce any embarrassment on Eleanor's part, though
she was not showing any, I started arguing, and threw some right-
wing jargon at her. Eleanor zestfully returned a torrent of talk from
the *New Masses,* while I felt her here and there, and she paid me no
more mind than I ever did to Vyvyan Finkel. This sort of thing went

on for some months before petering out. I remember little of it except that first orbital pass. I took Eleanor to dances and the theatre, but the nub of the matter was political contention on a sofa; the agitprop by Eleanor, the fondling by me.

Mr. Theodore Kraft, coming on me and Eleanor in the parlor, would make a noisy approach, giving me time to unhand her and let her straighten up. I suspect he was hoping something would come of the shenanigans on the sofa. These he tolerated, clearly figuring that no girl was ever made pregnant by a hand on her bodice; and he gave me a summer job as an office boy. Hanging around with the clerks, I discerned that the cases they worked on were much like Talmud issues, except that a legal point which the Talmud would put in a diamond-hard line would be diffused in a brief over twenty pages. Sometimes I joined the discussions, the clerks treating me as a sort of mascot.

At one point Mr. Kraft called me into his office and said he could see I had a mind for the law. He would write a letter to the Columbia Law School admissions office, and would consider bringing me into the firm when I graduated. Then, in a more confiding tone, he said he worried a lot about what Eleanor, addled by her Communist nonsense, would do with a quarter of a million dollars. She would all too soon be inheriting at least that much, he confided, in view of his own terrible health. Mr. Kraft looked in the pink, and in fact he lived another thirty years. I do believe he was trying to give old Eleanor a paternal assist. No chance. Eleanor was an undefended bosom and a Marxist broken record, not a love. But I did find out that summer how much I liked the law. It was my game, my oyster. Vyvyan Finkel's Molière talk faded to a pallid fantasy. I was going to be a rich lawyer like Theodore Kraft.

So despite putting out a *Jester* every month, I charged head-down through my senior year toward admission to law school, plugging and plugging for A's. Then one day the Varsity Show alumni chairman dropped into the *Jester* office. No usable script had yet been submitted, he said. If I would please write one, the committee would undertake to produce it. Imagine! A short year ago I had leaped trembling at a telephone, to hear this withered little dentist speak as from a burning bush to say *Oliver Obverse* had been accepted. And now this! Mark Herz was out of town, so I called Peter Quat. He

invited me to the San Remo apartment, and we worked up a plot for
the Varsity Show. I wrote it very rapidly. It was called *Pincus Forever,*
and it was pure Quat in vein.

Basic idea: Columbia is going broke in the depression. Along comes
Mr. Abie Pincus of Pincus Pot Cheese, and he makes a deal to "sponsor" the university. Pincus commercials interrupt every lecture; the
football team wears pictures of the pot cheese jars on its uniforms;
the alma mater song becomes "Pincus Forever." His daughter, Faiga
Pincus, falls for the captain of the football team, Kelly O'Kelly. And
so on. Well, between the Jewish and Irish jokes, the fun about a
bankrupt Columbia, and the burlesque commercials, the thing did get
laughs. In the writing, I romped along unself-consciously in the Quat
style. Abie Pincus, his wife, and his daughter were in fact a scabrous
lampoon of my own family. Mom afterward said bravely that *Pincus
Forever* reminded her of Sholem Aleichem. Pop was silent. After *Oliver
Obverse* he had remarked that I might consider becoming a writer.
He said not a word about this show. Nothing, ever.

I took Dorsi to the opening night, fool that I was. There were no
white orchids this time, but tea roses, and we went in my father's old
car. She was as bright-eyed, sweet-scented, and magnificently gotten
up as she had been at the *Oliver* opening. In fact there was nothing
the least bit different about her. She had always been the same. "*So,
you're the Vicomte de Brag,*" she had greeted me, and that was all I
had ever been to her. She had never pretended otherwise. The dips
and zooms of my hopes, the sinking spells, the dizzying exaltations,
I had generated all by myself, with my infatuated roller-coaster ride
around and around an inert object.

At her door, after congratulating me on the show, she said — by
way of summing up a discussion we had had in the car — "Well,
David, whether you become a writer or a lawyer, you'll accomplish
a lot, that I know. You're gifted. Good luck." With that, she shook
my hand, awkwardly put her cheek to mine as though we were dancing, and slipped into her apartment; leaving me dazed, with a feeling
on my cheek of a radium burn. Dorsi was not given to such bursts
of wild passion.

I was admitted to law school. Vyvyan Finkel was desolate. "But
David," he mourned, "you're a pewet. Lawyers are common as cabbages. Pewets are comets."

"I won't be an ordinary lawyer."

"No, you'll be another Morris Pelkowitz." He had not mentioned Pelkowitz before. "Oh, yes," he responded to my inquiry, "Morris was one of my best students, and now he's on the *Law Review*. His papers were always so thorough, and so dull! You're a corner-cutting scamp, David" — Vyvyan patted my knee, in arch reproof of my wicked ways — "but you're *never* dull."

"I'll be glad to make *Law Review*," I said.

"A pewet on *Law Review*," sighed Vyvyan. "What a waste!"

Walking out of Philosophy Hall on that beautiful day late in May, I wandered the campus at loose ends. It was Shavuos. I had gone to the temple with Pop the night before. I had taken my very last exam that morning, in Comparative Religion. Vyvyan was a fine teacher of comparative religion, but I doubt he knew Shavuos from Shrovetide. I might have cut the exam, but that didn't seem courteous to old Vyvyan, who had gone all out for me in Phi Beta Kappa's smoke-filled room, without success. *Pincus* had taken its toll of my senior marks.

Now there was only commencement ahead. The vacant rows of yellow folding chairs already filled the sunlit plaza in front of Alma Mater. The campus wore a holiday aspect. The Barnard girls in light dresses, strolling arm-in-arm with shirt-sleeved students, all looked seductive. Springtime and freedom were in the air, an inchoate ache was in my heart, and that radium burn tingled on my cheek, or seemed to. I had to stop at the law school to pay an advance fee. The check lay in my pocket. I dropped into a chair near the gilded Alma Mater, which I had first glimpsed as an awed Bronx yeshiva boy. Last thoughts before the plunge.

"Davey, I know you want to get the hell out of here," I heard Mark Herz say, "but commencement isn't until Tuesday." He sat down beside me, peeling tinfoil off a chocolate bar. "Lunch," he said. He looked as though he needed it, skinny and hollow-cheeked, with knobby wrists sticking far out of a shrunken seersucker jacket. The old battered hat, a mere rag, was tilted on the back of his head. "I hear your show was a hit. Nice going."

"Did you get that California scholarship?"

"Dunno yet. Why are you loitering here?"

"What do you think of my going to law school?"

"What's there to think about?"

"Three more years of classroom drudgery. I've been going to school since I was five years old. Has Peter told you about Harry Gold-handler? Peter says I might be able to get a job with him."

"I don't know." Mark hungrily ate chocolate. "Peter Quat, now, will never be anything but a writer. Never has had any other idea. He may fail, he may loaf, he may just live on Dad's money when Dr. Quat dies, but he'll write or do nothing. It's life to him." Mark looked at me sharply. "Are you asking my advice?"

"Yes."

"Get a profession. Put money in your purse. If you're a writer, it should burst forth one day. I suspect it will. Meantime you'll eat."

"Well, then, walk me over to the law school," I said, unaccountably cheered up. "I have to check in."

Outside Avery Hall, Mark offered me his bony hand. We held the handclasp, looking each other in the eye. Mark Herz had been perhaps my best encounter at Columbia, I thought, yet what did I really know of the Man in the Iron Mask? He lightly struck my shoulder. "Stay in touch, Godol."

That startled me. Once when we had gotten drunk on needle beer, I had amused him by describing the Minsker Godol era of my life, but he had not referred to it since. Off he strode, down the brick walk outside Philosophy Hall, past the big bronze replica of Rodin's *Thinker*.

One Columbia moment after that has stayed with me. The night after commencement, a very warm night, a block party is going on under the street lights in front of Alma Mater. To the music of a small college band, students in shirt sleeves are dancing in the gutter with their girls. Among them is Bob Greaves, doing all his smooth dips, slides, twirls, shuffles that he performed in white tie and tails; his left hand is stiff and high, but of course has no white kid glove on it. I have never seen Bob Greaves again, or heard what became of him; and I cannot tell you why, but in truth my long Columbia adventure fades out with that picture — Bob Greaves being ultra-smooth in shirt sleeves, in the gutter under the street lamps, a little ridiculous and a little sad.

55
Quat's Phone Call

I WAS working at a boys' camp in the Berkshires as a dramatics counsellor, to earn money for my law school expenses, when a wire came that Bobbeh had died. Within the hour, I was on my way to New York.

Pop and my uncles observed the seven days of strict mourning, shoeless and unshaven on low stools, in Aunt Rivka's apartment where Bobbeh had passed on in her sleep. I rode the Bronx Park Express every day to the old Simpson Street station, descended the old staircase to Westchester Avenue, and walked under the booming El and down 163rd Street. There the marketing Jewish housewives thronged as always, and there as always the fruit and vegetable hawkers, the fishmongers, the butchers at open stands heaped with bloody meat, raucously cried their wares in Yiddish. I even thought I recognized some of them, in their unchanging ragged aprons and three-day beards.

Condolence callers streamed in and out of Rivka's apartment. Mirrors were swathed with sheets, and there were no hellos or goodbyes, everything according to the book. Yet it was not a grim week, after all. It had some aspects of a reunion. Everybody in the Mishpokha showed up, even the uncle from Bay Ridge. The Brodofskys came, and the Grosses, and the Elfenbeins, and most of the Minsker Congregation members. Cantor Levinson showed up, strangely small and deflated in a street suit. Holy Joe Geiger paid a call. Mrs. Frankenthal one evening walked in through the ever-open door, all gray and hangdog, for her husband was already in jail. Paul was married (to a gentile girl, she whispered to me) and working in Florida.

Zaideh was there every day, studying Talmud passages with Pop

and the uncles in Bobbeh's memory. I joined in the learning. Time
rolled backward. I was speaking Yiddish, eating Bronx foods —
pickled herring, chick-peas, salted pumpkin seeds, sponge cake, honey
cake, halvah — praying regularly (though a self-proclaimed unbeliever, just to be sociable); and Zaideh beamed as I cut through tough
passages as in the old days. So did Pop, whose bristles were coming
in as white as Uncle Yehuda's beard. It is a damned strange thing to
write down, but I loved that mourning time for Bobbeh. I came home
again. The week was suffused with warm cheerful recollections of the
little lame old lady who had probably ended her long, bedridden decline — so my father put it — by welcoming the Angel of Death with
the inquiry, "Nu, what kept you so long?"

We talked about her old-country ways, her homemade sauerkraut
and wine, her wintergreen liniment, her blue spells, her family memories. I stumbled into a hornet's nest by praising her fried matzoh, a
Passover dish all Jews know. Some call it *matzoh brie*. It is a simple
fry-up of broken matzoh soaked in egg. I am mad for the stuff, always have been; and nobody ever made it the way Bobbeh did. I said
as much, and only ruffled all the women's feathers. Mama went out
to 163rd Street forthwith and bought some matzoh; fried it up, and
brought me a heaping plateful. Meaning no disrespect to the deceased's blessed memory, she demanded, wasn't this as good as Bobbeh's? Pop and the uncles had to eat some, too. Naturally we ex-
tolled it; but the melancholy fact is — and always has been — that
my mother doesn't begin to know how to fry matzoh. It comes out
all dry and stuck together. My mother is a remarkable woman, as you
may have gathered, but she is not a universal genius, and this is one
of her weak points.

Well, that was only the start of it. Aunt Rivka wanted to fry some
for us, too. Pop managed to talk her out of it, but next night, by
God, we had to eat Rivka's fried matzoh, and Aunt Sophie's as well.
At this point a matzoh-frying frenzy seemed to seize all the women
who came to that apartment. Before the mourning period was over,
Pop, my uncles, and I had fried matzoh coming out of our nostrils.
Aunt Faiga fried matzoh; Mrs. Brodofsky fried matzoh; Cantor Lev-
inson's wife fried matzoh; I swear, my sister Lee herself caught the
madness and fried matzoh. Hers wasn't all that bad, actually, for an
American-born girl. But you can eat only so much fried matzoh. It

is amazingly indigestible, and my insides were in chaos for a month thereafter. Still, it was an orgy to remember. I would do it again, anytime.

But nobody managed to fry the matzoh the way Bobbeh did. I will never taste the like again, and I know it. She took the secret with her to the Garden of Eden, to her unquestionably honored place at the feet of the zaideh I never knew, the shammas of the Soldiers' Shule in Minsk.

"Davey! What are you doing in New York?" Peter Quat, on the telephone. "I just called to find out how to reach you at that dumb camp."

The suitcase was open on my bed. I was packing to go back, though in the worst way I did not want to. The law school library was open, and I would have preferred to get at the books, but I had to finish the season to collect my two-hundred-dollar fee. The camp owner, an old alligator, had given me a week off, and no more.

I told Peter about the death of Bobbeh.

"Oh! Well, sorry about the old lady, but the thing is, Davey, we have a crisis here, and Harry Goldhandler wants to see you."

I was speechless. It was like a brilliant sunrise; like a woman surrendering; like a drawbridge lowering to a blast of trumpets, and the portcullis thundering upward with a rattle of great chains, to welcome the gallant Vicomte de Brag to the Castle Perilous. It was the call of the Outside, loud and clear.

Harry Goldhandler wants to see you!

"Davey, did you hear me? Hey! Are you on the line?"

"Look, Peter, I start law school in three weeks."

"Sure, I told Goldhandler that. He said, 'Tell your friend law school is for shitheads, and to get his ass up here.' Davey, I started at fifteen bucks a week. I'm already making thirty. He's busted up with Henny Holtz, and he's got three new programs starting September first."

Here was explosive news! Henny Holtz's Sunday evening hour outdrew the President's fireside chats. On a warm Sunday evening, the Holtz show wafted out through all the open windows in America. You could stroll down any street and hear the jokes, and the happy bellows of the studio audience. Holtz had been Goldhandler's major client. Peter hurried on, "The place is a madhouse. I can stall Goldhandler a day or so, but you'd better make up your mind fast, because there are ten other guys — shit, he's yelling at me — Davey, call me back here at midnight."

"Midnight? I'll be asleep, for God's sake."

"Set your alarm. We quit then to go out and eat. Listen, Davey, everything we do here is horseshit, the worst, but it pays. It's an experience. We'll be able to rent an apartment together. We'll write a farce and crack Broadway. You don't want to go to law school. You never have. Fuck the law. Bye."

Pop came home to dinner that day, his first at the laundry since Bobbeh's death, looking poorly. Those white bristles — he would not shave for a month — added twenty years to him. Losing his mother, for all his talk about her welcoming the Angel of Death, had hit him hard. When he went to recite evening kaddish for her, I came along, assuming he would just cross the street to the temple. But he walked down the hill toward Broadway.

"Where are we going, Pop?"

"Chopsuey."

I had heard him refer, by that peculiar name, to a small nearby shule where some of his Orthodox friends prayed, but I had never been there. We entered a Chinese restaurant, turned through a side door, and ascended steep dimly lit stairs on which Pop paused several times. Inside, Chopsuey — it had a long Hebrew name, but nobody ever called it anything but Chopsuey — was just like the Minsker shule: same arrangement of seats, tables, and reading platform; on the Holy Ark, same worn purple velvet curtain decorated with sequined lions; along the walls, same sagging shelves of Talmud volumes leaning this way and that; same handful of elderly men, same odor of dust, snuff, and old books. Except for the clangor of Broadway traffic and the Oriental cooking smells, it might have been the same place.

After services Pop had to go to a Zionist meeting. It was a steamy August night. As we strolled very slowly down Broadway together, I told him about Goldhandler.

"You're considering this? You don't want to go to law school?" It was a calm inquiry, but I knew my father's voice.

"Well, I'd start supporting myself, at least."

"Did I ask you to support yourself? Did Mama?"

"Pop, can you afford law school for me?"

We were waiting for a light to change. In the glow of a restaurant neon sign, Pop's frown scored black lines on his face.

"Yisroelke, your Cousin Harold wants to apply next year to a medical school in Canada or Switzerland. Here he's afraid he'll be turned down. Jewish quota. There they will admit him. All week long at Rivka's, Uncle Hyman was crying to me about what it would cost. I told him to go down on his knees and thank God he has a son who wants to be a doctor. I told him to borrow the money when the time comes, and if I had to, I would go on the note."

The light changed. As we crossed he went on, "Make up your mind. Do what you want. Don't look for excuses. Straight! What is your aim? Writing jokes, is that the ambition of David Goodkind? Do you really want to write? Like Mark Twain? Like Sholem Aleichem? Something great?"

"Do you think I can?"

"As a lawyer, I think you can be the best. A writer is something greater. Pindar said, 'Let me write a nation's poems, and I care not who writes its laws.' " Pop now and then came out with these ragtags of learning from his heavy reading, mostly in Yiddish, in his young days.

"I don't hope to be a poet," I said, with an inward grin refraining from saying *pewet*.

We halted outside the meeting hall, on the steep slope of Ninety-sixth Street. I was a head taller than Pop, and he was downhill from me. He had to crane his neck to look me in the eye. His bristly face was drawn and perspiring. "Well, make the right decision for my son, and don't think about money."

When the alarm got me up at midnight, I sleepily called Goldhandler's office. No answer. I lay in the dark, thinking. Suppose I worked for Goldhandler just one year? I might save almost enough to pay my own way through law school; I would cease being such a burden on Pop, and I would still be younger, when I went back, than most of my classmates. I tossed and worried, and fell asleep with nothing solved. The telephone woke me to the blazing sunshine of late morning. A sweet voice said, "David?"

"Yes?"

"Surprised to hear from me?"

God in heaven! *Dorsi?*

"Ah, who is this?"

"Why, it's Puss Puss Biberman," she said, in one of the letdowns of the ages.

Monroe had married Puss Puss in June. She was inviting me to dinner. They had just moved into their apartment in Washington Heights. Puss Puss said devilishly that she wanted to try out her cooking on me, before she risked poisoning other friends. I called the camp and told my assistant to start rehearsing *Jerry Sees the Gorilla;* and I spent the day walking up and down Riverside Drive, pondering my future. The Hudson was lined with gray warships at anchor. Ugly costly toys, I thought them, useless relics of a barbarous past. Who would ever fight another war?

Mama looked into my room as I was dressing to visit the Bibermans. "Say, Papa tells me that you're thinking of not going to law school. Of making money instead, writing jokes. That you want to make money is very nice. It's about time. But you can go to law school, you know, and still make money writing."

"Oh?" I peered at her image in the glass as I knotted my tie. "How?"

"Write the advertising for the Fairy Laundry. Go to law school, and do that in your spare time. I talked to Papa about this. You would make more money right away than that fool Felix Brodofsky."

Now there was a temptation, I grant you, to outearn the fat fuck on the Fairy Laundry payroll. I successfully fought it off. "Forget it, Mom. I'll probably forget this radio thing, too."

"Fine. You'd only get into partnership with this fellow Peter Quat. Don't ever go into partnership, David. Remember Brodofsky and Gross."

While Puss Puss pottered in the kitchen of the newlyweds' cramped little flat, Monroe and I talked in the living room. In two months he had put on many pounds. He was in a sport shirt, jowly and relaxed; I was dressed up, gaunt, and ill at ease. Why had they invited me, really? He and I had never been close, and now an abyss yawned between us; to wit, he was getting it regular, and I was not. He told me he was working in a mail-order business run by an uncle, but his real plan was to write a novel in iambic pentameter, based on the Book of Ruth. Meantime, he was making a living.

"But no smugness yet, Davey," he said. "Absolutely no smugness.

Every afternoon when I get home from work, I'm out playing ball with the guys in the park."

In our graduating class, you see, there had been much sentiment against getting married and settling down to a smug existence. *Smug* had been the operative word. Yet old Monroe was smug, mighty smug. He oozed smugness, as a ripe olive oozes oil. Smugness rather became him, actually. Getting it regular seemed to do it to a man; and for that matter, to a woman. Puss Puss came in, taking off her frilly little white apron, to announce that dinner was on; and she looked even smugger — if that's a word — than her hubby.

Puss Puss was a well-organized sort, and we had soup, salad, and lamb chops cooked on an electric grill, there on the tiny table. What stays with me as though I were there now in Monny's flat, smelling those chops broiling under my nose, is Puss Puss's offhand remark, "I'm going out of my *mind,* Davey, trying to decide what to wear to the wedding. September is so changeable, isn't it?"

"What wedding?"

"Why, Dorsi Sabin's. You've been invited, haven't you?"

And that, I suppose, is why I had been asked to dinner. Monny and Puss Puss were staring hungrily at me. The knitting women at the guillotine had nothing on the newlywed Bibermans for macabre enjoyment of another's discomfiture. Keeping my face as straight as I could, considering that it was on a lopped-off head lying bloodily beside the broiling lamb chops, I said, "Oh, is Dorsi getting married? To whom?"

"Why, Morris Pelkowitz," said Monny. "Didn't you know?"

"Pelkowitz!" gasped the severed head, its eyes widening, then closing forever.

I couldn't help it, couldn't control it. It is no surprise to the reader, of course. To me, it was an unimaginable surprise. Morris *Pelkowitz?* Why, the man was an antique, a fat old thing of twenty-six or so!

"I'm sure they'll be happy," said Puss Puss. "He's going into his father's bank."

Nothing else remains of that scene. It closed with the words, "his father's bank," and the eyes of the Bibermans feasting on the bleeding trunk of the decapitated Vicomte de Brag, last of the noble house of the de Brags, tracing back to Charlemagne.

When I got home about midnight I telephoned the Goldhandler office again. Peter Quat answered.

"Where the hell were you, Peter," I asked angrily, "when I called last night?"

"Who knows? He got hungry early, I guess. What's up?"

"When can I come to see him?"

"Hey, great. How about two-thirty tomorrow afternoon?"

"I'll be there."

"Terrific."

Once in my high school chemistry class, the instructor let fall a single droplet into a glass tank full of cloudy white liquid; the liquid magically cleared, and a white powder precipitated out. So it was with the news about Dorsi Sabin and Morris Pelkowitz. It cleared my mind, and precipitated my decision to see Goldhandler.

Pelkowitz!

That Dorsi Sabin, my first love, the radiant frost queen of Barnard, the untouchable Artemis of my innocent and desperate adolescence, should end up "giving it regular" to the dull shambling Morris Pelkowitz! All right, I had not won her. But Pelkowitz! What then was the point of going to law school, of drudging to make *Law Review*? So as to follow in the footsteps of Pelkowitz, the despoiler of the dream? Vyvyan Finkel's terrible words came back to me: *"You'll be another Morris Pelkowitz."*

Never! Let my lost Dorsi give it to Pelkowitz regular, night and day! Let copulation thrive! Let them beget a dozen dull thorough Pelkowitzes, and be damned to them. I was a PEWET! I had been the Minsker Godol, I had metamorphosed to the Vicomte de Brag, and now I would become the new Molière! And it might take five years, or ten, or twenty, or fifty, but the day would come when Dorsi Sabin would look at me with those heartwrenching blue eyes; and that contrite look would say, if her faded lips did not, "It should have been you, Davey. It really was always you. I'm sorry."

And so it was that I made my first major erratic move, in an adult life of erratic moves. The academics, who love ten-dollar words as I love fried matzoh, call such a random zigzag course "stochastic." Now, and only now, begin the stochastic adventures of I. David Goodkind.

56

Goldhandler

"I HAVE an appointment with Mr. Goldhandler."
The black girl in a starchy uniform made way. Before my eyes,
beyond a narrow foyer, a scene of opulence opened; a blurred picture of vast spaces and millionaire furnishings, bounded by great
windows which looked out past green vistas of Central Park to
downtown skyscrapers. In the foyer, on a straight-backed carved settee, a woman in plain black sat, holding nearsightedly to her nose the
Modern Library edition of *The Brothers Karamazov*. She was about
eight months pregnant; her stomach humped gigantically on her lap.
The book dropped to disclose a long attractive oval face with not a
trace of paint on the girlish skin, and unplucked fair eyebrows arching at me over sharp gray-blue eyes. "My husband will be down shortly
for his breakfast. Please wait in there." She put the book back to her
nose, and I walked into the living room.

Breakfast at two-thirty in the afternoon? Yes, that sounded like the
man Peter worked for. This was a tower penthouse, and the room
stretched clear across the whole structure, with windows on three sides.
The carpet — well, I have never since seen anything of that size and
beauty outside a museum. The antique tables, armchairs, sofas, set-
tees, breakfronts, side tables, and bric-a-brac that crowded the enormous room dazzled even my untutored eyes: possessions of a Gould,
furnishings of a lord's château. At an onyx table inlaid with check-
ered squares, two boys were hunched in polished spindly chairs over
red and white ivory chess pieces. One wore a baseball suit, the other
a crimson velvet bathrobe.

"Hi," said the one in the bathrobe. He looked about thirteen, and
very much like the woman reading *The Brothers Karamazov*. "Did you
write *Pincus Forever?*"

"I did." I came to the table and sized up the board, a close endgame of rooks and pawns.

"I'm starting Columbia in September. I'll write a Varsity Show one day. I'm Karl. This is my brother, Sigmund."

Sigmund, smaller and younger, was studying the board with thin-lipped intensity, his eyes in deep sockets bright and hard. "I'm going to City College in September," he said. He made a rook move that looked like a blunder; on second thought, a wily trap. He glanced at Karl, gnawing a knuckle. Karl thought a moment, took the rook, and in a fireworks exchange of pieces came out a pawn ahead. "It was unsound," he said. "Resign?" Sigmund shook his head, lips tightened, eyes glaring at the board.

I sat down in a nearby armchair, picking up a copy of the *New Masses* that lay on it. The lead article, blazoned on the cover in big black letters, was "Roosevelt, Pied Piper of Capitalism," by John Strachey. Now what was this Communist magazine doing in these baronial surroundings? And were those two chess-playing prodigies pulling my leg about their college plans? Peter Quat, in shirt sleeves and stocking feet, looked into the room and beckoned. I followed him to the foyer. Down a narrow carpeted stairway came a paunchy unshaven man with tousled scanty hair, offering me his hand. His face was deathly pale, his eyes commanding and crafty. "My name is Goldhandler. Come and have coffee."

I followed him into the dining room. Mrs. Goldhandler came in and sat down at the foot of a long table covered with a lacy cloth. It was Chippendale, I later found out; the entire dining set was pristine Chippendale. There were twelve chairs, twelve settings of fine china and silver, and at every setting a half of Persian melon. Goldhandler put me on his right at the head of the table. All the places filled up. Opposite me were the two boys, a little redheaded girl, and Peter Quat. Alongside me were three young men. Two had to be junior advertising executives: dark suits, pinned shirt collars, narrow ties, neatly barbered hair, Deke faces. The third was a sad balding jowly fellow, shoeless and tieless like Quat. He looked even paler than Goldhandler. "I'm Boyd," he said, as he sat down beside me. Peter had told me about Boyd and also about Mrs. Goldhandler's parents, who came shuffling from a back room and took chairs on either side of her.

Harry Goldhandler sat with his head bowed on a hand. Everybody else looked toward him in silence, not touching their melons. I thought, with some surprise, that he was about to say grace. What he did say with a glance at Boyd was, "Did the cocksucker call?"

I think my hair stood on end. I know my scalp tingled. There across from me were those three charming children; down at the other end was the pregnant pretty mother and the sweet-faced old Jewish grandmother. This was 1934, mind you. The revolution in American language had not even begun. In front of ladies, let alone children, one did not even say, "son of a bitch," and "shit" was utterly unthinkable. *Lady Chatterley's Lover* was still contraband. So was *Fanny Hill* and all the other hot stuff that has since flooded our land, for better or worse, thanks in part to my own legal efforts. But even today, in such company, his words would have startled me.

If Boyd could have turned paler, he would have, but he looked ghastly enough: eyes popping, lips trembling. "Not yet."

"He is a rat," said Goldhandler. "He is cowering in his hole." He cut into his melon, whereupon we all did, too. I had never eaten a melon so rich, so sweet, and so large. "He even looks like a rat," said Goldhandler. "Why, his nose twitches like a rat's." Here he did a vivid rodentlike nose twitch. "He has little pointy hands like a rat's." He dropped his spoon to hold up both hands like rodent paws. "Pointy hands, for thieving. Tiny pointy hands."

"He sleeps late, you know," quavered Boyd.

"He won't call," said Mrs. Goldhandler. "I warned you against Eddie Conn the day you hired him."

"So you did," said Goldhandler, devouring his melon. "You didn't mention the pointy hands, though. That was your mistake."

"He has gone to work for Holtz," she said. "Holtz would never have let you quit, otherwise. He hopes Eddie will steal everything. He'll learn better. Henny Holtz will be off the radio in a year. Without you, he's a ventriloquist's dummy that can't talk."

Goldhandler ate the last large spoonful of melon with relish. "Little pointy hands," he said. "I should have paid more attention to those tiny pointy hands." He turned on me abruptly. "So you're going to law school."

"I'm not sure."

"Better do that," said Goldhandler. "This is work."

"I can work," was my instant stung response.

Goldhandler addressed the advertising men. "When is that frog-voiced cunt coming?"

Nobody turned a hair; not the mother, not the children, not the grandparents, not the two black maids who were smilingly bringing in silver trays of food. Obviously I was the only one at the table jarred by Goldhandler's language.

"In fifteen minutes," said one of the men.

"She insisted," said the other. "Sorry, Harry. She has to cut a recording at four."

"She'll have to wait," said Goldhandler, "while I have my morning shit. Doesn't she ever shit? Maybe she doesn't, at that. Maybe that's where she gets that frog sound of hers. Like a damned fool I thought it was her voice. I never thought it might be backed-up farts."

I burst out laughing at the sheer outrageousness. I couldn't help it. Goldhandler crookedly grinned at me. The maid put before him, so help me, a heaping dish of fried matzoh ringed by pork sausages. "This is the most terrific dish in America," he said. "Have some."

"Ah, no, thank you, sir."

Like Peter and most of the others, I was served a thick rare filet mignon and a glass of milk. Mrs. Goldhandler, her parents, and the little girl had fried matzoh and pork sausages.

"What was your major at Columbia?" Goldhandler asked, forking up a sausage and some matzoh.

"Literature," I said.

"What is the funniest work in all literature?"

I glanced down the table at Peter Quat. He was busily cutting into his filet mignon, a faint sarcastic smile wrinkling his mouth.

"*Don Quixote?*" I ventured.

"One joke," he said. "An old lunatic getting his bones broken because he thinks he's a knight, for a thousand pages. Great, but tiresome."

"*Gargantua and Pantagruel?*"

"A museum piece."

"I think *Tristram Shandy* is the funniest work in all literature," spoke up the boy in the baseball suit.

Goldhandler turned on him, growling, "You do? How much Molière have you read?"

"You mean in French, Father?"

"What else, you little shit? In Sanskrit?"

"In French, only *Le Bourgeois Gentilhomme* and *Le Misanthrope,*" Sigmund replied, turning pink. "I've read most of the rest in English."

"You'll read every play of Molière in French this summer, and report to me after each play."

Sigmund glared straight ahead. "Yes, Father."

"Who is the funniest character in Shakespeare?" Goldhandler shot at me.

Across the table from me, Karl's mouth silently formed "Falstaff." I was going to say that anyway, so I did.

"Falstaff? Why, what the hell is funny about Falstaff?" Goldhandler demanded, with an amused sidewise glance out of those puffy deepset eyes. "What is Falstaff but a lazy fat old purse-snatcher and coward? A liar, a glutton, a drunk, a layabout, a whoremaster, a braggart, a bully, a cheat, a corrupter of the young? Is there a vice he doesn't have? Is there a virtue he does have? What is Falstaff but a useless, worthless, contemptible, repulsive nobody? What's funny about Falstaff?"

I had the sense to keep quiet. All the others were looking expectantly not at me, but at Goldhandler. Clearly this was how he enjoyed his meals, playing to his private audience.

"Well, it's one of the great topics of Shakespearean criticism, and of course you're right," he said. "To begin with, Falstaff is a man of powerful, elemental appetites. Of *zest!*" He struck the table with a fist. "Fat, old, worthless, on the brink of the grave, he loves life. And we love him, because we recognize ourselves in him. We love life as he does. We only wish we had the honesty to live it as he does. If we only dared to be truly ourselves — as he does — we'd all be gluttons, layabouts, drunks, cheats, screwing whores and not paying them, running away from fights and lying about winning them. Falstaff is earthy human nature, far more than Sancho Panza. He is *us.* And it hurts so much to see ourselves in that bulging fun-house mirror, distorted and yet our true secret selves, that we laugh so as not to cry."

While delivering this harangue, he finished the matzoh and sausages. I was nervously nibbling the filet mignon. I had little appetite. Nobody said a word in Goldhandler's pauses to eat. Boyd leaped to a sideboard when Goldhandler finished his food, and brought him a box of enormous cigars. As he carefully selected one, smelled it, and rolled it at his ear, he went on, "Now in writing radio comedy for the masses, you have to reach for just such elemental values, for those few things the entire American public, coast to coast, will understand, and recognize in themselves. There are therefore only three proper topics for radio comedy. They are pissing, shitting, and fucking."

With that, he struck three wooden matches at once, from a box Boyd offered him, and lit the cigar like a torch, in bursts of yellow flame and blue smoke.

"You write a joke on any other subject when you work for me, and I'll throw you out of a window. But of course, I forgot, you're going to law school, aren't you?"

He glared at me, as Sigmund had glared after his reproof. All the others were now laughing. I was so flustered that I drank milk by way of stalling. It may have been the first time I ever drank milk with meat. Though I had gotten careless about the food rules, milk and meat together still put me off, and in fact through all the free April House years I never did indulge in that specific abomination.

Goldhandler pushed himself out of his chair, "Boyd, show him around the place. Peter, come with me. That Penner script needs jokes."

I followed Boyd up the stairs. "Boys' bedroom. Liza's room. Master bedroom," he said on the first landing, like a tour guide. Through the half-open door of the master bedroom I saw a marble fireplace and a four-poster bed with blue silk curtains. The office on the next floor also stretched across the tower. The largest desk I had ever seen stood in one corner, an antique topped in green leather. There were steel filing cabinets all along the walls, two other desks, two typewriters on stands, a switchboard, and a very long green sofa.

"Stinks in here," said Boyd. It did, mainly of the dead cigars jammed into Perrier bottles on the big desk. "We worked all night, then kept going and quit about two hours ago. Well, there's one more floor." We climbed a steep winding stairway to a square unfurnished room with three sides of tall glass windows, one of rough masonry, and an arched, rough-plastered ceiling. The floor, carpeted wall to wall in thick soft white, was littered with old books and bundles of magazines. "They haven't decided just what to do with this room," said

Boyd, over the wind roar. It was gusting strongly, and one casement window, not quite fastened shut, was wailing, *Waa — oo! Whoo!*

The solid wall blocked off uptown. Through the glass one looked out at the park, at downtown Manhattan with its skyscrapers, bridges, and wharfs, at the East River and Brooklyn, at the Hudson River, and the blue glittery New York Bay; and beyond the Palisades, New Jersey stretching green to a far hazy horizon. Close by, much closer than I had ever seen it, and just about at eye level, was the APRIL HOUSE sign, big neon tubes in metal casings on a massive rusty frame. "They'll probably make a kind of music room and library out of it," Boyd yelled, "a quiet retreat where he can think. But they'll have to do something about the wind."

Back in the office, he rolled open drawer after drawer of file cards. "The jokes," he said, waving at the entire wall. Ye gods, I thought, they have thousands and thousands! Along another wall he pulled out drawers crammed with mimeographed scripts. "The Henny Holtz show. The Joe Penner show. The Russ Columbo show. Every show he has ever written. I'm supposed to be indexing them. They accumulate faster than I can index."

"What would my job here be?"

"Digging jokes." He threw open a closet door. Old comic magazines were stacked inside waist-high: *Judge, Life, College Humor, Screen Gems, Captain Billy's Whiz Bang;* also paper-covered joke books, hundreds of them, piled up and tied with string. "You dig through these, and the stuff upstairs. Any joke that looks usable, you type on a card, classify it, and file it."

"How, classify?"

"Well, you know, alphabetically. Animal jokes, baby jokes, cheap jokes, doctor jokes, and so on. About forty categories. Kissing jokes, insult jokes, undertaker jokes. Any funny topic."

I stared at the heaped-up magazines. The closet smelled of old disintegrating paper. "Wouldn't I do any writing?"

"Oh, sure. Peter dug jokes for a while. Now he writes drafts." Boyd smiled at me in a soft wistful way. I had never met such a soft-seeming man — soft white jowls, soft white hands, soft gestures, a soft slumped posture. "The boss will give you a quick two-week trial. Fifteen dollars a week."

"When would I start?"

"Now."

"Boyd, I have a job. It won't end until September first."

"Then, I'll have to telephone somebody else."

"Let me think about it."

"Take your time."

He left me alone. I stood at a window, staring out at the April House sign. Two weeks, thirty dollars, and my summer salary would go down the drain. "Digging jokes" out of the piled rubbish in the closet was a stupid prospect. Still, I had never been in an apartment like this, or met a man like Goldhandler, or such a family. I had been figuring I had nothing to lose. Now I stood to lose two hundred dollars.

Well, then, what to do? My fit over the Pelkowitz news had been mostly chagrin at the Bibermans' pleasure in my decapitation. Dorsi was gone. The Vicomte de Brag was dead. Dorsi had to marry some man, and why not Morris, the banker's son? To change my life's direction in a spasm of petulance would be childish. I had no deep-down impulse to write radio jokes.

Peter Quat now rushed into the room, exclaiming, "Shit." He went riffling through the gag files, snatching out a card here and a card there. I said, "Peter, this job is not for me."

"Of course it is. You made a great impression on him." He pushed a chair and a typewriter beside the green desk, spread out the jokes, and rolled paper into the typewriter. "You only got a taste of the Falstaff routine. He can go on for an hour about Falstaff. And Molière. And Shaw. And Freud. And Marx. Karl and Sigmund are named after Freud and Marx, I guess you spotted that." (I had not.) "He's an extraordinary bastard."

"Why does he do this crap?"

"Ever hear of money?" Peter began typing frantically with two fingers.

I went downstairs to decline the job and exit from this seductive phantasmagoria. It would take me three months of work here just to make up my loss; even assuming that I wanted to give up law school to "dig jokes," which I did not.

I heard uproarious laughter in the living room. From the stairway I could see Goldhandler sitting in a suit and tie, shaved and well groomed, reading from a script. He noticed me, and waved to me to come in. "Here's a young fellow who's trying to decide whether to be a lawyer or a writer," he said.

Two people, a mustached man and a woman with beautiful crossed legs, sat opposite him on a sofa, still laughing. "Maybe you can help him," he added to the man with a grin.

My knees knocked and my mouth went dry. The man was Ernest Hemingway, and the "frog-voiced cunt" was Marlene Dietrich. The two ad men sat at some distance, frozen with awe.

"Do you think you can write?" Ernest Hemingway asked me.

"Not like you," I gasped. "Never like you."

"You have to find that out," he said gently. "Hammering out a style takes work."

Marlene Dietrich said to Goldhandler, in a voice that seemed to be issuing from a cinema screen, so moviesque and Dietrich-esque did it sound, "It's an awfully amusing skit, Mr. Goldhandler." She turned to Hemingway. "Don't you think so?"

"Perfect for you," replied Hemingway.

"Well, I'll do it," she said to Goldhandler.

The two ad men jumped up and ran to Goldhandler, stammering congratulations. Nobody paid me any further attention. I walked out and went back up the stairs. Karl and Sigmund came gambolling out of their room stark naked, snapping towels at each other. "Oh, hi there," said Sigmund. As I slipped by them they went right on with their towel fight, snap snap snap, raising red welts on each other's bodies. In the office Peter was typing away, and Boyd lay on the sofa, a cigarette drooping from his mouth.

"I guess I'll try it," I said.

Peter shot me a smile, not pausing in his work. Boyd waved a languid hand at the closet. "Start digging. We need fresh jokes."

I hung my jacket and tie on a hook in the closet, took off my shoes — since that seemed to be the custom — and dragged out a bundle of *College Humor*. I was not sure I could do any work. I was still numb, and not only from the encounter with Hemingway and Dietrich. Coming on the two Goldhandler boys naked had shaken me up almost as much. They were the only uncircumcised Jews I had ever seen.

PART III

April House

57

Jazz Jacobson

Friday, September 14, 1973

I sit in an armchair in a suite on the eighteenth floor of the Sheraton April House, a yellow pad on my lap. Yesterday afternoon I saw Jan off to Israel.

Sandra telephoned us a couple of nights ago, startling us out of sleep about one A.M., to let us know that she has decided to stay in Israel, become an Israeli, and join the army at once to get her draft service over with. We induced her not to commit herself until one of us could come over to discuss it. "Not that it'll make any difference," she finally said. "Come if you like, but you'll be wasting your time." I couldn't leave my job so soon for another trip to Israel, so Jan threw together a travelling bag, and I told my secretary to reserve our usual suite at the St. Regis. I have never stayed in April House since, three days after Pearl Harbor, I walked out through its revolving door into a snowstorm. But it turned out that an auto dealers' convention had jammed the Manhattan hotels, so we landed in this haunted place. I spent the night here with my wife and sundry ghosts, and yesterday I took her to the airport.

Everything in April House has changed. In the lobby the carpets and wallpaper are all different. The style is obliterated. The magic odor of opulence, achievement, and romance is gone. Nothing is recognizable when you come in except the brass art-deco elevator doors, through which people like Max Schmeling and Claudette Colbert used to emerge. Yet by a morbid long-shot coincidence I find myself in the very suite Peter Quat and I occupied, and I can recognize it, though all has been thoroughly Sheratonized and nothing is the same.

Outside the bedroom window, you see, is a broken brick, which Bobbie Webb once named Peeping Tom, claiming it looked like the profile of a little man peering in at us. We had months of pillow-talk jokes about Peeping Tom, better imagined than resurrected. It's just a broken brick, of course. It doesn't look like a little man. Never did. Well, was I ever startled yesterday morning when I drew the curtain and saw that brick! It was Peeping Tom, not a doubt in the world of it, still there outside the bedroom where I first found out what love was, and what a woman was — a long chalk, may I say, from Dorsi Sabin. Jan lay there in the bed grumbling and moaning as is her wont before getting up, while remembrance flooded in on me with the gray rainy daylight.

"For God's sake, bring that idiot home," were my parting words at the airport, as she went off through the metal-detector hoop, "or else stay there."

"Who knows?" Jan returned over her shoulder. "If she makes sense, I may stay and join the Israeli army myself."

She is a small woman who wears big hats, quite visible in a crowd. As she went off amid a throng of jocund Jews, she glanced back and blew a kiss, and I had a flash of poignant love for her. Now I am waiting for two telephone calls: one from her in Israel, and one from an alien life form named Jazz Jacobson.

Everybody has read about Jazz Jacobson, the Hollywood wonder man, but few have had a close encounter with him. It is five P.M. in Israel, eleven in the morning here. Jan can still ring me before the Sabbath, if she has anything to report. I swear, I thought when I passed fifty that I was falling into the sere, the yellow leaf, but lately life seems to be breaking open faster than I can handle it.

On my way back from Kennedy Airport yesterday, Lee and I met at Pop's grave. Her husband, Bernie, is buried in that same Jewish cemetery, out near the racetrack. Yesterday was Bernie's *yahrzeit*, the anniversary of his death. Lee asked me when he died to observe kaddish for Bernie; so I do, since her sons are not interested. I said the graveside prayers for Pop and for Bernie, and we drove back into Manhattan so that I could recite Bernie's kaddish at Chopsuey.

Alas, Chopsuey no longer exists! Finished. The Chinese restaurant has become a cheap dry-goods store. The stairway is dusty and full of litter. The loft is dark. So we went to another synagogue, and then Lee and I had dinner at April House.

I told her I was writing about the West End Avenue days, and she came up with surprising things. She had no recollection, for instance, of the way she saved the situation at Faiga's wedding; and as she remembers it, Peter Quat was warm and gracious, a perfect gentleman; danced with her, and made a hit with everyone. Moreover, she thinks the wedding in *Onan's Way* is "a scream." Of course, Lee dines out on the Peter Quat connection. It impresses her suburban Jewish friends much more than my White House job. She and her friends cluck over Peter's books, their rabbis denounce them one by one as they're published, and everybody reads them. "Oh, sure, he's a swine," she once said, "but he's so clever!" She is agog about the new book, and says she can't wait to read it, though she's sure it's *awful*.

At one point I asked Lee how she had met Bernie. She peered at me incredulously. "But don't you know? I met Bernie at the temple. A men's club dance."

"You did? But how come? You wouldn't set foot in the temple, once you brushed off E. F. Kadane and Holy Joe."

"It was when I first came home. Remember? Holy Joe invited me. Just to snub old E. F., I said I'd go. Bernie never went to temple dances, either. It's a long story how he happened to be there, but anyway, that's how I met him."

"At the temple, then!"

"Oh, yes, at the temple."

"And through Holy Joe."

"Definitely, through Holy Joe."

"Then the move to West End Avenue worked, Lee. You owe your married life, and your three sons, to Holy Joe Geiger."

"I owe them to Pop. Pop killed himself, but he got me a nice Manhattan Jewish doctor."

"Don't say that. He lived for years after you married, his happiest years."

"He killed himself to get Bernie for me," Lee said sharply.

"Also, Lee, to give Mom the ploika."

Lee's mouth wrinkled in a sour smile. "Ah yes, the ploika. There you're wrong. Mama never got the ploika. She's still looking for it, over there in Jerusalem."

Then she told me about Moshe Lev. . . . But there's my phone call, one of them. . . .

Okay, that was Jazz Jacobson. I'll have to stay here another night, instead of returning to Washington. Imperative Hollywood interest in Peter Quat's new book, to my utter amazement. I considered it unfilmable, and still do.

When Peter Quat's agent told me that even the title of the new book would "knock my tits off," he was scarcely exaggerating. The title obviously cannot be put even on an X-rated movie. Yet Jazz Jacobson says he has an idea of how to handle it; also that his star, Mort Oshins, loves the book, and wants to make a film of it. Maybe it is true. Jack Warner was ready to do *The Smelly Melamed.* Those Hollywood people jump off in unpredictable directions, like fleas.

The title knocked the tits off both the Book-of-the-Month Club and the Literary Guild, I can tell you that. Because of all the hot trade talk, even the Reader's Digest book club unexpectedly asked to look at the novel. I received the manuscript back by messenger the same day I sent it over, with a short note in red ink scrawled on the title page by the editor, an old friend: *"Christ on a bicycle!"* When Peter first sent me the typescript and I saw the title, I myself nearly fell out of my chair. I thought Peter was playing a practical joke on his publisher. But he was and he remains serious about it.

"Either truth matters in art, or it does not," he wrote in his already celebrated ultimatum to the Book-of-the-Month. *"Either Joyce and Lawrence freed the artist from the obsolete shackles of Victorian prudery, or they did not. Now, thirty years after James Joyce died, let us find out. The title stands."* The letter is in this month's *Penthouse,* reprinted on a whole page in big type, with a handsome scowling picture of Peter on the porch of his Fire Island house, hunched barefoot on a rocking chair in Italian slacks and a sport shirt, narrowing his eyes at the world. A sensational plug, weeks before publication; and it comes right after a much-talked-about centerfold of a spread-eagled Chinese girl, captioned, *"See, it isn't true, what they say."*

I'm embarrassed to proceed, but I can't possibly continue unless I come right out with it, so I'll just have to worry about the family trade later. Well then, Peter's title is nothing more or less than *My Cock,* and that is what his novel is entirely about, too. It is a dialogue two hundred and thirty-seven printed pages long between the hero of the book and his penis. How on earth is such a book possible? Well, let me quote the blurb on the jacket: "*Peter Quat is the ultimate candid modernist. We are in the world of Joyce and Kafka, of expressionism and nightmare, where polite linear reality dissolves into the cloacal phantasmagoria that the human predicament actually is, and Victorian artificialities of taste dissolve before raw elemental truth.*" I strongly suspect Peter wrote that himself. Somebody else should do his blurbs. That makes the book sound heavy and worthwhile, whereas, like all the Quat books, it's just raucous fun in horrible taste, but quite easy to read. Either Peter Quat amuses you or he doesn't. Peter has always made me laugh. Mark Herz is bound to throw his worst fit yet at Peter's "traducing of his own people," for Peter has rolled the ball down the middle this time for a ten-strike.

The book is about a Jewish college professor, of course. All American Jewish novelists are college professors, and they all write about Jewish college professors, who are writing novels about Jewish college professors. It is a strict literary convention of the genre, like the fourteen lines of sonnet form. This professor is named Yehezkel Dienstag, and one day Dienstag's penis starts talking to him, as he is taking a shower. No explanation, it just does. The professor has recently been divorced by his shiksa wife for seducing too many female undergraduates, and so he is lonely and depressed and can't work on his novel. Yehezkel is surprised, with the mild inadequate dreamlike surprise one finds in Kafka, at being so spoken to, and he asks his appendage to explain itself.

"I am the Jewish people," the member replies. "I am the Wandering Jew, the Eternal Putz, and I have decided to speak out and tell you my story, so that you can tell it to the world."

With that, we are off to the races. I tried and failed to get Peter to change or cut that monumentally tasteless "eternal putz" phrase, but nothing is sacred to Peter; he maintains that it's his whole theme in two words, and it stays. Dienstag's thing goes rambling through history, starting back in Egypt, jumping around in time. Its identity sometimes melts into individuals like Joseph, Samson, Solomon, and Job, sometimes becomes the whole people, as at the Spanish Inquisition, again coalesces into two persons, as in an argument between Spinoza and Maimonides. Spinoza was actually his scrotum, says the appendage, "bearing all the seeds of the future, and I was Maimonides, the rigid old theology." I'm not describing the novel well, but try describing *Finnegans Wake* or Virginia Woolf's *Orlando* sometime! The book is one of those. It turns out that the "stiff-necked" people is a Biblical double entendre for the eternal Jewish character; that anti-Semitism is actually penis envy, and so on. The book is short, which is fortunate, because it is basically one unnerving literary joke. But of course, leave it to Peter; he has fleshed it out with plenty of steamy episodes. Potiphar's wife, and Delilah, and the Queen of Sheba, and Esther all make appearances, and there is stuff about Golda Meir, too, which may shake up the old Prime Minister some. Still, it takes a lot to faze her, and she'll probably just laugh her head off.

The problem of the clubs was, naturally, how could they offer a book with such a title? How could they even prepare their brochures? Both clubs were mad for the novel itself. After *Onan's Way* sold two hundred thousand copies, Peter Quat could do no wrong. Anyway, they both regard *My Cock* as a towering artistic breakthrough; in the words of a letter I got from a Guild official, "a marvellously original and sensitive tribute to the historical resilience of the Jewish people." In this same letter the Guild proposed instead, as a title, *Dienstag's Dingus*. They said they could live with that, and it would cushion the shock a bit for middle-American Guild subscribers. Peter remained adamant.

The Book-of-the-Month then weighed in with a truly ingenious alternative. They suggested that Peter call his book *The Putz and I,* pointing out that the parallel to *The King and I* would give it "respectability," since everything Rodgers and Hammerstein did was so wholesome. Also, gentile subscribers might take the word to be the monarchical title of some exotic Asian ruler. This suggestion came with an offer of a handsome advance on club royalties; contingent, however, on changing the title.

Maybe I shouldn't disclose this, in view of all the kudos Peter is now getting for his noble reply in *Penthouse,* but he was ready to take the offer. He thought *The Putz and I* wasn't bad, laughed out loud when he heard it, and said the money was terrific. But just then two paperback offers also came in, both munificent; and when I checked with the editors, they were both aghast at the thought of changing *My Cock.* "Why, it's the best-selling book title since *Gone with the Wind,*" said one of them. So Peter hardened up — though in this context that term may be slightly inappropriate — and wrote his famous letter, and the book will be known as *My Cock,* down the ages.

The Guild gulped and took it. I've seen their advance brochure. PETER QUAT'S NEW MASTERPIECE in huge type fills the cover. The subscriber has to look inside to find out the title, and then either turns purple and cancels his membership, or sends off the acceptance card with a drool.

Jazz Jacobson has seen the brochure, and says it is "pusillanimous." Jacobson is an articulate man. Maybe I should describe him, for those few backwoods readers who haven't seen his picture in news magazines. He is just under five feet tall, skinny as a stick insect, entirely bald, no eyebrows, round face, and strangely shaped ears. He does not have a green head or bug eyes or anything, but he really does not look quite terrestrial. His outstanding earthly feature is, in fact, not human; it is thick black-rimmed glasses. In *Variety*'s Christmas issue, where the Hollywood big-timers advertise themselves, there is always a full page with nothing on it but a picture of the Jazz Jacobson glasses, with no face behind them. Long ago Jazz Jacobson was an agent. Today he is what they call a packager, putting together a star, a director, a producer, a bank loan, and a hit play or a bestseller, to create a sure box-office success before the cameras even turn.

"Mort Oshins is dying to do it," Jazz Jacobson said to me this morning. We were breakfasting in the Gay Nineties Room, where Bobbie and I used to eat when it was just the April House coffee shop, and the waitresses wore plain brown uniforms, not black net tights and scarlet tutus, which afford you glimpses of waggling behinds with your orange juice. Jacobson was devouring ham and eggs as he talked. "It's a major work of comic art, Goodkind. Based on Quat's track record, it should sell three hundred thousand copies hardcover, three million paperback, and a million book club. We are talking of a vast pre-sold motion picture audience, a potential box-office gross, *going in,* of fifty to seventy million dollars. I can close a bank loan today to make this film — providing Oshins and Quat reach a meeting of the minds — of eleven million dollars, with payment to the author of one million dollars. Up front!" A guillotine chop of one stiff little palm marked off *up front*.

If I can convey how Jazz Jacobson utters the word "dollars," I will give you the whole man. You and I, and most people, even TV commentators, naturally say "*dollers*," throwing away the second syllable. Not Jazz Jacobson. Jazz Jacobson says doll-ARS, with a protracted powerful *a:* doll-AARS. When he says that, you hear dollars spoken of as we would all speak of them, if we put into our voices the yearning and reverence that we feel for dollars.

Probing a bit at this strange notion of making Peter's book into a film, I said, "I can see that the character of Professor Dienstag is quite an actor's challenge. But —"

"The professor?" Jacobson stared at me through those thick glasses, as though *I* were the insect presence from outer space, with no hair and pointy ears. "The professor? I don't follow you. Of course Mort Oshins is going to play his prick. *That's* the part."

Some statements are called conversation-stoppers. That one qualified. I shut up while he finished his ham and eggs with a glass of milk.

I was still not sure what Jacobson wanted of me. He had telephoned for this meeting in New York from London, where Mort Oshins is promoting his new hit movie, *Nailed, By Christ,* about the Jewish thief who was crucified alongside Jesus. Oshins first leaped to fame with his comic record of the thief's monologue, in heavy Yiddish dialect, based on the humor of his discomfort at being nailed up, and his impatient queries to Jesus about when they would go to Paradise together, and so forth. The hammering noise during the record got to be horridly funny — if you were going to laugh at this sort of thing — and the running gag, "OY! Easy mid det hemmer," became a national byword. Now it is the title of the theme song in the feature movie.

Oshins is no fool, and Jesus is never seen or heard in the film. Crowd reactions and the lines of the other actors convey that presence. Some churchmen have approved the film as "bringing the Gospel story to the mass audience through the medium of humor," though most of them have thrown the sort of fit that Peter Quat induces in Mark Herz and the more serious rabbis. Matching Oshins and Quat shows the Jazz Jacobson flair. Nobody else has thought of it, yet they go together, shall we say, like ham and eggs. Mort Oshins leans hard on Jewish humor in his movies, always playing a low Jew himself.

"It's all going to hinge on one thing," Jacobson said, delicately patting his mouth with a starchy napkin, "and that is whether Quat will give Oshins a free hand. Mort has written all his films himself, you realize. Never bought another writer's material before. I gave him the galleys to read on the plane coming home. He'll meet us here for lunch tomorrow."

A business lunch on Saturday? Out of the question for me, as the reader knows, but I said only, "He hasn't read it? Then how can he be crazy about it?"

"I described it to him. He fell for the idea, and began to improvise like mad. I've never laughed so hard in my life, Goodkind. He did twenty minutes in Yiddish dialect, right there in his hotel room, impersonating a prick getting circumcised. I had to beg him to stop. I was streaming tears. I thought I'd get sick from laughing."

"But how does he do that, exactly? I mean, such an impersonation seems impossible."

"Why?" Jazz Jacobson asked. "Did you see Zero Mostel in *Rhinoceros?*"

"Of course."

"Did he look like a rhinoceros?"

"Not at all."

"Did he convince you that he was a rhinoceros?"

"Absolutely."

"There you are. And Mort Oshins convinces you that he's a penis. I could *see* him standing there, all five feet seven inches of him, a big whang. It was uncanny."

"Tomorrow is impossible, sorry," I said. "Can we meet in Washington on Sunday?"

Jazz Jacobson looked grave. "I can call Mort in London and ask him." He glanced at his watch. "But let me advise you to move your appointments around and make this lunch date right here, tomorrow."

"Can't be done."

Jazz Jacobson dropped his voice. "Suppose it means losing the deal?"

Familiar Hollywood talk; on the other hand, there was my obligation to Quat.

"Well, would it?"

Jazz Jacobson dropped his voice still further, to a hollow dry outer space whisper. "Dreyfus."

"I beg your pardon? Dreyfus?"

"Mort has a hilarious angle on the Dreyfus case. Paramount is ready to go with it, and actually I flew to London to finalize the deal. I picked up the galleys of the new Quat for something to read on the plane. It just hit me, this conception of Mort Oshins doing the book. It's of the moment. It's thrilling. But Mort is a whimsical fellow,

Goodkind. He's passing through New York overnight" — again, Jacobson lowered his voice — "his girl friend is here, and his wife is waiting for him in Beverly Hills. You're not going to get him to Washington. If he returns to the coast without any further action on Quat, he'll sign for Dreyfus on Monday. I beseech you to meet him here tomorrow. I'll bring him right to this suite. It won't take more than an hour. Surely you can work that out, for the sake of a brilliant deal."

Of course Peter would pick an occasion like this to be incommunicado. False urgency is a staple of Hollywood trading, and your position strengthens once you shrug off the pressure. But I could not risk it without telling Peter. His agent is hospitalized with a kidney stone, and the whole thing is in my hands.

Peter is on a chartered yacht at anchor off Staten Island, I'm forced to mention, boffing the wife of his new publisher. She is a former fashion magazine editor, past forty but lissome and full of the old pizazz. She would be recognized in any halfway elegant New York hotel they might check into. So Peter has chartered this yacht, and she slips away when she can, hires a speedboat and goes aboard, and they make the beast with two backs. You would think Peter was getting old for this sort of thing, but not a bit of it. He is estranged from his fifth wife, so he doesn't have the jealousy problem; on the other hand, he is suing to get custody of their son, on the grounds that she is living in adultery with an expatriate South Vietnamese poet, so he has to watch his step. The long and short of it is, I couldn't pick up the telephone and call Peter about this. He told me he would come ashore and be in touch with me sometime next week. You wouldn't believe how hot he was to get aboard that yacht. He was fairly jigging with eagerness.

So either I had to accept a business meeting on the Sabbath, something I haven't agreed to since I started my own law firm, or — if I could believe Jazz Jacobson — I would be jeopardizing Peter Quat's chance at a rich film contract. Jazz Jacobson is one of Hollywood's most eminent and reliable personalities; the chance that he was lying was not more than eighty percent. The margin of possible truth was not to be ignored. An awkward situation!

"I'd appreciate it," I said, "if you'd phone Oshins."

Jazz Jacobson ordered a table telephone and called London. The operator there said Mr. Oshins was expected back in an hour. So Jazz left, saying he had an appointment with Heifetz.

"Jascha Heifetz? Isn't he on tour in Europe?"

"Sammy Heifetz," he said. "Best composer of movie scores in America. I want to tie him up for our project now, if I can. Fox is trying to get him for *Franklin and Lucy,* their big World War II movie about this woman Roosevelt was screwing on the side. That script was offered to me first, but I turned it down. There's such a thing as taste. I'll phone you as soon as I get through to Mort Oshins, but I implore you to stay for this meeting tomorrow."

So he left.

It is now well past noon; in Israel, after six at night. Jan will not be telephoning any more. She has lit her candles. Jacobson called to say Oshins refuses to go to Washington, so I'll arrange to stay over here. Drat Peter, anyway. Davey Goodkind, doing the Sabbath bit in April House! Peeping Tom will not believe his eyes. But Bobbie Webb would not be so very surprised. At heart she always knew.

58

Mort Oshins

September 15, 1973

THE airport is fogbound. The last shuttle to Washington sits outside the terminal window in drifting floodlit mist. We're promised a takeoff within the hour.

Peter Quat is going to become a very, very rich writer. The Almighty will have to forgive me for talking money on the Sabbath. It felt damned odd. I committed no technical violations, no writing, no telephoning. Still, I may well end up with a fat fee from this day's money talk, and if so I'll donate that fee to charity and skip all the contrition.

At the moment Peter is broke. That never bothers him. If he wants to charter a yacht for the somewhat special purpose of fornicating at anchor, why, he just does it, and then scrambles here and there for the money. Despite his big earnings, the price of pleasure past keeps his purse lean. Peter pays alimony to three ex-wives (the fourth has remarried), and he is putting several kids through school, one a byblow. He avoided a paternity suit by settling a lump sum on the mother, a twenty-year-old receptionist in the office of his previous publisher. Peter is a creature of impulse, no doubt of that.

Now and then, I'm bound to state, I envy Peter's gamy goulash of a love life. Since I married Jan there has been not one other woman. Nothing even close. If variety is the spice of life, I have been on a bland diet for thirty years. So has poor Jan, for that matter. The faithful creature eats up red-hot novels and sighs over them, and that — to my best knowledge — is that. Clearly monogamy agrees with me, and I must hope it does with her. I am as happy as they come in this vale of tears, partly because Jan is an enigmatic, shifty, and durably adorable little package, and I never know quite where I stand with her, or what is coming up next. Still, that is not the same as rogering your publisher's wife on a chartered yacht, one more score in a lifetime of random rogering. Let us not kid ourselves.

And as I sat writing yesterday in that haunted suite, which I once shared with Peter Quat and then with Mark Herz, my pen came to a stop. I fell to reliving the Bobbie Webb years, and thinking of Peter out there off Staten Island, and Jan and Sandra in Israel, and I spiralled down into a grim mood. So I telephoned Mark Herz in his physics lab at Columbia. He came over, I ordered up a bottle of bourbon, and that helped a lot.

Mark has little reason to be jealous of Peter, what with two ex-wives and many sporadic fooleries. But he is a different sort; faintly melancholy about his womanizing, and you sense that he deeply loves women, and to this day yearns for a lasting love. Peter seems determined to stab the whole sex to death with his prong, or beat it to death with typewriter keys. The females in his books are interchangeable lay figures (so to speak); Jewish college girl, Hollywood starlet, Vietnamese whore, French sculptress; they all say and do the same things, especially between the sheets, and they leave a stale taste about matters erotic. Maybe all that rogering down the years causes womankind in the end to merge into dull blurs, with hairy creases between their legs. Such is the School of Quat woman, more or less. I don't know, and I will never find out. You play the game once according to your nature, and there is no second deal.

Well, Mark and I got colossally soused Friday afternoon, so that my lone Sabbath eve in April House went by in a merciful fog. As I was pouring our first round he inquired, "Say, Davey, are we really going to be in-laws? After all these years?"

"What are you talking about? Cheers."

"Cheers." We settled down in the living room. "About Abe and your daughter. Who else?"

"You're misinformed."

"Are you sure? Just this morning I had to telephone Nahum Landau in Haifa about something. He said he heard they were going steady, and I'd have a nice daughter-in-law. I agreed."

"How did he hear that? From whom?"

"Who knows? In Israel everybody hears everything."

I told Mark about Sandra's bombshell phone call, and Jan's trip to Israel. At the news about Sandra he did not blink; said he had been through it all with Abe.

"Israel can do that to a youngster. The more noble-spirited and bright, the more likely. However —" With a sigh close to a groan, and a long pull at the bourbon, he gave me a dejected look and changed the subject. "One of my graduate students left this month's *Penthouse* in the lab."

"Oh, dear," I said.

"So old Peter is in again, eh? With *that* title? Truly?"

"Afraid so."

"I've never looked at *Penthouse* before, but I saw Peter's name on the cover." Mark shook his head. "Christ, that poor Chinese girl."

"A San Francisco tart, Mark, no doubt, who got paid plenty."

"Yes, and no doubt she's done almost everything else for money, but not exposing her privates to the millions. It had to hurt. Orientals have resistant standards of modesty, Dave. I've worked with them. Well, it was all in the spirit of Peter's letter."

Mark drank again, a large gulp that made him cough.

"Honestly, this wrapping himself in the mantle of artistic integrity! The teller of truth, James Joyce's heir! What rot!" He finished his drink in another gulp. "The literary Jewish Uncle Tom, he means. Reassuring the gentiles that — Israel's war prowess notwithstanding — we Jews are just as low and dirty and laughable as all the Hebe jokes have always made us out. Our very own Stepin Fetchit Yid, doing his funny servile shuffle with his dick hanging out, to give the goyim a giggle."

I said, to get him off this topic, "You're not in a good mood, either."

"I'm in a rotten mood. But in the best of moods I can't stand this self-righteous posturing of Peter's."

I hadn't anticipated that Mark Herz might have seen *Penthouse*. He lives in a shut-off research world. Peter Quat is his King Charles's head, and we might have had that broken record all afternoon, complete with reproaches for my representing Peter. I didn't need that, so I told him I had been reading Nahum Landau's *Quantum Mechanics for Everyone,* and couldn't make head or tail of it.

Mark brightened. He is at heart a teacher. He has never tired of explaining the new physics to me: general relativity, quantum mechanics, atomic theory, the lot. He even started to teach me calculus once, telling me, "That's the language God speaks, you'd better learn it." I've always understood Mark while he was talking. The trouble is that the new physics goes against common sense; or as Mark says, it's "anti-intuitional." What he tells me stays with me for a week or so, then fades away again. Anyhow, the distraction worked. I got him off Quat, and he was holding forth on quantum theory when a pink oblong of light hit the long wall of the living room, as it always did in the old days before sunset.

"Well, well," he said. "Sundown is upon you. I leave you to the Sabbath's ministering angels. Maybe one more tot of bourbon, eh?"

As he poured for both of us, I told him about Lee and General Lev.

"*What!* Why, I saw Moshe the day before he returned to Israel. He didn't say a word about it."

"I found out only yesterday, Mark, when I had dinner with Lee."

"But how serious can it be? They're both past sixty."

"All I know is, he visited her in Port Chester. They got to talking about this and that, and he asked her to come over there, and she's going."

"I'll be damned." Mark wryly grinned. "That's kind of wonderful."

"Do you remember how they met?"

"Of course. I gave you Moshe's address in Palestine, when you told me your sister was going there."

"Remember what you wrote it on?"

"No."

"A safety match cover. Do you realize" — I was feeling the bourbon in my head and knees as I walked him to the door — "what an upheaval that bit of cardboard made in several lives? What destinies it affected? Mark, can a man ever foresee the consequences of his lightest action? Can you truly call any human action free will? Lee's whole life was altered by that match cover. Who knows whether you had the choice *not* to write that address forty years ago, or whether you were not fated to do it?"

"Cocktail party profundity," Mark said with good-natured contempt. "Spare me." He stood at the door, glancing back into the suite, his face an iron mask, with sad remembering eyes looking through. "We've said nothing about Bobbie Webb."

"No."

"Or about Monica."

"No," I said. "Poor Monica."

"Jan is a terrific woman, Davey. How I've envied you, down the years! Bobbie would never have worked out. The specific gravity wasn't there. But my God, she was beautiful."

"That she was. So was Monica."

"Yes. They were both beautiful. That was their stock in trade. Happily, in those days there was no temptation to sell pictures of their cunts."

Nobody is shocked by words nowadays, but Mark Herz caught me unaware. It was a few seconds before I could say, "They'd never have done it."

"Who knows? Times change, manners change. I'm glad that they were young and beautiful then, and that we loved them."

He struck my shoulder awkwardly with a fist, and left.

Now for my slightly loony encounter with Jacobson and Oshins. When they arrived in my suite for lunch, I was wearing my yarmulka. I was reviewing the Torah reading, and I figured, why remove it for a couple of Jews?

Jacobson gave me a wary stare, very much like a voyager from Betelgeuse encountering a strange being in eerie headgear. Oshins astounded me. He took in the skullcap and the Hebrew volume, and threw his arms around me. "*A froomer Yid!*" he exclaimed in homey Yiddish. "*A shaymer shabbess!* (A religious Jew! A Sabbath observer!)" He swung into a syncopated Sabbath hymn, snapping his fingers, and began to dance as men sometimes do in the synagogue, not burlesquing it at all, moving with fluid grace. Then he pulled me into the dance, and there we were, this famed low comedian and a nobody of a tax lawyer, doing an honest-to-God *rikkud* — Hassidic dance — in the room where Bobbie Webb and I declared our love decades ago. Jazz Jacobson stood there, goggling at us through his trademark, not knowing quite how to react, I guess, but pleased that we seemed to be hitting it off.

As we danced, Oshins began to vary the hymn's words, slipping from the liturgical Hebrew into Yiddish. "*This pig here,*" he sang, rolling his eyes at Jacobson, "*lays his mother-in-law. That would not be so bad, but she is a cockroach.*"

In Yiddish it rhymed. I don't know whether that seems funny in

English on paper, but I broke up and fell on the couch, roaring with laughter.

"*This pig here*" — Oshins continued, dancing on alone —"*eats dog turds on Yom Kippur, without a yarmulka, and doesn't make a blessing.*"

Then he reverted to the sacred Hebrew words and went on singing and dancing while I tried to gasp myself back into seriousness. Jacobson might have recognized the Yiddish word for pig, *hazzer*, for it has crept into show-business slang, but Oshins called him a *dover akher*, "other thing," the Talmudic euphemism for a hog. Jacobson hadn't a clue. He just stood there, vaguely smiling.

"What did I tell you?" Jacobson said to me. "He is the world's greatest improviser. What amuses you so? What is he singing? A funny song?"

"*Ut der dover akher, der amaretz,*" sang Oshins, capering faster, "This pig here, this ignoramus, wipes my ass with his tongue, on request."

Well, enough. It went on and on, and I lay on the couch, laughing and laughing. The incongruity between the old hymn, Oshins's authentic rikkud, and the obscene insults to the oblivious Jacobson was just killing. What ended it was the arrival of the lunch. I had ordered it Friday, signing the bill in advance so that there would be no need to write. As the waiter rolled in the table, Jacobson said, "Niçoise salads? Why? I can't stand Niçoise salad."

Oshins spoke English for the first time. "Asshole," he said to Jacobson, "he's kosher, and it's Shabbess."

"What's Shabbess?" asked Jacobson, wrinkling his face unhappily at the salads.

"Saturday," I said.

"Is it Saturday?" said Jacobson. "I guess it is. Are you religious, Goodkind? Is that why you wear that thing on your head?"

"You can order something else," I said. "But you'll have to pay cash. I can't sign the bill."

"You're kidding." Jazz Jacobson picked up the telephone and asked for room service.

"Asshole," said Oshins, "he doesn't write on Saturday."

"Why not?" asked Jacobson.

"I went to a yeshiva for six years," Oshins said to me. He chanted perfectly half a dozen opening lines of the Talmud treatise *Benedic-*

tions, while Jacobson discussed the lunch menu with room service, and settled on fried clams with Canadian bacon.

Once we talked business over lunch, it went quickly. Peter is in for one glorious surprise when he drags himself back from Staten Island! The million "up front" is for real, an advance against handsome percentages of the profits. The sole stipulation is that the book reach the top of *The New York Times* best-seller list, as *Deflowering Sarah* and *Onan's Way* both did. For that money it's a reasonable proviso. I couldn't argue them out of it, though I tried. "Suppose it never becomes Number One?" I asked.

"Suppose the sky falls down?" said Jacobson. "I am buying success, and that is what Quat has to sell."

"It's his funniest material," said Oshins. "Can't miss."

Jazz Jacobson went into the bedroom after lunch to take a business call from Sammy Heifetz. Oshins told me he had started as a gagman, and to him Peter Quat had always been a legend, the joke-writer who had graduated to serious literature. Now he was going to do a Quat book as a film, and couldn't be more excited.

"Frankly, I still can't picture the thing," I said. "It seems impossible to adapt."

"Not in the least. The talking prick is a challenge, a *tour de force.* Any hairy-ass comedian would love to take a shot at it." Mort Oshins became the serious technician. "Once you get into Samson and Delilah, Joseph and Potiphar's wife, and all that, you're home free. You were once a gagman, think about it. Six sketches about screwing, with the cock itself as the narrator! That's what it boils down to. No contest!" A wave of concern passed over his mobile young face. "Not that there aren't problems. Look, do you mind if I smoke? I respect you, though I'm a shaygets. If you'd rather I didn't, say so."

"It's between you and Him, not you and me."

"*Goot gepaskent* (well ruled)." He pulled an enormous cigar out of a breast pocket and lit it. "You can get Havanas in London. Delicious. I'll tell you my problem. You'll understand. Jazz would think I was talking Chinese. Some Jew he is, that *dover akher!* Last month I did a promo appearance in Brooklyn and I visited the old yeshiva. The kids got a charge out of it, and so did I. I loved it. It was old home week. Before I left, the Rov and I were drinking tea alone in his office. He said appreciative, astute things about my films. He's

seen them all. Then, quite gently, he said, 'But, Mordechai' — that's
my name, Mordechai — 'even though Hitler, may his name be erased,
is gone, aren't there enough Hamans still in the world? Does Mordechai have to give Haman rope to hang Jews with?' "

Behind the door, Jazz Jacobson's vehement negotiating noises were
reaching a crescendo. I said nothing. Oshins puffed nervously at the
big cigar.

"The thief on the cross was an accident," Oshins burst out. "You
know how it happened? I did it one night at a party. I just made it
up as I went along. It worked. They fell around laughing. I kept doing
it at parties, improving it. I made the record more or less as a gag.
It sold over a million copies, and so I was stuck with the thief. That's
my persona. I play him in every film. You know that. But I plan to
make my break with Dreyfus. I'll play Dreyfus as a Chaplin figure,
pathetic, gallant, uncrushable. No Yiddish accent! A noble sweet human being. The humor will be about the *anti-Semites*. They'll be
Chaplin heavies, ridiculous Hamans. I can't pass up this Quat thing,
though. Jazz has lined up a fortune of bank money and I need it."

Jazz Jacobson popped exulting out of the bedroom, his whole
naked head bright pink. "We've got Heifetz for *My Cock!*"

* * *

WELL, the shuttle finally did take off, and I've had a pretty good
night's sleep here in this lonesome Georgetown house. When
Jan woke me at six, phoning me from Jerusalem, the sun was up and
she sounded cheerful, which started the day right. "There's hope,"
she said.

"Hope for what? That she'll come home?"

"Well, you'll soon know. She's written you a letter."

"A letter from Israel can take weeks!"

"You'll have it in a couple of days. This kibbutz chairman, Dudu
Barkai, gave it to a foreign ministry type who's leaving for Washington tomorrow."

"What's in the letter?"

Jan hesitated, then said uncertainly, "Just read it. It's pretty good."

"Is she all right?"

"Why, she's great, though impossible. Speaking of impossible people, your mother is okay. She made me take her to a kosher Chinese restaurant. She cross-examined the head waiter for half an hour, then ordered a plate of steamed water chestnuts, and a double gin and orange juice."

"What's the story on Abe Herz and Sandra?"

"Sandra is standing right here. Ask her."

"Jan, when are you coming home?"

"I'm trying to get reservations now."

Sandra came briskly on the line. No sense spending money on long-distance chatter, she said, until I had read her letter. Then we could talk.

"Say, what about you and Abe?"

"Abe who?"

"Come on. Are you two engaged, or something?"

"What on earth makes you ask?"

"There's a rumor going around Israel to that effect, and it's crossed the ocean."

"It's nonsense."

"You're not seeing him?"

"Look, now you're sounding like your mother. I couldn't eat my kosher egg foo yung for all her questions about the nice American lawyer. Abe's back on reserve duty, down at the Suez Canal. Read my letter."

That's that, and I'm off to the White House. Whatever awaits me there will not be fun. Any day now the Vice President, who still hangs on like a leech, will be skewered by an indictment. The grand jury is indicting one Presidential Assistant after another. As the first week in October rolls toward the President, it looks more and more like curtains. He's battling like a tiger in the courts against handing over those tapes to the Special Prosecutor. The Supreme Court reconvenes October first. If he hasn't already yielded to the lower courts, it'll undoubtedly order him to surrender the tapes. If he defies the Supreme Court, he'll be impeached. If he obeys, and the Special Prosecutor goes rooting through the tapes, he'll be impeached anyway. They must be fatal. His string is running out.

But I am not quitting. In New York I visited my law office. My junior partner has it humming on profitably. Once I leave the White

House I will never write another word of *April House*. I know that. I love writing it. Come hell or high water, I will get to what happened with Harry Goldhandler and Bobbie Webb, and write it all down.

* * *

59

Digging Jokes

M Y two-week tryout for the Goldhandler job sped by like two minutes. I uncorked, to my own surprise, quite a knack for digging jokes. My first move, not half an hour after I went to work, was to put aside the stacks of *College Humor* I had started on. A couple of hundred durable japes circulated endlessly in those magazines, and I figured that they must all be in the files. I checked. So they were. Samples, for readers curious about undergraduate wit in the 1930's:

SHE: Where did you learn to kiss like that?
HE: I used to play the tuba.

HE: Marry me, darling. If we make a mistake, we'll separate.
SHE: Yes, but what'll we do with the mistake?

Et cetera.
Poking in the closet, I came upon a pile of an extinct magazine called *Truth,* dating back to the turn of the century. The brown brittle pages, crumbling in my hand as I turned them, were fascinating for their illustrations of women in hobble skirts and bustles, men in boaters' and pipestem trousers, and the preposterous advertisements for cure-all medicines. I started moiling through *Truth* just for the fun of it. I remember the first nugget I came upon, because Goldhandler used it. The illustration showed a Gibson girl with her straw-hatted swain in a rowboat; he giving her a lovesick look, she very bored.

MARMADUKE: Alas, Gwendolyn, I fear you regard me as a perfect simpleton.

GWENDOLYN: Oh, no, Marmaduke. Among us poor mortals, perfection is so seldom to be found!

This clearly needed updating. I typed it out so on the card:

INSULTS
HE: I suppose you think I'm a perfect idiot.
SHE: Oh, no, nobody's perfect.

I must have gone through forty issues of *Truth* to cull a dozen such jewels. Peter left. Boyd and I had dinner with the family, and went back upstairs to work. About eleven at night Goldhandler staggered wearily in, chewing on a cigar. He slumped into his swivel chair, and began to look over my cards. "Boyd," he said. Boyd padded to the desk. Goldhandler gave him the cards. Boyd shuffled through them and looked strangely at me.

"Where'd you dig these?" Goldhandler demanded. I pointed to the magazines piled beside my chair. "What? *Truth?* Cut the shit."

"Well, I did shorten them, sir. That old style tends to be periphrastic."

Goldhandler and Boyd exchanged a glance. "Tired?" he asked me.

"I've been at it a while."

"Go on home."

I gratefully put on my shoes, tie, and jacket. "What time do I come back to work tomorrow?" I asked Boyd.

"Whenever you want to," said Boyd.

That joke from *Truth* made its way into Marlene Dietrich's skit on the Rudy Vallee show. When Dietrich said in that husky, sugary Teutonic drawl, "No, Rudy, nobody's perfect," the audience bellowed and broke into applause; and I was almost as proud as if I had written *Le Bourgeois Gentilhomme.*

Riffling through the cards day by day, I kept coming on familiar old dirty jokes, laundered to innocuousness, much less funny, but there they were. "Oh yes," said Boyd, when I pointed this out, "by all means, whatever you can think of. Just make it with kissing." I was then a walking bank of dirty jokes. My Talmudic memory, idling without that ancient learning to soak up, had absorbed scores of them at Columbia, and I was the life of any all-male party. So when the digging did not go well, I would fatten up my card stack by recalling a few of these and making them with kissing. Goldhandler used some of them, too.

I had been there about a week, and was digging away late one night while Goldhandler, Peter, and Boyd rewrote a script for Kate Smith (older readers will know the name), a burlesque of the opera *Aïda*. The singer had said there weren't enough jokes, and they were pumping in anything from the files that seemed to fit.

"Maybe you could do something about that name, Aïda," I ventured.

Testy and worn down, Goldhandler snapped, "Like what?"

"Well, since she's so fat, she could say, 'I am a princess of the royal house of Norfallot.' "

Boyd played a perfect straight to me, wrinkling up his sad white face. "*Norfallot?*"

"Sure. Aïda Norfallot."

Nobody laughed. Boyd, Peter, and Goldhandler looked at each other, nodding.

"It's in," said Goldhandler.

Next day I heard from Boyd that, though Kate Smith usually hated fat jokes, she had burst out laughing at Aïda Norfallot. For a year after that, whenever we ran into a block on a script, Goldhandler would turn to me and say, "Finkelstein, let's have another Aïda Norfallot." He called all of us Finkelstein, except when he called us Liebowitz.

What endeared me most to Harry Goldhandler, I believe, was the following. Drudging through old vaudeville booklets, I came on this gem and typed it up:

INSULT

PAT: Here's a picture of me, taken with a herd of pigs.
MIKE: I see. Sure, and you're the one with the hat on.

Goldhandler pounced on it and put it straight into a script. "Big joke, Finkelstein," he commented. Evidently, then, to imply that a man was an animal constituted a big joke. It did not seem too recondite an art form. I spent hours thinking up a few of these. To wit:

How many toes does a monkey have?
Take off your shoes and let's see.

How many ribs are there on a jackass?
Open your coat and we'll find out.

How many hairs are there on a pig's face?
The next time you shave, count them.

When Goldhandler shuffled through my cards that night, with me at his elbow, his heavy eyebrows went up, and he gravely nodded, pulling out the animal insults one by one. "Big jokes, Liebowitz. Where from?"

"I made those up," I said. "Variations on a theme."

Half-shut eyes appraised me through a veil of cigar smoke. Selecting the one about the pig's face, Goldhandler carefully laid it among cards spread on his desk for an all-night writing session. "Go home. Take a good rest."

Among the office chores that fell to me from the start was indexing the joke files, using little green celluloid tabs. Peter had done it for a while, and had got about as far as GIRLS, GOUT, and GUNS. Each category had to be typed on a tiny white slip that was inserted behind the green celluloid window, which, however, was so dark you could hardly read the typing through it. I was inspired — don't ask me how — to try an experiment. I typed MOTHER-IN-LAW in red, and slipped it under the small green tab. Magic! MOTHER-IN-LAW stood out bold and black and clear! Consult your neighborhood Nobel physicist for the basis of this marvel of optics. All I know is, it worked. Peter Quat was the first to remark on how readable my index tabs were.

"Slide out the label," I said.

He did. Exclaiming that he would be damned, he showed it to Boyd. Boyd gave me a stupefied stare. Goldhandler came into the office about then, and Boyd showed him how my wonderful red labels worked. Goldhandler summoned his wife and children to see the thing. Mrs. Goldhandler's parents came straggling along. So did the two maids and the cook, a very large fat black woman named Sardinia. The old folks chattered excitedly about it in Yiddish, and Sardinia and the maids, rolling their eyes at me and shaking their heads in amazement, chuckled and gabbled in black talk. Even Sigmund and Karl regarded me with new respect. They had been crushing me at chess and Ping-Pong, and had me sized up as a poor specimen; but here I had done something like inventing the wheel or discovering the fourth dimension. My trial period then and there was over. I belonged in the Goldhandler madhouse. I seemed born for it.

That same night — it must have been after one A.M., because we were about to go out to eat — Boyd took me aside. "The boss wants to talk to you. He's shaving."

Hesitantly I entered the huge sumptuous master bedroom. Mrs. Goldhandler was on a chaise longue in a negligee, a book to her nose. Goldhandler, stripped to the waist, his face thick with shaving cream, beckoned through the open bathroom door with his razor. "Well, Finkelstein, you want to work with us?"

"You want to hire me?"

Goldhandler reached out a thick naked hairy arm, and his brief powerful hug sent a wave of happy warmth through me.

The next day was my very last for registering at the law school. I woke around noon and walked up to the Columbia campus in warm September sunshine. My pre-law classmates were passing in and out of Avery Hall, loaded down with thick tomes. I sat on a stone bench in the shade, watching them come and go. I must have sat there for an hour. Then I returned home, ate something, and slept until dinner time.

"I'm going to work for Harry Goldhandler," I announced at the table. "Even if I enter law school next year, I'll be younger than the others in my class. I'm starting at twenty dollars a week."

Boyd had mentioned that figure to me in a near-whisper, just before I had left the penthouse at dawn.

Pop wrinkled his mouth and nodded. Nothing more.

"Well, maybe it's a good thing for you to grow up a little," said Mom, "before you start something serious like law school. Twenty a week isn't bad, only maybe you ought to do the advertising for the laundry, too. Pop spends a fortune on it, and it's no good."

"I told Bernie what you're doing," said Lee. Bernie was her pediatrician cavalier. "Bernie thinks you're a fool to take up something fly-by-night like gagwriting instead of a profession. Maybe you should talk to Bernie. Bernie has a head on his shoulders."

I let that pass. Bernie was not a bad fellow, as Lee's *shleck* went. (*Shleck* is the plural of *shlock;* which means misfortune, and by extension, as used by Zaideh, all of Lee's and Faiga's boy friends. I would have included Bernie, then; but he made Lee a fine husband, he was no shlock, and may he rest in peace.)

"Yisroelke is grown up," Pop said to Mom. "He knows what he's doing."

Pop ate nothing of the lamb stew that night, though it was a favorite dish of his. He said it was too hot for stew.

When I walked into Goldhandler's office at about nine that night,

Boyd and Peter Quat were furiously typing, and Goldhandler was just stretching out on the sofa, with a piteous groan. "Hi, Finkelstein," he said in a faded faint voice. "We need freshies. Get to work. Boyd, wake me in fifteen minutes. We have to do that Penner thing before we go out for coffee."

He was snoring before I had my jacket and tie off. Peter Quat made one of his most distorted faces at me. "Welcome to the pirate crew, Finkelstein."

60

The Pirate King

I HAD been on the Goldhandler merry-go-round for a month or so
when Aunt Faiga produced a boy. Mom and Pop pleaded with
me to come to the *bris,* the circumcision, at Zaideh's Bronx flat, so I
broached the subject at the Goldhandler dinner table. "But surely you
don't want to watch the savage mutilation of a helpless infant," said
Mrs. Goldhandler. Her figure was now fetchingly slim. She too had
had a boy, Charles Darwin Goldhandler, whose foreskin was quite as
intact as Sigmund's and Karl's and likely to remain so. "It's so barbarous, so primitive."

"As a matter of fact," I said, "this kid's parents are very up-to-date.
They're both Communists."

Mrs. Goldhandler frequently declared that she was a Communist,
so I hoped this might mitigate my relatives' backwardness.

"Parlor pinks," she sniffed.

"Oh, no," I persisted. "My Aunt Faiga was jailed for cold-cocking
a cop in a Union Square riot. She's the real thing."

The moment had come to point with pride to this bit of family
history. You never know.

Mrs. Goldhandler frowned at me, possibly because I said "cold-
cock." It was a curious convention that only the master could talk
rough at the table. Nobody else ever said as much as "hell" or "damn";
not Mrs. Goldhandler, not her children, and not the staff. Up in the
office we talked as we pleased, and Peter Quat pleased to talk most
of the time like a bilked whore. Boyd and I were milder.

Goldhandler said, "Look, go ahead to the bris, Liebowitz. Just make
sure they haven't hired a nearsighted rabbi. He might cut off the rest
of your cock. You might want it some day, though you wouldn't understand why."

Goldhandler knew that rabbis don't perform circumcisions, that was just his joke. He spoke a flawless colorful Yiddish, in which he told paralyzingly funny dirty stories about rabbis, Jewish observances, and Bible figures, often with Talmudic nuances. His late father had contributed to a Yiddish socialist newspaper under the pen name *Shloimkeh Apikayress,* that is, Solly the Atheist. Pop had been much impressed to learn who Harry Goldhandler's father had been.

"Solly the Atheist, eh? A very clever writer. So! No wonder Mr. Goldhandler is a success. The son of Solly the Atheist! Went a little bit too far, Solly, but the public licked their fingers."

I knew it would upset Zaideh if I didn't show up at the bris. On the other hand, it was happening on Sunday, and listening to Henny Holtz on Sunday night was a Goldhandler must. Afterward we would dissect the program, and you never heard so many synonyms for failure. It was an education of a sort, an alphabet of epithets with few gaps from A to Z. Every Henny Holtz program was one or more of the following:

an Abortion, a Bagel, a Bomb, a Botch, a Catastrophe, a Clunker, a Debacle, a Disaster, a Dog, an Emetic, an Enema, a Fiasco, a Fizzle, a Flop, a Hash, a Hodgepodge, a Jumble, a Lemon, a Louse, a Mess, a Nothing, a Pancake, a Stinker, a Turd, a Turkey, a Washout, a Zero, a Zilch

. . . or a Light Fart. This was Goldhandler's own coinage, a light fart, and it was his favorite dismissive term. Whatever else a Holtz broadcast was, it was invariably a light fart.

Caught once again between the Inside and the Outside — as with exams on Shavuos, and the Varsity Show on Passover — I decided to go to the bris, leave at the knife slash, and speed back downtown. It did not work out that way. Our entire Mishpokha, and Boris's too, jammed Zaideh's flat to see a child of two Marxists enter the covenant of Abraham. *"A generation goes, a generation comes,"* Pop happily quoted in Hebrew from Ecclesiastes, as we pushed our way into this boil of our family and of Boris's outnumbered but fleshy relatives, who took up about the same cubic volume as our crowd did. Zaideh's flat reminded me of the famous Marx Brothers' stateroom scene, except that people weren't squirming and stepping on each other's faces. It was all very merry and good-tempered. Once in, I had little chance of getting out fast. Zaideh made it impossible by awarding me the honor called *kvatter*. I protested that I had never carried a baby and might drop him, but I was laughed down. Actually there was no way that baby could have hit the floor. If I had let go of him, he would just have levitated on relatives until rescued.

So I went to get the baby from Aunt Faiga, who sat with him in the kitchen. Very plump and womanly, little resembling the firebrand in a Lenin cap who had cold-cocked a policeman, she handed over the infant with a worried maternal sigh. I worked my way with him through the kinfolk to Zaideh's bedroom. The swaddled infant lay very calmly in Zaideh's lap, blinking big blue eyes at the *mohel*, a bearded little man in a white medical smock, with a gauze mask over his mouth and nose.

And that was how I got my first look at a circumcision. I have since seen several, including my own two sons'. I do not recommend it as light entertainment. Nor am I about to regale the reader with a description. But maybe I should mention that the circumcision scene in *Deflowering Sarah* is one of Peter Quat's crazier inventions. What happens is about as likely as that a surgeon would leave his umbrella in an appendix incision. I suppose the drunken circumciser with the shakes is sort of funny, also the mother who faints when she sees ketchup spilled all over the rug, but as to the Jewish content, it is just pure Quat. Peter has never seen a circumcision, any more than he has seen the dark side of the moon.

After much ado with surgical instruments and antiseptics, and a lot of Hebrew chanting, the mohel all at once just went and did it, whiz! There was very little blood. The boy — then and there given the inside name Yitzhak, outside name Ivan — uttered one sharp yip, subsiding at once when the mohel put a wine-dipped cloth to his lips. Boris carried him off, the family broke into a joyous tumult, and my plan to rush off was kaput. I had to sing and drink with the rest. Fortunately, in Zaideh's book-crammed study, which was closed off from the party, a very ancient radio gathered dust. With some squeals and whistles, it still worked. I slipped in there to catch the Holtz show, while the relatives were falling to on the food.

How many hundreds of hours I had spent in this musty room, studying the Talmud with Zaideh! It occurred to me that Harry Goldhandler's irreverent jokes, no doubt learned from Solly the Atheist, must be the bitter lore of old-country yeshiva boys chafing at their bonds: a mordant inside-out tradition, handed down in parallel to the Talmud. I was the only one in the penthouse who could laugh at those jokes. Boyd and Peter knew no Yiddish. Mrs. Goldhandler and her parents knew no Talmud. As for Sigmund and Karl, they would never have an inkling of what that luxuriant acid humor was all about. The parallel lines seemed to meet, and both traditions to come to an end, in the former Minsker Godol, the unbelieving joke-digger, Finkelstein.

On came the familiar brassy voice, full of overwrought pep:

> *Keep your Henny side up, up,*
> *Here comes Henny to you.*
> *If you're feeling dismal and low*
> *I've got lots of jokes on my show!*
> *So keep your Henny side up, up,*
> *Let the laughter come through.*
> *Be like frisky colts*
> *Laugh with Henny Holtz —*
> *And keep your Henny side up!*

Well, I must say, away from the Goldhandlers, the program sounded like any other Henny Holtz shows I had heard down the years, the same old frenetic foolery; not a lemon, a turd, a bust, a pancake, or a bomb, but the familiar mélange of songs and jokes. Eddie Conn was doing a perfectly good job. So I was thinking, when Cousin Harold came in with a plate of chicken salad.

Cousin Harold was now definitely applying to medical school in Switzerland. To increase his chances of admittance, he had changed his name. We still all called him Harold, but he was legally Mr. Harley Granville. Later on, by the by, since the fashionable thing for psychiatrists was to be Jewish, he changed it back. In fact, today Cousin Harold is Dr. Chaim Goodkind. Anyway, we were keeping up a desultory correspondence, and his letters, of course, were about his various fornications. My sex life being a zero, I wrote about my entry into show business via Harry Goldhandler.

Chicken salad on his lap, Harold, or Harley, ate in silence until the next commercial. Then he asked me in a confidential man-to-man tone, "Say, Dave, have you ever screwed a chorus girl?"

"No, Harold. In fact, I haven't screwed anybody."

"Dave, I'm surprised. Not yet? Don't you know any girls?"

"I know lots of them."

"Well, why don't you screw them?"

"They won't let me."

"I never heard of anything so ridiculous. You just have to be firm, and screw them anyway."

"Even if they say no?"

"Especially if they say no. They always mean yes."

Henny Holtz came back on, and Cousin Harold went out, shaking his head. He had been wasting his good counsel on me since we were fifteen. Then Zaideh himself came in, all in a glow. Faiga's first! A boy! And Marx or no Marx, brought into the Jewish fold according to law and rite! Holtz was joking with a girl singer, and the audience was in a roar.

"Nu! I thought you were sitting in here and learning."

"Zaideh, excuse me, I have to listen to this."

"What are they saying? What are they laughing at? Translate it for me," said Zaideh.

It was a card from the files:

GIRL: Henny Holtz, I wouldn't marry you if you were the last man on earth.

HENNY HOLTZ: Of course not. You'd be killed in the rush.

I translated. Zaideh wrinkled his broad peasant nose at me, with a wry sad smile. "That's how you make your living? A Yisroelke thrown away." He went out, shaking his head like Cousin Harold.

When I got back to the penthouse, they were still sitting around the radio in the living room. Goldhandler, who was lighting up a long Belinda, malevolently grinned. "Did you hear it?"

"I did."

"What did you think?" Mrs. Goldhandler shot at me.

All eyes were on me: the Goldhandlers, the sons, the old parents, Boyd, Peter Quat, who was making a hideous face, and even the little daughter.

"A light fart," I said.

"A light fart?" thundered Goldhandler. "It was the bagel of the ages! The entire nation rose up as one man, from coast to coast, and shit on their radios! Except the constipated ones, who puked."

"It wasn't very good," I said. I went upstairs to dig jokes. We needed freshies.

We always needed freshies, to keep that money cascading in at two thousand a week. You may wonder how the son of Solly the Atheist had come to stake out this goofy Klondike. I did at first, too. Boyd gradually told me the main facts.

Harry Goldhandler's college graduation picture, which hung in our office, showed a slim dark-haired intense Jewish youth, sporting a Phi Bete key. In a photo on the book jacket of his early short stories, published not long after he graduated, you saw the same Byronic young fellow. That our rotund, balding, cigar-chewing, ribald boss had metamorphosed from this young litterateur passed belief. Yet so it was, and this was the story.

Henny Holtz, a Lower East Side boy, was an admirer of Solly the Atheist. When he was starting in radio and needed a writer, Solly recommended his son, then living on poverty's edge selling magazine stories. Harry Goldhandler got the job. To feed Holtz with surefire laughs he started to keep the joke files. When Holtz made a hit, other comedians came to Goldhandler for scripts. Eddie Conn, a veteran writer of vaudeville acts, joined him, and the big money began to roll in. They took on program after program, and hired full-time joke diggers. Boyd was the first. Thereafter, desperate work under multiple deadlines, snatched sleep and rich feeding at odd hours, continuous smoking of Havana cigars, and constant juggling and coddling of several comedians at once, had transmogrified the slim sensitive writer in a few years to the weary heavy gagman.

Henny Holtz had put his foot down, however, about their writing for a comic named Lou Blue, who blatantly imitated Holtz. To be sure, Holtz himself blatantly imitated Al Jolson, but that was another matter. Goldhandler defied Holtz and took the Lou Blue job. Blue's sponsor was Ex-Lax, it was the first time a laxative was going on the air, and the money was enormous. Goldhandler figured that Holtz must be bluffing. Who else could write Holtz programs?

Next thing he knew, Eddie Conn failed to show up at the penthouse, and did not return any telephone calls. It was on the third day of Conn's defection that Peter Quat had telephoned me. Of course Conn had gone to work for Henny Holtz. That Holtz was an ingrate, and Eddie Conn a Judas, were now articles of the Goldhandler loyalty oath. Peter Quat snickered at all that, and sympathized with Eddie Conn for quitting. Conn was now getting all the Holtz money, and no longer had to keep up the insane Goldhandler pace. More power to him!

Toward our boss, Peter Quat was altogether ambivalent. Goldhandler's Rabelaisian roarings could convulse him, and the celebrities who visited the penthouse awed him. At parties Peter would fascinate our college friends with tales of the colorful joke czar, well salted with casually dropped star names. Peter had another social life in cafés and automats, where he would talk literature with other aspiring writers. Once or twice I went along. In such company Peter would sneer at gagwriting as mere thievery, and at Goldhandler as a sellout and a barbarous kike. In the office a favored contemptuous gesture of Peter's was to shut joke-file drawers with his behind, and he liked to go around whistling "For I Am a Pirate King."

Peter had his future all planned. He would allow himself one more year of this prostitution. If by then he had not sold any stories he would go back to a university, get a doctorate in English, and teach until he made it as a writer. Goldhandler saw through Peter Quat, of course. He put up with him because Peter did honest work, but he rode Peter hard about his pretensions. "Finkelstein here" — he would wave his cigar at Quat — "has a picture of William Faulkner's ass in his room. Every time he walks past it, he kisses it like a mezuza."

Peter laughed off this kidding, but on one weak point he proved touchy. He would glower when I laughed at the boss's Yiddish jokes. "What? What's the point of that one?" he would exclaim. "I thought I was following it. What was the punch line?" He liked to use showbusiness Yiddishisms, but he usually got them wrong. I've mentioned that English has no sound like the Indian's "*ugh*." That guttural runs through Yiddish, and Peter couldn't pronounce it. Take "*tugh-ess*," meaning posterior, rump, or ass, as you please. It would come out "toke-us" as Peter said it, and he said it often. When Goldhandler thought Peter was being slow or dense, he would call him "Mister Tokus."

Meaning no harm, I once mentioned as we were eating in a Chinese restaurant, about two in the morning, the great Yiddish writer in Peter's family tree.

"You're kidding!" Goldhandler exclaimed. "That's impossible.

Mendele Moykher S'forim?" He turned on Peter Quat. "*Your* grand-father? Liebowitz is full of shit, isn't he?"

"What's the difference?" Peter said.

"But is it true? You're related to Mendele?"

"Oh, he was my great-granduncle or something. I don't know. I don't care." It was a surly response, and Peter was making a danger-ous face, his mouth all twisted up on one side.

"For Christ's sake, Mister Tokus! You are related to Mendele Moykher S'forim, and you can't even say a Yiddish word! What's with you, anyway?"

"Nothing's with me, and *fuck* Mandalay Mohair Serafin," snarled Peter, looking Goldhandler straight in the eye, "and fuck you, too!" His face crazily distorted, he slammed his napkin on the table and stalked out of the restaurant.

Goldhandler was baffled. "What's eating Finkelstein?" he asked me.

Peter showed up at work the next day as though nothing had hap-pened. Nobody referred to Mendele Moykher S'forim again. Gold-handler joshed him no more in that vein, nor ever called him Mister Tokus after that. Peter went on using Yiddishisms and mispronounc-ing them.

I did not share Peter Quat's disdain for our outlandish employ-ment. To me it was rare fun in a dream world. George and Ira Gershwin came to the penthouse, for instance, to talk over an idea for a musical show. Goldhandler ordered a vast platter of delicatessen sent in from Lindy's. The Gershwins smiled at us as we came troop-ing down the stairs behind Goldhandler. "The rebbe and his Hassi-dim," George Gershwin said, and there we were, lunching with the great Gershwins! Goldhandler knew publishers and editors, for be-sides his own short stories he had ghostwritten Henny Holtz's best-selling humorous books. He knew bankers, novelists, playwrights, and opera stars. They all came there just to listen to his rough fantastic humor. He never used old jokes in conversation. His talk was all original. He would stand in front of the mantelpiece and hold forth on the Broadway shows, or the new movies, or literature, or the ra-dio business, or politics. The visitors would prod him with a ques-tion or two, and he would soar off in a brilliant tirade, jamming the huge cigar into his mouth while his listeners guffawed at his sallies.

Peter used to growl, "If only he'd get it down on paper!"

At Lindy's, the all-night Broadway delicatessen restaurant, Gold-handler held court. We would march in at one and two in the morning to eat garlic steaks, or thick corned beef sandwiches, or heavy cream pies, whatever we desired. Goldhandler paid for everything. We ate and drank much more each week than our salaries would have bought. Show business is abuzz at that hour, and Goldhandler's table was the center of attention as though he were the mayor of New York; possibly more so, because he was funny, and people always want a good laugh.

I know I loved the man, and I felt at home with the Goldhandlers. After all, the boss and I were both atheists who revelled in Yiddish. Mrs. Goldhandler was a sort of plutocratic Aunt Faiga. Her parents were like Boris's relatives, totally Jewish and totally irreligious. Sigmund and Karl were freakish prodigies, zestful and funny like their father. Maybe the heart of the matter was that, unlike Peter Quat, I didn't take myself seriously as a writer. I was quite willing to be an apprentice or a Hassid to this gagwriting Gargantua for a year or so. Deep down, I had a sense that it was all a fantastic interlude, before I returned to the law.

And anyway, at the time neither writing nor law were on my mind as much as *something else,* to use Mama's words; and to use Goldhandler's word, something mighty elemental.

61

An Understanding Woman

O NE day a Broadway producer named Billy Rose was having lunch in the penthouse with Goldhandler and his Hassidim, to discuss the skits for a revue. Mrs. Goldhandler looked in to say that a young woman was down in the lobby, asking to see Mr. Rose. He glanced at his watch.

"Oh, yes. Tell her to come up." And to Goldhandler, "This won't take a minute."

In walked a tall redhead in a tailored gray suit, with a magazine-cover face and a voluptuously curved figure. Eyes wide and shining, she answered with anxious eagerness Rose's questions about her experience in the musical theatre, staring at him as though he held life and death in his hands.

"All right, dear," he said. "Let's see your legs."

"Yes, Mr. Rose."

With both hands the girl slid her gray skirt and lace-edged white slip up and up, above her knees, above her stocking tops, above white-gartered pink thighs to the lacy edge of peach-colored silk panties. And so she stood, waiting. I thought my heart would stop at the sight, so hard and painfully did it thump against my ribs.

"Okay, thank you," said Rose. Down came the skirt. The girl peered at him with a piteous desperate smile.

"Very nice, dear," said Rose. "Report back to Lenny. I'll talk to him."

"Oh, Mr. Rose, thank you. *Thank you.*"

As she joyfully rushed out, he picked up a telephone on a side table. Through my thunderstruck daze I heard him say, "Hello, Lenny?

Grade B showgirl. Tell Al I saw her. If you've got room for her in the second row, take her on."

Back in the office, Boyd and Peter said nothing about it. Boyd never showed any interest in sex that I can recall, or in anything or anybody but Harry Goldhandler; slavish devotion to that magnetic man was his life. As for Peter Quat, he was having a plodding affair with his father's receptionist, a scared mousy little woman I met once. They would rendezvous at the office when the doctor was out, and on the waiting-room couch, under a large disapproving portrait of Dr. Quat, they would bang away. I guess that getting it regular, or irregular, dulled for Peter Quat the incandescence of the showgirl's uncovering, as unforgettable a sight to me as a total eclipse of the sun. I have seen three total eclipses in my life. I remember them all well. I have uncovered more female thighs than you are going to read about in these pages. But that glimpse stays with me as the triggering of my young manhood. From that moment I was on the prowl for a woman.

But how to go about it? Inept though I was, I had already been on the verge with one or another of the girls I had trifled with. I have decided not to tell you about a dozen such episodes. Reread *Deflowering Sarah,* if such stuff amuses you. Eleanor Kraft was probably available at a push, but I hesitated at such an entanglement, despite the bubbling of my blood. Why, when we were having our brief fling, she took to telephoning me, reproaching me for not calling her, complaining that she was hot, or cold, or bored, or lonesome, suggesting that we do peculiar things like go to the zoo, or ghastly things like hear Earl Browder lecture. And mind you, the only claim that girl ever had on me was that I had pawed the bumps of her sweater, or in a fit of mad carnality reached inside her blouse. The prospect of giving a girl like Eleanor Kraft the righteous plaint of having yielded me her virtue appalled me. What a loss of freedom, what chains! Even Peter Quat had trouble with his receptionist. Meek mouse that she was, she still got on the phone to him, complaining in a squeaky voice, and he would say soothing things like, "Yes, dear, maybe tomorrow," and "I'll try my best, dear," rolling his eyes in exasperation.

Clearly, Cousin Harold had figured out an answer to all that. He could not have gone through so many women without a handy solution to the disposal question. I am sure that he just had his will of them, and then told them to bugger off; whereupon, having no real alternative, they buggered off. Most girls could discern in five min-

utes what sort of fellow Cousin Harold was, and they would either
do it with him because they felt like it, or they would refuse him, to
avoid being told to bugger off. Simple.

Well, I knew that I was different, that I would be the softest of
soft touches for a girl. If even a tough egg like Peter Quat had to put
up with telephoned squeaks from his mouse, what would become of
me once a girl sank her talons into my conscience? The price would
be fearful, *because I would feel I had wronged her.* Being the son of my
father and the grandson of Zaideh, I could not help that.

And yet — that showgirl! Those round perfect thighs! Those long
white garters straining over camellia-petal skin, those lacy edges of
peach silk! To seek such a showgirl for myself, even a Grade B
showgirl, I knew to be utter insanity; and what the hell had Rose
meant by "Grade B," anyway? What on God's earth then could a Grade
A showgirl be like? But since my hormones were boiling me alive, I
had to find some female who would let me do it, and yet not go
whining and squeaking and dragging me thereafter to Earl Browder
lectures, and demanding and demanding and never ceasing to demand, because she was giving me her all. In short, what I wanted
was a lady of easy virtue.

Now everybody knows that New York City teems with ladies of
easy virtue. There may well be five of them to every taxi driver in
Manhattan, especially on a rainy night. I was always reading about
big vice raids, and roundups of hundreds of ladies of easy virtue. In
college everyone but me seemed to know and visit them. And yet I
had no idea of how to scare one up.

I tried walking up and down Broadway at night. None approached me. I tried a taxi-dance hall. One lush blonde in skin-tight
red satin did snuggle up to me and strongly hint that she was a lady
of mighty easy virtue. Would I meet her after the music stopped and
take her home? I blew about twenty dollars on tickets, dancing with
her until four A.M. "Meet me outside, honey," she cooed. "I have to
change, won't be a minute." I waited in front of that darkened dance
hall for an hour, in a cold drizzle. Either the blonde in skin-tight red
satin was no lady of easy virtue, after all; or having collected that huge
stash of my tickets, she preferred just to go home and get some sleep.
But I was as much relieved as annoyed. I was pretty sleepy myself by
then, and she had smelled strange.

Well, then I ran into Earl Eckstein at a party. Earl and I had done

some pre-law studying together. He was a short sober straight-A grind
with thick straight sandy hair, very round-shouldered and humorless.
Earl is today one of the richest lawyers in New York; he is bent over
like Winston Churchill, and he still has all that sandy hair and no
sense of humor. We got to talking, Earl and I, and he cautioned me
against ladies of easy virtue: risk of disease, of being mugged or rolled,
and such conservative thoughts. He himself, he confided, visited a
certain understanding woman two or three times a week. She was
not a lady of easy virtue or anything like that, just an understanding
woman. For instance, she served coffee and cake, or tea, if you preferred. When he left her apartment he tucked a five-dollar bill under
her telephone, but money was never mentioned. He had gotten her
name and phone number from a fellow he played handball with. Was
I interested?

Yes, thanks, I said, that sounded just perfect. Her name was Mrs.
Gertrude Ellenbogen, and she lived on West Ninety-eighth Street, a
mere stroll from my home. That same night I telephoned her. "Oh
yes, Earl, I know him well. Are you a law student, too?"

"Ah, yes, ma'am."

"I like law students. They're sweet, and serious. Come at about half-
past ten. By then the children will be asleep."

Children? I hadn't pictured children as part of this lewd adventure.
It only went to show, on reflection, that Mrs. Ellenbogen wasn't a
lady of easy virtue, but an understanding woman.

I made the date for a Friday night, when I usually had dinner at
home. I figured that I could readily consummate my manhood with
the understanding woman after dinner, and still get back to work in
plenty of time for our all-night session on the Lou Blue show. I did
not foresee that Uncle Yehuda would come to dinner, so that Mom
would make a big stuffed veal roast; nor that the dinner would get
into such a long discussion of Uncle Velvel and shittim wood.

I suppose I had better explain that. To everyone's amazement in
the family, Uncle Velvel had prevailed over that soft-drink company;
that is, the company had settled the nuisance suit out of court and
had carted away the mountains of soda bottles from his premises. So
Uncle Velvel was flush, and he had plunged the proceeds into a new
venture: exporting religious books bound in shittim wood. Shittim
wood is what went into the tabernacle and ark in the desert. Palestine bookstores sold Hebrew holy books bound in that biblical wood;

my sister Lee had brought back such a prayer book for Pop. A wood-bound book is an unhandy thing, so he admired it but never used it.

Well, Uncle Velvel had bought up a whole lumberyard full of shittim wood real cheap, the owners having gone bankrupt or something. His idea was to bind Christian books in shittim wood: New Testaments, hymnals, psalters, and what have you. He had already ordered a large stock of these from a local bookbinder, so all his soda-bottle windfall was committed. He had written to Uncle Yehuda, and persuaded him to go into business importing these books. Uncle Yehuda thought it was the greatest idea since the electric lamp. Look at all the Christians there were! Hundreds of millions! If selling shittim wood books to Jews was a good business — and obviously it was, it had been going on in Palestine for years — then the Christian market had to be an absolute bonanza.

Uncle Yehuda took a long time to get to the point, meantime putting away a lot of stuffed veal. At last he said that, though one shouldn't talk about money on the Sabbath, he required a bank loan of two thousand dollars at once, and simply wanted Pop to guarantee it.

"But with promissory notes this time," said Uncle Yehuda in a new grandly businesslike way. "I'll sign any promissory notes the bank wants or that you want, Alex. Who cares about promissory notes? I'll pay them all off with the profits from Velvel's first shipment."

He was approaching Pop at the wrong time. My parents had just signed a lease for a smaller apartment off Riverside Drive. Lee was all set with her pediatrician, so the move to Manhattan had worked, and it was high time to retrench. The wedding would be costly, and Bernie had to be set up in his own office, too. I was contributing twenty dollars a month to the rent, but it had hurt Pop to agree to it. If I went back to law school, he said, every penny I had paid would be at my disposal. He was keeping an account.

So Pop equivocated; what did Yehuda really know, he inquired, about shittim wood? At once Yehuda flew into one of his old-time touchy rages. What? *Shittim* wood? Was there a six-year-old Jewish schoolboy who didn't know what shittim wood was? Noah's ark! The tabernacle! But — Pop mildly persisted — he was asking about shittim wood as a modern commercial material. Was it durable? Would it stand the damp of shipment by sea? Was the price stable? Was there a reliable supply? At that Uncle Yehuda really saw red. Supply? Shittim wood grew all over Palestine! You couldn't walk under a tree that wasn't a shittim tree! Price? Velvel had bought enough shittim wood to last them ten years. Stand the damp? What about Noah's ark? Had that stood the damp, or hadn't it? Would God have entrusted Noah and the animals to wood that wasn't durable?

I interposed that Noah's ark was gopher, not shittim. The ark in the tabernacle had been shittim wood.

"Gopher, shittim, so what?" snapped Uncle Yehuda. "Bible wood is Bible wood, and an ark is an ark."

Lee went and hunted up the prayer book she had bought for Pop. The wood binding was already warped and cracking. "I think maybe it isn't practical, Uncle," Lee said, trying to help out Pop. "It's just a tourist thing. Anyway, what do Christians know about shittim wood? It's a Hebrew word." She squinted at an old label inside the cover. "Yes. It means acacia."

His white beard quivering in triumph, Uncle Yehuda produced a gilt-edged Bible with a big cross on the soft black leather cover. He opened it to a bent-down page and read in his thick accent, " 'Und de Lord spake unto Moses, and dey shall make un ark of SHEETIM VOOD'! You hear dot? SHEETIM VOOD!" He slammed the Bible shut, pointed to the cross, and brandished it under poor Lee's nose, like a priest in a movie exorcising Satan. "A Christian Bible! You see? Vit a cross! Vit de Gospels! Vit everyting! Und it says SHEETIM VOOD!"

My stomach full of veal, and my mind of forebodings about this shittim-wood business, I set out for Mrs. Ellenbogen's apartment. Uncle Velvel and Uncle Yehuda had been burdens to Pop over the years, but he had handled them separately. Operating in tandem, Uncle Velvel and Uncle Yehuda could bankrupt a Rothschild, for sure. Yet I knew Pop would guarantee that loan. And another worry: it was already time for me to be back at work. Altogether, the assignation was proving inconvenient, but I was not about to pass it up, not in my libidinous state. Veal, Goldhandler, uncles, shittim wood notwithstanding, the fire burned on, unsmotherable. Truth to tell, I had spent most of the dinner fantasizing about Mrs. Ellenbogen, and what I would do with her.

The children were far from asleep. That was the first jolt. Three of them were milling around the dingy apartment eating jam-smeared bread, and one of them was a large girl with a bosom, perhaps fourteen. Mrs. Ellenbogen shooed them into the back of the flat. She received me in an orange kimono very like one my mother wore, and she decidedly did not look like a lady of easy virtue; more than anything, with her plump Slavic face, square-cut black hair, and billowy proportions, she looked like an aunt of Boris's from Worcester, Massachusetts, the one who always came late to family affairs. I could not tell whether she was Jewish. There were no candles, or mezuzas, or other clues. In the kitchen where we sat down to get acquainted, I saw cans of pork and beans and a canned ham.

She offered me tea or coffee, and I asked for tea. "Have it first, or later?" she wanted to know, setting a kettle on the boil.

"Ah, oh, first, I guess." I was very nervous, and I could hear her children off in the back, making a lively racket.

"And how is Merle Bickstein?" she inquired.

"Earl Eckstein? He's fine."

"He's the redheaded one, isn't he?"

"No, ma'am. I think he plays handball, maybe, with the redheaded one."

"You're right," she said. "Earl is the round-shouldered one."

"Yes, yes," I said, "exactly! Earl is the round-shouldered one."

She served me tea and a slice of store cake, and had some herself, chatting the while about her husband. They were divorced, and he was off somewhere in California; a nice man, but a drinker.

"Well!" she said, after all this, in a no-nonsense tone. She crossed her legs so that the kimono fell away, clear to her hips. I was looking at a pair of fat flabby yellow thighs and a very tightly stuffed, bulging pink girdle. Lusty lad that I was, I felt only dismay, as though I had barged into a women's john by mistake. The kitchen clock read twenty minutes past eleven. I was overdue at the penthouse.

"Mrs. Ellenbogen —"

"Oh, call me Gertie, dearie," she said in a Mae West tone, with a leer. The leer was clearly intended to drive me over the edge with desire, but it did not come off. Boris's aunt from Worcester was just making a funny face. I could still hear the children quarrelling in the back. I mentioned this.

For a moment, her voice hardened and saddened. "Don't worry about them. They know better than to come out. Shall we go to my room?" She stood up, slipping off the kimono. Her figure was very like Mom's; in fact Mom's was less lumpy. I don't remember what feeble excuse I made. I only know that in no time I was out on

Broadway hailing a cab, having left my sweaty rumpled five-dollar bill under her telephone. A lot of money for tea and store cake; but driven though I was, there was no way I could consummate my manhood with Boris's aunt from Worcester. I had learned something for my five dollars: no understanding women for me.

Well, then, what? A lady of easy virtue, after all?

Now I had heard that one dead-sure way to pick up a lady of easy virtue was to cruise around at night in a snazzy car. So I borrowed the shiny Buick in which Lee chauffeured Pop; and very late one night, after finishing up at the penthouse, I went cruising. I hadn't driven along Broadway for more than a few minutes when I spotted her, dead ahead on the deserted dark sidewalk. She was waggling along swinging a shiny oversize purse, in a bright baby-blue hat with two long dangling ribbons. The hat clinched it, as antlers in the bracken betray the quarry. At last, at last! I stopped the car and leaned over to roll down the window and commence negotiations. She beat me to it, pulling the door open. "Fi'dollizz," she said, poking in the blue hat, ribbons and all, and a heavily painted puttylike face.

Wow! Fi'dollizz! And smell that perfume! Attar of Woolworth's! The real thing! No understanding woman, this; a lady of easy virtue, no contest. I nodded, and she climbed in. "Turn right on Eighty-third Street," she twanged. Terrific! Actresses who played whores in Eugene O'Neill plays always twanged just like that.

"Park here."

I stopped the Buick at an old brownstone, and followed her through a door below the street level into a small cellar room with a dingy bed.

"Fi'dollizz." She held out her hand.

I gave her a creased fiver. She took off the blue hat, hoisted her skirt, and whipped off pink cotton underpants, all in one fluid set of motions. She had clearly done this before. She sat on the bed, skirt up around her waist, and lay back.

"Well? What are you waiting for?"

"Right, right."

Fumbling interval.

"What's your problem?" she inquired after a while.

"No problem, no problem," I said irritably.

She raised up on an elbow. "Say, have you ever done it before?"

"Well, to tell the truth, no. But —"

"Shit, boy! I'm not supposed to teach you how to get laid. I'm busy." Off the bed, on with the underpants and the blue-ribboned hat. "I have to go back out now."

And there we were on the street once more. "Give me a lift to the corner of Broadway," she said, and of course I did. Off she went down the sidewalk, swinging the purse. The whole episode could not have taken five minutes.

End of my quest for a lady of easy virtue.

62

Goldhandler in Hollywood

"Hollywood!" exclaimed Zaideh. "Yisroelke, you're going to a saloon."

"I'm not much of a drinker, Zaideh."

I had come to say goodbye. He laughed uncertainly. We studied a patch of Leviticus with commentaries — we always studied something when I visited him — and I was off to the saloon. Observe that Zaideh did not call Hollywood Gehenna, or Sodom, but a saloon, a "*shenk*": the ultimate unthinkable place for a good Jew to be found.

Goldhandler was going out there to write a movie called *Earl Carroll's Vanities*. He had contributed a few skits to this Broadway girlie revue. Metro-Goldwyn-Mayer had bought the title, and the film needed a story. When an MGM producer came to the penthouse to discuss it, Goldhandler soared off on an improvisation about a millionaire backer for the *Vanities* and a Bowery derelict who by chance was his double. He rang changes on this ancient joke of identical twins, with much popping in and out of showgirls' dressing rooms, and mistaken identities in bed, that had us all guffawing, the producer more than anybody. As soon as Goldhandler finished, the producer jumped up and shook his hand, saying that was the exact story he wanted, and Goldhandler could name his terms to come out to the West Coast and write it. Goldhandler closed the office door on the departing producer, and whirled on us in a conspiratorial crouch. "We are in the ground, boys," he stage-whispered. "We got nothing."

"Why, it's great stuff," Boyd said.

"Really? Write it down, Boyd. I have no idea what the fuck I said." It might have been almost true. Goldhandler could spin these wildly entertaining ad libs, airy as cotton candy, but once hired, he would usually write something else, turning off the wistful inquiries about "that funny thing you told us" with some offhand dodge.

By Goldhandler's terms, we were all going out in a body at MGM's expense: Boyd, Peter, myself, Sardinia, the two maids, and the whole family except the old folks. Boyd told us that Goldhandler's starting salary was something unbelievable, and if the *Vanities* job went well, he might even consider moving for good to Hollywood, family, staff, and all; for the big money obviously was in pictures. It was July, and we had only one modest summer program going, a Greek dialect comedian who called himself Nicholas Panilas (penniless, if you don't get it). I think his name was Ginsberg. Panilas was on "sustaining"; that is, he had no sponsor, and was hoping to attract one. Pretty small stuff, and Quat and I were drafting the Panilas scripts, using files of a German dialect program Goldhandler had written years ago. Our task was to switch the dialect to Greek and update the topical lines. This may strike the severe reader as sharp practice, but the Greek was enchanted with the scripts, the trade papers gave him good reviews, and nobody remembered the German comedian, who was dead. What else mattered?

Goldhandler was also bringing along at MGM expense one Morrie Abbott. This was the first time Goldhandler was travelling west of Newark, and he had Abbott along as a sort of Hollywood consultant and guide. Morrie Abbott was a slight gingery little man with curly reddish hair, and a bouncy way of walking and talking. Morrie had a brother I knew, an Orthodox rabbi named Applebaum, but Morrie had shucked his Jewishness. He liked to throw a Talmudic phrase at me now and then by way of persiflage, but Morrie was pure show-biz, nothing else. He had done a little sketch-writing, a little directing; and having recently married, he had subleased his small April House flat to the famous Skip Lasser. Most of his work had been done on some Lasser movie or Broadway musical. Aside from Irving Berlin or Cole Porter, few men were bigger in the musical field than Skip Lasser, and Morrie was more or less a hanger-on of his.

Morrie Abbott became mentor to Peter and me as we went rattling westward, ho, on the Superchief. *Savoir faire* was Morrie's thing. It was he who ordered the Kansas City steaks, the Denver beer, the Taittinger champagne, the Rocky Mountain trout, and the fresh celery. He knew where to get off to buy Indian blankets and jewelry, and how to haggle with the Indians, and how much to tip waiters and porters. And he knew all the variations of poker, and had read all the new books and seen all the new plays, and had authoritative views on these. And as for screwing showgirls, if one believed Morrie Abbott, he had left few unscrewed in Broadway or Hollywood. Making poor Peter and me slaver over his tales of showgirl conquests was Morrie's favorite late-night amusement, once the poker was over.

On the whole, I would say that Morrie Abbott was more full of shit than anyone I have ever met. Since I have worked in show business, the law, and the literary world, that is no small distinction. An instance: the three of us went together once to a preview of *Gone with the Wind*. When we came out, Morrie said oracularly, "They should have made it two hours long, and shot it in black and white. It won't go." That is a fair sample of Morrie's expertise. Peter and I were young, though, and he impressed us.

Morrie did know his Hollywood. He rented a house in Beverly Hills for the Goldhandlers with the obligatory giant swimming pool, also two tennis courts, a billiard room, a library that turned into a screening room; also sitting rooms, patios, dens, open porches, glassed-in porches, and gardens and lawns splashed with flowers, and shaded by high palm trees. Soon Karl and Sigmund, as to the manor born, were playing fierce tennis, or frolicking in the pool, or intently becoming billiard sharks, practicing by the hour. We checked in with Morrie to The Garden of Allah, an array of villas around a big pool where one saw people like Somerset Maugham, Gene Fowler, and Skip Lasser lounging in the sun. Lasser came out later; he was then in New York, working on a musical adaptation of *The Good Soldier Schweik*.

Well, Harry Goldhandler entered Hollywood like a lion. At their first dinner party in the fancy house, to which we were not asked, the guests were the Gershwins, Aldous Huxley, Joan Crawford, Franchot Tone, and Marlene Dietrich. "The gag czar" was an exciting novelty. He had written radio spots for many film stars, and had an advance reputation as a brilliant original. We saw little of him or Boyd. Morrie, who was advising Goldhandler on the *Vanities* screenplay, reported that the studio was ecstatic over the start of the script. The Panilas show was catching on, and that money kept sluicing in. The Goldhandlers were riding a crest. They swam, and played billiards, and went to dinner parties and the races, and were made much of. Mrs. Goldhandler hit it off so well with Joan Crawford that, according to Morrie Abbott, they were even going shopping together.

At The Garden of Allah we too were living the sweet life. Peter and I fell into Morrie Abbott's routine: breakfast by the pool at ten or so, or else at Musso and Frank's on Hollywood Boulevard; a little tennis, a little lunch at the Brown Derby on Vine Street, then out to the horse races, and then some leisurely script work until dinner. "Tonight we eat Chinese," Morrie Abbott would decree, or, "Let's try Eaton's Steak House again," or, "It's time we went to Perino's." Rarely, he might even say with a giggle, "I feel like eating kosher," and we would go to a place called Mama Levy's, which wasn't kosher, but served things like gefilte fish and chicken soup with matzoh balls.

It goes without saying that Morrie Abbott was a Communist. So was Skip Lasser, Morrie told us. Everybody we met in Hollywood, almost, seemed to be a Communist. But you have to understand about those Hollywood Communists. In those days out there it was like jogging, or group bathing in a redwood hot tub. They would talk revolution around their swimming pools, or while driving to Malibu Beach in white Buick convertibles, or while dining at Chasen's or Don the Beachcomber's. They were as politically menacing as butterflies. Not one of them had so much as cold-cocked a policeman.

In such company Peter Quat tended to bait them, striking a Noël Coward pose of the amoral man of pleasure, bored by politics and cynical about ideologies. This went on for hours beside The Garden of Allah pool. Morrie and his sharp-tongued wife, and a woman called Sugar Gansfried, Lasser's girl friend, kept trying to make Peter see the light. They would become terribly earnest, playing all the old Aunt Faiga records at him. Nobody could attend Columbia in the thirties without knowing the Marxist clichés by heart, and the arguments to oppose them if one wanted to bother. I stayed out of it, for Peter was matchless at this. Morrie finally lost his temper when Peter so tied him up in knots that even the women tittered at his discomfiture. "Shut up, I say," he yelled at Peter. "You're an ignorant kid. Just shut your mouth!" Morrie's voice went soprano, and his face scarlet. Peter and I retired to our villa and rolled around on a sofa, laughing.

But Morrie got his revenge. A man named Fokety, with a slight European accent, one day telephoned our villa: a free-lance director who had heard that we were staying at The Garden of Allah. He had an idea for a movie, he said. The studio was hot for it, he needed writers, and he had heard that we were the brightest new writing team around, fresh out of Columbia College, the real writers of Goldhandler's Panilas show. He made a date to meet us at a bar in Beverly Hills to get acquainted, and said he would bring along three showgirls for some laughs. Showgirls! Peter and I fell for it. Peter had been too long away from his receptionist, and the prospect had him dancing around the villa. Fokety never showed at the bar. Next day he called with some excuse, to make another date. We bit again. This happened several times. The cream of the jest for Morrie and the ladies was to hear us complain about this elusive Fokety, and to discuss the mystery at length with us. Morrie Abbott, of course, was Fokety.

He even took to letting us talk to the "showgirls." Purring in bed-room tones, they would say they were dying to meet us. However, Sugar Gansfried and Morrie's wife pressed us too much about whether the showgirls sounded real, and we caught on. When Fokety made a call at midnight, proposing we drive out to Malibu Beach to go wading by moonlight with three Goldwyn girls, Peter kept him on the line, while I crept through the darkness to Morrie's villa. There I could hear "Fokety" nattering away, and the two women giggling. Peter and I never let on, but just let Fokety keep calling until Morrie tired of it. The residue of the episode was an on-going joke about the way "the boys" hotly hankered for showgirls.

Notwithstanding all that nonsense, how enchanting Hollywood was then! What a dream life it was, brief and transient as a dream! What you find out there now resembles what was once there, as a dead cat resembles a frolicking kitten. The green-brown hills stood out sharp and clear in translucent air, morning after morning. The word *smog* had not been coined. Everywhere there was the spicy smell of fresh grass and tropical flowers, and all the Beverly Hills mansions were new. I missed New York, but though I was so out of it in Hollywood, such a nobody, I loved this fabulously beautiful place. The film colony itself seemed to me (and for that matter still does) to be a rainbow-hued soap bubble, forever shimmering on the verge of bursting. In fact from time to time it does burst. They call that re-trenchment. After a while one or another movie is a huge hit, and the bubble gets blown up again, and the whole magic scene springs into life, and so the crazy cycle goes. If a lawyer has author clients, he has to keep an eye on that cycle. Sometimes the turn can be startlingly swift.

We had been in Hollywood three weeks; Peter was off getting his morning tennis lesson, and I was alone in the villa, when the telephone woke me around noon.

"Hello?" I said sleepily.

"Hello, it's Boyd. Goldhandler has been fired."

And so it was. The producer had abruptly dropped the option, an event as inconceivable to all of us as the sky falling. Boyd had told us that Goldhandler was there on a thirteen-week contract. Not exactly, it now turned out; a three-week contract, renewable for ten more weeks. Goldhandler had not been able to put his cotton-candy improvisation on paper, so he had been writing something else; and at his price, the producer wasn't amused. Morrie Abbott, no whit concerned, said that other studios would quickly be bidding for the gag czar's services. "They're desperate for comedy out here," Morrie reassured us. "A blue chip like Goldhandler can choose his spot."

The next evening, Goldhandler and his wife dropped in at our villa, on their way to Grauman's Chinese Theatre for the grand opening of a new Joan Crawford film. The boss made no reference to losing his film job, and pretended to talk about the Panilas script, but they were obviously showing off their finery. "Joan" had invited them, Mrs. Goldhandler said, to the private party at Ciro's after the premiere. Goldhandler had on a white dinner jacket, and she wore a new evening dress with masses of glittery sequins. Off they went, buoyed by our compliments. They were back a couple of hours later, banging at our door. "We're famished," bellowed Goldhandler. "Any food in this joint?"

We ordered sandwiches from an all-night delicatessen and listened to their wrathful tale. They had been turned away from the party! The door attendant had said they were not on the guest list, and had rudely refused to let Mrs. Goldhandler talk to "Joan." Goldhandler made us guffaw with his angry description of the attendant, an old waiter with false teeth who spit copiously as he argued. Our laughter relaxed him. He wolfed a sandwich and recounted the soggy plot of the film with caustic exaggeration, making us laugh so hard we couldn't eat. He had come for just this, to cheer himself up by playing to his sure audience. Mrs. Goldhandler also laughed, but she did look forlorn in all those sequins. I had never seen her painted before, and the makeup was a garish sight. She was much prettier without it.

At this juncture, when Harry Goldhandler didn't need more trouble, I did a bad thing.

There was this dark attractive girl with whom I got friendly at the poolside; a petite, sleekly groomed graduate of Smith, with an endless wardrobe and a silver Lincoln convertible. She was a stockbroker's daughter, she told me; her brother had a job at a studio, and he was angling for a part for her in a movie. She and I hit it off marvellously well. At least, I thought so. I made her laugh. When we went dancing her eyes would sexily flash at me. She even began cooking for the two of us in her villa. There was a strange remoteness about this girl, all the same. I was soon head over ears infatuated with her, yet much as she seemed to like me, I couldn't break through the girl's cold crystal envelope. I decided drastic measures were called for, and I took her to Don the Beachcomber's.

Don's was then something new, and the specialty was an enormous drink served in a whole fresh coconut, called — I think I'm right about this — King Kong's Downfall. It was a mixture of several rums, coconut milk, crushed ice, and spices. It tasted like coconut ice cream, and the coconut was real, green husk and all. It was usually a mistake to have more than one King Kong's Downfall. You were apt to lose interest in the food, or to injure yourself by falling off your chair unconscious.

But this girl's capacity was phenomenal. On her third King Kong's Downfall, she finally did crack, and blurrily admitted that yes, she supposed she might strike me as a bit distant and odd. She was having an affair with her brother, she explained, and actually was a couple of months pregnant by him, so she had a thing or two on her mind. Hollywood was and is quite a saloon. Zaideh was right about that.

Well, all this is by way of accounting for the bad thing I did. It happened next day, when I was recovering from those Downfalls and that disclosure, and was scarcely *compos mentis*. At about four that afternoon, the telephone rang. I was lying in a darkened bedroom, still nursing a rough headache. Peter was in the pool. I stumbled to my desk. "Hello?" I moaned.

"FINKELSTEIN!" Goldhandler, a maddened bellow. "What script did you send to Nicholas Panilas?"

"Why, why, the script Peter and I finished yesterday."

"You did? Take another look at your desk!"

I obeyed. Oops. There lay the Panilas script, cleanly retyped by the stenographic service, ready to go. Then what script, I foggily wondered, could I have sent him? I remembered staggering out of bed around noon, my head pounding, when the bell rang. I remembered taking a script off the desk, slipping it into an envelope, and handing it to the messenger sent by Panilas to pick it up. Then I had gone back to sleep.

"Oh, my *God!*" A horrified gasp, as I realized what I had done. There had been only one other script in my room: the old German show, on mimeograph paper yellowing with age, from which we had copied the Panilas program. That script had gone to Nicholas Panilas. "Kee-rist," I groaned. "I'm sorry, boss —"

"Never mind. Is Liebowitz there?" asked Goldhandler, anger gone, all business.

"In the pool."

"Get him out."

While Peter was dressing, Boyd arrived with three men carrying typewriters. The men left. Working at frantic speed, Boyd, Peter and I doctored up another of the old programs, and commenced typing like fury. All three typewriters had the identical typeface that the stenographic service used. Within the hour, we batted out a new Panilas show, looking exactly like every other script we had sent him.

Boyd telephoned Goldhandler. "Is he still there?" he asked, sotto voce. Then, loud and cheery, "Oh, hello, Nick. Yes, they just got back five minutes ago from the beach. The script's been sitting here on the desk all day. Isn't it ridiculous? Sure, I'll bring it over right away."

Boyd hung up, lit one of his strong-smelling Turkish cigarettes, and sighed. "He's drunk as a pig. Let me have a scotch and water. Jesus, the boss was magnificent. He's a giant, a genius. Nobody else could have pulled this thing out."

He told us the story while he sipped the drink. Panilas had burst in on Goldhandler, brandishing the old script, a red-eyed foaming maniac, threatening a lawsuit, threatening to beat Goldhandler up, threatening to take a full-page ad in *Variety* exposing him as a fraud, a crook, a pirate, a bandit, and a plagiarist. Passing off old programs on him! Taking money that he had earned with his blood, with his health! Goldhandler let him rave himself out, then gave him a whiskey. He said he would explain, and then would accept Panilas's apology.

The explanation: "the boys," meaning Peter and me, were new to script writing. We had brought out a few old scripts to study the technique of dialect comedy — of which, by the by, Goldhandler declared, Panilas was the greatest master alive. All other dialect comics would be forgotten once Nicholas Panilas broke into network radio. Goldhandler would be glad to show him all the old scripts the boys had. If he found a single joke that had actually been used in a Panilas show, even *one* joke, Goldhandler would refund all the money Panilas had paid him to date. As for this week's show, it was all written, and it had nothing to do with the old script Panilas had received by mistake. It was the funniest Panilas program yet, nothing but yocks and boffs. He would send Boyd over right away to The Garden of Allah to get it. If there was the *slightest* resemblance to the old script, Goldhandler would write for him gratis hereafter. He wouldn't even mind that, because it was an honor for him to be writing for the greatest dialect comedian in the world.

"Actors are all born idiots," Boyd said. "Panilas fell down on his knees to apologize. He kissed the boss's hands. It was sort of pathetic, the way he slobbered on his hands, slurp slurp. He said he wouldn't dream of checking on the scripts. He loved and trusted Goldhandler like a brother. But of course, he's dying to see the script, so I'd better get it over there." And Boyd steamed off.

I was never penalized for what I did, never even called on the carpet. The next time I saw Goldhandler he shook his head at me, and said in a tone of amused paternal reproach, "Oy, *Liebowitz!*" That was all. Maybe that helps you understand my affection for the man.

Skip Lasser showed up in The Garden of Allah a day or two after the Panilas crisis, dressed much like Bob Greaves. He was a grayish stocky Jew of forty or so, not a tall lean blond Deke of twenty, so the effect wasn't the same. But it was all right: tweed sports jacket, gray slacks, button-down shirt, figured tie. All the Hollywood revolutionaries dressed so, more or less; but Lasser brought it off better, with his British-cut cashmere jacket and flannel slacks, and calm superior air, based quite justly on his Broadway hits and money-making films. When Morrie Abbott introduced us, Lasser grinned impishly, almost boyishly. "Ah, yes, the boys who are dying to meet showgirls."

"We wouldn't mind," said Peter.

"That shouldn't be hard. When I get back to New York, I'll introduce you to showgirls."

Lasser had returned to Hollywood to polish a screenplay he had written for Fred Astaire; and Goldhandler, through Morrie Abbott's mediation, accepted the job of doctoring the script with jokes. It paid less than his MGM employment, and was quite a fall in status, but it was an eight-week contract, and he had the summer lease on that big house to pay for. He and Boyd took over the Panilas scripts, and he paid our fares back to New York. If business picked up in the fall, he said, he would be in touch with us.

Peter said to me as we boarded the train — not the Superchief — "I'm glad to be getting away from this creepy place and those god-damned old jokes. We'll write a farce, Davey, and clean up. You'll see."

"Liebowitz! I need you. I am in the ground."

Goldhandler on the telephone, on a sizzling day late in August; the first I had heard from him since our long hot sad ride back from Hollywood, sleeping in upper berths. On my desk, in an airless room of the small flat Mom and Pop had taken off Riverside Drive, lay a pile of first-year law books, and two acts of the farce Peter and I had been sedulously cooking up. The books depressed me; to think that my classmates had absorbed them and pulled ahead of me by a year! The farce depressed me: a hollow echo of the Kaufman and Hart style.

"I'm planning on law school, boss," I said. "I can still get in."

"Why, sure. This won't interfere. A quick two-week job. Where the hell is Finkelstein? Boyd's been trying to call him. Get over here as soon as you can."

When I walked into Goldhandler's office again, and saw the vista of the park, and the rivers, and the skyscrapers, and that ever-haunting April House sign, and smelled the stale effluvium of cigars soaked into the curtains and carpet, and he tiredly hailed me, "Hiya, Liebowitz," I sensed that I was back for more than two weeks. And

whatever regrets I have on looking back over my patchwork existence, I have no regrets about the years of Goldhandler and Bobbie
Webb that followed. Certain cups must be drunk to the bottom,
whether to taste sugar or lees. In this case, both.

*   *   *

63

Sandra's Letter

September 1973

Sandra's letter arrived yesterday, and my first coherent thought after reading it was that I had better resign from this White House job at once. I am clipping her letter to these yellow scrawls exactly as it came: four long, coarse blue sheets of messy single-spaced typing, all spotty with inked-in letters.

Kibbutz Sde Shalom
September something

Dear Dad

I don't know where the kibbutz got hold of this decrepit Underwood with two keys missing, but it'll have to do. *Zeh mah sheyaish.* Israeli byword, "That's what there is." Time is short. Dudu Barkai is going up north in an hour or so, to report to his unit for thirty-day reserve duty. He's a tank captain, as well as a laundryman, kibbutz leader, and violinist. Dudu will give my letter to a man who's flying to Washington. This is Mom's idea, that I explain myself to you direct. It took me a couple of days to get through to her, and I don't know how I'll do with you in a couple of typed pages, but all right, I'll try.

I put off my return, as you know, to hear Professor Landau lecture, and to finish some kibbutz work. When the two weeks were up I travelled by bus to the airport, all set to go home, but feeling rotten about it. When I walked into the terminal, I decided — or rather, realized — that I wasn't going to leave. So I asked a girl at an El Al desk where I could cash in my ticket. She advised me to hang on to it and keep the return date open. When I told her that I was staying indefinitely, making aliya, she gave me the kind of smile you've never seen on the face of an Israeli, old Dad, and she directed me to the refund office on the mezzanine.

I have to tell you what followed, because it's another face of Israel. The girl in that office wouldn't give me the refund. Said it was too close to plane departure time, or something. Her English wasn't very good, but her obstinacy was Class A. She kept saying, "*Ain lee somchoot.*" When I got mad and hollered at her to translate, she hollered back, "I dunt hev *somchoot,*" which wasn't much help. We got into a real shouting match, I yelling at her that I wanted to make aliya, and she screeching that she didn't have *somchoot.*

Then in walked this dark lean young Israeli guy and asked what the problem was. I explained, and he gave me that special smile, and said, "Come with me." I turned in the ticket for a fistful of Israeli money. "You really want to make aliya?" he asked. "Are you crazy?" And then he inquired where I was staying, and what I was doing that night. He looked sad when I said I was returning to Sde Shalom. He said that was very far, and everybody was crazy there, but it was a nice place.

Abe Herz says *somchoot* means authorization. He says this country is infested with creatures in offices who "don't have *somchoot.*" These are called *pakidim,* office-holders, and the whole bureaucracy is in fact wryly known as Pakidstan. It is the curse of Israel, he said. It has worn him down. It almost drove him back to the States. The only hope, according to Abe, is if enough Americans come here, stick it out, and change things.

From the airport I went up to Jerusalem and saw Grandma. Another spur-of-the-moment decision. I spent the night with her, and she regaled me with reminiscences of her childhood. Even after we turned out the lights she went on with her stories.

Did she ever tell you the one about a sort of Boston Massacre they had in Minsk? The Czar announced some liberalization measures, and the Jews went pouring out in the streets, rejoicing and carrying on, and troops appeared and started mowing them down. She was out there in the mob, and she fell and was trampled. Later she crawled out of the main square, which she says was all covered with bodies, and went home, where they had thought she was dead. "It was the only time in my whole life that I was ever afraid," she said. "That was what really made me decide to go to America. I was never afraid before, and I've never been afraid again. I want you to remember that, about me."

I believe her. In that respect Grandma is like the people here. They aren't afraid. They are mighty concerned about the Egyptians and the Syrians — the intelligent ones are, others are off on a euphoric binge — but their ability to defend themselves gives them, I don't know, straight backs. That was what first attracted me about Abe Herz. He's American to the bone and always will be, but he's acquired that air. The Jewish fellows I knew back home didn't exactly have it, and if you'll forgive me, old father, despite your war service you don't have it.

When I told Grandma I was making aliya, she said, "Oh, I knew you would. You like that American lawyer." Exasperating! I think I convinced Mom there's more to it than that. Whether I can convince you I don't know, but that's your problem. Actually Abe has extremely mixed feelings about my staying. He is terribly worried about the military situation. But I saw how it cheered him up, when I told him I'd turned in my ticket. "You're even dumber than I thought," he said, "and I thought you were pretty damned dumb." Those were the words, but the music was nice.

If despite all the problems, I do stick it out and find my place, I'll certainly miss America. Nobody has to tell me that. In my most radical phase, I only wanted America to live up to itself. I hated the Vietnam war, and the vile creep you incomprehensibly work for in the White House. God knows you made me aware of being Jewish, soaked it into me, but the result was only obdurate resentful negativism that spilled over into all my thinking. Your friend Peter Quat expresses how a lot of my generation feel. In my radical crowd, we anti-Zionist and anti-Israel Jews were doing straight "School of Quat" politics, as Abe's father would call it. It's natural, I assure you, if you're disgruntled at what seems to be the unfortunate accident of being born Jewish in America.

Now that I know a bit about Israel, it is a social and political labyrinth unlike anything else one studies in political science. So I've lost interest in my thesis, or in any M.A. thesis right now, though Abe urges me not to give up the idea. One thing I might do here some day is teach, he says, if I do stay on, and a Johns Hopkins M.A. would "sweeten" my résumé.

A thesis I might do eventually is an in-depth comparison of the Israeli hawk and dove views. It's a genuine study. I'm just beginning to grasp that, starting from identical facts of geography and population, with logic on both sides very hard to fault, they come to opposite conclusions. Curiously, they agree on only one point. Israel needs another million Jews — preferably Americans, because they have the highest level of know-how — but in a pinch any warm bodies, a million more of them. Then, says the hawk Landau, the

Arabs will give up the hope of erasing a country of four million, and Israel can settle the territories in peace. Then, says the dove Lev, with no fear of being overwhelmed, Israel can make peace and give back all the territories.

Surprisingly my Arab gentleman friend (whom I presume you remember, old Dad!) said that, too, in a different way. With thirteen million Jews outside, and only a small fraction inside "the Zionist entity," he argued, what kind of "Jewish homeland" is that? And even those inside are mostly refugees, and a lot of them leave if they can go elsewhere. Zionism is a fraud, he said, a vestige of British colonialism, a mere intrusion of the west into Islam like the Crusaders. Just an episode, and it will be liquidated the same way in the end. Another Holocaust, though he didn't use the word.

Listen, old Dad, the Holocaust bores me. Shocked? That's God's truth. I mean the Holocaust studies, all that academic going on and on about it. Either you do something about it, or you forget it. They're dead and gone. I wasn't alive then. You were. What were you doing, Dad, when the Germans were killing the Jews? Do you wish you'd done more about it? And if they could talk from the grave, those dead six million, don't you think they would say, almost with one voice, "Go to Israel, make it work, make it safe"? I'm quoting Abe again, but that argument of his hits home to me. How does it strike you?

Dudu just looked in, quite spiffy in uniform, and asked me to hurry up. I love the man, Dad, and I love these people, and I love this little land. What else can I tell you? I have to give it a shot. It's a very rough existence, after America. I have no idea what I'll end up doing. Teach? Could be, but learning Hebrew that well, what a job! I'm not a kibbutznik type, that's for sure. So far all I know is, I'm marvellously happy here. No negativism, no alienation, much pain in the ass from *pakidim*, otherwise sunny joy of life. Also, a hope of doing something with my life that can matter and make a difference. That's a brand-new feeling.

Do you know why I went to see Grandma? Because when we first arrived, and I saw her standing there in the airport, I was hit by a wave of relief and admiration. You had told me she was at death's door. That was why you were making the trip. And by God she was not only there, she was on her feet! In a muddled way I can't spell out, that feeling about Grandma and my feeling about Israel overlap. She's where I'm from, and so is this place.

Abe's main argument for what he's doing boils down to this: if world peace ever comes it'll start here, with the peace between the

Jews and the Arabs. He believes that, and I'm beginning to believe it. He says that's really why he has hung on. Peace is what the whole human predicament is now all about, and Zion is the place where it will start happening. Geopolitics and theology both point that way. He can give you two solid and rather mystical hours about this, and I can't give you another line. Dudu is standing over me, and I still have to ink in all the missing r's and m's. Then I'll be going back out to the *lool,* the turkey pen, where I work. It has the godawfulest stink in the world, that lool. Mrs. Barkai has assigned me there to earn my bed and board. Not much Zionist idealism about the smell of a lool! But to repeat, *zeh mah she-yaish.* I've batted this out all backwards and shallow, left out so much! But there was no time. Thanks, old father, for the Jewish awareness you drummed into me. You gave me the best thing you had.

I love you,
Sandra

T HAT'S Sandra's letter. Now what?
My game here is played out. In this paralyzed administration my "cultural and educational liaison" has become a joke. To educators and artists this White House is a leprosarium. I am still in charge of the President's box at the Kennedy Center: that is, I decide which big shot gets to use that flossy cubicle, with its own toilet and bar, to watch operas and ballets. I attend board meetings of the Smithsonian and the National Gallery and so on, but nobody ever seems quite sure who I am or what the hell I am doing there.

Otherwise, all day at the White House, except for my rare confabs with the Chief, I've been scribbling or typing away at *April House.* I was up at dawn yesterday and wrote; went to my office and wrote; came home, and found Sandra's letter. It was like a hammer blow on the head, but I staggered on, fueled by coffee and bourbon, and wrote.

After a nap between midnight and two A.M., more coffee, more bourbon, and I resumed scrawling. Now outside my library window, the dawn is just painting soft pink brushstrokes across the clouds over the Potomac, like the soft pink skin of a Grade B showgirl's uncovered thighs. I've been back in the Goldhandler frame of mind, working as though night and day were time divisions for other people, and we just kept at it until the boss collapsed on the couch with an exhausted groan to Boyd, "Wake me in fifteen minutes, Liebowitz."

I once asked Peter why he never wrote about the Goldhandler days. "That opinionated vulgarian? What's there to write? Who gives a fuck about a thieving radio gagman in the thirties?" Such was his verdict, delivered with a frightening face. Nobody can sneer like old Peter. Well, he may be right but I can't help it; this Goldhandler stuff has been pouring out.

"What did you mean," I asked Jan this morning, telephoning her at three A.M. — in Tel Aviv it was nine in the morning, and she was packing to fly home — "when you said, 'There's hope'? She's not coming back."

"No, she isn't."

"Hope for what, then?"

"Oh, I forget. See you tomorrow."

From time to time Jan does the Delphic business.

The Vice President is going at last. He is still proclaiming that he will never step down, that he is the innocent victim of nefarious plots, clean as the Lily Maid of Astolat. This fellow, mind you, has been tub-thumping up and down the land for years about law and order, and decency, and honesty, and clean government, and patriotism, and all that time he has been a crook on the take. The blatant hypocrisy of it would boggle the mind, if further mind-boggling were possible these days. But the American mind has already been totally — and perhaps irreversibly — boggled. We may be a hundred years getting over the drop from George Washington and Abraham Lincoln to this administration. We may never get over it. The nature of our land may have been changed once for all, as is a virgin lad's after he is had by a whore.

But I wander drunkenly, while pink streaks mount in the buttermilk sky. The hue and cry after the Vice President has given the Chief a respite. If ever I am to quit, without seeming the last of the rats diving off the wreck, now is the time. The media will gnaw the bones of the Vice President for a couple of weeks. I have stayed on mainly because I did not want to desert a man in a jam. His sensitivity for such things is acute. In this lull, he will not see me as putting distance between myself and a falling President.

Why then don't I do it?

All right. I am tired enough, and drunk enough, to write down exactly why I will not quit today or tomorrow. My reason is this:

every time I try to nerve myself to resign, a voice says to me, sounding clear and crisp as Jan talking on the telephone from Tel Aviv this morning: "NOT YET." I will let it go at that, because that is the truth of it. I looked myself in the eye in the bathroom mirror awhile ago, splashing cold water on my face, and I was thinking that I must resign today, and I heard that voice say again: "NOT YET."

Very well then, "not yet," but damned soon. And to hell with that lonesome bedroom upstairs, me for this library couch.

Wake me in fifteen minutes, Liebowitz.

* * *

64

Johnny, Drop Your Gun

GOLDHANDLER had put in the emergency call to us because he needed an audition script for Panilas in a hurry. Campbell's Soup had suddenly shown interest in putting the Greek on prime-time network radio! But by the worst luck, Campbell's Soup had also sponsored that now-dead German comedian, so the old programs were useless. One of those soup fellows might just recognize the material, and blooey would go pots of money, not to mention Goldhandler's reputation for strict probity. Goldhandler already had his hands full, hence he had called us in to do a first draft while he attended to other things.

All he was sure of, for the coming season, was the Lou Blue Ex-Lax show. Two programs had unexpectedly been cancelled, and there was trouble about Becker and Mann, the husband-and-wife comedy team. In fact, there was trouble about Lou Blue. The Ex-Lax people were toying with the notion of dropping him, and going for "class" by sponsoring the Metropolitan Opera. The opera directors had voted against such sponsorship, in fact were aghast at the thought; but the opera treasurer was fighting for it, arguing that laxatives were, after all, healthier than cigarettes, and Lucky Strike was the current sponsor. For the moment the Lou Blue show was safe. In that penthouse we operated from moment to moment.

The acute crisis concerned Becker and Mann. The sponsor, a shoe company, had notified them that their act was worn out, and that unless Goldhandler could provide a fresh format, the show would be dropped. On the very day Peter and I returned, the shoe executives showed up in the office to hear Goldhandler's new program idea. It was one of his masterly performances. Becker and Mann would play

Hansel and Gretel, he revealed, not themselves, and would have all kinds of hilarious adventures in the woods with the wicked witch, and elves, and wolves, and evil woodcutters. Mann as Hansel would be the blundering fool, and Becker as Gretel the smart resourceful one.

Not such a blinding inspiration, you may say. But I swear, not five minutes before those shoe executives arrived with the two worried comedians, Goldhandler was pacing like a caged grizzly bear, begging us and Boyd to think of something, *anything,* that he could tell them. Once they arrived and settled themselves to listen, he was cool as a test pilot, lighting up a fresh Belinda and then launching into this Hansel and Gretel thing. God knows how it came to him — probably while he lit the Belinda — but you would have thought he had worked on it for weeks. He could perfectly mimic the team; and he rattled off one mad scene after another that had the shoe men guffawing, and the two comedians weeping with joy. The program was renewed on the spot. Sardinia brought champagne, Becker jumped up on Goldhandler's desk in her stocking feet and did a fandango, and you never saw such happy carrying-on.

When they were all gone Boyd asked Goldhandler, "Will it work?"

"Are you kidding?" snapped Goldhandler. "With those two dummies? How the fuck can they play characters? They can barely read lines."

"Then what'll we do?" Boyd persisted timidly.

"Do? What's the matter with you? From now on when they tell the jokes, it'll be" — here Goldhandler did the comedians' intonations — " '*Gretel,* how many ribs has a monkey got?' — 'Well, take off your coat, *Hansel,* and I'll see.' — That'll be Hansel and Gretel." That was it, too.

Well, so Peter and I drafted the Panilas audition script, drawing expertly on the card files. Goldhandler was pleased with it, and so was Panilas. But the overeager comedian fell apart during the audition, and in the middle of the show he actually stopped and begged the watching sponsors in a quaking voice to let him start over. Of course the audition failed. Goldhandler's ribald abuse of the Greek, as we all rode back in a cab from the disaster, made us scream with laughter; but in sober fact the flop meant Goldhandler remained in real financial difficulties.

Still, he kept turning up more prospects. There were shoals of vaudevillians frantic to break into radio and willing to pay anything for audition scripts. He put Peter and me to work on these, while he and Boyd ground out the Lou Blue show and "Hansel and Gretel." So the weeks went rolling by, and when law school started I was scarcely aware of it. Peter too was glad to be back earning money again, for all his grumbling about the demeaning nature of the work. His father had read our incomplete farce and called it worthless, which it was. Matters were sticky in the Quat household, until Peter resumed contributing to the expenses. Dr. Quat was not a skinflint at all, he just held stern views about a man past twenty-one not paying his way in life.

Early in December Skip Lasser came to the penthouse. By then there was real trouble. None of the auditions had caught on. Becker and Mann were gone, the Hansel and Gretel a fiasco. Lou Blue, the only show Goldhandler had running, had been renewed at the last minute by Ex-Lax on a week-to-week basis. The Ex-Lax officials were still dickering with the opera. Goldhandler, his back to the wall, at a meeting with them had proposed that, if they really wanted class, what they should do was sponsor the Barrymores — Ethel, Lionel, and John — in a serialization of *War and Peace*. What a breakthrough in class! The book was in the public domain, he pointed out; the rights would cost nothing. He said he knew the Barrymores well and would undertake to interest them.

Boyd told us that it was just a brainstorm, a straw the boss had clutched at to stave off the immediate cancellation of Lou Blue. The Ex-Lax men had gone into ecstasies over it, and now Goldhandler was committed to line up the Barrymores to do *War and Peace* on the radio. Peter and I were trying to compress the first chapters of the Tolstoy book into a half-hour audition script, with appropriate pauses for selling Ex-Lax; Goldhandler had an agent cautiously approaching the Barrymores; and all this had to be done in the strictest secrecy, because Lou Blue had somehow heard — though the sponsors had promised not to talk about it — that he was being threatened with replacement by a classy *War and Peace* show. Goldhandler kept assuring him at length over the phone that it was absolute nonsense, who the fuck would want to listen to *War and Peace*? But the comedian was calling up all the time in a great sweat about his script, and about the Tolstoy menace. I sometimes felt a little awkward, picking up the phone while typing some dialogue between Pierre and

Natasha, and connecting Lou Blue to the boss, and listening to Goldhandler once more tell the comedian that the *War and Peace* rumor was absolute horseshit.

Well, what with all this turmoil, Goldhandler had given no mind to the libretto of Lasser's new show for Broadway, *Johnny, Drop Your Gun,* the musical adaptation of *The Good Soldier Schweik.* He had brought the libretto back from Hollywood, but it had just sat on his desk. Now a reading for backers was two weeks away, and Lasser was coming to find out what he had done. Goldhandler's job was to gag up the show, as he had the Lasser screenplay. Goldhandler called Skip Lasser "a titter man"; he could think of whimsical show ideas and write cute lyrics, that is, but he couldn't make people laugh.

There was a huge delicatessen platter from Lindy's in the living room, awaiting Lasser's arrival. Goldhandler went to answer the doorbell himself, more nervous than we had yet seen him. He was desperate for the Lasser project, because of the growing trend in radio toward "class." Another Broadway credit was just what he needed now, and Lasser had promised to bill him as a collaborator.

Lasser greeted Peter and me with bare nods as he walked into the magnificent living room. "Terrific place you've got here, Harry," he said, with a note close to awe.

"Why, thanks, Skip."

"And to think," Lasser went on, "that it's all built on shit." Goldhandler's proud smile faded. "How's the shit program coming, by the way, Harry?"

"It's all right."

Lasser pointed a thumb at the platter. "What's that for?"

"I thought we'd eat while we talk."

"No time. I have to talk to directors and choreographers."

Goldhandler showed him through the apartment as we went upstairs. Looking into the dining room, Lasser said, "Just imagine, how many people had to take a shit to furnish this room!" When we came into the office, Lasser whistled at the view. "Fantastic. Never seen anything like it, Harry. It needed an Empire State Building of shit to pay for all this."

Such was Lasser's genial vein. When Goldhandler acknowledged that he had not yet done any writing on the libretto, and started to ad-lib ideas, Lasser turned harsh. "Harry, save that bluffing for the shit sponsor. I know you. *Tokhas af'n tish!* (Put your ass on the table!) You've got nothing, and how come? You're not doing anything but that shit show, are you? Do you want to do this libretto, or don't you? Eddie Conn wants to work on it. He hasn't had a Broadway show yet."

Naming Eddie Conn to Goldhandler was like poking him with an electric prod. He leaped out of his swivel chair and slammed a hairy fist on his desk, so that the ashtrays, the Perrier bottles, the cigar humidor, and the scripts jumped. "You want Eddie Conn? Go ahead! Take your libretto to him!"

Having administered the prod, Lasser backed off. It was agreed that Goldhandler would deliver a revised libretto in ten days.

"You fellows still want to meet showgirls?" With that beguiling grin of his, Lasser addressed us for the first time as he was leaving the office.

Peter said, "Hell, yes."

"Well, I can do better than your friend Fokety." A wider grin. "You're going to meet showgirls."

That night Goldhandler was as low as I had ever seen him. Partly, I suppose, it was the weather. A blizzard was whirling and howling outside, big flakes splattering and sticking on the windows. At dinner he cut only a bite or two from the triple lamb chops on his plate, then pushed the food aside and lit a cigar. For Goldhandler, I thought, Skip Lasser had coated the whole penthouse with a thick layer of stinking ordure.

"It's no way," he said, breaking his long oppressive silence. "Running around all day, writing all night, how can anything good get done?"

"Balzac wrote all night," said Mrs. Goldhandler, "just like you."

Goldhandler replied sadly. "Balzac was only the greatest writer of his time."

"You're a great writer. Maybe the greatest of your time. *Poor Rosalie* is sheer greatness, isn't it? It should have gotten the O. Henry prize, not that lousy honorable mention. *Poor Rosalie* is Maupassant. It's Chekhov. It's great, GREAT!"

Poor Rosalie was an early Goldhandler short story, one of the best. Mrs. Goldhandler had to reach back over six years of Lou Blue, Henny Holtz, Nicholas Panilas, Becker and Mann, and so on — ten file cabinets full of such stuff — to make her point. But when she said "great, GREAT," her pale face reddening, her eyes flashing, a small white fist flailing, you could see the faces of her sons light up, and Goldhandler's spirits revive. He sat up straight, grunted a laugh, and ate more lamb.

"We need sun," he said. "That's what we need, boys. A little sun. We'll go to Florida. Five days. None of this night work, we'll sit around in the sun, get some exercise and fresh air, and do that libretto with our ass. Nothing to it."

We caught a midnight train to Miami, the four of us and Mrs. Goldhandler, and we checked into the Roney Plaza, where luminaries like Walter Winchell and Eddie Cantor got their winter tans.

It happened that Mama, Papa, and my sister Lee were already in Miami, at the kosher hotel where we had stayed years before, when we drove down in the twelve-cylinder Cadillac. I managed to visit them just once, for Friday night dinner. At the Roney Plaza, all ablaze and festooned with Christmas lights and decorations, with the loudspeakers blaring carols day and night, I had quite forgotten that it was also Hanuka. Pop had brought the old menorah from home. He said the blessing and lit the candles in their suite just before the Sabbath fell, when I waved aside his invitation to me to do it. We sang the Hanuka hymn, "Mighty Rock of My Salvation," to the old melody of his father, the shammas in Minsk. All this felt awkward and odd, and so did eating in the big dining room, where Sabbath candles burned on the tables, and most men sat in skullcaps. Some young sparks were bareheaded, but when Pop produced a yarmulka for me, I put it on. Nothing brought home more strongly to me the distance I had travelled. I was more at home in the Roney Plaza than in this kosher hotel, and if I had a father to look up to, it was Harry Goldhandler.

By then, you must understand, I was seeing very, very little of Pop. Back at home, he would leave in the morning for the laundry while I slept. Once I woke I would go to the penthouse and stay on until dawn. On Friday evenings I would come home for dinner, and hold forth about Goldhandler and the celebrities I was meeting. Mama ate that up. She was telling her friends that I was having fun and making some money in radio before settling down seriously to law school; for of course I was going to be a lawyer, nothing flimsy like a writer. My sister Lee too was avid for the show-business gossip. The laundry talk, what I heard of it, was normal; idiocies of the partners, cliffhanging money troubles and respites. In that small flat, a decided

comedown from our West End Avenue layout, these things seemed
as remote and dim as Aldus Street, compared to the adventurous
brilliance of life in the Goldhandler penthouse.

Pop had joined the Orthodox synagogue and was chairing its
building fund drive for a new Hebrew high school. He was president
of the Manhattan Zionist chapter, too. One Friday night I went with
him to a meeting. A fiery speaker, flourishing a smoking cigar, roared
defiance of the British mandate and spoke of taking up arms against
its decrees. This struck me as the most vaporous possible foolishness.
Jews, fighting like soldiers? Pop's other preoccupation, the Nazi threat
to the Jews, seemed just as farfetched to me. Hitler had been in power
for a couple of years, and nothing much had happened, except that
German Jewish refugees were swamping Manhattan hotels and eating places.

Pop would take in with quiet wry amusement, half-proud and half-
sad, my talk about Harry Goldhandler on Friday night; his sagacious
brown eyes on me, his mouth compressed in a small smile as he listened and said nothing, while Lee and Mom would ply me with
questions until the Sabbath candles burned down and I went back to
the penthouse for the night's work. Pop seemed to be waiting for me
to come out with something, and I never did. Maybe it was this book.
A little late, Pop, if so, but I'm doing my best.

"Finkelstein," said Goldhandler, thrusting currency into my hand,
"bet this on Idle Dreamer to show, quick. It's two thousand. I've got
to go to the can before I shit in my pants."

We were at the Hialeah racetrack. Goldhandler had taken me to
the races for company, because his wife was getting her hair done.
All afternoon he had been devouring hot dogs heaped with mustard
and sauerkraut, maybe six or seven of them. In his childhood on the
Lower East Side, he said, he had had a hot dog about once a year;
and he intended to eat as many hot dogs as he wanted, whenever he
wanted to, for the rest of his life. The money looked strange in my
hand; a sheaf of new stiff bills like stage money. I don't believe I had
ever seen hundred-dollar bills before.

Goldhandler had a new infallible system for beating the odds. He
was betting only on favorites, and only to show. The return was small,
sometimes no more than one dollar for fifteen or twenty wagered.

But as Goldhandler explained the system, it was as riskless as picking up pennies in the street; just pick up enough, and you were a millionaire. A mathematical certainty! His neighbor in Beverly Hills, a retired film director, had played the system for years, and was fifty thousand dollars ahead. You just had to have the nerve, said Goldhandler, to venture big sums for modest returns. In point of fact, Idle Dreamer came in second, and paid Goldhandler two hundred and five dollars. I bet on the horse to win, and lost two dollars.

The Goldhandlers were going to Hialeah every afternoon, to the dog races in town every night; and after the dogs they would drop in on a casino for an hour or so of roulette. Miami was wide open in those days, and Mrs. Goldhandler seemed to relish gambling as much as he did. We would get to work about midnight for a couple of hours, then "go out for coffee"; that is, at an all-night delicatessen or Chinese place we would eat huge meals, and return to the Roney Plaza to work until dawn. We would sleep till lunch time, and start over. It was our penthouse routine, unchanged. The only sun any of us got, in the five days we were there, was in the box at Hialeah, which was so close to the track that you could smell the horses thudding by, and sometimes get hit by the flying dirt.

Yet in five nights Goldhandler redictated the entire Lasser libretto. One of us sat at a typewriter writing down his ad libs, another scrawled them into a script, and a third would catnap while Goldhandler plowed ahead like an iron man. He was not inserting old jokes at all, but improvising lines and whole scenes. I never admired Harry Goldhandler more. It was an astounding burst of creative work. Lasser had switched Schweik to an American army camp in the World War, a sound notion, but the libretto was long on antiwar sentiments and short on laughs. Goldhandler knew *The Good Soldier Schweik* by heart. When he was through, the libretto had recaptured the coarse and pathetic fun of that great book, and was the more effectively antiwar because there was no antiwar talk in it. Only the Lasser songs, like "Oh, What Fun To Die" and "The Doomsday Rag," retained the social significance vein. Goldhandler had nothing to say about the lyrics.

The sun was coming up over the ocean when Goldhandler stumbled off to bed, the job done. Peter lay on a couch, out cold. Boyd and I sat looking at each other, Boyd hunched over a scrawled-up script, I at the typewriter, both utterly exhausted.

"My God, Boyd," I said, "it's marvellous."

"He had something to go on," said Boyd in hoarse weary tones, lighting perhaps his thousandth Melachrino of the Florida stay.

"He's a much better writer than Lasser. There's no comparison."

"Lasser isn't very funny," Boyd said with professional calm, "but he's inventive and smart. It's his show, his idea, don't overlook that. He went to Czechoslovakia, and got the rights to the book. It wasn't easy. Goldhandler's working on something Lasser's already created."

"Why doesn't he just write shows himself, and forget the radio garbage? Aside from anything else, he'd make more money."

Boyd gave me a strange look and said, "Let's get some sleep."

Our trip back to New York was gloomed over by a foray to Hialeah before train time. In two races, the favorites failed to come in third. I have never seen a man look more amazed and stunned than Goldhandler, watching the favorite of that second race shamble in last. Boyd later whispered that the boss had dropped eight thousand dollars. Mrs. Goldhandler, who had been down on the infallible system right along, somewhat repaired matters by taking a flyer of fifty dollars on a forty-to-one shot that came in. All the way to the railroad station, they bickered in the limousine. Why hadn't she bet a hundred dollars, Goldhandler wanted to know; or better yet, five hundred or a thousand, as long as she had a good hunch? They would now be in *forty thousand dollars!* And why hadn't they stayed for one more race? There was plenty of time. Actually, we made the train with about thirty seconds to spare. We absolutely had to be back in New York for the Lou Blue broadcast rehearsal.

As the Goldhandlers disappeared into their drawing room, Mrs. Goldhandler was snapping, "Just like picking up pennies on the street! Ha! A mathematical certainty! Ha!" I had never before seen them testy with each other, and I don't recall that I ever did again. They were a strange pair, but one thing is sure, they were crazily in love with each other to the last.

"I once saw them go at each other worse than that," Boyd said, as we sat drinking in the club car, "over the stock market. They're both plungers, and they had to swear off. They made a big ceremony of it. I was the witness. They took off their wedding rings and gave them to me to hold. Then each one put a hand over mine, and they swore on their marriage, no more stock market. They've stayed out, too."

"My father lost everything in the crash," Peter said crossly. "He doesn't have to swear off. It turned him into a nut about money, a conservative nut."

"Gambling makes me nervous," I said. "When I lose money I'm sick at the waste of it. When I win, which is seldom, I feel I've stolen it."

"Jewish conscience," sneered Peter.

"It was the gambling," said Boyd, "that got him going on the libretto. He didn't come to Florida for the sun, he hates the sun. He says the sun gives you cancer."

Peter Quat said, "Why does he need those fucking card files, anyway? He can make things up. He's original. That libretto is funny now, brilliantly funny."

"Make up three programs a week?" said Boyd.

"Wouldn't she rather see him write one Broadway show a year? Or every two or three years?" I asked Boyd. "What's it all about?"

Boyd's oval puffy white face went blank; his bald brow wrinkled up like an accordion and unwrinkled to blank smoothness. He slashed open a fresh box of Melachrinos with a thumbnail. "Another time," he said, and he signalled to the waiter for more drinks.

Lasser liked Goldhandler's revisions, and Bert Lahr was overjoyed. The great comic star was cast as Schweik. He was too old to play a doughboy, so Lasser had cannily premised the show on the drafting, through a clerical error, of a middle-aged grocer, who kept protesting to the army bureaucracy that it was all a mistake, that he didn't belong in uniform. Lahr had signed to do the show on the basis of Lasser's successes and the book's fame. But he was bored by all the social significance, and threatening to pull out. Lasser did not invite Goldhandler to the reading for the backers; however, he telephoned that they had laughed, applauded, and even cheered, and that Bert Lahr had hugged him. "I gave you full credit, Harry," I heard Lasser say. I was manning the switchboard. "Your name goes into the program, and on all the signs and advertising. Great job."

And so *Johnny, Drop Your Gun* went smoothly into rehearsal at the Winter Garden, starring Bert Lahr. I don't remember who else was in the cast, except for a singing showgirl named Bobbie Webb.

65

Backstage at Minsky's

"LIEBOWITZ, have you ever been to Minsky's?" Thus Goldhandler, with a leer at me, a week or so after we got back from Miami. "Sure."

"Ever been backstage?"

"Me? No, of course not."

"That's where you're going right now."

"Wait, I volunteer," said Peter Quat, halting his typing at an audition script.

"Not you," said Goldhandler, "you'll be jerking off for a week, and it'll affect your work." He was always making such remarks. He often accused me of abusing myself, too; and he had a whole routine about Dr. Quat trying to catch Peter and me doing it to each other, and always just failing to break in at the right moment.

My instructions were to take a cab to the Minsky burlesque house in Brooklyn. Joey Mack, a comedian, would give me the script of a skit called *Dr. Schneidbaitzim,* Yiddish for "Dr. Cutballs," which I was to bring to Goldhandler backstage at the Winter Garden. Like every other adolescent frequenter of burlesque houses, I had seen "Dr. Cutballs" any number of times. I did not exactly see how Goldhandler could make it with kissing, but mine not to reason why.

Nowadays naked girls shimmy and squirm and wriggle for a living in every other neighborhood bar, topless and bottomless, but in those days any disrobing as public entertainment was against the law, unless it was part of an "artistic dance." Thus the striptease was born. Minsky's was its home. The carnal glimpses of uncovered female hide went with sitting through terrible old movies, harangues by candy butchers, and wearily drawn-out skits by comedians under orders to kill time, and lots of it. But there were kernels of classic comedy in those skits, and Joey Mack was a steady supplier for Goldhandler. Marlene Dietrich, for instance, never knew that she had played in a rewrite of a Minsky standard bit entitled, *Oh, Doctor, It Feels So Good.*

I set off for Brooklyn with a racing pulse and sweaty palms. This chance to peek backstage at Minsky's was a teenager's sex fantasy come true; and the reader knows what a teenager in attitude and experience I still was. What might I not see back there! I couldn't wait, and the Brooklyn Bridge, crowded with traffic, seemed a hundred miles long. The metal stage door of Minsky's squeaked open a crack, and a gray-bristled jowly face peered at me. "Whaddya want?" I quailed at the snarl. This watchdog obviously knew I was slavering to peek at naked breasts and buttocks without paying. That was all anybody wanted who knocked at that stage door, and it was his job to make sure that I damned well didn't see a goddamned thing.

"Joey Mack is expecting me."

"Who are you?"

"I come from Harry Goldhandler."

He glanced at a scrap of paper from his pocket, opened the door enough to let me slide in, and slammed it shut. "Up two flights," he said, pointing at an iron staircase. "First door left."

I ran up the stairs and knocked at what I thought was the first door left. A young woman in a dressing gown, with a heavily painted face, opened the door. "Whaddya want?" She clutched the dressing gown tight over a full bosom, clearly reading my mind, too. It was discouraging to be so transparent to these people. I was there, after all, on an honest errand. My fantasies were my own business.

"I have an appointment with Joey Mack."

"Joey's on after Anne. He's backstage."

I trotted back down the stairs. Now I could hear the pit band playing the bump-and-grind music of a striptease, beyond the flats, ropes, and curtains.

"He's down here somewhere," I said to the old bruiser at the stage door.

"Shit, yes," he said, suddenly much friendlier, like so many watchdogs after the first bristly encounter. "Come with me." He locked the door and led me around backstage. There was nothing to see but props, tinselly settings, spotlights, and such, all very sleazy, grimy, and battered.

"Joey, here's that kid from Goldhandler."

"Hi, kid." A pudgy man with a red-painted nose, in baggy pants and an oversize jacket, was playing cards with a stagehand on a wooden prop box. The striptease music here was louder.

"Ladies and gentlemen," a loudspeaker proclaimed, "Miss Anne Darling."

WHUMP, whaa, WHUMP, whaa, WHUMP, whaa went the drums, trumpets, and trombones. I could see Miss Anne Darling in my mind's eye, but that was hardly the idea.

"I'm supposed to pick up *Dr. Schneidbaitzim,*" I said.

"After the bit, kid," said Joey Mack, yawning and playing a card.

(WHUMP, whaa, WHUMP, whaa.)

"Say," I blurted, "can I, you know, can I watch?"

Joey Mack shrugged and gestured at the wing, where I could see the glow of footlights. I darted there and looked out at the stage. I was not alone. A stagehand in overalls and a bald man in a dark suit already stood there. Miss Anne Darling was flirting with the audience as strippers do, smiling, bridling, flashing her eyes, doing the standard strides, dips, and whirls. She was a tall blonde girl, very intent on her work as she went about peeling off a blue costume studded with rhinestones. It was an odd angle for viewing a stripper. Seen from backstage she was much less a fantasy object than a hard-laboring performer.

The French developed a whole intellectual mystique about strippers, way back then; "*déshabilleuses tentatrices,*" they called them, and also "*les strippers,*" and I do believe Jean Cocteau or Jean Paul Sartre eventually wrote a book about them. Some heavy Frenchman named Jean; or on second thought, maybe it was Albert Camus. Anyway, all that was about a stripper seen from out front by a heavy Frenchman. But there was something industrious and dogged about Miss Anne Darling, observed from backstage, that pretty much dissipated the good old hot erotic miasma of Minsky's. I went on watching the free show, gulping and wetting my lips, but that was a Pavlovian reflex to the WHUMP-whaa music, rather than to Miss Anne Darling's increasingly visible integument. There she was after a while, flailing her naked pretty breasts hither and yon and undulating her hips and belly, and she could hardly have provoked less indecent thoughts in me had she been a seal blowing "God Bless America" through her nose on a rack of horns.

She caught sight of us in the wing, as she half-hid herself coyly behind the curtain for her first encore. She gave us a horribly dirty look, then sailed out again to take off her rhinestone-bordered pants. As she danced around some more, all but naked, with very little protection on what Laertes describes to Ophelia as her chaste treasure, she managed several disgusted glares at us, between sultry ogles at the audience. It was quite a feat of facial mobility. When her act ended she snatched a robe hanging in the wing and pulled it on angrily. "Well, you creeps," she said, her voice dripping venomous contempt, "did you get an eyeful?" And off she flounced. My ears and face burned. She might as well have caught us spying through a keyhole. Her outraged modesty was every bit that real. A strange business!

Then I watched Joey Mack, and an aging straight man I had seen in Minsky shows for years, do an interminable version of *Boy, You Sure Look Natural,* one of the dreariest of the time-killers. I spare you the details. The idea seemed to be to drive out of the theatre all but the most obsessive voyeurs, and the customers did go streaming up the aisles. As the curtain closed, the house lights came up, and a candy butcher began barking his wares: various candy bars and — so he assured the audience — incredibly obscene books from Paris, France, all in English, with very illegal pictures.

"Well now, let's see," said Joey Mack, in his dressing room atop the iron stairs, opening a worn suitcase full of flimsy scripts. "It's here somewhere. Hmm. *His Tale Touched My Heart . . . The Crazy Dentist . . . Who'll Ride My Sister . . . Boy, You Sure Look Natural . . . Flugel Street . . . Slowly I Turned . . . She Wants Cream In Her Coffee . . .*"

Joey Mack was such a valuable resource to Goldhandler because he alone among the burlesque comics had written down these "bits." They were an oral tradition in *commedia dell'arte* style, the lines and business changing with every performance. Mack had laboriously committed skeleton versions to paper, and it was these that Goldhandler bought from time to time for good money.

"Ah, here we are." Mack handed me a dirty dog-eared script of ten pages or so. "*Dr. Schneidbaitzim.* There's too much kack in there," he said. "Mr. Goldhandler will have to clean it up. You can't compete with tits, except with kack."

A rickety Taj Mahal set was being slapped up on a broad shaky turntable when Mack and I went downstairs. Girls were milling around it in Hindu dress; and boy, oh boy, here were my bare bosoms and cleft rears, sure enough! Everywhere I looked! Nipples! Buttocks! I guess my eyes popped, I don't know, but I do know the vision was a disappointment. The girls were fussing with each other's costumes or with their own, or looking for props, or fixing their hair. These were Grade C or D showgirls, to give them the best of it; some with lumpy legs, others with protruding stomachs, working women making a tough living, bustling about their jobs; so uninterested in sex, and so uninteresting! The nipples and behinds "looked natural," but totally unprovocative. Women had these things, and what else was new?

"This Taj Mahal scene is nice. Stick around and watch it," Joey Mack said. He spoke to one of the girls, "Hi, are we having dinner?"

"Sure, I guess so, Joey."

Something like a gilt leaf hung on each breast, not concealing much. With a grin at me he lifted a leaf. "Don't be funny," she said sharply, giving me an embarrassed sad look, and she walked away.

I won't burden you with the whole Taj Mahal scene. After some wooden pantomime by a rajah and his queen (Miss Anne Darling, robed to the ears), the rajah sang "Pale Hands I Loved" over and over, the turntable turned, and the Taj Mahal slowly and unsteadily revolved, I guess to give the customers every possible view of the showgirls posed all over it. The law was that they could display their charms in tableaux, providing that they didn't move. They did their best to stay within the law, poor things; but keeping their balance was hard, and they had to hang on the scenery and each other, and their breasts would bob and their behinds quiver. No judge would have punished them for that, they were taking punishment enough. This was the dead of winter. It was cold in Minsky's, and very drafty backstage. Most of the audience sat in overcoats. When I left, the turntable still creakily revolved, the showgirls were shivering, their breasts and behinds were turning blue, and on and on the baritone rajah bawled "Pale Hands I Loved." The Taj Mahal number had to kill its allotted time.

One more fantasy blasted. On to the Winter Garden.

66

Grade A Showgirls

I CAME to that stage door, which for months would be my haunt, thoroughly de-fantasized — if such a thing is possible, like being deloused — turned off sex, expecting nothing, intending to give Goldhandler the script and go back to the penthouse. It is there yet, the Winter Garden stage door, forty years later. It has hardly changed, for theatres outlive actors and actresses and their loves. Showgirls pass through the door now as then; young men bring them there and wait for them to come out; and so they live again and yet again the old tale of young love in the big city, where the beautiful girls come to go on the stage, and the bright young men come to make their fortunes, and to love the beautiful girls. That Taj Mahal forever turns.

"Yes?" said the grizzled man who opened the door. He wore a suit and a tie, he had a thick wrestler's neck, and he looked just as capable of kicking me into the street as the Minsky's watchdog, but less disposed to.

"Harry Goldhandler is expecting me."

"Over there, second door."

In a long dressing room lined with mirrors and lights, Goldhandler sat alone at a typewriter in a fog of smoke. He read *Dr. Schneidbaitzim* and shoved it into a portfolio. "Terrific. Come with me, and" — he got up, shuffling papers together and giving me the old foxy smile, a Belinda clenched in his mouth — "mum's the word."

We hurried across the stage. Girl singers were huddled around a piano in slacks or skirts and sweaters, listening to a man play and sing "The Doomsday Rag." In a large dressing room, Bert Lahr and Skip Lasser were having sandwiches and coffee. I had never seen Lahr up close before. He appeared older than on stage, and extremely worried. Yet the man was funny just to look at. He was funny biting into a sandwich, funny sipping coffee, and don't ask me why.

"It's that friggin' hospital scene, Harry," mourned Lahr, his face creasing into a thousand comical wrinkles. "We got to do something about that friggin' hospital scene."

"It's a fine scene," said Lasser, sitting with his feet up on a low table piled with scripts. "It's a very meaningful scene, Bert, and you're terrific in it."

"It's no scene," said Lahr. "It's a friggin' hole. The show goes down that friggin' hole."

"I have an idea about that," said Goldhandler, and he began to ad-lib. He had not gotten far when Lahr's face, until then a funny mask of gloom, metamorphosed to a funny mask of joy. "You mean *Dr. Schneidbaitzim!*" he exclaimed. "Fantastic! Why didn't I think of that?"

"What's that?" Lasser asked. Goldhandler managed to throw Lahr a huge warning wink. "Something you did in another show, Harry? Now, none of that crap!"

Lahr hastily said he'd just been reminded of an old doctor joke. "Keep going, Harry. It sounds okay," said Lahr with ludicrous solemnity. Goldhandler went on, working "Dr. Cutballs" adroitly into the show's hospital scene, a confrontation between Schweik and an army psychiatrist. Lasser said he'd like to see it on paper, and he left. Lahr threw his arms around Goldhandler. *"Dr. Schneidbaitzim!* Couldn't be better! But the way I used to do it, Harry —"

"Wait for me, Liebowitz," said Goldhandler, waving me to the door. "We'll go home for dinner together."

On the stage a choreographer was shouting at boys and girls dancing to the piano music. I saw the singing girls lounging in orchestra seats, and I went and sat down close to them. They were absorbed in their talk, and I could stare at them all I wanted; and I realized that at last I was looking at Grade A showgirls.

Now, how do you go about describing beauty? I am not a describer. I have enough trouble just putting down what happened. Maybe I can write something of the effect those girls had on me. They were very different from each other, but each one was dazzling in her own way. They were all big slender girls, that they had in common; some with the broad shoulders of swimmers, others slighter and more delicately formed; some faces strong-boned, others softer and sweeter; and — another common feature — they all had huge eyes. They wore almost no makeup. Their working clothes were unglamorous. They were there to do a job, like the Minsky girls; but unlike the Minsky girls, they stirred the passions at sight.

Oh, Lord, the careless queenly desirability of those singing girls! They laughed, they sprawled about with shapely long silk-clad legs, they smoked cigarettes, they made unseemly faces at each other as they gossiped; but none of that could dispel the aspect of allure, the sense of their own beauty, that was their mark. The Minsky girls had been pathetic creatures; that Grade B girl of Billy Rose's had been pitiable too, in her trembling eagerness to snatch up her skirt and land a job. The unaffected self-regard of these girls was what smote you. They knew their worth.

I had once despaired of ever laying eyes on a girl as beautiful and desirable as Dorsi Sabin. Fool! I was looking at ten girls, each one ten times more seductive than Dorsi Sabin. Dorsi was for the likes of Morris Pelkowitz. A monarch, a president, a billionaire, could fall for one of these girls and become her slave. That was a matter of luck, for such catches are few, *but it was possible!* They were a chorus of Theodoras, of Madame du Barrys, of Nell Gwynns. They were Grade A showgirls. And I might never win one of them — God in heaven, how *could* I? — but I could forget about Dorsi Pelkowitz, the lost goddess. She was a lost housewife.

"Let's go, Finkelstein."

I must have jumped two feet off the chair. Goldhandler glanced with amused comprehension at the girls, and I expected a coarse joke, but he said nothing. We went out to catch a cab on Broadway. Over the marquee, men on scaffolds were obliterating the name of the last show with white primer. "It'll be nice at that," said Goldhandler, "to see my name up there again. It's been a while."

We rode in silence in the cab. He puffed a Belinda. I stared out at Broadway, bemused, confounded, despondent. "Pretty girls," Goldhandler said, startling me again.

"Yes. Pretty girls."

"You'll get a pretty girl, Liebowitz. In the end you'll want one that's smart. That's the main thing."

"You won't believe this," Boyd said as we came into the office. He sat at Goldhandler's desk, looking as stunned as I probably had, contemplating the girls. "You missed him by two minutes."

"Missed who?" Goldhandler asked.

Peter, batting out a script at a typewriter, made a disconcerting face at me.

"John Barrymore."

"*Barrymore?*"

"He's interested in doing *War and Peace.*"

Goldhandler stared at Boyd, for once in his life speechless.

"I picked up the phone, and it was Barrymore, I tell you," Boyd said. "I almost died of the shock. They're all interested, Ethel and Lionel, too. John's coming east on business, and he wants to talk to you about it."

Goldhandler fell into an armchair, cast his eyes up to heaven, and slowly breathed. "Holy . . . shit." Then suddenly and sharply he said, "You didn't tell him it was for Ex-Lax?"

"*God,* no," said Boyd.

"Well," said Goldhandler, addressing Peter and me, the old foxy grin breaking out on his fat face, "you two fuckers better get hot on the Battle of Borodino."

John Barrymore actually came to the office, what's more.

Talk about the difficulty of describing! Who is like John Barrymore today, that great Hamlet, that chiselled profile, that peerless movie idol? I had never missed a film of his since in *Dr. Jekyll and Mr. Hyde,* a silent movie, he had scared the daylights out of me at age ten. Barrymore's Dr. Jekyll was a man as celestially handsome as a Raphael angel, as elegantly turned out as the Prince of Wales. His Mr. Hyde was a stooped pointy-headed leering horror, dressed in flapping funereal black, with writhing lips, claws for hands, and mad murderous little eyes. That story has been done to death since, but as a show it has always hung on the charm of Jekyll. Anybody can be tricked up as a monster; I could play a creditable Hyde, if there were any point in it, and there is no comedian who hasn't parodied Mr. Hyde. But there was only one great Jekyll, one perfect figure of a man to contrast to the horrible Hyde, and that was John Barrymore.

And it was Dr. Jekyll who came to Goldhandler's penthouse. Stories were rife about Barrymore's decline, his drunkenness, his temper, his pranks and whims; but this was a quiet-spoken gentleman in a gray double-breasted suit and a gray homburg, who did not look thirty-five. He might have stepped out of *Topaze* or *Twentieth Century,* recent movies in which he had played a modish man of the world. He talked about the Tolstoy project with calm astute professionalism, and at last put the main question: what sort of money was in it, and who would be the sponsor?

When Goldhandler named the Lou Blue budget, one Barrymore eyebrow went up, and the head appreciatively tilted, just as in the movies. About the sponsor, the situation was delicate, Goldhandler said, involving the cancellation of a big program. Barrymore nodded, and did not press him. Goldhandler promised to submit sample scripts for his approval, and he left with the star, who was going to another appointment on Broadway. Boyd had been telephoning the Winter Garden every day about the sign. It had just been finished, and Goldhandler's name was on it. No doubt he wanted to show it casually to Barrymore, and he was pretty eager to see it himself.

Peter Quat exclaimed when they were gone, "I feel I'm working in an insane asylum. This thing is preposterous! Dave and I have been beating our brains out uselessly for weeks. You *can't* stuff Tolstoy into a series of radio half-hours, that's all. It can't be done, Barrymores or no Barrymores."

"It's class," said Boyd serenely. "If the boss gets a twenty-six week contract, what else matters? We have to buy some more copies of *War and Peace* right away and start assembling half a dozen scripts. Boss's orders."

Goldhandler returned to the office with a face dark as thunderheads. He opened a fresh box of Belindas, held them to the light, and barked at Boyd, "Black! Coal black! I might as well smoke tarred ropes! Where are the mouse-colored ones?"

"Those are the mouse-colored ones," said Boyd.

Goldhandler believed that mouse-colored cigars were the mildest, so that the thirty he smoked every day wouldn't affect his health. With a grouchy mutter Goldhandler lit one, and sank in his swivel chair, puffing.

"Didn't they put your name on the sign?" Boyd ventured.

"Yes, they did," said Goldhandler, "in fly shit. 'Book and lyrics by' " — he let out a frightening roar — " 'S. K. LASSER, and' " — he dropped his voice to a weak whisper — " 'additional dialogue by H. Goldhandler.' " He jammed the cigar into a Perrier bottle. "Faugh! It tastes like I'm smoking my cock."

Next day was his birthday. He was only thirty-six. I could hardly believe it. Rotund, double-chinned, almost bald, a tooth missing, hollow-eyed, he looked twenty years older than Barrymore. I came to the penthouse refreshed from a long sleep, and seeing him breakfasting, I marched in and said, "Happy birthday, boss."

"What's happy about it?" he snarled. I was set back on my heels. What had I done wrong? Or was he still upset over the fly shit? Mrs. Goldhandler was looking white-faced at her food. Her parents, though eating heartily, might have just come back from a funeral. Peter never glanced at me as he cut up a steak. Boyd and the children weren't there.

"Sit down and have coffee," growled Goldhandler.

I lied that I had had a big breakfast, and took the stairs two at a time to the office. Boyd was attacking a copy of *War and Peace* with shears. Other copies were stacked on the big desk and by the switchboard. I did not think Boyd could look any paler, but he did. There was a hint of green in his gray-white face.

"What in hell is wrong down there, Boyd?"

"The stock market."

"The *stock* market?"

"She wanted to surprise him. She bought U.S. Steel on margin this morning. She had a hot tip that it was going to zoom up, something about a big navy steel order. Since she bought it, it's dropped eight points. When he woke up he was out forty-eight thousand dollars. That was his birthday surprise."

67

Double Trouble

NEW switchboard orders came through: until further notice Goldhandler was talking only to Lou Blue, Barrymore, Lahr, and Lasser; no brokers, no bankers, no bill collectors; and Mrs. Goldhandler was talking to nobody at all.

"Not even Mrs. Fesser?" I inquired.

"Not even Mrs. Fesser," said Boyd.

Peter Quat looked grave. "You mean he won't talk to Klebanoff?"

"Oh, yes. He's *always* in to Klebanoff."

We had been through tight times before, with such switchboard orders. Sooner or later things would loosen up, and the calls would go through again. The Goldhandlers, in the manner of the rich, were just slow pay. When a cash bind came along — as upon dropping forty-eight thousand dollars, for they had decided at that birthday breakfast to cut their loss and sell at once — the paying could slow yet more. But never, since I had come to work, had they yet shut off Mrs. Fesser.

Mrs. Fesser was an interior decorator specializing in antiques, and the penthouse was wholly furnished with bargains she had picked up from a liquidation of a big estate on Long Island. I had often wondered about those furnishings. No matter how much money Goldhandler was raking in, he hadn't been doing it for long. How on earth could they have amassed such treasures? Simple answer: Mrs. Fesser had sold them the stuff on credit. Putting down very little hard cash, paying off a bit at a time, the Goldhandlers could live in these princely surroundings. Such things were possible in the depression. Mrs. Fesser kept urging more and more antique purchases on them, because the pieces could be bought so reasonably, and were such marvellous investments.

In fact, so Boyd once told me, a bank owned the apartment building, which had gone bankrupt (those were rough times, friends) and to inveigle a tenant into that quadruplex tower, the bank had given the Goldhandlers an enormous "concession" on the lease, I believe a whole year. In short, the Goldhandlers were really arriviste ex-paupers, camping out precariously in the ruins of other people's wealth; and the penthouse was a ploika, after all, on the most fantastic imaginable Aladdin's lamp scale, with Mrs. Fesser as genie; except that — a crucial exception — Mama never bought anything except for all cash.

This Mrs. Fesser looked something like a genie, and seemed to come and go like one. She always wore a turban with a long feather. The turbans varied in color and shape; but there was inevitably this huge plume slanting up and away, lending her an air of great dash. And she was always smiling, always bubbling, and she always talked with apostolic authority. Cutting off Mrs. Fesser was a distress signal that gravelled us all.

To wrap up that stock-market episode, it turned out that the Goldhandlers sold at the low point of a sag. Before the market closed that same day the stock recovered two points. Next day it struggled back up to the price she had paid. In two weeks it did climb eight points on a big navy order. Mrs. Goldhandler's tip was accurate, but it required more staying power than they had. That incident, and a few others I observed at the penthouse — for neither of them could ever quite lay off the market — burned a fear of Wall Street into my soul. I have missed all the bull markets, keeping my money virtually in my sock, while my friends have made fortunes, lecturing me in vain about how inflation was shrinking my dollars. Lately my friends have been fretting and borrowing, and having strokes and ulcers, and selling off their Bentleys and Caribbean condominiums; and you still can't get me to buy all those nice dirt-cheap stocks with my shrunken dollars.

As for Klebanoff, the Alaskan mining engineer, to whom Goldhandler was *always* in, he comes into the story later. Right now I have to tell the double catastrophe that burst on Goldhandler, with remarkable consequences for me.

Goldhandler had gone to Boston, where *Johnny, Drop Your Gun* was trying out. Boyd and I were hard at it early one afternoon patching up a *War and Peace* script, using Tolstoy snippets from several cut-up books that lay about the office, plus some Quat and Goodkind dialogue typed on loose pages. Peter had not yet come in to work. The house telephone buzzed. Boyd answered it, and said in surprise, "Mr. Barrymore? Which Mr. Barrymore? But Mr. Goldhandler is out of town. . . . I see. Very well." He hung up and said to me, with a puzzled frown, "It's John Barrymore. He's coming up in the elevator. The doorman says he seems upset."

"What about?"

Boyd shrugged, and lit a Melachrino. "Go down and meet him, Dave. Tell him the boss isn't here. Feel him out a bit. Then I'll come and handle it, whatever it is."

"Okay."

As I trotted downstairs I heard the elevator arrive and the doorbell ring. I opened the door, and there stood Mr. Hyde.

Mr. Hyde to the life, I tell you, stooped over in a black chesterfield, and a black homburg tipped to one side, his hands curved in claws, his eyes bloodshot and murderous, his lips writhing. "I have come to kill him," said Barrymore, hoarsely, calmly, and distinctly.

"Who?" I stammered.

"The Jew Goldhandler," said Barrymore. "The Ebrew Jew Goldhandler." He stepped in and closed the door behind him, then faced me, breathing powerful whiskey fumes.

"He isn't here," I said, "he's in Boston."

"I have no quarrel with you, boy," said Barrymore. "Stand aside, and live."

Again I said, "But he isn't here, sir, honestly. May I ask what the trouble is?"

With a sweep of an arm, he knocked me aside. "He cannot hide from me," he said. "His hour has come." Stooped in that black coat, grinning maniacally, he went thumping up the stairs. I followed him, but he moved fast and got to the office ahead of me. When I came in he was approaching the desk, behind which sat Boyd, staring at him with some concern.

"I am going to kill you, Goldhandler," said Barrymore. "Make a short shrift, my fingers long for your throat." The talons wriggled in the air.

Boyd stood up, saying, "I'm not Mr. Goldhandler, Mr. Barrymore. I'm Boyd. I work for him, and he's in Boston, so —"

Exactly like Hyde in the movies — this whole thing was eerily like a movie, what with the actor's resonant diction and theatrical gestures, though it couldn't have been more real and frightening — Barrymore went scuttling like a huge black crab around the desk, and grabbed Boyd by the throat with both hands.

"You degenerate pen-pusher! How DARE you plot and plan and propose that the Barrymores be purveyors of *excrement?*" He shook Boyd by the throat. "Promotors of *bowel movements?*" Another shake. Boyd was holding Barrymore's hands, trying to pry them off his neck. If you ask why I didn't intervene, all this was happening in seconds, and I was stupefied. "Hawkers of *feces?* Costermongers of *shit?* Down on your knees, and DIE!"

At this Boyd pulled off those claws from his throat and said, "Really, Mr. Barrymore, I'm not Mr. Goldhandler. I work for him. I'm Boyd. You remember, he's much fatter, and has a tooth missing."

Barrymore peered into Boyd's face, blinked several times, and straightened up into a semblance of Jekyll. "Quite right. You are not the Jew Goldhandler. I owe you an apology. I am slightly nearsighted, the ravages of age. I beg you to forgive me."

"That's all right," said Boyd. "Can I offer you some black coffee?"

"No, thank you. Where is your employer, Boyd? It is extremely important that I kill him."

"Mr. Barrymore, he's out of town with his show. In Boston."

Barrymore shook his head as though to clear it, and blinked. "On the road? In Boston?"

"Yes, sir."

"Well, what a pity." Barrymore sank into an armchair. "That is very disappointing." Leaning his head on a hand, he fell asleep.

"Whew!" Boyd dropped into the swivel chair. "How do you suppose he found out?"

"Did he hurt you?"

"Not at all. It was stage throttling," said Boyd. "Not that it wasn't a scare. I'll have to phone the boss. He'll take it hard." He looked around at the mutilated copies of *War and Peace.* "All that work for nothing. One of those idiots at Ex-Lax must have talked."

Barrymore opened his eyes. "Boston, you said? The Ebrew Jew Goldhandler is in Boston? Boston is a terrible place to die. Which hotel is he staying at, if I may ask?"

"I truly don't know, Mr. Barrymore, I'm waiting for a call from him this evening," said Boyd. "Perhaps you would care for a drink?"

"I shall return to my hotel," said Barrymore, "throw a change of linen in a bag, and go to Boston to destroy the man."

"Would you like me to call a cab for you?"

"My limousine is waiting," said Barrymore.

He tried to stand, and couldn't make it. We helped him down the stairs and into the elevator. He was pleasant and even genial, saying he needed something to eat before proceeding to Boston to kill Goldhandler, so he would lunch at the Players Club. He insisted, in a charming courtly way, that Boyd join him. He wanted to drown the inadvertence of almost strangling him in a bottle of good claret. All this happened in the elevator, and we assisted him out to the street. A large black limousine parked at the corner started toward us, but a taxicab swooped in front of it and drew up at the canopy. Out of that cab stepped Lou Blue.

"Boyd, you son of a bitch," said Blue, not recognizing Barrymore, whose black hat was down over his face, "where's my script? And what the hell are you doing?"

"I called the messenger service three times, Lou," said Boyd. "The program's up there in an envelope, waiting." That was the truth. The envelope lay in the foyer on the settee.

Blue went into the building as we were boosting Barrymore into the limousine. "Oh, God," said Boyd, "*War and Peace* is all over the place. Don't let him go upstairs, Dave. Get him into the living room and keep him there. I'll be right up."

"No, you won't," said Barrymore. "I throttled you, and you must drink claret with me."

I scampered into the building and saw the door of the elevator to the penthouse close. I rang and rang, but the lights kept flashing upward to the top. Then the elevator came down for me.

"Where is he?" I shouted at the poor maid who opened the door. I could see the envelope still lying there in the foyer.

She stammered, shrinking away from me, "He, he go up to de offus."

Galloping up the stairs, I charged into the office, and came on Lou Blue sitting in Goldhandler's swivel chair holding our patchwork *War and Peace* script, staring around at all the copies of the book on the desk, and crying. Big tears were rolling down the man's cheeks.

"Look at this! He isn't human," Blue sobbed. "He's something terrible. He's a monster. He would sell his grandmother for dog-meat. People like him shouldn't be allowed. Look at how he lied to me! And I believed him. He's a horrible thing, like a vampire."

"Mr. Blue, whatever you may be thinking, you're wrong," I said. "Mr. Goldhandler doesn't know anything about this. He's in Boston."

"What are you saying?" He brushed away tears with both fists. "Sure he's in Boston, but so what? Don't you go lying too, kid. Isn't this his office? Don't you work for him?"

I told him, making it up frantically as I went along, that Boyd and I were the traitors. We were taking advantage of the boss's absence to do a *War and Peace* audition, hoping to sell it to Ex-Lax and screw Goldhandler. We deserved to be fired, but I hoped he would take pity on us and not tell Goldhandler. As Blue listened skeptically, drying his tears, in walked Boyd, carrying the envelope. "Now, Lou, all this is easy to explain, however peculiar it may look, and here's your script," he said.

"Well, I'm certainly willing to listen," said Lou Blue. "Go ahead, Boyd. Explain it."

Naturally, Boyd told a different — and much better — story. It had not occurred to him that I would attempt a Goldhandler-scale lie, and with Blue's eyes on me, there was no way I could warn him. Ex-Lax had given Goldhandler no rest, said Boyd, pestering him for a *War and Peace* show. In desperation he had at last ordered us to put together a rotten script, so as to sabotage the idea and protect Lou Blue. All Lou had to do was read the script to see how bad it was. The man who had just left was John Barrymore himself. He had rejected the project, once for all. Goldhandler's plan had worked brilliantly, and the Lou Blue show was safe at last.

Now there was a story worthy of a disciple of Harry Goldhandler. It might even have worked, but for my own amateur fibbing. As it was, Boyd was just blundering deeper into a quagmire with every word.

"Well, you are both pretty good liars," said Lou Blue when Boyd finished, "but not like Harry Goldhandler. He is the biggest liar I have ever known. It frightens me to think what a bad man you work for. Now I want you to tell him something. Eddie Conn has got a great new classy idea for my show. Who doesn't know that Ex-Lax is out for class? Why didn't Goldhandler think up a classy idea for me, instead of trying to stab me in the back with *War and Peace?*"

"I'm sorry you don't believe me," said Boyd. "I'll swear to it, Lou."

Lou Blue picked up his script and walked to the office door. "Eddie's idea is to do *Gulliver's Travels*. None of these hokey old jokes off the cards any more. I'll be Gulliver. I'll have all kinds of hilarious adventures with giants, and midgets, and Japs, and Chinks, and like that."

Oh Lord, I thought, Hansel and Gretel again.

"Lou," said Boyd, "you can easily get another sponsor, even if Ex-Lax lets you go. You have good ratings. Don't do *Gulliver's Travels*. It's a stupid idea."

Lou Blue paused, his hand on the door, and looked at me. "You're just a kid. Get away from him! Get away from these cards!" He shook the script envelope at Boyd. "You just tell him I'm switching to Eddie Conn. Our lawyers can handle the details."

Exit Lou Blue.

Boyd and I looked disconsolately at each other over half a dozen ruined copies of *War and Peace*.

"I'd better take the next train to Boston," said Boyd. "He forgot to pack some pills. I can bring him the pills."

Boyd departed forthwith for Grand Central, leaving me drudging listlessly at an audition script. Peter Quat didn't appear until almost dinner time.

"Where in the lousy hell have you been?" I snapped.

"Moving out of my father's house," said Peter. "We had the fight of our lives. I'm quitting Goldhandler."

Well, as the fellow says, it never rains but it pours. Peter was impatient with my account of the Barrymore and Blue disasters. He paced around the office, making faces like a drunken monkey and talking a blue streak. Two of his short stories had at last been accepted, and by two very prestigious magazines, the *Antioch Review* and the *Kenyon Review!* The two letters had come in the same morning mail. He had rushed over to his father's office, to say he would leave Goldhandler now and concentrate on literature. He had saved some money. He asked only to live at home until he got on his feet as a writer. But when Dr. Quat heard that Peter had gotten eleven dollars for one story and nothing for the other but a free subscription, he had laughed and told Peter to stick with Goldhandler for a while yet. Peter had defied his father and stormed out.

"I'll move into a fleabag hotel or into the YMCA," Peter fumed, "but I'm quitting this madhouse, that's for sure. TONIGHT! *War*

and Peace finished me. What a fraud! I'm glad it's off. I never want
to look at those cards again."

"Peter, don't be a fool," I said. "Work to the end of the week and
get paid. One thing you need now is money."

"Where will I sleep tonight?"

"Come home with me. Sleep in Lee's room. She's visiting her future in-laws in Miami Beach."

Peter groaned, "We'll see. What are you working on?"

About midnight Boyd called from Boston. "Is Peter there? Put him
on."

"I'm on," said Peter, at the switchboard.

"Peter, were you with us when we did Lord Piffle?"

"Lord Piffle? Sure. I did the draft with Eddie Conn."

"Okay. Dig out Lord Piffle, and read the scripts over, both of you."

"What's up, Boyd?" I asked, on the other phone. He sounded
ebullient.

"He's done it!" Boyd exclaimed, laughing joyously. "He's pulled it
out! He's the bloody champ. But I can't go into it now. Just read
over Lord Piffle, and start thinking about Leslie Howard."

Peter and I stared at each other across the office, and we said with
ludicrous simultaneity, "Leslie *Howard?*"

And Boyd did go into it. He was bursting with the news, with
relief, and with adulation for Goldhandler.

The reader has seen old Leslie Howard movies on television, and
knows what a charmer this suave British star was; not flamboyant
like Barrymore, but talk about class! He was then at the height of his
vogue. Like many an actor whose forte is light comedy, he had at-
tempted Shakespeare; nothing less than *King Lear,* which had opened
in Boston, and was about to close down after bad notices and poor
business. On getting Boyd's calamitous report, Goldhandler had
clapped on hat and overcoat, had trudged in a snowstorm to the theatre where *King Lear* was playing, and had talked with Leslie Howard backstage about going on the radio. The star, so heavily out of
pocket, had been receptive. At the disclosure that the sponsor might
be a laxative, he shrugged. As long as he didn't have to read the commercials, he said, what did it matter who paid for the show?

Thereupon Goldhandler had rushed back to the hotel and telephoned a Mr. Menlow, the president of Ex-Lax, to tell him that he

could get Leslie Howard to replace Lou Blue. This was a lucky shot. Menlow was such an admirer of Howard that he had put some money in the *Lear* production, and still insisted that Leslie Howard was a great Lear.

"It's in the bag," Boyd exulted. "Howard wants it, the sponsor wants it, and the money will be fantastic. Now all we need is a show. The boss thinks Lord Piffle will work fine. So get hot, boys, and update a couple of scripts."

The Lord Piffle programs had been hectographed in purple on a slick paper that had turned brownish. The jokes were as aged as the script, and the idea was just as aged: a silly-ass lord and an impudent butler trading wheezes, nothing more.

"Who on earth were Rawlins and Stone, Peter?"

"Oh, a couple of British vaudevillians. They did a few weeks on sustaining and flopped."

"No wonder. The stuff's garbage."

Peter swept both arms around at the office. "It's all garbage."

"Goldhandler's forgotten," I insisted, "how crude this material is."

"Oh, what does he care? Christ, he could do something with Leslie Howard, too. Something Noël Cowardish, an international jewel thief working the ocean liners or something, charming the rich ladies, stealing their bracelets and their panties. Anything like that, something light, something gay. If he'd once forget about these damned cards! He's a *good writer!*"

"Peter," I said, "let's try that."

"Try what? The jewel thief?"

I rolled a sheet of paper into the typewriter. "Let's just draft it out. No jokes. No cards. You dictate. Let's see what happens. Lord Piffle can't work. It's nothing."

"Dave, it's one o'clock in the morning." Peter sounded peevish, but his face took on life. "Anyway, I don't give a shit about any of this, you know that — Goldhandler, Leslie Howard, Ex-Lax, the whole nightmare. You do it if you want to. He should narrate it, Howard himself. It should be like the memoirs of Raffles, just dramatize the high points."

"Are you sleepy, Peter?"

"No."

"Come on, then. I can't do it myself. Lord Piffle is worthless, and I'm not quitting Goldhandler."

Reluctantly, Peter said, "Well, I'll help you get started, then I'm passing out on that couch, and when you're ready to go home, wake me."

At three o'clock Peter was still dictating, pacing in his stocking feet, in his hunched posture of concentration. We had both pitched in, and the idea of a competing beautiful woman thief was mine, but Peter had done much of the draft; all very obvious stuff, but better than Lord Piffle, and even — I thought — with a bit of class to it.

"Liebowitz," I interrupted him, "let's go out for a cup of coffee."

He stopped in his tracks, looked at me, and broke out in a wry laugh. "Why, you serpentine little bastard."

We ate at Lindy's, then went back to the penthouse; worked till dawn, and finished the script without a card joke in it.

68

"Apiece?"

"WHAT have you two fuckers been up to?" Goldhandler grated as Peter and I came into the office. He picked the script off his desk and rattled it at us. "What is all this titter-titter crap? Where's Lord Piffle? Leslie Howard will be here in half an hour."

He was in his purple cashmere bathrobe, unshaven and haggard. He had returned on a midnight train, almost unconscious with fatigue, and had gone straight to bed. It was now about one in the afternoon. Peter was sullenly silent, so I tried to explain what we had done, and why. Goldhandler's face clouded and he kept glancing at his watch. "All right, all right," he broke in, "let me have the Piffle stuff."

He headed for the bathroom, with the faded hectographed scripts and our draft. "Tell my wife I want to talk to her." She came up and, not seeing him, went straight into the bathroom. They were that close, and he was usually that pressed for time.

Boyd had telephoned my home, just before he left to pick up Leslie Howard at Grand Central, to summon us to the penthouse quick-march. He had read our Leslie Howard draft and was appalled. "It's not radio. Where are the laughs? And where do you get off ignoring instructions?"

"Is it any good?" I asked.

"Oh, it's slick and facile, sort of fake Noël Coward. What good is that? I don't want to be around when he reads it."

Mrs. Goldhandler came out of the bathroom with the Piffle scripts and went downstairs, giving us in passing the look of contempt with which she would speak of Eddie Conn. Goldhandler followed her, slinging our draft on his desk. Not long afterward Boyd arrived with

Leslie Howard, who greeted us with a shy smile and a soft "Hello, there." Casually dignified, his chalk-stripe black suit unmistakably Savile Row, his sensitive long face calm and slightly wary, the slender blond star did almost make you feel in the presence of a lord. Goldhandler came hurrying in, smooth-shaven with some bloody nicks, wearing his double-breasted dark blue "bar-mitzva suit," as he called it, intended to make him look as unlike a gagman as possible. It was not an impenetrable disguise. After the pleasantries he sat down in his swivel chair and lit a cigar with long flaming puffs.

"What we do here," he said at last to Leslie Howard, "as you may have heard, is create radio programs with three or four audience laughs per minute."

"Your reputation goes before you," Leslie Howard said amiably.

Goldhandler acknowledged this with a gracious nod. "Coming from you, that's something. There has never been a star of your calibre on the radio, you know. For guest spots, yes. For a show, no. Just vaudevillians, who live or die, from minute to minute, with the laughs they get. Nobody who can sustain a comic idea of any quality, a *Scarlet Pimpernel*, a *Berkeley Square*."

Leslie Howard's face subtly hardened, and he made a brusque gesture. "What do you have in mind?" He had not come to hear a gagman praise him. It shut Goldhandler up. He puffed at his cigar, looked at Howard through half-closed eyes, and got on his feet.

"We can give you your three or four laughs a minute," he said breezily, beginning to pace. "That's no problem. But what would you say to a truly bold departure? A show without a studio audience, without those moronic yapping laughs? A comedy of manners, light as champagne, in your inimitable farceur style?"

Peter and I exchanged a swift glance.

"Let's say there's this elegant Lord Algernon Throop, crossing the Atlantic aboard the *Queen Mary* in a first-class suite . . ."

My God, I thought, he's cornered, he's utterly desperate, he can't think of anything!

". . . as charming and suave a young nobleman as you'd want to meet," Goldhandler went on, "only as it happens he's not a nobleman at all, but an international jewel thief."

The actor's mouth twitched in amusement. Whether he was smiling with pleasure at the notion, or with disdain at the banality of it, who could say?

"Let me read you a page or two," said Goldhandler, picking up our script, "of a little thing we've thrown together. Stop me any time you'd rather hear something cruder, or as we say in the gagman trade" — here he grinned at Howard — "more on the nose, up the alley, meat and potatoes, sure pop."

"Go ahead," said Howard, laughing at Goldhandler's disarming self-mockery. Howard did not stop him at all. Goldhandler warmed to our lines, and even did elephantine imitations of Howard's mannerisms which made the star chuckle. When he finished, Howard rubbed his mouth thoughtfully. "Ah, does this — ah, this laxative sponsor — like it?"

"Whatever Leslie Howard cares to do, any sponsor in America will jump at," said Goldhandler, "but I need your okay first. Otherwise it's too fresh, too innovative, for the kind of minds I deal with in radio."

"Why, it seems all right. As you say, quite light. It might do. I'm not disappointed."

At this foaming British enthusiasm, Goldhandler leaped up. "Then shall we go and talk to them now? They're waiting to hear how this meeting went."

"Why not?" Howard stood. Goldhandler lumbered to him, and seized him around the waist. Howard had to lean his willowy body away from him, holding a cigarette high in two fingers to keep from burning him, smiling in embarrassment at this close contact; and also, it seemed to me, at the irrepressible animal magnetism of Harry Goldhandler.

"We'll kill them, Leslie!" Goldhandler hugged him tight and released him. "We'll knock them dead, and start a new era of quality in this tawdry medium!"

The switchboard buzzed, and Boyd plugged in. "It's Mrs. Fesser," he told the boss, "for Mrs. Goldhandler."

"*Put her through*," roared Goldhandler, "and let's get going, Boyd."

When Peter and I were alone he said, "That script we did is thin crap. What's the matter with Howard?"

"Peter," I said on a heady surge of self-confidence, "we're going to ask for a raise."

He only blinked at me.

"I mean it. Howard wants the radio money. He was agreeably surprised that it wasn't a string of old gags. He's going for it, so Ex-Lax will go for it. Class! Peter, Goldhandler will get a fortune from Ex-Lax."

"By Christ, you're a pushy bastard, aren't you? It's that Bronx up-bringing. All right. What do we ask for?"

Now remember, this was deep in the depression. At the time he was getting forty a week, I was making thirty, and it was good money for both of us. "A hundred for the team," I said, "split any way you say."

Peter shook his head at me, half in exasperation, half in admiration.

"Okay, if you want to try, go ahead. If you get it, we'll split fifty-fifty." Peter slipped into his shoes and put on his jacket. "Only I don't want to be around, Davey. You handle it. A hundred! Christ, if you pull it off we can even rent an apartment, can't we? I can get some real work done."

About an hour later Boyd telephoned. "Well, Menlow danced around the room. I still say you two had some crust, but anyway, it's in. Congratulations. The boss is on his way home. I'm going to bed, I haven't slept for two days."

Goldhandler strode victoriously into the office, puffing on a half-smoked cigar. "Where's Finkelstein?" he inquired with a high-spirited grin.

"He had to go home."

"Presumptuous pricks, both of you." The tone was admiring. He sat down, rocking in the swivel chair. "Thanks."

"It was all in the way you presented it."

He nodded, still savoring the triumph. "No, you're a good team. You made a hell of a contribution."

What an opening! "I'm afraid I can't keep Peter, though," I said, "unless you give us a raise." Goldhandler's happy look faded into a cold hard stare. "He wants us to get an apartment together," I rushed on. "He's had a fight with his father. Right now he's staying with me. He's had two short stories accepted. I had to talk him into working on this jewel thief thing."

Goldhandler knew very well of Quat's literary aspirations. "What magazines?"

"*Kenyon Review* and *Antioch Review*."

"Ha! I had stories in both of those when I was still in college. They pay in glazed farts. Nobody reads them."

"He's really ready to quit, however."

Long silence. Goldhandler inquired soberly, "What are you two asking?"

"A hundred."

He opened wide eyes, then squinted at me through the smoke. "Apiece?"

My stomach knotted, but in the tone and with the self-assurance of The Green Cousin, I replied, "Of course, apiece." It was a pure Mama moment. He had said the word first, I hadn't.

Frowning, Goldhandler picked up his phone and jabbed at an intercom button. "Come up, I want to talk to you." Mrs. Goldhandler vaguely bleated on the phone. He barked, "I know Blue's lawyers will be here any minute," and he went into the bathroom.

She came trotting in, beaming at me as though I were Joan Crawford or Aldous Huxley. "Isn't it lovely about Leslie Howard?" she carolled, heading for the bathroom.

When she emerged in a few minutes I got the Eddie Conn glare, and she slammed the office door.

"It won't do," Goldhandler said, wiping his hands on a towel as he came out. "Suppose you up and decide to go back to law school? Or Peter takes it in his head to quit and write a novel? For that salary you'll have to sign a two-year contract, both of you."

I could scarcely believe it. As nonchalantly as I could, I said, "I'll have to talk to Peter."

Goldhandler heavily nodded. "Yes, you do that. He's a talented asshole, but too unpredictable. As for you —" He sized me up ruefully. "I don't know. Beneath that yeshiva boy innocence, there's a broad streak of ghetto cunning." He looked at me in silence, then ambled to me and hugged me as he had Leslie Howard. "I think a hell of a lot of you, Liebowitz," he said, and he went out to talk to Lou Blue's lawyers.

Peter was stunned. "*Apiece?* Wow!"

He talked no more of quitting. Goldhandler's lawyer drew up a contract full of hooks, but Peter laughed them off. I pointed out to Peter, for instance, that by the wording Goldhandler could claim to own any stories, plays, or novels we might write while under contract.

"Look, Davey, who cares? We'll sign the goddamn thing, and then do as we please."

Peter Quat's attitude toward contracts has not changed to this day. That's it, and it makes for problems. Wives can have writs out against him, publishers may be suing him, the IRS and New York State may be after him for back taxes — in fact, all those things are happening at the moment — but he pays my office charges punctually, no matter what, and leaves all that to me. He is the fun-lover, and I am the fixer. With that "Apiece" coup I won his confidence, and it has not wavered. I more or less respect him as an artist, if a horribly screwed-up one; he more or less respects me as a man of business and law; and that equation has held since "Apiece."

Peter took a vindictive joy in letting his father know. He dropped unannounced into the doctor's office. The poor receptionist, his mistress and doormat, let him walk over her, ahead of the waiting patients. Dr. Quat congratulated him, took credit for convincing him to stay with Goldhandler, and invited him to return home. Peter responded that he would never come back; but he would go on contributing to the rent if his father needed it. Dr. Quat, "vastly humiliated," declined the offer. Such was Peter's account of the meeting.

I felt sorry for Dr. Quat, then and always. He was an eminent surgeon and a thoughtful, decent man. Peter was and is a handful. His portrait of the doctor father in *Deflowering Sarah* is one of the rougher passages in the Quat version of the American Jewish experience. I heard that Dr. Quat talked about it on his deathbed, and said Peter had never been a happy boy, and he bore him no ill will. I heard this from the doctor who attended him.

"Are you crazy?" Mom said. "Why move out? Now you can really save up money! Why pay it to some stupid landlord? Listen to me for once. You have a nice room, you can eat here all you want to, it's home. Don't go into partnership with that Peter Quat! Partnership means only trouble."

"It's so silly," Lee said. "Bernie lived at home until he finished his residency."

As usual, Pop let the others talk first. He just listened with his tough business look to my account of the Leslie Howard deal, and my negotiation with Goldhandler; which Mom kept interrupting, to say it was obvious I ought to be a lawyer. Then Pop asked, regarding me with softened pride and concern, "You'll come home Friday nights?"

"Yes, I will."

He nodded. This place would remain my home, he said, but he would not accept any rent money from me hereafter. My own feelings, upon informing my family that I was moving out on my own, on a salary of a hundred a week, I remember as though it had just happened. Never since have I had quite such a sense of power, of manhood, of setting myself free. There is only one first flight out of the nest.

Yet in my rosiest fantasies I had not dreamed of where I would alight.

69

I Arrive

MR. Lucius Horan telephoned us one afternoon when I was at the switchboard. "Would you fellows be interested," he whined, "in April House?"

Through the office window I could see the sign close by, that sign to which I had been drawing nearer year by year. "Why, we can't afford that," I said, as my pulse thumped hard.

"Well, this woman is crazy, she's asking Chinese telephone numbers, but she has to go to Hollywood for a while, and she's very anxious not to leave her suite empty. She's a divorcée and needs money. Take a look at it."

"Okay, we will."

Horan was a little whiny gray-headed man holed up in a tiny office over a kosher delicatessen on Seventy-second Street. He subleased furnished apartments. Seldom have I met a man who so hated what he was doing. The human race, said Lucius Horan, were basically swine. They fell into two great groupings, landlord swine and tenant swine. The landlords were greedy swine, who quoted their rental prices in "Chinese telephone numbers." The tenants were dirty thieving swine, who left apartments wrecked, welshed on the rent, stole towels and cutlery, and passed bad checks. Still, that was his living, and in offering us flats he was pushing us toward luxury. The surprise was how cheap even the fancy places were, in those depression days. One Friday afternoon, returning to my own home, I realized with a little shock that Peter and I wouldn't consider renting it. Too small and dark, the furniture too old-fashioned. Pop was not making anything near our combined salaries of two hundred a week.

We saw the divorcée only once, when we closed the deal and she handed over the keys; a raddled blonde, very Hollywood in her talk, and inclined to show a lot of pretty leg. Her face was thickly painted, and her tailored gray suit had the football-player shoulders made modish by Joan Crawford. The apartment faced south. The sun shone straight in on her copious jewelry, and she sparkled like an art-deco chandelier.

"I'm being awfully nice to you boys," she said in a gravelly voice. She had come down from a hundred thirty to a hundred a month. When Jan and I stayed in that suite recently, I paid a hundred fifty dollars *a night.* (On the other hand, we don't have twenty-five percent unemployment nowadays.) The lady was in an almighty hurry to go out west.

"Remember," she said, "I'll be back June thirtieth, and you'll have to find yourself another place."

That short inconvenient chunk of time was the reason she was being so obliging. But Peter and I had fallen for the place, and Peter was ready to pay her price. I did the bargaining. Morris Elfenbein would have been proud of me.

"I will never be without a partner from the Bronx hereafter," said Peter, when she departed, and we sat there in our April House apartment, still scarcely believing we belonged in it. With that edge of snotty condescension, the usual Quat note about Jews, there was also a respectful, even wistful, undertone. A complicated fellow, old Peter.

The place had its drawbacks: only one bedroom and one bath. I had not shared a room since, back in Aldus Street, Lee and I had slept together on a davenport. There was no place to work. Peter and I had to set up our typewriters on card tables. Nor were there any bookshelves. The only evidence we ever found that the lady could read was a copy of the *Hollywood Reporter* lining the garbage pail. We bought cheap bookshelves and put them in a big gloomy useless foyer.

What then was so hot about the place? Well, the view, to start with; it was on a high floor, and we saw the downtown skyscrapers — great gray spikes against the clouds by day, towers of golden light under the moon and stars — much as we did from the Goldhandler office; except of course that we were *inside April House,* a few floors below the sign. An exalting thought!

The living-room furnishings were starkly modern, as in Manhattan penthouses in the movies. Let me tell you about just one armchair. It was big and deep, with severely squared-off lines, and it was upholstered in what looked like peach-dyed mink. It hit you in the eye as you entered the place; so soft, so luxurious, so modern, so obviously waiting for Astaire and Rogers to come waltzing in! I was a goner as soon as I laid eyes on that peach mink armchair. I had to have that apartment. I'd have paid the woman full price, if she had held out, just for the privilege of sinking into that peach mink armchair whenever I pleased, until June thirtieth.

Soon after we moved in, we encountered Skip Lasser in the lobby. *Johnny, Drop Your Gun* had left Boston to go on to Philadelphia, and he was back in New York for the day. We invited him up to see our suite. "A lot nicer than my place," he commented, with genuine envy, and so it was. Our suite was a real bargain. Long ago we had visited Morrie Abbott's flat, which Lasser had sublet: one small room and bath, looking east at other tall hotels. "Perfect place to have parties. You boys are in luck." He did not renew his offer to introduce us to showgirls. I had been haunted for weeks by thoughts of the singing girls in his show, but he had weightier matters on his mind, no doubt.

Important people like Lasser, and women almost as beautiful as those singing girls, passed through the April House lobby all the time. From the Orchid Grill, dance music drifted day and night. To come from my parents' side-street home, or even from Goldhandler's penthouse, into this posh lobby, to smell that magic April House smell — gone now, gone forever, obliterated by the ubiquitous Sheraton lobby odor, but strong in my nostrils as I write, the spicy odor of Manhattan wealth, Manhattan fashion, and young love in Manhattan — well, it was to have made it, to be on top of the world, to have arrived at last in the Goldena Medina. In all my life, I myself have never come any closer to seizing the ploika.

Almost as remarkable as the way I had risen from Aldus Street to April House was the rapidity with which I became used to it, though of course, there was an ongoing low power hum of self-satisfaction in my spirit. For Peter Quat it was less of a change. April House had been in sight from his bedroom since childhood, and Dr. Quat was a man of taste and means. But now Peter was living in luxury by the sweat of his own brow, not his father's. That was a leap, too. What a lordly sensation it was, when for the first time we bought orchestra seats for $3.30 apiece, instead of our usual standing room, and walked down the aisles past the standees for the new Kaufman and Hart comedy, and sat among the old gray fat cats and their be-furred and be-gemmed women! Or when we went into restaurants like Dinty Moore's or Henri's, and ordered up what we pleased, and not on Harry Goldhandler's tab! That was the life, let me tell you.

Having a place of our own subtly changed our status at the penthouse. We were no longer of the inner circle. We would taxi or walk to the penthouse around noon, and leave for dinner. Sometimes we came back for a night session, sometimes not. We worked better, away from the joke files. We found ourselves writing fresh, usable lines. The switchboard was not buzzing, Goldhandler and Boyd were not hurrying in and out, and we were not getting called to meals, or summoned to play Ping-Pong or Monopoly with a weary boss seeking a respite, or with whiz-kid sons wanting victims. Before Leslie Howard went on the air we managed to draft several episodes in advance, and even so Peter progressed faster in his literary labors. And of course we plugged away at first drafts of the joke shows as before.

Never think, though, that Harry Goldhandler sold our apprentice work for thousands, and was merely throwing us the bones, even at a hundred apiece. Whatever we did — Lou Blue, an audition, a Howard show — he would tell us what to write. Then he would take our draft and redictate it start to finish. He was the master, he was the source, he was the funny man, and he was the final editor. Even the jewel-thief drafts, including our first effort, he brightened. His "Noël Coward" dialogue was much better than ours. He didn't need Peter and me to write that stuff, and my demand for a raise had been brash and risky. But his besetting problem was time. We saved him time. Big as our raise was, I think we gave him value for his money. His attitude remained warm, and we were still interchangeably Finkelstein and Liebowitz. But to the rest of the family our name was mud — or should I say, Eddie Conn? Karl and Sigmund turned cool. I'm not sure Mrs. Goldhandler ever smiled at us again, once we moved to April House. We had committed lèse-majesté by even desiring freedom from the presence of Balzac, not to mention our swinish greed for money.

As for the unfathomable Boyd, he perhaps became a shade more distant. Maybe not. We never knew what Goldhandler paid Boyd, but it must have been plenty. The whole machine would have ground to a smoking ruined stop without Boyd. Yet he remained ever-present or on call, vanishing to some side-street brownstone hole he slept in for a few odd hours, but otherwise still eating all his meals there, shadowing Goldhandler wherever he went, covering for him, and even responding patiently to the grandparents' handy-man orders. He worshipped Goldhandler, he was totally committed to the adoration of one man, and when we left the household, I think we lost Boyd.

The desk clerk handed me an envelope with the return address:

> *Johnny Drop Your Gun*
> Winter Garden, New York

Inside were two opening-night tickets, first row center, mezzanine, perfect seats for viewing a musical; with a card clipped to them, *Compliments of S. K. Lasser.* I was amazed. We had not seen or heard from Lasser since his visit to our suite. Goldhandler had gone to Philadelphia, and had returned seething again over "fly shit" credits on the theatre sign. But the show looked like a hit. Dr. Schneidbaitzim was a high point. Lasser had wanted to cut it in rehearsal, but he had desisted, seeing Lahr get roars with it night after night.

"Hey, mezzanine! Great!" Peter exclaimed, when I brought the tickets up.

"Why do you suppose we rate, Peter?"

"Who knows? Maybe he wants us to joke up his next libretto," sneered Peter, "so he can put up *our* names in fly shit."

He resumed clattering with two fingers at a short-story typescript. Peter has turned out a million words, maybe, and he never has learned to type. I can do eighty clean words a minute; Goodkind words, alas, not high-priced Quat prose.

Next day the hotel phone rang. Lasser wanted to know whether we had received the tickets.

"I left a note in your box, Mr. Lasser," I said "We'd like to pay for them."

"Nonsense. Now, I haven't forgotten about introducing you to showgirls. I'll be up in a minute."

Peter and I leaped around like crazy men. We were very young, both of us. Lasser came in and told us that he had put our names down for the opening-night cast party on the stage. "They'll all be there. You'll meet every last girl in the show."

"That's just marvellous," Peter said, in a congested voice.

Peter suffers from a kind of sex dementia, as you may have gathered from his writings. To some extent he has turned it into art, but it has driven him into quagmires, clinical depressions, narrow escapes through windows, four divorces, a paternity suit, and a Section Eleven bankruptcy. Peter has paid for his fun, plenty. He may remind you of my Cousin Harold, but once Cousin Harold married his nurse and settled down, that was the end of it. You never saw such a hearth-hugger and TV-watcher as Cousin Harold. I don't think Cousin Harold has so much as smelled another woman's perfume since, except for the mothers of his teenage kooks. Peter Quat started late, but turned into a perpetual Cousin Harold. I don't pretend to understand these quirks. It's just how people are.

"The only trouble is," said Lasser, "that cast parties are a madhouse. I'm having a little private party afterwards for a few friends. Bert Lahr, Moss Hart, Johnny Mercer, just a dozen or so people. I wonder, could I hold the party up here? My place is too small. I'll provide the food and liquor, and I'll invite two great girls from the show. I've already mentioned you to them, and they'd love to come."

Peter and I looked at each other, smiled, and broke into loud laughter.

"You're on," Peter said.

"Good."

"I suppose," I said, "that you'll invite the Goldhandlers."

"Well, I'm sure Harry will be having his own party," said Lasser, and he left.

"Shit," said Peter.

"Maybe we should back out of it," I said. But that was just talk, and we both knew it. *Those girls!*

Peter said, "No, let's ask the boss anyway, and fuck Lasser."

When we diffidently mentioned the party to Goldhandler and invited him, his face toughened. His reply, omitting the obscenities, was that he would not attend a Lasser party, even if Skip Lasser performed some physically unlikely acts in order to induce him; and anyway, the Goldhandlers did not go where they were not asked.

70

She Arrives

"PETER," I called from the living room, "we'll be late." The clock on the Paramount Building showed a quarter to seven. Curtain was at seven-thirty. The growled reply from the bedroom was not suited to the family trade.

I stood at the window, looking out at the dark towers patchy with gold: the Chrysler Building, the Empire State Building, the forest of skyscrapers all the way down to the Battery. It was one of those clear starry New York nights in early March; snow predicted, a strong wind blowing, a full moon sailing through torn clouds, a faint whine at the window sash. I put my forehead to the chilly glass, and murmured, "She's out there somewhere." Moonlight did that to me. I was expecting nothing of this night, except the thrill of brushing unattainable glamor. A man about to be presented to the Queen of England has no idea of making her, the awesome thing is just to be meeting her. It was Peter Quat who was prancing with anticipation of "having a nice affair," as he put it, with one of those two showgirls.

Peter's receptionist was getting difficult. He had never brought her to April House. She did not like that. She knew that he was in funds and had broken free of the formidable Dr. Quat, and she was muttering about marriage. That horrified Peter. He did not want to be tied down to any woman, let alone to his doormat. She was "a nice Jewish girl," in Mama's way of talking, that is, she wasn't a gentile. For a year she had been hoping that Peter would get so used to her that he would marry her. Now she was trying the desperate old game of withholding sex, which made Peter all the more eager to be off with the old and on with the new. What better replacement than a Grade A showgirl from *Johnny, Drop Your Gun?*

My frame of mind was different. I was weary of fooling with easy girls I did not love; weary, too, of the former college beauties still circulating, decorative but unresponsive dates, picked-over Dorsi Sabins who had not yet landed their Morris Pelkowitzes. What did I want? What was I asking of the moon? I wanted a passionate romance with a beautiful girl. It was that simple, and I felt that she was "out there somewhere." She had to be. Sex would be a natural and radiant part of such a romance, once such a girl miraculously liked me.

As for marriage, I had no thought of it. I had not yet turned twenty-one. What I had in mind, if you come right down to it, was also "a nice affair," I guess, though I would never have put it that way. Vaguely I envisioned a romance out of Hemingway novels, Millay poems, Cole Porter songs, and Coward plays; an amusing bittersweet amour of young lovers who gave no thought to such grubby practicalities as weddings, housekeeping, budgets, and babies, but laughed and loved around the clock for a month or two, and bye-bye. Ideally, of course, this would happen in Paris. I was a long way from Paris, but I was in Manhattan, which wasn't bad either, and I was in April House.

She's out there somewhere!

Yet the farthest thing from my mind was that she could be one of the two Nell Gwynns who were coming with Skip Hartman that night to April House. I thought Peter was kidding himself. They were not for the likes of us.

A hand on my shoulder. "Well, let's go." Peter peered out at the night. "I bet it snows. Romantic. Got the tickets?"

From our perch in the mezzanine, we saw the Goldhandlers come down the aisle. She was wearing that sequined thing from the Joan Crawford premiere. Bad luck seemed to dog that dress. An usher stopped them, looked at their tickets, and pointed to empty seats near the end of a crowded side row. To avoid squeezing past a dozen people already seated, they had to go back and come down the side. I could see that Harry Goldhandler bled as he trudged up the center aisle, and that his wife was red with rage.

In the first ten rows center sat everybody who was anybody: the producer, the composer, movie stars, the mayor, Noël Coward, the Lunts, Irving Berlin, and so on. Read an old show-business book of 1936, and fill in that seating diagram yourself. There too, of course, sat Skip Lasser, with Sugar Gansfried. The farther one's seats were from that glittery section, the more agonizing were the Proustian pangs at being snubbed or downgraded. We were up on the mezzanine among the nobodies in street clothes. That didn't matter. Status mattered only in the orchestra, among the black ties and the long dresses.

And it was a real outrage that the Goldhandlers were not sitting in that front center section. Why not? And why the fly-shit credits? And why was Lasser not inviting them to his party, in the apartment of Goldhandler's own staff? Jealousy, vanity, an itch to hog the credit? Not altogether, not quite. On the Broadway bourse of reputation, Lasser rated as a "serious" writer, you see, concerned with social significance. Harry Goldhandler was a gagman. Lasser wanted to keep his distance from the gagman. *Johnny, Drop Your Gun* played the Winter Garden for a while, a modest success. You never hear any of the songs. They are lost to memory — though never to my memory. Lasser had several Broadway and movie hits, but this was a forgettable musical. Harry Goldhandler sat way over on the side of the fifteenth row, while the jokes I heard him dictate in Florida rocked the Winter Garden, and his ingenious variation of "Dr. Cutballs" brought down the house.

There's no business like show business.

"That redhead is for me," hissed Peter during the opening number, "second from the right. See? Oh, wow! Oh, Christ! Oh, I hope Lasser's bringing *her*."

Well, I thought all the singing girls looked unearthly there under the lights. This was not the Ziegfeld sort of show, where tall silent beauties paraded wearing glittery nothings to display their nudity. These girls had pleasant voices and they chirruped in simple harmonies, and they wore charming finery. Yet the main thing about them, too, was their looks.

Oh, what's the use? I tried before to describe them, and gave up, and now they were ever so much more beautiful in the radiance of the stage. What can poor print convey of the brilliance of those young eyes, the curves of those young bodies, the grace of those young movements, the enticement of those young stage smiles? God Almighty, a beautiful girl is and will always be the most enthralling sight a man's eye can look upon, and ten of them were up there on the Winter Garden stage. For trying to figure out which two Lasser would bring to April House, Peter Quat and I could hardly keep our minds on the songs and the jokes; except, I must say, for that hospital scene incorporating Dr. Schneidbaitzim.

It came along midway in the first act, that point in a musical on opening night when the ice must break or the show dies. That stiff show-me audience at last melted, broke up in laughter, guffawed, clapped, and so did we. Lahr was marvellously ludicrous, scuttling in terror around the stage to evade the crazy psychiatrist. The foil who played the doctor did a superb job of gradually changing from a dignified Viennese savant to a menacing lunatic, convinced that Lahr urgently needed castration at once, brandishing glittering clashing scissors almost as big as hedge-clippers as he pursued him. I don't know how Lahr managed the business of shinnying halfway up the proscenium, but it was a great comic surprise; and when he gibbered like a monkey from up there, and pelted the crazy doctor *with coconuts,* at this mad touch — not in the original Joey Mack scene; very little of this was — the Winter Garden exploded in applause, and Skip Lasser had a hit going, thanks to Harry Goldhandler. The show never reached that high point again, but it didn't have to.

The cast party was a mob scene, all right. Peter and I found ourselves in a jostling buzz of people who all seemed to know each other, who hugged, and kissed, and shook hands, and waved, and shrieked greetings, and pushed. We saw Skip Lasser with Sugar Gansfried, and walked right up to them, but they ignored us, busy as they were greeting the mayor, and Ethel Merman, and George S. Kaufman, and other hot shots from the first ten rows center. I said to her, "Hello, Sugar," but she looked through me and past me unseeing, her heavy long tan satin skirt bunched in one hand, her eyes glassily glittering as she hurried past me toward Governor Lehman.

Peter Quat's redhead was in the crowd, still in a fetching 1918 garden-party costume, cartwheel hat, and garish stage makeup. Peter elbowed me. "That's her! Christ, isn't she something?" and started toward her. Just then a tanned lean man with well-groomed heavy gray hair, in a tuxedo with big diamond cuff links, an apparition straight out of a *New Yorker* advertisement for Cadillacs, came toward her through the crowd. She flung herself into his open arms, clutching at her hat. "Why, that old shitface," snarled Peter. When we left about half an hour later, we saw them outside the stage door, getting into a chauffeured limousine. She then wore a chinchilla coat over an evening dress, and her eager laughter and her amorous roll of great eyes at the tanned grayhead strongly suggested that this was not an old married couple going home for hot cocoa and ladyfingers. "Have fun, old shitface," sneered Peter through his teeth. As I've said, he was and is a poor loser.

I remember some good things about that cast party. When Bert Lahr appeared in black tie, his face pink from the towelled removal of makeup, a burst of applause greeted him. He made straight for the Goldhandlers and shook hands with them first. "Harry, you saved our ass with that hospital scene," he said quite loudly, "and those god-damn coconuts." He stayed beside the Goldhandlers, so that whoever came up to him — and everybody wanted to — had to greet the Goldhandlers, too. Goldhandler looked flustered and happy, and as for his wife, why, she perked up like a wilting flower put in water. If Skip Lasser was aware of any of this, he took no notice, busy as he was responding to compliments.

Lasser was late to his party in our suite. Everybody else had already showed up, including, to our astonishment, Leslie Howard. Lasser and Howard had become friendly in Boston, and there was talk of their doing a musical show based on *Berkeley Square*. Nothing came of that, but it gives you a notion of Lasser's knack for seizing opportunities. Anyway, I went to answer the doorbell, and there he stood between two girls taller than himself. "Hi, meet Monica Carter and Bobbie Webb."

Sugar Gansfried came trotting up to him, all in a glow. A spy at the *Times* had telephoned to say that the review was already being set up in type, and was a rave. I helped the blonde girl off with her coat, and Peter darted up to assist the black-haired one. I recognized the blonde from the rehearsal, but not the black-haired girl. In our foyer, they seemed less supernatural, less fallen from the stars, but make no mistake; from the outset they looked far too mature, pretty, and high-powered for me, and, I thought, for Peter Quat, too. If Leslie Howard was looking for a romance, one of these might do.

"*I get the blonde!*" Peter snapped, as they went off with Lasser to the living room. That was his way. When we had first moved into the apartment, he had said, "I get the two top drawers, you take the bottom ones." Though we were now receiving equal pay, there was no doubt who was senior between us. He was still the great PDQ, I was still the humble Vicomte de Brag, and that was how the thing stood until we broke up. To a certain extent that's how it still stands.

I cannot think of four words ever spoken to me that made a greater difference in my life. Nothing could have happened between me and Monica Carter, and Bobbie always told me that Peter repelled her with his grimacing and his ego. If Peter had picked the brunette, that would have been that. Fate spins slender threads sometimes, but I offer this as some kind of uniquely fine spiderweb stuff on which to hang crucial years of a man's life. *"I get the blonde!"*

The black-haired girl stood at the window, holding a drink and looking out at the view. I remember that she wore a purple satin suit. She seemed ever so much older than me, and very quiet and on her dignity. I could see Peter on the sofa with the blonde, talking away and making her laugh. Monica Carter had magnificent legs, glorious thick wheat-colored hair piled on her head, and the kind of strong-jawed pretty face that in these days of television would have made her fortune. As for Bobbie Webb —

Am I supposed to try for a description now? She is here before me, more real than all the fleshly scurriers in the White House corridors; a haunting presence, as poignant and intense as I can bear. But okay. Black hair to her shoulders, large eyes set far apart under a broad brow, very white, very smooth skin, a snub nose and thin finely cut lips; Bobbie Webb was in fact an archetypical Irish beauty, a colleen out of the magazines. And I remember her hands, slender and white and long-fingered. But when I try to project myself back to call up my very first impression, I return to those eyes: gray-blue, huge, sparkling, very alive, with a look in them of sweetness, of an eager appetite for fun, and of femininity as powerful as all the electricity out of Boulder Dam. And this was when Bobbie Webb was not trying, when she just looked at you and talked. When she used those eyes — well, we will get to that.

The other thing I think of is her teeth, and the odd way she smiled. She seemed terribly solemn and unwilling to laugh. I was pelting her with badinage out of sheer self-consciousness, out of a sense that I was beyond my depth and had to amuse, since I could not possibly attract, such a beauty. Any wit can tell whether he is registering. I knew I was amusing her, it was in the flash of those eyes, and in the quick coming and going of her smile; but it was a compressed, controlled smile that did not show her teeth.

71

Consummation

"You will?"

She just nodded. Molly Bloom says, you will recall, "Yes yes I will Yes," but in this real event nature did not imitate art. Just a nod. We looked in each other's eyes, with that glittering nakedness of purpose and disclosure that comes once, and only once, at the beginning of an affair. "You fiend!" she said. "As though you ever doubted it. From the first minute!"

Bobbie Webb pushed down the black silk skirt over the most beautiful gartered thighs in the known universe, and got out of the peach mink chair with a resigned sigh, hitching one shoulder. "Give me a bathrobe or something." I rushed and snatched Peter's red-and-yellow silk Sulka dressing gown from a closet. By the happiest of chances, Peter was in the hospital with double pneumonia. "Mm, swanky," she said, and with a wryly amused look she disappeared into the bedroom.

And now, while Bobbie is disrobing, let me fill you in on the events leading up to this seismic occurrence a few minutes past midnight on the first of April, 1936, in April House, three weeks and four days after she walked into my life.

I will spare you the poems I wrote to Bobbie and left at the Winter Garden, excruciatingly embarrassing doggerel. Nor will I trace the course of the growing intimacy between us, which the whole world can imagine, more or less. The story of me and Bobbie Webb begins only on the far side of this glorious night.

"I'm going to learn how to make gefilte fish," said Bobbie on our third date, bringing her dainty fist down on the tiny nightclub table, "and I'm going to marry you." I laughed and she laughed, and I forgot it; nor indeed have I thought of it again until just now, when out of the Pandora's box of this long shut-away love, the memories come flying like bats at dusk. It was beyond conception that this stunning siren whose photograph hung in the Winter Garden lobby, who appeared on stage every night for men to goggle at, could possibly be interested in marrying a gagman of just twenty-one, Jewish at that, the pimples that had put off Mrs. Dorsi Pelkowitz barely fading from his face. As it happened, Bobbie was dead serious, and that remark about the gefilte fish was the run-up of her colors. Seeing the way I took it, she laughed, too.

And I must say that as I start to tell our story, I find that my sympathies are all with Bobbie Webb. My picture of her now is enormously different from the way I saw her then. How I convey my stereoscopic view of this female of females — one eye that of an infatuated boy, the other that of a chilly old tax lawyer, with little in common but the name Israel David Goodkind and the same social security number — is a literary dilemma beyond me, but I can only crash on.

My intentions, on the other hand, were totally unserious: not dishonorable, exactly, but romantic. I wanted to seduce Bobbie, and have that bittersweet Hemingway-Porter-Millay-Coward passion with her; poignant, delicious, magical, with a reasonably early cutoff date. It was a cardinal point with me, the legal mind functioning even then, never to utter the words, "I love you" to Bobbie — stage name Violet — Webb, though that negotiating posture in time collapsed. So you see, we entered into the thing at cross-purposes, not a wholly uncommon occurrence in young love.

As to the first step, the seduction, there was no deep disagreement. I was bent on seducing this goddess; for though I could scarcely have been denser or less experienced, instinct had arisen from my male depths, broken through my Minsker Godol inhibitions and Columbia philosophizing, and growled to me to get going and have this woman. She was giving me enough inviting signals, I would say in retrospect, to arouse a career eunuch. But that is not how I saw it then. I thought I was being shockingly daring and dashing and forward with my letters, my poems, my sweet talk, and my heavy passes at her in taxicabs, and sometimes in the front seat of Pop's Buick, when I could borrow it. Bobbie went along with all this not only willingly, but encouragingly. If she had a game plan, as we say now-adays, it clearly included a seduction some time early on, so that she could let me see and feel how much she loved me.

Because that Bobbie Webb did love me was the key to the whole business. In Bobbie's view, a short bittersweet amour was for the birds. She decided very quickly she wanted me for life, but it was up to me in the first instance to seduce her. For she was actually a very proper young woman, in her fashion; lived with her mother, had genteel ways, liked to go to church now and then, and often carried a good book under her arm, something like Thurber or Steinbeck. She was not going to seduce me, no way. Since she could not expect a proposal of marriage from this queer fish she had hooked, not yet, she just had to wait and leave progress up to me.

Now any sensible woman, if she levels with you, will tell you that two things are necessary for a seduction, assuming the lady in ques-tion is not dead set against it: a private place where you can lie down and do it, and a loving yet firm masculine hand to remove the lady's pants. Bobbie was eminently sensible, and she was waiting — I can now see, with tender patience — for me to provide these simple re-quirements for sin. But I hadn't a clue. I went on wooing her like mad with flowers, and ballades, and letters, and horseback riding in Central Park, and taxicab foreplay, and double-entendre talk, and passionate declarations; a little like a nearsighted boxer, maybe, who jabs and weaves and ducks and bobs all over the ring, unaware that he has already landed a lucky punch and his opponent is out cold on the canvas. I will never know what Bobbie really thought of all this. With perfect female instinct, she was forever protective of my ego; until the time came to hurt it, that is — a long way off, but hell on earth when it arrived. I now suspect that once in a while in those wooing days, when she excused herself in a restaurant or cabaret to go to the powder room, she really retired and laughed her head off in there for a bit, then returned with a straight face to be wooed some more.

I say she was protective of my ego; and as an example, how about those unforgettable words with which she yielded? Once Peter Quat was accommodating enough almost to die of pneumonia, so that he had to be rushed to the hospital, that selfsame night the thing hap-pened, since finally I could provide at least uninterrupted privacy and a bed. *"You fiend! As though you ever doubted it. From the first min-*

ute!" Fiend, mind you. I was the saddest excuse for a fiend on the island of Manhattan; and not only had I doubted it right along, I couldn't believe my ears when she said she would. I was working her over, you see, in my inconclusively fiendish fashion, and the practical girl realized that Quat wouldn't have pneumonia forever, that the time had come. She could also perceive, since she was getting to know me, that it would be a cold day in hell before Noël Hemingway would be so forward as to take down her pants. So she gasped that she couldn't endure my entreaties and the touch of my hot hands any longer, that she would do anything I wanted; and she phrased it so that I was not at all a postadolescent fumbler, but a devilish Don Juan who had overcome her, sensing her weakness with my worldly wisdom from the start. Bobbie was a good and sweet thing, and female to her very neurons.

"Hi, honey."

There she stood in the bedroom doorway, with Peter's dressing gown dragging on the floor and the sleeves hanging below her fingertips, making a funny face at me. My first thought was how much shorter she looked. I had never seen her out of high heels. She was still a big girl, but as I went up to her and embraced her I was half a head taller; whereas until now we had been dancing and kissing almost eye to eye. There was something very appealing about this sudden diminution of Bobbie.

"I've changed my mind," she said.

"The hell you have," replied the fiend, and he swept her into the bedroom to have his will of her.

I think I should explain how Peter Quat happened to get double pneumonia, before I proceed. Peter went to the wedding of a classmate, and there met a Dorsi Pelkowitz to end all Dorsi Pelkowitzes; a toothsome and carnally inflaming Jewish girl of medium height, ashblonde, infernally bright, and only nineteen. Her name was Marilyn Levy. She lived in New Rochelle, her parents had a lot of money, but the main thing about this girl was her sexual charge; it could throw out electric relays in her neighborhood, so to speak, and draw down the lightning. She really was something, this Marilyn Levy; she had to be, to affect a hard-nosed cynic like Peter Quat as she did. And she was virginal and unconquerable as the snows of Kilimanjaro. Naturally.

He had gotten nowhere with Monica Carter, I should mention. They never had another date. Bobbie told me that while he amused Monica, the faces Peter made had frightened her off. Monica suspected that he was not quite sane. It may have bothered him, and heightened his vulnerability, to watch the callow Vicomte de Brag making time with a showgirl where PDQ had failed. But falling for Marilyn Levy needed no other explanation than Marilyn. You can read all about it in *Deflowering Sarah,* for Sarah is Marilyn to the life, except that Peter doesn't tell the truth, which is that he had to marry her to get her; that they stayed married for five years, and that it was she who divorced him, tired of his persistent screwing of the poor little coeds in his English lit courses. *Deflowering Sarah* is his revenge book.

Apparently he and Marilyn quarrelled on their second date — my guess is, over an unsuccessful attempt by Peter to deflower her up there in New Rochelle — and he walked two miles to the train station, and got caught halfway in a drenching rain. In those days pneumonia was still a killer disease, and when Peter next morning awoke with the shudders, chattering his teeth, I called Dr. Quat and he came and at once took Peter off to the hospital. And that is how I came to my consummation with Bobbie Webb. It's an ill wind, or rainstorm.

"My God, how beautiful you are, Bobbie!"

The bedroom was dark, but the moon shone on her breasts as she shrugged off the dressing gown, hopped into the wrong bed, Peter's, which she had neatly made up, and pulled the blanket half over herself.

"I'm too small," she said, "there's not enough there."

I already knew that that was her professional opinion of her bosom. In my early fiendish passes I had once sent a couple of rubber pads flying and bouncing all over the place, and Bobbie had been somewhat miffed and embarrassed. And maybe by Broadway standards these girlish breasts were not hefty enough; but by the God that made Bobbie and me, those breasts — lit by the moon, bared for me on my first night of love — were the prettiest, the most alluring, the most wondrous sight I had ever looked upon. To this day I think slight breasts are the sexy ones; the watermelons leave me cold, and conceivably the taste traces to that night.

We were naked in each other's arms, messing about ecstatically but very clumsily, and not getting much of anywhere. I thought I knew all about it, but my ignorance was still beyond belief; certainly, it will be for present-day readers, for whom I understand active sex begins shortly after learning to ride a two-wheel bike, more or less. But it didn't matter. I wasn't anxious or worried about my manhood. I was in a trance of bliss, a dazzle of heavenly sensation, embracing America the Beautiful, Bobbie Webb, the transcendent avatar of the Outside, in a flood of moonbeams in April House, in my first real act of passion.

"Darling," she said, "I'm sorry I'm such a *langeh loksh.*"

There was Bobbie Webb for you in one blinding "epiphanic moment," as the creative-writing professors put it these days; apologizing to *me* for my own ineptness as a fiend, and using a bit of showbiz or garment-center Yiddish to make me feel more at home. *Langeh loksh* is slang for somebody tall; literally, "long noodle."

Seductions have a way of working out, and this one of course did. How many times? Think back to your own first night, reader, or at least your honeymoon night; if you're a man never mind exaggerating, if you're a woman don't be too wistful about what you read in books. We are nearly all pretty close to average. Who wants to be a freak of sexual prowess, anyway, the ace barnyard cock, racking up the orgasms like billiard scores? Peter Quat is Priapus's fool. Love is the thing, and love was a white radiant blaze that enveloped Bobbie and me that night until the window showed not moonlight but lilac dawn.

"Oh, my God. Mother will be having kittens. Take me home, darling." Bobbie leaped naked from the bed.

The magic trailed us down the elevator, through that deserted red-and-gold lobby, into the taxicab, and all the way to Ninety-fifth Street, like a shower of stars all around us. We kept looking deep in each other's heavy-lidded eyes, spent, content, drained, still rapturous in the afterglow, in the new intimacy, in the one-time and all-time wonder of first love.

But I had played it straight. Through the torrent of endearments, all that night long, I had never once told Bobbie Webb that I loved her. That, I had managed to avoid. For that would have been misleading the girl. I was not that much of a fiend.

72

The Hemingway Pillow

COUSIN HAROLD's mother, Aunt Sophie, was the Walter Cronkite of the Mishpokha Broadcasting System, so taking Harold to the Winter Garden lobby to show him Bobbie Webb's picture was an insanity. What a red-hot news break for Aunt Sophie! Why, this was *Yisroelke,* Zaideh's pet, the big yoxenta's jewel, the Minsker Godol, going out with a *shiksa* in a Broadway show! I tell you, it was a family Sputnik shock. Yet that possibility never crossed my mind when I dragged Cousin Harold to the Winter Garden. I was in an amorous daze, a blissful sleepwalk.

Cousin Harold stood gaping at that picture like a believer at a wonder-working saint's statue on the saint's day, expecting it to start bleeding. "Wow," he breathed.

It was an old-time shadowy glamour pose, tilted head and naked shoulders, with a slight smile barely parting her lips, so that you did not see her teeth. Among the showgirl pictures Bobbie's was not the most striking, but it sure struck Harold. "Are you —" Cousin Harold hesitated, then dropped his voice, as befitted conversation about a holy object, in a holy place, "— are you, ah, having an affair with her?"

Note Cousin Harold's delicacy; not "fucking her," or more circumspectly, "screwing her," which would have been his secular style.

I laughed. "Ye gods, no. Nothing like that. We're just having great fun."

Not taking his eyes off her, Cousin Harold heaved a deep, deep sigh; and that sigh balanced out, for me, ten years of listening to the tales of this copulating Sinbad. He was back from his Swiss medical school between terms. At lunch he had been recounting his conquests in boardinghouses, train compartments, and one in a funicular car; and I had sat quietly, a disguised billionaire letting a beggar ramble on, waiting to show him Bobbie's picture. He also told me about the whiffs of anti-Semitism drifting across the Alps from Germany, the scrawls of *Juif* on store windows, the spreading rash of Hitler pictures and swastikas, but none of that dented my somnambulist serenity.

"Think you'll end up marrying her?"

"No, it's not like that, but she couldn't be lovelier."

"I'll bet." Harold looked respectfully at me, as he had used to before we reached puberty. Then he had sprouted that extraordinary member, framed in a bush like a gorilla's topknot, and set off on his precocious career, while I had languished behind, an inept virgin with morbid concerns about being an invert. Bobbie's picture ended all that, without Harold even knowing what the true situation was. So perhaps you can understand why I did such a damn fool thing. Believe me, it was a satisfying moment, though I paid for it.

Peter Quat returned from the hospital, talking once more about quitting Goldhandler. But it was no time for Peter to desert. We were carrying a heavy work load. Goldhandler was riding high again, grinding out two new comedy shows as well as the Leslie Howard program, and also drafting a libretto for a Gershwin musical. The quadruplex penthouse was becoming crammed with Mrs. Fesser's antiques, Karl and Sigmund were getting straight A's at college, and the Klebanoff mine in Alaska was actually starting to produce some gold. I was dickering with our landlady for a full year's lease, and it appeared feasible; not, however, if Peter left. And that brings me to the unfortunate matter of the Hemingway pillow.

Admirers of Ernest Hemingway will surely recall that when a Hemingway hero is doing it to one or another woman, he is likely to put a pillow under her loins. Hemingway makes a big deal of women's loins. As between loins and lions, it is a close-run thing in Hemingway, and with the loins there generally goes a pillow, underneath. Now as I've said, in my mind this relationship with Bobbie Webb was a mishmash of Hemingway, Coward, and other literary influences, maybe above all Edna St. Vincent Millay, as in her definitive quatrain:

> *My candle burns at both ends;*
> *It will not last the night;*
> *But ah, my foes, and oh, my friends —*
> *It gives a lovely light!*

There you had it. Passion was an evanescent delight, to be enjoyed and then given up with a little agony, a little sadness, but on the whole mutual good feeling and thanks for the memory. Certainly that was my idea of what was happening between me and Bobbie Webb. All this took place long ago, before the sexual revolution made such bohemian posturing very old hat. You have to project yourself back into a former quaint set of values, almost as when you read *Anna Karenina*, to understand that for our Yisroelke, in the 1930's, these were exceedingly liberated notions.

It followed that the closer I could approximate my literary models, the better. Edna Millay offered no suggestions as to how to go about doing it, just lots of lyrics declaring how sweet, short-lived, painful, and precious the whole business was. Ernest Hemingway, however, had this highly specific suggestion of a pillow under the loins, which would greatly heighten mutual rapture.

"A pillow?" said Bobbie. "Why a pillow? Everything's fine this way."

I insisted we ought to try it, and Bobbie was nothing if not compliant, at this stage. Taking Peter's pillow to put under Bobbie's marvellously shapely loins did not seem quite the thing, somehow. So I went into the living room and fetched a cushion from the couch. Well, Bobbie was right, it made no perceptible difference. Bobbie, though, was so anxious to please me that she said afterward, why yes, it was just marvellous, we would have to use a cushion more often. And I was so happy in bed with her that I only wanted her to be half as happy; so I was delighted with her reaction, and greatly obliged to Ernest Hemingway, and we did use that sofa cushion now and again when I thought of it. It didn't harm anything, there was just the nuisance of going to get it. Finally Bobbie held me back one night and said irritably, "Darling, look, do me a favor and get on with it, forget that goddamn cushion, will you?" Exit Ernest Hemingway from our romance.

As it happened, that couch was Peter's favorite reading spot, as the peach mink chair was mine. It was upholstered in shaggy brown material like a grizzly bear's hide, and the cushions were a smooth bright yellow; altogether a gaudy item, much in keeping with our Hollywood decor. Peter loved to lie propped on the cushions with one of his far-out books: Carl Van Vechten, Laura Riding, Ezra Pound, or what have you. One evening he was settling down to read when he froze. He held a cushion up to the reading lamp and picked something off it.

"There's hair on this cushion," he accused me. I was in the peach armchair.

"So? You're the one who uses the couch," I said. "It's your hair." I had not told him about Bobbie and me, and wasn't about to.

"My hair?" He brought it over to me: a very short black curly wiry hair. "What kind of hair do you call *that?*"

I might better have kept my big mouth shut, but I was feeling pretty foxy, and I said, "Could be an eyebrow."

"An eyebrow?" Peter snarled, with the ghastliest face he had ever made, and a roll of his eyes like a mad dog. "Some fucking eyebrow!"

Next day he told me his mind was made up. He was going to get his M.A. in English literature at Harvard, starting in the fall, then go into university teaching; and as soon as he had enough stuff published, he would apply for a Guggenheim fellowship and write novels. It wasn't until the early fifties that he got the Guggenheim on which he wrote *Deflowering Sarah,* but otherwise he lived by that plan. And so far as that goes, my hat is off to him. Anyway, after the pillow episode I was on notice that come the summer layoff, Peter Quat was out. As for the contract with Goldhandler, Peter just ignored it, as he ignores all contracts until the law closes in.

Peter was never surly to Bobbie, I'll say that. When she would call up after the show and we sweet-talked, he would sit listening with a sardonic smile. "You, my friend, will marry that girl," he would say. But I knew better, of course. Bobbie and I had agreed that our thing was a shining palace built upon the sand, a trip to the moon on gossamer wings, etc. Peter and I even double-dated sometimes with Bobbie Webb and Marilyn Levy, and it was a caution to see how swimmingly those two got along: the high-powered, heavily moneyed, big-bosomed nineteen-year-old Jewish Bennington sophomore, and the tall thin professional Irish beauty in her twenties, sparsely educated, poor as a rat. They would go off to the powder room together, chatting and chortling like lifelong friends. All they had in common was that they were both in love with eccentric Jewish gag-men. I guess this peculiar fate made them sisters under the skin, pro tem.

When I came home for Friday night dinner, a few days after my lunch with Cousin Harold, my sister Lee collared me and pulled me into her frilly pink bedroom. "Tell me about the showgirl!"

"What showgirl?"

"Oh, *please*. Mom and Pop are up in arms. Pop hasn't slept for three nights."

I woke out of my somnabulism as though I had walked under a waterfall. "Cousin Harold," I said. "Damn."

Lee's eyes snapped with excitement. Here was high Yiddish-theatre drama, in the poky Goodkind flat! She was safely engaged to her Jewish pediatrician, Bernie Cooperman, and their marriage was only a month off; and "my David" was in the hottest of hot water.

"She isn't Jewish, is she? Not a showgirl."

"She's not Jewish. She's a darling, and we're having a marvellous time."

Lee gave me a penetrating sisterly look. "I'd love to meet her."

"Why not? I'll take you to the show."

It was an unusually quiet and glum Sabbath meal. The candles seemed to be burning blue.

"Who's been manicuring your nails?" Mom said abruptly. "They look so nice and clean."

"I just cut them," I said. "Nobody's manicuring them."

"Your nails never looked as clean and shiny as that. Somebody's been manicuring them."

"Leave him alone," Pop said. "If he says nobody manicured them, nobody manicured them."

That was as close as we came to discussing Bobbie Webb; except that when I left to go back to April House — where in fact I was meeting Bobbie — Pop said with weighty meaning, "Take care of our son."

"Don't worry, Pop," I said, and off went the jewel for his rendez-vous with the Outside.

You may ask, since Quat was over his pneumonia, and since Bobbie lived at home with her mother, how were we managing? Well, in seduction the first slice off the loaf, the first olive out of the bottle, is the whole thing, you know. After that you are lovers with one desire, which much simplifies things. There were times when I knew Peter wouldn't be in. He was an obsessive bridge player, and every Monday night he invariably played until two in the morning. So Monday night was regular management night, so to speak. I would sit in the peach mink armchair on Monday night, trying to write funny jokes on a pad, but forever glancing downtown with an eye for only one of those light-spangled skyscrapers, the Paramount tower with its illuminated clock.

The show let out at eleven, but she had to take off her makeup and change. When it reached ten minutes to twelve on other nights, the telephone would ring, and it would be Bobbie wanting to chat. But on Monday nights it would crawl past that mark, past twelve, and about five or six minutes after midnight — seldom later; Bobbie was if anything more passionately into this thing than I was — the doorbell would ring, I would fly to the door, and there she would stand glowing, my Grade A showgirl, with a love gleam in her eyes and an inviting, intoxicating smile. I would pull her inside and there at the door we would commence crazy kissing; and she would do her best to hold me off, to laugh at me, to ask for a drink, to insist she was hungry. But on Monday night that was just talk.

Ah me, those Monday nights in April House! "Youth is a crown of roses," says the Talmud, "old age a bed of thorns." Poor grizzled tax lawyer! Dear God in Heaven, Bobbie Webb, how the roses became you!

73

Lee's Wedding

M Y sister Lee, Dr. Bernie Cooperman, and I watched the show from house seats. Over the footlights Bobbie threw us bewitching smiles, and when at one point the singing girls raised those long World War I skirts to show their legs, Bernie Cooperman's eyes popped at Bobbie and he hissed "Kee-rist!" My sister Lee, with a tart little grin, laid a possessive hand on his arm. Afterward we ate in a seafood restaurant. Like Lee, Bernie loved abominations. We all ordered Uncle Yehuda's South African lobster tails — I doubt that I can cram in here the loony but true story of Uncle Yehuda's striking it rich in lobster tails — and Bernie Cooperman peppered Bobbie with leaden doctor badinage, which she fielded with frolicsome ease. You'd think my sister Lee would have been disapproving, but not a bit of it.

"Why don't you marry her?" said Lee next day. She was shopping for her trousseau, and she dropped in to our suite.

"Hell, Lee, you know the answer to that."

"Oh, look, she can convert, can't she? You won't do much better. I've never seen you look at a girl like that, and she's obviously crazy about you."

Coming from Lee, that threw me. I carefully explained to her that Bobbie and I were enjoying the lovely light of a candle burning at both ends, but she couldn't grasp this difficult concept. She seemed all set to teach Bobbie how to make gefilte fish; except that she couldn't make it herself. Lee has never liked gefilte fish, so she never learned how. Anyway, my sister Lee clearly perceived Bobbie as a wife, not as a pair of transient Hemingway loins.

Goldhandler weighed in as matchmaker. I had been bringing Bobbie to occasional rehearsals and programs. "Taking kid, that black-haired girl," he remarked when we were working together late at night in the penthouse. "Rabbi's daughter, I presume?"

I laughed uneasily.

"You ought to marry her, Finkelstein. She's nice."

"Why, I barely know the girl."

He gave me a shrewd squint through cigar smoke, and dropped it.

One Friday night after dinner, Pop came to me with a Bible open to a chapter in Proverbs about "the strange woman," the wanton who lures a young fool into her bedchamber and seduces him with her wiles, assuring him that her husband is off on a trip. The simpleton ends up with an arrow through his liver. One gathers the husband got back too soon. I could see in this no relevance to my own liver. After all, I was seducing Bobbie, not the other way around, and anyway she was single. I brought the Bible back to Pop.

"Okay, Papa. Forget it."

"It's not serious?"

"No."

"Mama and I wouldn't interfere with your life, you know. We could move to Palestine, or maybe Hawaii."

"Papa, for crying out loud, that's absurd."

"Lee is having a very big wedding." His weary wise eyes searched mine. "Maybe too big, but that's what Mama and the Coopermans want. Zaideh will marry them. You're the best man. Nothing should interfere."

"Nothing will interfere."

He held out his hand. I shook it.

Bobbie was sweetly tactful about not being invited. "Of course I understand, dear," she said. "It wouldn't do, would it? With your grandfather, and whatnot." Bobbie liked my sister Lee, and she knew that Lee liked her, for one night in Bernie's flat Lee had put on for the four of us a jolly meal of turtle bisque, oysters Rockefeller, shrimps Creole, sea urchins in wine sauce, and Uncle Yehuda's lobster tails. Lee had committed herself to keeping a kosher kitchen, you see, out of consideration for Mom and Pop, who were giving the happy pair the dowry for Lee, saved up probably since the day she came out a girl baby: a honeymoon in Europe, and ten thousand dollars to set up a pediatric office on Central Park West. So she and Bernie were cramming in home-cooked abominations while the cramming was good.

Bobbie wanted to know, when I told her about the wedding, where it would be held ("Wow, the Algonquin!") and how many guests there would be — she had one very mobile eyebrow, and it went up high when I said over three hundred — whether Lee's dress had a train, what I would wear as best man (top hat, white tie, and tails), and such girlish inquiries. And who was coming, that she knew? Peter Quat? Yes. Marilyn Levy? Um, yes. The Goldhandlers? Yes. Boyd? Yes.

"Even Boyd? I didn't think he was Jewish. I guess everyone's coming but me."

The arrow sailed through my amorous fog and got me in the liver. Bobbie and I were together in the peach armchair. She put both arms around my neck. "Oh, honey, don't look like that. It's all right, truly it is."

Rough. I was twenty-one. Again, I paid.

As our family weddings went, Lee's was a sedate affair. The large Cooperman contingent from Port Chester was a university-educated crowd, elegantly turned out, good dancers. Tuxedos and evening dresses had a sobering effect on the exuberant Goodkinds and Levitans, salted as they were among the Port Chester people and my parents' Manhattan crowd. Uncle Yehuda's gold strike in lobster tails had remarkably tamed him. His white beard was trimmed and his manner was mild to all.

Still, there was one disorderly interval. Lee had sworn that she was not going to circle Bernie seven times. Never. Not even once around, to keep the peace! She had laid down the law to Mom and Pop. She had defied Zaideh, too, telling him that if she had to get married by a judge, she was not going to walk around Bernie. Zaideh had given in with cheerful resignation. God forbid Lee should be married by a judge! Lee came back in a glow from that talk with Zaideh. By God, she had beaten the system.

But, in the bride's room at the Algonquin at the last minute, Aunt Faiga, now a plump rubicund mother of two, worked hard on her. After all, hadn't Lee herself prevailed on Faiga to walk around Boris? And now, said Faiga, she was glad she had made Zaideh happy, with such a simple thing. Next came Holy Joe Geiger, resplendent in lilac robe and pompom hat. Lee and Bernie had met at his temple, so they had invited him to join in the ceremony. Geiger suggested that Lee compromise and go around Bernie three times; tradition should be altered tenderly, said Holy Joe, not brutally. And as Lee was being beset on all sides, who should walk into the room but Aunt Rose, our rabid Mishpokha unbeliever, all ablaze with jewels and a splendid dress, Uncle Yehuda's lobster-tail bonanza on display.

"I tell you what," my sister Lee barked at Mom and the other besiegers, "I'll do whatever Aunt Rose says. All right?"

She put the thing up to Rose.

"Oh, Lee, the idea at a wedding is to make everyone feel good," said Rose. "Go around him seven times and the hell with it."

Lee had not reckoned with the mellowing effect of riches, and she had to cave in. She went around and around Bernie beneath the canopy, counting under her breath as though she were cursing. At six she halted. A tractor would not have dragged her around again. Zaideh knew that, and he proceeded to marry them. The way Lee tells the story, she is the only member of the family who ever successfully balked at circling her bridegroom seven times. That is true enough. She does not mention those first six circuits. Nor do I.

Well, this took place on a Sunday night, and the Winter Garden was dark on Sundays. While the Cooperman-Goodkind nuptials went merrily on, Bobbie Webb had plenty of leisure to picture her Noël Hemingway in top hat, white tie, and tails, charming three hundred guests at the Algonquin Hotel, while she washed and set her hair, and did some laundry, and read some Thurber, in the tiny flat she shared with her mother and her dog, on the top floor of a rundown tenement on West Ninety-fifth Street.

Next night, I sat writing at the window in April House, watching the Paramount clock. The telephone rang at ten minutes to twelve.

"Hello, honey, I'm famished," chimed that high delectable voice. "Let's meet at the Golden Horn."

"Darling," I said, "it's Monday, you know."

"I know it's Monday." The voice became brisker. "I have something to tell you. We have to talk."

The sands suddenly quaked under the shining palace.

"What is it, sweetie?"

"Not over the telephone."

The Armenian headwaiter said to me as I walked into the restaurant, "Your wife is here."

Good God! Even this Levantine clown was in on the conspiracy to marry us! True, we ate here often, Bobbie liked the lamb and pilaf, but why should he assume she was my wife? Didn't Armenians read Edna St. Vincent Millay? Or did Bobbie already look so swellingly pregnant that it was an understandable mistake? I was in panic, I admit, and not thinking too clearly.

"How was the wedding?" were her first words, with an odd look in those enormous eyes.

"Oh, you know weddings," I said. "It went off okay."

"Did Lee walk around Bernie?"

I did not want to get into that tangled tale. I was on tenterhooks for Bobbie's news. Also, I yearned to hurry her back to April House. She wore an enticing light gray spring dress, and looked not in the least pregnant, of course. How could she, after a mere six or seven weeks? But Bobbie was not her ardent Monday-night self, no doubt of that. She was dawdling, one slow chewy mouthful at a time. It was getting on to one o'clock, Peter would return at two, and there she sat chewing and chewing, and asking about the wedding.

"Why are you bolting down that lamb?" she shot at me irritably. "You'll get sick. What did Marilyn Levy wear?"

And so it went for nearly an hour, before she came out with what she had to tell me.

"Well, you needn't look so relieved," she said, "and for God's sake stop looking at your watch! Do you have to catch a train, or something?"

It was twenty after one, and she was touching a napkin to her mouth like an arthritic dowager.

"I'm not relieved at all, I'm devastated, Bobbie. How can the show be closing so soon? Shall I pay the check?" I sawed my arms in the air at the headwaiter, who was contemplating the ceiling in a religious reverie.

"No, I want some dessert. Order me a pear Hélène." Bobbie made off for the ladies' room.

There had been empty rows when I saw *Johnny, Drop your Gun* with Lee and Bernie, but that it was closing came as a jolt. As of June fifteenth Bobbie would be out of a job. Monica Carter had invited her to drive to Amarillo, her hometown. Monica had a cousin,

a rich land developer, who had seen the show and fallen hard for
Bobbie. This cousin was eager to entertain both of them, and he knew
everybody in the oil business. That was Bobbie's news.

"What on earth did you think I was going to tell you?" she asked
when she returned at twenty-five to two, and dug into the pear
Hélène. "That I was pregnant? Honestly, dear, you're so *transparent*.
With the precautions *you* take?"

Well, she sort of had me there. I was sincere in my careless head-
long Monday night raptures with Bobbie, truly I was. I did wear my
crown of roses atilt with a bacchant's abandon, I did soar on wings
of heaven-brushing ecstasy. All the same, I never quite forgot what
happens when spermatozoa meet ovum, and I was now damned glad
of it. She proceeded to chatter about the journey. She had never been
to Texas. She had to pay only her share of the gasoline, and she would
stay with Monica. "So, my dear," she said brightly, "it looks like this
is it, eh? Fun's fun and all that, but don't you think that'll be our
time to say goodbye?"

How could I disagree? It was standard Hemingway-Millay. Bobbie Webb was the strayer from fairyland who had shared fleeting magic
with me. Now she would dance off on a moonbeam, and I would
hold her in my heart for ever, a Grade A Tinker Bell who had briefly
loved me, then tinkled away in a shimmering cloud of fairy dust. Such
had always been the scenario, and here was the reasonably early cutoff date. Only, I didn't like that detail of the land developer, some
gross old Texas moneybags, fooling with my Bobbie in Amarillo. But
there it was.

"Look, June fifteenth is years and years away," I said.

She gave me a maternal caress on the cheek. "That's how let's think
of it. Years and years."

After taking her home I walked down Central Park West to April
House, aching with unsatisfied Monday night longing. The pull between Bobbie and me was something tidal, yet she had kept her distance in the cab. Well, I thought, she is cooling it, and that is as it
should be, since this is just one of those things.

74

Such Sweet Sorrow

THE crowd almost blocked the sidewalk in front of Bergdorf Goodman. When I pushed through, the amazing sight that greeted me was Bobbie, no more than one foot tall, smiling and waving at me. It was a novelty window display of summer dresses, a trick of mirrors and lenses, which reduced several beautiful girls to living miniatures. Talk about your Tinker Bell! There she was to the life. The little figure beckoned to me to come into the store. The lifesize beauty met me at the back of the display, painted up like a doll, her eyes brilliant, her figure in the thin frock a piercing joy to remember embracing.

"Surprised, dear?"

"Astounded."

It was a daytime job for a week, she said, a hurry-up call from her model agency, a lot of fun and very good pay. "All right, now go back to your typewriter. I just thought you'd enjoy it."

"I love it. You look enchanting."

"Oh, do I? Well, in that case, what are you doing tonight? Do you suppose we could have a date?" The sudden glint of her eyes set my blood racing.

"You're on, by God."

"On one condition," she said.

"Name it. Anything. Anything!"

Bobbie laughed at me. "Remember how you used to send me a flower every day? Buy me a flower."

"Ten dozen!"

A low laugh, a warm squeeze of my hand. "Just one. A gardenia. Like before."

She darted back into the window.

That was the night she named the broken brick Peeping Tom. And since it was Tuesday, you will inquire, where was Peter Quat? Luckily, off in Martha's Vineyard, looking for a summer place to rent. There was no hurry, no oppressive two o'clock deadline. We had all night. At midnight Bobbie was ringing the bell. I tell you, the attraction between us came crashing through the literary taffy that night, an affinity strong as death, clamorous to go on and not to die. A trip to the moon on gossamer wings, a candle burning at both ends, my ass; this was the power that rules the earth and all that is in it, manifesting itself in the shattering shuddering embraces of two discordantly mismatched young people. The lightning had seared and welded us; but I did not understand, and that is what the rest of my story is about.

"We are observed," panted Bobbie, in her comical baritone huskiness after much wild lovemaking. "See? A Peeping Tom." She pointed to the brick, which by a freak of the moonlight, did look a bit like a man's profile.

"Well, let's give him something to peep at." I wearily gathered her to me again.

She held me off with a chuckle. "Honey, nix, you'll hurt yourself. Enough! Anyhow, I am dying for a lobster tail."

So we ate a couple of Uncle Yehuda's largest size at a late-night Broadway restaurant, laughing all the time at nothing at all. Next, we found ourselves in an open hansom cab, plop-plopping through Central Park in the violet silence before the dawn; a morning twilight in May, the brighter stars still twinkling, blown cherry blossoms along the road raining petals down on us. We passed Cleopatra's Needle, and I remember thinking that in all the centuries since those hieroglyphs were first carved, nobody could have been any happier than we two were at that moment.

When she got out of the hansom cab at her door, she gave me the bruised gardenia. "Something to remember us by," she said. "Us, and this night."

A gardenia drying and crumbling over thirty-seven years retains a ghost of its fragrance. Do you believe that? I know it.

In those days I used to keep a diary. Once not long ago I went to a cracking dusty cardboard carton in the cellar and dug under the jumble of photograph albums, diplomas and yearbooks, yellowing Goldhandler scripts, UJA and Israel Bond plaques, law society citations, Air Corps service files, Varsity Show programs, and bundled-up *Jesters*; and down at the bottom where I had buried it I found the diary. Two objects fell out: a picture of Bobbie, and a disintegrating brown fragment of a flower. I put it to my nose and so help me, there I was back in Bobbie's arms in April House, both of us looking out at Peeping Tom in the moonlight and laughing in joyous exhaustion.

Lord, lord, how young Bobbie was! That's what I keep forgetting. The girl in the picture could be a friend of Sandra's. Yet to me at the time she was an older woman, much older, formidably more worldly and more experienced. I could not have been her first man, though she was coy and evasive about that, but I know I was Bobbie Webb's first love. We were both young blunderers in the gardenia-scented dark.

The hell with it, let me tell you about Uncle Yehuda and the lobster tails.

A remote relative of ours, Uncle Haskel Goodkind, who had long ago migrated from Minsk to South Africa, was the abomination czar of Cape Town. Uncle Haskel had been trying for years to get Pop to import his lobster tails to the United States. Europe had been consuming them all, but the depression had ruined that market. Pop was far too tied up in the Fairy Laundry. Uncle Yehuda, though still struggling along with Uncle Velvel's shittim-wood books, took on Uncle Haskel's abominations, too. Now, by the sheerest luck, at that very time some crustacean disease hit the Maine lobster catch. The Maine supply dried up, and Uncle Yehuda found himself sitting on oil land. Cable after cable blitzed across the Atlantic and the equator: HASKEL SEND MORE TAILS YEHUDA. He liquidated his Bible stock, and went all out for South African lobster tails, and the money rolled in hand over fist. So now you know why Aunt Rose was so richly decked out at Lee's wedding. Yehuda always put his money on Aunt Rose's back when he had it.

But South Africa was not sending nearly enough to meet the demand. A seafood dealer showed up from Tasmania, with sample lobster tails just like Uncle Haskel's, and somewhat cheaper. Aunt Rose cooked and ate them and said they were fine. That was good enough for

Uncle Yehuda. He ordered some gigantic amount of Tasmanian tails, several refrigerator-ship loads, sinking every cent in them that he had or could borrow. This was to be the killing that would set him up for life.

Ah me. Victrolas or lobster tails, Uncle Yehuda just had that withering touch. Tasmanian lobsters, he found out too late, fed on copper oxide reefs or something, and under ordinary refrigeration they went queer. Unless cooked fresh and alive, or kept hard-frozen, they turned black when boiled, not red; and their meat became dark brown, like pot roast. That seafood dealer had carried his samples hard-frozen halfway around the world, so that they cooked up red and white, all nice and normal.

Yehuda sued him for fraud, of course. Getting at him in Tasmania took some doing. The thing did come to trial at last in New York, and the fellow claimed that the whole seafood industry knew about refrigerated Tasmanian lobster tails, which was why they were so cheap; moreover, that the brown lobster meat was perfectly healthy and tasty. The judge in the case ate a couple of the tails. He ruled that they were in fact a great delicacy, and the brown color a piquant novelty, and he decided against poor Uncle Yehuda.

All this took years and years, you understand. Meantime the Maine lobsters came back. So did the European market for the South African tails. Uncle Yehuda was left hanging, with several tons of Tasmanian tails in a freezer warehouse. Over the years he very, very slowly sold them off, to the limited market for brown lobster meat. Maybe you can even still buy a case of frozen Tasmanian tails from my Uncle Yehuda, now well into his nineties, if you are curious how black lobsters with brown flesh taste. Free-thinker though I was way back then, I never did try them. I was not that inquisitive.

"Oh, my God," Bobbie breathed huskily in my ear, "I can never leave you now." It was the night before her departure for Amarillo, and we were making a Monday night farewell edged with tenderness and rue. This hoarse gasp of Bobbie's gave me a turn. But as it got on toward two o'clock and we dressed, and for the last time — as I was certain — that exquisite body disappeared into that delectable 1930's underwear, and then into a blouse and skirt, she was talking cheerily about the trip. "Well, dear, is this it? Do we stay in touch at all?" she said. "I mean, are we still friends?"

"Good Lord, of course. I want to hear from you, Bobbie."

"All right, then, I'll call you from Richmond tomorrow night. That's where we're stopping."

She did call from Richmond, and she sounded all pepped up, very affectionate, and a bit lonesome. I was glad to hear her warm voice, though reconciled to her opening distance between us. If it hurt like hell to lose such sweetness from my life, why, that was just as it should be, according to all the books and poems and songs. What was my alternative? Declare myself in love and marry Bobbie, after all? Don't think I hadn't wrestled with that one. My heart was not elephant hide.

Zaideh had astonished me, on my last visit to him, by taking down the *Shulkhan Arukh,* and running through with me the section on conversion, for no apparent reason. Zaideh had a sort of Zen approach to instruction; often what he did told you more than what he said. He was letting me know in his way that for him Yisroelke's falling in love with a gentile showgirl wasn't the end of the world. It would depend, so the laws clearly spelled out, on the truth about Bobbie, our relationship, and her genuine interest in being Jewish. It was no mere matter of learning to make gefilte fish, but I had always known that.

Well, all right. What *was* the truth about Bobbie Webb? Starting with the most vital of vital statistics, her name, she was a puzzle. In the show program she was listed as Violet Webb. Why, then, Bobbie? I didn't know. She had never explained. Her age? Twenty-three, twenty-four, or twenty-five, depending on what conflicting clues she had let fall. Place of origin? Florida. I knew no more. Education? She claimed one year of college; name of college not specified. Her conversation was not really educated; charming, sure, but those brilliant big eyes wordlessly supplied most of the fun and nuance. Family? A faded little mother, no father in evidence, no brothers, sisters, relatives. Past? Vague; and she was decidedly cagey about it. Religious views? Very vague. Occupation? Professional beauty. Interest in Judaism? She had once quoted her mother, that Jews made good husbands. Otherwise, nil. It did not add up, no matter how I added it, over and over and over.

Peter Quat answered an early-morning telephone call a few days later. I jumped out of bed, sure it was Bobbie and prepared for his snarls. He hung up, his expression blank.

"Goldhandler had a heart attack."

"My God. How bad?"

"Boyd wants us to come over there right away." Peter looked around at his strapped-up suitcases, shaking his head. He had planned to leave for the Vineyard that morning.

The office had the old familiar reek. Empty Perrier bottles were scattered on the desk with dead cigars jammed in them. The diathermy machine which had relieved Goldhandler's shoulder pains still glowed red over his swivel chair. The seizure had come at dawn, after an all-night session with Boyd polishing our first draft of an Al Jolson script, a program Goldhandler was just taking on. Al Jolson had signed for the summer in Henny Holtz's Sunday night slot, and Goldhandler saw him as his long-sought means of crushing Holtz.

Turning off the machine, Boyd dropped into the chair, his face chalky, black rings under his eyes, "Look fellows, when they carried him out he was in such pain he couldn't talk. He barely managed to whisper, 'Tell Liebowitz and Finkelstein to go on doing Jolson. *Don't lose Jolson!* They can name their price. I'll be all right in a few weeks.' "

"Boyd," said Peter Quat, "I'm quitting. You know that."

Boyd laid his head on his arms on the desk. "Jolson knows Goldhandler's in the hospital," he said in a muffled voice, "but I read your draft to him and he loved it. He's flying in from Hollywood. It's the biggest writing budget we've ever had. Name your price, the boss meant that. The doctors say he can come back to work in four or five weeks. Talk it over, and let me know."

Peter and I did talk it over, long and hard, walking back to April House. I telephoned Boyd to tell him our price — doubled salaries — and Peter's condition: as soon as Goldhandler came back to work, he would quit. Boyd agreed to everything with such alacrity that I suspected we should have asked for more money. The question arose: what about our April House suite? Our landlady had offered to extend the lease. Should we do that, give it up, or what? And for me, another shadowy question: what about Bobbie?

Bobbie had written me one lighthearted letter from Texas, and I had shot back a casual reply. I had not felt quite lighthearted about a snapshot she sent me: she and Monica on either side of a paunchy man in boots and a ten-gallon hat. This was "Roy," the land developer. Bobbie wrote that Roy was "lots of fun, and a perfect gentleman." The arm around Bobbie was tight, and she was snuggled up against Roy, whereas Monica stood off from him like a proper cousin. But what did I care, after all? Tinker Bell had danced away on a moonbeam, had she not? And had I not been figuring on moving back home, and piling up my earnings for one last year?

Well, I signed a month-to-month lease, for Peter would have no part of it, saying he would merely split the rent until he left. I couldn't let Goldhandler down. I didn't believe that Peter would really quit, not at that salary. It was the most practical decision. So I told myself. It had nothing whatever to do with Bobbie Webb, who had written that she was returning by bus, and would arrive on July twenty-fifth.

＊　＊　＊

75

War!

I AM alone in a hotel suite overlooking blacked-out Jerusalem, drawing my first relaxed breath in days, having just listened to the evening news on the "Voice of Israel" English-language broadcast. On this third day of the war, the army chief of staff, General David Elazar — the universal nickname for him here is "Dado" — finally held a press conference. The Israeli army is now advancing north and south, throwing back both the Syrians and the Egyptians! I wonder if military annals record, anywhere, in any war, such a lion-hearted recovery and turnabout.

My mind will not be easy until I find out where Sandra is. Nobody seems to be sure. As for Mama, the word from the doctors is that the next twenty-four hours will tell whether she will make it this time or not. The crushing heart attack which brought me here yesterday, on an El Al plane full of Israelis returning from all over America and Canada to fight, sent her back to the Hadassah hospital. But she is putting on a pretty lion-hearted show herself. They allowed me to see her in her oxygen tent, for five minutes this morning. "I only hope I'm not interfering with the war," she gasped to me in Yiddish. "I don't want to be in their way. The Angel of Death is welcome to come for me, anytime." She was staring straight ahead, her vestigial vision gone — though the doctors say it can come back, if she pulls out of this — but her handclasp was firm. "Yisroelke?" she said when I first arrived. "You're here? Go and fight."

The Jerusalem Savoy is a fifteen-story hotel on a hill overlooking the Old City. The lobby glitters in gilt and glass, the purple plush-lined elevators whoosh and glide, the swimming pool is huge, the food in the three restaurants — coffee shop, delicatessen, and grill room — is lavish and kosher. The Savoy is a transplant of Miami Beach flourishing in the Holy Land, watered by the dollars of rich retirees. Abe Herz calls it "the Colossus of Toads." When I managed miraculously to reach him by phone at his army base last night, I said, "I'm in the Colossus," and he laughed and said, "Enjoy, enjoy." He has no idea where Sandra is, nor do the people know at Fields of Peace. I had hell's own time getting through to the kibbutz, and then all they could tell me was that they thought she had gone to Tel Aviv. She vanished a couple of hours after the Egyptians attacked.

I am in bad shape. Jet lag always hits me hardest when I fly eastward. I drank all night on the plane and kept writing about Bobbie, since sleep was impossible amid those excited returning expatriates. A horde of standbys milled around to the last, desperate to go and get shot at by the Arabs. And what a motley crowd made it aboard! Sunburned California types in snappy sportswear; East Coast pale-faces in ties and business suits; religious ones wearing yarmulkas and studying small Talmuds; hippie-looking characters all hair, beards, and jeans; and even a few in Texas hats — a number of girls and older women, too — and all of them chattering a mile a minute in Hebrew. I can read the Book of Isaiah at sight or cut through a column of Talmud, but I hardly understand Israelis talking quickly among themselves, any more than I can follow the Hebrew newscasters. It's frustrating.

I asked nobody's permission to fly here, I just informed the President's appointments secretary I'd received word my mother was dying in Jerusalem, and I was on my way. I had come home from the synagogue the moment Yom Kippur ended; and there was the cable, and I went straight to the White House to tell the secretary. He looked disconcerted and mentioned the war, which had then been on only a few hours. I came home and was packing a suitcase when, wouldn't you know, a gray faceless State Department figure showed up at my door. He said the Department felt that a hurried trip to Israel at this time by a Presidential Assistant, even a relatively, ah, inconspicuous one, might send a wrong message to the Arabs. He even made vague noises about my passport being held up. I said I would travel incognito, would remain truly, ah, inconspicuous in Israel, wouldn't check into the King David Hotel, which is the goldfish bowl of Jerusalem, wouldn't let anybody in the government know I was there, and when I wasn't at my mother's bedside would hole up in some secure place. I guess if he has no face he has a mother, because I encountered no passport hitch.

Possibly the Jerusalem Savoy doesn't quite fill that "secure" bill, but I'm not registered at the desk, and nobody knows I'm here but Mark Herz and Abe, and my sister Lee. Mark's uncle — that furrier he was working for when Peter Quat quit Goldhandler, and I got Mark to come on the job — owns this terraced penthouse. He and a few of his friends built the Jerusalem Savoy. He switched long ago from the fur business to Manhattan real estate, and in his nineties he's still back there, trading skyscrapers like Monopoly tokens. He comes to the penthouse on Passover, otherwise when he has a board meeting of some Israeli company. He's very religious, and he just gave a couple of million dollars to some hospital here for a cancer institute named after his wife, who died of it. I've never met the man, but Mark, who has been using the penthouse and invited me in, says he's a "dotty old bastard." All Jewish children should be so dotty.

Mark was back in Israel because of a woman he got to know during his lecture series here. Mark is no Peter Quat, but at sixty he's still a susceptible old dog, keeps questing for the girl he never found, or found and lost. I haven't met this one. She's some army big shot's wife, and she has several kids, and all in all it's a classic Mark Herz mess. She can't come to the Colossus because she'd be recognized. Of course he can't go to her house. For all I know they make out in his rented Subaru; though, even setting aside his gray hairs, Mark's pretty tall for hanky-panky in a Subaru. He is very gloomy company, partly, I suppose, because of that; also, though no such word has yet passed his lips, out of concern for his son.

I don't know whether he heard General Elazar's press conference, or if so took comfort from it. Mark has been saying ever since I arrived that it's all up with what he calls the "ephemeral episode of the Jewish State"; and while he's always been against the whole Zionist idea, and has regarded the eventual military collapse of Israel as foregone, he is troubled to see it happening as it were before his eyes.

"I didn't think it would come so soon," he said last night. We were sitting on the terrace. Jerusalem was all darkened, and a nearly full moon lit up the scene below in great splashes of silver and velvety black. The Old City is so small, seen from above! The zigzag Crusader walls stand out clear, and the ancient gates, and the mosques on the Temple Mount; and you can see down into the broad plaza that was bulldozed at the Wall after the Six-Day War. The picture is like the Celestial City in *Pilgrim's Progress* woodcuts, or like the Jerusalem of medieval paintings; also, a bit like a Hollywood set for a Bible movie, too much like one's childhood image of the Holy City to be the real thing. And of course it's only a small museum patch of the real thing. Modern Jerusalem stretches all around the Colossus, a panorama of thousands of new buildings and broad avenues on many hills, at the moment all dark under the moon.

"Israel is an egg with a tough shell," Mark went on. "The shell is the army. Break through the shell, and there's nothing inside but rich yolk to be devoured — the farmlands, the wealth, and the women. And the shell is cracking. A surprise attack on Yom Kippur was a damned smart play. It worked."

I did not reply. I was exhausted, I had no idea what was going on in the war, and I still had not seen my mother. I was in no shape to argue.

He peered out at the darkened city, his bony face scored with melancholy black lines in the moonlight. After a while he said, "I was sitting on this terrace, right in this chair, when it started. It was about two in the afternoon, very sunny and beautiful. You never saw anything so eerie as Jerusalem, five minutes before the alarm. The streets were empty. I mean empty. No traffic whatever. All deserted and silent, not a bus, not a taxi, just a few people strolling down the middle of the roadways in the sunshine —"

"It's always that way on Yom Kippur," I put in.

"Ah, but then! Sirens and madness! Men rushing everywhere with prayer shawls streaming, army trucks, buses, cars pouring into the streets, and the noise, the noise! It sounded up here like ocean surf in a storm. God!" Mark shook his head and drank a large gulp of his uncle's kosher Israeli brandy.

"In Washington it was ten in the morning," I said. "The whisper ran all through our synagogue that the Egyptians were crossing the Canal. Later we heard about the Syrians. Nobody was upset, we assumed they'd be turned back and slaughtered. That's what all the news commentators back home are still predicting."

"What do American TV drivellers know?" Mark snapped. "The

Syrians are clear through in the north. There's nothing between them and Haifa right now, and the Egyptians are approaching the Sinai passes."

"How do you know all that?"

He left it unanswered, with a somber look that said his source was sure. "Dave, Israel has a tiny standing army. The reserves are the real power. They need three days to mobilize. They're still struggling to do it, under heavy attack." He poured more brandy into his glass, and the night was so quiet I heard the splash. "The BBC said this morning the Syrians are attacking with three thousand tanks, and the Egyptians have about four thousand. All together the Israelis have fifteen hundred tanks, and most of them aren't deployed, even yet."

"They've always been outnumbered," I faltered, "and they've always won."

"Not this time, not against these odds in a surprise attack. Zionism has failed, Dave, and this is the moment of truth. The Jews never came. Not enough of them. They aren't here. They're everywhere but here, hanging on their TVs all over the world, waiting for the news that the handful of super-Israelis have done it again. Meantime the greatest soldier in this country, and don't ask me his name, told an army command meeting today, *'The Third Temple is falling.'* And don't ask me how I know. *I know.*"

Well, try to picture such talk on the marble-tiled penthouse terrace of a luxury hotel, with a breathtaking view of blacked-out Jerusalem under a high-riding moon! "What, then?" I said, forcing facetiousness out of sheer nerves. "Are the Arabs going to march in north and south, cutting throats as they go, and join up here at the Jerusalem Savoy for the final bloodbath?"

"No, nothing like that." Mark managed a sad smile. "The superpowers will stop it on terms, of course. But the Russians will let it drag on long enough to make it a total defeat for the Jews. You'll end with a disarmed rump Israel cut back to the 1948 borders. How long that will last, how long any Jews will want to stay here, is anybody's guess, but it won't matter. There were Jews in Palestine before this nationalist madness got going, and I suppose there will always be a remnant, praying at the Wall and waiting for the Messiah. After this they'll have lots of elbow room on that plaza, until the Arabs build over it again."

His woman telephoned him and he left. Such was my welcome to

Israel, on the second night of what they're starting to call the Yom Kippur War. Thank God things look better tonight. Israeli generals don't lie. "*I'm happy to say,*" General Elazar told the press, "*that we are already at the turning point, and we are on the advance. We will break their bones.*" That has the old super-Israeli ring, after three very worrisome days. These people have an expression, *yih'yeh b'seder,* which means approximately, "It'll be okay." That was the gist of Dado's words, and I believe him.

Meantime, what can I do with the slow hours until I can see Mama again, but go on with *April House?* Thank God for it. The ultimate time-killer is writing a book; though to tell the truth, here in the Colossus Bobbie Webb seems almost as unreal as Thuvia, Maid of Mars, with whom I fell wildly in love at thirteen. But Bobbie is no storybook enchantress. She happened.

Strangely, the telephone lines to the USA still work, hardly any worse than in peacetime. I assured Jan that Moshe Lev is tracking down Sandra. My sister Lee asked him to. Moshe is down in Tel Aviv in central staff command, a senior adviser. He told Lee there's no way the army would use a volunteer American featherbrain like Sandra, so that's one worry the less. But where *is* she?

Jerusalem Savoy
Wednesday, October 10, 1973

Mama is still hanging on. So is Israel. About both, I know little more than that, except that Dado was dead wrong at his press conference.

Mama made it through those crucial twenty-four hours, and then for a while the doctors wouldn't let Lee or me see her at all. This morning we were allowed in for a glimpse of her. She is a wasted wraith, but her eyes were alive, glinting at us. She did not talk. She wrote on a pad with trembly skeletal fingers what looked like wandering marks, just random scratches, until I realized that her hand was moving from right to left. She didn't finish the second Hebrew word, dropped the pencil and closed her eyes. She was writing *yih'yeh b'seder.*

Did Dado deliberately lie to the press? No. Not in Israel. Maybe he believed overoptimistic field reports. Or the urge to maintain the super-Israeli image may have carried him away. At any rate, five days after it started, this war is looking worse and worse. There was consternation here yesterday when Brezhnev suddenly called for a ceasefire, a signal that the Arabs are ready to cash in their chips on a won gamble, a sensational victory. What's more, the Soviets have been mounting a gigantic airlift to the Egyptians and the Syrians, so that for all their battle losses they are now *more heavily armed* than they were when they started the war. There has been some talk of an American airlift to counter it, but so far, only talk.

Abe Herz has turned up in the big army hospital, Tel Hashomer. I went along with Mark to see him. He is in bed with an arm in a sling, a bandaged head, and some minor burns. His tank was hit, and a flying metal fragment severed some tendons in his left hand. These army doctors here are marvels at patchwork, and he expects to return to the Sinai tomorrow. The wounded are going back into action, Abe says, as fast as the doctors release them. Many leave the hospital and hitchhike to their units without permission.

"Haven't you had enough of this?" Mark asked him.

"Why? The war is just getting rolling," Abe said, talking with some difficulty through a bandage. "We're going to cross the Canal and smash the Egyptian army. Then there will be a real peace. I'm not missing that. Some of my tank crew were cut up worse than me and they're still fighting. I'm being coddled. The American."

As we walked out through the long ward of wounded, Mark Herz kept looking around and shaking his head at these bandaged youngsters, some of them greenish-pale and moaning, some asleep, but most of them lively, talking, reading, smoking, listening to the radio.

I said, when we came out on a smooth flower-bordered lawn in brilliant sunshine, "They're a different breed of Jews."

"Not so different. Surviving, surviving, surviving, that's been the Jewish game for thirty centuries. Survive for *what?* The Jews have always been historically crazy. These are suicidally crazy, and if you call that a difference, okay."

My sister Lee had a dustup with Mark about the war at lunch. We ate out on the terrace. The food in the Colossus continues excellent. The room-service waiter was a kid with two bandaged hands and an eye patched shut. He couldn't open the wine after fussing and fussing with the corkscrew. Mark opened it and asked why he wasn't in a hospital. The waiter seemed surprised. "This is my job," he said, "while I study aeronautical engineering. In the army I'm a jeep driver, and I can't drive with this wound, so I'm working. The hotel is shorthanded."

He was a sabra, a native-born Israeli. When he left Lee began to reminisce about the first time she had heard the sabra accent, and she drifted to her usual rhapsodies about Jerusalem under the British Mandate: how charming it was, how elegant, how cosmopolitan, how peaceful. All she is really saying is that she was young and in love in Mandate Jerusalem, just as I've been weaving my own rainbows about April House. But she tells a good story and keeps coming up with fresh details, like her flirtation with the German consul who denied being a Nazi and said he really loved Jews; until Moshe Lev found out that he was a Gestapo officer with a horrendous British dossier on him. I had never heard about this consul before. Lee produced him complete with a thin blond mustache, piercing blue eyes, duelling scars, the name Klaus, and a flair for dancing. Lee said she and Klaus went on a junket to Cairo and won a bottle of champagne doing the tango at Shepheard's Hotel. I sometimes think Lee should be writing *April House*. She would jazz it up more than I can.

Mark asked how Moshe Lev would have had access to British intelligence. "Oh, he was very important, even then," she said airily. "He knew everybody worth knowing in Jerusalem."

"How come? Moshe was only a history instructor at the university."

Lee does not like being challenged about her whoppers, or unusual true adventures. "He was a sport flyer, wasn't he? Well, the head of British Intelligence also was a sport flyer. They were like *that*." She held out pressed-together fingers. "They used to take up two planes and dogfight."

"What does Moshe say about the way the war's going?"

"None of your business."

Silence. Mark raised gray eyebrows at me. "As a matter of fact, he says the worst is over," Lee said with a glare, "and we're about to smash them. First the Syrians, then the Egyptians."

I *know* Lee was just making that up. I've taken to guessing how the war is going from the sound of her voice over the telephone. She's in Ramat Gan, staying in an apartment house near General Lev's home, and I talk to her every day. Her voice has been falling in key and energy, and taking on concern, all week.

"Did he really say that? Didn't he tell you that the southern front is in a shambles? That the generals aren't talking to each other and are disobeying Dado's orders? That the whole command structure is coming apart? That Moshe Dayan is in paralyzed shock?"

"Where'd you get all that nonsense," sneered Lee, "from that tootsie of yours?"

Mark is a gent, and he let it pass, but Lee's blood was up. "Good God, how can you face yourself, with her husband down there fighting the Egyptians? How can you look in the mirror to shave?"

"I don't know what you're talking about."

"Oh, please. We're in *Israel*. Shall I mention her name?"

"When the war broke out they were arranging a divorce," Mark said with a rare hard note. "How about dropping it?"

Lee and Mark had scarcely left the penthouse when the telephone rang, and a girl sabra said, "Please hold for the Prime Minister." After a wait which gave me time to digest my surprise, I heard that strong cigarette-roughened voice.

"Doovidel, what's the matter? You're in Israel and you don't come to see Golda?"

I have been Doovidel — little David — to Golda ever since that tour we made together for Israel Bonds.

"Madame Prime Minister, I figured you might be busy."

She made a melancholy noise, half a laugh, half a grunt. "Is that what you figured?" Pause. A heavy breath or two. "Doovidel, I'm sorry about your mother. How is she?"

"Thanks. The doctors were more encouraging today."

"And how long are you planning to stay?"

"Well, that depends on Mama's condition. It's very serious."

"Yes. I know. I saw a report. Still, Doovidel, maybe you can help us by going back."

"When, Madame Prime Minister?"

"Tonight."

A wave of pins and needles washed over me; along my arms, down my back and down my legs to my toes.

"Madame Prime Minister, whatever I can do, tell me."

"I'm in a conference. You'll be at that number for a while?"

"Yes!"

"Doovidel, it will be all right," she said, and now she sounded grave, talking as though each word were a dropped stone. "We can use help. But if we don't get help, it will still be all right."

How did she know I was here? How did she know about Mom? Well, as Lee says, we're in Israel. I hope to hell the grapevine discloses, before I leave, where Sandra is. I don't want to face Jan with no clue about her.

And that is why I sit here on the terrace, trying my best to resume writing *April House* as I wait, to quiet my whirling mind.. The clock has since inched through two hours. My bag is packed.

* * *

76

Bobbie's Teeth

As the twenty-fifth of July approached, and I was missing Bobbie more and more, it occurred to me that when she got back it would be nice to give her something to remember me by. Now, about Bobbie's teeth; I have mentioned the peculiar way she smiled. Bobbie's two upper front teeth were discolored in contiguous patches; and her odd way of smiling, and her habit of curling her tongue over her upper teeth, were due to that blemish. She was silently, horribly self-conscious about it. My gift, I decided, would be caps for those teeth.

Well, she telephoned me from the bus terminal the minute she arrived, sounding amiable, if tired and rushed. When I asked her to come to the hotel (I wanted to tell her about the teeth, of course), she said hesitantly, "You mean right now? Are you sure you want that? Aren't you and Peter working?"

"Peter went to Jones Beach."

"Oh." Thoughtful pause, buses snorting in the background. "Well, maybe just for a minute, then. I'm all grimy and mussed, but I do want to show you my tan. Roy had this Olympic pool, and Monica and I just lived in it. But I've gotten so fat! You won't recognize me."

I recognized her. She wore the light gray dress, and as for being fat, the gain of a pound or so had only curved her more lusciously. There she stood in the doorway with that controlled smile. "Hi, honey."

"Hello, Bobbie. That's quite a tan."

We had a cool polite kiss, bodies well apart, in the gloomy foyer. "How is Mr. Goldhandler?" she inquired with real concern. "Will he be all right? I've worried a lot about him."

"It'll be a long pull. He may not come back to work for months."

"Oh, my! How awful. Well, let me look at you." We were strolling into the sunlit living room. "You should be at Jones Beach yourself, dear. You're pale."

"I'm glad I'm not at Jones Beach," I said thickly. I was having trouble breathing. The familiar smell of her perfume, the way her hips and skirt swung with each step, the sway of that black hair around her face, were having the effect on me of a severe asthma attack. I was also very light-headed, as though I had gulped a whole bottle of wine since she walked in. I was altogether in a peculiar state, and could not for the life of me think of a tactful way to bring up the caps for her teeth.

She glanced around. "Place looks just the same. And you've leased it again, have you? Well!" She sat down in the peach mink armchair, crossing her legs. "Tell me about Al Jolson. I once tried out for a Jolson show, but didn't make it. How do you like working for him?"

My response was not much to the point. I sprang on her like a leopard.

The reader will not approve, and this one false move unquestionably turned the current of my years. But let me explain that when Bobbie sat down she carefully lifted up and spread her gray skirt, so as not to crease it — any more than it had been creased in the bus ride from Texas — and in so doing she accidentally flashed her thighs in a clinging rosy half-slip afoam with lace; and as I say, she crossed those long legs of hers, and because of the spread skirt they happened to be in sight well above the knees. Hence my abrupt act, which had little to do with capping her teeth, any way you look at it. She did her best to fight off the leopard, but was overpowered, being fatigued from her journey, and the rest followed.

"Darling," I said, when the hammering of my heart subsided enough so that I could talk without panting, "have you ever thought of doing something about your teeth?"

"*Thought* of it?" She blinked up at me in weary astonishment. "Dear, it's my life. But I can't afford it."

"I can."

Her eyes rounded, and that one mobile eyebrow went up high. "Why, I can't let you spend that kind of money on me."

"I've got the money, and you're going to do it."

She studied my face, then said archly, "A farewell gift?"

"Something like that."

"Honey, I thought we made our farewells back in June."

"So did I."

She had arrived in New York by bus at two in the afternoon. By the Paramount clock it was now a quarter to four. By the time she left April House she had agreed to get the dental work done, and her grateful affection knew no bounds.

"Why, that's what I do," said Dr. Malman, Harry Goldhandler's dentist, to whom I had been going for a year or so. He was cleaning my teeth. "I gave Margaret Sullavan a whole new mouth. And I worked on Ethel Merman, and Henry Fonda. .Why, it's my specialty."

"I hardly know this young lady," I said. "I met her at a party the other day. She's just a singer, and she hasn't got much money."

Dr. Malman grinned at me, and the grin said, more plainly than plain English, "Don't worry, sonny, I won't overcharge you." His spoken reply was, "Of course. Have her make an appointment."

She telephoned me some days later. "It's impossible, honey, he wants seven hundred dollars."

"Go ahead and get it done. How long will it take?"

"A week and we won't be able to see each other till he's finished. I won't let *anybody* see me. I had the most awful dream last night. I dreamed he put in these two new teeth, and I saw myself in the mirror and I looked like a gopher. Now can you *truly* afford it, darling?"

When the job was done, Bobbie insisted on meeting me for dinner at the Golden Horn. "I just can't face being alone with you, dear. There have to be people around. Anyway, I've got to try out these fangs on a nice crusty roll." Her laugh was very shaky.

I waited quite a while in the restaurant, at our usual table. At last, led by that fawning headwaiter, here she came, walking tall and straight in a lightweight lilac suit I hadn't seen before, and a pearl choker. Her black hair was up in soft rolls around a face as shy and shining as a bride's.

"Hi, honey."

She slowly smiled. It was something of a shock. Those pitifully discolored teeth were gone, and she had a perfect white upper row. There had been a faint winning pathos about that blemish, but she was undeniably prettier.

"Bobbie, it's marvellous."

She grasped both my hands. Hers were damp and cold. "Aren't they too big? They're not tusks? You don't hate them?"

"They're beautiful. Perfect."

I handed her a gardenia, and the headwaiter brought the champagne I had ordered. Soon the confused Armenian served us another bottle on the house, and then still another, surmising that this was our wedding anniversary, or something. So we were awash in wine, and had a high old time. Convinced at last that I approved — I had to tell her so, over and over — Bobbie confessed that she was wild with joy, and her only concern had been whether I would be pleased.

"Oh, darling, no," she chortled when I offered to order brandy after dinner. "I'm loopy as it is. Whatever is going to become of us? Have I had my goodbye present? Is this truly the end?" So saying, she put her hand on mine, and turned lustrous eyes at me. Her look penetrated to my bones. She added, with a knowing grin, very tender and beguiling, "Listen, I don't mean *tonight,* of course. And, oh hell, I can't go on calling you *that,* can I? It's icky."

She had just used her original pet name for me, which the reader knows not and will not know. I have left it out of all her talk in this book, though she said it as often as "dear" or "honey." It was unutterably ridiculous. Peter Quat recently asked me out of nowhere, "What the hell was that idiotic name Bobbie Webb used to call you?" He was the only other person who knew it, except Monica, who is dead. I said I'd forgotten, and the secret will go with me to the grave.

Bobbie went on, "I've never liked 'Davey,' either. Maybe it's the way Peter says 'Davey,' with that little sneer in it. What does that 'I.' in your name stand for, anyway?"

No reason not to tell her, I suppose. "It's Israel."

She smiled, her face lighting with surprise. "Israel? That's nice. That's *you.* . . . Izzy . . ." She said it slowly, and her hand tightened on mine. "Yes! You're Izzy, from now on. And isn't it time, Izzy dear, that we went to April House, and looked at the moon?"

Well, in that context, Peter being away for the weekend, I was not about to start an argument about "Izzy," though when she uttered the name an old forgotten Aldus Street chill hit me. But she said it in such a caressing way that it did not sound so bad.

When we came out of the hotel, weary though we were, Bobbie wanted to walk. The warm starlit night was fading, with streaks of dawn over Fifth Avenue. We strolled up Central Park West arm in arm, moving like one person, bathed in physical gratification, saying nothing for a long time.

"Ah, Izzy," she burst out, "it was all supposed to be so casual and Noël Cowardish. It isn't working out that way, is it?"

"It isn't, Bobbie, no."

"Then what will happen to us?" She clung to my arm with abrupt fierceness. "I love you so much I can't eat, I can't sleep, I can't think. You *must* know that! In Texas I dreamed about you, about us, every night. I tore up letters I wrote to you. Monica would find me crying, and I'd lie about it. But she knew. Even Roy knew I was going out of my mind. I was supposed to stay till Labor Day. We were all going to spend two weeks on a yacht out of Galveston. I cut it short. I couldn't bear being away from you. You make me happy, and nobody and nothing else does."

I stopped at a bench, and made her sit down beside me. We were under a street lamp, but it was behind her and her face was in shadow. Now and then a taxi went by with hissing tires, otherwise the avenue was quiet. The traffic lights were changing — green, red, green, red — decorating the night but directing no traffic.

Minsker Godol, your move! I was dumbfounded. In a lightning turn, with that declaration, Bobbie was changing the rules, and throwing out the scenario. I spoke the truth, not knowing what else to do.

"Bobbie, I can't marry you," I said, forcing the words. "Both of us have known that, right along."

"Why? Tell me why. Is it because of the religion?"

I didn't respond.

"Or is it your parents? Why should they object? They've lived their lives. It's our turn now. I'm not a servant girl, I can hold my head up with anybody, and I'd be a good wife."

"What's the use, Bobbie? It isn't going to be, so —"

A hand with a wisp of handkerchief went up and touched the shadowed eyes.

"For God's sake, my sweet, don't cry."

"Oh, I'm all right. I'll be fine. It's just that I've never been jilted before."

Zing! Arrow into liver again, sharp and agonizing. Offhand, nothing came to mind from the works of Hemingway, Coward, or Edna Millay to deal with that red-hot pain.

"Call us a cab, Izzy," Bobbie said, "and don't look so sad. We'll both live. I'm just tired and cranky."

On the telephone next day, her voice was a jubilant chime. "Honey, I made it! Believe it or not, the Rodgers and Hart show. I'm IN!" At the tryout she had met old friends, and compliments had been showered on her about her teeth. "The chorus boys are falling all over me, dear, fair warning," she laughed. "And listen, I feel so stupid about that dismal scene I put on last night. I was so beat! I'm perfectly happy, everything's peachy, and would you take me somewhere to eat right now? I'm starved."

How to keep up with this creature? I telephoned Boyd, who was showing admirable generalship, keeping the troops marching on all fronts of the precarious Goldhandler empire. In a dead voice he agreed to my coming an hour late to a Jolson rehearsal.

"Look, Izzy darling," she said to me at Lindy's, turning serious after bubbling about her new job, "let me just say this, and then let's forget it. You've made me happy. You've changed my life for the better, and I couldn't be more content and grateful just as things are. Okay?"

And once more we agreed that our romance had no future, that our beautiful times together were all we wanted or expected of each other, and that our new cutoff date would be the departure of her show for the Boston opening. "It's perfect timing," said Bobbie with airy good cheer. "I'll be away for weeks, I'll be busy as hell, and I'll have all these new friends in the show." We shook hands on it and kissed, and she hurried off to the theatre.

Two weeks later she was threatening suicide.

She was unnerved at the possibility of being fired from the show. A few girls were due to be axed and paid off, and we had a ghastly blowup the night before the ax was due to fall. Bobbie had been moody right along during the rehearsals, lustful and hostile, sugar-sweet and crabby, by turns.

"I don't care if I'm axed! I don't want to go to Boston. I don't want to leave you, I can't bear the thought of it. I'd rather die! Maybe I'll just quit the show. Don't you want me to? Don't you care that I'll be leaving you? What's the matter with you, aren't you human? What are we doing in this bed anyhow?" On and on she raged, then turned ominously still. A stony look froze on her face and her eyes nastily glittered as she dressed in silence.

We had a grim wordless taxi ride to her house. "All right," she broke forth when the cab stopped. "I'll show you. You want me out of your life, that's plain. So be it. You'll be rid of me much sooner than you think."

"Oh, come on, Bobbie, what's that supposed to mean?"

"You'll find out." She got out of the cab, her face white and set as a corpse's, not looking at me at all.

"Good night, Bobbie. I'll call you tomorrow."

"Goodbye," she said in a strained far-off voice.

Why do I remember that I was carrying a rolled-up umbrella that night? I was, I know that. I walked to my parents' flat to get some sleep, a straight five-minute walk from Bobbie's tenement past the synagogue where Pop was a trustee. I didn't really think Bobbie was going to defenestrate herself, but it would be false to say I wasn't shaken up. My Tinker Bell fantasy had exploded in my face. I had on my hands a changeable fury of a woman, and I was a boy in these things, less able to handle her than to face down a charging cow elephant.

"Bobbie Webb? Hold on," said the janitor's voice next day, with no more than routine surliness. Bobbie lived on the top floor and the telephone was in the lobby. I heard him buzz her apartment, and after a few seconds, the whine of the elevator. Relief! Had Bobbie splattered herself all over Ninety-fifth Street, the man would probably have mentioned it.

"Hello? Who is this?" Alive, yes, but not perky. "Oh, it's you." Short silence. "Hi, honey."

I asked, "Are you all right?"

"I didn't get much sleep."

"Neither did I. Let me take you to lunch."

"Uh-uh. Me for a long cold shower, dear, and straight to the theatre."

"Dinner, then."

"Izzy, I'm coming home right after rehearsal and falling into bed.

I look awful. If I don't have one good night's sleep I'll get the ax. I'll call you, dear."

Okay, I thought. Bobbie's move.

But after a week of silence I decided it was preposterous to prolong this nonsense, and I called Mrs. Webb. Bobbie was fine, said the mother, but very busy. Oh, yes, she was still in the show, getting ready to go to Boston. Mrs. Webb sounded odd; not cold to me, but watching her words.

"Hi, honey, Mother said you called." Bobbie telephoned at midnight, sounding blithe as a robin. "Oh, my gosh, has it really been a week? How awful of me." She gave a guilty little laugh. "Just a second, dear . . . Eddie, will you turn down that radio? I'm on the telephone."

"Who's Eddie?" I inquired. "Where are you?"

"He's in the show, he's the lead baritone in the chorus. I'm in his apartment. Honey, I've been picked to understudy Doris Gray! Eddie's a voice coach. He coached Monica for years, and he's coaching me for nothing. We're working right now on my first-act solo."

Rumbling baritone voice in the background: "Hey, Violet! Want it straight up, or on the rocks?"

77

New Girl in Town

I would have been most cold-blooded of me not to feel a stir of jealousy at Bobbie's midnight call from a man's apartment. I did feel it, but I recognized that it was wounded ego, nothing more. Bobbie was clearly going to survive. There would be no diving under trains or other Tolstoyan gestures, and a chorus boy in the same show was a logical rebound. Still, wounded ego, however unworthy a feeling, does need to be assuaged. Enter, providentially, a new girl in town.

Pop's synagogue on Ninety-fifth Street had recently engaged a tall imposing rabbi from Belgium, a Dr. Hoppenstein, with a Ph.D. in Semitics from the Sorbonne, a full brown beard, and an elegant French accent overlaying his slow precise English. On Sabbaths and holy days Rabbi Hoppenstein wore a cutaway coat, striped trousers, and a high hat. Real class. His daughter Rosalind had class in her own way; still in college, she spoke French, Spanish, German, Flemish, and Hebrew, and her conversation was bookish but briskly engaging. She had a sweet if slight figure, and an alert fresh-colored face; no Bobbie Webb, Rosalind, but not bad, not bad. On Rosh Hashana I went with Pop to the synagogue, and that was how I met Rosalind.

Bobbie's show was trying out in Boston; and however sensible and inevitable our breakup, I was enduring withdrawal pangs, after all. Every love song on the radio seemed to be about Bobbie, and every sad love movie, too. She kept coming around street corners in strange girls' bodies. Night after night I dreamed about her. I found myself reading poetry — not Edna Millay any more, but heavyweights like Keats, Byron, Swinburne, Yeats, Donne — and all of English lyric verse seemed to be coalescing into one vast anthology, *The Golden*

Treasury of Bobbie Webb. I had not heard from her; not a call, not a postcard, nothing. As my troubled mind wandered during the long Rosh Hashana service, I became more and more aware of Rosalind Hoppenstein in the women's balcony. Glances shot between us, up and down across the large empty space to the first balcony row, where she sat beside a battleship-shaped mother.

Yom Kippur I spent with Zaideh, in the old Minsker Shule. Usually Aunt Faiga stayed with Zaideh on the great fast day, but she was sick, and I volunteered to keep him company. Well, it was a shocking passage, I tell you, from April House back to that Bronx synagogue, scene of my bar-mitzva triumph. How it had shrunk! I was entirely at home the moment I walked downstairs and smelled that cellar smell, and the odor of the shelves of old Talmuds along the back wall; at home, and yet as much a stranger as Gulliver in Laputa, the island floating in the air, peopled by queer inhabitants with bizarre beliefs. It was strange and familiar to hunger through the day, to keep glancing at the clock as I had in my boyhood, to watch the sunlight fade to red on the brick tenement wall outside the windows, and then, as the cantor chanted the *Closing of the Gate* prayers, to see that wall slowly darken to lilac, to purple, and at last to the black that spelled release and food.

All through the long fast, as I sat in a heavy prayer shawl of Zaideh's, I was thinking far less of atonement than of the many childish flirtations I had had in this shule. I could picture the girls, remember their voices and their dresses, recall what innocent liberties I had scored with them; all this, you understand, in flashes between haunting visions of my nights with Bobbie Webb, and hopeful thoughts of Rosalind Hoppenstein. True, Roz wore long drippy earrings, her dresses covered her from throat to wrists, and her heavy blonde hair was tied up in schoolgirl braids. Nevertheless, she had possibilities. Her sleepy slant eyes had a certain smolder to them. It was an aberrant way to spend the Day of Atonement, I grant you, thinking of girls, girls, girls, but that was how it was that year.

Zaideh, of course, was his usual cheery and informative self, breezing through the fast as though food were only for lower animals, pointing out to me charming subtleties in the poetry of the liturgy, and delivering a complicated sermon in his gentle voice to a half-filled synagogue. Even on Yom Kippur, when most temples and synagogues are jam-packed, the Minsker Congregation each year drew fewer worshippers. Zaideh was too old-country even for the Bronx people, who could hardly follow his elegant interweavings of Scripture verses and hard Talmud logic. I had to, because I knew he would ask me to repeat the whole thing. Anyway, I enjoyed it.

"Look," he said to me with a rueful gesture, as the day was ending, "an empty shule."

Whether he understood why that was, I don't know. Nor, as far as I could tell, had he guessed at my inappropriate state of mind. Then again, I'm not sure. When we broke the fast together in his flat, I joked about feeling confident that the boiled chicken was kosher. Zaideh's face all at once settled into sad stern lines. "My child," he said, "never eat forbidden food." That was all. It was a passing moment, and he was jovial again, but it sank in deep. Why? Uncle Yehuda's lobster tails? Bobbie Webb? I only know that after nearly forty years I can still see his grave old face before me, as he said it.

I returned to Manhattan all on fire for a date I had with Rosalind. When I called for her the battleship mother straddled me with broadsides of questions. Pop had chaired the rabbi-selection committee, and that was in my favor, but she clearly thought that writing jokes was a flighty trade. She kept probing around for something solid in me. When I mentioned — or rather, when it was bombarded out of me — that I might be going to law school one day, she ceased firing and offered me Cherry Heering with a smile. Rosalind walked in and behold, her dress was chic, her arms and throat were whitely visible, and her hair was modishly done. However, the earrings still dripped low, and her toes turned out. I had become too accustomed, I thought, to Bobbie's professional grooming and carriage. I had to make allowances.

But soon I was captivated, earrings and toes forgotten. Talking to Rosalind was like being back at a Columbia seminar, for quickness of repartee and range of thought. Yet she was all girl, and quite willing to flirt — with words. I would no more have made a pass at her than at her mother. Not that Rosalind was distant or forbidding, she just flashed an unmistakable "No Handling" sign in those clever smoky gray eyes. But we would touch, and there would be currents between our skins; not the galvanic magnetism that made it almost impossible for Bobbie and me to dance decently together, but then, it had not been that way at first with Bobbie, either.

And I liked Roz's father. Rabbi Hoppenstein was as different from

Zaideh as he was from Holy Joe Geiger; strictly Orthodox, yet carrying lightly a freight of western philosophy like Vyvyan Finkel's. He
befriended me, no doubt noticing my interest in his daughter. We
walked miles along Riverside Drive, talking religion. He had a sharp
wit, a warm tolerant way with strayers, and an absolutely first-class
mind. The way I live now began to take shape in those talks with
Rabbi Hoppenstein, as I tried to sort things out after Bobbie Webb's
tornado passage through my life.

Work was my best anodyne in that chaotic period. The hurt over
Bobbie throbbed on and on. Goldhandler was back in the penthouse, sneaking cigars, eating prohibited stuff like Lindy's cheesecake
and fried matzoh with pork sausages, and popping glycerine pills for
chest pains. Boyd, Peter, and I were working like dogs to keep up
with Jolson, Howard, and two low-comedy shows. The newspapers
and networks were in tumult, for Roosevelt was running against
Landon. Lee and Bernie returned from their honeymoon and got in
a nerve-wracking mess remodelling an apartment. Pop came down
with a kidney stone. Peter Quat's crazed passion for Marilyn Levy
half-disabled him, for she had become engaged to the son of a rich
cotton converter. The only bright ray in all this gloomy turbulence
was Roz Hoppenstein. Interest in Roz, I well realized, meant marriage and nothing else. Well, I sometimes thought, okay, so be it, *a*
rabbi's *a* daughter. Like father, like son.

"He's so mature, so thoughtful, so wise, Izzy, and he gets all his
philosophy from this one book."

"What book, Bobbie?"

We were supping at the Golden Horn a couple of nights after her
show opened on Broadway. Of course I went to see it, and took her
out afterward. Every trace of amorousness was gone from Bobbie
Webb's manner. Not long ago I had feared this girl might jump out
of a window for love of me. Ha! She could hardly stop talking about
this Eddie, and I pieced together a picture of an impressive chap. Not
only had he appeared in other Rodgers and Hart shows, he was also
a high-earning radio soloist, as well as a sought-after voice coach. He
read intellectual literature, and wrote plays; he was even working on
a new one during rehearsals.

"*The Prophet,* by Kahlil Gibran," she said. "It's so deep, and he reads
it aloud so beautifully." I had never heard of *The Prophet* or Gibran,

but said I would get hold of it. "Oh, do, Izzy. You'll learn so much. You need that book. I wish you had a mind like Eddie's."

That remark irked me. I was trying to be a genial sport, since at bottom I was relieved that Bobbie was happy, and off my conscience. Still, I doubted that I would be better off with any chorus boy's mind. On stage he had looked rather a ripe chorus boy, perhaps thirty-five. Bobbie assured me in the cab on the way home — not that I inquired — that it was just a friendship, because Eddie was married. A sisterly good-night kiss in the cab, and she was gone; very possibly, I thought, from my life for good. To sit with this dear familiar perfumed beauty in a taxicab and not touch her had been a trial. But it was over, it was the only way, and after all there was Roz Hoppenstein. Thank God for Roz!

Next day I asked Peter Quat about Kahlil Gibran. Oh yes, he said, his doormat mistress had treasured *The Prophet,* and could reel off whole pages by heart.

"What's it all about?"

"It's utter horseshit," Peter snapped. The cotton converter's son was still ruining his disposition. So I hunted up a copy and read it, and Peter was right on the mark. I wondered whether Bobbie had been playing a deadpan joke on me.

But I forgot about it, and tried to forget about her, and went out with Roz Hoppenstein several more times, growing ever fonder of her. Life improved. Roosevelt was elected, Pop passed the kidney stone, Lee's apartment turned out magnificent, Goldhandler seemed more and more his old powerhouse self, and Marilyn Levy threw over the cotton converter's son; so Peter calmed down, and decided to stay on the job and pile up more money, the academic year being shot anyhow. For all I know, I might sooner or later have proposed to Roz Hoppenstein, such was my mood; and we'd have lived happily ever after, and there might be nothing more to tell here. But out of the blue Bobbie Webb telephoned me, after some weeks, wondering how I was; and the fool I am writing about made another date to meet her at the Golden Horn.

78

A Moment of Truth

OVER her lamb and pilaf Bobbie blithered away again about Eddie, mostly about their work together on her understudy part. I put up with it, saying very little, waiting for a chance to break it up and go home. At last she asked why I was so quiet. Was I going out with someone? She hoped I was, because she didn't want me to be miserable.

"Oh, there's this rabbi's daughter, Bobbie. But she's just pleasant company."

A strange look came over Bobbie's face. She wanted to know all about the rabbi's daughter. She plied me with questions, almost like the battleship mama. The more I tried to dismiss the subject, because there was something unsettling about Bobbie's fixed gaze and set jaw, the more she dug and prodded for details. What color was her hair? How tall was she? How old? ("My God, an adolescent, Izzy!"—"Yes, Bobbie, but very smart.") Hm! Did she dress well? Could she dance? And so on, and suddenly, with our food only half-eaten, Bobbie jumped up and insisted on going home.

I have said Bobbie Webb was changeable, and now listen to this. As I had sprung at her on her return from Texas, so she pounced on me in the cab. "Oh, God," she muttered, kissing me again and again and again with those inflaming lips, "why do I love your mouth so much? The inside of your mouth is like honey. Take me to April House. Is Peter there?"

"I don't know," I gasped, forgetting that Peter was in New Rochelle, whence he seldom got back before three or four A.M.

"Well, dear, I don't care if he is. We'll throw him out. We'll tell him to go and see a late movie."

Thus Bobbie, brazenly laughing, all her gentility by the board. We did go to April House. I had a strong feeling — I could hear a voice in my brain telling me — that this time I was making a mistake for which I would pay very steeply. But resisting that onslaught of Bobbie's was absolutely beyond my power, and any reader who does not understand that lives in another world than mine.

"You know, Izzy," she said, as we lay there in spent lazy bliss, loosely embracing, "you were wrong about the deerfly, after all."

I was not sure I was hearing her right, being in a half-stupor. "What? What, Bobbie? The deerfly?"

"Yes, it's a problem of relative motion, you see. So only Einstein's theory of relativity can give the answer."

I sat up and stared at my love, lying there in the moonlight like the Nude Maja. We had not talked about the deerfly in months. I asked her where she had gotten all this. From Eddie, she replied. Eddie was a genius at problems, and Eddie said my answer was nonsense. There was no arithmetical answer. That was the whole trick of the question. The answer was that the deerfly's length of travel was a problem that had to be solved by the Einstein theory.

A reader here and there may not know the old deerfly chestnut, and it's vital to my story, so here is a quick run-through. A deerfly, fastest of flying creatures, zips back and forth between two railroad trains travelling toward each other. They start twenty miles apart, and both go forty miles an hour. The deerfly does sixty miles an hour. How far does the deerfly travel before the trains collide and crush the fly?

Another girl had brought the puzzle into the chorines' dressing room at the Winter Garden, causing great arguments. Nobody had figured it out. So Bobbie asked me, and I gave her what I thought was the answer. Bobbie carried my solution back to the Winter Garden, and tried to explain it to the other girls, but being muddled herself she couldn't state it clearly, and got hooted down; not without some comments that her supposedly smart Columbia Jew boy friend must be a real jackass. And that was the last I had heard of the deerfly, until this moment.

"Bobbie, listen carefully," I said, still dazed. "The trains start out twenty miles apart. Right? They each travel at *forty* miles an hour. Right? So the gap is closing at *eighty* miles an hour. So it will be

closed in *a quarter of an hour,* sweetie. Won't it? So the deerfly flies
for a quarter of an hour. One quarter of sixty miles is fifteen miles.
That's it. I think that's the answer. I'm pretty *sure* of it. Certainly it
hasn't got a goddamned thing to do with Albert Einstein."

"You don't have to swear and raise your voice," she said. "I must
bring you and Eddie together to argue it out. I bet he'll convince
you. I know he's right. Now come here and kiss me."

But a combative squirt of adrenaline was waking me up. I asked
her whether she had been kidding me about *The Prophet.* She appeared puzzled. Why, of course it was a great book, she said, but
Eddie had predicted that I wouldn't understand the philosophy, because I was too young. Next I inquired about the play Eddie was
writing. She hemmed and hawed, and said Eddie had made her
promise not to tell me the idea, because I might steal it, since all gag-
men were notorious thieves. "But I guess you can't steal it, at that.
It's beyond you," said Bobbie, "it's a very serious play." She revealed
that it was about reincarnation. Three great men were all actually the
same person, and the three acts would show how the three lives were
really one. The three men were Napoleon, Edgar Allan Poe, and Bix
Beiderbecke. Eddie hoped to star in the play himself, as these were
his three heroes.

Well, somehow that did it. It was a moment of veil-ripping truth.
This Eddie might be a good voice coach, I knew nothing about those
things, but he was a preposterous ass, that was certain, and my Bobbie lapped up his mindless drivel. She lay there naked in body, mind,
and soul, the glorious Avatar of the Outside, my poor dear first love,
as fair as the daffodils of April, a hopeless, gullible ninny.

"Let's go, Bobbie. Peter will be getting back," I said.

"Oh, dear, yes." Bobbie happily yawned, stretching. "And I did
tell Mother I'd be home early. We must do this more often, Izzy."

And as she tucked her exquisite breasts into a lacy brassiere, it came
to me with pain like acute angina that whatever she was, I loved this
girl, loved her as I could never love Rosalind Hoppenstein; that I
was bound to this one girl, of all living girls, with unseen steel cords;
and that I had had to find out just what a lightweight fool she could
be, to strike down to the bedrock fact that I loved her.

"For Christ's *sake!*" groaned Peter the next night, looking at his
glowing watch dial. "The phone, three in the morning?"

"Probably a wrong number." I leaped out of bed. I had not closed my eyes all night, lying there tossing in bedclothes redolent of Bobbie's perfume. I shut the bedroom door and answered the phone.

"Hello, Izzy dear." Gay tipsy note. In the background, laughter, loud talk, music, clinking of glasses. "Is this awful of me, to wake you up?"

"I wasn't asleep."

"Oh, working late again? How are you, honey? Look, this whole place is in an uproar over the deerfly. I did my best to explain your fifteen miles, but everybody thinks Eddie is right about the Einstein theory. Why don't you talk to Eddie? Here he is — come on, Eddie, he wasn't asleep."

Rich rumbly baritone: "Hello, there, Izzy. This is Violet's idea, calling you up. But anyway, Izzy, you're wrong about the deerfly. What's all this about fifteen miles?"

I was too numbed, I guess, to do anything but run through the answer again.

"Well, Izzy, your methodology is fundamentally mistaken. You see, you've got a series of smaller and smaller relative motions there. So you just can't work the problem without the Einstein theory of relativity. Albert Einstein's down there in Princeton, you know. I've met the man, we've talked for hours."

Poor, poor bubble-headed Bobbie! "I didn't realize you knew Einstein," I said. "Of course that settles it."

"Okay, Izzy. I hope Violet didn't wake you, just for this. . . . Violet, want to talk to the guy again? I've got to go to the can."

"He calls me Violet," she giggled. "He says Bobbie is a childish name. So, it's all straightened out about the deerfly? Good. That was fun last night, Izzy. Call me."

Click.

I sat there in my pajamas, looking out of my April House aerie at the downtown skyscrapers, dark against the stars except for a few yellow patches of windows, and at the Paramount clock that had once kept the time of our shining palace. No use going back to bed. I felt that I might never sleep again, or eat, for that matter. The arrow in my liver this time was poisoned.

A snowy night in February.

I have been walking for hours. Starting from April House, I have wandered in the white silent park, and then gravitated downtown to Broadway. Circling aimlessly, I have stopped twice at the theatre where Bobbie's show is playing, and have stared and stared at the cast pictures, picking her out of the chorus scenes, twisting the dagger in my gut.

Just to do something with myself, I drift on to the Radio City Music Hall, where the box office is about to close for the night. I am in time to see the last stage show. When the forty Rockettes line up and do their kicks, I see forty Bobbie Webbs kicking perfect, unmatchable, maddeningly exciting Bobbie Webb legs. The sight is unendurable. I walk out to the foyer.

I am in an exceedingly bad way. Peter Quat has put up with my collapse and is doing the work of both of us, even agreeing to my taking a ten-day cruise to Cuba, which has helped not at all. My trouble is an all too simple and common one. The reader who has not been through such an ordeal has enjoyed a sheltered youth. After enduring tortured weeks of Bobbie's moody, peevish, whimsical veering between me and the man who knows Einstein — her evasions, her broken dates, her brazen lies, her blowing cold and hot — I have become a disintegrated wreck; and to end the humiliating torment, I have written her an ultimatum. Her reply has been silence. It has now lasted more than three weeks.

In the grotesquely grand and ornate lobby of the Music Hall, I am almost alone. The voice in my brain speaks. *I know where she is. I am going there. It will be the worst experience of my life, but I must go.* Nobody can ever tell me that there is no such thing as a presentiment; and incidentally, I have never again been inside the Radio City Music Hall.

Bobbie stares at me, shocked, round-eyed and open-mouthed, as though she is seeing a ghost. Probably I look like one, hat and coat caked with snow, my face maybe whiter than the snow, bursting into the bar out of the night. She is sitting on a bar stool beside the man who knows Einstein, in the small sleazy bar of the Broadway hotel where he lives.

"Good lord," she says to him. "It's Izzy."

The man who knows Einstein turns and grins at me. Close up, he appears to be forty, with a lined jowly face. "Hi, there, Izzy. What a surprise. Come and have a drink."

I go and sit beside her. There is nobody else in the bar. "Bobbie, I want to talk to you."

"Well, go ahead and talk."

"Will you come with me somewhere?"

Bobbie hesitates. Her abundant black hair is carelessly pinned up. I have seen it that way often, late at night, when she has just gotten out of bed. She is sitting between me and the man who knows Einstein. She deliberately puts her hand high inside his thigh and rubs affectionately near his crotch. "Anything you want to say to me, you can say in front of Eddie."

"All right. I love you. I want you to marry me."

Whatever Bobbie is expecting, she does not expect that. She looks as though I have knocked out her wind with a punch. She peers at me and glances at the man who knows Einstein. He is smirking over his beer as he sips it.

"Well!" she says, speaking very slowly and primly, with a slight stammer, "I see. Of course I'm proud and happy that you feel that way, but . . . excuse me."

Off she goes into a powder room visible in the lobby, leaving me with the man who knows Einstein. He gabbles about the hard lot of gagwriters, who have to be thieves for a living. I pay no attention. I am in deeper shock than Bobbie. That unmistakable, unspeakable gesture of her hand!

She returns. "Oh, you're still here? I thought you'd gone by now. Well, have a drink, then. Or are you leaving?"

"Bobbie, I want an answer," says the damned young idiot who was then called David Goodkind.

Bobbie's face takes on an expression I have never seen before and have never since forgotten — half-closed glassy glittery eyes, contracted black brows, and a cold smile showing all her teeth. She glances at the man who knows Einstein, lays her hand again high inside his thigh, and looks straight at me. "Don't you know when you're done, Izzy? That's not characteristic of your race."

So at that I collect myself, and what is left of my self-respect, and walk out of there. Right? Wrong. That is not how things go in real life. What she has said, I scarcely grasp; not just then, not yet, as they say one does not at once feel the penetrating knife or bullet. I cannot remember what I reply, but there are more words. Bobbie jumps up, very agitated, puts on the beaver coat I bought her, and angrily ties a red shawl over her hair and under her chin. "I'm leaving, if you're not. Come on, Eddie," and she plunges out into the night. He follows her. I dumbly start to follow, too.

"Look," the man who knows Einstein says to me at the door, with more condescension than malice or menace, "she really doesn't want to talk to you, don't you know that?"

But I come out anyhow, and I watch them fade off side by side in the whirling neon-lit snow of Broadway.

79

Bobbie's Second Thoughts

"IZZY, are you *all right?*"

That voice, that unforgettable voice — that voice I can hear in my mind now, thirty-six years later, as plainly as I've just heard a patrolling jet fighter break the sound barrier out over the Mediterranean — that voice was on the telephone again after a long terrible month and more, sounding rushed and shaken. I had jumped from my typewriter to the phone, not expecting to hear from her, yet still in that state of excruciating tension when every telephone ring was like a gunshot.

"Hello, there, Bobbie. I'm fine, why?"

"I had the most *horrible* dream about you last night. I couldn't stand it, I had to find out how you were. You really are all right?"

"Perfectly okay. How are you?"

"Oh, not bad."

Long pause. Then Bobbie, in a different sheepish tone, "It sounds sort of *obvious,* dear, my calling like this, but I did have this truly awful dream about you."

Overwhelmingly sweet as it was to hear that light crystalline voice again, the pain at least equalled the sweetness, and through my tumbling emotional murk a single idea shone through, an Eleventh Commandment booming at me out of fire and cloud, HAVE NOTHING MORE TO DO WITH HER.

"Well, it's nice of you, Bobbie, but I am quite okay."

"I'm so glad. How is Mr. Goldhandler?"

"Pretty well recovered. I see your show's still running."

"Oh, sure." Another awkward pause. Then, gaily and a bit shyly: "Are you doing any horseback riding?"

And there it was. The dream ploy was feeble enough, but this was as close as a girl like Bobbie Webb could ever come to backtracking.

In our magic springtime, one of the many things we had done was ride together in Central Park. I had bought her a fetching riding habit, and we had trotted, or rather plodded, around the reservoir now and then on placid old hired nags. Now here was the olive branch. I had only to say the word. It was late March, the park was greening, and the riders were out.

"Well, I've been sort of busy, Bobbie. A lot of work."

"I see. I hope I haven't interrupted you."

"Not at all. It's nice to hear from you."

"Nice to talk to you." Slight pause, and she added cheerily: "Well, goodbye, then."

"Bye, Bobbie."

Between that famous encounter in the bar, with the man who knew Einstein as witness, and this call, exactly four ghastly weeks and five ghastly days and nights had elapsed. It was by chance that I was in April House when Bobbie called. I had been living at home in Lee's old room, and coming to the suite for a few hours to work with Peter. I couldn't sleep a wink in April House, couldn't endure looking out at Peeping Tom, seeing the Paramount clock at night and that whole downtown panorama. Peter Quat surmised my trouble, more or less, when I temporarily moved out. "I'm not paying the whole rent," was all he said, and when I assured him I would go on paying my share, that was that.

But Mama asked so many questions when I came home with a suitcase that I was inclined to give up the idea, until Pop snapped at her in Yiddish, "What's the matter with you? The boy comes home, and you ask questions? Don't ask. The boy came home, and finished." That silenced Mama.

I had read somewhere that one slept best in a cold room, and it was a bitter winter, so I took to turning off the radiators in Lee's room, opening the windows wide, piling on the blankets, and downing stiff slugs of neat whiskey. I still didn't sleep much, but there was something primally comforting about air icy in the lungs, booze warm in the stomach, and a heavy swaddling of blankets. Mama did some muttering when she came in some mornings and found snowdrifts on the floor, but she made no trouble about it. She did bother me a lot, however, about a large sign I pasted in my bathroom, the day after my date with Vyvyan Finkel's secretary.

Seeking relief from my agonies over Bobbie, you see, I went up to Columbia to talk to Vyvyan in his office. Vyvyan was delighted. He put his arms around me, gave me several damp friendly kisses, and offered me sherry from a bottle lying on a shelf behind the collected works of George Santayana. I kept pouring out my heart as he poured the sherry. He was most sympathetic about Bobbie, assuring me that all this would be grist for the mill, once I entered on my true calling as a pewet.

"I seem to be the fool of the world," I said. "Maybe I should start my education over again."

"You have." He recommended several books, including — I remember — *The Education of Henry Adams* and *The Memoirs of Casanova.* "Just to get the range," he smiled, and he invited me to come to a concert with him, as in the old days.

Well, on my way out, there sat at a desk in an outer room this big blonde girl in tweed, busy with papers and books. Any port in a storm! I introduced myself, and was surprised by a friendly smile, a warm large-boned handshake, and the disclosure that she had seen my Varsity Shows, and read my Vicomte de Brag columns while at Barnard. I took her to the theatre. The date cheered me up more than my talk with Vyvyan had. Here was a girl with a brain, a Columbia education, and a Phi Bete key; catch her falling for a chorus boy who knew Einstein! I was enchanted, and tried necking with her in the taxicab afterward. That was not so hot. She had a way of staring wide-eyed at me as I kissed her, and she smelled soapy.

Still, when I got home from that date I was a new man, or thought I was. I printed in crimson crayon on a piece of cardboard, *IT WAS THE LUCKIEST THING THAT COULD HAVE HAPPENED* — referring, of course, to my rejection in the bar — and propped it in my bathroom, so that when I got up and went to bed, this consoling thought would confront me. I forgot that Mom would see the sign. She pestered me about it. "What was the luckiest thing that could have happened? Tell me. Tell me what was so lucky! Why can't you tell your own mother?" Et cetera. Papa had to intervene again and order her to leave the boy alone, if something lucky had happened to the boy she should thank God, and finished.

That sign was all very well, but one more date with Vyvyan's secretary, and I gave up. No soap. Or rather, soap, yes, brains, yes; but ah for black hair, huge eyes, and dopey gullibility about Kahlil Gibran! The ordeal of icy sleepless nights went on. I was keeping my sanity by concert-going with Vyvyan Finkel, burying myself in work for Goldhandler, and seeing more and more of Zaideh — as Vyvyan put it, to get the range. Bobbie's ineradicable words, *"That's not characteristic of your race,"* had thrown me back a long way. During those insomniac whiskeyed-up nights they reechoed and reverberated in my mind. Naturally I told Zaideh nothing of all this. Nor did he ask questions, except, as I would be leaving, "When will I see you again?" We studied Talmud, and he told me about old times in Russia, and he also talked a lot about Uncle Velvel's latest quagmire, a matter of peanuts.

Last and maddest of the Velvel stories, true as sunrise. Briefly, a cousin of Velvel's worked on a kibbutz that grew peanuts and shipped the raw product abroad. Velvel had some money, though the shittim-wood scheme was finished, because his wife had finally divorced him, and his father-in-law had given Uncle Velvel a nice lump sum to get lost, permanently. Uncle Velvel invested in machines that salted and packaged peanuts, and built a small processing plant near that kibbutz. The markup from peanuts off the vine to the packaged article was of course enormous, and Uncle Velvel saw his ship coming in, after a lifetime of thwarted visions.

The ship might well have made port, what's more, except for the unforeseen problem of vibration. The floor of the processing plant had been poorly set down, so it vibrated. The whole plant vibrated. In fact the entire kibbutz vibrated, or so the kibbutzniks claimed. In a nearby kibbutz machine shop, the ceiling fell down, knocking cold some idealistic Americans working there. The kibbutz council blamed Velvel's peanut plant, and there was hell to pay.

That was bad enough, but the main problem was with the product. The vibration threw the salting process out of whack. A large shipment of heavily oversalted peanuts went to France — though it was news to me that Frenchmen ate anything as normal as salted peanuts — and set fire to a lot of Gallic insides and caused no end of trouble. Most of the shipment came back. The French importer was suing Uncle Velvel. Velvel was suing the contractor who had built the processing plant. The council that ran the kibbutz, fearful of getting involved, had given up on Velvel and resumed shipping peanuts abroad.

So Uncle Velvel was left high and dry with a peanut-processing plant that vibrated, and no peanuts. Far from taking this lying down, he was importing peanuts from Liberia, and suing the kibbutz council for not supplying him with peanuts. He had nothing on paper, so he was suing in a rabbinic court, where an oath of a pious man, and Uncle Velvel was visibly pious, would have weight. It was a Marxist kibbutz, not pious at all, so the council was countersuing Uncle Velvel in a secular court for trespassing, since the vibrating plant was on their land and they wanted it off. The council claimed that Uncle Velvel had built the plant too close to their dairy barns, and the vibration was making the cows nervous, drying them up and causing them to fight like bulls. I am summarizing a mess that went on for years. Zaideh would read me Uncle Velvel's letters, naively rejoicing over his son's reports of triumphant turns in the lawsuits, which always concluded with pleas for more money to pay his lawyers.

It was a study in contradiction in one man's personality; Zaideh's sword-sharp mind for Talmudic profundities, and his uncritical swallowing of Uncle Velvel's reports. Zaideh lived on air, or so it seemed, and sent Velvel every dollar that came his way, whether through fees for weddings or divorces, or gifts by younger rabbis who studied with him, or money Pop would give him to buy new clothes and better food. Zaideh's ruling principle, which I guess overrode his penetrative intellect, was family affection. There are worse weaknesses.

The night after Bobbie telephoned me I slept nine uninterrupted hours. My first thought on opening my eyes was sheer astonishment that it was broad day. Then the pain flooded back in, from the void in my life torn by the loss of Bobbie. It was as sharp as ever, and yet I had slept. Why? I understood nothing then. I just stumbled along, day by day and week by week, in the dark even at noonday. But now it seems simple. Most of my insomniac anguish was over the loss of a beautiful girl, but the rest was stabbed ego. Bobbie's one hint about horseback riding closed that stab wound as by a miracle at a shrine. Night after night I slept, though the loss still hurt so much. I moved back to April House, and there too I could sleep.

Peter said to me, one afternoon when I returned in boots and jodhpurs from a ride in the park, "Wasn't your birthday in March?"

"Yes, why?"

"Bobbie called, and said to wish you a happy birthday."

It was April first. I knew what she meant. By the gargoyle face Quat made, I gather that he did, too. A few days later, a book came for me in the mail: *Second April,* poems by Edna St. Vincent Millay; inscription, *For IDG, happy birthday, with best regards to P. Tom, from BVW.* I thought it would be churlish to ignore this. After writing and tearing up half a dozen attempts at a noncommittal note of thanks, I telephoned Bobbie. Not for months had I heard those elevator whines and door crashes and footsteps. The pain came on strongly.

"Hello, who is it?"

She sounded muffled and weak, and went into a coughing fit.

"What's the matter, Bobbie?"

"Oh, it's *you.* Hi, there." Cough, cough. "Excuse me. I've had pneumonia."

"My God, Bobbie."

"I'm getting better now. I hope to be back in the show next week. I guess you wish I'd *died* of it."

The bitterness of her tone! I did not believe I could feel any worse about Bobbie Webb, but this made me feel worse, and yet in a crazy way a little relieved. Whatever her present attitude toward me, it was still intense, still, like mine, running with heart's blood.

"Darling," I said, using the endearment deliberately — and rustily, for it had been a long time, "thanks for the book."

"Oh, that. Don't mention it." More bad coughing. "Look, Izzy, there's an awful draft in this hall, I'd better go back upstairs or I'll have a relapse."

"Bobbie, will you call me when you're better? Let's have dinner at the Golden Horn."

"That'll be fine." Through harsh coughs she said goodbye and hung up.

80

Quat Quits

"WELL, this does it!" All sweaty, Peter Quat burst into the suite, waving a letter and a tennis racket, waltzing around the room and then handing me the letter. "I'm quitting. *Now.*"

The publisher was not exactly offering to buy *Mother's Milk*, Peter's fragment of a novel, but his letter did say that if the rest of the book lived up to the promise of the beginning, he would be interested. Peter Quat's multitudinous admirers may wonder at a title of his that they haven't come upon; but the fact is, *Mother's Milk* was eventually rejected by nineteen publishers. Peter wisely shelved it.

The book was a youthful first effort, a steamed-up memoir of a summer he spent in Mexico. The central character, a lady school-teacher of forty or so from Minnesota, is on a tour, and meets a college senior vacationing in Taxco. At first she seems a dried-up wistful prude, but she soon turns into a prophetic Quat foreshadowing of the heroine of the film *Deep Throat*. Old Peter broke fast from the starting gate. However, all that part was pretty tiresome, and certainly much ahead of its time. *Ulysses* was barely legalized then, and considered red-hot reading. The funny scene in the Tijuana whore-house which closes *Deflowering Sarah* was, in an early crude version, the start of *Mother's Milk*, and the best thing in it. Peter Quat usually salvages his good stuff, sooner or later.

Anyway, Peter packed up and left that same weekend, to hole up in his father's cottage in Maine and work on *Mother's Milk*. So ended abruptly our years of collaboration and living together. His parting words were much in the Quat vein. His eye fell on a porcelain cat from Hong Kong that Bobbie had given me, sitting on my desk. "Well, at least I'm seeing the last of that frigging Chinese dust-catcher," said Peter, and he picked up his suitcases and departed.

That same week I ran into Mark Herz at a *Jester* reunion dinner, and he looked so gaunt and seedy, and ate the leathery roast beef so hungrily, that I figured he might be wanting employment. He said he was interested, being dead broke. The furrier uncle had recently sold his business, and Mark was on his uppers, though promised an eventual fellowship at Berkeley. Harry Goldhandler was skeptical of my notion of recruiting Mark, but said he would talk to him. Mark came when Goldhandler was very grumpily eating breakfast. A comedy program the night before had flopped, the stock market was down, and Henny Holtz's audience rating was up. The main trouble, however, as Boyd managed to whisper to me, was the Alaskan gold mine. Klebanoff was in town again.

"Pass the shit," Goldhandler said to Boyd, pointing to a platter of scrambled eggs. Mark winced and glanced at Mrs. Goldhandler, who sat placidly smiling beside her pretty little daughter. Goldhandler had had another, less severe heart episode and was no longer eating fried matzoh with his pork sausages, just plain scrambled eggs. He was taking it hard. He asked Mark only a few perfunctory questions. His face was as gray as the stubble besprinkling it, he had lost more teeth, and though he was thirty-seven, Mark would have believed me if I had said he was fifty.

"Well, Finkelstein," Goldhandler said to me later in the office, while Mark waited downstairs, "it's up to you. Bright guy, but an amateur."

"Let me try Mark," I said.

Klebanoff came into the office just then, a burly bewhiskered man in corduroys and a sweater. "Good news, the syndicate has come through," was his gravelly greeting.

Goldhandler's tired face lit up in a surprised gap-toothed smile. He dismissed me with a nod. "Terrific! Really? When did this happen?"

"I talked to Juneau this morning. None of us have to put in another cent. What happens after this —" As I went out, Goldhandler was listening to Klebanoff with the beaming look of Zaideh reading aloud Uncle Velvel's letters about his legal successes.

"I thought you said he was amusing," Mark remarked as we walked downtown.

"He was in a bad mood."

"Oh, come on, Dave, honestly. '*Pass the shit!*' The man's a barbarian."

"You don't want to do this?"

Mark walked along in silence, in that peculiar hitching gait of his, almost a lope. He wore the old brown tweed jacket of Columbia days, patched at the elbows and frayed at the sleeve ends. "I'm in no position to pass it up. I just don't know if I can be of any use to you. Anyway, I'm counting on that fellowship, so it will only be until the summer."

Mark moved into the suite, and went to work on gags. It was an awkward situation. Here I was, ever so junior to the Man in the Iron Mask, yet making more money, and in charge. The Man now had a job by my sufferance, and was living in a luxury suite at my cost, for I refused his offer to contribute to the rent. Nor was he much of a joke-writer. He was a university wit, and there is a difference, of which he was well aware.

"You're doing it all," he said to me after a couple of weeks. "I'm not contributing, and I feel like a leech."

But I urged him to stay on. He did have funny notions, and it was useful to talk out the drafts with him. Though the Bobbie anguish had abated — I had found other girls, nobody like Roz Hoppenstein and none of consequence to this story — I did not yet want to live alone in April House. For one thing, I did not trust myself not to ask Bobbie back there, in a weak moment. Besides, Mark Herz was a mighty pleasant roommate after Peter Quat.

I haven't complained here about old Peter, but now I can mention that he had been rather a trial to live with. For one thing I have never known a person who farted so much, or who so perversely regarded farting as an accomplishment, rather than a weakness. Peter would crow happily after letting an explosive fart, like a hen upon laying an egg. You can tell from his books that he retains some odd fixation on breaking wind. Also, he was very strange in the mornings. He would wallow around in the bedclothes for about two hours, singing snatches of old songs and giggling to himself. He would then get up and shave, laughing crazily and making sounds like "Breep breep! Poop de broop poop!" But he was not really merry. On the contrary, if I spoke to him before he had eaten breakfast and read through *The New York Times,* he would give me a frightful snarl, uncovering his teeth like an attack dog. You had to get used to Peter Quat. I've often thought that may be one reason why he keeps changing his women every couple of years, like cars. The girls may plain wear out.

Returning from a morning walk under the blooming cherry trees, I let myself into the suite and heard Yiddish being spoken a mile a minute; and it was nobody but Mark Herz talking! In the living room with him sat a bearded little man in a yarmulka and a plump gray-headed woman, who was mopping her eyes.

"*Meine elter'n,*" said Mark with a harassed look at me; that is, *my parents.*

Mark had never before used a Yiddish word in my hearing. Only because he had been a Beta Sig had I known he was Jewish. To the observances and holidays he had been indifferent; not hostile like Peter, not satiric, just blank; in this, as in speech, dress, and general air, a very Deke. His attitude toward all religion was like Vyvyan Finkel's; totally detached, condescending, and cold. Vyvyan had called Mark "his best student ever" in comparative religion.

His father started to greet me in broken English. Mark abruptly interrupted, "*Er farshteit,*" that is, *he understands;* and he went on to me in Yiddish, "Can you lend me a hundred dollars?"

"Glad to do it, Mark," I replied, same language.

The father said excitedly, "Why do you bother your friend? The bank will lend us the money, you only have to come home and co-sign the papers."

Mark told his father he was not going to drag out to Coney Island to get involved with that bank again; he already owed too much there. I sat down at my desk with the checkbook. The mother asked me shyly how it was I knew the language. Hadn't I been born in America? Answering her, I could not but note how halting my Litvak talk was, compared with Mark Herz's natural Galician flow. He endorsed my check and gave it to his father, saying, "Now, Papa, you can bury Aunt Rose. My mother's sister died this morning, Dave. A benevolent association is supposed to pay for her funeral and her grave, but the records are all messed up. The money isn't forthcoming, and there Aunt Rose lies in a Far Rockaway funeral parlor."

"Such a scandal, such a disgrace!" said the father. He put the check in his pocket and shook my hand. "You have a great mitzva. Burying the dead is a holy thing, and you've taken a part in our family duty."

When Mark came back from seeing his parents to the elevator, he said, "Well, I guess that's that. I stay on the job and work it off."

"Your Yiddish is damn good," I said in candid wonder.

Mark made a wry face. "It ought to be." He rattled off in Aramaic, in perfect yeshiva chant, the start of the Talmud order *Damages: "The major categories of damages are four: the ox, the pit, the grazer, and the fire-setter."* Then in his natural sardonic English: "I'm off to see Aunt Rose planted. That draft of the Fanny Brice skit is on your desk. I suspect it's worthless."

That night we were both typing away when Bobbie Webb telephoned me in tears and panic. This time it was no ploy, she was clearly distraught about her dog. Mark paid no attention to my conversation, though he gave me an odd glance as I went on trying to soothe her. On an impulse, when I hung up, I pulled out Bobbie's picture — the one in my diary now — from under a lot of scripts in a drawer, and showed it to him.

"That's her?" All he knew was that I had problems with a girl.

"That's her."

He shook his head over the picture. I put a bottle of scotch and glasses between us, and told him my story as we drank. It took a while.

"Question," I wound up, "do I help her with the dog?"

Mark just looked at me, musing.

"Well, Mark?"

"The student prince and the barmaid," Mark said.

"What?"

"The oldest of old stories, Davey. Pure operetta."

"I don't follow you. Bobbie's no barmaid, she's a dazzling Broadway beauty, and I'm no student prince, I'm a wretched gagman."

Mark poured very stiff drinks for both of us. "You're the Minsker Godol."

"Ye gods, I told you that only once, when we were drunk on needle beer. How can you remember?"

"Davey, I was a Godol."

And Mark opened up and talked about himself and his family. He did it that once, and never again. Nor did he speak Yiddish again, not around me. Just that one night, the iron mask came off as we finished the bottle of scotch.

Mark was born in a Polish village outside Cracow, he told me. His father was the town *shokhet,* the kosher slaughterer. The family came to America when he was four, and his father started as a shokhet in Far Rockaway. But he was so embittered by what he considered irreligious fraud in the American kosher meat trade that he put away his knives, opened a candy store in Coney Island, and gave Hebrew lessons. He remained rigidly pious. Mark, for a while the apple of his eye, rebelled, left the yeshiva, and applied on his own for a scholarship to a Manhattan private school. The school took in a few poor bright boys to broaden its outlook and raise its average, and Mark was a natural for admission. He went through Columbia on scholarships, too. The fraternity waived his initiation fee. He never had any money at all.

His break with his father came over a triviality. Our Sabbath afternoon liturgy includes a long recital of sixteen psalms, beginning with Psalm 104; opening words, in Hebrew, *Borkhee Nafshee,* "Bless the Lord, O my soul." The entire recital is therefore called by that name. Mark one afternoon neglected to say the sixteen psalms, and absorbed a beating; then deliberately refused to say them, and got another beating. Then he did say them, for the last time in his life. Next day he ran off to the flat of a married sister. She took him in, and it was years before he entered his parents' home again. The father was now resigned to Mark's apostasy, and even took a sour pride in his academic honors and awards, but they had never been really reconciled.

"So, due to *Borkhee Nafshee,*" I said, with a scotch-loosened tongue, "the world lost a Godol, and gained an out-of-work physics prof."

"Not at all. I'd been sick of it all for a long time. *Borkhee Nafshee* is the greatest nature poem ever written, but my father made me detest the very sound of those two words. The lickings were a handy excuse to break free."

"You don't miss it?"

"Miss what?"

"Talmud? Bible? Yiddish?" Mark kept shaking his head. "It's all meaningless to you? I'm not observant myself, but still —"

"You'll be observant," said Mark. "You're just misbehaving." He pointed a thumb at Bobbie's picture. I laughed uncertainly and he went on, "You'll see. You had a different upbringing. If my father had been wiser and kinder, I could conceivably be a very advanced

Talmudist now and nothing else. A sterile pursuit, but I used to love it. He did me the greatest favor of my life, by beating me up for not saying *Borkhee Nafshee*."

"You don't believe? Not in anything?"

With a chilly stare, Mark poured himself the last of the scotch, half a glassful, and took a long gulp. "Believe? I know things. Not much, not enough, but what I know, I know."

"What can you know about God?" I was drunk enough for such talk. "You either believe or you don't."

"You're quite mistaken," said Mark, somewhat slurring his words. "You can know almost anything about God, providing you put the right questions to Him. You have to learn how to put the questions, and they have to be accurate and airtight."

Mark finished his scotch, hicccupped, and went on, "Now my father, for instance, doesn't know that two atoms of hydrogen bind with one of oxygen to form a water molecule. Yet it's God's truth, and an important one. You don't know it, either, Davey. You believe it, because you read it somewhere, or a teacher told you. I know it. I've put the question, and He answered, straight out. God will answer a high school boy. He asks only that you use common sense, pay very close attention to Him, not be sloppy, and count and measure correctly. God ignores sloppy questions. Sloppiness is the opposite of Godliness. God is exact. He is marvellously, purely exact. Theology is all slop. Moses gave the best answers you could get, three thousand years ago, and he was no theologian." Mark stretched and stood up. "Christ, am I drunk. Poor Aunt Rose, I liked her. I'll miss her. Good night. How was my Fanny Brice sketch, by the way?"

"I fixed it up some, and sent it to Goldhandler."

"I see. You passed the shit. Well done," said Mark. "And look here, you've got to help the barmaid with her dog. Noblesse oblige, prince." He stumbled off to bed.

81

I Flee

AND now about that damned dog.

His name was Toby, and he was something like a wire-haired terrier, except with a long collie tail. A messy creature, altogether. Toby's hair was fuzzy and ragged rather than truly wiry, and to me he looked like an overused Fuller brush; but then, I was no fan of his. He yapped, he bit people, and he threatened every dog he saw, straining at his leash and barking his head off. Still, the other dog had only to make a move toward Toby, and he would put that collie tail between his legs and defecate on it. It is not easy for a dog to do that, and the feat was a distinction, but otherwise Toby was a very ordinary coward, incompletely housebroken.

Bobbie could not leave Toby by himself in her flat. Usually her mother was there, but if Mrs. Webb had to go out the dog would yap without cease until she or Bobbie returned. The neighbors took to telephoning the police, and once Bobbie barely snatched Toby from the dogcatcher's truck. She had called me this time because the dogcatcher had come and actually taken off Toby. Toby had bitten a neighbor, an old irascible lady, for the fourth time; the neighbor had called the animal society, and Toby was gone. Bobbie desperately wanted me to do something about it.

I'm afraid I had a hard-hearted reaction to the news. I had reason not to like Toby. Against my earnest pleas she had brought him to April House twice, on both occasions causing trouble. The first time, Peter Quat returned to the suite sooner than expected. Bobbie and I were out of bed and dressed, so that part was okay. We were at the bedroom window, mooning over the sunset colors on the Hudson, when we were startled by a crazed human scream, and ferocious growling, followed by anguished *ki-yi-yi-ing,* and Toby came scuttling into the bedroom with Peter after him, yelling, "Whose the fuck dog is that? I'll kill him! He bit my leg half off!" Toby had not drawn much blood, but he had torn open Peter's trouser leg. We had an embarrassing scene, and Bobbie promised Peter not to bring Toby again.

However, she did. She could not bear to risk another close call with the dogcatcher, so she showed up one Sunday afternoon with Toby. We never got to make love that afternoon. On arrival, Toby jumped up into the peach mink armchair and puked all over it. That annoyed me, and I bawled him out, possibly a bit harshly. Thereupon he ran all over the place, frantically pissing and shitting as he went. You never saw anything like it. Bobbie would try to catch him, and he would dart to another spot and let fly some more. At last we did corner him, and locked him in the bathroom, where he howled, whined, whistled, scrabbled, unrolled all the toilet paper, emptied what was left in his bladder and bowels, ate up Peter's shaving cream, and then fell asleep in the bathtub, in a puddle of foaming vomit.

Bobbie took off her dress — which for once excited me no more than if she had been a crone of ninety — and went down on her hands and knees to clean up, while I scoured the neighborhood for a shop that sold dog-stain remover and strong deodorant on a Sunday. That took a while. When I returned I found Bobbie still in her underwear, exhausted and perspiring on the couch, in a rage against Peter Quat for being such a pill about dogs, and at me for panicking Toby. The mess was all my fault. Why had I been so cruel? Hadn't I ever up-chucked, myself? She bathed Toby, showered and dressed herself, and departed in unforgiving dudgeon, leaving me to finish the cleanup.

For the next day or two Peter was eyeing blurry spots on the carpeting, sniffing the air, and glancing suspiciously at me. Once I came on him down on hands and knees, smelling at a spot. He got up, looking silly, and that was the end of it. As for Bobbie, on Monday I sent her roses and a box of candy at the theatre, and by Monday night all was forgiven, and our idyll was back on track.

And now a year later Bobbie was sobbing over the phone. "Izzy, I hate to trouble you, but I have no one else to turn to. Poor Toby! Eddie is so darned ineffectual, I don't know how he stays alive."

Well, here was an unexpected negative note, the first I had yet heard from her, about the man who knew Einstein. "Okay, okay, Bobbie. We can't do anything tonight. I'll talk to you in the morning."

And in the morning I taxied with her to the animal shelter, but we had no success there. My heart was not in my advocacy for Toby. The upshot was that Bobbie might try to get a court order for his release, but it would take time and money, since Toby was a four-bite loser, and the neighbor was determined to press the complaint. The man in charge advised Bobbie to buy another dog and forget Toby.

Bobbie cried a bit as we left the shelter, but as we taxied uptown she recovered her spirits, asking about my sister Lee, Peter Quat, and Mr. Goldhandler. I must say she looked alluring as ever. This was the first time I was setting eyes on the girl, remember, since the turndown in the bar. That scene was strong in my mind, and how could it not be haunting her, too? But her aplomb was remarkable. She was perfectly at ease and very smartly gotten up, considering how distracted she was over Toby. She wore the lilac suit with a white blouse, and the pearl choker, and her hair was carefully coiffed in lustrous black rolls. Well, then, was it a ploy, after all, and have I just figured that out, half a lifetime later? No, Bobbie was in genuine distress over Toby, I'll swear to that. But she knew I would respond to her SOS. Bobbie could always see through me; her only problem was nailing me down. It suited her purpose to look beautiful, and by God did she ever.

HAVE NOTHING MORE TO DO WITH HER, thundered the Eleventh Commandment in my brain.

"Stop the cab, driver," I said. The taxi drew over to the curb at a large pet shop, with a window full of leaping puppies, and I bought her a dog to finish the matter.

"Izzy, she's adorable," Bobbie was telling me on the phone, two weeks later, "and growing like a weed. She must be twice as big as when you bought her. The neighbors all love her. Mother does, too. I just had to call and thank you."

"Why don't I come over and see her?" I heard myself say, and was immediately both sorry and glad that the words had escaped my mouth.

I had Pop's car, and after viewing the little Scottie — an improvement over Toby as the light is over the darkness — I offered Bobbie a drive in the country. We lunched in the screen porch of a New Jersey roadhouse, where lilac scent from tall old bushes filled the warm air. I felt my soreness over the bar episode ebbing. Bobbie was being as sweet as the lilac-perfumed air itself, and I was doing the magnanimous forgiving man of the world. There were no recriminations and no fencing remarks. I talked about Mark Herz, and she told me all about Monica, back in town after an affair with a married oil man.

"Take all you want," said the proprietress, when I asked if I could break a branch or two of lilacs for my friend. And so on the drive back, Bobbie sat beside me with a double armful of lilacs. She left me some when I dropped her off, and I brought them up to the suite.

"What are you looking so happy about?" Mark Herz wanted to know, as I came in with the lilacs.

"Do I look happy?"

"The barmaid," said Mark, "for a thousand dollars."

"I went to see the dog I bought her."

"I'd like to meet that girl sometime."

"You would?" I picked up the telephone. "Nothing easier."

"Oh, hi," Bobbie said with cheery surprise. "You again? Wasn't that fun? Mother is crazy about the lilacs."

I proposed a double date with Monica and Mark Herz.

"My stars," said Bobbie. "Are you sure? Isn't that Mark Herz some kind of genius? Monica is just one of the girls, like me. We were going to the movies tonight, but okay, let's meet at the Golden Horn."

The headwaiter said to me *sotto voce,* as he bowed us to a table, "We have missed you and your wife, sair. Madame looks charming."

Mark kept us laughing all through the dinner, in his dry deadpan way. He was in great form, and Monica's eyes gleamed at him. Bobbie was as grateful as I was, I'm sure, that he made us laugh off the crowding memories. I dreaded the cab ride afterward, but needlessly. She was cool and collected, and I found myself talking of my current dilemma; still the old one: law school in the fall, or one more year with Goldhandler? My old classmates would be third-year men now, and I would be an entering student among them, a depressing prospect. Next year, they would all be gone, and I could make a fresh start, still about the age of most first-year men.

"Dear, if you're asking me," said Bobbie, "by all means go on making money to pay for law school. Your daddy's health isn't good, and you don't want to be a burden on him. Anyway, you love Mr. Goldhandler, and you're having fun — that is, when some dumb girl isn't making life hell for you."

We looked at each other in the intermittent light of street lamps. This girl knew me pretty well, I was thinking. About me she was no ninny. "Nobody's complaining," I said.

"Oh well, Izzy," she said with resigned good nature, "you gave as good as you got."

When the cab stopped we shook hands. "This was a nice idea," she said. "Your friend Mark cheered up poor Monica. He's fun. Not like that screwy Peter Quat."

When I read in the *Times* that Bobbie's show was closing, my first notion was to telephone her and offer her a consoling dinner at the Golden Horn. "Whoa there, boy!" said the Eleventh Commandment voice. Right, right. Well, then, I would call the unhappy creature, but no Golden Horn, no sir; and no Cellar Door afterward, either, the murky little nightclub where we had so often sat drinking until the dawn. Just a consoling meal in some brightly lit place. Mark Herz was working in the living room when I called Bobbie. She said dolefully sure, she'd be glad to have dinner. Mark glanced at me over his typewriter, squinting one eye in the cigarette smoke. "I thought you weren't going to see her any more."

"Her show is folding," I said, with compassion.

"Well, let's make it a foursome, if you like."

Mark and Monica apparently had hit it off famously, and were having just the sort of thing that Bobbie and I had botched. He had never talked about this, except to give me the telephone number of Monica's place. Mark seldom slept in April House now.

"No, thanks," I said. "She may not be in the mood."

"Hm. Okay."

At Lindy's, where she downed a big steak like a carnivore, Bobbie's mood was sad but stoical. She had to make money, so Eddie was working up a solo singing act for her. Above all things, she did not want to go back to modelling. That would spell defeat. In the cab going home she began to weep. "Oh, Izzy," she mourned, "why did it have to turn out like this? You'll probably end up marrying that rabbi's daughter or someone, and I'll probably marry Eddie, and we loved each other so much!"

So I gathered her in my arms and kissed her, but she pushed me away hard. "No, no, for *God's* sake let's not start that. I can't go through it again, truly I can't, and I don't want to."

The repulse was for real. I released her and said, "I'm going to Europe this summer." I had been thinking of a European trip, and I made the decision as I spoke, or the Eleventh Commandment voice made it for me.

"Are you? Well! Bon voyage. I wish I had that kind of money."

"How are you fixed, Bobbie?"

"Oh, it's only the recordings. They cost so much! If I had my own machine I'd be fine."

"What does a machine cost?"

My genteel Bobbie would not accept money from me, except as a loan, so a loan it was. Next morning I mailed her a check, adding enough to get her through a workless summer; sending a copy of the check, so to speak, to my conscience. A week later she called in high spirits. The machine made marvellous recordings, almost studio quality. She sounded immersed in her new work, happy, and quite uninvolved with me. But this time I was determined to put a heaving ocean between us for a long summer of forgetting.

That Friday night I told my parents about my trip; and I said I would live at home next year, and asked Mom to fix up Lee's room in a less girlish style. "Hooray," said Mama. "Mazel tov! Eat some more veal." Pop said nothing, he just reached out and grasped my hands in both of his, joyously laughing.

Mom and Pop were aging away in their small apartment off Riverside Drive, going on with their Jewish activities: work for the synagogue and the Hebrew school, Zionist meetings, fund-raising for yeshivas, and the like. Pop had a driver now who brought him to and from the Bronx. The Fairy Laundry was gasping on, always with some new crisis to grind him down between the millstones of the money men and the partners. Lee and I had flown the coop, and had been educated away from their Jewish interests. They were proud of us, and uneasy but resigned about our drift from Jewishness. I think my Mom and Pop much more nearly represented "the American Jewish experience" than Peter Quat's diverting sex-mad college professors, but Pop couldn't write a book. I'm not sure his son can, but I'm giving it the old try.

"Is that from *her?*"

Mom picked up the Hong Kong porcelain cat, wrinkling her nose. She had swiftly transformed Lee's room: maroon wallpaper, draperies to match, folding couch instead of a bed, leather armchair and ottoman with reading lamp, and a walnut desk. I was bringing my stuff home piecemeal from April House.

Mom's "Is that from her?" came out less approving, even, than Peter Quat's remark about the frigging Chinese dust-catcher. The inquiry was a hard one to field, since Mom had never acknowledged that Bobbie Webb existed. Still, on very rare occasions, Mama would refer to "her." This contradicted the policy stance that there was no such person, but that was Mama for you. Cutting Gordian knots was her specialty.

"I picked it up somewhere," I said. "Wherever did you get that Columbia banner, Mom?" The blue-and-white football pennant hung on the wall with my diploma, some other college mementos, and a very large framed picture of Mama. It was as though I had just graduated. The bad April House time had never existed.

"Oh, I save things," said Mama, "not like some people."

Mark Herz's fellowship came through about then, and he packed up his meager belongings, mainly books, while the Goldhandler programs were still running. "Let's not kid around," he said, tightening straps on his worn suitcases, "you won't miss me. I've been taking money under false pretenses. Except for burying Aunt Rose, I've spent it all on Monica. Never used money more wisely, and never will. It's been an experience, prince. I commend your flceing Bobbie. Very wise. I hope it works. Enjoy Europe."

The bon voyage party in my first-class stateroom was reasonably jolly. Goldhandler sent a basket of champagne, and my sister Lee and Bernie made considerable inroads on it. So did Mama and I, while Papa ate fruit from a basket he brought. At one point he walked out with me on the deck, and said, leaning on the rail and looking out at the Hudson, "Your mother and I came over steerage. For food they threw bread and potatoes to us, like dogs. You're going back to Europe in style."

"Thanks to you," I said.

"You're getting away from her?"

It was no use playing dumb with my father. "Trying to."

"It will be hard." He shook my hand and hugged me. I had to lean down for the hug. "Have a good time, son. Keep your eyes open, and learn what you can."

A first-class crossing on a luxury liner in the thirties was a wallow in elegance and creature comfort such as the world will not know again. A billionaire today cannot know it. The ambience is gone, like the court of Louis the Fourteenth. It didn't seem all that hard, getting away from Bobbie Webb, when I stood at the back rail and watched the glittering blue ocean widen between us.

A young man travelling with money in his pocket collects girls as a blue serge suit picks up lint. I had adventures, none of consequence and all forgotten, in my lone European summer. As you can guess, when I heard songs from Bobbie's show on a hotel radio or in a nightclub, or walked alone in St. James's Park or the Tuileries Gardens, and saw young couples arm in arm, the ache would come back. But there were always diversions. On the boat I met an old art history professor, with whom I junketed around for a while, visiting museums in London and Paris, and arguing religion with zest, for he had studied for the ministry and was a real Christian. We went together to the Folies-Bergère, too, and such. It felt eerie to be so much closer to Nazi Germany, and to talk to gentile travellers who had just come from there and had had a great time. The hoarse rantings of Hitler on shortwave radio, and the worrisome headlines about war scares, I tried to shrug off. I wandered as the mood moved me, and drifted to the French Riviera. In Marseilles I thought of taking a boat to Palestine, since Lee had liked it so much; but there was a *Bataille des Fleurs* at Cannes, a carnival with a parade and fireworks, and I went there instead.

With that distance and diversion I did a lot of cool thinking about Bobbie. Poor girl, in that sad bar encounter! She had won her game, brought me down on a knee; but there she sat with the man who knew Einstein, to whom she had rebounded, into whose bed she evidently had bounced, with whom she had no doubt shared long hours of berating that awful Jew gagman Izzy Goodkind; and out of the night and the snow bursts this same Izzy fellow, if you please, after weeks and weeks of silence, and springs the long-sought proposal on her then and there, under the nose of Einstein's pal. Talk about a hopeless, exasperating predicament for a girl! The kick in the teeth she gave me was, at this distance, at least understandable. Close the books, I thought. Forgive and forget.

I returned to America and to the Goldhandler job without having written her a line, and I made no effort to get in touch with her. The trip had worked.

82

The Recapture

BOYD came hurrying through the control room of Studio 8H, the biggest in Radio City, with an armful of mimeographed scripts. He still had the cadaverous look which had shocked me on my return from Europe. A liver ailment contracted in Alaska, where he had gone with the boss, had turned him all skinny and yellow. Goldhandler, on the other hand, was glowing with energy and good cheer. The Alaskan trip had evidently been a great success, though I knew no details. Goldhandler was on the phone night and day with Klebanoff, excitedly talking mining, stock deals, and money.

"Friend of yours out there," Boyd said to me, jerking a thumb at the door. I went outside to the eighth-floor foyer, where technicians were shoving wheeled equipment from studio to studio, and musicians, actors, actresses, and advertising people were hurrying to and fro. There on the couch sat Bobbie, legs crossed, white-gloved hands folded. I had not seen or talked to her in half a year.

"Hello, Bobbie."

"Why, hello there, Izzy." She looked very surprised. She said she was waiting to audition for a job, but I thought she might be waylaying me. Her gloves were yellowish from too much cleaning, and one was split along a seam. Her lilac suit was threadbare, she was thinner, and her eyes were dark-ringed.

"How was Europe?"

"Not bad."

"I'd like to hear about it. Take me to dinner some time."

"Sure, Bobbie."

"Let's see, I'm free this Friday evening," she said. "But that's right, you're always home on Fridays, aren't you? I haven't forgotten."

"I'm living at home now, Bobbie."

"Are you? Well!" She took it, not wrongly, as a suggestion of her past power over me. Coquettishly she pulled her skirt down over her knees. "My, your parents must be happy about that."

I said I would call her, and I returned to the studio shaken. She looked so down, so poorly, that I could pity her; but God Almighty, what did it take to pull free of that gravitational field?

A few days passed.

"Hi, Izzy. I thought you were going to take me to dinner."

Though Mom and Pop were in Florida, Bobbie's call to our home rattled me, and I stalled.

"Izzy, if you don't want to see me it's perfectly all right."

"Oh, Bobbie, don't be ridiculous." I proposed one evening and another. No, no, she was busy. I could call her again sometime, or maybe she would call me. Brief, cool, huffy, she hung up. Okay, Bobbie, I thought, the hell with you, and what a relief!

"Do you still love me?"

Bobbie and I are dancing at the cavernous New York version of Don the Beachcomber. She has called me after a week or so, this time all sugar and spice and everything nice, about the deferred dinner date. This is it. We are in each other's arms for the first time since my return home, a return in more ways than one. I have been reading Yiddish with Pop, seeing Zaideh regularly for Talmud, and working through the Hebrew prophets on my own. The discontinuity between the Inside and the Outside is becoming acute. Yet Bobbie knows, by the way we dance, that she risks little by asking.

"I won't answer that," is my stupid response.

"Well, do you still desire me?"

Some question! "The hell with this," I say, and I lead her back to the table. She laughs and squeezes my hand.

At the doorway of my parents' apartment she holds back, seeing the mezuza. "I feel funny about this."

I feel damned funny myself, but I say, "Come on." I am powerless to do otherwise, or think I am. I open the door and switch on the light. Confronting us, staring straight at us, is the tinted blowup of Zaideh's passport photograph on the foyer wall.

"Who is that?" Bobbie quavers, at the sight of the lifesize stern bearded patriarch in a black round hat.

"My grandfather."

We go into the living room, Bobbie hugging herself in her beaver coat as though we are still outside in the zero weather.

"Is that your father? You look like him."

It is a poor painting, done long ago by an impecunious artist in Pop's Bronx Zionist chapter; and it too looks straight out at you.

"He's aged a lot since then." I gesture at photographs on the piano. "That's my grandmother. She's gone. Of course you know my sister Lee."

"I feel surrounded by eyes," says Bobbie. "Give me a drink."

"We'll put you in the Columbia room," I say. "That's my lair."

I am so used to Mama's picture that I don't think of it. When I bring the drinks, Bobbie is sitting in my armchair, still bundled in her coat, staring at Mama, who is regarding her with a territorial glare I have not noticed before.

"Eyes, eyes, *eyes,*" says Bobbie. "You look like her, too. Around the eyes." Bobbie peers at me. "You have such strange eyes, both of you. Like a Tartar's."

"Take off your coat, for crying out loud."

As we kiss, Bobbie keeps her eyes open like Vyvyan's secretary, looking past me at The Green Cousin. I understand, I sympathize with the girl, and my kisses are all tenderness and no passion.

"This isn't going to work, honey," Bobbie says. "It was a mistake."

"Okay, Bobbie."

Still, it has been a whole year, and on the dance floor we were locked in mutual longing. After more kisses she says with pathetic defiance, "Oh, I don't care about the eyes, come on," and she honestly tries to throw herself into it. But the effort sputters and dies, and we laugh ruefully, knowing each other well. The long time lapse has melted away to nothing. I take her for a look through the apartment. "It's so homey," she says. "Your mother is an excellent housekeeper. You're better off here than in April House, dear. You must be saving tons of money."

"There are drawbacks."

Those huge eyes glisten at me. "Oh well, I guess you'll have a place of your own again, one of these days."

Fighting is sometimes useless. I will spare the reader the resolves I make, the oaths I take, in the long days that ensue. I have never been caught in anything like that powerful undertow back to Bobbie Webb. I call her. We do the Golden Horn and the Cellar Door. About three in the morning we get into a cab and I tell the driver, "The Park Central."

Bobbie tightens a chilly hand on mine and says in a charged whisper, "No. No."

"Why not?"

"Not a hotel, that's nothing but lust. I won't be a party to it."

The taxi stops at the Park Central. I get out, and hold my hand to Bobbie. She hesitates, then she descends with an angry look. In the elevator she stands silent and grim. "I hate the smell of hotel corridors," she snaps as we walk to the room. My hand trembles and fumbles with the key. Once inside she lets her fur coat drop to the floor.

"Izzy," she gasps in my arms, "are you very, very sure you want to do this? I don't, I truly don't, it's a bad idea. I beg you, I implore you not to, unless you're absolutely sure."

"Never call me Izzy again," I say. "My name is David."

She leans back, and looks into my eyes. "But why, dearest? And if you didn't like it, why didn't you say so sooner?"

"Never mind. Those are the orders."

Her puzzled look metamorphoses into a slow coarse smile. "Yes, David," she says. "Yes, my lord and master, yes."

We were dining at the Golden Horn not long afterward and she abruptly asked me, "How much money have you got in the bank?"

Caught off guard, I just looked at her.

"Well, are we friends or aren't we? How much money have you got in the bank?"

"Bobbie, even my father doesn't know that. Why should I tell you?"

She cocked her head at me wryly. "You've learned how to parry a question."

Her singing act hadn't gone over, she said, and she had decided to learn shorthand. She needed a steady living, Broadway was uncertain, she hated modelling, and she knew she could be a right-hand woman to an executive. She had to pay the rent while she studied shorthand, and a wonderful opportunity had opened up. Eddie had dropped singing and coaching to raise chickens in New Jersey, and the money was just piling in. Now he needed a partner with capital, so that he could expand. If I would lend her two thousand dollars, she would invest it with Eddie. He would pay her a salary of thirty a week, and when he eventually sold the farm at a profit, she would get half, and she would pay me back the two thousand with ten per-cent interest.

Well, here for once I was on familiar ground. Shittim wood, lob-ster tails, New Jersey chickens, same idea. It occurred to me that, liv-ing in New Jersey, Eddie could drop in more often on Einstein at Princeton. I refrained from mentioning this. I said I would be glad to give or lend her fifty a week while she studied shorthand.

"Oh, I don't like that, David," said Bobbie, disappointed. "You'll just be my sugar daddy, then. This other is an investment."

She accepted it, but getting a weekly check from me must have really bothered her. She kept saying she felt like a concubine, and gradually she turned ornery as only a woman can. I pass over a thou-sand rotten recollections of my months in Morrie Abbott's April House flat — which I had rented, so I told my parents, as a "studio" — and ask you just to believe me. She became a demanding, difficult, sar-castic teasing harpy. Her sex games were the very worst. She would provoke, refuse, taunt, lie there cold, turn hot when I was tired or had to write, and work and rework all that ancient universal bag of Eve's tricks. Of those, she showed herself a world virtuoso. Even at this distance of cooling years I cannot figure out exactly what she was up to. At a guess, she too was caught like me, but she had the com-plication of being broke. That was obviously why she had tracked me down at Radio City, and perhaps she was ashamed of her poverty and her motives. I'll never really know.

Oh, those long hellish months that followed Bobbie's recapture of me, to call what had happened by its right name! I remember only a dim montage of torment, up to one snowy night late in January; the night I threw her out of Morrie's flat and told her to be damned to hell and never to trouble me again. On that night, we ate a royal dinner at the Oak Room of the Plaza, then went to a Kaufman and Hart comedy, and then had a boisterous snowball fight in the park across from April House, ending in our rolling and wrestling in each other's arms in the snow. Just terrific! We went up to the flat, drank hot buttered rum, and were shedding our clothes when — at the point

of discarding her lacy satin underwear — she started up the old concubine nagging, forced a quarrel, and dressed again. That did it. That
was when I threw her out. Whether the reader thinks I was a monster, or a poor sap who should have done it sooner, that is how it
happened.

Still, I didn't give up the flat. Goldhandler had hired another gagman, a nimble-witted fellow named Sam something. This Sam was
quite a character. He flew his own airplane. He took me up once and
stunted around the Statue of Liberty's spiky head and upraised torch
arm, scaring the hell out of me. This same Sam became an Air Force
ferry pilot during the war; went to Israel in 1948 to train pilots, and
survived a crash, badly burned up; and ended as a prosperous TV
writer on the West Coast. Sam Abelson, now that I think of it. Well,
I couldn't work with Sam at home. Mom would make him stay to
dinner, and Sam would eat like a horse and fall asleep. At the penthouse we couldn't write at all. Lawyers came and went, and Klebanoff kept showing up, bringing assayers, investors, and mining engi-
neers. Goldhandler and his wife were altogether in a lather about
Alaskan gold, and at Morrie's flat Sam and I could at least get things
done. Otherwise it was a dingy little hole, to be sure, compared to
my lost paradise on the eighteenth floor.

My sister Lee at this juncture had a baby boy, a joy to Mom and
Pop beyond describing; inside name after Pop's father, Shaya, outside name Sherman. Today Sherman is a successful brain surgeon out
in Beverly Hills, where you would think he would starve for lack of
anything to operate on; but no, they keep him busy, perhaps with
transplants. Sherman was a big beautiful baby. He yelled like anything when he was circumcised; none of your Jewish instinct to endure and be mute, not an American Jew like Sherman. It was the last
time the Mishpokha came together in anything like its old numbers.
Mom had the bris catered in Lee's apartment. She was past the time
of stuffing forty-foot kishkas, though Bobbeh had helped her stuff
my bar-mitzva kishka in her eighties. Different generation. There was
no kishka, but plenty of rich kosher food and an open bar, and everybody had fun except Sherman. Maybe he enjoyed the screaming, too,
in his inscrutable newborn way.

And yet, the bris was kind of a sad affair under the jollity. You could see the Mishpokha coming apart. There had been deaths. Relatives had moved all over the map — Florida, California, Canada, Texas — and we were diluted by Bernie's family. Of the uncles and aunts who still hung on, some of their children had scattered, and the rest who came were for the most part grown-up strangers; they hardly knew the old family songs, and tended to cluster apart, making New Yorkish talk and jokes. Cousin Harold was there with his wife, a nice Jewish nurse, and in that crowd he stood out as real family. He even seemed strongly Jewish, which gives you an idea, maybe. If not for the indomitable Aunt Faiga, the party might have died. But she got the singing going despite all, and Mom and Pop — who had the spirit but lacked her energy — and Cousin Harold and I backed her up, and after a while the young crowd thawed, forgot what cool cats they were, and put on a passable performance as Jews.

What didn't work was Zaideh's effort to introduce a note of religion. He tried to make a speech, but his weak voice didn't carry. So he told me to expound a patch of Talmud we had just learned, on the circumcision of Isaac. For his sake, I spoke in Yiddish. Half of them didn't understand me, and of those who did, few could follow Talmud logic or wanted to. But I didn't care, I bulled through, ignoring the inattentive chatter. It saved the day for Zaideh. While I talked his face shone.

As I was typing away at a draft that night, Pop came into my room. "Your Yiddish is improving," he said. "That was a good *vertel.*" The word denotes a short learned talk with an elegant point.

"I've had good teachers."

"Tell me, Yisroelke, why that hotel room, that studio? What for?" He gestured at my typewriter, and the papers piled on my desk. "You write here."

Happily, I could look him in the eye and explain about working with Sam.

"And the girl?"

It was his first reference to Bobbie since the bon voyage party. "It's over, Papa."

"You're sure?"

"Yes."

"Not after Europe, it wasn't?"

"Well, no, not entirely."

"She won't make a life for herself, you know, as long as she has any hope."

"It's over, Pop. Truly it is."

"I was proud of you at the bris." He gave me a brief squeeze on the shoulder and walked out.

Weeks passed. The snow was gone, and the forsythia was bursting out in the park in golden splashes.

"Sorry, Bobbie, I've got a script to turn out today. Thanks, some other time."

She was calling to invite me to lunch. "Oh, come on, David. You have to eat, don't you? Meet me at the Palm Court of the Plaza. It's just across the street from where I'm working, Bonwit's. So I can't stay long. And I'm buying. Please, David."

Since she was back at modelling, which she so detested, I could expect a lunch nasty, brutish, and short, but her "Please, David" had a pathetic note.

"Okay, Bobbie, but you're not buying me lunch."

Of all my mental pictures of her — and the photo album is endless — the way she looked that day walking into the Palm Court, remains the quintessential Bobbie Webb. She wore a tailored outfit as usual, this tall slender brunette with a petal-white, delicately rouged face, striding in with her trained queenly walk, making heads turn. This was the Bobbie Webb I had fallen in love with, the sort of woman that men will break their lives and fortunes to possess, and still not really possess. All she wanted to tell me was that she was sorry; that she had been driven by "her devils," a mean streak stirred up by the hated shorthand course and her worries over money. Now she had a fine job. She loathed garment-center modelling, but working at Bonwit's was prestigious and fun, and she was all set.

"I don't know if you'll ever take me back, but I wish you would think about it, David. I'm asking only to be with you, as long as you want me, and absolutely nothing more. I know how badly I behaved. It's over. If you give me a chance, you'll find out that I mean it. What we've had, what we can still have, is too beautiful to give up, just because it can't be forever." Not her exact words, but that was the idea.

She did pay for the lunch, too, which we hardly touched; snatched the check, made a little joke about it, and paid. Bobbie had never acted more calm and under control. She jumped up gaily, said she felt twenty years younger, and had better get back to work. And she was gone, leaving a stunned student prince sitting there over the uneaten salads and the cold tea.

83

Quat's Wedding

PETER QUAT never wrote letters, so the invitation to the wedding reception at the Waldorf was a bolt from the blue. When Peter quit, he and Marilyn had long since broken off. He had even stopped talking about, that is, reviling her. A year had gone by, and now this! A scrawled note on Harvard stationery was clipped to it:

> *How about coming to the ceremony at my father's apartment before the reception? A small nonsense, it won't take long. The rabbi wants ten guys. Phone me.*
>
> *Peter*
>
> *P.S. I guess I owe you the thousand.*

Peter had once jeered, after a lovey-dovey phone talk I had with Bobbie, that I would end up marrying her. I had retorted that I would not, but he would probably marry Marilyn Levy; and he had sworn that the day he married Marilyn Levy he would pay me one thousand dollars. I called him in Boston.

"Congratulations, Peter. My wedding present is a thousand dollars."

A relieved chuckle at the other end: "Very big of you, Davey. Thanks."

"And of course I'll come to the ceremony."

"Great. I'm asking Goldhandler and Boyd. It'll be fast and painless. We'd have been married by a judge, but she has this halfway religious grandma."

"All right if I bring Bobbie to the Waldorf party?"

"Aha!" Sardonic lift in Peter's voice. "That's still on, is it?"

"Sort of."

"Of course, bring Bobbie. Why not? It'll be a mob. . . . What's it up to now, dear, four hundred fifty?"

Marilyn's voice faintly in the background, "Four hundred seventy-seven."

"She's there?" I said. "Let me congratulate her."

"Sure she's here. We're jumping the gun." Angry female noises, Peter laughing complacently. "I'm kidding, of course, Davey. I still can't get to second base with her, I assure you."

Marilyn came on the line, annoyed but giggling. "He's absolutely impossible."

"He's a screwball, Marilyn, but probably a genius."

"So you'll bring Bobbie, eh? Will you two be next?"

It was a more complicated question than Marilyn Levy knew. "Not right away, anyhow."

"Hmm! Well, give her our best."

I had been very cautious about taking up with Bobbie Webb again. It was weeks before I brought her back to April House. We walked in the park, we met for lunches and dinners, we went to shows and concerts. I kept it placid and friendly, or tried to. But the fire was there, just banked, and in a natural course it leaped up. Bobbie kept her word. All the whims, games, changes, moods, wiles, tricks, were gone. Bobbie could not have done it with willpower, or by calculation. She had turned some corner in her inner life, and was another woman. Both of us were older. Both were growing up, in different ways. It remained a fugitive love affair, for in those days "moving in together," as we now call it, was a thing only very free spirits did. The less free called it "shacking up," or even living in "sin," if the reader recognizes the word. Bobbie invariably left Morrie's flat and went home to sleep, while I returned to my "Columbia room" or slept over at April House. Mrs. Webb must have known what was happening, just as Mom and Pop did, but what was unspoken did not exist, or did not have to be faced. "Mother must never know," Bobbie said soberly, more than once.

One night she broke down and told me, laughing sheepishly, that Eddie's poultry venture had gone up in smoke. I had done her a great favor by keeping her out of it. Nobody had cautioned Eddie that because of some ghastly plague in the New Jersey soil, the chickens had to be kept off the ground on wire netting. All his three thousand

chickens had died in one night. Shades of Uncle Yehuda! The man
who knew Einstein could not even sell the carcasses for fertilizer. He
had had to burn them, and the stench had brought in state troopers
and health inspectors for fifty miles around. Eddie was ruined, and
was back coaching girl singers.

"He has the gift of blarney," she said. "Eddie can talk the birds
down out of the trees. The shorthand was his idea, and I was a fool
to listen to him."

"I met him only that once, in the bar," I said. "Remember? *'Don't
you know when you're done, Izzy? That's not characteristic of your race.'* "

Bobbie cringed and spoke softly. "Did *I* say *that?*"

When I told her I was taking her to the wedding reception of
Peter and Marilyn, she was excited as a child.

The rabbi kept winking and giggling at Peter and Marilyn, telling
them that the ceremony wouldn't take long. He seemed less like a
rabbi than a dentist, reassuring the couple that he wasn't going to
hurt them a bit. He had brought a stack of purple skullcaps, and a
square of purple velvet on four sticks. Somewhere off in Dr. Quat's
apartment a phonograph struck up a scratchy Lohengrin wedding
march, and Peter and Marilyn came arm in arm into the living room
in street clothes, smirking. Goldhandler and Boyd, holding up two
canopy sticks, looked preposterous in purple skullcaps. I held up a
stick, and the fourth was in the hand of Marilyn's brother, a six-footer
with a crew haircut, who played football for Cornell, and appeared
much embarrassed by these alien goings-on. The happy pair halted
under the velvet, and the rabbi welded them in nothing flat, ripping
off the blessings at greased speed. He collected the skullcaps, folded
up his canopy and sticks, and whistled out, having several other such
jobs in the neighborhood. Sunday, he said, was his busy day. During
the week he was the chaplain of a mental hospital.

The reception was different. The reader has been at big wedding
receptions, and if you picture as fancy a one as you ever saw, you've
got it. It was not the usual sort of lavish kosher family festivity, of
course. There were hams and lobsters in the buffet, and white-gloved
waiters passed around shrimp and crab claws. The champagne was
Veuve Clicquot, four musicians played Schubert and Beethoven, and
the flowers were banked solid and high on all the walls. There wasn't

an Aunt Faiga in the place, and nobody sang or danced. Bobbie attracted many glances of the men there, and she kept remarking how nice the reception was, and how much at ease she felt, after dreading to come to her first Jewish affair. Well, this wasn't Sherman's circumcision, exactly. She was just one more non-Jew among many, and the Jews at the party were not caftaned Hassidim.

"Hello, Bobbie, lovely of you to come," said Marilyn as we moved past the couple on the receiving line. The polite words dropped a glass curtain between her and Bobbie, but if Bobbie sensed it she said nothing. Peter gave her that faintly lewd grin of his, and waggled his eyebrows at her like Groucho Marx. To me he said, "What a zoo, hey?" We landed at a table with Boyd and the Goldhandlers, who kept talking about Klebanoff's mine with animated absorption, paying no attention to us. Bobbie and I left early.

"You're the one who should be getting married, David," said Bobbie, as we sat in the April House bar drinking stingers. "You're a family man. Peter isn't. I'll bet it doesn't last."

She was talking straightforwardly, like a friend, not in the least like a mistress seeking to improve her status. She looked me in the eye and added, "Why don't you go out with some Jewish girls? I have other friends, you know."

"I do, Bobbie, now and then. It's meaningless."

Brushing her fingers across my mouth, she said, "Honey, that's my problem."

It happened to be the first of April, so I had made a dinner reservation at the Golden Horn, ordering a special meal and special wine. I made the mistake of telling the muddled Armenian headwaiter that it was "sort of an occasion." After the meal he came marching up to our table with a spotlighted cake inscribed in pink icing:

> *Mr. and Mrs. David Goodkind*
> *Happy Anniversary*

He offered Bobbie the knife to cut it, while the people in the place applauded. "Oh, David," Bobbie laughed. "You're really being cornered, poor dear, aren't you?"

"I tell you what, Liebowitz," said Goldhandler, "stick around for dinner and we'll discuss it."

I had not eaten at the penthouse since Mark's unfortunate "pass the shit" lunch. Only Boyd still kept up the feudal custom of eating at the master's table. When Sardinia passed around a large brown clove-studded ham, I regretted agreeing to stay. It was Shavuos, and that morning I had gone to the synagogue to hear Pop chant *Akdamos,* a cabalistic Aramaic poem in the liturgy. Having learned the subtle chant from his shammas father, he did it every year; it was much admired, and for me it wakened poignant childhood echoes. Zaideh's "My child, never eat forbidden food" had by now sunk in. Amid the tortures I had endured over Bobbie, there had been heavy soul-searchings about religion and identity, which I trust the reader can imagine. I was no longer ordering the prohibited creatures in restaurants, and I waved off Sardinia.

"What's with you, Liebowitz?" growled Goldhandler, busy devouring a thick red slice of pig's rear with much of his old gusto.

I said I had had a big late lunch.

"This sneaky fucker is getting religion, that's what," Goldhandler said. "Any time now he may stop jerking off. I mean, of course, on Saturdays."

"He was Professor Finkel's pet," said Karl, who now had a bass voice and dark shaved jowls, and was looking more and more like Goldhandler. "There's no way he can be getting religion."

I ate some salad. After putting away a large meal, Goldhandler demanded a cigar.

"Harry," said his wife, in a tone both pleading and warning.

"While I live," declared Goldhandler, as Boyd brought him the box, "my motto is, fuck 'em. And after I die, surely fuck 'em." He lit the cigar with a torch of three wooden matches, and puffed with immense satisfaction. "Sweet as sugar," he said defiantly.

Later we sat in the office, just the two of us. Beyond the windows I could see the APRIL HOUSE sign, haloed by the misty night.

"So, what's going to be next year, Finkelstein?" Goldhandler rocked in his big swivel chair, chewing on the cigar. "Game to fumble along with us for another year?"

"I'm not sure yet."

"Things will be different in the fall, me boy. We're going to take it easier and make more money. All of us."

One successful Broadway farce, he pointed out, could earn more than all the money he had ever made as a radio writer. We could certainly turn out amusing plays, he and I. He smiled at me, and the missing teeth made me warm to him, perhaps because Pop too had lost the same teeth. I was a funny fuck, he said. Radio was a treadmill on which he could run in place till he dropped. He had gotten on it through Henny Holtz, and had never since been able to pause and catch his breath to do better things. But his situation had now radically changed. Next year money would be no problem. He might take on one or two radio shows just to keep the business going, but Sam and Boyd could draft those, while we wrote a play. It would be a collaboration. There would be a raise for me, and I would share in the royalties.

I did believe that Harry Goldhandler could write successful plays, or movies, or books, if he could ever break free of the life-consuming radio rubbish. Obviously he was counting on the income of the Klebanoff mine, though he did not speak of it. And I could help him write plays, I thought, by being someone to talk to. If I was a "funny fuck," it was on a plateau of competence due to his training. Increasingly, in this gaudy Goldhandler circus, I was feeling like a misplaced colorless lawyer. I was no longer the wide-eyed Vicomte de Brag, I was three years older, and I was ready to get back to my studies, more than ready. But Bobbie was right, I loved the man, and to work on a Broadway play with Harry Goldhandler — well, I walked to the desk and offered him my hand. "I'll think about it, boss, and it's terrific that you want me."

"We'll kill 'em, Liebowitz!" Laying aside the cigar, he clasped my hand with both his fat paws, laughing as Pop had done when I said I was moving home, and he roared, "We'll kill 'em, and we'll both make a cocksucking fortune!"

I pass over the charm of the second April Bobbie and I had, and ask you to take my word for that, too. Everything that we did together was right — horseback riding, dancing in Harlem, driving to the ocean for walks along the deserted beach, a day in Coney Island taking all the scary rides, a trip in a Goodyear blimp — whatever we did was fun. There always seemed to be more things we wanted to do. It was another fair spring, after all; the second time around, and therefore less thrilling and brilliant, maybe. On the other hand, we weren't confused, groping, out of our heads. We knew each other. We knew our situation.

"Could I see your sister's baby?" she asked one day.

"Sherman?" I hesitated only for a second. "Why not? Any time."

"I don't want to intrude. I just want to see him. Does he look like you?"

So I had to disclose to Lee and Bernie that I was still seeing Bobbie. It was no shattering news to them, and Lee invited us to dinner. When we came to the apartment, Lee led us straight into the nursery, where Sherman lay all swaddled in blue, gurgling at a toy monkey hung over him. Bobbie started to cry. Lee put her arm around her.

"He's just so beautiful," Bobbie said, wiping her eyes. "Sorry about this."

"He doesn't look so beautiful," said Lee, looking proud enough to explode, "when he gets you up at three in the morning."

"I wouldn't care if he never let me sleep."

It was a pleasant, even intimate meal, though Lee and Bernie hadn't seen Bobbie for two years. When Sherman's feeding time came, while Lee warmed the bottle she let Bobbie hold him, to quiet his shrieking for instant service. Though the whole evening was an embarrassment, indeed an agony, for me, the sight of Bobbie with the baby in her arms cut me up more than anything else. April was ending. I had reapplied to the law school. An era in my life seemed to be slipping away, the era of Goldhandler and Bobbie Webb. But I found myself wanting to cling to both of them. Why not? *Why not?* Bobbie Webb was a quiet pretty woman, I loved her, and I knew her as I knew myself. All the bad times were dimming from mind. She was behaving. The Goldhandler money would enable me to live well even with a wife, if I wanted that. Not smart or educated enough? Not Jewish? That man who knew Einstein? *Why not, despite all?*

The weather was mild and warm when we left Lee's apartment. We walked downtown through Central Park in the darkness. One could do that then. At the lake we sat down on a bench, under a lamp. The night was so quiet that the April House sign was reflected upside down in the black water.

"Maybe we should get married," I said.

She took a long time to answer, looking at me with enormous eyes glistening in the lamp light. "What about your faith?"

"Couldn't you learn it?"

"Is this something you want, David?"

"I think maybe so, Bobbie."

"My, you're sweeping me off my feet." She kissed me lightly and said, "It's wonderful that you've asked. I won't hold you to it, just because you've said the words. Let's give it some time. There's no panic."

Next morning, when the telephone woke me in the Columbia room, my first sleepy thought was that by God I had proposed to Bobbie again, incredible as that was, and I had better talk right away to Pop. As I reached for the phone, my head was in a whirl. How could I put it? How would he take it?

It was Boyd calling. "Goldhandler died," he said.

✳   ✳   ✳

84

Airlift!

Aloft, en route from Lajes Field, Azores, to Lod Airport, Israel
October 14, 1973

I AM writing in the crew rest area of a C-5A Galaxy aircraft, now roaring eastward on a hairline course down the middle of the Mediterranean Sea. This Brobdingnagian cargo plane of the Military Air Transport Command is the biggest flying machine in the world. The main deck below looks like a long sawed-off chunk of the Holland Tunnel; a space with curving walls and rows of lights stretching off into startling distance. That space is crammed with tanks, guns, and ammunition, and a troop-carrying compartment on this upper level is full of stuff, too. The first C-5 Galaxy that took me to the Azores is still grounded in Lajes with a "crump," a mechanical problem. I'll miss that flight commander, a chatty lieutenant colonel from Ohio. He invited me into the cockpit, put me in the jump seat, and we talked all the way across the Atlantic Ocean. It made the time go, I'll say that.

This pilot is more taciturn, in fact strictly business, for we are now heading straight into some scary unknowns. America's European allies have denied transit rights to the airlift. So all the planes will be forced to fly through the Straits of Gibraltar and along the exact jagged dividing line over the sea between European and North African airspace; a route this C-5A I'm in is the first aircraft to traverse. For six hundred miles we will be flying within range of the Libyan lunatics and the Egyptian air force, all armed with MiGs. We're supposed to be escorted past the trouble spots. But we are alone now.

Air rendezvous over water is a chancy exercise, as I know well from my own war days.

What a collapse was there in Europe! What a failure of nerve! The Soviets are openly sending a giant airlift to Egypt and Syria. The whole world knows it. Yet the European powers, great and small, prohibited even landings to refuel, for an American airlift to Israel. The Arabs merely said "Oil" in a loud voice, and all Europe cringed. Why, where else could the Arabs sell oil, if not to Europe or America? Who else has the money to buy, money that means anything? Russian rubles are colorful toilet paper, worthless except where people are forced to take them. Think of England, France, Italy, Germany, Austria, Greece — yes, and Spain and Portugal too — the great old centers of western civilization, some of them so recently masters of the world, trembling like frightened old ladies before a few robed sheikhs! Until Portugal relented at the last minute and let us use the Azores, the Air Force was working on a desperate plan for refueling in the air in mid-Atlantic. That chatty flight commander went first because he's one of three C-5 pilots who can refuel in the air. It's a new evolution for these behemoth aircraft.

Well, six and a half nervous hours to Tel Aviv. I am as jumpy as I ever was flying bombing missions over Germany and Italy; more so, because now I'm a passenger with nothing to do, and my nerves have had thirty more years of wear and tear. Maybe I can kill the time by scrawling out what happened in Washington when I got back from Jerusalem. I certainly can't sleep, nor can I just sit here for six hours, waiting for the thumping of gunfire, as this flying Goliath skirts Europe's airspace and approaches the war zone. As for *April House,* there's little left to tell, and forget it for now. I am riding a typhoon.

I arrived in Washington at eleven at night in a downpour, and I had no housekey. Jan poked her head out of the bedroom window to see who was banging the brass knocker.

"My God, *you?*"

Standing there in the rain, I called up to her, "Yes, and I'm okay. Let me in."

When I came inside the peerless woman saw that I had no luggage. She looked into my drenched face and inquired, "Can you tell me anything?"

"No."

"Will you be going back?"

"Yes."

"What about Sandra?"

"I don't know. I couldn't track her down."

"I see." Only I could read Jan's calm tones and know how hard it hit her. "And your mother?"

"Hanging in there."

"The war isn't going well, is it?"

"No."

"Will we lose?"

"I don't know, Jan."

The telephone rang.

"Ah, good, you're here," said the Israeli ambassador. "How was the flight?"

"Okay. What do I do now?"

"Wait."

While I was wolfing an omelet Jan whipped up, she told me that Peter Quat, in a huge dither over his novel, had been vainly trying to telephone me in Israel. It had come out shortly before Yom Kippur to the usual ecstatic reviews, but it wasn't selling. The piles in the bookstores were "beginning to stink like stale fish," so Jan quoted a frantic Peter.

The telephone rang again; this time the White House, to say that a car would come and take me to the helicopter. The blades were already noisily spinning white spirals of glittery raindrops when I got to the pad. We lifted off in the jerky ungainly fashion that always scares me, and thudded and thrashed to Camp David. In the darkness I saw nothing of the camp except a lit-up heated pool outside the big lodge, steaming clouds of vapor into the rain.

The President sat in shirt sleeves, the usual yellow pad in his lap, by flaming logs in a stone fireplace, in a large sitting room with exposed ceiling beams. He looked awful. The firelight deepened the hollows of his eyes and the downthrust lines of his mouth, and highlighted his sagging jowls. He inquired about my mother's health as I handed him Golda's letter. With a glance at me from under those heavy eyebrows, the cartoonists' delight, he opened it, and read it slowly, twice.

"Do you know what is in this letter?" he asked, dropping the pages in his lap.

"No, Mr. President."

"No idea at all?"

"No, sir." This was simple truth. All the possibilities were so bad that I had tried hard to shut them from mind.

"What did she say when she gave it to you?"

"That it was for your eyes alone, and that nobody should know of its existence."

"Does anybody know?"

"The Israeli ambassador knows I brought a letter."

"Yes, he notified me."

Sunk low in the armchair, he stared at the fire, then he sat up and put the handwritten sheets into the flames. "Forget you delivered it, or that it existed."

"Yes, Mr. President."

A handwritten letter from a Prime Minister to a President, burned before my eyes! Maybe she made a copy, in which case it will survive in Israel's secret archives. Otherwise I believe the letter is gone from the world and from history.

He took off his glasses and rubbed his eyes. "How's the war going over there?"

"Sir, I've been out of touch since I left."

"I'm interested in your impressions."

So I described Dado's too-optimistic press conference, and the dark plunge afterward in the Israeli mood. I recounted, too, Mark Herz's inside army gossip of disaster. He kept nodding, slouched down in his chair, his eyes glazed and hooded. Then I told him about my visit to the young American lawyer and tank captain in the hospital, and about Abe's determination to get back into the war; also about the wounded soldiers going AWOL from the hospitals to rejoin their units. It was something to see, the way the President straightened up, and his face brightened, and his eyes cleared.

"They are going to win, and thank God for that," he said. "They deserve to."

"Mr. President, the Prime Minister said they need help. The Soviets have got a vast airlift going to Syria and Egypt."

"We know. We're not going to let Israel go down the tubes." He gestured with his highball glass at a movable bar. "Have a drink."

In the unbuttoned vein that he sometimes falls into with me, he began to ramble. I suspect he cannot sleep, and dreads lying down

in the dark. Uppermost in his mind was a bill Congress is about to
vote on, the War Powers Resolution, which he considers a historic
national calamity. He says it hobbles a President's power to use the
armed forces in a sudden foreign crisis. "They are cutting the balls
off the Presidency," he put it, "and our enemies will know it, and
will act accordingly." If the bill passes he will veto it. He expects to
be upheld, but it will be close. He talked of this as the major failure
in his Presidency, his inability to persuade Congress that this bill is a
catastrophic move. Imagine! With all the failures, mistakes, foul plays,
and crimes of which he stands accused or has even admitted, he blames
himself for this, something the media ignore.

Then he circled back on worn tracks. He had ended the Vietnam
war by having the guts to do unpopular things like invading Cambodia and bombing Hanoi. Now Congress, with this resolution, was
inviting the North Vietnamese to blitz the south. They would do that
in short order if the bill became law. All those thousands of American boys, after securing an honorable peace with their lives, would
have died in vain. As to Watergate, he was definitely going to fire
the Special Prosecutor, a Kennedy man with a staff of Kennedy loy-
alists all out to get him. He was still waiting for a court decision about
the tapes, and if it went against him he would take it to the Supreme
Court. Such an invasion of executive privilege would really gut the
Presidency, and if it meant being impeached, he would not yield.

As he went on, he drifted into a new, wistful key. He loves football, and football analogies. Most games were decided in the fourth
quarter, he said; and his whole aim in seeking the Presidency had
been to do something about world peace in the fourth quarter of his
life. That would fix his place in history. He had been elected in the
thick of the Vietnam mess, not of his making. He had brought home
the troops, initiated détente and disarmament with the Soviet Union,
and achieved the rapprochement with China. He had abolished the
biological warfare section of the army, and ordered the stockpile of
such weapons destroyed, a serious unilateral step toward peace. "Catch
the media ever mentioning that," he said. (It was news to me, in fact.)
He had had a grand plan in mind for a start on world peace; but
now between Watergate and this War Powers Resolution, it would
probably die, a blasted dream.

Peculiarly, he never once referred to the big story of the hour. The

Vice President had resigned, and for the first time in our history a President was going to appoint his own successor. The media were frothing with guesses and rumors about who he would designate. The story overshadowed the Middle East war and Watergate, but on this topic he said not a word. At two o'clock his voice was fading, his eyes drooping shut. All at once he sat up and told me I could go, and I might hear from him about midday.

Coming so abruptly, his dismissal jolted me into talking before I thought. I had been waiting and waiting for him to say something more about the war than that vague, "We're not going to let Israel go down the tubes." Nothing. Yet everything depended now on the word of this one distracted, dejected, hounded, played-out, incredibly hated man in shirt sleeves, the President of the United States.

"Sir," I blurted, "may I say one thing before I go?"

He barely nodded.

"You spoke about the figure you'll make in history," I said. "Mr. President, the people with the longest historical memory in the world are the Jews. The Israelis can hold off the Arabs, though they're outnumbered in manpower twenty-five to one. They can match them. They can beat them. The one thing they can't match is the output of the Soviet Union's munitions plants. They're only three million people. The Russians have pushed the Arabs once more to die trying to destroy Israel, so that Soviet communism can move in and grab the Middle East. It's happened before and now it's happening again, Mr. President. It's *all* that's happening."

"I'm aware of that," the President said in a dry tone.

"Sir, my point is that it's truly touch and go in Israel. I don't know the latest intelligence, but I know how I felt when I saw Golda Meir's face. If you order an airlift now to match the Soviet shipments — *now,* sir — then the world's longest historical memory will honor you forever." In those remote, infinitely tired eyes, I thought I saw a dusky glimmer. I plunged ahead. "It will honor the man who showed greatness, by rising above his own desperate political predicament and coming to the rescue of the Jewish State."

The President said nothing for a while, staring at the dying fire, then he tiredly pushed himself up out of his armchair. "Well, I may have to kick some ass, at that. The thing has been batting back and forth all week between State and Defense." He sighed, glanced back at the fireplace, and said indistinctly, as though to himself, "Anyway, she doesn't leave me much of an alternative." I wouldn't swear to those words, but that's what I think I heard.

He walked with me to the door and shook hands. "You've stayed aboard while some others were jumping ship. It's been appreciated. Get some rest. You may be flying again soon."

A gentle shake woke me up. "I hate to do this to you, but Peter Quat is here."

I opened my eyes, and found myself lying dressed, except for shoes, tie, and jacket, on the library couch. I had no recollection of going to sleep. Jan drew open the drapes, and sunlight blazed on me.

"Peter Quat? What the hell?"

"He telephoned at nine o'clock, and like a damn fool I told him you were here. I didn't expect him to hop the next Eastern shuttle, but he did."

"Has the White House called?"

"No."

"The Israeli Embassy?"

"No."

"What's the war news?"

"No better."

Peter Quat looked sulky the first time I ever laid eyes on him, in the bus to Camp Eagle Wing; a sulky face was his normal mien at college and in April House; and he has looked sulkier and sulkier in his book-jacket pictures, as they have gotten older and older and his hairline has kept receding. But never have I seen him looking quite so sulky as he did today, glowering at me over the coffee and cake Jan served us in the living room. That grizzled widow's peak of his has now receded behind his ears. Yet he still has the old air of the eternal sneering bad boy, plus a certain prideful bearing, because after all, he is Peter Quat. This time he was also in great rage.

"I want you to start a lawsuit against my publishers."

"What for?"

"They're not advertising my book, the sons of bitches."

"Peter, I saw several ads before I left for Israel. I saw a full-page ad in the *Times Book Review*."

"Why wasn't it a double spread?" He brandished a folder. "Look, don't argue with me, Dave, I've got the reviews here. A book with such notices should be selling five thousand a week. They say there are no sales, and a lot of returns. They can't explain it. Didn't the bastards contract to *sell* my book, not just print it? What they need is a red-hot poker up their ass."

"The book's been out only a couple of weeks, Peter."

"Goddamn it, Dave, the first weeks are crucial for a novel! If it doesn't get roaring in thirty days it's gone. I've been in story conferences with Mort Oshins in Malibu for a month. He's been snooping in the bookstores ever since pub date, and I *know* he's cooling off already. I can feel it. Meantime I bought a house in Bel Air. Gigantic mortgage, all the cash I had or could borrow, and if Oshins drops this project I am up shit creek."

His voice dropped and he sourly grinned.

"What's more, and for Christ's sake keep this to yourself until my custody suit over Stephen is settled, I've been screwing a movie star out there. I can't mention her name, she's got a husband and two kids, but she's read all my books, and she's the most astounding quiff I've ever experienced. We went to bed the same night we met. It's a new country, Dave, a new *universe* of quiff — and, besides, she has all the money there is. We could even end up getting married. Wouldn't *that* solve all my problems! But not if I have a fucking flop! You know how movie people are. Unless I hit number one with this book I am *creamed,* and it's a *great book,* and I want you to make those stingy shitheads advertise it."

All the time he was talking, my ear was cocked for a telephone ring. What in God's name was happening with the airlift?

"Peter, the book is probably starting slow because of the war, that's all."

"What war?" Peter Quat honestly and truly asked that question. Then, "Oh, you mean the war in Israel? So what? What's that got to do with my book?"

"Look, Peter, the Jews are your main audience, you know that. Ordinarily they love to laugh at themselves, and the more savage the jokes are, the better. That's been your secret. Only right now they're not in the mood. They're worried. I'm worried. I've just returned from Jerusalem, and I assure you Israel is in trouble."

Peter did not quite get my point. He may not have been paying close attention, being so upset. "Fuck Jerusalem, and fuck Israel! *My*

book isn't selling!" He waved both arms up in the air and then down
to the floor, pounding Jan's oriental carpet with both fists. "MY —
BOOK — ISN'T — SELLING, do you hear, Dave?"

"Well, I can't start a lawsuit for you, Peter, but if you insist I can
suggest some good litigation lawyers. I'm busy."

"Doing what?" Peter inquired, making a magnificently horrible face.
"Working for that depraved lying criminal who's destroying America?"

"Mainly he's destroying himself. It's pitiful, and he's done some
fearful things, but I think he's going to help the Jews."

The telephone was ringing in the library.

"Christ, what a narrow point of view," said Peter Quat.

"Wait a couple of weeks, Peter. Your book will start to sell."

I darted into the library. The President's appointments secretary
told me that I should plan on flying to Israel tomorrow.

"I may have trouble getting on El Al," I told him.

"I don't think you'll be flying El Al," he said. I hung up and sat,
bemused. Not flying El Al? *Airlift?* Peter Quat came into the library,
and this will sound odd, but I had forgotten that he was in the house.

"Dave, why do you think my book will start to sell?"

There was something touching about his anxious tone. Peter Quat
is a major author, if a monstrous muddlehead; he has long leaned on
me for counsel; and the great PDQ once took a Bronx boy under his
wing. So I assured him once more that he had a solid following, that
My Cock was vintage Quat, and that they would be coming around
to the bookstores. "Whether you'll be number one, Peter, is in the
lap of the gods," I said. "That *Willy the Whale* book unfortunately
seems to be all the vogue. Even Jan went out and bought it. Just
don't go starting a lawsuit. You'll land on the front pages trumpeting
that your book is a flop. That can be very damaging."

Peter hesitated, then said uncertainly, "Well, okay. I'll sweat it out
for two more weeks. If there are still no sales, I'm definitely suing
the bastards, and I want you to handle it."

"Maybe by then the war will be over."

"Fuck the war."

Peter left for New York. His literary vocabulary is luxuriant, but
his conversation has a certain repetitive spareness. I fear he's in trouble
with the Bel Air house. That whale book, a tenuous whimsy a hundred
pages long, is selling like the Bible. Such freaks come along in pub-

lishing. Old Peter's timing has been bad, and his new universe of astounding quiff may, alas, dissolve into thin air

> *And, like this insubstantial pageant faded,*
> *Leave not a rack behind.*

Jan and I had an incongruously peaceful Friday night meal: candles, wine, gefilte fish, chicken soup, the works. As we sang the Sabbath songs, I kept thinking that it was getting on toward sunrise in Israel, and that more tank battles must be already thundering in the Sinai and the north.

Afterward I walked down to the White House through bleak drizzle, because I'd been invited to the announcement of the President's choice of successor. It was no surprise. The ceremony was very incongruous in its way, too; a lot of happy laughing and congratulating under blinding blue television lights, just as if the Administration was not foundering and all-out war was not exploding in the Holy Land. I came and went unnoticed. I might have skipped it, but you never know with the President. Jan said an Air Force major had called in my absence. We disregard telephone rings on the Sabbath, but that's off. He was coming for me early in the morning, no other details.

Well, as the world knows, wartime lends a golden edge to lovemaking; it is one of the corrupt charms of mankind's chronic insanity. My unexpected night with Jan brought back old times, for we met and fell in love during the war, while I was serving in the Army Air Corps. I've written hardly anything about Jan, nor will I, but she is the woman poor Bobbie was not, the love of my life, the woman that lasted; and I am not putting Jan in any book, she is my private love, not for publication. The Air Force major telephoned at six in the morning and said he'd come for me within the hour, so I reluctantly disengaged myself from rapture and tumbled out of bed. "No heroics, now," said Jan. "You're a creaky old thing, and the Israelis can take care of themselves."

"Me?" I said. "I'm sitting it out in the Jerusalem Savoy."

When we parted at the door her eyes were wet. "I know you. You're having fun," she said. "Not too much, do you hear? And when you find Sandra, call me."

At Dover Air Force Base things were jumping. All sorts of machines were noisily crisscrossing hither and yon: jeeps, trucks, forklifts, half-tracks, small cranes, and huge flatbed vehicles piled high with crates on pallets. Galaxies like this one were parked helter-skelter, with cavernous openings at nose and tail, into which the trucks were wheeling to unload and driving out again, to the shouts of loadmasters and work parties, and roars of arriving aircraft. It was like old times on bomber bases, but our Flying Fortresses were Piper Cubs to these open-ended leviathans.

The trip to the Azores passed pleasantly in all that cockpit talk. When we were coming down through night clouds the pilot let fall a disconcerting fact. The backbone of the airlift will be the smaller C-141, and a number of them are all loaded and ready to fly. But the recent crosswinds in the Azores were and still are beyond the C-141's capacity to land. So some Galaxies were loaded up in a hurry, because they can lock their landing gear off-center, and do hairy crosswind landings. Well, it was a damnably queer sensation, I tell you, sitting in that jump seat and watching the lights of the landing strip coming up at an angle to the plane, instead of straight ahead. "This is what we really get paid to do," the flight commander said, calmly chewing gum as his titanic machine went crabbing into the ground, smooth as glass, and rolled on the tarmac along the strip of lights at that same acute angle.

"Pretty nifty," I said, in a shaky voice.

"Just lucky," he said.

But then, as I've mentioned, that Galaxy was grounded by a "crump." This one came flying in, refueled, and took off, and I thumbed a ride. I had no notion of the risky flight plan, and deserve no credit for intrepidity; though even if I'd known the worst, the President's letter in my breast pocket would have spurred me to get aboard. . . .

The flight commander has just sent for me. What now?

What indeed!

When I came into the cockpit he gestured at the windows. On both sides of the Galaxy, six U.S. Navy planes were flying formation on us; half a dozen silver and blue needle-nosed fighters, flashing along in the sun. He motioned at the empty co-pilot's seat, and pointed downward. I clambered into the seat, and through the clouds I saw below a carrier and its escort vessels, tiny and gray on the purple sea. I glanced at him and ventured a smile. He smiled back like a barefoot boy, and made a thumbs-up. Next moment his round freckled face froze into its hard cast. So on we go. Three reassured hours to Tel Aviv. However, two hundred miles out, the U.S. fighters will peel off. The Israeli Air Force is supposed to take over and escort us in. There's the crunch.

I think I'll be able to take a nap meanwhile. I haven't slept much in the past two days. Six U.S. Navy fighters are a soothing presence.

* * *

85

Sandra Found

F ROM that deep peaceful snooze in the rest cabin of a thundering C-5A Galaxy, I was harshly awakened by alarmed shouts up forward: "Fighters! Fighters! Not ours!"

And there they were outside the windows as I came stumbling into the cockpit: four F-4 Phantoms in the red light of a setting sun, with the blue and white Star of David on their fuselages, the six-pointed star that I first saw at the age of three on a paper flag I was given in the Minsker Synagogue, to wave as I marched during the Rejoicing of the Law. I muttered in Hebrew, *Blessed are you, Lord Our God, Ruler of the Universe, who have kept us alive, and sustained us, and brought us to this time.* Standard blessing on good news. Judging by the cheers of the Galaxy crew, I was saying it for them, too. They were already kidding the copilot about his panicky yell, on spying fighter shapes with unfamiliar markings.

After that, even hearing the Russian airlift pilots talking on the international air control channel was an anticlimax. Those Phantoms stayed with us until the Israeli air controller said, "Shalom, C-5 Galaxy, you are cleared to land." Then they flipped away into the starlit night. The stupendous flying machine came winging past darkened Tel Aviv, settled toward the lights of the landing strip, and touched down. It was still rolling when work parties and trucks came swarming out to commence unloading. The crew and I were rushed into a VIP lounge, where the prettiest El Al stewardesses I ever saw gave us bouquets of roses, and drinks, and food, and a lot of kisses and hugs, too. I did not rate such a welcome, but I was thoroughly enjoying it, when a young fellow in an open white shirt came sidling through the girls to me. "Doovidel? The car is here."

That was three days ago.

The Israel Defense Force has since crossed the Suez Canal, and is counterattacking on Egyptian territory. Golda announced it in the Knesset. In the north too they have broken the attack, and are grinding forward into Syria. There's no question any more of premature optimism. We are going to win this war. The Israelis have brought off another military miracle, a recovery and turnabout after a multiple surprise attack that could have ended the Jewish State. For that is the problem of Israel, and perhaps the secret of its military power, too. The slim margin for error compels the fighting capacity the world wonders at, whether with admiration, or with gnashing of teeth. I believe both sentiments are now being felt, here and there around the planet.

Well, then, is the airlift superfluous, now that it's coming to flood out there at Lod Airport, we believe surpassing the Russian effort? Not on your life. A general about to shoot off his last bullets fights a different battle than one who knows replenishments are on hand or coming. The Israelis crossed the Canal on their own with what they had, but the start of the airlift gave them a terrific shot in the arm. I saw that on Golda's face. She was not the same woman. She looked half her age, smiling and greeting me, "Nu, Doovidel, did you have a nice time in America?"

The word from the President was that I can stay here until my mother's condition stabilizes. The doctors at Hadassah hospital say that it is still touch-and-go. "She is an old, old lady," expostulated the doctor on duty when I pressured him for a glimpse of her. "Anything can happen, at any moment. Don't disturb her again until she's out of the oxygen."

Meanwhile, by sheer chance, I have located Sandra. Israel's a small place. I went to the Colossus after seeing Golda, and in the lobby I ran bang into, of all people, Earl Eckstein; the lawyer who, you recall, recommended me in my hot adolescence to the understanding woman. His mother is in an old folks' home outside Tel Aviv. He came to Israel to visit her for the holidays, and got caught like thousands of other tourists.

"What a nice daughter you've got," he said. "My mother loves her."
And it turned out that Sandra is working in that home, and that's
my daughter's heroic war service, wheelchairs and bedpans for ancient Jewish wrecks. I went to see her.

"My God, *you?*" was her filial greeting, as she stood there in a dingy
corridor in jeans and a sweatshirt, a sloshing basin in hand. She said
half the people in that home know my mother, and all agree that
Mom's a ball of fire. Sandra is sure she'll pull through once again.
She wouldn't agree to come to the Colossus for a meal. "There's nobody here under seventy-five but me," she said. "The whole staff had
to go to the war. I'm managing the place with a few inmates who
can still walk."

So I picked up my stuff at the Colossus, and moved down here to
the almost deserted Hilton. I want to be near Sandra. Her sanato-
rium is ten minutes away from the hotel by car.

I did not like the way Sandra looked at all. Her hair was in disorder, her face was white, and her eyes were bloodshot. I ventured to
ask her about Abe Herz. "He's back in Tel Hashomer hospital. He
was blinded, the day they crossed the Suez Canal. The doctors can't
tell yet how much of his sight he will recover." She said all this without visible emotion, but I know Sandra, and her look and voice lac-
erated me almost as much as the news about Abe. The bandages are
coming off in two or three days, and then we may know what his
chances are. Sandra said Mark has spent much time at his bedside,
talking and reading to him, and Abe's spirits are not bad, considering.

As for the war, my sister Lee tells me that Moshe Lev expects it to
last another week, unless the Russians rescue the Arabs from a complete debacle by forcing an earlier cease-fire. Now or never, here in
this luxury suite overlooking downtown Tel Aviv and the serene
Mediterranean, let me push on and finish *April House.* One more hasty
pile-up of yellow pages, and farewell forever to Bobbie Webb, and
to my young days. And, I strongly suspect, farewell to this second
bizarre technicolor interlude in the drab black-and-white of a tax
lawyer's career. When the President shook hands with me and said
goodbye, there was a final note in his manner. I think instinct told
him that my service is done.

*   *   *

B OBBIE Webb, Bobbie Webb! Gone from my life thirty years and more! Yet the tones of her voice in differing moods, the way she shrugged into and out of that beaver coat, how she lit a cigarette, how she held a pocket mirror and painted her mouth, how she pulled on her stockings, how she flipped her hair out of a coat collar with both hands and shook her head — such things are as present to me as the rippling blue sea below.

Before the computer there was the human brain, with its vast storage capacity, and a merciful shut-off mechanism called forgetting. That shut-off has failed me with Bobbie Webb. All those memory tapes have been spewing out their contents. The rest of *April House* will be an exercise in flood control; for the story draws to its close, a familiar old tale, after all. Not of a student prince and a barmaid — that was a mere collegiate wisecrack of Mark Herz's — a simple story of lost innocence and found identity.

What happened then, and what is happening to me now, begin to merge as two sides of one coin.

86

A Tribute of Tears

HARRY GOLDHANDLER lay in a richly polished silver-handled walnut coffin, overflowing with plushy pink linings and banked about with flowers. We Orthodox Jews wrap our dead in white shrouds and, where the local laws allow, put them into the earth that way, dust to dust. If there has to be a box, we use as plain and rough a box as we can get, and the very pious bore holes in it to make a way for the dust to return to the dust it came from. Such is the old tradition. Not all Jews do that nowadays, of course.

From my place on the long queue shuffling past the bier, only his pale face was visible. When my turn came to peer down into the coffin, I saw that he was in black tie; in fact, in the same old double-breasted tuxedo he had worn at opening nights. Eyes closed, face still sunken with fatigue, he looked much as he had, stretched out on the long office couch, snatching an hour's sleep at three or four in the morning; except for the clean shave, that is, and the formal attire. Almost, I could imagine my shaking him, and the dead man opening one eye and hoarsely pleading, "Wake me in another fifteen minutes, Liebowitz." But Harry Goldhandler had to plead for sleep no more. For the first time since he struck it rich writing jokes, he was going to get enough rest.

There was no rabbi. There were no prayers, no hymns, no music. A well-known publisher, who had frequented the penthouse to guffaw at Goldhandler's routines, gave the eulogy: fine family man, amusing friend, brilliant wit, etc. "Harry would not want to exact from us the tribute of our tears," he concluded, and indeed no tears were shed that I noticed. Many star comedians, wearing incongruous solemn expressions, were there: Bert Lahr, Jimmy Durante, Al Jolson, Fanny Brice, also a lot of smaller fry like Nicholas Panilas and Morrie Abbott. Henny Holtz came, too; Mrs. Goldhandler later complained angrily about that. Skip Lasser sat near me, and I saw Billy Rose and the Gershwins amid a knot of Broadway people; and what with friends and relatives of the Goldhandlers, and a large turn-out of the broadcasting trade, there was standing room only at the farewell to the gag czar.

Wearing the only skullcap in the place, and not wanting to flaunt it, I sat in the back row. As Mrs. Goldhandler, veiled in black, walked out escorted by her sons, I was whispering a kaddish for Goldhandler. Once the family left, the hushed crowd strolled out in a buzz of greetings, handshaking, chatter, and laughter. Boyd remained by the open coffin, making notes on a pad. When the place had emptied, leaving just Boyd and me, a soft-walking attendant in black closed the coffin, and wheeled it briskly out through a side door; possibly straight to the flames, for Goldhandler was being cremated. Boyd followed his dead boss out, wiping his eyes; the eulogy notwithstanding, giving Goldhandler the tribute of his tears. A different attendant wheeled in another fancy coffin, containing a heavily rouged old lady in an evening gown, and I left.

As it happened, I was scheduled to speak at Pop's synagogue that Friday night, when Rabbi Hoppenstein ran his after-dinner cultural forum. I told Bobbie that I would talk about Goldhandler, and she asked diffidently if it would be wrong for her to come and hear me. "Not at all, do come," I said. I saw her walk out on the balcony and sit down in a rear pew. Thereafter only her tilted green hat was visible, behind the solid rows of hatted ladies.

It was a sizable audience. The Goodkinds' raffish gagman son had a certain notoriety in the Orthodox crowd, for I had gone out with several of their daughters; and there had been that romance with the conspicuous Rosalind Hoppenstein. My talk promised to be a light interlude between lectures on substantial topics like Maimonides and Moses Mendelssohn. No doubt I startled the audience by saying that my boss, the gag czar Harry Goldhandler, had just died; that my time as a joke-writer was over, and what I had to say was a *hesped,* a eulogy of a man I admired. Anyway, there was not much dozing off.

It is thirty-five years since I gave that speech, but I remember that I started with some heavyish Friday forum talk about the sense of humor, calling it God's comfort to mankind for the tragic human predicament. So far as that goes, I still hold to the notion. It is why I represent and defend Peter Quat; whatever his ignorant neurotic hangups about being Jewish, he has transmuted them to redeeming laughter. The world's best-loved authors, I pointed out — Mark Twain, Molière, Dickens, Cervantes, and our own Sholem Aleichem — were writers who made people laugh. Harry Goldhandler was under no delusions, I said, about gagwriting; he was a man of exceptional gifts, but he had been content to coin them into fleeting amusement. "Our fathers came to the Goldena Medina believing you could pick up gold in the streets," I recall saying at the end. "My boss found out that it was true, but he wore himself out picking up too much too fast. Millions of people laughed at famous radio comedians, and never knew the name of the man who actually made them laugh. If they had known Harry Goldhandler, they might have loved him the way I loved him, may he rest in peace."

As I came out of the synagogue to a sidewalk crowded by the departing audience, Mom pounced on me. "You were wonderful! Come on home, we've invited a lot of people. Papa will read some Sholem Aleichem in Goldhandler's memory."

"Maybe he has something else to do," Pop said, catching my momentary glance across the street, where Bobbie stood in the shadows. It was the only time he ever laid eyes on her.

I said I might come home after a while, and I hurried to catch up with Bobbie, who was starting to walk off. "Oh, hi," she said. "Don't you want to go with your mother and father?" For answer I took her arm. "It's a shame Mrs. Goldhandler and her children weren't there. It was a lovely talk, what I got of it. Of course you kept losing me, with all those Hebrew expressions."

"What? I only used one or two, Bobbie."

She stopped short, freeing her arm, and looked at me. "Are you serious? David, you kept throwing them in all the time. Your audience understood you, but I sure didn't."

I thought back over my speech, and realized I had been free with Yiddish interjections, which in that setting I hardly thought of as another language. Bobbie of course could not tell Yiddish from Hebrew. "Did you hear well?"

"Oh, sure. The ladies were very quiet. You're much admired up there in the gallery, dear. I heard some nice compliments. Also I got some funny looks. Or maybe I was just self-conscious."

In Morrie's flat Bobbie kicked off her shoes and curled up in an armchair. We talked quietly over drinks, far into the night. I told her about Goldhandler's total rewrite of *Johnny, Drop Your Gun* in a few days in Florida. It was news to her. The word around the show, she said, was that Goldhandler had kept trying to put in crude stale jokes, and Lasser had cut them all out. She had no idea that the hospital scene, which had saved the show, was Goldhandler's work.

That got us going on Skip Lasser; and so, on reminiscences of the start of our love affair. Bobbie remarked a shade sadly that she missed Peeping Tom. Morrie's flat was an unromantic rendezvous, to be sure; one room with a double bed, a desk, and two chairs. As we talked of our good and bad times up on the eighteenth floor, and I remembered the Paramount clock, the grand view of the skyscrapers and the river, the Hemingway pillow, and the gardenias, I was overwhelmed with yearning for that lost time, and with desperate affection for this outsider of outsiders in the green hat and stocking feet, to whom I had again proposed marriage. Neither of us said a word about that. There was no chill between us, but an odd constraint. She went home about two in the morning, with a tranquil goodbye kiss at the elevator, and I sat down at the typewriter to dredge a Jimmy Durante script from a void and distracted brain.

Next night when the Sabbath ended I telephoned Pop and said I had to talk to him. I caught him on the way out to a Zionist meeting. He was the chairman, he said, and couldn't miss it. If I would come there, he would turn over the chair to someone else as soon as possible. It had to be a night of lashing rain and high winds, naturally. I had hoped to take a slow walk with Pop, and break the news gently. All Saturday I had walked and walked around the Central Park reservoir, racking my brains for the best way to handle the thing. The day had been glorious, and I had hit on an approach which, in the sunshine amid the blooming cherry and crabapple trees, had seemed considerate and mature. In that wet windy night misgivings whipped at me, and I taxied to Pop's meeting, not knowing what the hell to do or say.

"Not one dunam!"

A short swarthy man was addressing about eighty men and women on folding chairs, in a bleak meeting room thick with smoke. Pop sat up front at a table with a gray-haired man.

"Not one dunam, and if we have to fight, we fight!"

I am not stopping my story for an excursion into Zionist history in 1938, but in a word, the topic was a British plan to partition Palestine. A "dunam" is about a quarter of an acre. I did not know then what it was, nor had I heard of the Peel Commission, which the speaker berated at length. The gray-haired man, a professor from some seminary, then spoke in favor of accepting partition. The little dark man bitterly argued that the British had already partitioned the Jewish homeland once, reneging on the Balfour Declaration and awarding the Palestine Arabs the entire huge Transjordan. To partition again the remaining fragment of Palestine west of the Jordan would leave no Jewish area that could survive Arab assaults. Any Jewish state, however tiny, the gray professor persisted, where European Jews would have a haven from the menace of Hitler, was better than no state at all. The dark man retorted that the European Jews were not worried enough about Hitler to be arriving in Palestine in any numbers, though they were free to do so.

My mind was on Bobbie and Pop. The debate, insofar as it penetrated my inattention, seemed to me mere chatter in a vacuum. I classed the idea of a Jewish state, when I thought about it at all, with such futuristic imaginings as rockets to Mars and world utopias. These people discussed it like a Czechoslovakia ready to raise its flag. As for the menace of Hitler, I thought it must be greatly exaggerated, probably for the purposes of Jewish fund-raising.

God help me, how I want to strike out those lines! But they are the truth.

I write on my balcony facing the Mediterranean, on a brilliantly sunny morning. The news is as brilliant as the day. The tiny Jewish state, which — thirty-five lightning years ago — I considered a nutty fantasy, has routed the armies of Egypt and Syria, and is on the march to Damascus and Cairo. The Egyptian Third Army is trapped west of the Suez Canal. The Russians are frantically pushing a cease-fire to save that army from annihilation and Sadat's Egypt from collapse. The American Secretary of State has flown to Moscow to work out the deal.

As for my skepticism about the Nazis, I will die regretting it. So will every Jew of my generation who disbelieved until it was too late; and that is ninety percent of us, including the European Jews themselves, those few who survived. The little dark man and the professor were talking stern reality. It was my head that was in a soundproof vacuum of obsession with a girl, and that part doesn't bear thinking about.

"HAVE you been with her as man and wife?" Pop quaintly put it, hardly able to get the words out. At the answer he leaned his head on an arm resting on his knee, and covered his eyes. We sat in the chilly lobby of the building, both of us in raincoats.

Pop, in muffled tones: "And you're sure you want to marry her?"

"I love her, Papa."

He uncovered his eyes and scanned my face. "Well, then, that settles it. She'll be a Jewish daughter."

All this must have been in Yiddish, because I can hear him saying "*Yiddishe tokhter*" (Jewish daughter) in a warm, even affectionate way, as plainly as I hear this pen scratching. Pop habitually talked Yiddish about serious matters.

"And when do you plan on getting married?"

"That's what I have to talk to you about."

87

The Shoot-out

WHAT followed between Pop and me I have long thought of as the shoot-out at the O.K. Corral. It took place in Morrie's flat in April House, and there was no shooting, or even raising of voices. Not with my father. But it was a confrontation that brought a swift denouement, and here is how it went that night.

The considerate and mature scheme I had worked out, walking amid sunlit cherry and crabapple blossoms, was to get engaged to Bobbie, but not married. Not straight off, certainly. Rationale: I would have hard adjustments to make, returning to law school. So would Bobbie, what with conversion and all. Marriage now would be a complication. Having proposed marriage, I had to do something about it, and that is what I would do at the moment, get engaged. I told all this to Pop in April House. He sat in the same armchair Bobbie had curled up in the night before, his large brown eyes soberly fixed on me, and heard me out.

"Have you put this plan to the young lady?"

"I wanted to talk to you first."

"I appreciate that."

He asked about Bobbie's family, her religion, her work, her education; and as I answered candidly I began to realize, picturing her through his eyes, that the religion was all but a red herring. Quite aside from that, Yisroelke had himself a pretty girl with no background, limited education, and at best average intelligence; facts that I knew, but that left out the tenderness, beauty, and hard-knotted bond of our love. My hope was that Pop understood that, he was a man.

"Yisroelke, you told me at first it was not serious," he said at last. "You told me that over and over."

"Yes, I did."

"Then you told me it was finished."

"I know."

"And now you say you want to marry her."

"Yes."

"*Hayitokhon?*" inquired Pop.

We looked at each other in the eye, and believe it or not, we both sadly laughed.

Hayitokhon is one of those great Yiddish words taken over from Hebrew, into which are packed four thousand years of Jewish experience. You can translate it, "Can it be?" or "Is it possible?" or "Does it make sense?" or "How come?" or "Come on!" or "Gimme a break"; or even — when used as a profane incredulous expletive — "Jesus!" All those are overtones or harmonies of *hayitokhon*. With that one word, Pop bridged the gap between us in a rueful chuckle.

I did my best to respond. I dwelled on Bobbie's warmth to me, her practical sense, her devotion to her mother, and the stouthearted way she was supporting both of them in a depression. Given my education, I argued, how could I be preoccupied, as he and Mom were, with being Jewish? And what other education could I have had? Zaideh's notion of making me into an iluy, an anachronism like himself, had always been doomed. I was an American, making a living in America, and I had fallen in love with a beautiful girl out there. I had tried to break it off and had failed, and here I was. Such was my pitch, more or less, stumbled through incoherently and ending up in the air.

Pop looked puzzled and unsatisfied. "You've known her how long now?" he asked when I had talked myself out. "Two years?"

"A little more."

"You have broken up, you say, and gotten together again?"

"A couple of times."

"And now what? Have you had a fight? Has she given you an ultimatum?"

"No, nothing like that."

A silence. Pop was a pacer when he was thinking hard — as I am to this day — and he got up and paced, hands clasped behind him.

"During the time you broke up, she had other men friends?"

"Yes."

"That doesn't bother you?"

A direct stab to a deep abscess: *the man who knew Einstein.* "No
. . . it doesn't."

"Would she really want to become Jewish?" Pop asked.

A deeper probe.

*Bobbie's green hat in the ladies' balcony; Bobbie baffled by the Yiddish
in my talk; Bobbie in the shadows, across the street from the synagogue;
Bobbie and I in April House afterward, constrained and sitting apart.*

"She would do it."

Papa paced, then halted and spoke deliberately. "I'll tell you what,
Yisroelke. I have never been in England, but Disraeli once said, 'The
only truth is race. There is no other.' He said that out of experience,
and he was the Prime Minister of England. You must be sure to understand exactly how the young lady feels. Not about you. She loves
you. We know that. But about being Jewish. You're talking about
the rest of her life."

How much deeper will Pop cut?

*"I'm going to learn how to make gefilte fish, and I'm going to marry
you."*

*"Don't you know when you're done, Izzy? That's not characteristic of
your race!"*

"Whose Izzy Izzy, Izzy yours or Izzy mine?"

"Hollooeen!"

"Clip cock! Clip cock!"

"That doesn't worry me."

"All right." Papa's tone changed to that harsh straight business voice
of his. "Now I want you to tell me, what made you ask her to marry
you just at this time? And no bluffing, Yisroelke, out with it! What
has happened?"

I told him. I described the visit to Lee's house, Bobbie's weeping
at the sight of the baby, the intimate yet awkward dinner, the unbearably distressing moment when Bobbie held the baby in her arms.
I tried to explain how I had felt at that sight.

"I see," Pop said, "and now I think I understand you."

He took a long pause, pacing and pacing. Then he sat down in the
armchair. I see him now before me, and I realize — it seems, for the
first time — that the Minsker Godol's follies may have aged him and
worn him out as much as all his other burdens together.

"Yisroelke, you have treated this girl very badly," he said with slow melancholy, in his clear rich Yiddish. "You have done her a great wrong. She's older than you, and she's a worldly person, but that makes no difference. Because you're a *mentsch* you hate feeling so guilty. That much is all right. Still, to get married so as not to feel guilty, just to apologize for doing a woman wrong, is not good. Not for her, and not for you. It's not a basis for a life together. It's a mistake. Now is that your main reason, or isn't it?"

A moment for truth.

"That's my main reason."

"What is her name?"

If I did not remember his asking this, I wouldn't mention it, it seems so unbelievable. But for two years and more, Bobbie had been "the girl" or "the young lady."

"Violet," I said, and I'll never know why I didn't say "Bobbie."

"Violet? All right." He switched to English. "I think maybe you should say, '*My dear Violet, I asked you to marry me, and I meant it. And since I said it, I will do it. But the more I think about it, with all the problems, I'm afraid it might be a mistake for both of us. We should talk about it, and if after all you agree, then I want to give you money. It's the best thing I can do. That way you can be free to make a life for yourself, and you won't be hard-pressed in the meantime.*' You should consider saying something like that, Yisroelke."

"Buy her off, you mean," I snapped.

"Don't twist my words," said my father, shaking his head at me. "I think she won't be offended, Yisroelke, and she won't accuse you of buying her off. She sounds like a down-to-earth person, and if she is, she'll be sad but also relieved. Becoming a Jew isn't such a bargain nowadays, believe me."

We talked a lot more, we talked until the windows turned gray in the dawn, but that was in essence what happened in the shoot-out at the O.K. Corral.

I picked Bobbie up at Bonwit's. As we walked arm in arm across to the Plaza for lunch, I said, "You know, I asked you to marry me."

"Yes, so I seem to remember."

"Well, I've been thinking a lot about it."

She slowed in her walk. Her arm tightened on mine. It was the only emotion she showed at the disclosure, in the words and in my tone, that it was over.

"Yes, David?"

"We'll talk inside," I all but shouted. We were crossing Fifty-eighth Street in a traffic jam, and the auto-horn cacophony was horrendous.

Well, in brief, Pop was right on all points. Bobbie released me with a note of relief, sad though she was. At first she said she didn't want the money; we had been happy together, and I owed her nothing. But I pressed her, and in the end she accepted my offer. It was about half of what I had saved in the Goldhandler years. "The truth is, honey, your faith scares me," she confessed, with a regretful smile, "because you take it so seriously! You and your whole family. All those *eyes*. I do love you. There's never been anything like this for me before. Maybe for both of us, there never will be again. But it's best this way." She put both her hands over mine, and looked at me with the same shining eyes that had astounded and thrilled me when she said, "*You fiend! As though you ever doubted it. From the first minute!*" We were at one of the conspicuous middle tables of the Oak Room, but we might have been alone on a bench in the park. "Anyway, I'll never forget that you asked me." A mischievous little grin twitched that lovely mouth. "Twice."

The penthouse was gutted. Boyd wandered the vacant spaces like a ghost, except that his footfalls made noise; but no ghost ever haunted a more desolate ruin. Mrs. Fesser had showed up with two vans and a squad of moving men, Boyd said, and had cleaned the place out. How could she do that? Well, on Goldhandler's death she had demanded immediate payment of the balances due, an option in the small print of her invoices. Of course Mrs. Goldhandler couldn't pay, and so La Fesser had descended and repossessed all those bargains.

In the office the cigar smell was still spookily strong. The boss's big desk and swivel chair were gone; but the joke files, the steel cabinets of old scripts, the typewriters, the carpeting, and the switchboard had survived the Fesser raid. Boyd and I had undertaken to get the files moved to a new apartment the widow had rented. She considered those files a treasure, but without Goldhandler's crafty ingenuity and wit, the treasure was worked-out waste paper. For her sake Boyd tried to keep the business going, but we lost the programs, one by one, writing in Morrie's flat, or Sam's apartment, or the new place. When the work dwindled to nothing, Sam flew off in his airplane, I gave up the April House room and dove into my law books, and Boyd went on to another job, writing and directing a soap opera.

Let me finish up about Boyd. He lived only a year or so after that. He was doing well at his job, but then he up and died of something called an embolism. I found this out by running into Karl in a theatre lobby. Boyd's sister notified the Goldhandlers, but for one reason and another none of them could go to the funeral. When Karl told me about it, Boyd had been dead a good while. Boyd couldn't have been more than thirty when he died. Maybe grieving dogs die of an embolism.

It was Boyd who gave me some inside facts about Goldhandler's sudden death, as we tried afterward to cope with the collapse of the joke factory. Goldhandler had died in the tub, taking his morning bath. The Alaskan mine entanglement had brought on the fatal heart attack; that was Boyd's bitter certainty. The Goldhandlers had plunged in way over their heads when, according to Klebanoff, the gold began coming through in Klondike quantities. Goldhandler had gone on the board of directors, and he had countersigned with Klebanoff guarantees for large capital outlays which a syndicate was supposed to provide. The venture had suddenly turned sour. There was no syndicate. Klebanoff was facing an indictment for fraud, he was missing, and a warrant was out for him. An investors' committee had formed to sue Goldhandler; and on the morning he died he was scheduled to meet that committee in his lawyers' office, to explain how he proposed to pay off a quarter of a million dollars in guarantees.

The last time I ever saw Boyd we talked about Goldhandler's career, which in retrospect began to seem the falling flash of a brilliant meteor. Boyd said the clue to it all was that the Henny Holtz show had been Goldhandler's base for his rich living, and he had lost it too soon after occupying the penthouse. All the mad doings thereafter had been clutches at straws to arrest his fall, and keep up that dream aerie overlooking Central Park. "Maybe they loved each other too much," Boyd said about Goldhandler and his wife. "They wanted each other to have the moon, and by God they had it."

Thus Boyd. Maybe there is something in that. But the truth is, I think Goldhandler was ready for his long rest, even without the failing programs and the Klebanoff disaster. The boss had a great heart but he had broken it, trying too hard to make the Goldena Medina laugh, for money.

The apartment the family moved to was on the ground floor rear of an old building near Columbia, dark and dowdy, but commodious. I visited the Goldhandlers often during my law school years. The first time I came to dinner, Mrs. Goldhandler in deference to me baked a salmon. She had noticed at the funeral that I was praying for Goldhandler. "Harry never missed a trick," she said. "You are getting religion, aren't you? I don't believe in it, of course, but I appreciated your sentiment."

Mrs. Goldhandler is still alive, over seventy but full of zip, doing administrative work in a Tucson hospital. She never remarried. She was a very handsome widow, but what man could follow Goldhandler? Sigmund became a physicist, and Karl, after some strange shadowy doings in international currencies, is now, of all things, an eminent scholar on Byzantium. He attends an annual conference in New York of Byzantians, or whatever you call such rare birds, so I see him and get the family news.

A son of Karl's, a rock musician, aged twenty, passed through Washington not long ago and called on me, seeking advice about going to Israel to work on a kibbutz. He said he was interested in exploring his origins. He had never been inside a synagogue or a temple, knew no Hebrew, not even the alphabet. He did not know that Hebrew was what Israelis spoke. It gave me a turn to see how much — except for his shoulder-length hair — he resembled the book-jacket picture of the slim, aesthetic short-story writer, Harry Goldhandler.

88

The End

I DID not hear from Bobbie for about a year.

The first year of law school is less a course of instruction than an ordeal of passage, like adult circumcision among the aborigines. The intent is to cull out the weak. Never have I worked so hard. College by comparison had been kindergarten play. Rusty at the books after such a long layoff, competing against the sharpies who chose Columbia as the high road to Wall Street jobs, I tunnelled through the weeks and months like a mole, blind and deaf to everything but the next assignments and examinations. The Munich crisis came and went, Hitler occupied all of Czechoslovakia, the war talk kept mounting, but it might all have been happening on Pluto. I was holding my own, even beginning to forge forward with some hope of *Law Review,* and what else mattered? When the summer vacation came, I just studied harder. Attendance in the law library dropped low, but I was there straight through July and August, still making up those lost years.

The day England declared war, Bobbie called me. She wanted to chat about the big news, and to give me her latest address and phone number. She was rehearsing in a new musical, and feeling perky about that. I went to the opening night, and we had a date after the show, and then in the months that followed, a few more. Once again the chronic weakness threatened. To fend it off, I almost married Rosalind Hoppenstein, and here is how *that* happened.

Pop went into a real decline when France collapsed in May. He had worked himself half to death, gathering those "affidavits" which enabled refugees to come to the States. He signed many himself and got me to sign some too. Pop assured me the Jewish agencies would take care of everyone who came, and so it was. I never even met the people whose lives I saved by scrawling my name on those pieces of paper, not enough by a long shot. The fall of France and the Low Countries meant a clang of iron Nazi doors on thousands of refugees, some of whom held Pop's affidavits. Shavuos came around, late in May, and Pop asked me to chant *Akdamos,* he wasn't up to it. I said a shaygets like myself ought not to do *Akdamos.* "Never mind," Pop said. "You're all right. You know it. Do it."

So I did. Afterward Rosalind came up to me, shook my hand with her vigorous grip, and invited me to *La Traviata* that night, the synagogue opera benefit. That poor betrayed self-sacrificing courtesan, dying of a broken heart to the most gorgeous of Verdi's melodies, brought Bobbie Webb poignantly to mind. I started calling up Roz again. My attentions were welcomed, and the romance was once more on. My summer job in a law office was a lark compared with the school. We went to shows, and rode horseback, and swam at Jones Beach. I even spent a weekend at a hotel where the Hoppensteins were staying. The rabbi and the fearsome mother were all smiles. Early in the fall they invited me for Sabbath dinner at their home; a rare honor, and a decided signal of encouragement, for they were reserved Europeans.

Now you have to get the historical picture, to believe me when I say I was considering marrying Roz. The Battle of Britain had brilliantly enlivened the summer. For the first time, Hitler was not having things his way. It looked more and more as though we would get into the war. There was talk of a draft. In a burst of patriotism not unmixed with cunning, I went to an Army Air Corps recruiting office. Not for me the mud, the lice, the rat-infested trenches of *All Quiet on the Western Front!* Me for the wild blue yonder, like those RAF heroes in Spitfires and Hurricanes! I found out that I might get into a reserve officers course when I finished law school, if I could restore a physique worn down by the Goldhandler working hours, Bobbie's regular recycling of her beloved Izzy through the meat grinder, and the law school ordeal.

So I did three things: I took up boxing, I signed for flying lessons, and I began to think seriously about Rosalind Hoppenstein. Program: I would get myself into martial trim. I would return to the recruiting office not a mere lawyer, but a licensed pilot. I would meantime marry somebody pure, right, lovely, and Jewish, who would cheer my parents while I battled in the skies, and who might even produce a child or two to keep my memory green, were I to go down in flames. Not wholly absent was the dim notion that a wife might keep me out of the draft.

The boxing did harden me up, but the flying was a failure. I never got to solo. My instructor, a lantern-jawed flying fool named Jiggs, couldn't persuade the owner of the school to turn me loose. I overheard them arguing about it. Jiggs said that the worst I could do was smash the undercarriage. The owner said I might also die, which would hurt business. My depth perception, you see, was off. I would come in for perfect landings, twenty-five feet above the earth. The plane would then pancake straight down, and the owner would come cursing out of the hangar. When I tried to correct the fault, I would fly straight at the ground, and Jiggs would sob through the intercom, "Christ, no, no, I've got it," and would send us zooming. So I gave up the flying idea.

But about that fatal Sabbath dinner with the Hoppensteins. It all went merrily as a marriage bell — in fact, very much like a marriage bell altogether — until the dessert, a pink pudding made by Mrs. Hoppenstein. Rosalind had cooked the rest of the meal (the day before the Sabbath, of course, and kept warm in an oven), and it was excellent, and well advertised as her handiwork. The rabbi forked up some pink pudding as he chatted with me about a fine point in the Sabbath Scripture reading.

"Rabbi," said his wife sharply, interrupting his discourse, "use the spoon." Her Germanic origin was evident in the pronunciation. She said *shpoon*.

He smiled at me, and at her, and observed that it really didn't matter, did it, what utensil he ate it with? It was a gentle reproof of the interruption of scholarly talk, with a touch of Gallic irony at the ways of women.

Well, her response! The turrets of that woman's main battery trained at the rabbi, and the salvo rattled windows all over mid-Manhattan. "Yes, it does matter," she roared, with a great belch of flame, "because *I made it, and I want you to use the SHPOON!*"

As she said *SHPOON*, she struck the table with three earthshaking fingers. I glanced at Rosalind and suddenly noticed how much she looked like her mother; noticed too that Rosalind took this exchange quite for granted, normal byplay in a happy household. The rabbi laid down the fork, took up the spoon with another ironic smile at me, and ate the dessert. That *SHPOON* rings in my ear as I write. I might or might not have married Roz anyway — I admired her, she was a sweet and accomplished girl, although we were never in love — but that was the moment when I knew that I wouldn't.

"David, I don't know who else to turn to." Bobbie again, calling after nearly a year when I hadn't seen or spoken to her. "I'm pregnant."

"Good God, Bobbie!"

"Don't take on, dear. It's not the end of the world, truly it isn't, but I do want to talk to you."

Bobbie waded through the standard dinner at Lou Siegel's with vast enjoyment: chopped chicken liver, fricassee of chicken wings, matzoh-ball soup, sweet and sour tongue, and a garlic steak, with unlimited pickles and rye bread. She was quite cheerful, though decidedly plumper. About the baby's father she would say scornfully only that he was an animal, she had been a terrible fool, and she would have nothing to do with him. "This is an excellent steak," she observed. "I didn't know kosher food could be this good. May I have another beer? What will you do in the Air Corps, David? You won't get kosher food."

We had been catching up on each other's news. I had been accepted for a reserve officers' course, starting after I graduated from law school.

I said, "I'll survive. You're sure you want this baby, Bobbie?"

"Of course. Abortion is wrong, dear. It's a sin, and anyway, you know how I've yearned for a baby, for years and years. That's my decision, and I won't change it. Mother has been a brick. She completely agrees with me."

"When are you due?"

"Mid-October."

Rapid mental arithmetic: this was late March, so she was finishing her third month, the outside safe point for an abortion. Probably she had just made the decision, and as a first order of business was acquiring a protector. That would be old Izzy, and fair enough.

"If ever I can help, Bobbie, call me."

Her eyes glistened. "I'm fine, honey, but I appreciate that."

When I returned her to her small apartment in the Village, Mrs.

Webb's warm greeting, and then the cynical, faintly salacious smile with which she quickly withdrew to a back room, wrung my heart. A woman with another man's baby growing inside her was nobody I cared to make a pass at, but as far as Mrs. Webb was concerned, the protector was entitled to whatever he wanted of Bobbie. True, the façade of propriety lay in ruins. Still, who could say? Perhaps under the gray ashes lay a live coal somewhere!

Not until after I graduated did I tell my parents about the Air Reserve course. Sufficient unto the day, I thought. Mama's reaction was to exclaim, "Air Corps! Good boy!" and go sailing around the room making airplane noises, holding out her arms like wings. "B-R-R-R! V-R-OO-M! Another Lindbergh!" My father just looked at me, and whatever color was in his face fled, leaving him greenish as a dead man. To reassure him, I said I couldn't qualify as a pilot, and probably would end up in an Air Corps legal office, but meantime I was signed up for a navigator course.

"Why the Air Corps?" Papa asked hoarsely. "It's the most dangerous service."

"It beats washing army barracks floors, Pop." More than once Papa had said he would do that if we got into the war, or anything else he was fit for.

A bleak smile lightened his face. "I see. Well, leave washing the floors to me. Just take good care of our son."

At the Louisiana airfield where they gave the navigator course I was something of a freak: a New York Jew, a lawyer, a former gagman, in with ROTC types and assorted volunteers, mainly deep Southerners. It was my first total immersion in non-Jews. I suppose these prewar volunteers were for the most part screwballs like me, and at all events I got along. There were a few "clip-cock" types, but I had no truck with them, and that was that. The navigation was a challenge, we flew a lot, and the peacetime Air Corps was far from an intolerable grind, especially after law school.

In August, when I flew home for my first leave, I was shocked at the change in my father: the feebleness of his motions, the way the skin of his face hung in folds, the baggy looseness of his clothing. Yet he was so glad to see me, so full of eager inquiries about the Air Corps, and so quick with his old Yiddish joking — moreover, he clearly was so proud of me — that I buried my uneasiness. Mama insisted that he was all right. If I could only persuade him to take a two-week vacation he would come back a new man. I went straight to him and told him to do it.

"Is that a military order?" Pop inquired.

"Right," I said. "Failure to comply will result in washing barracks floors for thirty days."

Pop laughed and agreed to go.

I did not see Bobbie, but we talked on the telephone. Her obstetrician was worrying her about the baby's position and heartbeat. She wanted to go to another doctor. Everything was costing more than she had expected, and her savings were running low, but her mother was working in a tea room, and they would be all right. When I returned to the base I sent her a check, anyway. Bobbie wrote back a strangely articulate and moving letter about our relationship, going back to our first days in April House. I tore up that letter, with a pile of other mementos, the night before I married Jan.

The call came on October 15. "It's a girl, darling." Bobbie's voice was high and muffled, as when she was tired or sleepy. "You're the first to know. Mother went home at four A.M., all worn out."

"That's great news, Bobbie. Congratulations! Are you okay?"

"Well, dopey from the anesthetic, I guess, but sure, fine, very happy. I had a rough time, but she's just perfect, she's adorable. And so big! Nine pounds! I just saw her for a little while, then they took her away, screaming bloody murder."

The telephone at the gunnery school hung on the wall in the lobby of the officers' quarters; not much privacy, with the fellows trampling past me on the way to breakfast. "Is there anything I can do, Bobbie?"

"Just come and see us next time you're in town." Bobbie wearily chuckled. "She's something, honestly."

"Of course I'll come."

But I never did see Bobbie's baby, and I did not see Bobbie again until after Pop died.

"It's about your father."

The duty officer shook me awake at three in the morning. I stumbled to the telephone. Lee told me shakily that Pop was in the hospital, and the doctors thought he might make it, but they had advised her to summon me. I put on my second lieutenant's uniform, thinking it might facilitate travel. An Air Corps plane was leaving the base at dawn for a field outside Washington, so I caught a ride on it and flew on to New York from there. The uniform did help, especially when I told the ticket salesman at the air terminal why I was travelling. I got aboard a sold-out plane.

Mama was sitting on a couch in the hospital corridor near his room. "You can't see him for very long," she said, "but he knows you're coming, and he's waiting for you."

"How is he?"

Mama shrugged, and smiled in that tough way of hers under stress. "They give him a fifty-fifty chance."

I had never seen oxygen apparatus before. Papa sat propped up on pillows, with a tube from his nose to a plastic bag hanging over his head, which collapsed and inflated with each breath. He turned his head to me. At the sight of the uniform his face lit up, and he murmured, *"Ut is Yisroelke, der Amerikaner offizier."*

"Papa, hayitokhon?"

That brought a ghostly little laugh. Beside him lay a pad and pencil, and a pile of scribbled notes. His secretary came from the laundry every day to collect these and report on business. He wrote those notes until he died.

In Yiddish he whispered, "What do you think, Yisroelke? Will I be a *laydig-gayer?*" The word means idle-goer, do-nothing, loafer; a heavy term of Yiddish opprobrium.

"Not you, Pop. Never."

He nodded, and lay his head back on the pillow with a weary smile. He held out a hand, barely lifting it from the coverlet, to gesture at the uniform.

"Nu, mein offizier, zye a mentsch." (Well, my officer, be a man.)

"I'm trying, Pop."

Again he nodded, and he shut his eyes. Mama and I left. I did not see him again alive. The doctors said he was doing well, and told us to go home and get some rest. We were awakened after midnight by a call from the floor nurse, who said to me, "It looks very bad." When we got there he lay with his head to one side. I took his hand, still warm and sweaty, and recited the final confession for him, not knowing whether he had managed to say it, for he died alone.

I do not mean to dwell on sad things, but that much is part of my story. I have described the graveyard scene, and the partner Brodofsky leaping to pile the first shovelful of earth on Pop's rough wooden coffin. I will remember that till I die. Nor will I write here a eulogy of my father. I have written it already, such as I could.

We were sitting *shiva,* the seven days of mourning, when the Japanese bombed Pearl Harbor. That Sunday, December 7, was the last full day of our shiva. I called the navigation school and talked to the deputy commanding officer. He said I should complete my mourning and get back as soon as possible. When I mentioned that I had a seven-day growth of beard, and that my tradition required me to let it grow thirty days from my father's death, he hesitated and then said, "Well, come on back, Lieutenant, and we'll see about that." In the event the school let me grow the beard.

So there we were on Monday morning, terminating the shiva. The members of Pop's synagogue who had come every day to the apartment for services, so that Lee and I could say kaddish without leaving home, had all had their coffee and cake and departed. Mom was taking down the sheets that had swathed the mirrors; I was stacking the prayer books, and Lee was collecting the low mourning stools, when the phone rang.

"It's Bobbie Webb," Lee whispered to me, with a side-glance at Mom.

I closed the door of my bedroom and picked up the phone. Bobbie said she had called me at the school to talk about how our getting into the war might affect me. They had told her where I was.

"Can I see you before you go?" she asked gaily. "Heaven only knows when we'll meet again, flyboy, you're off to the wars, aren't you? You're entitled to a going-away present. I'm in April House, Room 729."

"What? April House?" I spoke slowly and stupidly, not able to handle this alien note striking into my changed life.

"I couldn't get Suite 1800, dear," she said. "I asked, but Peeping Tom is booked up." I said nothing. Her tone altered. "David, is everything all right? You sound odd. If I'm disturbing you, or embarrassing you —"

"No, no, Bobbie. Room 729? I can't stay long, I'm on my way back to base."

"Oh, it shouldn't take long, honey." Her voice lifted again into arch flirtation. "You might have let me and Angela know you were on leave, and dropped in to see us."

"Who was that?" Mom asked when I came out of my room. They don't come more alert than my mother, and to this hour, nearly blind and deaf as she is, that is still true.

"Somebody I knew when I was a boy, Mom."

When Bobbie opened the door of the hotel room and saw my face, and the growth of beard, she knew.

"It's your father, David."

"Yes. He died a week ago."

It was a small room, smaller even than Morrie's, with a rather dingy hotel bed, a couch, and some nondescript chairs. Bobby and I had had many a tryst in such rooms, but not in April House. A bottle of champagne stood in a cooler on the bed table, with two glasses.

"I'm awfully sorry. I've been sitting here thinking it must be your father. Ever since I heard your voice on the telephone." She touched the beard. "For how long?"

"A month, if the Air Corps will let me."

"Gray hairs, David. Have you noticed? Just two or three."

"I noticed. How is Angela?"

"Unbelievably cute. Sleeps straight through the night, a sheer joy. Wait till you have a child of your own, David. Life starts over again, truly it does." She glanced at the wine doubtfully and said, "I don't know. Want some?"

"Why not? This is thoughtful of you."

"Well, dear, I didn't know about your father. Why didn't they tell me? They just gave me the phone number."

I opened the wine, and we drank, Bobbie sitting on the couch, I on a chair facing her. We talked of the war, naturally. She was solicitous about Lee and my mother. I told her something about our mourning practices, and how my father had died.

"I only saw him across the street that once, outside the synagogue, and then the painting in your home. I wish I could have known him."

"He knew about you, Bobbie, and always wished you well."

We had been drinking the wine rather fast, in this awkward conversation, and I poured the last of it in our two glasses.

"May I drink to his memory?"

"Of course."

We raised our glasses and drank. Bobby crossed her legs. She could do that casually, as women do all the time without thinking, or she could do it as an offer of love. This was an offer. My eyes went from the legs to her face. Seeing what she saw in my eyes, she pulled her skirt over her knees, and that was the end.

She left first, with a gentle goodbye kiss. I had to make phone calls, and I said I would pay the bill. When I walked out of April House for the last time, it was starting to snow.

*   *   *

89

The Beginning

Lod Airport, Israel
El Al Engineering Building
Sunday, November 4, 1973

THE late afternoon sun is so dazzling in this room that I'm wearing sunglasses as I write. They've taken down the blackout cloths but haven't yet put back the blinds, though the war's been over for more than a week. The U.S. Air Force colonel running the airlift invited me to use this room, set up by the Israelis for the rest and recreation of his crews, while I wait for my El Al flight home. I jumped at it. These reclining chairs from El Al's first-class cabins are a lot more comfortable than the seats in the terminal. Moreover the silent desolation of that once-boisterous waiting room, the row of dark airline offices, the empty benches, were giving me the willies.

The triumph cost the Israelis two thousand dead in twenty days. Proportionately, that is about four times the losses the United States took in all the years of the Vietnam war. There is no dancing in the streets here over one of history's most astonishing military feats. The Arabs and Soviets are already trying to fish political gain, as usual, from military disaster, as our Secretary of State shuttles around to nail down the cease-fire. How the Secretary, a Jew who talks a lot about being Jewish, feels as he twists the Israelis' arms while they are still burying their dead, is an interesting question, but let me not dwell on that. This service to the Administration has been my last. The President is doomed to fall soon, after that incredible "Saturday night massacre" of successive attorney generals who refused to fire the Watergate special prosecutor. But that is not why I will resign. This war and — to some extent — writing *April House* have changed me.

I started on my goodbyes early this morning by taxiing to the Hadassah hospital in Jerusalem. The highway traffic was as thick and clogged as I have ever seen it; to that extent life here is normal again. I was half an hour late getting there, and consequently enjoyed at a distance a remarkable sight: my mother, walking out of the hospital entrance into the pellucid white Jerusalem light under her own power, leaning on a cane and indignantly shaking off my sister when Lee tried to take her elbow. Mom's Puerto Rican companion trailed discreetly behind. Later Lee told me that when the companion tried to help her walk out, Mom hit her over the head with her cane.

"Where have you been?" Mom said as I hurried up to her. "Why weren't you here to check me out? Were you fighting in the war?"

"The war's over, Mom."

"I know the war's over," Mom said testily, covering the fact that she had forgotten. "I asked whether you fought."

"Mama, I'm fifty-eight years old."

"So what? Wasn't Lindbergh an old general, and didn't he fight in the war?" She laughed. "My Lindbergh! I'll bet you were fighting up there" — she pointed at the sky — "you just didn't want me to worry. Papa worried himself to death when you joined the Air Force. I said, 'Another Lindbergh,' and I went flying around the room. Brrr! Brrr!" Mama made weak airplane noises and flapped her arms, striking the companion with her cane, for once unintentionally. Mom's companions are well paid, but she has a way of taking it out on their hides. Why they develop a sort of reluctant affection for her is beyond me.

The four of us had trouble getting ourselves into the little Peugeot with General Moshe Lev at the wheel. "How do you like your new brother-in-law?" Mom asked me as we drove.

"Oh, Mom, don't be preposterous," said Lee, blushing as though she were sixteen instead of sixty-two, and looking nearer sixteen for radiant prettiness. Moshe Lev, grim as a rock in his rumpled uniform, turned to give her a brief smile.

I asked General Lev what he thought of the Secretary's putting the heat on Israel, in the disengagement talks, to let the trapped Egyptian Third Army escape, with no *quid pro quo* from the defeated Egyptians. To my surprise he said it was a very good thing. Israeli politicians would never of themselves do what had to be done to bring about a peace. If the Americans pushed them to it, using the leverage of the airlift, there might be a chance for a real deal with Egypt, for the first time since Israel existed. I commented on the Secretary's being Jewish. Moshe Lev shrugged and said, "The man works for the American President. He's doing his job."

Zaideh's grave is in a cemetery outside Tel Aviv. He went to Israel at the age of eighty-eight and lived there another seven years in perfect health. Then he became too feeble to do much for himself, and there was no room for a companion in his tiny apartment, so the family decided to move him to a nursing home, the best in Tel Aviv for the Orthodox elderly. Zaideh visited the home, said it was very nice, and consented to the arrangement. On returning to his apartment he lay down and died. He is buried near a great Talmud luminary in a grave he bought as soon as he arrived in Israel.

"Papa, here is Yisroelke to say goodbye to you," said my mother in Yiddish, standing at the graveside in the beating sun, perspiring from her long hobble among the tombstones. "I'm not going. God gave me a little more life, and I'll live it out here and be buried here. Poor Alex lies alone in America, so maybe the children will bring him here, but I will not leave the Holy Land, Papa, ever again." With her almost sightless eyes she managed to find a rock on the dusty ground, and she put it on his tombstone, an old custom.

"Goodbye, Zaideh," I said. "I'll be back."

Mama allowed Lee and me to hold her elbows as we slowly made our way back to the car. She was done in. She dozed until we reached the Ramat Gan apartment house where Lee has rented a flat, near the building that General Lev lives in. She plans to look after Mom, and keep on the companion, who is a very religious Catholic and adores being in Israel. Lee has said nothing to me about an understanding with the general, if she has one, and he never says much about anything. Anyway, we got Mom up to Lee's flat and I said a dozen goodbyes to her. "Just remember I'm here now," she said as I was making it out of the door. "In Eretz Yisroel."

"Right, Mama," I said. "You got the ploika."

She looked surprised, then burst out laughing. "The ploika! Yes, that stepmother of mine, I showed her, didn't I?"

Mama also "showed" the partners and the money men of the Fairy

Laundry. I once intended to write up the whole lawsuit and Mama's crushing victory; but by now you have the idea about The Green Cousin. They tried to manipulate the stock voting so as to cut her off from a living Papa had set up for her. Ha! They ended paying her everything Papa had provided, with legal costs and punitive damages. As I wrote long ago, they spat in the wrong lady's kasha. She can live on in Israel in comfort till the age of one hundred twenty, and I hope she does.

The American Air Force colonel who is boss man of the airlift just dropped in and bent my ear for a while, evidently hoping I'd pass it all on to the President. He wanted me to know how the pilots had pushed themselves to exhaustion to keep the airlift going; how the Air Force had transformed the moribund Lajes Island airfield in the Azores almost overnight into a major facility; how a twenty-four-hour Air Force watch at the Pentagon had kept supplies flooding from all over the United States into the pipeline of the airlift; and, in short, what an altogether bang-up performance the Military Air Transport Command had turned in. I've heard the same story from the Israelis, with awed wonderment and admiration, and I don't know why the colonel shouldn't blow the horn of the Air Force. They have done one hell of a job.

"And I'll tell you one other thing," he said, "and every pilot who is flying this mission will tell you the same. This is the most satisfying thing I've ever done in my military career. The gratitude of these people — the feeling that the Air Force is helping a small country, in big trouble against huge odds — great, just great, nothing like it in my life."

Now the recreation room again is empty and quiet.

* * *

WHEN I next saw Bobbie Webb, four years had gone by. The Germans had surrendered; the war with Japan was still on. My war record was minimal. I flew some B-17 missions as navigator, mostly over Italy, then the Air Corps pulled me back as an instructor, to the States and then to a special course set up in England. Late in the war I did a stretch in the legal section of a base in California, working on Air Corps contracts with manufacturers. That was awful, but I met Jan at a party in the officers' club on that base. I asked her to lunch next day and before the lunch was over I was pretty sure I would marry her. After two weeks of seeing her day and night, I thought I had better mention it to her. It turned out that she had the same idea, though she was engaged to some guy over in France. She wrote him what we then called a Dear John letter, and I wrote about Jan to Bobbie.

The B-29 assault on Japan was getting going about then, and I was ordered to the Marianas base on Tinian as a navigator. Jan and I agreed to get married after the war, and back I went to New York, for a week's leave before flying to the Pacific. While I was there I called Bobbie, and we met in the Palm Court of the Plaza.

Well, four years will show their mark, and I won't say that Bobbie hadn't changed, but she looked smart and well. Carriage does so much for a woman, and she came striding in with that old erect yet very feminine walk, her head held just so, wearing her style of tailored suit and elegant hat, tilted just so. Bobbie Webb, who had once been all the Outside, all the Goldena Medina, to me, was now just herself, a tall woman past thirty, yet I felt a throb of the old affection for her. That was, of course, exactly what Bobbie intended that I feel.

Over tea and cakes I talked some about my war experiences and Bobbie chattered about Angela. Bobbie had taken time off from her modelling job, and I had much to do, so it was a hurried encounter.

"Well, now," says Bobbie, laying a hand on mine, "Tell me about this Jan. Is she really that pretty and clever? With such a responsible job, and she so young, she must be brilliant."

Well, nearing sixty, I still know very little about women, but even then I knew that candid praise of one woman to another, especially if the latter is or has been your love, is not the world's smartest idea. I kept my words about Jan very dry and short, or thought I did. Even so, I could see Bobbie's sunny mood fading, her eyes widening and beginning to moisten. So I broke off, and we looked at each other in silence.

"Tell me," says Bobbie, in a sad tone that cuts at my heart as I hear it again, so clearly, almost thirty years later, "why is it that I could never have the one thing in the world that I really wanted?"

I saw her just once more.

* * *

90

He Will Make Peace

"ZAHAL" is the Hebrew acronym for "Israeli Defense Force," and Zahala is the classy northern suburb of Tel Aviv where army generals live. Moshe Dayan has a big house there. The general's wife whom Mark has been seeing took Abe into her home, and has put Sandra up, too, with the general's genial consent. These Israelis, the secular ones, tend to be what some might call adult about marriage and divorce. The general showed up during my visit, and there was no visible awkwardness among him, Mark, and the wife, who isn't much to look at, but otherwise is quite a woman. She works in aeronautical designing, and has an engineering degree from the Technion in Haifa. The general is in love with somebody else's wife, I think a bank manager's, but I didn't delve into all that. Mark has accepted a lecture post at the Technion; just temporarily, he assures me; there's no way he'll settle in Israel.

When I got there I saw Sandra feeding Abe lunch in the garden; so I let them alone and went inside, where I found Mark chuckling evilly over the foul review *Time* had given Peter Quat's book. Its heading was *My Eye,* and it went on from there. The issue was several weeks old, for the war had delayed the mails.

"Well, this is the end of Peter's kike comedy," said Mark, "and high time. The joke is over. School of Quat fiction is dead. The Jews are a threatened species, probably doomed, because how many more military miracles can Israel pull off? It ain't funny any more."

Though I wasn't in an arguing mood I fired up at that. "We aren't a threatened species, and we aren't precisely because Israel exists," I retorted. "If we ever stop laughing at ourselves, then we'll be a threatened species. As for the military miracles, they will go on, don't worry, until the Arabs wise up, and get tired of dying for the Soviet Union. Then there'll be peace."

"He's your client," said Mark sourly.

Actually Peter isn't in such bad shape. This book has to be written off as a muff, and his publisher naturally has gone sour on Quat merchandise, but Peter went to another publisher with a new book idea; and he telephoned me the day after the war ended, all in a happy fizz about, believe it or not, the Gilgamesh epic. He came upon this pre-Biblical flood story, and started reading up like mad on Mesopotamian religion, which was, I gather, very licentious and scatological. Peter has this vision of a tremendous Mesopotamian book ending in the great flood. "The ultimate disaster novel, a mighty parable of our times," he calls it. Apparently the new publisher agreed and is talking big figures. The Noah of the Gilgamesh epic is named Utnapishtim. Peter will have to do something about that, but I daresay he will. You can't keep a good man down.

I said my farewell to Sandra in the garden. She and Abe are being as reticent as Lee and Moshe Lev about their plans. I'm asking no questions. Abe's blindness isn't total. When they took off the bandages he could see light and shadow with one eye, and the other eye reacted to light stimuli. Now he's bandaged up again. The best man in the world for this sort of thing, the Israeli doctors have told Mark, lives in Florida. Sandra and Abe will go there when he has healed enough to travel. He will be in Florida for a year, and Sandra says she will enroll in law school in Miami. "I'll be his eyes," Sandra said to me, "if he needs me for that, and anyway I may practice law. He makes it seem interesting."

"*He's* interesting," I said.

"Oh, go on home," said Sandra. "Mom must be climbing the walls, all alone there in Georgetown."

When I shook hands with Abe, I found it very hard to get out any words. "I hope it goes well," was what I managed to produce.

"It has gone well," he said with a melancholy yet spirited smile, turning his bandaged sightless face up at me. "We won."

The general then invited me in for a drink. His liking for old scotch is exceptional; most Israelis don't drink at all, or sip sweet liqueurs. This is a big bluff career army man with a heavy jaw, large fists, and a brisk hearty manner. Before the war broke out, he was administering the Gaza Strip. I told him what Moshe Lev said about the disengagement talks. He disagreed tersely and violently. The Secretary is an opportunist, he growled, selling Israel down the river to snatch favor with the Arabs, when resolute American support of the Israeli victory could seal a secure peace right now in the Middle East.

"The Arabs are in a shambles," he said. "Syria is finished. Egypt is broken. The Soviet Union made noise and sent arms, but failed them. With total surprise and total war, they still lost. The airlift gave us a moral boost, no doubt of it, but we were crossing the Suez Canal before it got going. We turned the war around in the field, with the stuff we had on hand. The Americans have been great. The way they mounted that airlift was awesome. But the Secretary is a damned court Jew, negotiating away the advantages we won for the United States and ourselves to make himself look like Metternich."

"Golda herself has publicly said," I ventured, "that the Americans saved Israel."

"Golda and Dayan wouldn't allow a preemptive air strike the day the Arabs began the war. They were afraid of what the Americans would think. That cost us two thousand dead boys and two weeks of fighting. She has to maintain that that price was necessary. It wasn't."

And that's the kind of stand-off you come to, in most discussions in Israel; the old rabbinic break-off on so many issues, down the centuries: *"This needs further study."*

They're calling my flight. . . .

And the thought of that further study is beginning to draw me. What really happened? Would a preemptive strike have stopped the Arabs in their tracks? Would it have alienated the Americans? The Arabs alienated nobody by striking first, that's self-evident. What about the blowup among the Israeli generals on the southern front, hints of which are just surfacing in the press?

But over all looms the question that more and more haunts me: how did a people that thirty years ago marched docilely into gas chambers by the millions, women, children, and all, turn around in a generation to become one of the most impressive armed forces on earth? *There* is the true astounding reversal, the military miracle that still stuns the world, and that I don't begin to fathom.

Who does? Where are the books? What is the answer? If I can't find a book that tells me in plain English what I want to know, maybe I'll dig for the truth and write one myself. After all, I'm now a man who has written a book — or almost.

The plane is taking off, and joggling my pen . . .

Airborne . . . I would have to come back to Israel, and maybe even live here, to write that book, but why not? Jan and I have money. Helping big utility companies to screw the Internal Revenue Service out of millions no longer seems to me a fun thing, as they say. Jan thinks Israel is fine for the Israelis, and for Sandra if that's what she wants — though about that she's skeptical — but that we would be nuts to live here. We'll see.

The lights of Israel are blazing in the twilight as the plane circles and climbs, and the music tape is playing an old liturgical song, the last words of the kaddish, which has become a sort of marching song for the Israelis:

> *He who makes peace in the Highest*
> *He will make peace, for us*
> *And for all Israel, amen.*

Every time I leave Israel and look back at the coastline and the lights, I feel a tug, but now! Mama is there for good, and perhaps Lee, and at the moment Sandra, too, and even Mark Herz. That song's refrain goes on and on, a rousing melody repeating just two Hebrew words, *Yaaseh shalom*, that is, "He will make peace."

> *Yaaseh shalom*
> *Yaaseh shalom*

Let me write my last glimpse of Bobbie Webb, as I take my last glimpse of Israel, and then get stone-drunk, but one more thing first, before I forget. This morning as I said my prayers, alone in my hotel room, I recited this passage from the daily liturgy; and it is sounding in my brain as I watch those receding lights.

> *Look down from Heaven and see that we have become a scorn and a derision among the nations. We are considered as sheep bound for the slaughter, for murder, for extermination, for smiting and for shame. Yet with all this we have not forgotten Your name. Do not You forget us.*

We spoke those words, I and my father and his father, and their fathers before them, for two thousand years — and even in my own time, alas — as a terrible statement of fact. Now there are the lights of victorious Israel below.

Yaaseh shalom . . .
Yaaseh shalom . . .

S OME years after we were married Jan and I went to a Broadway show, and ahead of us, passing the ticket-taker, I glimpsed Bobbie Webb. More by her carriage, and the way she held her head than anything else, I recognized her, because her back was to me. The man who apparently was with her, handing over the tickets, was a greasy-looking, swarthy little person about sixty years old. I thought with horror, ye gods, is this what Bobbie has fallen to? But when we came out into the lobby at intermission, there she stood with a very tall, good-looking man in rimless glasses, so that had been my mistake. She saw me and smiled, and I saw her lips form the words, "There's David Goodkind."

The obscenity trials were getting a splash in the papers just then. No doubt she had told her husband something about us. The tall man said, when she introduced us and we shook hands, that he admired what I was doing in the trials. His manner was cordial, his clothes excellent, his speech cultivated. So Bobbie had landed well, after all. She was plumper, but still good-looking, still straight, still striking. Only her eyes were dulled. "I've followed you in the papers, David," she said. "It's wonderful, everything that's happened. I'm so proud for you." Her mother was gone, she said, and Angela was doing well in boarding school. "Angela's a beauty," the tall man said, with a touch of fatherly fondness.

I was so stirred I almost lost awareness of where I was and what I was doing. I had not heard from Bobbie Webb since that last meeting in the Palm Court. The four of us went back into the theatre together, still chatting. Bobbie walked past the aisle like a blind woman, and her husband had to take her arm and turn her. "This way, dear." I watched them walk down to two of the best orchestra seats. Yes, Bobbie had landed well. Thank God.

"Maybe we can meet them afterward for a drink," I said to Jan.

"As you wish," Jan said.

I did not look for Bobbie after the show. Bobbie Webb's last best gift to me was to vanish from my life.

Yaaseh shalom
Yaaseh shalom

The plane still climbs in the darkness, and the old kaddish song goes on, sung in full-throated chorus by young Israelis.

Bobbie and I always talked of going to Lake Louise together. We never did. We should have gone there at least once, and danced under the stars, but the time went by in our quarrels and reconciliations, and we did not manage it. I have never yet been to Lake Louise, and if I ever get there, it will not be to dance with Bobbie Webb under the stars. I do not know what has become of Bobbie; I did not catch her married name, and I have no idea whether she is alive or dead. She would be only sixty or sixty-one, so there's no reason why she should not still live. But if this book is published and she reads it, I will not hear from her, and I will never know what she thought. She and Jan smiled and spoke fair to each other, but Bobbie has sense, and her last best gift stands.

He will make peace,
For us, and for all Israel, Amen.

The lights of Israel are gone. The kaddish song has ended. So has my book. It is a kaddish for my father, of course, start to finish; but in counterpoint it is also a torch song of the thirties, a sentimental Big Band number that no one has ever heard till now, and its name is, "Inside, Outside."

The stewardess comes up the aisle of the first-class cabin, taking drink orders. The man sitting beside me is a young American, perhaps a war volunteer. "Arthur Susman," she reads from her list.

"That's me," he says.

"What will you drink, Arthur?" Warm smile, Israeli first-name informality. He asks for a martini.

"Israel David Goodkind," she says.

"Right. Double bourbon and water."

She blinks at the hairy-chested order, and makes a note. Then, with that El Al smile: "And what do they call you, Israel or David?"

Slight pause. Then Pop's Yisroelke, enjoying a wry Yankee joke she may not get, smiles back.

"Call me Israel."